Praise for Katie Lane and
The Deep in the Heart of Texas Series

MAKE MINE A BAD BOY

"Katie Lane is a wonderful new voice in Western romance fiction."

—Joan Johnston, *New York Times* bestselling author of the Bitter Creek and Hawk's Way series

"I absolutely loved Colt! I mean, who doesn't like a bad boy? Katie Lane is truly a breath of fresh air. Her stories are unique and wonderfully written...Lane, you have me hooked." —LushBookReviewss.blogspot.com

"A delightful continuation of *Going Cowboy Crazy*. There's plenty of humor to entertain the reader, and the people of the town will seem like old friends by the end of this entertaining story." —*RT Book Reviews*

GOING COWBOY CRAZY

Also by Katie Lane

The Overnight Billionaires

A Billionaire Between the Sheets
A Billionaire After Dark
Waking Up with a Billionaire

Deep in the Heart of Texas

Going Cowboy Crazy
Make Mine a Bad Boy
Small Town Christmas (anthology)
Catch Me a Cowboy
Trouble in Texas
Flirting with Texas
A Match Made in Texas
The Last Cowboy in Texas

Holiday novels

Hunk for the Holidays
Ring in the Holidays
Unwrapped

The
Heart
of a
Texas
Cowboy

The Heart of a Texas Cowboy

2-in-1 Edition with *Going Cowboy Crazy*
and *Make Mine a Bad Boy*

KATIE LANE

FOREVER

New York   Boston

Forever
Hachette Book Group
1290 Avenue of the Americas, New York, NY 10104
read-forever.com
twitter.com/readforeverpub

Going Cowboy Crazy and *Make Mine a Bad Boy* originally published in 2011 by Forever.

First 2-in-1 edition: January 2021

Forever is an imprint of Grand Central Publishing. The Forever name and logo are trademarks of Hachette Book Group, Inc.

The publisher is not responsible for websites (or their content) that are not owned by the publisher.

The Hachette Speakers Bureau provides a wide range of authors for speaking events. To find out more, go to www.hachettespeakersbureau.com or call (866) 376-6591.

ISBN: 978-1-5387-3727-9 (mass market 2-in-1)

Printed in the United States of America

CW

10 9 8 7 6 5 4 3 2 1

The Heart of a Texas Cowboy

Going
Cowboy
Crazy

To James, the boy from Texas
who gave me the dream

Acknowledgments

It takes a village to get a first novel published. At least it took a village for this one. From Mrs. Hart, my fifth-grade teacher who had me write my very first fictional story, to the charming and hospitable people of West Texas. Unfortunately, I have only one page to show my appreciation.

That said...

Thank you, Alex Logan, my wonderful editor, for this page and for all the pages after it. My book couldn't have found a more nurturing and loving home than Grand Central. And a very special thanks to my amazing agent, Laura Bradford, who believed in me and refused to stop searching until she found that home.

Speaking of home, I need to thank my husband for his patience and understanding. Jamie, I love the "rubber" chicken you make for me on the nights I work late and your unwavering belief that my book is going to be the next Pulitzer Prize winner.

And how do I thank the most beautiful and intelligent daughters in the world? Tiffany for the hours spent working on my website, and Aubrey for her support and advice. And then there are my sisters, Christy and Sandi, who went over story lines and read rough drafts without complaint. What a sisterhood of love I have!

Finally, I'd like to thank my mother and father, Helen Marie and Joseph Abner, for giving me the kind of safe and loving childhood where a skinny kid could wander around "in her own little dream world."

Chapter One

IF YOU THINK MY TRUCK IS BIG...

Faith Aldridge did a double take, but the bold black letters of the bumper sticker remained the same. Appalled, she read through the rest of the signs plastered on the tail end of the huge truck: DON'T MESS WITH TEXAS; REBEL BORN AND REBEL BRED AND WHEN I DIE I'LL BE REBEL DEAD; I LIVE BY THE THREE B'S: BEER, BRAWLS AND BROADS; CRUDE RUNS THROUGH MY VEINS.

She could agree with the last one. Whoever drove the mammoth-sized vehicle *was* crude. And arrogant. And chauvinistic. And a perfect example of the rednecks her aunt Jillian had warned her about. Not that her aunt Jillian had ever met a redneck, but she'd seen Jeff Foxworthy on television. And that was enough to make her fear for her niece's safety when traveling in a state filled with punch lines for the statement—

You might be a redneck if...

You have a bumper sticker that refers to the size of your penis.

The front tire of her Volvo hit yet another pothole,

pulling her attention away from the bumper stickers and back to her quest for an empty parking space. There was no defined parking in the small dirt lot but, even without painted lines, the occupants of the bar had formed fairly neat rows. All except for the crude redneck whose truck was blatantly parked on the sidewalk by the front door.

Someone should report him to the police.

Someone who wasn't intimidated by law enforcement officers and didn't worry about criminal retaliation.

Faith found an empty space at the very end of the lot and started to pull in when she noticed the beat-up door on the Ford Taurus next to her. Pulling back out, she inched closer to the cinder block wall, then turned off the car, unhooked her seat belt, and grabbed her purse from beneath her seat.

Ignoring the trembling in her hands, she pulled out the tube of lip gloss she'd purchased at a drugstore in Oklahoma City. But it was harder to ignore the apprehensive blue eyes that stared back at her from the tiny lit mirror on the visor. Harder, but not impossible. She liberally coated her lips with the glistening fuchsia of Passion Fruit, a color that didn't match her plain brown turtleneck or her conservative beige pants. Or even the bright red high heels she'd gotten at a Payless ShoeSource in Amarillo when she'd stopped for lunch.

A strong gust of warm wind whipped the curls around Faith's face as she stepped out of the car. She brushed back her hair and glanced up. Only a few wispy clouds marred the deep blue of the September sky. Still, it might be a good idea to get her jacket from the suitcase in the trunk, just in case it got colder when the sun went down. Of course, she didn't plan on staying at the bar past dark.

In fact, she didn't plan on staying at the bar at all. Just long enough to get some answers.

After closing the door, she pushed the button on her keychain twice until the Volvo beeped. Then, a few feet away, she pushed it again just to be sure. One of her fellow computer programmers said she had OCD—Overly Cautious Disorder. Her coworker was probably right. Although there was nothing cautious about walking into a bar filled with men who paraded their egomaniacal thoughts on the bumpers of their trucks. But she didn't have a choice. At seven o'clock on a Saturday night, this was the only place she'd found open in the small town.

As Faith walked past the truck parked by the door, she couldn't help but stare. Up close it looked bigger...and much dirtier. Mud clung to the huge, deep-treaded tires, hung like stalactites from the fender wells, splattered over the faded red paint and blotchy gray primer of the door, and flecked the side window. A window her head barely reached. And in the heels, she was a good five-foot-five inches. Well, maybe not five inches. Maybe closer to four. But it was still mind-boggling that a vehicle could be jacked up to such heights.

What kind of a brute owned it, anyway? Obviously, the kind who thought it went with his large penis. The kind who didn't think it was overkill to have not one, but two huge flags (one American and the other who knew) hanging limply from poles on either side of the back window. A back window that displayed a decal of a little cartoon boy peeing on the Toyota symbol, two blue-starred football helmet stickers, and a gun rack with one empty slot.

Faith froze.

On second thought, maybe she wouldn't ask questions

at this bar. Maybe she would drive down the main street again and try to find some other place open. Someplace that didn't serve alcohol to armed patrons. Someplace where she wouldn't end up Rebel Dead. Not that she was even close to being a rebel. Standing in the parking lot of Bootlegger's Bar in Bramble, Texas, was the most rebellious thing she'd ever done in her life. If she had a bumper sticker, it would read: CONFORMIST BORN, CONFORMIST BRED, AND WHEN SHE DIES SHE'LL BE CONFORMIST DEAD. But she just didn't want to be Conformist Dead yet.

Unfortunately, before she could get back to the leather-upholstered security of her Volvo, the battered door of the bar opened and two men walked out. Not walked, exactly. More like strutted—in wide felt cowboy hats and tight jeans with large silver belt buckles as big as brunch plates.

Faith ducked back behind the monster truck, hoping they'd walk past without noticing her. Except the sidewalk was as uneven as the parking lot and one pointy toe of her high heel got caught in a crack, forcing her to grab on to the tailgate or end up with her nose planted in the pavement. And as soon as her fingers hit the cold metal, an alarm went off—a loud howling that raised the hairs on her arms and had her stumbling back, praying that at least one of the men was packing so he could shoot the thing that had just risen up from the bed of the truck.

"For cryin' out loud, Buster. Shut up." One of the men shouted over the earsplitting noise.

The howling stopped as quickly as it had started. Shaken, Faith could only stare at the large, four-legged creature. With its mouth closed, the dog didn't look threatening as much as . . . cute. Soulful brown eyes looked back at her from a woolly face. While she recovered from her scare, it ambled over to the end of the truck and leaned its head out.

Faith stepped back. She wasn't good with dogs. Or cats, gerbils, birds, hamsters, or fish. Pretty much anything living. She had a rabbit once, but after only three months in her care, it died of a nervous condition.

"Hope?"

The name spoken by the tall, lean cowboy with the warm coffee-colored skin caused her stomach to drop, and she swiveled around to look behind her.

No one was there.

"Baby, is that you?" The man's Texas twang was so thick that it seemed contrived.

Faith started to shake her head, but he let out a whoop and had her in his arms before she could accomplish it. She was whirled around in a circle against his wiry body before he tossed her over to his friend, who had a soft belly and a chest wide enough to land a 747.

"Welcome home, Little Bit." The large man gave her a rough smack on the lips, the whiskers of his mustache and goatee tickling. He pulled back, and his blue eyes narrowed. "What the hell did you do to your hair?"

"She cut it, you idiot." With a contagious grin, the lean cowboy reached out and ruffled her hair. "That's what all them Hollywood types do. Cut off their crownin' glory like it's nothin' more than tangled fishin' line." He cocked his head. "But I guess it don't look so bad. It's kinda cute in a short, ugly kinda way. And I like the color. What's that called—streakin'?"

The man who still held her in his viselike grip grinned, tobacco juice seeping from the corner of his mouth. "No, Kenny, that's what we did senior year."

"Right." Kenny's dark eyes twinkled. "But it's like streakin'. Tintin'? Stripin'? Highlightin'! That's it!" He whacked her on the back so hard she wondered if he'd cracked a rib. "Shirlene did that. But it don't look as good as yours. She looked a little like a polecat when it was all said and done. Does she know you're back? Hot damn, she's gonna shit a brick when she sees you. She's missed you a lot."

His eyes lost some of their twinkle. "Of course, we all have. But especially Slate." He grabbed her arm and tugged her toward the door. "I can't wait to see his face when he sees you. Of course, he ain't real happy right now. The Dawgs lost last night—twenty-one to seven—but I'm sure you'll put an end to his depression."

Faith barely listened to the man's constant chatter as he dragged her through the door and into the dark, smoky depths of the bar. She felt light-headed, and emotion crept up the back of her throat. Did they really look so much alike that these men couldn't tell the difference? It made sense, but it was still hard to absorb. All this time, she thought she was an only child and to realize...

"Here." Kenny slapped his black cowboy hat down on her head and tipped it forward. "We don't want to start a stampede until Slate gets to see you. Not that anyone would recognize you in that getup." He shook his head as his gaze slid down her body to the tips of her high heels. "Please don't tell me you got rid of your boots, Hope. Gettin' rid of all that gorgeous hair's bad enough."

Faith opened her mouth with every intention of telling him she never owned a pair of western boots to get rid of, or had long gorgeous hair, for that matter. But before she could, he tucked her under his arm and dragged her past the long bar and around the crowded dance floor with his friend following obediently behind.

"So how's Hollywood treatin' ya?" Kenny yelled over the loud country music, then waved a hand at a group of women who called out his name. "It's been way too long since you came for a visit. But I bet you've been busy knockin' them Hollywood directors on their butts. Nobody can act like our little Hope. You flat killed me when you was Annie in *Annie Get Your Gun*. Of course, you did almost kill Colt—not that I blame you since he was the one who switched out that blank with live ammo. But the crowd sure went crazy when you shot out them stage lights. I still get chills just thinkin' about it."

Chills ran through Faith's body as well. Hollywood? Actor? Live ammo? Her mind whirled with the information she'd received in such a short span of time.

"Yep, things sure ain't been the same without you. I can barely go into Josephine's Diner without gettin' all misty-eyed. 'Course those onions Josie fries up will do that to a person. Still, nobody serves up chicken-fried steak as pretty as you did. Rachel Dean is a nice old gal, but them man hands of hers can sure kill an appetite."

Kenny glanced down at her, then stopped so suddenly his friend ran into him from behind. From beneath the wide brim of her hat, she watched his dark brows slide together.

"Hey, what's the matter with you, anyway? How come you're lettin' me haul you around without cussin' me up one side and down the other?"

Probably because Faith didn't cuss—up one side *or* down the other. And because she wasn't a pretty waitress who was brave enough to get on stage and perform in

14   Katie Lane

front of a crowd of people. Or move away from the famil-
iarity of home for the bright lights of Hollywood.

Hollywood.

Hope was in Hollywood.

For a second, Faith felt an overwhelming surge of disappointment, but it was quickly followed by the realization that all the hundreds of miles traveled had not been
in vain. This was where Hope had grown up. And where
Faith would find answers to some of the questions that
had plagued her for the last year.

Except once Kenny found out she wasn't Hope, she
probably wouldn't get any more answers. She'd probably
be tossed out of the bar without even a "y'all come back
now, ya hear." She'd become a stranger. An uppity east-
erner with a weird accent, chopped-off ugly hair, and not
one pair of cowboy boots to her name. A person who was
as far from the popular Hometown Hope he'd described
as Faith's Volvo was from the redneck's truck.

But what choice did she have? She had never been
good at lying. Besides, once she opened her mouth, the
truth would be out. Unless...unless she didn't open her
mouth. Unless she kept her mouth shut and let everyone
assume what they would. It wouldn't be a lie exactly, more
of a fib. And fibs were okay, as long as they didn't hurt
anyone. And who could possibly get hurt if she allowed
these people to think she was someone else for just a little
while longer?

Hope wasn't there.

And Faith wouldn't be, either, after tonight.

Swallowing down the last of her reservations, she
tapped her throat and mouthed, "Laryngitis."

Those deep eyes grew more puzzled. "Huh?"

"My throat," she croaked in barely a whisper.

His brows lifted. "Oh! Your throat's hoarse. Well, that explains it." He gathered her back against his side and started moving again. "For a second, I thought I had someone else in my arms besides Miss Hog Caller of Haskins County five years runnin'." He chuckled deep in his chest. "'Course, Slate's gonna love this. He always said you talked too much."

"Hey, Kenny! What ya got there?" A skinny man stepped off the dance floor with a young woman in a tight T-shirt with the words "Keepin' It Country" stretched across her large breasts and an even tighter pair of jeans that pushed up a roll of white flesh over her tooled leather belt.

"None of your damned beeswax, Fletch." Kenny winked at the young woman. "Hey, Twyla."

She scowled. "I thought you was goin' home, Kenny Gene."

"I was, darlin', but I have to take care of something first."

"I got eyes, Kenny. And if this is the somethin' you need to take care of, then don't be callin' me to go to the homecomin' game with you. I got other plans."

"Now don't be gettin' all bent out of shape, honey," Kenny yelled at the woman's retreating back. "Man, that gal's got a temper," he chuckled. "Almost as bad as yours."

Faith didn't have a temper. At least not one anyone had witnessed.

"Now don't go and ruin the surprise, Hope. Let me do all the talkin'." He shot her a weak grin. "Sorry, I forgot about your voice. Man, is Slate gonna be surprised."

For the first time since allowing this man to take

charge of her life, Faith started to get worried. Surprises weren't always well received. Her mother had dropped a surprise a few months before she passed away, a surprise Faith was still trying to recover from.

But this was different. It sounded like this Slate and Hope had been good friends. He would probably whoop like Kenny had done, give her a big hug and possibly a little more razor burn—and hopefully a lot more information before she made her excuses and slipped out the door.

And no one would be the wiser. Except maybe Hope, if she came home before Faith found her. But that wouldn't happen. Faith had every intention of finding Hope as soon as possible. She might not be a rebel, but she was tenacious.

Tenacious but more than a little scared when Kenny pulled her inside a room with two pool tables, a gaggle of cowboy hats, and a sea of blue denim. The light in the room was better but the smoke thicker. The music softer but the conversation louder. They hesitated by the door for a few seconds as Kenny looked around; then Faith was hauled across the room to the far table where a man in a crumpled straw cowboy hat had just leaned over to take a shot.

Faith had barely taken note of the strong hand and lean forearm that stretched out of the rolled-up sleeve of the blue western shirt before Kenny whipped the hat off her head and pushed her forward.

"Lookie what the cat drug in, Slate!"

The loud conversation came to a dead halt, along with Faith's breath as every eye turned to her. But she wasn't overly concerned with the other occupants of the room. Only with the man who lifted his head, then froze with his fingers steepled over the skinny end of the pool cue. He remained that way for what seemed like hours. Or what seemed like hours to a woman whose knees had suddenly turned as limp as her hat hair.

Someone coughed, and slowly, he lifted his hand from the table and unfolded his body.

He was tall. At least, he looked tall to a woman who wasn't over five foot four in heels. His chest wasn't big enough to land a 747 on but it looked solid enough to hold up a weak-kneed woman. It tapered down to smooth flat cotton tucked into a leather belt minus the huge buckle. His jeans weren't tight or pressed with a long crease like most of the men in the room; instead the soft well-worn denim molded to his body, defining his long legs, muscular thighs, and slim hips.

The hand that wasn't holding the cue stick lifted to push the misshaped sweat-stained cowboy hat back on his high forehead, and a pair of hazel eyes stared back at her—a mixture of rich browns and deep greens. The eyes sat above a long, slim nose that boasted a tiny white scar across the bridge and a mouth that was almost too perfect to belong to a man. It wasn't too wide or too small, the top lip peaking nicely over the full bottom.

The corners hitched up in a smile.

"Hog?"

Hog?

Her mind was still trying to deal with the raw sensuality of the man who stood before her; there was no way it could deal with the whole "hog" thing. Especially when the man leaned his pool cue against the edge of the table and took a step toward her.

She prepared herself for the loud whoop and the rough

manhandling that would follow. But what she was not pre-pared for was the gentleness of the fingers that slid through her hair, or the coiled strength of the hand that pulled her closer, or the heat of the body that pressed up against hers. And she was definitely not prepared for the soft lips that swooped down to bestow a kiss.

It wasn't a long kiss or even a deep one. It was merely a touch. A teasing brush. A sweep of sweet, moist flesh against startled gloss. But it was enough. Enough to cause Faith's heart to bang against her ribs and her breath to leave her lungs.

Wow.

Her hands came up and pressed against the hard wall of his chest in an effort to balance her suddenly tipsy world. Her eyelids, which she hadn't even realized she'd closed, fluttered open. Unlike her, he didn't look passion-drugged. Just cocky and confident.

"Don't tell me I left you speechless, darlin'." The words drizzled off his tongue like honey off a spoon, with very little twang and a whole lot of southern sizzle.

She swallowed hard as Kenny spoke.

"She can't talk. She's got that there lar-in-gitis, prob-ably from all that actin' she's been doin'."

A smirk a mile wide spread across Slate's devastating, handsome face. "Is that so? Well now, ain't that an inter-esting state of affairs."

"Who cares if she can talk, Coach." A man behind him yelled. "You call that a welcome-home kiss?"

Two other men joined in.

"Yeah, Slate, I kiss my cousin better than that."

"That's 'cause you're married to her."

"And you got a problem with that?"

"Shut up, you two," Kenny said. "Come on, Slate, remind her of what she's been missin' out on. Give her the good stuff."

A look of resignation entered those hazel eyes, a strange bedfellow for the dazzling grin. "Sorry, Hog," he whispered, right before he dipped his head for another taste. Except, this time, his lips were slightly parted, and the soft kiss brought with it the promise of wet heat.

If it hadn't been a year since she'd been kissed, she probably could've ignored the tremor that raced through her body and the zing that almost incinerated her panties. But it had been a year, a year filled with loss, pain, and revelation. A year that made a cautious conformist want to be something different. Something more like an arrogant rebel, Miss Hog Caller of Haskins County, or Annie Oakley with a loaded gun.

Or just a woman who gave a handsome cowboy a kiss he wouldn't forget anytime soon.

With a moan, she threw her arms around his neck, knocking off his cowboy hat and forcing him to stumble back a step. A chorus of whoops and whistles erupted, but didn't faze her one-track mind. Not when his lips opened wider, offering up all the good stuff. Teetering on the tiptoes of her high heels, she drove her fingers up into the silky waves of his hair, encasing his head and angling it so she had better access to the wet heat of his mouth. She dipped her tongue inside and sipped and tasted. But it still wasn't enough.

She wanted to consume this man. Wanted to slide her fingers over every square inch of fevered skin and sculptured muscles. Wanted to press her nose into the spot between his neck and shoulder and fill her lungs to capacity with the smoky laundry-detergent scent of him. But most of all, she wanted to stare into the rich fertile earth and endless sea of his eyes and see a reflection of her own desires—her own wants and needs.

Slowly, her eyes drifted open.

But it wasn't desire she saw in the hazel depths. And it wasn't cocky satisfaction. This time, it looked more like stunned disbelief. Obviously, Slate's relationship with Hope didn't involve sexual assault.

Stunned by her uncharacteristic behavior, Faith pulled away from his lips and dropped back down to her heels. What had she been thinking? Had she lost her mind? How could she throw herself at a complete stranger? And not just any complete stranger, but Hope's close friend? Her gaze settled on those perfect lips—lips that were slightly parted, wet, and smeared with glittery Passion Fruit—and it became crystal clear why she had lost her mind. The man was beyond hot. He was one sizzling stick of yummy, and she was a deprived child with a sweet tooth.

"Thatta way, Hope," a man on the other side of the pool table yelled. "You can take the girl out of the country but you can't take the country out of the girl!"

"Ooooo—wee, Coach! It looks like you was missed," someone else joined in.

"Does this mean you're stayin', Little Bit?" Kenny's friend stepped closer.

"Stayin'?" A voice came from the back. "With enthusiasm like that, I wouldn't let that woman out of my sight!"

"Is that true, Slate?" Kenny asked. "You gonna let Hope go back to Hollywood after that kind of greetin'?"

Slate blinked. Once. Twice. Three times. Slowly, the

shock receded from his eyes, but his shoulders remained tense. He cleared his throat twice before he spoke, but it still didn't sound as smooth or confident as it had.

"Well, I guess that depends."

"Depends on what?" someone asked.

"On whether or not she still likes me after she finds out I let The Plainsville Panthers whup our butts."

The room erupted in laughter, followed quickly with grumbled comments about hometown refs. Then a man with a huge belly and an even bigger handlebar mustache pushed his way over.

"All right, you've had your turn, Slate. Give someone else a chance to welcome our girl home."

For a fraction of a second, those hazel eyes narrowed, and the hands at her waist tightened. But then he released her and she was passed from one big bear hug to the next, accompanied with the greeting "Welcome home, Hope."

She wasn't Hope.

But, strangely enough, it felt like home.

Chapter Two

SLATE CALHOUN SAT BACK IN THE DARK CORNER and watched the woman in the conservative pants and brown sweater take another sip of her beer as if it was teatime at Buckingham Palace. Hell, she even held her little pinkie out. If that was Hope Scroggs, then he was Prince Charles. And he was no pansy prince.

Still, the resemblance was uncanny.

The impostor swallowed and wrinkled up her cute little nose. A nose that was the exact duplicate of Hope's. And so were the brows that slanted over those big blue eyes and the high cheekbones and that damned full-lipped mouth. A mouth that had fried his brain like a slice of his aunt's green tomatoes splattering in hot bacon grease.

The kiss was the kicker. Slate never forgot a kiss. Never. And the few kisses he'd shared with Hope hadn't come close to the kiss he'd shared with this woman. Hope's kisses had always left him with a strange uncomfortable feeling; like he'd just kissed his sister. It had never left him feeling like he wanted to strip her naked and devour her petite body like a contestant in a pie-eating contest.

But if the woman wasn't Hope, then who the hell was she?

He'd heard of people having doubles—people who weren't related to you but looked a lot like you. He'd even seen a man once who could pass for George W. in just the right lighting. But this woman was way past a double. She was more like an identical twin. And since he'd known Hope's family ever since he was thirteen, he had to rule out the entire twin thing. Hope had two younger sisters and a younger brother. And not one of them was a look-alike whose kisses set your hair on fire.

The woman laughed at something Kenny said, and her head tipped back, her entire face lighting up. He'd seen that laugh before, witnessed it all through high school and off and on for years after. Hell, maybe she *was* Hope. Maybe his lips had played a trick on him. Maybe he was so upset about losing last night's game that he wasn't thinking straight. Or maybe, it being a year since her last visit, he was so happy to see her that he read something in the kiss that wasn't there.

It was possible. He'd been under a lot of stress lately. Football season could do crazy things to a man's mind. Especially football season in West Texas. Which was why he had planned a two-week Mexican vacation after the season was over. Just the thought of soft rolling waves, warm sand, and cool ocean breezes made the tension leave his neck and shoulders.

What it didn't do was change his mind about the woman who sat on top of the bar with her legs crossed—showing off those sexy red high heels. Hope didn't cross her legs like that. And she hated high heels. She also hated going to the beauty salon, which was why her long brown hair was down to her butt. This woman's hair was styled in a short layered cut that made her eyes look twice as big and was highlighted the color of Jack Daniels in a fancy crystal glass.

Of course, Hope had lived in Hollywood for five long years. Maxine Truly had gone to Houston for only two years and had come back with multiple piercings and a tattoo of a butterfly on her ass. So big cities could screw you over. He just didn't believe they could change someone from an outspoken extrovert to an introvert who hadn't spoken a word, or even tried to, in the last hour.

Laryngitis, my ass.

That couldn't be Hope.

But there was only one way to find out.

Pushing up from his chair, he strolled around the tables to the spot where her adoring fan club had gathered. It didn't take much to part the sea of people. Hope might be the hometown sweetheart, but he was the hometown football hero turned high school coach. In Bramble, that was as close as a person could get to being God.

As usual, Kenny Gene was talking to beat the band. Sitting on the bar stool next to her, he was monopolizing the conversation with one of his exaggerated stories.

"...I'm not kiddin', the man blew a hole the size of a six-year-old razorback hog in the side of Deeder's double-wide, then took his time hoppin' back in his truck as if he had all day to do—hey, Slate."

Slate stopped just shy of those pointy-toed shoes and trim little ankles. Slowly, he let his gaze slide up the pressed pants, up the brown sweater that hugged the tiny waist and small breasts, over the stubborn chin and the full mouth that still held a tiny trace of pink glittery gloss, to those sky blue eyes that widened just enough to make him realize he hadn't made a mistake.

The woman before him wasn't Hope.

But he was willing to play along until he found out who she was.

"Kenny, what the heck are you doing letting Hope drink beer?" He pried the bottle from her death grip as he yelled at the bartender. "Manny, bring me a bottle of Hope's favorite and a couple of glasses." He smiled and winked at her. "If we're going to celebrate your home-comin', darlin', then we need to do it right."

"I wanted to order Cuervo, Slate," Kenny defended himself. "But she didn't want it."

"Not want your favorite tequila, Hog?" He leaned closer. "Now why would that be, I wonder?"

Before she could do more than blink, Manny slapped down the bottle of Jose Cuervo and two shot glasses, followed quickly by a salt shaker and a plastic cup of lime wedges. He started to pour the tequila but Slate shook his head.

"Thanks, Manny, but I'll get it." Slate took off his hat and tossed it down. Stepping closer, he sandwiched those prim-and-proper crossed legs between his stomach and the bar as he picked up the bottle and splashed some tequila in each glass—a very little in his and much more in the impostor's. He handed her the salt shaker. "Now you remember how this works, don't you, sweetheart?"

"'Course she knows how it works, Slate," Twyla piped in. "She's been in Hollywood, not on the moon."

Slate didn't turn to acknowledge the statement. He remained pressed against her calf, the toe of her shoe teasing the inseam of his jeans and mere inches from his man jewels. His body acknowledged her close proximity but he ignored the tightening in his crotch and continued to watch those fearful baby blues as they looked at the salt shaker, then back at him.

"Here." He took the shaker from her. "Let me refresh your memory, Hog."

Reaching out, he captured her hand. It was soft and fragile and trembled like a tiny white rabbit caught in a snare. He flipped it over and ran his thumb across the silky satin of her wrist, testing the strum of her pulse. As he bent his head, the scent of peaches wafted up from her skin, filling his lungs with light-headed sweetness and his mind with images of juicy ripe fruit waiting to be plucked.

Easy, boy. Keep your eye on the goal line.

With his gaze pinned to hers, he kissed her wrist, his tongue sweeping along the pulse point until her skin was wet and her pupils dilated. Then he pulled back and salted the damp spot he'd left.

"Now watch, darlin'." He sipped the salt off, downed the shot, then grabbed a lime and sucked out the juice— all without releasing her hand. "Now you try. Lick, slam, suck. It's easy."

She just sat there, her eyes dazed and confused. He knew how she felt; he felt pretty confused himself. His lips still tingled from touching her skin, and his heart had picked up the erratic rhythm of hers.

"Go on, Hope," Kenny prodded. "What's the matter with you? Don't tell me you forgot how to drink in Hollywood?"

That seemed to snap her out of it, and before Slate could blink, she licked off the salt, slammed the shot, and had the lime in her mouth.

A cheer rose up, but it was nothing to what rose up beneath Slate's fly. The sight of those pink-glitter lips sucking the lime dry made his knees weak. And so did the triumphant smile that crinkled the corners of her eyes as she pulled the lime from her mouth. A mouth with full lips like Hope's but with straight even front teeth. Not a slightly crooked incisor in sight.

Relief surged through him. The hard evidence proved he wasn't loco. It also proved his libido wasn't on the fritz. He wasn't hot after one of his closest friends; he was hot after this woman. This woman who was not Hope… unless she'd gotten some dental work done like they used to do on *Extreme Makeover*.

He mentally shook himself. No, she wasn't Hope. And if it took the entire bottle of tequila to get her to 'fess up, so be it.

He poured her another shot and had her salted and ready to go before she could blink those innocent eyes. "Bottoms up."

She complied, demonstrating the lick-slam-suck without a flaw. She grinned broadly when the crowd cheered, but she didn't utter a peep. Not even after the next shot. Damn, maybe she was Hope; she was just as mule-headed. And could hold her liquor just as well—although she did seem a little happier.

"Do a Nasty Shot," Sue Ellen hollered loud enough to rattle the glasses behind the bar.

Slate started to decline, but then figured it might be just the thing to get to the truth. Besides, he'd always been a crowd pleaser.

"You wanna do a Nasty Shot, Hog?" he asked.

She nodded, all sparkly-eyed.

For a second, he wondered if it was a good idea. She'd almost set him on fire the last time she kissed him. Of course, that was when he thought she was his close friend and her enthusiasm had taken him by surprise. Now he knew she was a fraud. A sexy fraud, but a fraud nonetheless. Knowing that, he wouldn't let things get out of control. He would get just aggressive enough to scare her into speaking up.

"Okay." Slate lifted her wrist and kissed it, this time sucking her skin into his mouth and giving it a gentle swirl with his tongue. Her eyes fluttered shut, and her breasts beneath the soft sweater rose and fell with quick little breaths.

The man muscle beneath the worn denim of his jeans flexed.

This was definitely a bad idea.

Unfortunately, with the entire town watching, he couldn't back out.

Lifting his head, Slate cleared his throat. "Remember how this works?" He covered the wet spot with salt. "Same premise, but this time we lick and shoot at the same time. Just leave the sucking part to me. Here." He uncrossed her legs and stepped between them, which prompted a few sly chuckles from the men. "For this, we need to get just a tad bit closer."

Those long dark lashes fluttered, and her thighs tightened around him. Slate's breath lunged somewhere between heaven and hell, and his hand shook as he poured a full shot for her and a little for himself.

"Okay, darlin'." Luckily, he sounded more in control than he felt. "You ready?" He dipped his head and pressed his mouth to her skin.

She hesitated for just a second before she followed. The silky strands of her hair brushed his cheek as her lips opened and her tongue slipped out to gather the salt, only millimeters from his. Even though they didn't touch, an electric current of energy arced between them so powerfully that it caused them both to jerk back. Those big baby blues stared back at him, tiny granules of salt clinging to her bottom lip.

His mind went blank.

"Tequila, Coach," Rossie Owens, who owned the bar, yelled.

Snapping out of it, he straightened and grabbed up the full shot, then downed it in an attempt to beat back the rearing head of his libido. She followed more slowly, her wide, confused eyes pinned on him.

"The lime, Slate," Kenny laughed. "You forgot the lime."

Hell. He jerked up the lime and sucked out the tart juice, not at all sure he was ready to go through with it. But then people started cheering him on, just like they had in high school when they wanted him to throw a touchdown pass. And, just like back then, he complied and reached up to hold her chin between his thumb and forefinger as he lowered his lips to hers.

It wasn't a big deal. Slate had kissed a lot of girls in his life. Including one whose eyes were the deep blue of the ocean as it waits to wash up on a Mexican shore. Except he hadn't noticed that about Hope. Hope's eyes were always just blue. Yet this woman's eyes caused a horde of descriptive images to parade through his mind. All of them vivid...and sappy as hell.

Luckily, when he placed his lips on hers all the images

disappeared. Unluckily, now all he could do was feel. The startled intake of breath. The hesitant tremble. The sweet pillowy warmth.

"Suck!" someone yelled.

Her lips startled open, and moist heat surrounded him. Shit, he was in trouble. He parted his lips, hoping that once he did, she would pull back and start talking. But that's not what happened. Instead, she angled her head and opened her mouth wider, then proceeded to kiss him deep enough to suck every last trace of lime from his mouth, along with every thought in his mind. Except for one: how to get inside her conservative beige pants.

Slate pulled his head back. Get in her pants? Get in *whose* pants? He didn't know who the hell the woman was. And even if he did know, he sure wasn't going to get in her pants in front of the entire town. He liked to please people, but not that much.

Ignoring the moist lips and desire-filled eyes, Slate dropped his hand from her chin and lifted her down from the bar. When he turned around, the room was filled with knowing grins. He thought about explaining things. But if he'd learned anything over the years he'd lived in Bramble, it was that when small-town folks got something in their heads, it was hard to shake it. Even if it was totally wrong. Which was why he didn't even make the effort. He just grabbed his hat off the bar as he slipped a hand to the petite woman's waist and herded her toward the door.

It wasn't as difficult as he thought it would be. Which was just one more reason he knew the woman wasn't Hope. Hope was too damned controlling to let anyone herd her anywhere. Just one of the things he didn't particularly miss.

Once they were outside, Slate guided her a little ways from the door before he pulled her around to face him.

"Okay. Just who the hell are you?"

Her gaze flashed up to his just as Cindy Lynn came out the door.

"Hey, Hope. I was wonderin' if you could come to the homecomin' decoratin' committee meetin' on Monday afternoon. I know decorations aren't your thing, but everybody would love to hear about Hollywood. Have you met Matthew McConaughey yet? One of my cousins on my father's side went to college with him in Austin and—"

"Hey, Cindy." Slate pushed the annoyance down and grinned at the woman who, on more than one occasion, had trouble remembering she was married. "I know you're probably just busting at the seams to talk with Hope about all them movie stars, but I was wondering if you could do that later, seeing as how me and Hope have got some catching up to do."

"I'm sure you do." She smirked as she turned and wiggled back inside.

Realizing Cindy Lynn would be only one of many interruptions, Slate slapped his hat on his head and took the woman's hand. "Come on. We're taking a ride."

She allowed him to pull her along until they reached the truck parked by the door. "This is your truck?"

Slate whirled around and stared at the woman who sounded exactly like Hope—except with a really weird accent. He watched as those blue eyes widened right before her hand flew up to cover her mouth.

The hard evidence of her betrayal caused his temper—that he worked so hard at controlling—to rear its ugly head, and he dropped her hand and jerked open the door of the truck. "Get in."

She swallowed hard and shook her head. "I'd rather not."

"So I guess you'd rather stay here and find out how upset these folks get when I inform them that you've been playing them for fools."

She cast a fearful glance back over her shoulder. "I'm not playing anyone for a fool. I just wanted some answers."

"Good. Because that's exactly what I want." Slate pointed to the long bench seat of the truck. "Get in."

The sun had slipped close to the horizon, the last rays turning the sky—and the streaks in her hair—a deep red. She looked small standing so close to the large truck. Small and vulnerable. The image did what the Mexican daydreams couldn't.

He released his breath. "Look, I'm not going to hurt you, but I'm not going to let you leave without finding out why you're impersonating a close friend of mine. So you can either tell me, or Sheriff Winslow."

It was a lame threat. The only thing Sheriff Winslow was any good at was bringing his patrol car to the games and turning on his siren and flashing lights when the Bull-dogs scored a touchdown. But this woman didn't know that. Still, she didn't seem to be in any hurry to follow his orders, either.

"My car is parked over there," she said, pointing. "I'll meet you somewhere."

"Not a chance. I wouldn't trust you as far as little Dusty Ray can spit."

She crossed her arms. "Well, I'm not going anyplace with a complete stranger."

"Funny, but that didn't stop you from almost giving me a tonsillectomy," he said. A blush darkened her pale skin. The shy behavior was so unlike Hope that he almost smiled. Almost. She still needed to do some explaining. "So since we've established that we're well past the stranger stage, it shouldn't be a problem for you to take a ride with me."

"I'm sorry, but I really couldn't go—"

Kenny charged out the door with the rest of the town hot on his heels.

"Hey." He held out a purse, if that's what you could call the huge brown leather bag. "Hope forgot her purse."

Slate's gaze ran over the crowd that circled around. "And I guess everyone needed to come with you to give... Hope her purse."

"We just wanted to see how things were goin'." Tyler Jones, who owned the gas station, stepped up.

"And say good-bye to Hope," Miguel, the postmaster, piped in.

There was a chorus of good-byes along with a multitude of invitations to supper.

Then someone finally yelled what everyone else wanted to. "So what are you gonna do with Hope now, Coach?"

What he wanted to do was climb up in the truck and haul ass out of there. To go home and watch game film— or better yet, pop in a Kenny Chesney CD and peruse the Internet for pictures of Mexican hot spots. Anything to forget he'd ever met the woman, or tasted her skin, or kissed her soft lips, or stared into her blue eyes. Blue eyes that turned misty as she looked at the smiling faces surrounding them.

It was that watery, needy look that was the deciding factor.

"Well, I guess I'm going to do what I should've done years ago." He leaned down and hefted her over one shoulder. She squealed and struggled as the crowd swarmed around them. Then he flipped her up in the seat and climbed in after her.

"What's that?" Ms. Murphy, the librarian, asked as she handed him a red high heel through the open window.

After tossing it to the floor, Slate started the engine. It rumbled so loudly he had to yell to be heard.

"Take her to bed."

The woman next to him released a gasp while poor Ms. Murphy looked like she was about to pass out. Normally, he would've apologized for his bad behavior. But normally he didn't have a beautiful impostor sitting next to him who made him angrier than losing a football game.

He popped the truck into reverse and backed out, trying his damnedest to pull up mental pictures of waving palm trees, brown-skinned beauties, and strong tequila. But they kept being erased by soft white skin, eyes as blue as a late September sky, and the smell of sun-ripened peaches.

The town of Bramble, Texas, watched as the truck rumbled over the curb and then took off down the street with the Stars and Stripes, the Lone Star flag, and Buster's ears flapping in the wind.

"Isn't that the sweetest thang?" Twyla pressed a hand to her chest. "Slate and Hope—high school sweethearts together again."

"It sure is," Kenny Gene said. "'Course, there's no tellin' how long Hope will stay."

"Yep." Rye Pickett spit out a long stream of tobacco juice. "That Hollywood sure has brainwashed her. Hell, she couldn't even remember how to drink."

"Poor Slate," Ms. Murphy tsked. "He'll have his hands full convincing her to stay and settle down."

There were murmurs of agreement before Harley Sutter, the mayor, spoke up. " 'Course, we could help him out with that."

Rossie Owens pushed back his cowboy hat. "Well, we sure could."

"Just a little help," Darla piped up. "Just enough to show Hope that all her dreams can be fulfilled right here in Bramble."

"Just enough to let love prevail," Sue Ellen agreed.

"Just enough for weddin' bells to ring," Twyla sighed.

"Yep." Harley nodded as he hitched up his pants. "Just enough."

Chapter Three

FAITH WAS IN THE REDNECK MONSTER TRUCK. A truck with huge flags fluttering and snapping in the breeze, a dog's wet nose pressed up against the back window, and the radio blaring out a song about putting a boot in someone's ass. While the arrogant rebel, who flaunted the size of his privates and had crude flowing through his veins, hung one wrist over the steering wheel, completely unconcerned that the huge tires straddled the double yellow line.

She rechecked her seat belt, then placed both hands back on the dashboard. "Would you stay on your side of the road," she tried to speak over the music. When Slate shot a glance over at her, she cleared her throat. "Please."

One hazel eye squinted beneath the brim of the beat-up straw hat before he pulled his gaze away and continued to drive down the middle of the road. She probably should demand that he turn around and take her back to Bootlegger's, but there was something about the way his muscular body slouched in the seat that stole the breath from her lungs and the words from her mouth. Besides, it wasn't like the man was an ax murderer. He was a friend of Hope's.

Unless Hope wasn't in Hollywood after all, but buried beneath this man's double-wide.

Faith glanced behind her, checking for an ax in the bed of the truck. But all she saw were empty beer cans and the dog with his sad eyes.

"I think your Labradoodle is cold."

Slate's head snapped around, and his cowboy hat shifted up with his eyebrows. "My what?" He reached over and turned down the radio.

"Your Labradoodle." Faith pointed at the back window.

His gorgeous eyes popped wide. "Buster's not a Labra—" He cut off as if he couldn't bring himself to say the word "doodle." "He's a registered bird dog."

"Are you sure? He looks just like my friend's dog that is a cross between a Labrador and a poodle."

"Poodle?" His brows knotted. "He's no poodle. He's a purebred hunting dog."

"Oh. Well, I think he's cold."

"Cold?" He snorted. "It has to be at least seventy outside."

"Then why is he staring at me?"

"Probably because he's trying to figure out just who the hell the fussy woman is parading around as his Hope."

"Fussy? I'm not fussy." Faith's teeth rattled as Slate turned up a dirt road. The truck dipped and bounced over every rut and rock, jostling the empty fast-food cups and bags that littered the floor.

"Really?" He glanced pointedly at her fingers that were white-knuckling the dash.

Afraid to let go, she only shrugged. "I'm careful, that's all."

"Careful. Fussy. Same difference. I bet you haven't even been four-wheelin' before."

"Of course, I have—" The truck bounced down in a hole, jostling her reply right out of her, and she glanced over and caught him staring down at the front of her sweater. The heavy-lidded look he sent her made her heart race and her nipples harden. To hide both, she jerked her hands off the dash and crossed her arms over her chest.

For the next few miles, neither one spoke. It was hard to speak when your insides being jarred out. Without the dash to stabilize her, Faith felt like she had back in high school gym class when she was paired with a more aggressive teenager on the trampoline... never the bouncer, always the bouncee. She glanced behind her to see how Buster was holding up.

"Ohmygod! Stop!"

Slate slammed on the brakes, and the truck's tires locked up and skidded a few feet. "What?!"

"Your dog!" She pointed at the empty window. "Your dog fell out!"

After the confusion cleared from his eyes, he shook his head. "Geez Louise." He gunned the truck, and it took off again, this time in the direction of a copse of trees—a rarity in the barren Texas landscape.

"But your dog?"

"Is fine." He tapped on the back window with his elbow, and the dog's head reappeared. "He was just lying down."

"Oh." Her face heated up.

He flashed a cocky grin. "City girl, I take it?"

Faith nodded.

"East?"

"Chicago."

"Ahh, that explains the weird accent."

Before she could argue over who had the weirdest accent, Slate whipped around a large cottonwood and a cluster of wind-ravaged elms to reveal a breathtaking sunset. Vibrant orange flamed up from the horizon to merge with the deep grays and purples of the wispy clouds while the black silhouettes of fence posts, power lines, and the large duck-headed beasts that pulled oil up from the ground stood against all that color like charcoal drawings on an acrylic painting.

"What do you call those?" Faith pointed to one of the nodding oil pumps.

"A pumpjack." He turned off the engine, and Buster let out a howling bark and flew past her window.

She started to voice her alarm, but then thought better of it. If the cute dog got eaten by some wild animal, who was she to complain? Besides, his owner didn't seem to be too concerned.

Slate unfastened his seat belt and slouched back in the corner of the truck, stretching his legs out toward her. "So who are you?"

Unable to stop herself, Faith watched as Buster bounded through the dry, thick grass, scaring up flocks of birds, before disappearing into a jagged crevice lined with bushy vegetation. She pointed a finger at the windshield.

Slate groaned. "He's fine, but you're not gonna be if you don't start talking."

She pulled her gaze away from the spot where the dog

had disappeared, but it was hard to talk when facing such raw sexuality, so instead she stared down at the round scuffed toes of Slate's brown boots.

"Faith. Faith Aldridge."

"So, Faith Aldridge, what brings you to Bramble?"

"The weather." The smart-ass reply surprised her. She had never been a smart-ass. It had to be the tequila. Yes, that explained it. The tequila had to be responsible for all her inappropriate thoughts and behavior thus far.

"You like wind, drought, hailstorms, and tornados, do ya?" He took off his hat and flipped it up on the dashboard. "Let's try this again. What brings you to Bramble?"

She would've loved to wipe the smirk off his face with some whopping good lie, but she couldn't think of one. Not even a wimpy one. Besides, she had only herself to blame for being in this predicament. If she hadn't posed as Hope, she wouldn't be stuck in a king-sized truck with a king-sized cocky cowboy.

"My sister." Just saying the words caused her stomach to flutter.

Slate's eyes widened. "Hope?"

She nodded.

Pulling his feet off the edge of the seat, he sat up. "Twins?"

"Yes."

A slow whistle escaped through his teeth. "But how? I mean, it doesn't make any sense. I've known Hope and her family for years, and I never heard anything about some long-lost twin sister."

All the bitterness she'd felt over the last few months came back in full force. It didn't make any sense to her, either. How could a mother keep that a secret? And why would she want to? A person had a right to know if they had a sister. Especially a twin sister.

"Obviously," Faith said, dryly, "her adoptive mother failed to mention it. Mine didn't say anything until she knew she was dying."

His hazel eyes grew even more surprised. "Hope's adopted?"

It was her turn to be shocked. "She doesn't know?"

He turned away, then quickly turned back again. "And you know this for a fact? Maybe your mother was mistaken."

"Mistaken?"

His gaze ran from the top of her head to the tip of her red shoes. "No. I guess not." Releasing a long rush of breath, he ran a hand over the back of his neck. "Hope's adopted—damn, this can't be good. I'd like to think she knows and has kept it a secret all these years, but Hope isn't the type to keep secrets—nor is she the type who likes surprises."

"She has the right to know," Faith stated, although she couldn't help the quaver in her voice. She had been nervous enough about showing up on her sister's doorstep unannounced; the news her sister wasn't aware she was adopted tripled her apprehension.

"Yeah, you're right," Slate said. "Though I'd hate to be the one to tell her."

Faith swallowed hard at the thought of breaking the news to a woman who brandished a gun—onstage or off. Still, she had come too far to back out now. "So do you have her address and phone number?"

"I'd love to help you out with that, darlin', but I don't have either one."

"But I thought you and Hope were good friends."

"We are." He shrugged. "We've both just been a little busy the last year."

She leaned forward, stretching out her seat belt. "A year? You haven't talked to her in a year?"

He held up a hand. "Now calm down. I haven't talked to her much, but her mama talks to her every week, and from what I hear, Hope is doing just fine."

Relieved, she relaxed back against the seat. "Oh. Well, do you think her mother would give me her information?"

Slate hooked his arms over the steering wheel and stared out the windshield. "Hell, I don't know. The Jenna Scroggs I know wouldn't mind at all, but then again, the Jenna I know wouldn't keep a secret from her daughter. But it doesn't matter, seeing as how she and Burl are in Lubbock visiting Jenna Junior and won't be back until Monday." He glanced over at her. "Unless you want to wait."

"No." Faith shook her head. "I need to find her."

Finding Hope had become a relentless need—something that pulled her through her mother's diagnosis of pancreatic cancer, the nine months of suffering, the funeral, and the quiet loneliness that filled her life afterward. Besides her aging aunt, Hope was the only family Faith had left. And she wasn't willing to live without her sister for longer than it took to reach California. Even if Hope didn't like surprises.

"So I guess that explains why you're here," Slate broke into her thoughts. "Although it doesn't explain why you were impersonating Hope."

Embarrassed by the stupid charade, Faith turned away and looked out the side window. "I thought I would get more information that way."

He snorted. "Hell, darlin', all you had to do is ask—there are no secrets in Bramble...at least, I didn't think there were." He sat back against the seat. "So without her address or phone number, how do you plan on finding her?"

It was a good question. Finding her sister in a small town in Texas was nothing compared to finding her in a huge city with millions of people.

Suddenly feeling exhausted and defeated, she slumped back in the seat. "I don't know."

He nodded as if he somehow understood her irrational behavior, then stared at the sunset for a few moments before he spoke. "I guess if you give me your number, I can call you with the information when Jenna and Burl get back."

She glanced over. "You would do that?"

"I don't see why not. Any sister of Hope is a sister of mine." He flashed that sexy smile.

Slightly dazed, she took a while to locate her gel pen and notepad in her purse. After writing down her name and number, she carefully tore off the piece of paper and handed it to him. He studied it briefly before he folded it and stuffed it in the front pocket of his shirt.

"Well...." he said. The word just hung there until Faith realized he was waiting for her to finish it.

"Oh! Yes—well, I guess you better take me back to my car." She paused. "You are planning on taking me back to my car, aren't you?"

He rolled his eyes. "No. I plan on keeping you out here at Sutter Springs all night long."

"Sutter Springs?" She looked around. "Where are the springs?"

Slate laughed. It was almost as sexy as his smile.

"Mostly dried up by the overpumping of groundwater for irrigation, but if you walk down to that arroyo"—he pointed to the spot where Buster had disappeared—"you'll find enough water to get your feet wet. Although people don't come out here for the water."

Faith leaned closer to the windshield. "Can your dog swim?"

"He's a hunting dog, for God's sake. Of course he can swim."

She turned back to him. "So what do people come out here for?" Slate shot her a suggestive look, and her face heated. "Oh."

He chuckled. "You sure get flustered easy. I don't think I ever remember Hope blushing."

Faith wasn't surprised. It seemed she and her sister had nothing in common. Still, she refused to stop searching for similar traits.

"So tell me about her."

His eyes squinted. "Hope?" When she nodded, he shrugged. "She's Hope. Sassy and controlling. Smart and funny. Determined and stubborn." He smiled and stared off as if conjuring up her image. "I've never seen a woman who loves to set goals as much as she does—she was the busiest little bee you've ever seen in high school."

"Did she go to college?"

"She was saving up to, but then Hollywood distracted her."

The sun slipped farther beneath the horizon, replacing the vibrant colors with soothing pastels. The hours spent on the road finally caught up with her, and she leaned back and rested her head against the window.

"So I guess she's a talented actress." There was a long pause, and she glanced over.

Slate slouched back against the door, his eyes crinkled in thought. "Talented? I don't know if I'd go that far. Entertaining is probably a better word."

"So she's not any good—" A mournful howl brought her head up. "Is that a coyote?"

"Nope, just Buster. He must've found something."

Faith rested her head back and tried not to think about the somethings that were wandering around in the growing dark waiting to jump through the open window.

"You really do look like her, you know."

She turned. Slate stared back at her from across the worn leather, the last sparkle of sunlight highlighting his wheat-colored hair, dusting his long lashes, and reflecting off the gold flecks in his eyes.

"I do?" she asked.

"Identical." A corner of his mouth tipped up. "Except for the hair and those." He reached over and tapped her lips with his index finger.

"My lips?"

"No, your straight teeth. Hope has a crooked one."

The thought of a crooked-toothed sister made her smile. "I had braces."

"And a scissor-happy barber." Again his hand reached out, but this time it seemed in no hurry to leave. His warm fingers brushed over her forehead and slid through the strands of her hair. "But I guess it's not so bad."

"You mean it's kinda cute in a short ugly kinda way." She made a lame attempt at Kenny's country twang.

The grin got wider, revealing a set of perfect teeth. "Something like that."

The smile faded as his hand stopped stroking and rested against the side of her neck. Through the open window came the chirps and creaks of insects as the purple of dusk settled in around them. There were at least a million questions she wanted to ask about Hope and her life here in Bramble. But with the warmth of his hand pinning her to the seat, she couldn't verbalize one. All she could do was look back at him and try to memorize each feature so she would be able to recall it on her long drive to find her sister.

The unique color of his eyes that defied description. The nose that wasn't too long or too wide. The hard angle of his smooth-shaven jaw. And the curves of his perfectly shaped lips. Lips that were soft. And warm. And gentle. The gentle part was what intrigued her. The two kisses he'd given her didn't go with his cocky strut or flagrant flags and bumper stickers.

At the thought of those kisses, a chill tiptoed down her spine, and she shivered.

"You cold?" Before she could answer, his thumb brushed over her bottom lip. "Because I was thinking..." Suddenly his lips were only inches away, his breath hot and tinged with lime and tequila. "That if you *were* cold, I might be able to warm you up."

The old Faith would've pulled away from those hot fingers and asked to be taken back to her car, but the old Faith didn't have a twin sister or a pair of red high heels or a tube of Passion Fruit lip gloss. And she would never shoot tequila or suck lime juice from a man's mouth. Or have the strong desire to find out if the bumper sticker on the back of the truck was something more than false bragging.

But the new Faith still couldn't bring herself to voice

her desires. Thankfully, Slate was aggressive enough to take matters into his own hands.

His thumb tipped her chin up as he lowered his head and touched his lips to hers. They rested there, soft as silk and slightly parted, before he took a sip. "Mmmm, you still taste like Cuervo," he breathed, before he deepened the kiss.

His tongue slipped inside her mouth, all wet and lush and wonderful. It swept along the edge of her teeth, then settled into a lazy dance that curled her toes inside her red high heels. He took his time, his skilled lips sweet, the hand cradling her chin gentle. Then just when she had turned into a limp puddle of need, he pulled back. And her eyelids fluttered open to a pair of eyes that glittered in the growing darkness.

"Faith." He said her name in a way that made her stomach feel all light and airy, as if he was trying out the word to see how it rolled from his sweet Texan tongue.

It rolled nice.

But no nicer than what followed.

With a groan, he lowered his head again. But this time, there was nothing gentle or sweet about the kiss. It was deep, and demanding. And the hand on her neck no longer rested but moved up and manipulated her head to match the angle of his. He delivered one hot kiss after the other, until she grew light-headed and dizzy. Then his fingers slipped from her hair and caressed their way down to her breast. His hand encased her, molding and shaping the aching flesh until she whimpered deep in her throat and tightened the grip she had on the front of his shirt.

A snap popped open.

Intrigued, Faith tugged harder. *Pop—pop—pop*. The

rest of the snaps came apart. Hesitantly, she slipped her hand inside the opening, trailing her fingers down the deep hollow between his rib cage, over the rippled muscles of his stomach and back up. His skin was smooth and hot, his muscles tight and hard—his textures so vibrantly male they made her tremble. She slid her hand over the well-developed swell of his pectoral, cupped its sculptured perfection, then brushed a thumb over the tiny nipple.

A deep growl rumbled up in his throat, and he jerked the shirt off his shoulders to reveal what only her touch had known—ripples of hard muscle cast in the deep blues of twilight. As her gaze clung to the exposed skin, he reached down and released her seat belt, enfolding her in his waiting arms.

"Better," Slate breathed as he settled back against the seat and pulled her onto his lap.

It seemed like an eternity since she'd been held by a man. She turned her head and burrowed into the spot where neck met collarbone, breathing in the scent of him. Smoke and soap collided with the strong foreign smells that wafted in through the open window, and unable to stop herself, she swept her tongue over his salty skin.

"Jesus, Faith." His lips brushed the top of her head as she gently sucked. "You're killin' me, darlin'."

The passion-thickened *darlin'* made her stomach flutter, and her mouth went slack as his hand skated up her thigh and two fingers slipped between her legs. She'd been sexually active with two of her boyfriends, but not one had the ability to take her from steamy to sizzling in only two strokes. This redneck seemed to know exactly what to do and where to do it. He brushed and strummed over the wool of her pants until her head dropped back on his shoulder and her breath pumped in and out of her lungs. Until her hips flexed against the hard knot of his fly and her legs dropped open in invitation.

An invitation he quickly accepted. Before a moan could work its way up her throat, her pants and panties were off, and she was lying on her back on the cool truck seat with her high heels hiked up on either side of the man who knelt between her legs. A tiny flicker of panic wiggled past the mental exhaustion and shots of tequila, but was quickly snuffed out when she lifted her gaze.

Kneeling before her, Slate was every woman's cowboy fantasy all rolled up in one: James Dean's swaggering sex appeal in *Giant*—Robert Redford's squinty-eyed toughness in *Sundance*—Brad Pitt's ripped boyish charm in *Thelma and Louise*. As an awkward adolescent who was allowed only two hours of television viewing a week, Faith had easily fallen prey to these sexy silver-screen studs and whiled away many hours fantasizing about them.

Which was probably why she was in no hurry to stop the scene that played out before her. It had all the markings of a really great daydream. This wasn't reality. At least, not any reality she'd ever experienced. So she relaxed back against the cool leather seat and allowed her gaze to slither over the well-defined shoulders, the hard sculptured chest, and the flat, lean stomach.

Tipping his slim hips forward, he reached for the button on the fly of his worn jeans. All the moisture left her mouth as the gold teeth of the zipper eased apart to reveal something that looked an awful lot like naked skin. But before she could get her mind around the fact that her sexy stud didn't wear underwear, bright lights flashed across the back window.

"Shit." Slate's head ducked down next to her.

"What? Ohmygod! Is it the cops?" Faith struggled beneath him, her legs flailing. The toe of one heel hit the steering wheel, and the horn blasted. Slate jumped up and bumped his shoulder on the gun rack at the same time that she pulled her foot back and dug her spiked heel into his side.

"Sonofabitch!"

"Sorry." She jerked her foot back, only to honk the horn again, but this time he grabbed the heel before she could pull it back and knife something a little more sensitive than his side.

Feeling completely exposed to his gaze, she struggled to sit up, but it was difficult when his body was between her legs and her foot was in his hand.

"Sit still," he ordered as he jerked her deadly shoe off and dropped it to the floor.

She flopped back down and glared up at him. He didn't look so gorgeous now. In the light from the oncoming car, he looked mean and surly.

"Sit still?" she fumed. "I'm half naked."

His gaze traveled over her lower body as he zipped and buttoned his jeans. "I can see that, but if you'll sit still a minute, nobody else will."

For some reason, she trusted him. Probably because she didn't have much of a choice. Stretching her sweater down, she made a vain attempt to cover herself as he jerked on his shirt. He left it open and slipped back over to the driver's side, pulling her legs across his lap just as the lights grew brighter. In a cacophony of rumbling engine and blaring country music, the vehicle pulled up next to them.

"Hey, Bubba!"

Slate cringed slightly before he leaned out the window. "Did you need something, Billy Ray?"

"Coach?" The boy's voice hit a high note and was followed with another boy's "shit."

"What are you boys doing out here?" Slate's deep authoritative tone surprised Faith. Probably because she'd already pegged him as a good old boy—a friendly cowboy with a killer smile who teased everyone he met. Although in the last few seconds, he hadn't been so friendly.

"Nothin', Coach. We was just gonna sit and talk."

"You know the rules during the season. Curfew's eight on the weeknights, ten on the weekends. No drinkin' and no dates. Now you get those girls home before their mamas call Sheriff Winslow, and I decide to bench you the next game."

"Right, Coach. Sorry."

The vehicle left in a shower of gravel, the music fading in the distance.

Once they were gone, the awkwardness set in.

But it was hard not to feel awkward when you were half naked, with your legs sprawled all over a man's lap. A complete stranger, no less. She tried to scramble up to a sitting position, but his hands slid up her thighs, trailing a line of fire that took her breath away.

"Hey, now." The grinning cowboy was back. "Where do you think you're going?"

"I really—" Faith squeaked and grabbed his hands in an attempt to stop the marauding fingers from getting any closer to the needy pulse between her legs. "I-I really need to get back to my car."

His fingers froze against the tops of her thighs, and

there was a long, uncomfortable silence as he stared down at her. Thankfully, it was now dark enough that she couldn't see his eyes. Those hazel peepers had some weird mind-altering effect on her.

"Excuse me?"

She swallowed. "I need to go."

He removed his hands and shifted around in the seat. "You're kidding?"

Refusing to look at him, she sat up. "Actually, no. I'm sorry, but…" She jerked her pants up from the floor and tried to locate her panties. "This was a mistake. I-I don't even know you—I mean, I know who you are, but I don't really know you…personally."

Slate reached up and unhooked her panties from the rearview mirror. "And I was about to remedy that, darlin'."

Her face heated up as she pulled the cotton panties from his hand. Now that she'd found her clothes, she couldn't bring herself to put them on. Not when he watched her every move. So instead she held them over her lap and proceeded to do what she always did when she got nervous.

Ramble.

"Yes, well…I've got this goal to find my sister, and only a few weeks to do it in, and I really can't be distracted by a good-looking cowboy who kisses really great. I need to stay focused until I find her. Then after I find her, I need to get back to my life in Chicago because with my mother's illness and the funeral and this trip, I don't think my boss is exactly thrilled by my productivity—and everyone knows how competitive technology is. And besides work, I need to sell my parents' house. And I just bought a new condo that still isn't decorated—so getting involved with someone right now would be really stupid." She turned to him. "I'm sure you can understand."

"I'm not sure I can, darlin'. But I liked the part about a good-looking cowboy who's a great kisser."

"Oh." Faith really liked that part, too, which made it hard to get the next words out. "I need for you to take me back to my car . . . please."

"That's what I was afraid of." He studied her for a few seconds more before he opened the door and the cab filled with harsh light.

She gripped her pants tighter. "What are you doing?"

"I need a little air, sweetheart." Slate lifted his eyebrows at her. "I don't exactly cool down as fast as you do."

Her gaze dropped down to the bulge in his blue jeans, then quickly back up to the smile that tipped one side of his mouth. If her face got any hotter, it would incinerate.

Faith watched as he jumped down and closed the door, then waited until his shadowy form disappeared into the darkness before she slipped on her panties and pants. She found her purse on the floor and searched through it for anything that might improve her appearance before he got back. It wasn't hard to locate her brush, or her peach-scented hand lotion, or the small square container of dental floss. But after brushing, flossing, and moisturizing, she couldn't find her tube of lip gloss.

It wasn't a big deal. Up until this afternoon, she'd never concerned herself with makeup. Just a few swipes of mascara and a neutral-colored matte lipstick would do her. But for some reason, the gloss had become more than just makeup. She wasn't sure what; all she knew was she wanted it on before Slate returned.

She had to click on the overhead light before she discovered it in one of the side pockets. Looking for a mirror to apply it with, she flipped down the visor, but all she found were two ticket stubs to an Alan Jackson concert and a condom. The condom was like a cold, hard slap of reality. She'd almost had sex with a complete stranger. A man she had known for only two hours. Three tops. A man who owned so many guns he needed a rack for them. Bragged about his penis size. And kept an extra large condom in his visor.

An arrogant redneck.

Her aunt Jillian would be horrified. And her mother was probably turning over in her grave, along with her dear old dad. And none of her friends at work would believe it.

Not Faith. Not sweet, rule-abiding Faith.

She screamed.

Not because she was so upset about what she'd done, but because Buster had returned and jumped up on the truck, his large front paws curved over the bottom edge of Slate's open window. Blood dripped from his woolly muzzle.

"What the hell?!" Slate came charging around the front of the truck with his open shirt flapping.

"It's Buster!" She jerked out the small package of disinfectant wipes she never left home without and pulled out three. "Something attacked him!" Sliding across the seat, she grabbed the dog's head and stuffed the wipes into his mouth, searching for the source of the blood so she could apply pressure. But the dog jerked his head loose and hopped down, cowering behind Slate's legs.

"For the love of Pete." Slate took the wipes out of her

hand and tossed them into the bed of the truck. "Buster didn't get attacked, he attacked something. More than likely a prairie dog."

"A prairie dog?" She looked down at Buster, who was now pawing his nose. "Do you think the prairie dog is badly hurt? Maybe we should call someone."

"Like who? The Prairie Dog Ambulance?" He walked to the back of the truck and pulled the tailgate down so Buster could hop in. By the time he jerked open the door, the grin was back.

"You're sure a worryin' little thing."

Faith slid back over to her side of the seat as he climbed inside. The awkwardness was back, so she busied herself closing the wipes container and putting it in her purse. But when he didn't start the engine, she glanced over at him.

His eyes twinkled in the overhead light. "You sure you don't want to get to know me personally?"

Nodding her head was harder than she thought it would be.

"All right then." The smile faded as he leaned forward to start the truck. "But if you're ever in Bramble again, be sure to look me up."

His words brought with them a sense of deep regret. With Hope in Hollywood, there would be no reason to return to Bramble. Which meant Faith would probably never again view the world from the high perch of a monster truck. Or do a Nasty Shot. Or watch a West Texas sunset paint the skies in vibrant shades. Or kiss a redneck with sparkling hazel eyes.

It was sad.

Chapter Four

SEXUAL ATTRACTION WAS A FUNNY THING, Slate thought as he drove back to town. He had been around Hope for close to twelve years before she moved away and not once in that time had he wanted to have sex with her. Not even the couple months they'd dated in high school. Yet here was a woman who looked exactly like Hope, and he was so sexually attracted to her, he felt like he had the time that he ran a hundred and four temperature—all shaky and disoriented.

It was the darnedest thing. And hell if he could figure it out.

Damn Billy Ray. The kid was going to run at least twenty laps for his inopportune timing.

"Are you hot?"

The softly spoken question caused him to glance over, something he'd been avoiding. It was a mistake. The lights of an oncoming semi reflected off the glitter gloss of her lips, and all he could think about was pulling over and kissing them clean. Yeah, he was hot. But Slate Calhoun had never forced himself on a woman in his life. And he certainly wouldn't start now. She'd made her choice.

Now Slate had to live with it.

"Hot?"

Faith touched the spot right below her cute little nose. "You're sweating."

After wiping the sweat off on the shoulder of his shirt, he rolled the window up and turned on the air-conditioning. But the cold air that blasted out of the vents didn't cool him down a lick. Geez Louise, he needed to get a hold on himself. There wasn't a woman alive who'd ever made him sweat like he'd just taken a big bite of a jalapeño straight off the grill. Obviously, he needed to spend less time watching game film, and looking at Mexican resorts online, and more time with women.

Willing women.

"Is it always this warm in September?" she asked.

Thankful for the distraction, Slate nodded. "Usually. Of course, tomorrow we could get a cold front and freeze our rears off. West Texas weather is pretty unpredictable."

When Faith didn't comment, he looked back over. She sat all prim and proper, with her knees together and her hands folded on her lap. It was hard to believe that this was the same woman who'd ripped apart the pearl snaps on his shirt and looked at his chest like it was a cloud of sweet cotton candy she wanted to dive into. The same woman who sprawled out on the truck seat, with those sexy red high heels riding his waist, and her hot, wet center all ready and waiting.

"Watch out!"

Slate jerked the steering wheel, coming dangerously close to taking out the WELCOME TO BRAMBLE: HOME OF THE STATE CHAMPION BULLDOGS sign. Which wouldn't have been such a bad thing. The sign was a constant reminder of his failure as a coach. Four years and he hadn't led the team to one state victory.

Pitiful.

He steered the truck back to the centerline and mumbled something about a skunk in the road. After he'd almost killed them, it was a stupid thing to say. But his mind wasn't working on full capacity. The blood needed for coherent thinking had pooled elsewhere.

He cleared his throat and tried to clear his mind. "So, darlin', you planning on leaving tonight?"

It took a moment for Faith to answer, probably because he'd scared her speechless. "I thought I'd drive until I got tired."

"If I were you, I'd get on twenty-seven, and maybe stay the night in Amarillo. That will give you a good start for the morning."

"Thank you, I might do that." She released the dashboard but kept her eyes pinned to the road. "And I was wondering if you might keep my identity a secret until I've had a chance to talk with Hope. It's just that I—"

He held up a hand. "I understand. This is between you and your sister." The smile she flashed him made his heart do a crazy little jig, and a few minutes passed before he could think clearly enough to make another stab at conversation. "So do you have any other sisters or brothers?"

"No. Do you have a big family?"

"A younger half brother and sister, but they live in North Carolina with my dad," Slate said.

Faith glanced over at him. "So your parents are divorced?"

"Since I was eleven."

"Were you born in North Carolina?" she asked.

He shook his head. "Savannah, Georgia."

"That explains the weird accent."

Her comment made the tension in his shoulders ease, and he looked over and smiled. "Yeah, I guess it does."

She smiled back at him. "So your mom moved here after the divorce?"

Slate thought about saying something clever to distract her from a conversation he really didn't want to have. But smothering the sexual desire took most of his energy, so he couldn't think up a clever retort to save his soul. It didn't matter. She was leaving Bramble and would soon forget any conversation she'd had with some hick cowboy from Texas.

"My mom didn't move here. I was the only one who came to live with my aunt and uncle." Something that felt an awful lot like pain twisted his gut. But you had to care about someone to feel pain, so he attributed the feeling to the rare hamburger he'd eaten for lunch.

"Oh." The one word held enough pity for an entire orphanage.

Slate shrugged, trying to make light of it. "I don't blame her. After my dad left, I was a pretty hard kid to handle. Of course, any kid was too hard for my mom. Mothering wasn't her thing." Men were her thing. Just one of the reasons his father had left.

"At least she kept you for a while," Faith said. "Mine gave me up at birth."

"Maybe your mother had a good reason. Maybe she thought other people would do a better job than she could. Lord knows, my aunt and uncle were better parents than my own." He glanced over. "Were your adoptive parents good people?"

"Very. They were close to fifty when they adopted me. But what they lacked in youthful energy, they made up for in love. You couldn't ask for parents more proud of their only child's accomplishments."

"And what are your accomplishments, Miss Aldridge?" he asked, hoping to bring a lighter note to the dark road their conversation had traveled down.

Faith laughed and counted out on her fingers. "Well, I walked before I was one. Was potty trained and talked in full sentences before I was two. And by three, could read simple words."

And by thirty, knew how to make a man burn.

"A real honest-to-goodness prodigy," Slate said, trying not to think about how badly he burned.

"Not really, but my parents thought so. They were academics. My father taught at the University of Chicago and so did my mother before they adopted me."

"Did you graduate from there as well?"

"Yes."

He took his eyes off the road long enough to study her. "You don't sound real happy about it."

"I'm glad I got a degree, but college was stressful."

"Because you had to live up to your parents' expectations?"

In the lights from an oncoming car, her eyes looked thoughtful. "Yes. I guess I didn't want to disappoint them."

"Expectations will do that to a person." He snorted. "I used to love football, until I started coaching it. Now it just stresses the hell out of me."

"So you're telling me there's an A-type personality beneath that easygoing smile?"

Slate looked over, and their gazes locked. "Maybe."

It was strange this connection he felt with a complete stranger. Or maybe it wasn't so strange, given that she looked exactly like a person he'd known for most of his life.

At any rate, Bootlegger's neon sign appeared much too quickly.

"We're here." Faith sounded as disappointed as he felt.

"It looks that way." As they neared the honky-tonk, he eased his foot off the accelerator. "Look, are you hungry, darlin'? Because there's this all-night truck stop that serves the best steak and egg—"

"Where's my car?"

He glanced at the empty parking lot. Where *was* her car? Hell, where were *all* the cars? It couldn't be much past ten o'clock. And nobody left Bootlegger's before eleven on a Saturday. Not even Moses Tate, who was close to a hundred. Which meant something wasn't right.

As he turned into the lot, Faith pointed a finger. "My car was parked right there by that wall."

"Don't panic," he said, although he felt a little panicky himself. "There has to be a good explanation." He reached over and jerked the glove box open and pulled out his phone: 10:24. Something was definitely wrong. He found Kenny Gene's number, and after only two rings, Kenny started in.

"Hey, Slate. What's goin' on? What happened to Hope? Did you drop her off at her house? You know Jenna don't ever lock the door, so she can get right in. You want me to come over and watch some game film with—"

"Where is everybody, and where is Faith's car?"

"Whose car?"

Shit.

"Hope's car. Where's Hope's car?"

"Sheriff Winslow impounded it."

"What?!"

"Yeah. It's all part of the town's grand plan to get you and Hope together again." He laughed. "Ain't it a doozy?"

Slate groaned and dropped his head in his hand.

"What happened?" Faith leaned closer. "It's my car, isn't it? My car got stolen. I knew I should've checked the locks again." Her eyes widened. "Or did someone hit it? That's it, isn't it? Someone ran into it in the parking lot and totaled it."

"Hey." Kenny's voice came back over the line. "Is that Hope? Put her on; I've got this great story to tell her."

Slate closed his eyes and took a deep breath, trying to pull up an image of a white sandy beach with a hammock stretched beneath two palm trees. "Look, Kenny. Hope doesn't want to hear a story. She just wants her car back. So do you think you could tell me where it is?"

"Gee, Slate, I don't know. But Sheriff Winslow probably does. So can you put Hope on—"

Slate hung up and dialed Winslow's number.

In the parking lot lights, Faith's worried blue eyes stared back at him. "So where's my car?"

He held up a finger as he waited for Winslow to pick up. "You need to give me a minute, darlin'. I'm working on it."

"Sheriff Winslow."

Slate rolled his eyes. The man was too full of himself. "Hey, Sam, it's Slate."

"Hey, Slate. Hope with ya?"

"Yes." He continued to take deep, even breaths. "And we were wondering if we could come get her car."

"Her car? I don't have her car."

Slate gritted his teeth and at the same time tried to shoot Faith a reassuring smile. "You don't?"

"No, I don't."

"Do you know who does?"

"Yes, I do."

He gripped the phone tighter. "You think you could tell me, Sam?"

"I could, but then you'd tell Hope. You never could keep a secret from her. Remember on her fifteenth birthday when we wanted to surprise her with a party and you went and ruined the surprise by—"

Slate put his hand over the receiver. "Listen, Faith, I realize you don't want a lot of people knowing who you are until you've had a chance to talk with Hope. But if you want your car back, I think we're going to have to tell Sheriff Winslow."

Those full glittery lips pressed together for a few seconds, before she nodded. "Fine. But only the sheriff."

Slate didn't have the heart to tell her that if Winslow knew, by morning the entire town would. He put the phone back to his ear and listened to the conversation that had gone on without him.

"... 'Course we were stuck with all those ceramic pigs that Sue Ellen made in ceramics class for centerpieces. Although they looked real nice at the Christmas Ball with red ribbon and holly around their little fat—"

"Sam." Slate butted in. "I need you to listen for a minute. That car isn't Hope's. It's Faith's."

"Faith? Who's Faith? Is that that little waitress from that truck stop near Odessa? The big ole gal with all that red hair?"

"No." Slate closed his eyes. "Faith is Hope's twin sister."

"Twin sister?" Sam's laughter rang out. "That's a good one, Slate. You can sure come up with 'em."

"I'm being serious, Sam."

The laughter died. "Now, Slate, I realize that Hope's puttin' all kinds of pressure on you to get her car back. But you need to be as tough with her as you are with your team. In fact, women are a lot like teenagers. They don't know what's good for them unless you show them. So take the bull by the horns, boy, and show that girl that the best thing for her is stayin' right here in Bramble and marryin' you. And tell Hope not to worry about her car because I got it in a real safe place. Although once you two get hitched, I'd be buyin' her an American-made if I was you. Vole-Vo. What the hell is that?"

The phone clicked.

There were times when Slate considered moving to a bigger town. One where people kept their nose to the grindstone instead of up their neighbor's ass. This was one of those times.

He closed the phone and slipped it in the breast pocket of his shirt as Faith's eyes remained riveted on his face.

"So where's my car?"

"Well, darlin', there seems to be a little misunderstanding." He tried to keep his voice as upbeat as possible.

Her brows lowered. "What kind of misunderstanding?"

How could he explain it when he couldn't even understand it himself? Damned small-town mentality. "It's kind of complicated, and something we really don't want to get into until we've both had a little shut-eye."

"I'm not tired. And I need to get to California."

"I'm afraid you'll have to wait until morning to leave." He reached over to pop the truck into gear but she grabbed his arm.

"Oh, no, you don't. Not until you tell me what you did with my car."

"What *I* did with your car? How could I do anything with your car when I was making out with you at Sutter Springs?"

Her face flushed a cute shade of red. "I know where you were, but that doesn't mean you aren't responsible for my car missing."

She was probably right. In a roundabout way, he was responsible. Years ago, he should've let everyone know he wasn't interested in Hope, instead of going along with the entire jilted boyfriend scenario. He just hadn't wanted to crush their dream that someday the homecoming queen would return to the football hero and they'd live happily ever after.

That and the fact that being thought of as Hope's man worked out pretty well for him. He got to enjoy his freedom and not worry about matchmaking mamas and overzealous women whose biological clocks were ticking. All the women who spent time with him knew it wasn't forever.

Not when he was saving forever for Hope.

It had seemed like only a little white lie.

Until now.

Now someone else was involved. An innocent victim who didn't deserve to be caught in the sticky web he'd helped weave. Unfortunately, he couldn't see a way out of it. Years of lying made for a pretty tangled mess. Especially when the mess included the stubborn people of Bramble. People who had spent their lifetimes believing what they wanted to, rather than the truth. Still, it was his responsibility to set them straight, and he planned to.

First thing in the morning.

"Look, darlin', your car's been towed, and there's no way you can get it back until the morning."

"Towed? But why would—" She blinked, and her hand slipped from his arm. "Because I was drinking?"

Relief washed over him. "Exactly. We have real strict drinking laws here in Texas."

She nodded, but still looked adorably confused. "Then I guess I'll need to get a hotel room for the night."

"I'm afraid there aren't any in Bramble."

"No hotels?"

He shook his head, feeling almost as good as he had when an unexpected ice storm canceled all his high school classes on the first day of finals. He didn't try to figure out why he suddenly felt so damned happy. Happiness was something to enjoy, not analyze.

With a smile tugging at his lips, he popped the truck in gear and made a big circle in the empty lot before he drove off the curb. Faith's body jostled back against the seat, and he glanced down at the jiggling dollops of her breasts.

His smile deepened.

"But where are you taking me?" she asked.

"With me, darlin'. You're coming with me."

Chapter Five

Faith woke with a start and stared in confusion at the dingy sheet that was thumbtacked over the small window. She would've remained confused for at least a few seconds more if a sloppy wet tongue hadn't slid from her chin up to her forehead.

"Yuck!" She sat up and wiped the back of her hand across her face.

"Now, sugar pie." A honey-drizzled voice came from the doorway. "He's just kissin' you good mornin'."

Her gaze snapped up, and her breath caught.

Slate stood in the doorway dressed in nothing but a pair of faded jeans with a frayed hole in one knee and what looked like blue paint on the other. The loose waistband rode low on his lean hips, displaying a curved line of pale skin that made her heart trip faster. His body didn't have the bulging muscles of the bodybuilders who worked themselves into a sweaty lather at her gym. Just smooth, defined hills and lean valleys that flexed and released as he moved around the bed.

"Good mornin'." He leaned down, and his lips did a

lazy sweep over hers. He pulled back and sent her a dazzling smile, his hair sleep-tousled and his eyes drowsy.

Everything inside her melted, completely obliterating the valid excuses she'd spent most the night coming up with. It wasn't the long trip, the pain of losing her mother, the stress of trying to locate her sister, or the three shots of tequila that had turned her from an introverted prude to an immoral slut.

It was this man.

This golden-haired redneck with his smooth southern drawl and devilish grin that had kept her up for most of the night fighting against the strong desire to strip naked and join him on the tiny plaid couch he'd too readily occupied. She'd won the battle. Except staring at the tempting piece of manhood before her, she didn't feel like much of a winner. In fact, she felt like The Biggest Loser—starved and deprived.

"Don't tell me, you've got laryngitis again, darlin'." His gaze sizzled its way down the T-shirt he'd loaned her and stopped at the words written across the front. And since it was his T-shirt she figured it wasn't the phrase *Women Want Me, Fish Fear Me* that caught his attention.

Faith tried to pull the sheet up over her breasts, but it was tucked under her leg. She tugged, and the 10-count fabric ripped.

Horrified, she stared down at the long tear. "Oh! I'm so sorry!"

Slate stared, too, but not at the ripped material as much as the bare leg it exposed. "No harm, no foul, darlin'. Bubba needed new sheets anyway."

"Bubba?" She slipped her leg farther under the sheet. "These aren't your sheets?"

His hot eyes followed the line of her leg beneath the thin material. "Nope."

She glanced around the room, its only furniture the sagging mattress and a scarred chest of drawers with the bottom drawer missing. "Just what do they pay a high school coach?"

"Not nearly enough, sweetheart." His gaze drifted up to the valley between her legs. "Not nearly enough."

Faith's breath caught as he lifted his head, and she stared into twin pools of heat. But before she could turn into the immoral slut, Buster bumped against Slate's leg and whined pitifully.

"You just went out, boy," Slate said, his eyes never leaving Faith. But the whining grew louder until he was forced to acknowledge the dog. "All right, all right." He moved toward the door in a wondrous display of lean back muscles. Glancing over one smooth, tanned shoulder, he sent her a sexy wink. "Don't go anywhere, darlin'. I'll be right back."

Once he was gone, Faith scrambled off the bed and headed for the tiny bathroom. The room was smaller than an airplane's and twice as cluttered. The edge of the sink was crammed with a can of shaving cream, a razor, a bar of Dial soap, a cup with a toothbrush and toothpaste, a bottle of Tums, a bottle of aspirin, and a half-empty bottle of Pepto-Bismol. There were rolls of toilet paper stacked on the back of the toilet and at least three towels stuffed on the rack. Towels that looked like they belonged in the garage.

Of course, Slate didn't have a garage. Or a carport. Or even a driveway.

Slate had a dirt lot.

And on the dirt lot, he had a trailer. Not a double-wide, more of a twin-wide that wasn't much bigger than a motor home without the motor. It did have tires. Last night, she'd counted at least two on the roof. It also had two bedrooms, although the other one was filled with boxes, fishing equipment, and more guns.

She used the toilet she'd cleaned with her disinfectant wipes the night before—along with the sink, floor, and doorknob—then washed her hands. On the second lather, she glanced at her reflection in the tiny mirror and groaned at her bedraggled appearance. In the sunlight that poured through a large hole beneath the shower window, she looked like something a cat would refuse to drag in. Of course, there was no help for it now. All her hairstyling products and makeup were locked in the trunk of her car.

She grabbed the toothpaste and squirted some out on her finger. She still couldn't understand how a sheriff could get away with towing a car without a sobriety test, but she figured small towns were different from big cities. Besides, the man had probably done her a favor. If a cop had stopped her on the highway, not only would her car have been towed, but she probably would've spent the night in jail.

Instead of with a red-hot redneck.

Not that she ever got the chance to see how hot her redneck was. But regret was something she'd have to live with. Her life was complicated enough without adding a man to the mix. A man who belonged in her world about as much as she belonged in his. No, the sooner she got her car and got out of there, the better. Every second she stayed with the man, self-restraint seemed more and more overrated.

Especially when she pulled open the door to Slate's bare chest. She took a step back until her legs came in contact with the cool plastic of the toilet.

With his hands on either side of the door frame, he leaned in and brushed a kiss over her lips. "Mmmm, minty fresh."

Closing her eyes to block out the steamy image of bulging biceps and smooth, hard chest, she tried to sound like a tough, determined woman instead of the quivering, needy wimp she was. "I need to go."

Slate's breath ruffled the hair on her forehead. "Later." He kissed her again, but with sheer determination, she held her lips firm. After a few seconds of some very skillful attempts to get them open, he pulled back and heaved a sigh.

"Fine. I'll see if I can find your damned car." Slate picked her up and set her out of the way.

"Find my car? What do you mean, find my car? I thought you said the sheriff had impounded it because I had too much to drink."

"That's right." He leaned over to turn on the shower, his tight buns flexing beneath the soft denim. "But Sheriff Winslow is an absentminded old guy and sometimes he forgets where he puts things."

"Forgets where he puts things? A car?"

"Cars. Trucks. You name it." Slate glanced over his shoulder. "You mind closing the door, honey? I don't want to catch a draft."

She wanted to point out that the draft wasn't coming from the open door as much as the hole in the wall, but she didn't want to hurt his feelings. He couldn't help it if the economics of the town were so bad that their football coach's income was below poverty level.

She walked out and pulled the door closed behind her.

There were still a lot of questions she wanted to ask—mainly how a man who had trouble remembering things could get elected sheriff—but she figured she would have plenty of time to get answers on the way back to town. Besides, she could think a lot clearer after Slate was fully dressed.

"Faith, darlin'." He didn't even have to yell to be heard through the paper-thin wood of the door.

"Yes," she called back.

"Could you come here for a minute?"

She cracked open the door and peeked in. "What?"

He looked back at her from around the edge of the shower curtain, his thick blond hair plastered to his head and the corners of his eyes crinkled. "I didn't mean for you to leave."

She blinked. "Excuse me?"

His brows lifted. "I thought you might want to take a shower."

Her face heated up. "With you?"

"Considering we only have about two more minutes of hot water, I'd say it's now or never."

All the moisture left her mouth. "I can't fit in there with you."

"You're probably right." He jerked back the curtain to reveal a thin stream of water trickling down miles of hard, luscious flesh. Hard, luscious flesh that was just as impressive as a monster truck. "But I think we should give it a try."

She stared for a second, or maybe more like thirty, before she pulled her head back and jerked the door closed. Then she stared at the door for a good five minutes more as her immoral slut struggled to get out. But the introverted prude won out and she walked back to the bedroom to get dressed.

Unfortunately, the image of his naked splendor was burned into the back of her brain and remained there all the way into Bramble.

"You okay, darlin'?" he asked as they passed the WELCOME TO BRAMBLE sign. "You look almost as green around the gills as Buster."

At the mention of the dog, she finally looked over at Slate—something she'd been avoiding even after he was completely dressed. "I'm so sorry about Buster. I didn't realize the disinfectant wipes would make him sick."

"He'll live. But that has to be the worst case of the runs I've ever seen."

"Do you think he'll be okay? Maybe we shouldn't have left him." She looked out the back window. "What if he gets dehydrated?"

"With all the bowls of water you put out, I don't see that happening. Besides, he's a dog."

She tried to relax back against the seat, but it wasn't easy. She couldn't live with herself if she was somehow responsible for another animal's demise. Her rabbit Powder Puff's had been devastating enough.

"Hey."

Faith looked over into a pair of twinkling hazel eyes.

Slate reached over and smoothed a strand of hair off her cheek. "Old Buster will be just fine. He has a stomach of steel."

His kind words coupled with the warmth of his fingers made her feel all tingly inside. It wasn't a sexual feeling as much as a feeling of connection. The feeling that someone on the face of the earth cared about her. Even if it was only for a moment. This feeling bothered her much more than her sexual ones had, and she turned away and tried to change the subject.

"So how are you going to find my car if the sheriff doesn't remember where he put it?"

"I'm sure he'll remember now that he's had a good night's sleep."

"How did he take the news that I was Hope's twin sister?" She couldn't help but feel nervous about meeting a man she'd more or less lied to.

"Pretty well, actually."

"He wasn't mad?"

"No...I wouldn't say he was mad."

Relief washed over her. Obviously, small-town people were a forgiving bunch.

"What are you doing?" Faith asked a few minutes later when he pulled into the parking lot of Josephine's Diner, a faded pink train caboose with a lopsided, smoking building attached to the back. It seemed the entire town was sitting in booths in front of the windows—all waving.

"We're talking to the sheriff." He drove around back and rolled up next to the Dumpsters.

"The sheriff's office is in a diner?"

"Sort of." He got out and came around to her side of the truck, opening the door and helping her down. But once her feet were on the ground, he didn't seem in any hurry to move.

In the late-morning sun, he was even more handsome. His thick hair glittered like ripe wheat and the faded green of his western shirt turned his eyes a deep moss.

Eyes that suddenly looked extremely serious. And since they rarely looked serious, she started to get worried.

"Look, Faith. Before we go in there, you need to understand the type of people you're dealing with. Small-town folks are different." Slate paused and ran a hand over the back of his neck. "They don't see things like most people. In fact, sometimes they don't see things at all."

"What do you mean?" Obviously, whatever he was trying to tell her was difficult for him.

"I mean, sometimes they get something in their heads, and they just don't want to let it go. Like you being Hope."

"Of course, they think I'm Hope. You said yourself that I look just like her. And I wasn't exactly truthful with them." Faith glanced around at all the cars in the parking lot, and guilt washed over her. "But maybe I should be."

"Well, I've been thinking about that, and I don't know if that's a good idea."

"Why not? I thought the sheriff was happy about it."

"Maybe happy is the wrong word."

She frowned. "He was mad?"

He held up a hand. "No. He wasn't mad. He was just . . . surprised! That's it, he was surprised. And I don't think it would be fair to leave Hope out of surprising the rest of the town."

"Oh." She hadn't thought of that. Of course, it should be left up to Hope to tell her friends and family. "So you think I should keep acting like Hope until I leave?"

"I think that might be for the best. Hope would blow a fuse if everyone found out before she did."

Faith nodded. "Okay, I'll only talk to Sheriff Winslow."

He placed a hand at the small of her back as they walked to the door. "Actually, honey, I thought I'd talk to the sheriff. He gets nervous around strangers. And when he gets nervous his memory gets worse."

"Oh." She stopped. "Then maybe I should just wait in the truck."

"That might work in other places. But in Bramble, if you don't show your face, they'll come out and get you." He pulled open the door. "So just have a seat and do what you did last night—smile and don't say a word."

The strong smell of fried onions brought tears to her eyes as she stepped through the door. They were still watering when a man sitting at the table to their right greeted them.

"Mornin', Hope. Slate."

"Hey, Little Bit." Kenny's friend sat next to the man. "You sure disappeared fast last night, Coach."

"So fast it makes a person wonder what you were up to," a woman with a baby on her lap said.

"The water still low at Sutter Springs?" someone else asked.

"Hell, they weren't worried about no water. Not from what Little Billy Ray said," a man in a booth clear across the room yelled.

There were snickers and a few sly winks. And Faith would've turned back around and headed out the door if Slate hadn't blocked her way.

"Mornin', y'all." His hand pushed her forward. "You're sure looking bushy-tailed this morning. Must be the extra sleep you got. Funny thing, the parking lot at Boot's clearing out so early."

The room filled with excuses.

"My arthritis started actin' up."

"Bunions."

"Had to get the babysitter home."

"Early church."

"Stomach didn't feel right."

Slate ignored the excuses. "Anyone seen Sam?"

"Yeah, he's back in the kitchen talking with Josie," said the woman behind the counter.

He guided Faith to a chrome and red vinyl bar stool. "Sit down here, darlin', and I'll be right back. Rachel Dean, will you fix Hope and me some pot roast and eggs? Plenty of gravy."

"Ain't he sweet?" Rachel Dean moved up to the counter with a stained apron over her broad hips and her large hands holding a kitchen towel. "Sorry I missed you at Boot's last night. We had a big crowd for dinner, and I was dead on my feet. But you sure look good, honey—well, except for that hair. I don't know why a gal who can grow it would ever cut it off." She plucked at her thin salt-and-pepper strands. "Twyla tried out a new perm on me and left another bald spot. You'd think I'd learn, but she sure gives a good shampoo. You don't want pot roast and eggs, do you, honey? Why don't you let me fix you up your usual."

Even though she didn't have a clue what the usual was, Faith nodded.

Rachel's small, dark eyes narrowed. "I heard about your throat. Have you tried gargling with Epsom salt? Granddaddy Morris used to swear by it. Of course, Granddaddy always had a few screws loose." She turned and picked up a pot from the commercial coffeemaker on the counter behind her and poured Faith a cup. "I'll have your food right out to you, honey. After spending most of the night at Sutter Springs, you must be starving to death." She winked before she walked back to the kitchen, filling coffee cups on her way.

Faith stared at the dark liquid in the white cup and tried not to blush. Hope didn't blush, and she drank coffee. Thick, black coffee. Faith didn't like coffee, at least, not coffee that didn't come from Starbucks with multiple flavors and a huge dollop of whipped cream on the top. She reached for the little metal pitcher of cream.

"Why, Hope, I thought you drank your coffee black." The man from the night before with the handlebar mustache took the stool next to her.

She set down the pitcher and, to cover the blunder, grabbed up the cup and took a sip. She grimaced as the bitter hot liquid slipped down her throat.

"So I take it your throat's still sore." He didn't wait for a nod before he continued. "Bad stuff, laryngitis. You probably need to rest up from something like that. And there's no better place to recover than your hometown." He patted her hand with his large, calloused one. "It was all fine and dandy that you ran off to Hollywood to sow a few wild oats. But five years is long enough to be away from the people who love you."

He nodded at the kitchen door. "That there boy has missed you so much he's barely been able to keep his mind on coaching. The Dawgs are due a state championship, Hope. And I'm sure you'd want to do everything in your power to make sure they get it."

Faith didn't have a clue what the man was talking about. So she was relieved when Rachel Dean slipped back through the kitchen door with her food.

"Now, Harley, don't be bugging Hope." Rachel gave him a stern look as she set down two plates. "A flower garden won't bloom if it's fussed over."

Harley seemed to get the analogy. He nodded and gave

Faith a quick peck on the cheek before moving back to his seat.

"Josie made it just the way you like it." Rachel Dean nodded down at what looked like some kind of red meat sauce with two over-easy eggs floating in it. "Go ahead, honey, tell me what you think."

Faith thought she was going to be sick. She hated over-easy eggs with their runny whites and yolk. But there wasn't much she could do with the woman staring down at her. So, staying away from the eggs, she took a forkful of red sauce and slipped it between her lips.

It wasn't bad.

She swallowed.

Kind of sweet and spicy.

Her eyes widened.

And hot.

Really, really hot.

As her throat burned, she looked around for water but there was only the cup of bitter coffee.

"Water." She motioned at her throat. "I need water." When Rachel Dean just stared at her, she yelled louder. "I need some water!"

That got the woman moving. She turned and splashed some water in a glass, then handed it to Faith, who drank it, then held it out for more. By the second glass, the main fire was out, though the back of her throat still burned.

"Oh, thank you." She handed the glass back to Rachel Dean. "I'm sorry I yelled, but that was extremely hot. What is that—"

Faith's mouth snapped shut as she looked around the room. Every eye was on her, and all of them looked confused. Except for Slate. Standing in the archway that led to the kitchen, he seemed more exasperated than anything.

"What happened to your voice?" Rachel Dean was the first to speak.

"Yeah, Hope. You sound funny." Kenny's friend stood up. "And what happened to your laryngitis?"

Panicked, she looked at Slate.

"Well"—he strolled into the room—"that's kind of a funny story."

"I bet I can figure it out," a woman piped in. "I bet Hope didn't have laryngitis at all."

"You mean she lied?" Rachel Dean looked confused.

"Of course she lied, but only because she was embarrassed."

"Embarrassed? Of what?"

"That Hollywood has taken her Texas talk."

A gasp raced around the room, followed quickly by head shaking and whispered disbelief.

Finally Harley stepped up and slung his big meaty arm around her. "Why, Hope, you didn't have to go and lie. We don't care if you sound all weird and citified. You're our hometown girl, and we love you."

There was a chorus of agreement.

"'Course we love you. You're our ray of Hope."

"Our Little Bit of Sunshine."

"As bright as the star of Texas."

The hot food wasn't entirely to blame for the tears that welled up in Faith's eyes. The devotion of this town was almost too much to bear, and it seemed the worst sort of betrayal to allow them to keep thinking she was their hometown girl.

"I'm not Hope," she whispered.

"What did you say, honey?" Rachel Dean leaned down closer, while Slate covered his eyes with one hand and shook his head.

"I'm not Hope." Her voice grew stronger. "My name is Faith Aldridge." She decided to leave out the part about her being Hope's sister. Hope could explain that.

"Faith All-ridge?" Rachel Dean rested her hands on the counter. "What do you mean?"

Again the crazy woman chimed in. "Oh, I get it. That's her stage name."

"Stage name?"

"Yeah, you know, like Faith Hill."

"Oh," Rachel said, although she still looked confused. "But I thought Faith Hill was Faith Hill's name."

"Of course not. Every famous person changes their name."

Rachel Dean's eyes stared straight through Faith. "Well, I like Hope Scroggs better."

Faith opened her mouth to try and explain things, but Slate stepped up and tossed some money on the counter before she could. "Come on, darlin', we need to get going." He took her elbow and helped her up from the stool.

"Goin'," Rachel Dean said. "Hope—I mean Faith— hasn't even finished her breakfast. And you haven't even touched yours."

"I'm sorry about that, Rachel, but you know how Hollywood stars like to starve themselves. And I've got a lot of game film to go over if I want to win next week's game." He flashed the entire room a cocky grin as he pulled Faith toward the door.

"Game film?" Harley chuckled. "We're not fallin' for

that, Calhoun." He winked at Faith, and the entire room erupted in laughter before the door closed behind them.

Stunned over what had just taken place, Faith allowed Slate to haul her back to the truck without saying a single word. Once there, he jerked open the driver's side door and helped her up—or more like tossed her in. Then he climbed in after her and gunned the truck. He backed out, almost hitting the fender of the beat-up Taurus before he hit the accelerator, and they shot out of the parking lot in a spray of gravel. With the indifferent look on his face, he didn't look upset. But his actions said something else entirely.

Once they were back on the highway, Slate reached down and pressed the button for the CD player. The song that blared through the speakers had a definite Caribbean sound although the male singer's voice was country.

"I think we need to go back and talk with them," Faith finally found her voice. "There has to be something we can say that will convince them I'm not Hope."

"Convince them?" He snorted. "This is a group of people who still think the South won. That driving after three beers improves your reflexes. That the Dallas Cowboys football team doesn't represent a city but the entire United States. And that Tim McGraw lied about being born in Louisiana and was actually born only miles away. Knowing those crazy beliefs, do you think we're going to convince them of anything?"

Faith opened her mouth, then closed it. She sat there digesting the information as one upbeat song ended and another began. It was strange how determined the town was to hang on to the belief that she was Hope. Strange and kind of sweet. It must be nice to be loved by an entire town so much.

"Well, I guess it doesn't matter." She glanced over at him, relieved that his shoulders were no longer so tense. "Since I'm leaving today anyway."

He released a long breath. "About that..."

Her eyes widened. "Don't tell me the sheriff still can't remember where my car is!"

"I'm afraid so. Although he did say the town will reimburse you if you want to buy some clothes and personal items."

"I want my car back!" She flopped against the seat and crossed her arms.

A grin split his face. "You in that big a hurry to get rid of me, darlin'?" Faith sent him an annoyed look, but it only made the grin bigger. "All right, we'll find your car. It shouldn't be that hard since in Bramble a foreign-made car sticks out like a hooker in church." Slate stretched his arm along the seat and his fingers brushed her shoulder. "But first let's go on down to the truck stop and have some breakfast. I can't think real well with a hollow stomach."

Since her own stomach growled, she agreed. "Fine. But no coffee or runny eggs or really hot red stuff."

"Why, Hope," he teased. "You used to love Texas chili."

She smiled and relaxed back against the seat.

Faith might not love Texas chili, but she sure loved being with a certain redneck.

Chapter Six

THE FRUSTRATION SLATE FELT AFTER TRYING TO convince Sheriff Winslow that Hope wasn't Hope—and that even if she was Hope he didn't want to marry her—didn't last long. It was hard to be upset when Kenny Chesney was singing about loose señoritas and stiff margaritas. And when it was a beautiful Sunday with only mild West Texas winds and enough sunshine to make up for what wind there was. And when a pretty woman spent the day with him. A woman with eyes that matched the very peak of the September sky and skin that smelled like the ripened peaches they sold just south of Austin.

Even a stubborn sheriff and loony townsfolk couldn't ruin a day like that.

His enjoyment of the day was probably why Slate didn't put too much effort into finding her car. He checked out a few vacant barns on the way back from breakfast—where he'd learned she liked veggie omelets and orange juice— then when the barns didn't turn up anything, he made a few calls. It came as no surprise that not one person was willing to offer up any information about Faith's car.

Satisfied he'd given it his best shot, or at least a mediocre one, he decided to give up the search for the rest of the
day and work on getting Faith in bed. Which was almost
as difficult as finding her Volvo. For some reason—
probably lack of tequila—she wasn't as accommodating
as she'd been at Sutter Springs. In fact, instead of melting
every time he touched her, she stiffened up like a pool
cue. And it was starting to worry him. Especially since
he'd spent his life surrounded by women who seemed to
like his touch, if not downright loved it. Not that he'd
touched a whole lot of them, but the ones he had touched
always came back for more.

He figured Faith's reaction had to do with the short time
they'd known one another, which meant his best chance
of getting those sexy-as-hell high heels wrapped around
him was to spend the day becoming her friend. So he did
his utmost to charm the hell out of her as he escorted her
around town, buying toiletries, new sheets for Bubba's
bed, and clothing. He had never been much on shopping,
especially with an indecisive female, but it turned out to
be fun sitting in a chair in Duds 'N' Such, waiting for
Faith to parade out in her new clothes.

She listened intently as Justin Jr. filled her in on western wear—from pearl-snap shirts to button-down, Rockies
jeans to Cruel Girl, western-style boots to square toe—
before deciding on a couple of pearl-snap shirts, Wran-
gler jeans, and a flamboyant pair of red leather boots with
chocolate stitching. The fetish she had for red footwear
intrigued him. Especially when coupled with those baby
blues that looked at everything in wide-eyed wonder as if
it was the first time she'd ever seen it. It probably was. Few
people got to witness a sideshow as freaky as Bramble.

The freakiness got even worse as the day progressed. Even though they referred to her as Faith, the insane towns-folk continued to believe she was Hope. The sly winks and mile-long smirks gave them away. Slate sat back and let them do their thing until they started in on stories about him and Hope; then he stepped in and steered them to another topic. Faith didn't need to hear about his relationship with Hope. Even if it was mostly in their deluded minds.

After they shopped, he took her back to the trailer where he washed her clothes and the new sheets while she called her aunt and fussed over Buster until the dog hid under the trailer. He thought about taking her into town for dinner, but he'd had enough of the sideshow. So instead, he picked up BBQ and took her out to Sutter Springs, where they ate on an old Indian blanket beneath the cottonwood while Buster raced around chasing any-thing that moved.

Slate enjoyed talking with Faith. She was intelligent, interesting, and knew exactly when to laugh. Although it was hard to keep up a conversation when that sweet mouth turned a dinner of barbecue chicken and ribs into a hot sexual fantasy—every time she slipped those lips around a saucy piece of meat his body grew tighter and tighter. And by the time they were on their way back to the trailer, Slate felt as if he'd been ridden hard and put away wet. He couldn't think of one more Hope story or any more clever quips. All he could think about was getting Faith beneath those nice crisp sheets.

Unfortunately, her mind was not on the same track as his.

"I think I should get a hotel room."

The words brought his gaze up from the soft swells of her breasts.

"A hotel room? Now why would you want to do a thing like that when there's a perfectly good bed back at the trailer?"

"I couldn't impose again."

"Impose? Why, it's no imposition to give a bed to a friend." He sent her the most whupped-puppy look he could muster. "Unless you don't see me as a friend."

"Of course, I do. I mean…" She waved her hand around in that cute flustered way of hers. "I just thought it would be better if I stayed somewhere else."

"Well, darlin', you thought wrong. My aunt would skin me alive if she thought I wasn't hospitable to a friend in need."

"Oh, well, in that case…"

Slate smiled and leaned back in the seat. He didn't try to pull her back into a conversation. After talking all day, he was pretty talked out. So he popped in an Alan Jackson CD—because there wasn't a woman alive who Alan couldn't get in the mood—while his mind feverishly worked on his strategy. Unfortunately, by the time they got to the trailer, he had worked himself up into quite a lather.

"Here, darlin', let me get that for you." He reached over her shoulder to pull open the screen door, but instead tripped on the metal step and ran into her from behind, planting her face into the screen. His knee struck the sharp corner of the step, and it took a second before he could talk around the pain. "Y-you okay?"

"I think so." Faith stood on the top step with a hand over one cheek.

"Here, let me take a look." But just as he pulled her hand away, Buster nudged him in the back of the legs, causing him to poke Faith in the eye with her own finger.

"Dang it, Buster!" Slate pushed the dog away with his knee before he turned back to Faith. "I'm sorry, honey. Let's go inside, and I'll get you something to put on it."

"I'm okay," she said.

He shook his head to try and clear it. She might be okay, but he wasn't. After twenty-four hours of suppressing his sexual urges, he felt like a Brahman bull penned in a chute with his flank strap cinched too tight—his entire body tensed in anticipation of the chute opening so he could release all his pent-up energy with some good, old-fashioned bucking.

Now all he needed was a rider.

Not just any rider, but the petite, stubborn woman who didn't seem in any hurry to saddle up.

"Here." He switched on the light and limped over to the kitchenette. Opening up the small refrigerator beneath the counter, he pulled out a can of Budweiser. He walked over to her and tipped up her chin. Her injury wasn't as bad as it had sounded. The screen pattern embossed on her cheek would fade, and her eye didn't look all that red.

As he held the can to her cheek, Faith stared up at him. Looking into her eyes was like fishing on a deep mountain lake. The view was just as nice as the catch. Although he was looking pretty forward to the catch. He ran his thumb over the smooth skin just below her bottom lip.

"You sure you're okay?" he asked.

She nodded, and he slid his thumb a little higher. There was no glitter pink on her lips, just a natural rose that made his heart beat faster. He stroked her lip, pressing the supple plumpness first one way and then the other. When he couldn't take it anymore, he lowered the cold can and bent his head.

The plan was to hook her with a few simple kisses, then slowly reel her in with deep, wet ones. Except the plan went to hell in a handcart when he touched those sweet soft lips, and there was nothing simple about the kiss he gave her. The can of beer fell from his fingers and rolled away as he jerked her up to her toes so his mouth could better devour her. For a few seconds, she answered him back, her mouth welcoming, her tongue hot and friendly. Then suddenly she slipped off the line and got away.

Faith pulled from his hands and stepped back, her breathing rushed, her eyes confused. "I-I really need to take a shower."

He blinked. "Huh?"

"I thought I'd take a shower."

The image of her all naked and soapy almost brought him to his knees, but she didn't seem to notice his drunken sway.

"I-I thought it would be a good idea if I took one tonight so there would be plenty of water for you in the morning." Her eyes skittered down to the toes of her red high heels.

A better idea would be if they shared a shower in the morning after a long night of sweaty sex. Still, if she took a shower now, she'd be a lot closer to naked.

"You go right ahead, darlin'." Slate made an attempt to even out his breathing. "I'll be right here waiting when you get out."

She looked kind of distressed by the notion, before she hurried off to the bathroom. If he didn't know better, he would think she was trying to give him the brush-off. But that didn't make any sense. Not after the way she'd melted into his kisses the night before. Of course, she'd been pumped full of tequila the night before.

He hurried over to the cupboard to check his supply.

Thank God, he had a good half bottle. Of course, there was not a lime in sight and only one little packet of salt that he'd brought home from a fast-food restaurant. But he wouldn't need all the frills when a couple of straight shots should do the trick.

After he arranged the bottle of tequila and two mis-matched glasses on the bar, he turned on the clock radio on the windowsill and scrolled through the stations until he found one he liked. Since Alan hadn't worked so well, he stayed away from country and chose the only classical station he could find. With Buster bouncing at his heels, he rushed around the room, trying out different lighting. He settled on the small light over the range. It was easier to get a woman's clothes off in less light than more. And since she hadn't bought any pajamas at Duds 'N' Such, there would only be one thin T-shirt and a pair of panties between him and nirvana.

Slate glanced down at his jeans and boots. It would be a shame to slow things down. Hearing the water shut off, he bolted toward the bedroom. He toed off his boots and flipped them in a corner, then struggled out of his jeans. He didn't wear undershorts—a habit he'd gotten into when he kept running out of clean pairs—so he grabbed some gym shorts out of the chest of drawers and slipped them on. He thought about removing his shirt, but he liked the way she'd ripped the snaps apart the night before so he left it on—although he unsnapped a few snaps, then, not wanting to look overzealous, snapped them back up. Remembering the condom in his wallet, he retrieved the leather trifold out of the back pocket of his jeans and stuffed the little square package in the side pocket of his shorts.

By the time he got back to the kitchen, he'd worked up a sweat. Buster danced around his sock-covered feet, confused by his master's behavior. Slate felt pretty confused himself. In all his born days, he'd never gotten this worked up over a female. It was pretty pathetic. Jerking up a dish towel, he mopped the sweat off his forehead as he moved to the door to let Buster out.

By the time the bathroom door creaked open, he was back at the bar, trying to look as nonchalant as a sweaty heavy-breather could. Faith's head peeked out, her hair all towel-dried and spiky. When she saw him, her eyes widened.

"All squeaky clean?" He tried to act casual, but it was difficult when his nerves were nothing but a jangled mess.

Her eyes darted to the bottle of tequila and glasses, then back to him, then back to the tequila. He started to offer her some, but before he could, she darted across the hallway like a barn mouse to a pile of hay and slipped inside the bedroom.

"Good night." The door shut with a decisive click.

It took a minute for his mind to comprehend what had just happened. He moved around the edge of the bar and stared at the closed door before he walked to the empty bathroom and looked inside. He looked back at the bedroom door and opened his mouth—then closed it.

Slate wasn't sure how long he stood there before he finally turned and walked back to the counter to pour himself a shot. It burned a path of fire down his throat, and by the time it reached his stomach, reality set in.

It seemed that Hope's shy, insecure twin from Chicago had just given him—the star quarterback of two state championships, the only football player in Bramble's history to receive a full scholarship to the University of Texas, and the man who could send most women in a tizzy with just a smile—the brush-off.

It just didn't make any sense.

No sense at all.

All the time spent on charming conversation and witty remarks, the effort put in on shopping excursions and sunset picnics, and the attention given to lighting and mood music was for nothing. He hadn't even made it out of the chute.

He moved through the kitchen and turned off the light, let Buster in, and then wandered over to the couch to make his bed for the night.

Damn fool woman, he thought as he spread out the tattered blanket. She didn't know shit from Shinola about seduction. He ripped open the snaps on his shirt, yanked it off, then wadded it up and threw it at the 12-inch TV. Hell, he was lucky he wasn't going to have sex with her. A woman like that probably didn't know one end of a man's johnson from the other. Sex with her would've been a major disappointment.

He flopped down on the couch and crammed the pillow beneath his head. And he didn't need any more disappointments in his life. Losing state championships was enough. Which was just another reason he didn't need to have sex with her. He didn't have time for a woman in his life right now. Not when he needed to figure out how to win football games with an inept quarterback, a mediocre defensive line, and a punter who couldn't kick his way out of a paper bag.

Buster whined at the bedroom door wanting to be let in.

Well, Slate wasn't going to whine. He wasn't the whining kind. Especially since he'd figured out that sex with some screwy broad from the East was the last thing he needed. And once he made up his mind about something, that was it. And he'd made up his mind about Faith. Hell, even if she stripped naked and came out and forced herself on him, he wasn't doing it. He didn't care how great her legs looked beneath his T-shirt or how nice her breasts jiggled under the thin cotton. He wouldn't have sex with her now if she was the last woman on the face of the earth.

Faith stood with her back up against the bedroom door and her hands pressed over her quivery stomach. She didn't know how long she'd been standing there. It felt like hours had passed since she'd peeked out of the bathroom and had seen Slate looking all sexy and rumpled in his untucked western shirt and gym shorts. Hours since she heard the front door open, then bang closed, and the creaks of the floor as he moved around the living room. Now, except for a few whines from Buster, everything was quiet.

If she was smart, she would let Buster in and go to bed.

Except she wasn't smart.

Beneath her straight-A report cards was a stressed-out C-student with a nervous stomach. An average little girl who studied for hours every night to get the grades that would make her above-average parents proud. She read every book her father suggested. Practiced her violin until she formed calluses. Joined the debate team. Was secretary of the Honor Society. And spent every weekend at foreign film festivals, the symphony, or some Save the Earth rally.

But it was all a façade.

Because deep down, she wasn't a child with a high intellect as much as a normal girl who wanted to spend her evenings reading celebrity magazines, watching romantic teen movies, and chatting on the phone with her friends. A teenager who longed to spend her weekends at slumber parties or on dates with guys who gave hickeys.

Of course, it wasn't her parents' fault that she didn't do these things. They had no idea what she liked or disliked because she never told them. Not wanting to disappoint them, she buried her desires way down deep and tried to become what they wanted.

Until now.

She didn't think her parents would want her staying the night with a man she barely knew. Or buying western clothes she would probably never wear again, or red high heels that would give her back problems later, or pink glitter lip gloss that supported an industry that put too much emphasis on physical beauty. And they would never understand the quivering need she had for a hot cowboy with sultry eyes who drove a gas-guzzling truck that probably deposited more emissions into the air than a textile factory in India.

They wouldn't understand that at all.

Faith barely understood it.

Sex with Slate was not a good idea. She didn't believe in casual sex. The previous night's behavior excluded, all her sexual experiences had been with men she'd known for at least six months. Men who lived in houses with foundations, good-sized tiled bathrooms, and at least 300-thread-count sheets. Men who drove conservative cars without gun racks and disposed of aluminum cans in recycling containers instead of in the bed of their trucks.

Yet even knowing this, she still wanted Slate, wanted him like she'd never wanted anything in her life. More than low-rise designer jeans or artery-clogging, chemical-infused pizza. She had spent the entire day fantasizing about kissing that cocky grin from his face, and nibbling a trail down the strong column of his throat, and ripping the snaps on his western shirt apart to expose all that tanned, smooth skin to her fingertips.

And what made it even worse was that Slate wanted that, too. It was there in his desire-steeped eyes and in every teasing note of his voice. In the heated brush of his fingers and his wicked grins. It was in his cheerful whistling as he did the laundry and the care with which he smoothed the sheets over the bed.

So why was she cowering behind the door when she could be drinking tequila with a gorgeous redneck who was an extremely good kisser?

Because it was hard to do away with thirty years of conditioned behavior in one day. Hard to throw her cautious nature to the wind and take a ride on the wild side. And she had no doubt that having sex with Slate would be a wild ride—one she would regret taking for the rest of her life.

The trailer was dark when she eased open the bedroom door. Buster greeted her with a wagging tail and wet tongue, following behind her as she hesitantly took the three steps needed to reach the living room. In the faint light spilling in from the cracked window, she could just make out Slate's tall form stretched out on the couch. It looked as if he was asleep, which was probably a sign from God. Unfortunately, her parents were more meta-physical than religious, so she took a step closer.

The floor creaked, and his head came up.

"Faith?"

"Oh...you're still awake." She tugged at her T-shirt and pressed one big toe over the other. "I thought you might be asleep. Although I don't know how you can sleep on that little couch, seeing as you're so tall—how tall are you? Six-one? Two? My father would've fit on the couch perfectly—he was short, like me—not that we have the same genes or anything but—"

"Did you need something?" His voice sounded nothing like the teasing cowboy who'd done such a good job of seducing her all day.

"Need something?" She hit an unusually high note. "Well, I was just thinking that maybe we could...umm... I thought that we could—I mean if you wanted to—"

"Look, Faith." Slate sat up. "Between finding your car and work, tomorrow's going to be a busy day. So unless there's something you want..."

Faith swallowed. "Yes...well...." She cleared her throat. "There is something I wanted."

"What would that be?"

"You." The word just popped out of Faith's mouth and hung there.

In the thick, painful silence that followed, she pretty much wanted to crawl out the front door and never look back. But before she could move, Slate sprang up from the couch.

"Well, that works out real nice, darlin'." Within two steps, he had her in his arms. He buried his nose in her neck and inhaled deeply, almost as if he wanted to breathe her in. "Because I'm about to combust from wanting you."

His fingers pressed into the muscles of her back, coaxing her up to her toes, as his lips found hers. The kiss was hot and greedy—one sizzling slide of wet heat followed by another—and another, until Faith didn't know where one stopped and the other began. She grew dizzy on desire—or perhaps from lack of oxygen—and her head fell back as he trailed kisses along her jaw and down her neck.

"I tried not to want you," she whispered. "We're so different...and I'll be leaving soon...and it will only make things more complicated—"

"Darlin'"—Slate sucked on the spot just behind her ear, sending a sensual shiver through her body—"you think way too much." He swept her up in his arms and carried her to the bedroom.

"But I don't know if I can have casual sex, Slate." She looped her arms around his shoulders and nestled against his bare chest. His skin felt like warm toast all ready for buttering. When he reached the bed, he let her legs slide down his body before pressing the hard evidence of his desire against her.

"There's not a damned thing casual about this."

Catching the hem of her T-shirt, Slate drew it up over her head. Thankfully, there was very little light in the room. She wasn't comfortable enough with her body to want it displayed to someone who looked like he did. As if sensing her shyness, he didn't grab or fondle, but instead cradled her face and gave her a leisurely kiss that had her hands gripping the lean muscles at his waist for balance.

The kiss deepened, his tongue caressing her mouth in sweet strokes as his hand slipped from her cheek to one trembling breast. He held it as if it was the most fragile keepsake, gently cradling the flesh against his palm as his thumb feathered over the pebbled peak. Then he pulled back from her lips and dipped his head to take her nipple in his mouth.

The feel of rough tongue and scorching heat caused her knees to buckle. His hands tightened on her waist and his biceps flexed as he lifted her up off the floor. Her legs instinctively wrapped around his waist, her quivering center riding the hard ridge that swelled beneath the cotton of his shorts as he continued his sweet torture of hot sweeps and gentle tugs. When she thought she couldn't take it a second longer, he lowered her down to the mattress and gave the wet, beaded tip one last gentle kiss before he released her to slip off his shorts. He came back for her panties, his hot fingers slipping beneath the elastic and slowly skating down her legs.

Then the mattress dipped beneath his weight, and for some strange reason the bumper sticker flashed through her mind—*If you think my truck is big . . .*—and apprehension reared its ugly head. But instead of the arrogant redneck, the gentle cowboy settled against her side. So close she could feel the solid wall of his chest against her shoulder, the rhythmic thumping of his heart, and the hard length of him nudging her thigh—a hard length that was impressive but not in the least intimidating.

As he bent his head to kiss her, the backs of his fingers trailed in a feathery soft caress down her throat, back and forth along her collarbone, then around each breast before he repeated the soul-tingling pattern. Faith melted beneath his skilled fingers, although when those hot digits deviated down her body, she couldn't help but cover his hand with hers and pull away from his lips.

"I'm leaving." She whispered the words more to herself than to him.

"I know." He kissed the tip of her nose, then each eyelid. "But for now, let me touch you."

It was too late.

He already had.

Closing her eyes, she released his hand. But his knuckles only stroked back and forth between her hip bones as he delivered one sweet kiss after another. Lulled into a blissful, hypnotic state by his talented lips and gentle caresses, she wasn't even aware of his hand moving lower until one finger dipped into her wet heat.

She tensed, but he soothed her with soft whispers as he adjusted his finger and his thumb came to rest on the pulsing nub at the top. Her legs quivered as a jolt of desire swept through her. But it was nothing compared to how she felt when his thumb began to move. There was a callus on the pad, like the finest grain of sandpaper ever made, and he brushed it around her pulse point in wispy little sweeps. On the upsweep his finger deepened; on the down sweep it receded. The circle grew tighter, becoming more of a stroke that pushed intense heat first one way and then the other.

Completely mindless, Faith could only dig her head back into the pillow as Slate manipulated the flame into a full-fledged bonfire that soon consumed her. Then with one final sweep and stroke, he brought her back to earth.

He brushed a kiss on her forehead before he shifted away. In a hazy mist, she turned her head and watched as he fumbled with something in the dark. It only took a second to figure out what it was.

"Do you think one will be enough?" she asked.

His head came up. "What?"

"One condom. Maybe you should use two."

"Two? You got something I don't want, darlin'?"

"No, I just thought..."

He slipped over her, his hands braced on either side of her head. "Don't think." He dipped down and kissed her lips. "Just feel."

Always the good listener, Faith closed her eyes and just felt. Felt the heat of his breath on her face. The brush of muscle and lightly furred skin as he guided her legs apart with his. The nudge—then stretch—of smooth, hard muscle as he pressed deep inside, touching a spot she didn't even know existed. She knew now. With each penetrating stroke, the intensity grew until her hips tipped and met him thrust for thrust.

Her second orgasm took her by surprise, coming hot and fast in jumpy little spasms. Slate followed closely behind, his head bent forward as he groaned out his release. His body was heavy as he sagged against her, but she didn't mind the extra weight pinning her down to the crisp sheets. She liked the feel of being beneath him. Liked it so much she actually giggled.

He came up on his forearms and looked down at her. "Is there a problem?"

"No. No problem at all," she said as she hooked her arms around his neck and pulled him down for another kiss.

Faith had just discovered something she liked better than red shoes and pink lip gloss.

And she planned to get her fill while she could.

Chapter Seven

SLATE STOOD NAKED IN THE DOORWAY OF THE TRAILER and stared out at the Texas sunrise. It wasn't as spectacular as a sunset, but it was nice in its own right. Of course, spectacular or not, he'd rather be back in bed. And if Buster hadn't had a bad case of the trots, he would be. Dang nuisance of a woman trying to kill his dog.

Buster ambled back up the steps and pressed against Slate's leg, staring up with soulful eyes.

"Sorry, boy." He scratched the dog behind his woolly ears. "She was just trying to be helpful. But in the future I'd keep a little distance if I was you."

The dog pulled away and headed inside. Slate followed him back to the bedroom only to shake his head when Buster flopped down on the floor right next to Faith's side. Obviously, the dog didn't care if she killed him. In a little over a day, he'd grown attached.

Slate looked down at the woman who slept on her stomach with one hand dangling off the bed and one small foot peeking out from the sheet. Damn, if he didn't know exactly how Buster felt. If Slate didn't get her out of there fast, she would be the death of him, too. Or at least, the death of his coaching career and his sanity. Except he didn't listen to his own advice, either. Instead of hopping in the shower, dressing, and getting on with the car search so he could then get on with his coaching responsibilities, he slid beneath the sheets.

The feel of his morning-chilled skin made her grumble but she didn't wake up, not even when he nuzzled his nose into the soft hair on the nape of her neck and ran a hand over the curve of her rear end. She smelled good, like his Irish soap and peaches. And she felt even better. All toasty warm and as soft as a downy chick. He pushed the sheet off, so he could look at the sweet flesh he caressed. Her skin was as lily white as his ass. Except all over. He traced the bumpy trail of her spine up to her shoulders, then down again, before he switched positions so that his head was down by her feet.

Leaning on an elbow, he lifted one dainty foot to examine it. The nails were clipped short and devoid of polish. He kissed her pinkie toe, no bigger than a pencil eraser, as he ran a thumb over her instep. At Duds 'N' Such, he'd learned her feet were size five. Cinderella's couldn't be smaller. He kissed the high arch. Or prettier. He licked his way around her ankle. She tasted good. Like warm peach cobbler, or maybe that was the way she smelled. His senses seemed to get all jumbled up when she was near.

Running a hand along her calf, he noticed how toned she was and wondered if she worked out at one of those stuffy fitness gyms or if she liked outdoor sports. He pressed his mouth to a spot at the back of her knee where a blue vein throbbed beneath the pale skin and for a second absorbed the rhythm of her heart. Then he moved up her firm thigh to her cute little curved bottom. He cupped the smooth hills, the tips of his fingers brushing the crevice between them.

With her leg bent, he could just make out a shadowy slice of heaven. The sight made him as hard as cherrywood. But instead of coaxing her awake and relieving his need, he was content just to look. It was like watching the sun come up over the flat expanse of a Texas cotton field. Or seeing the faces in a hometown crowd when you scored the winning touchdown. Or looking into this woman's face when she reached orgasm.

It was beautiful, and a sight he wasn't willing to miss.

The mattress shifted, and two sleepy eyes the color of Texas bluebonnets gazed over a creamy white shoulder.

Attempting to cover the jump of his heart, he smiled. "Good mornin', darlin'."

"What are you doing?"

"Just lookin'."

Her eyes turned concerned. "At what?"

He trailed his fingertips around each butt cheek. "At the most beautiful thing I've seen in a long time."

Her face flushed bright red, and she rolled to her side, pulling all that sweet flesh from his fingers as she covered herself with the sheet. "I'm not beautiful."

"Really?" He moved back up, lying on his side to face her. "And what makes you say that?"

Her gaze refused to settle on his. "Because it's the truth. I've never been beautiful. Just cute in an ugly kinda way."

"I disagree." Slate tipped her chin up and stared down into those deep pools of insecurity. "You're beautiful, Faith Aldridge. But if you can't take my word for it, I guess I'll just have to show you." He leaned down to settle his lips against hers, but she put a hand on his chest and stopped him.

"I have morning breath."

"Me too." He took the hand and hooked it around his neck. "Which cancels everything out."

She melted into his kiss with such a warm welcome that it made him light-headed. Her fingers lightly caressed the nape of his neck, and her breasts snuggled against his chest. He liked kissing her, liked it almost as much as he liked being in her—almost. Her lips fit his to perfection. But soon kissing was not enough, and he pressed her back on the bed with every intention of sliding on top of her and slipping deep inside all that warmth.

But just when he was about to sink into heaven, Buster jumped up and barked as the front door slammed. And before he could do more than slip under the sheet and turn around, Hope's mama—or adoptive mama—strode through the door.

"Well, it's about dang time."

Slate held the sheet up to his chin, while Faith dove beneath it. Thank God he'd bought thicker sheets the day before.

"Mornin', Jenna." He tried to disguise the horror he felt. This wasn't good. Not good at all. "I see you got back from Lubbock in one piece."

"We got back late last night." The woman's brown eyes sparkled with unsuppressed joy as she bent down to scratch Buster's ears. Slate had never noticed before, but Jenna was just as petite as Hope and Faith.

"We stopped to get gas only to discover my long-lost daughter has come home and was last seen driving off with our football coach. How could you, Slate Calhoun?" It was a weak attempt at outrage, especially when it was followed with a bright smile. "I wanted to stop by last night, but Burl wouldn't let me. He said this morning was soon enough." She grabbed the dainty foot that peeked out of the sheet. "Hope, honey, is that you under there?"

The sheet tightened.

"Now, honey, there's no need to be embarrassed. I could see it if you were fifteen. But you're thirty years old, and I have long since stopped worrying about your virginity. Especially since you and Slate have been sweethearts forever."

The sheet was jerked down to reveal a disheveled and confused Faith.

"Sweethearts?" she squeaked.

Suddenly Slate wished he was Buster and could just slink out the door with his tail between his legs. This was worse than not good. This was flat-out bad. He'd been able to stop the townsfolk from spouting off, but there was no way to stop this woman. She steamrolled better than her daughter.

Adopted or not.

"Oh, Good Lord, Hope, what did you do to your hair, child?" Jenna moved around the side of the bed. Except before she reached Faith, she froze in her tracks and her eyes widened with something that looked like wild disbelief. Since the hair had already been mentioned, Slate could only conclude that Jenna was more perceptive than the rest of Bramble.

And he didn't know if that was a good thing or a bad one.

"Faith?" Her voice shook with emotion. "Faith, is that you, baby girl?"

Faith shot a confused glance at Slate, but he felt as confused as she was. How could Jenna possibly know Faith's name? He grew even more confused when Jenna fell sobbing into Faith's arms.

"My baby," she wailed. "My baby's come home."

With the hysterical woman flung over her lap, Faith sat frozen in shock. She looked back at him, but the only thing he could do was shrug. He didn't have a clue what was going on.

"Jenna, darlin'." Slate tried to remain calm as his mind struggled to piece things together. "I realize you're upset. I know it's a shock to see someone that looks so much like Hope. It shocked me, too. But you need to get—"

Jenna pulled back, but this time there was fire in her eyes. "What I need, Slate Calhoun, is to get a gun and blow your fool head off." She tugged a bewildered Faith protectively to her chest. "Burl!" She screamed loud enough to knock some of the exposed insulation out of the ceiling. "Burl, get in here!"

Big Burl came charging in the door. "What are you hollerin' about, woman?"

Jenna pointed a finger at Slate. "I want you to whup his butt." She flicked her finger. "For violating our baby girl."

"Now, Mama," Burl said. "I realize this is kinda an uncomfortable situation." He cleared his throat. "I sure know it's uncomfortable for me. But isn't this what you've been praying for?"

"Not with our baby!" She yelled. "Not with Faith!"

"Faith?" Burl looked down at the woman in his wife's arms. "That's Faith? But how did she get—" He turned on Slate, and his eyes narrowed.

Now Burl Scroggs had been the meanest defensive end in Bramble High history. His record for most sacks in a season had never been equaled or even threatened. Proof still resided in large purple block letters on the wall of the gym. Slate knew he would never make it out the door without his bones being crushed in those large roughneck hands, but he refused to make it easy. And he also refused to go down naked as the day he was born.

While Burl's mind was still muddled with anger and confusion, Slate leaned over the edge of the bed and grabbed his gym shorts, slipping into them under the sheet. Once they were on, he stood up in the small space between the wall and the bed.

"Now, Burl, I don't exactly know what's going on, but I think we can discuss it like gentlemen."

"You think it was very gentlemanly to have sex with my baby girl, Slate Calhoun?" Jenna accused.

"Baby girl?" He ran a hand over his face. "You keep saying that, Jenna, but I'm not getting it." He pointed a finger at Faith, whose eyes were wildly darting back and forth between him, Jenna, and Burl. "You're right, that's Faith. And she's Hope's twin sister. But how does that make her your baby girl? Not unless . . ." His eyes widened as his brain kicked in. "Hope isn't adopted, is she?"

"Of course she ain't!" Burl yelled. "And I should kick your butt just for thinking it!"

"Then that means . . ." He stopped, unable to finish.

There was a long pregnant silence before Faith spoke.

"You kept Hope, but gave me away." She pulled out of Jenna's arms, her blue eyes filled with so much pain that Slate felt like he'd been sucker punched.

Jenna's anger drained, and she started sobbing again.

"I didn't want to, but I had already signed the papers…
and your mama was there…and we weren't married—
didn't even know if we wanted to get married…and both
of us were still in school—"

"So you gave me away?"

"Oh, honey." Jenna reached for her again, but Faith
tucked the sheet around herself and scrambled off the bed
next to Slate. He tried to hook an arm around her waist,
but she jerked away from him.

"Faith, sweetheart." Burl's blue eyes filled with tears,
eyes that were an exact duplicate of his daughters'. "Please
let your mama explain."

"My mother's dead," Faith whispered.

Jenna's sobs grew even louder.

But Slate didn't care that Jenna was upset. All he
cared about was the devastated woman next to him.
He'd never felt so helpless in his life. He wanted to pull
her into his arms and shield her from the pain of rejection that he knew only too well. But all he could do was
glare at the two people he'd thought were devoted, loving
parents.

"I think it would be best if you two left." For one of
the few times in his adult life, his tone was hard, his anger
evident.

"Why you scrawny little—" Burl reached over the
bed, but Jenna stopped him.

"No, Burl," she choked out. "He's right. We need to
leave." She stood on trembling legs, her makeup running
down her cheeks in thin black streams. "I'm so sorry,
Faith. I'm so sorry."

Burl put an arm around Jenna and tugged her against
his chest. "I'm not done with you, Calhoun," he warned

before he shot Faith a beseeching look. "Hopefully, some-day, you'll let us explain."

He led Jenna from the room.

After the front door slammed, Slate wasn't sure what to do. It was like a tornado had hit without warning, turning what had once been familiar into unrecognizable wreckage. Wanting to ease the tension, he made a stab at humor.

It was a lame attempt.

"So, darlin', you think there's room in that car of yours for another passenger?" He turned to her with a weak smile, but the image she presented caused the smile to drop.

She cowered in the corner, her hands clutching the sheet, her blue eyes huge and filled with tears.

"Faith, darlin'." He held out a hand, but she recoiled from it and shook her head.

"Don't touch me. Please don't touch me."

He held up his hands, afraid that if he touched her she'd fall apart like the fragile paper of a hornet's nest. And he didn't think he could deal with that. Not when just the sight of her all bunched up like a scared, trapped animal made him want to weep and sob like Jenna.

"That's all right, honey. If you don't want me to touch you, I won't."

"You and Hope"—her gaze dropped down to the bed, and she swallowed hard—"are . . . sweethearts?"

He cleared his throat and stared down at his bare toes. "Not exactly. It's kind of a funny story, really. You see—"

"Get out."

The hateful words caused his head to snap up. The woman that looked back at him wasn't the soft-spoken, mild-mannered woman he'd spent the last two days with. This woman still looked hurt but also madder than a cornered rattlesnake.

"Let me explain, Faith—"

"Get out."

Sometimes retreat was the wisest move. Especially when facing a woman who looked like she wanted to rip your head off and spit in your neck.

He backed away. "I can see you need a little time alone, so I'm just going to go scrounge us up something to eat. And while I'm doing that, why don't you take a nice, long shower. Don't worry about using all the hot water—I could use a cold shower to wake me up." He grabbed the doorknob. "And then after you're feeling better, we can sit down, and I'll explain things. How does that sound?"

She glared at him.

"All right then, if you need anything, you just call." He motioned to the dog that stood at the foot of the bed. "Come on, Buster."

But Buster was smarter than the rest of them. He didn't ask permission. He simply jumped on the bed and bumped his nose against Faith. Her arms wrapped around him as she slipped down to the bed, her sobs shaking her entire body.

With his own eyes stinging, Slate pulled the door closed behind him.

Chapter Eight

THE WEAK TRICKLE OF HOT WATER didn't make Faith feel better, but it did help her collect her thoughts. Thoughts that had been jumbled up from the moment she stared into the petite woman's brown eyes. Even if the color was wrong, the shape had been familiar. Along with the nose, the mouth, and the stubborn chin. A prickle of recognition had been there even before the woman called her Faith.

The woman.

Jenna Scroggs.

Her mother.

A mother who'd given her away at birth.

And Burl Scroggs.

Her father who had gone along with it.

The realization still brought pain, but not as intense as before. She no longer felt like she would break out in tears at any minute. Of course, she'd cried most of her tears out on poor Buster. By the time she had finally dried up, the spot on his neck was drenched. Did salt water hurt dogs? She hoped not. She would hate to do any more harm to the sweet animal.

She turned off the shower. She might not want to hurt Buster, but she wanted to hurt someone else. Like a certain deceitful redneck. If she was upset over her biological parents' rejection, she was absolutely furious over Slate's deception.

He and Hope weren't just friends. They were sweethearts. So close that even her parents weren't surprised to find them in bed together. Arrrgh! Faith had slept with her sister's boyfriend, and not just slept. She had practically thrown herself at him. And the dirty, rotten liar hadn't said a word. Not at Sutter Springs. Or all day yesterday. Or especially not last night. She squeezed her eyes shut. Obviously, to an egotistical redneck, there was nothing wrong with keeping it in the family.

The sleazeball.

She jerked open the shower curtain so hard that she pulled off two of the metal rings. A glass of orange juice sat on the edge of the sink. The sight only made her angrier. No, she didn't feel like crying anymore. Now she felt like hitting something. Really hard. Like a cocky cowboy's face.

She drank the orange juice only because she was thirsty and because ignoring it wouldn't prove anything. And she was ready to prove some things. Like she was through being a doormat. Not for a lying jerk. Or a sheriff with dementia. Or heartless biological parents. And certainly not for an entire wacko town that refused to accept the truth.

It had taken her thirty years, but Faith Aldridge, or whoever she was, had finally reached the limit of what she was willing to put up with. She was mad as hell, and she wasn't going to take it anymore.

At least not from anybody in this Podunk town.

With anger boiling in her stomach, she slipped on the new clothes Slate had washed the day before—the new pink lacy panties and bra, the tight Wranglers, and the pink and red plaid shirt with the pearl snaps. She looped the brown silver-studded belt through her pant loops, then tugged on the red cowboy boots. Unable to find a hair straightener in town, she fluffed her hair with the new blow-dryer, then sprayed it into a wild spiky array. Using a heavy hand, she applied her new cosmetics, then stepped back to study the results.

The woman who stared back at her didn't look like Faith Anne Aldridge, the conservative unassuming computer nerd from Chicago. She looked like a woman you didn't want to mess with—which was exactly who she wanted to be.

This time, Slate wasn't waiting outside the bathroom door. Just Buster followed her around the bedroom as she collected the rest of her things. As she moved around the room, she kept her gaze away from the bed with its rumpled sheets. Earlier she'd heard the sounds of banging pans and sizzling bacon. Now she didn't hear anything. If she was lucky, the jerk had run off, and she'd never have to lay eyes on him again. Unfortunately, she'd never been lucky, and once she got to the kitchen, a quick glance out the window proved her luck hadn't changed.

Slate stood next to a blue SUV, talking through the open window to Kenny. Her eyes narrowed on his casual stance and naked back. The man was too conceited for his own good. He stood there looking as if nothing had happened. As if he hadn't just had sex with his girlfriend's sister or witnessed her humiliation at the hands of her biological parents. He stood there looking like he always did—happy-go-lucky, confident, and gorgeous.

Jerk.

The aroma of bacon pulled her gaze away from the window and down to plates filled with scrambled eggs, bacon, and toast. She grabbed a piece of bacon and took a bite of it, debating her next move.

If her cell phone hadn't been dead and her charger in her missing car, she would call for a cab. Not that there was cab service way out in the sticks. Her gaze fell on a set of keys next to a worn black wallet. Of course; why did she need a cab when there was a vehicle sitting right in front?

Before she even had the front door completely opened, Buster squeezed past her legs and raced over to Slate, who glanced up in time to register shock.

He recovered quickly.

"Well, don't you look all spiffed up and ready to shine?"

"You sure do, Hope—" Kenny shot a quick glance at Slate. "I mean Faith."

She ignored both of them as she took the stairs and headed for the big monster truck. It was harder to get into without Slate's help, but she managed it and had the door closed and the seat adjusted before his shock wore off.

"Now, darlin'." Slate hurried across the dirt yard. "That's a pretty big truck for a little gal like you—"

When he stopped to pick a sticker out of the bottom of his bare foot, Faith started the engine. The loud rumbling startled her, but only for a second, the second right before Slate stepped in front with his hands held up.

"Now, Faith, honey. I don't think this is the time to

be driving. Not when you're so upset and all. Besides, I'll take you anywhere you want to go."

"Fuck you."

His hazel eyes widened, and his strong jaw dropped.

Faith was almost as shocked. She knew the word but had never said it. Surprisingly, it felt good. Real good.

"Slate?" Kenny called from his truck. "You sure that ain't Hope? 'Cause that's a Hope word if ever I heard one."

Slate remained frozen until Faith popped the truck into drive. But when the huge tires rolled toward him, he moved quickly enough.

"Faith!" His voice no longer sounded all southern sweetness as she maneuvered the truck around Kenny's SUV. "This isn't funny anymore. Damn it, Faith, you get back here right now!"

She gunned the truck, and it shot out into the road amid a spray of dust and gravel. As she fought for control of the beast, she glanced in the rearview mirror. Slate stood in the plume of dust with his eyes squinted and his fists clenched, while Buster stood next to him with his tail wagging. Ignoring the spark of sadness the sight evoked, she looked away and concentrated on driving.

It wasn't easy. She now understood why Slate had straddled the yellow lines. Any little movement caused the wheels to veer to one side or the other. But after a while, she got the hang of it and found there was something kind of empowering about being in control of something so big. High atop her perch, she stared out at the world in front of her, daring anyone to cross her path.

The feeling was so exhilarating that she considered driving all the way to California. But then she vetoed the idea. She might not want to be a doormat, but she wasn't a thief. Besides, she wasn't about to leave her Volvo and all her suitcases.

Thinking about California caused her to think about Hope. At least now Faith didn't have to worry about telling her she was adopted. Hope had grown up with her biological parents. Faith was the only disposable daughter.

Pain welled up again, but before it sent her into another sobbing fit, she reached over and turned on the radio. A twanging male voice came on singing some country song about sweet tea and bad directions. She changed channels. She'd had enough twanging voices to last a lifetime. Unfortunately, every programmed station turned out to be country, so she was forced to use the dial until she found something that didn't make her weepy or so angry that she wanted to smash the radio with her fist.

She had just found a pop station when the truck started to bounce. She glanced up to discover that she was driving on the shoulder of the road, flattening clumps of brown bushy grass beneath the huge, deep-treaded tires.

But the grass didn't concern her as much as the pedestrian.

With her heart in her throat, she laid on the horn just in time to alert the young man. He dove out of the way as she jerked on the steering wheel, the truck careening across the road to the opposite shoulder before she slammed on the brakes.

She jerked up the emergency brake, then opened the door and jumped down. "Ohmygod!" She raced around the back. "Are you okay?"

The teenage boy stared up at her from his spot on the ground. His ball cap had flown off, and he had one iPod earplug intact while the other hung over his dusty T-shirt.

"Have you lost your mind, lady?" He got up, his rangy body unfolding to a good three inches over six feet, and brushed at the dirt on his jeans.

"I am so sorry." Faith picked a chunk of sod off his shoulder. "I wasn't paying attention."

"No shit," he said, before he blushed. "Pardon me, ma'am. But cusswords have a way of slipping out during stressful situations. And almost being killed is a pretty stressful situation."

Since Faith had used the king daddy of all cusswords just minutes earlier, she couldn't say much. "Maybe we should take you to the hospital." She leaned closer. "Is that a cut on your forehead? Oh no, are you bleeding?"

"It's nothing." He reached down to pick up his backpack.

"Of course it's something. We need to get that cleaned before it gets infected. People can die from infection." She picked up his cap, then grabbed his arm and tugged him toward the truck, which wasn't an easy task with a kid that big. "Are you feeling dizzy or nauseous?"

"Geez, I'm fine."

But Faith refused to release him until she reached the truck and took out the disinfectant wipes. She pulled out two wipes as she examined the small cut. Actually, it was more like a scratch, which caused her to relax a little.

"So what were you doing walking along the highway? Don't you know how dangerous that is?" She handed him the wipes. "Don't put these in your mouth." By the confused look on his face, it was a stupid warning but she wasn't taking any chances.

"It wasn't dangerous until you showed up," he said as he swiped twice over his forehead. "And how else am I going to get to school when my mom refuses to buy me a car?"

She snapped the lid closed on the wipes and put them back. "Oh, so you're headed to school?"

"Unfortunately," he grumbled.

"You don't like school?"

"Hate."

She glanced up at him. "Hate is a pretty strong word."

He shrugged his bony shoulders. "So is this your truck? I thought it belonged to some guy named Bubba." He stuffed the wipes into the front pocket of his jeans.

Bubba? Who was this Bubba? She might've questioned him if it hadn't just dawned on her what was so different about the young man—he didn't talk with a twang or drop his *g*s.

"Where are you from?"

"Iowa."

She smiled and held out a hand. "Then we're neighbors—Faith Aldridge from Chicago."

His large hand engulfed hers as he gave it a quick shake. "Austin Reeves."

"Austin?"

"Yeah, I know; it's real funny that I should be named after a city in a place I hate. But that's what happens when you don't get a say in your name." Austin grabbed his cap off the seat where she'd placed it and tugged it down over his wavy brown hair. "I wish I could say it's been a pleasure meeting you, but almost getting killed ranks right up there with moving to this hellhole." He lifted a hand as he turned. "See ya around, Faith Aldridge."

He had only taken a few steps when she stopped him. "Wait. Why don't you let me give you a ride to school? It's the least I can do."

He hesitated. "That thing got seat belts?"

Faith laughed. "Yes. But I promise I'll be more careful."

It was easier said than done. As soon as they were back on the road, she fought to keep the big truck from straddling the yellow lines.

"So do you play sports, Austin?" she asked, trying to make conversation.

"Some."

"Basketball?" It seemed likely given his height.

"No, football. At least, I played football in Iowa where they didn't let buttholes coach." He shot a glance over at her. "Sorry. Like everyone else in this town, you probably love Coach Calhoun."

Love?

Her hands tightened on the steering wheel. "Not hardly."

Austin shot her a startled look before a smile spread across his face. A smile that transformed him from a gangly kid to a handsome young man. "So I guess you and I are the only people in Bramble who aren't members of The Slate Calhoun Fan Club."

"I guess so." She glanced over at him. "So why don't you like him?"

"Because he's a jerk."

She lifted an eyebrow.

"Well, he is!" He crossed his arms. "He bumped a darned good quarterback off his team just because I told him his rules sucked. He said I had an attitude problem."

"And do you?"

"Hell, yes, I have an attitude problem! Who wouldn't have an attitude problem when their parents get a divorce and their mother drags them halfway across the country, away from all their friends and family, to some lame town with a bunch of redneck hillbillies?" He slouched down in the seat, his ball cap sitting low.

His words sounded so much like her thoughts, she couldn't help but agree.

"Parents can be real buttholes."

He peeked out from beneath the brim of his ball cap and grinned. "I like you, Faith Aldridge, even if you did try to run me over."

She grinned back at him. "I like you, too, Austin. Even if you have a bad attitude."

He tipped up his hat. "So are you headed into town?"

"Yes. It seems Sheriff Winslow forgot where he put my car."

"So you're the woman everyone's talking about—the one going back to Hollywood."

Rather than explain, she only nodded.

"Lucky," he grumbled, then a second later perked up. "You wouldn't want a traveling companion, would you?"

She shook her head. "I don't think taking a kid across the state line is a good idea."

"I'm not a kid. I'm almost seventeen."

"Fine. I don't think taking a minor across the state line is a good idea."

"Bummer." He slouched back down in the seat.

Funny, but suddenly Faith didn't feel as upset and angry as she had earlier. In fact, Austin had made her realize she didn't have it so bad. She wasn't stuck in this lame town. In fact, in a couple of hours, she'd be on her way to California, and Bramble would be nothing more than a bad memory.

Or more like a nightmare.

The high school was on the outskirts of town, the parking lot filled with beat-up trucks as teenagers arrived for school. Afraid of taking out one, or two, on her way into the narrow driveway, Faith pulled off to the side of the road to let Austin out.

"Hey, thanks for the lift," he said as he scrambled down from the truck. "Sure you won't change your mind about taking me with you?"

"I'm sure."

He went to slam the door, but stopped and pulled it back open. "Listen, I probably shouldn't say anything because I don't always understand what these crazy Texans are talking about. But from what I overheard, I don't think Sheriff Winslow forgot where he put your car."

Faith's brows drew together. "What do you mean?"

"I mean, I think he hid it. All some grand scheme to keep you here. Although I thought the girl they were talking about was named Hope."

Words escaped her. All she could do was stare back at the kid until he shrugged and slammed the door. The jarring sound snapped her out of her daze, and her eyes narrowed as she gunned the truck and bounced back out on the highway.

Josephine's Diner wasn't as crowded as it had been on Sunday. Which was a good thing, since Faith barreled into the parking lot without paying too much attention to things like cars. She parked by the Dumpsters and jumped down, without giving one thought to her purse and unlocked doors. The front door banged against the wire newspaper rack as she threw it open and marched in.

Just like Sunday, every eye turned to her. But this time, she couldn't have cared less. Her narrowed gaze swept around the room until it lit on the man with the taupe felt hat and shiny badge.

"Where's my car?"

The man stood up, and hooked his thumbs in his loaded-down black belt. "Now, Hope, darlin'."

"The name is Faith." She pointed a finger in his face. "And if one more person calls me darlin' . . ." Her voice trailed off, because, having never threatened anyone before, she couldn't think of one good threat. But that didn't stop her from continuing. "So where's my car?"

He held up his hands. "Now Ho—Faith, don't go getting all fussied up. I didn't hurt your car. I just put it somewhere for safekeeping."

"Safekeeping?"

He nodded. "Just long enough for you to see the error of your ways."

Over the last two days, she'd figured out that the people of Bramble were two cards short of a full deck. Now she realized it was closer to fifty.

"What do you mean, the error of my ways?"

"Why, leaving poor Slate for five long years with only a few measly visits," the sheriff said.

"And thinkin' you'd ever find happiness in a sin-filled city like Hollywood," Harley joined in.

"But I'm not Hope!" She screamed louder than she ever had in her life.

"Why, of course you are, honey." Rachel Dean stepped out from behind the counter. "That proves it. Nobody yells like our little Hope."

Completely stunned, Faith stood there for a moment before she turned and headed back out the door. She wasn't a violent person. But desperate times called for desperate measures. The gun was a lot heavier than it looked. Once she had it off the rack, it nearly toppled her into the seat. But her anger gave her strength; that and her determination to get her car back and find her sister.

Besides, it was worth the effort when the sheriff's eyes bugged out.

"Now, Ho—Faith, don't go and do anything stupid." He backed toward the kitchen.

"I want my car back." She waved the long end of the gun around, but kept her finger completely away from the trigger. She was desperate, not delusional. "Now."

"Fine." The sheriff held up his hands. "Hand me the gun, and I'll see what I can do."

"No. Tell me where—"

Two muscular arms reached over her head and pulled the gun out of her hands. She whirled around to dark greenish-brown eyes. Slate no longer looked like the easygoing cowboy.

"That's enough, Faith. I know you're mad, but you can't be threatening people with guns."

"Fuck—"

He slapped a hand over her mouth and pulled her toward the door as she struggled against his chest. "If you folks would excuse us, Faith and I need to have a little talk."

"You mean Hope," Harley said.

"Of course he means Hope." Rachel Dean waved one man hand. "But he can't say that when Hope's packin' a gun and has her heart set on being called Faith."

"Well, I kinda like Faith, myself," a woman spoke up. "It has a nice ring to—"

The door slammed closed behind them just as Faith bit down on one of Slate's fingers.

"Sonofabitch!" He released her, shaking his hand.

"You sure she ain't Hope, Slate?" Kenny stood by his SUV, still looking confused.

Slate ignored him and reached for her again. "Now, Faith, just listen to me."

"Don't touch me!" she screamed. "Don't you ever touch me again!"

"Fine!" He glared back at her. "I won't!"

"Good!" Faith whirled and headed back to the truck.

"And just where in the hell do you think you're going?"

"To California!"

"Without a car?" He stepped in front of her. "Because you're sure not taking this truck." He pointed a finger. "Hell, you can't even park the damn thing."

"Go to hell." She tried to march around him, but he grabbed her arm.

"I realize this morning couldn't have been one of your better days. But if you would just settle down a minute, we could get some things worked out."

"Really?" She stopped struggling. "Like maybe why you failed to mention that you and my sister are..." She couldn't even bring herself to say the word.

"Friends," he finished for her. "Just friends."

"Friends?" She felt her temper rise, and she pulled from his grasp. "Is that why her mother wasn't surprised to find us in bed together? And why the entire town is holding me hostage? Because you and Hope are just friends?"

Slate's gaze flickered. "Now I can see where you might be confused, darlin'. It's a pretty complicated situation."

"Well, let me uncomplicate it for you." She shoved her way around him and jerked open the door of the truck.

"What are you doing?"

"I'm leaving." She pulled her purse out and hooked it over her shoulder.

"Haven't you figured out by now that the crazy people of this town aren't going to give your car back?" He ran a hand over the back of his neck. "Damned fools."

"Which means you fit right in." She turned and headed for the street.

"Just where do you think you're going?"

"To find a hotel, and then to find a lawyer who will sue the hell out of this town." Faith tossed the words over her shoulder as she marched across the dirt parking lot. When she reached the strip of asphalt that ran through the center of Bramble, it took her a moment to figure out what direction to head in—a moment that gave Slate a chance to climb in the monster truck and pull it up next to her.

"Damn it, Faith, get in the truck." He leaned down and spoke through the open window.

"When hell freezes over." She adjusted her purse strap and headed toward the WELCOME TO BRAMBLE sign.

"Would you stop walking and listen to me? The closest hotel is a good fifty miles away."

Fifty miles?

She hesitated.

"And that one fills up with roughnecks at night. Not a good situation for a pretty single woman. So stop being stubborn and get in the truck. You can stay with me until I find your car."

"I'm not staying with you."

"Fine. You can go stay with Jenna and Burl."

If his plan was to tick her off, he'd achieved it. "I'd rather sleep with a hundred sex-starved roughnecks."

He banged the steering wheel with his fist. "Then what the hell do you want me to do, Faith? Leave you here on the side of the road?"

She opened her mouth to tell him that was exactly what she wanted him to do, except the words refused to come out. Probably because as angry as she was with him, she really didn't want him to leave her. He was the only semi-friend she had in this town, and the thought of him driving away didn't exactly make her feel good.

Things would've been so much easier if Jenna and Burl hadn't shown up, and she had remained Blissfully Ignorant Faith. Instead of standing on the side of the road, she would still be snuggled up against Slate's hard, warm chest. Unfortunately, Jenna and Burl had arrived and with them the knowledge that this man wasn't hers to snuggle up against.

He was Hope's.

Faith's jaw tightened, along with her resolve. "Yes, Slate. I want you to leave."

He stared at her for a few seconds, his eyes gorgeous and sincere, before he nodded. "Fine. I guess I'll see you around."

Her good-bye got stuck behind the lump that had formed in her throat, and all she could do was stare back at him, completely unaware of the black Lincoln Navigator that pulled up.

"Well, I'll be damned. If I hadn't seen it with my own two eyes, I never would've believed it." A beautiful blonde came around the front of the SUV, and before Faith could take more than a step back, she was smothered against huge, soft breasts.

"Same dwarfy size. Same bony body." The woman

pulled back and studied Faith with sparkling eyes the color of wet spring grass. "Hair's different—very polished." The woman flashed white teeth and dimples before she tipped her head down and looked at Slate through the open window. "What's cookin', good lookin'?"

The smile Slate sent her lacked his usual charm. "Hey, Shirl. How was Dallas?"

"Filled with plenty of stores for me to spend Lyle's money in." Her gaze shifted between the two of them. "Did I interrupt something?" The smile deepened. "My bad—or maybe my good, since it looks like you two could use a little distance." She hooked an arm through Faith's. "Come on, honey. Let's go back to the house and you can tell Shirlene all about it."

Faith dug in her boot heels and glanced back at Slate.

Grudgingly, he nodded. "Go on with Shirlene, darlin'. She's a good friend."

Good friend to whom? Faith wanted to ask. But it wasn't like she had another choice. Go with Slate, stay at Jenna and Burl's, or walk fifty miles and become a roughneck's main squeeze. The beautiful blonde with the bright smile seemed like her best option. Still, once in the passenger side of the Navigator, Faith started to have second thoughts. The only reason the woman was so happy to see her was because she thought Faith was Hope. Which meant she needed to explain things before they went anywhere.

But before she could open her mouth, Shirlene surprised her.

"Welcome to Bramble, Faith." She winked. "You like margaritas? Because I make the best margaritas this side of the Rio Grande." She whipped the SUV around and headed in the opposite direction from Slate. "Did you know that the frozen margarita was invented by a Texan?"

Faith didn't know that. But she also didn't know how sad she would feel watching a truck with offensive bumper stickers and two flapping flags grow smaller and smaller in the side mirror.

Chapter Nine

THE SPANISH MISSION-STYLE MANSION Shirlene lived in was as far from Slate's trailer as a home could get. And it was all Faith could do to keep her jaw from dropping as Shirlene gave her a tour of the sprawling estate with its swimming pool, guest cottage, spa and sauna, and the media room the size of a small theater. Not that Faith hadn't been in gorgeous homes before—her boss had a multimillion-dollar home on the North Shore of Chicago—but she just hadn't expected to find a house this size in Bramble, Texas.

Of course, there were a lot of things she hadn't expected to find in Bramble. Things much more jaw-dropping than a big mansion. Things she couldn't think about without wanting to sling around a few good four-letter words. And since Shirlene had been the epitome of gracious hospitality since bringing her back to her home—offering her the guesthouse and a sumptuous breakfast prepared by her cook, Cristina—Faith kept her anger to herself and tried to be a grateful guest.

It wasn't hard given Shirlene's bubbly personality. The woman was like the neighborhood Welcome Wagon—

Texas-style. And sitting across from her in the large sunroom off the kitchen, Faith still couldn't get over the breathtaking combination of thick blond hair, sparkling green eyes, and bee-stung lips that were rarely without an impish smile.

"So you're from Chicago?" Shirlene sat back in the corner of the opulent white couch and sipped her margarita—her second before noon. "I've never been there, myself. I tried to get *Oprah* tickets once, but I swear that woman is harder to get in to see than God on Judgment Day. Of course, it's probably just as well, seeing as how Lyle thinks she's one of those liberals." She flashed a smile. "Not that there's anything wrong with being Liberal—I'm pretty liberal-minded myself."

"Liberal" wasn't the word Faith would use to describe Shirlene. Flamboyant and vivacious seemed to fit much better. Or possibly bountiful, considering everything about the woman was abundant—from her piles of blond hair to her ample breasts. From the lavishly decorated home to the copious diamonds that crowded her long, slim fingers. She was the complete polar opposite of Faith—a tall, passionate nonconformist who had no trouble speaking her mind.

"So you ready to tell old Shirlene all about what's been going on between you and Slate?"

Faith's face flamed, and Shirlene chuckled.

"It's nothing to be ashamed of, honey. You aren't the first woman to melt from just a glance of those hazel eyes, and you won't be the last. Lyle may have money, but Slate has what all Texans covet."

"An ego the size of the state." Faith's voice dripped with sarcasm.

Shirlene smirked. "Well, that, too. But I was talking about a quick wit—a tall, athletic body—dazzling good looks—and an arm that can throw a fifty-yard touchdown pass under the pressure of a full-out defensive blitz."

"Oh, brother." Faith leaned her head back on the couch, suddenly extremely tired. Or maybe just depressed over having had sex with some kind of a West Texas Casanova. How stupid could she get? Her first clue should've been the condom that dropped from his truck visor.

"That's it?" Shirlene set down her drink on the beautiful glass and wood sculpture that served as a coffee table. "That's all you're gonna say on the subject? Damn, you're as bad as Hope—she never did like talking about her love life." Leaning down, she slipped off her sky-high turquoise stilettos before she wiggled back on the couch and tucked her feet beneath her. "Still, she and I used to have some times. Of course, we didn't drink margaritas out of fancy crystal glasses in a fancy house—more like sloe gin out of a bottle in the front seat of her mama's old Buick. But it was still a hoot."

"So I guess you've known Hope a long time," Faith said.

Shirlene glanced over at her and cocked an eyebrow. "You say that like it's something wonderful. Believe me, honey, being friends with your sister can be extremely tedious at times. Besides, our lives haven't been all wine and roses. Not when we grew up on the south side of town—Hope with Jenna and Burl, and me with my mama and my big brother, Colt." Her smile dimmed. "Times were hard back then. We were what you might call trailer trash, although we didn't know it. We thought the broken-down vehicles in our front yards were put there for us to play in. And the tall weeds grown just for hide-and-seek. Hell, I didn't know I was poor until I started school and realized that most kids had shoes without holes in them."

The picture Shirlene painted wasn't exactly what Faith had visualized. Not only was it hard to imagine Shirlene, with her diamonds and designer jeans, living in a run-down trailer park, but also Hope—the town sweetheart. Faith knew Jenna and Burl weren't wealthy, but she hadn't realized they'd been so poor.

While Faith hadn't been spoiled, she'd had the best quality shoes and clothing, the best educational toys on the market, and a well-tended backyard with a little pink and white playhouse her father had built for her fifth birthday. Once she'd reached an age when she no longer used it, her father had stored his gardening tools in it. And when he passed away, she had gone out and sat amid the trowels and bags of fertilizer and wept for the man who'd spent so many hours building it for the daughter he loved.

A daughter he would never have given away.

"Of course, they didn't stay as dirt-poor as we were," Shirlene continued. "When Hope was six, Burl got a job on an oil rig, and Jenna got a job doing bookkeeping for the Feed and Seed. That's when they moved into town. Soon after, Tessa, Jenna Jay, and Dallas showed up."

Shirlene had mentioned Hope's siblings during breakfast, but Faith was still having trouble processing the information. She had always dreamed of being part of a big family—and now it seemed she had one. Of course, in her dreams, she hadn't been the outcast no one seemed to want.

"That house was always brimming with kids." Shirlene reached for her margarita again. "Slate and I practically lived there. Of course, Slate didn't show up until middle school." After taking a sip, she tipped her head in thought. "I remember the first day he swaggered into school. Even at thirteen, he was drop-dead gorgeous. And that charm. Man alive, he had charm. I thought half the girls were going to pass out the first time he spoke. Hope and I had our very first fight over who would get to sit next to him. Of course, Hope won." She shook her gorgeous blond hair. "That girl won any contest she entered, even if she didn't particularly want it."

Faith lifted her head up from the couch cushion. "She didn't want Slate?"

"Oh no, she wanted Slate. But she could've done without Miss Hog Caller of Haskins County. Burl was the one who entered her in that every year, and every year, I got to hear her complain about it. Of course, Hope didn't complain to anyone else. She's not a complainer—more of a pain-in-the-butt overachiever."

"So Slate and Hope were..." It was hard to get the word out. "An item."

"Were? Oh, honey, to this town Hope and Slate are still an item."

Fighting down a fresh wave of anger, Faith picked up her margarita and drained it. When she set the glass back down, Shirlene was smiling.

"It's not anything to get upset about. To this town I'm still Shirlene Lomax, the poor little white trash girl that lives out on Grover Road."

Brushing the salt from her lips, Faith glanced around at the tall ornate ceilings, the multipaned windows, and the intricate marbled floors. "White trash? Have they ever been here?"

"Every Christmas. But change is hard for them to accept."

"Obviously. No matter what I say, I'm still Hope."

"Well, you do look exactly like her." Her green eyes ran over Faith. "If Jenna hadn't called, I might've been fooled."

"I might physically look like her, but I certainly don't sound or act like her."

"Sound, no. Act?—Now there, I think you're mistaken. I think you act quite a bit like Hope. You're not as loud or as ornery, but you're just as pigheaded."

"I'm not pigheaded." The words came out sounding like a belligerent teenager's.

"Of course you are. Otherwise, you'd give up trying to change this town's mind and enjoy your stay. Bramble folks are good folks once you get to know them—including your mama and daddy."

"I don't want to get to know my—Jenna and Burl. In fact, I'll be lucky if I never see them again."

Shirlene topped off her margarita from the pitcher that sat in the middle of the coffee table. "If I've learned anything from this crazy life of mine, it's never say never. Besides, since your own parents are gone, you never know when you'll need an extra set." When Faith opened her mouth to argue, Shirlene lifted a hand. "I get it—you want nothing to do with them. All you want to do is find Hope. But I gotta tell you, honey. That might be easier said than done. Hope hasn't exactly been receptive to visitors since moving to LA. In fact, she's been downright evasive."

"Well, I'm sure she'll want to see *me*." Faith sounded a lot more confident than she felt. "And while I appreciate your hospitality, Shirlene, I'm going to California—even if I have to take a plane."

Unfortunately, before the words were even out, she realized her credit cards were in her suitcase, put there as a precaution against the rest-stop muggings Aunt Jillian had warned her about. She had a grand total of twenty-three dollars and change in her wallet. Certainly not enough for a plane ticket—or even a bus. She could always call her aunt and have her wire money. But if she asked for money, she would need to give an explanation. And there was no way to explain the Twilight Zone she had landed in, not without causing her aunt to call out the National Guard.

And she wasn't ready to do that yet.

At least not until she'd exhausted all other avenues of escape.

Shooting a quick glance at her hostess, Faith cleared her throat. "I was wondering if you could loan me some money, Shirlene—just until I get my car back."

"I'd love to help you out, honey. But—"

"I understand. You have to live in this town. No doubt they'd lynch you if they found out you'd helped me." Defeated, Faith flopped back on the couch.

Shirlene snorted. "That's doubtful, since Lyle employs half the town. Besides, that's not why I won't help you."

"Then why?"

"Because I'm as pigheaded as you are. And I think you've got a lot of unfinished business here to take care of before you go traipsing off to California."

"Great." At that point, Faith might've gotten up and left, if the tequila hadn't sapped the last of her strength. Besides, where was she going to go when the entire town seemed dead set on holding her hostage?

Leaning in, Shirlene sent her a bright smile. "Now don't look so downhearted, honey. West Texas might not be Hollywood, but we've got our fair share of entertainment—not to mention a pisspot full of smokin' hot cowboys."

"Are you ladies talking about me?"

A short, balding man walked in, dressed in creased blue jeans and a western shirt so starched it could stand on its own. At first, Faith thought it was one of Shirlene's older relatives. But then he leaned over the couch and kissed her, and Faith reevaluated the situation.

"Hey, Lyle, honey." Shirlene patted his round cheek before pointing at Faith. "Look who's here." As the man turned, she sent Faith a wicked wink.

"Hope?" His eyes widened. He tossed his cowboy hat down to the coffee table—almost knocking over Faith's margarita glass—before he jerked Faith up off the couch and enfolded her in stiff cotton that reeked of cigar smoke. "Lord have mercy, girl. Aren't you a sight for sore eyes."

"I'm not Hope," Faith tried to explain.

"What?" He set her back down on her boots, his gaze running over her features. "Well, you're right. You don't look like the Hope I remember. Not with that short hair, but those baby blues are the same."

Shirlene giggled, obviously enjoying her little game.

"I'm really not Hope. I'm her twin sister, Faith."

Lyle chuckled as he leaned down and gave her a kiss right on the tip of her nose. "You and Shirlene—always playing tricks. Remember the time you two took my Cadillac for a joyride?" He shot a smile over at Shirlene, whose giggles had turned to out-and-out laughter. "That taught me never to leave the keys in the ignition. Hell, you two remind me of Lucy and Ethel with all the mischief you get into.

"And speaking of mischief, I've got a hardheaded foreman to attend to before I head to Houston." He reached down and grabbed his cowboy hat off the table, then addressed Shirlene. "I'll be back on Saturday, sugar. If you need me, call me on the cell." Still giggling, she only nodded.

Before Lyle left the room, he shot one more glance at Faith and shook his head. "Twin sister."

Once he was gone, Faith flopped back down on the couch and glared at Shirlene. "That wasn't funny."

"Oh, yes it was," she got out between fits of laughter.

Faith watched her for a few seconds before a smile tickled the corners of her mouth. It was impossible to stay mad at a woman with such a love of life. "Okay, so it was pretty funny. But you didn't help matters, Lucy, making Ricky think I'm Hope."

Shirlene caught her breath. "Oh no, I'm not Lucy. Hope's Lucy. I'm Ethel." Her green eyes widened. "Which means Lyle is Fred."

Since Lyle was a dead ringer for Fred, Faith couldn't help but laugh.

"So the margaritas are finally kicking in?" Shirlene asked.

Faith shrugged, even though Shirlene was probably right. She didn't feel as angry as she had. In fact, she felt pretty relaxed.

"Good." Leaning forward, Shirlene filled their glasses back to the top before handing Faith hers. "So here's the plan. We'll get you settled into the guesthouse and then we'll head on over to the high school for the homecoming decorating meeting. I can't wait to watch that show. Cindy Lynn has always wanted to step inside Hope's skin—so it should be real entertaining."

"Oh no, I'm not—"

Cutting her off, Shirlene lifted her glass. "Here's to Lucy and Ethel—may they ride again." She clinked Faith's glass and took a deep drink before holding up the glass again. "And to Lucy's twin sister and Ethel—may they get into just as much trouble."

Unable to refuse Shirlene's offer of friendship, Faith clinked glasses and resigned herself to one more day in Bramble.

Besides, how much trouble could you get into at a homecoming decorating meeting?

Chapter Ten

"SO IT'S DECIDED. Hop—I mean, Faith—will be in charge of paper plates and cups. And Shirlene will be in charge of the punch." Cindy Lynn, president of the Women's Society for the Betterment of Bramble, sat at a table in the front of the classroom with her overprocessed hair curled in a style that had been popular...never, and with so many layers of mascara on her top and bottom lashes, they resembled fuzzy black spiders.

"Would that be slutty or virgin punch?" Shirlene yelled from the back of the room where she sat—or *leaned* would be a better description—next to Faith.

While Faith had only sipped on her second margarita, Shirlene had polished off the rest of the pitcher.

"Virgin, of course," Cindy said. "After all, it's being held in the school gymnasium. Now, if there are no more questions about the dance, we can move on to the Parade of Queens."

"I think I saw one of those in San Francisco once," Shirlene blurted out. "The costumes those guys wore were spectacular."

Faith coughed to cover her laughter.

Cindy's spiders narrowed. "Yes, well, most of us can't afford to travel as much as you, Shirlene." With a slight upsweep of her pointy nose, she moved on. "So I assume everyone knows that the parade takes place before the game with a shorter version at halftime. All homecomin' queens, past and present, will meet at the town hall by five thirty and, during the game, sit in the designated first two rows of the stadium so it will be easier for them to get down to the field. Last year, Emma Jean sat up with her kids and husband and held up the entire procession because she got stuck behind the band when they were takin' the field."

"Oh, yeah, I remember that," some woman in the front row said. "Didn't she get stuck in the tuba section?"

"Right behind Ernie Clines," another woman cut in. "And you couldn't move that boy with a John Deere front loader—"

"Ladies." Cindy Lynn tapped a tiny mallet on the table. "We need to keep on track or else we won't get anything accomplished." Her eyes scanned the group. "All queens will sit in the first two rows. Now moving on to the next order of business—Darla, how's the float comin'?"

A plump woman with rosy cheeks stood up and turned to the group. "I'm happy to announce that the float is finished and is the cutest thing you've ever seen. As you know, after last year—when the students chose that filthy rap song—Principal Garner insisted they choose one this year that was an oldie but a goodie." At this point it looked like she tried to roll her eyes, but her eyes were so small it was hard to tell. "So of course, they chose another weird song that no one has heard of—'Welcome to the Jungle.'"

Faith and Shirlene burst out laughing, but the women didn't have a clue what they were laughing at.

"I know," Darla continued. "Can you imagine? I could just see our lovely queens dressed up like monkeys swingin' from a bunch of ugly vines. Anyway, I was forced to use some creative thinkin', and I can't wait for y'all to see it." She waited for the round of applause before she took her seat.

"Good job, Darla," Cindy Lynn said before she addressed the entire group. "As a homecomin' queen myself, I will be contactin' the other queens to make sure they know where and when the parade will start. Twyla has been kind enough to offer her services on Friday so all queens will have matching updos."

Shirlene cringed. "I don't envy you, honey."

Before Faith could ask what she meant, Cindy Lynn stood up and motioned in her direction.

"So now, without further ado, I give the floor to Hope— I mean, Faith—so she can tell us all about her time in Hollywood." She moved out from around the table, and all eyes turned to Faith.

"Oh, no." Faith shook her head. "I-I can't—really."

"What do you mean?" Darla asked, looking at Faith as if she had just killed her favorite dog. "You mean you ain't gonna tell us any Hollywood secrets?"

Faith swallowed. "W-well, I—"

"Of course she's going to answer all your questions," Shirlene butted in, seeming not quite as drunk as she had been a few moments ago. "Lord knows, we'd never get out of here if Hope didn't say a few words." And when Faith sent her a desperate look, she added under her breath. "Just fake it, honey. This group won't know the difference."

But her reassurance didn't make Faith feel any less sick to her stomach. Public speaking terrified her, but no more than disappointing a room filled with expectant faces. She thought about telling them the truth, but realized that even if she spelled everything out for them—starting with her conception and ending with Jenna and Burl's visit to Slate's trailer—they still wouldn't believe her. Like ghost hunters in a deserted house, they only saw and heard what they wanted to.

And what they wanted was Hope. Therefore that's who she was, no matter what evidence she offered to the contrary. Which meant she had no choice but to go along with the charade.

"So what would you—y'all like to hear about?" The accent was all wrong, but not one set of eyes registered confusion.

"Matthew McConaughey!" someone yelled out.

"Yeah." Darla held her pudgy hands over her ample chest. "Please tell us you got him into bed, Hope."

Faith's eyes widened, but she swallowed down her panic, and using everything she'd learned in the one high school drama class she'd taken, tried to channel Hope.

"Well"—she cleared her throat—"there was that one time..."

It was funny how a few lies could snowball into an avalanche. An hour later, Faith was completely buried beneath the façade she'd conjured up. Gone was the shy woman who blushed at every sexual reference, and in her place was a chatty slut who had fake affairs with every Texas actor—from Tommy Lee Jones to Sandra Bullock.

"I can see that about her," Darla said. "Wasn't she like a lesbian in that beauty pageant movie?"

"She wasn't a lesbian." Cindy Lynn's globby eyes narrowed in thought. "I think she was a klutzy cop."

"I loved that movie," another woman piped up. "But enough about her. Did you get to meet any country entertainers while you was there?"

"Hundreds," Faith lied.

"Don't tell me you met Tim."

"Oh, you mean Timbo. Of course I did. And I guess y'all knew that he was really born and raised in Texas." Faith thought it was a nice touch and, if the look on the women's faces was any indication, so did they.

"Ohmygod!" Cindy Lynn gushed. "I always knew that."

"Well, so did the rest of us, Cindy Lynn, so don't go actin' like you was the first," Darla huffed.

"I was not actin' like I was the first—"

Suddenly Shirlene stood up and headed toward the front. "I hate to break this party up—Lord, I can't remember when I've had such a good time—but Faith and I need to be getting back to the house for supper." She hooked her arm through Faith's. "Come on, honey, I think you've done enough damage for one day."

As they moved toward the door, the women called out their good-byes.

"I'll call you, Hope."

"We're glad you're back, Hope."

"Sheriff Winslow said you lost a few screws in Hollywood, but he never did know his butt from a hole in the ground."

"That's right. You haven't changed a lick."

"Same old Hope."

"Sure enough, the same old Hope."

Cindy Lynn held open the door for them. "Hope, don't forget you need to be at Twyla's by four to get your hair done." The door shut before the light went on in Faith's brain.

"Oh no." She looked at Shirlene. "I'm not going to be in the Parade of Queens."

"No?" Shirlene tugged her down the hall lined with lockers and large banners advertising the homecoming dance. "An hour ago, I might've agreed with you. But after that performance, I'd say you're pretty well screwed. You have now convinced those women that you're Hope Scroggs. A Hollywood Slut Hope Scroggs, but Hope Scroggs nonetheless."

Faith stopped and stared at her. "But I thought that's what you wanted me to do."

Shirlene rolled her eyes. "I didn't realize you were going to love the part so much. I thought you'd go up there and answer a few questions—truthfully, I might add. 'No, I don't know Matthew. No, I've never met any Hollywood stars. No, I don't kiss women.' Instead, like Forrest Gump, you took the ball and ran and ran and just kept running until you were so far out of sight there was no calling you back."

Feeling like she'd been thrown under the bus, Faith pointed a finger at her. "But you laughed."

"Of course I laughed, honey. I laughed when Hope swung off the clothesline pole and broke her arm. Sometimes even train wrecks can make you laugh, until you survey the damage. And, girl, you just did a whole lot of damage."

Faith looked back over her shoulder. "Maybe I should go back in there—"

"Nope. I think we should call it a day and leave it at that. Besides, nothing you can say will change their minds now." She tugged her through a set of doors and out into the late afternoon.

The temperature had to be close to eighty; nowhere near the fifties and sixties of the Chicago autumn Faith had left behind. From the distance came a strange clapping noise. She looked at Shirlene for an explanation, but Shirlene only smiled and headed in the direction of the sound.

The football stadium was much larger than Faith's old high school stadium and better cared for. The locker rooms, box office, and concessions looked freshly painted, as did the huge gray snarling bulldog that glared down at them from the side of the stands. When they reached the first set of bleachers, Shirlene headed up to the top.

The stands weren't entirely empty. A few men sat close to the bottom, a group of giggling teenage girls sat in the center rows, and a young boy in a baseball cap sat close to where Shirlene chose to sit. If Faith hadn't held that ball cap in her hand, she probably wouldn't have recognized him.

"Austin?"

He turned away from the field. "Hey. You kill anyone today?"

She grinned as she took a seat next to Shirlene. "Almost, but Slate took my gun away."

"Just another reason to dislike him."

"Who's that?" Shirlene asked.

"Austin," Faith called. "This is Shirlene...." She paused when she realized she didn't know the woman's last name.

"Dalton," Shirlene supplied. "I'm pleased to meet you, Austin. How come you're not playing ball?"

"Dalton of Dalton Oil?" Austin asked.

"That would be my husband."

"Geez, you must be rolling in it."

She flashed her signature smile. "Pretty much. So answer the question, why aren't you playing?"

"Personality conflict." He turned away as if the conversation was over.

Faith followed his gaze to the field where young men in football gear were practicing. It didn't take her long to pick out Slate. With the sun turning his hair a burnished gold, he was hard to miss.

"So how did you meet that kid?" Shirlene asked.

"I almost ran him over with Slate's monster truck."

"You mean Bubba's truck?"

"Who?" Faith glanced over at her.

"Are we talking about the honkin' big truck with all the stupid bumper stickers?"

Faith nodded.

"Yeah, that's Bubba Wilkes's truck. He showed up here a few years back to do some hunting, and I guess he liked it so much he decided to invest in some real estate." She snorted. "As if anyone but a redneck would want to vacation in Bramble. Anyway, I guess Bubba loaned the truck to Slate so he could haul materials out to the house he's building."

"Slate is building a house?"

Shirlene pulled her gaze away from the field. "Don't tell me you think Slate lives in that beat-up trailer Bubba uses as a hunting lodge." When Faith only stared back at her, she laughed. "And you still liked him? Man, you have been bitten by the Calhoun bug." She shook her head. "No, Slate is only staying there until his house gets finished."

The news she hadn't slept with an arrogant redneck should've made Faith happy. Instead she was furious. Not only had Slate lied about his relationship with her sister, but he'd also lied about his truck and his home. And if he'd lied about those things, there was no telling what else he'd lied about.

She looked around the huge stadium. "I guess Bramble pays their coaches pretty well?"

Shirlene looked offended. "Of course we do. This is Texas, honey."

Faith's gaze narrowed on Slate as he walked across the field. Obviously, the man had no honor whatsoever. She watched as he leaned down to scoop up a football and toss it back to one of the players. He had no honor, but in jeans and a polo shirt with the wind ruffling his sun-kissed hair, he had sex appeal in abundance. Yes, she had been bitten by the Calhoun bug, but she would get over it. For now, all she could do was sit there and try not to scratch.

"Damn you, Slate. Coach that kid," Shirlene said, extremely interested in what was taking place on the field. To Faith, it looked like mass confusion.

"What's he doing?" she asked.

"Nothing," Shirlene grumbled. "That's the problem. He's been coaching for four years, and in all that time, I've never once seen him communicate with a kid. He comes up with the plays, and he enforces the stupid rules, but he has no relationship with his team. None at all." She chewed on her thumbnail. "If he doesn't make the play-offs this year, he's gone. I don't care if he is the golden boy of Bramble. Lyle won't have a losing team."

"Lyle owns the team?"

"Honey, Lyle owns most of this town."

It didn't make any sense to Faith, but there wasn't much in Bramble that did, including Shirlene's enthusiasm for football. If she wasn't yelling at Slate, she was yelling at another coach or one of the players. While she ranted, Faith sat quietly and tried to keep her gaze from wandering back to Slate. She failed miserably.

Needing a distraction, she turned her attention to Austin, who watched the mass confusion of flying balls and smacking shoulder pads with such longing that she couldn't help but get up and walk along the bleachers to where he sat.

Sitting down next to him, she stared at the field for a few minutes before she spoke. "You know, sometimes people change their minds."

"About what?" Austin looked over at her from beneath the bill of his hat.

"I'm sure Slate would consider taking you back— that's if he thought your attitude had improved."

"It hasn't."

"Okay. I was just making sure you weren't cutting off your nose to spite your face."

"Funny," he grumbled.

"Come on!" Shirlene called as she headed down the bleachers. "I've had enough torture for one day."

Faith got up. "You need a ride home, or do you intend to sit here all night and wallow in self-pity?"

A grin cracked his face. "A ride would be good, although the self-pity was kind of fun."

She swatted the bill of his cap. "Come on, smart butt, before Shirlene leaves us." She trotted down the stairs, but was easily overtaken by Austin as he agilely took the bleachers. At the tinny thump of his feet against the aluminum, the girls looked over. One, a pretty brunette with wide blue eyes, smiled and waved. Austin blushed.

"Girlfriend?" Faith teased.

"No." He drew out the word even as his gaze flickered back to the girl.

When they reached the bottom, Shirlene was nowhere in sight, but Slate was. He'd moved from the other side of the field and stood on the black shiny asphalt of the track. A stopwatch hung around his neck, and he held a clipboard as he listened to one of his coaches.

It hadn't been easy to ignore him from thirty bleachers up—only yards away, it was impossible. Especially when those deep hazel eyes stared back at her with an intensity that took her breath away. Her heart did a crazy little flip, and her stomach tightened with an uncontrollable longing to run her fingers through his wind-ruffled hair and press her lips to the hollow spot at the base of his tanned throat.

Instead, she turned and walked away.

"Man," Austin said when he caught up with her. "You really do hate him."

Hate him? No, she didn't hate Slate. The feelings that assaulted her body weren't even close to hate. Which was exactly why she needed to stay away from him.

Worried that Shirlene was still slightly tipsy, Faith drove Shirlene's Navigator out to the house Austin shared with his mother and grandparents. It didn't take long, but it was long enough for him and Shirlene to get into a heated discussion about Bramble High football. By the time they pulled up in front of the well-tended little farmhouse, Faith was concerned they might come to blows.

"I think you're wrong. The offensive line is big enough; they just don't have the right kind of motivation," Shirlene leaned around the front bucket passenger's seat and looked in the back at Austin.

"Motivation?" Austin snorted. "And who's going to motivate them? Not that slow-witted senior they have for a quarterback."

"Jared isn't slow-witted as much as slow-footed. That boy couldn't get out of the pocket if his life depended on it—which it does since the line won't protect him. But still, he's not that bad."

"Not that bad? Did you see the game on Friday? It was his two intercepted passes that won the game for Plainsville. He's telegraphing his passes like a billboard in Times Square."

Shirlene's eyes narrowed. "What position did you say you played back in Iowa?"

"I didn't."

"Quarterback," Faith supplied, proud that she was finally able to enter the conversation.

"Quarterback?" Shirlene almost jumped out of her seat. "Varsity?"

"Look, I need to go."

Austin got out, but not in time to beat Shirlene. She jumped in front of him before he could even slam his door. Worried she was about to do bodily harm to the kid, Faith hopped out and hurried around the front of the SUV.

"I assume Slate knows this," Shirlene asked.

"Yes, ma'am." He stuffed his hands in the front pockets of his jeans and smirked at her.

"And are you any good?"

Austin only raised his eyebrows, which made Shirlene let out a whoop and fist-pump the air.

"Hot damn!" She did a little dance that had Faith laughing but Austin scowling.

"It doesn't matter," Austin grumbled as he hooked his backpack over his shoulder. "I'm not playing for Coach."

The smile died on Shirlene's face. "You're right. Slate can be pretty muleheaded when it comes to his rules. And if he kicked you off the team, then he'll have to be the one to let you back on." She chewed on a nail for a few seconds before her eyes lit up. "But maybe if you were to apologize..."

"Not a chance." He started for the porch.

"Oh, come on." She hurried after him. "How else can we get into the play-offs?"

"Not my problem." He took two porch steps before Shirlene grabbed his T-shirt.

"Not your problem? But it's your school."

Austin jerked away. "My school is back in Iowa." The front door slammed closed before Shirlene could finish her argument.

"Pigheaded people," she fumed on her way back to the car. "I am surrounded by pigheaded people." She circled around to the driver's side. When Faith shot her a questioning look, she lifted her hand. "Believe me, I'm sober."

"I assume I'm included in the pigheaded group," Faith said as she climbed into the passenger's seat.

"Actually, since the margaritas, you've gotten a little better. Not completely, but some." Shirlene shook her head. "No, I was referring to Slate and that stubborn kid."

"And you really think he'll make a difference in the team?"

"I don't know, but anything's worth a try." She glanced over her shoulder as she backed out of the dirt driveway. "Now if we can only figure out a way to get him back on it."

"Austin isn't going to apologize."

"I can see that." Shirlene clicked her bright red nails on the steering wheel as they drove along the dirt road. "So maybe we can get Slate to give in."

"That shouldn't be too hard. Slate seems like a pretty easygoing guy."

"Not about football." Shirlene stopped at a stop sign before turning right onto the highway.

"I thought your house was that way." Faith pointed in the opposite direction.

"It is, but we're not going home just yet."

"But I thought we had to get back for supper?"

"That was just to get out of the meeting. Tonight is half-off Ladies' Night at Boot's."

Faith shook her head. "Oh no. No more margaritas for me—or you."

"You're right, but we're not going there to drink, Faith. We're going there to Boot Scootin' Boogie."

Faith didn't have a clue what that was, but it didn't sound good.

Chapter Eleven

Damn crazy woman.

Slate wanted to toss down his clipboard and cuss a blue streak as he watched Faith's little blue-jeaned butt sway out of sight. But he didn't. Losing his temper only made things worse, something he had learned early in life when his adolescent tantrums had gotten him dumped off in Bramble. It didn't take long to figure out that if he wanted to stay someplace, he needed to control himself. It was a lesson he learned well.

Almost too well.

He couldn't remember the last time he'd really lost it. There were a few moments he'd wanted to. Like when his uncle had died, and when he hadn't been drafted by the NFL. But those moments had been few and far between. Besides an inept football team, his life here in Bramble was calm and uneventful. At least, it had been up until the last few days. Now, every time he turned around, something else was pissing him off—the town refusing to listen to reason—Jenna and Burl giving up their own daughter—Faith looking straight through him as if he wasn't even there.

Usually he could hide his anger behind a confident smile. But damned if he could smile when the crazy woman wouldn't even acknowledge him.

Slate shifted the clipboard to his other hand and tried to concentrate on what his offensive coach was saying, but it wasn't easy. Not when his mind kept returning to Faith.

In the last twelve hours, she'd turned into some kind of a chameleon. Where was the woman who looked up at him with big, blue, adoring eyes, the woman that melted into his kisses and went along with all his sexual suggestions? Where did that woman go? First, she tore his heart out by looking all weepy-eyed and crushed over her mama giving her away, and then she'd walked out of the trailer looking like some kind of cowgirl warrior with that huge bag flung over her shoulder and her hair all spiked. A woman who had no qualms about running him over with Bubba's truck, or threatening a law enforcement officer with a gun, or walking fifty miles, or sitting up there in the stands as if it was something she'd done every day of her life.

He'd almost lost it when he looked up and saw her laughing with Shirlene. Not his temper, but something else entirely. His stomach did a weird little somersault, and he had the overwhelming desire to run up those stairs, yank her into his arms, and kiss the daylights right out of her.

Which was weird. Just plain weird. Especially since she looked nothing like the sweet little thing he'd taken to bed the night before. That sweet little thing was long gone. But it didn't seem to make a difference. Even the new hairstyle and clothes didn't stop his libido from popping into overdrive or his heart from seizing up.

"...So what do you think, Slate? You think this new route will work on Coolidge?"

Slate blinked down at the clipboard his offensive coach held in front of him. "Yeah, Travis, I think it's a good one." He turned away not knowing what he'd agreed to. But it didn't matter; their quarterback couldn't hit a receiver on an old route, let alone a new one.

"Hey, Coach!" One of his defensive ends pointed at the stands. "Burl Scroggs says he wants to talk with you."

Slate glanced over at the huge, angry-looking man who leaned on the purple railing. Great. This was just what he needed. He handed his clipboard to Travis and walked across the field, trying his damnedest to keep a smile on his face as he climbed up the steps to where Burl stood.

Once he was standing next to the man, Slate didn't beat around the bush. "So? You here to whup my ass?"

"I'd like to, I can sure tell you that." Burl's fists clenched as he stepped away from the railing.

"Well, I know how you feel." Slate took a seat on the lower bleacher. "I wasn't real happy about you barging in this morning and upsetting Faith."

A blush ran up from the collar of Burl's work shirt. "Is she okay?"

"Okay" wasn't the right word. But since he couldn't think of a word to describe Faith's transformation, he ignored the question.

"I don't blame her for being upset." Burl sat down and studied his huge calloused hands. "Me and Jenna made a mistake giving that girl away."

"So why did you do it?"

He lifted his head and stared out at the field. "The only

person we need to explain that to is Faith." He paused. "If she ever lets us explain."

"Well, good luck with that, Burl." Slate rested his elbows on the bleacher behind him, even though his entire body was pulled as tight as a cramping hamstring. "After this morning, it doesn't look like she's going to talk to any of us. Which means, the best thing we can do for her is to convince Sheriff Winslow that she's not Hope so she can get her car back and leave." Except just thinking about her leaving made his chest hurt.

"Well, me and Jenna don't see it the same way as you."

That came as no surprise. It seemed no one in the town saw things the way he did, and he was getting pretty damned sick of it. Maybe he shouldn't wait to get fired for not winning a state championship. Maybe he should resign as soon as the season was over and head someplace that wasn't populated with a bunch of crazy yahoos.

"So how do you see things, Burl?" he asked.

"We think Faith needs to stay here—learn about her people. Once she gets to know us, it will be easier for her to forgive me and Jenna and accept us as her family."

"Accept you as her family?" Slate's fingers tightened around the cold aluminum of the bench. "Why would she want to do that when you never accepted her?"

Burl glared back over his shoulder. "It had nothing to do with accepting her. We loved her from the first moment we saw her."

He snorted. "Damn, Burl, you sure have a funny way of showing it. And now you think by keeping her here against her will, that she's going to forgive and forget?"

"It couldn't hurt."

"It couldn't hurt?" Slate sat up. "The woman is spitting mad at you for giving her up at birth and me for not mentioning I dated her sister. What do you think is going to happen if she finds out we're in cahoots with Winslow? You think that's going to make her like us, Burl?"

"Well, she doesn't have to find out. It's not like we made Sam take the car. Hell, Jenna and me weren't even in town."

"You do realize that the town's plan is to keep Faith—who they think is Hope—here until she marries me."

"Yeah, we figured as much. Harley's already organizing a painting committee for the town hall and pulling the pig centerpieces out of the boxes."

Two months. If Slate could only hang on for two months, he would be in a Mexican paradise—far, far away from this craziness.

"Look, Slate"—Burl turned to him—"I'm not asking you to lie. All I'm asking is that you don't talk to Sam until Faith's had some time to get to know us. We're not bad people. We were just doing what we thought was best."

There was probably some truth to that. People in this town were always screwing things up by doing what they thought was best. Besides, it was hard to stay mad at a man who looked as whupped as Burl Scroggs. Slate might not think there was a chance in hell his plan would work, but he couldn't fault the man for wanting to try. For wanting a chance to make things right.

Slate sure wanted that chance.

Releasing his breath, Slate got to his feet. "A week. That's all I'm giving you."

"That's enough."

It didn't seem like enough to Slate. Not with the glare

Faith had shot him that afternoon. But stranger things had happened. Especially in the town of Bramble.

"Hey, Coach," Travis yelled. "You ready to call it a day?"

Oh, yeah, he was more than ready to call it a day.

Which was exactly what he should've done. Called it a day and gone on home. Instead, he made the mistake of letting his coaching staff talk him into stopping by Bootlegger's for a beer.

Slate's day from hell continued.

"Hey, Slate." Kenny Gene yelled at him from across the crowded bar. Of course, the bar was always crowded, except on Sunday when it was closed. Not because people in Bramble were all that religious, but because Sunday was the day the owner, Rossie Owens, went fishing.

Slate paid for his Bud and took a deep drink as he waited for Kenny to make his way over.

"How's the team lookin'?" Kenny slipped onto the stool next to him.

"Ready to take on Coolidge." It was the standard reply with only the name of the opposing team changing. It was also one he was getting damn sick of making.

"That's great." Kenny slapped him on the back. "We wouldn't want to lose our homecomin' game."

"No." Slate took another drink. "We wouldn't want to do that."

"So have you seen Hope?"

"Hope?" The beer stopped halfway back to his lips.

Kenny grinned. "Yeah, she's back to being Hope." He pointed a finger in his face. "You sure had me going with that whole twin thing."

Slate lowered the bottle. "What do you mean, she's back to being Hope?"

"I mean, she's back to lettin' us call her Hope. Accordin' to some of the girls, it all started at the homecomin' decoratin' meetin'. Hope waltzed right up to the front and started talkin' about her life in Hollywood." He stopped, and his eyes got kind of dazed. "Did you realize that before she married Jesse, Sandra had sex with Hope in the bathroom of a Taco Bell?" He closed his eyes and released a long sigh. "It sorta makes me want to drive all the way to Odessa for a Taco Grande." His eyes flashed open. "Hey, you want to go with me? We could be back before midnight."

Slate couldn't talk. All he could do was stare down in the cavernous hole of his beer bottle and try to figure out why he was still living here. Or maybe still sitting here.

"So Faith—"

"Now," Kenny waggled a finger at him. "I'm not fallin' for that again."

Slate squeezed his eyes shut and gritted his teeth. "So Hope told people she'd had a lesbian encounter with a movie star?"

"I'm not sure if it was on the counter or in the stall, but it was definitely in the bathroom. Least ways, that's what I could get from the girls. Sometimes they talk so fast it's hard to make ends meet. But if you want to find out for sure, you should talk to Cindy Lynn."

Slate downed the rest of his beer and slammed the bottle down before he pushed past Kenny and headed to the pool room. Kenny called after him, but he was in no mood to listen to any more craziness. And it was craziness. Even if Faith had given up trying to prove she wasn't

Hope, there was no way that she would stand up in front of a group of women and make up stories about her sexual exploits.

No way in hell.

At least, that's what he believed through the first game of pool. But after an entire hour of listening to detailed descriptions of Faith's movie star fantasies, he started to believe that there was some kernel of truth to the stories. Bramble was good at elaborating, but they sucked at creativity.

"So how do you think you compare to that Matthew fella?" Tyler Jones asked as he knocked a solid into the corner pocket. "From the pictures I've seen in those star magazines, the guy looks pretty ripped."

"Yeah, but a ripped stomach don't mean he's ripped where it counts," Harley said.

Rye put in his two cents' worth. "From what I hear, Hope don't mind if you ain't ripped in that area. I hear she did it with a movie star midget in the electronics department in Wal-Mart."

"What do you mean?" Tyler chalked the end of his pool cue. "Just because midgets have short legs don't mean they have short everything else."

Slate tossed his pool cue down to the table and headed for the door.

"You leavin', Slate?" Harley asked. "Why, it's not even eight o'clock."

Rye chuckled. "More than likely all that talk got him riled up, and he's goin' lookin' for Hope."

"Well, he doesn't have far to look—she's been on the dance floor for the last half hour."

Harley's last comment caused Slate's head to jerk

toward the dance floor. And sure enough, there Faith was in all her bright red cowboy-booted glory attempting to line dance to a loud Brooks & Dunn song.

The track lighting reflected off the gold highlights in her hair, hair that didn't look as spiky as before—just sexy and bedroom-mussed. In Duds 'N' Such, he'd thought the western clothes made her look more like Hope. But now he realized that even with the new clothes, she looked nothing like her sister. And not just because of the short silky hair, but because of the hesitant, cautious way she moved and the softness of her smile and the delighted discovery in her eyes. She wasn't close to getting the country line dance right, but she didn't seem too upset by it. Her cheeks were flushed, and her eyes sparkled as she attempted to follow the other dancers.

Other dancers who all seemed to be men.

At least, there were no women around Faith. Just a bunch of horny cowboys who didn't seem to mind at all when they had to guide her with a hand or nudge her with a hip to get her back on track.

Slate's eyes narrowed, and he tried to remind himself to smile with indifference. Except he didn't feel that indifferent. After listening to all the sex stories, he felt a little bit wild-eyed. Like a deer caught in the headlights of a semi on a slick highway. He knew he should run for his life before he was splattered all over the asphalt and his head got mounted over a fireplace, but his feet were frozen. And so was his gaze.

Frozen on Travis's hand that had just encircled Faith's waist.

The sight seemed to get him moving. Just not in the right direction. His feet ate up the floor as he crossed the room, jumped up on the dance floor, skirted around the long lines of dancing fools, and grabbed Travis's arm.

"Thanks for warmin' her up for me, Trav." From the surprised look on Travis's face, Slate had probably used a little more force than was necessary to move him away from Faith. But he didn't care.

"Sure, Slate." Travis backed away. "Anytime."

Slate tucked a hand around Faith's waist and pulled her from the line of men and over to one tiny corner of the floor.

She tried to jerk away. "Just what do you think you're doing?"

"What am *I* doing," he hissed. "What the hell are *you* doing? Matthew and Tommy Lee? And now Travis! Have you lost your mind, woman?"

"Hey, Hope." Twyla did a grapevine in front of them. "Don't forget your appointment on Friday at four. I scheduled you for last because I've got big plans for that hair of yours."

"I can hardly wait," Faith gushed as Twyla did a stomp-kick and swiveled away.

Slate's mouth dropped open. "Where did you get that?"

"What?" She glared at him.

He waved a finger in front of her mouth. "That country twang."

Even in the dark bar, he could see her blush. "I don't know what you're talking about."

"You *have* lost your mind."

"Don't be ridiculous."

"I'm not ridiculous. That accent is ridiculous."

"I don't know why. It's exactly how you sound."

"I do not sound like that!"

His voice rose enough to cause all lines on the dance floor to pause in mid-boot scoot and stare at him. He made an attempt at an indifferent smile, but it must've fallen short because their eyes widened.

"Come on." Slate pulled Faith off the dance floor and toward the small hallway that led to the bathrooms. Once there, he sandwiched her between the pay phone and the door to the men's room. "So explain yourself."

"Me?" She shoved against his chest. "I'm not the one who needs to explain anything."

"Really? So I guess all the stories I've been hearing are a bunch of lies and that fake accent I just witnessed was all my imagination."

She stopped struggling, and her face flushed even brighter.

"So it's true." His hands dropped from her arms. "You are running around pretending to be Hope."

She smirked. "Not exactly."

It was the same wording he'd used when she asked him about his relationship with Hope. And he didn't believe for a second that it was only a coincidence.

"Hey, Slate. Hey, Hope." Emmie Leigh and her little sister scooted past them on their way to the women's bathroom. "Glad to see you two lovebirds back together." They giggled as the door marked COWGIRLS closed behind them.

Slate cringed as Faith's eyes narrowed. But before she could let loose with the four-letter word that set his teeth on edge, he reached out and shoved open the door to the men's bathroom and pushed her inside.

"What are you doing?"

"I'm giving us some privacy." He slammed the latch home before he turned and rested back against the door.

Those wide blue eyes darted around the room, hesitating on the urinal before bouncing back to him. "Open that door."

He crossed his arms. "No. Not until we've had some time to talk."

"I don't want to talk with you." Crossing her arms, she mimicked his stance, but the effect wasn't quite the same. He didn't have perfect little breasts to push up, and it took a real effort to pull his eyes away from those sweet swells.

"Well, darlin', you might as well talk to me because you're not getting out of here until you do."

Her arms dropped to her sides, and she took two steps closer, until that cute nose was inches from his chest. "So talk, darlin'. Nobody's stoppin' *yew*."

The fake accent grated on his nerves worse than any pig calling Hope had ever done, and he gritted his teeth and pushed away from the door, forcing Faith to take a step back.

"First, stop talking like that."

"Like what?" The accent was twice as thick.

"Like a bad Dolly Parton impersonator."

Faith smiled up at him and batted her eyes.

"Second, what the hell do you think you're doing parading around like Hope, spouting off all kinds of nonsense about having sex with Hollywood movie stars?"

Her lips pressed together—lips that were coated with that glittery pink stuff—and he figured she was about to give him some smart-ass reply. Instead, she surprised him.

The stiffness melted from her shoulders as she drooped back against the counter of the sink. "I figured if I couldn't beat them, I'd join them. But I may have over-done it a little."

"A little?" Slate shook his head. "Darlin', if half of what I heard tonight is true, you more than overdid it. You dug a hole so deep you've got one foot in China."

"Well, what did you expect me to do?" Her hands flailed around, missing his chest by mere inches. "I tried telling the truth, and no one paid the least bit of attention to me. And then those women started asking me all these stupid questions about Hollywood, and after Shirlene's margaritas, I just started talking, and before I knew it, I'd had sex with half the movie stars in Hollywood."

It was a relief to see the angry, hostile Faith replaced with the cute, insecure Faith. Especially when he thought he'd lost that woman for good.

He took a step closer and grinned. "But did you have to screw midgets?"

Her hands hung in midair as she looked up at him. "Midgets?"

"Ahhh. No midgets, I take it. I figured that was prob-ably an exaggeration. Along with the whole lesbian Taco Bell thing."

Her gaze dropped to the toes of his boots. "Well, actually..."

Heat filled the crotch of his jeans, and when he spoke his voice hit a note it hadn't hit since the sixth grade. "You came up with that one?"

Her head lifted, her face as flushed as his body felt. Damn, he had never realized how hot the little bathroom was, probably because he'd never been in there long enough to notice. And because he'd never shared it with a woman with sexy hair, a sweet little body, and a hot lesbian fantasy.

Needing some fresh air, he glanced at the small window to the right of the sink. Unfortunately, it was painted shut.

"Well." Slate cleared his throat. "It sounds like you had quite an afternoon." He looked around, desperately searching for something to get his mind off Taco Grandes. "So you're staying with Shirlene?"

Faith blinked at the quick subject change. "Yes."

He nodded. "Good. She'll treat you right. Although Shirlene has been known to have a wild streak a mile long, so you might want to keep that in mind when she makes suggestions—like line dancing at a country honky-tonk with a bunch of rowdy cowboys."

Her face scrunched up in confusion. Of course, she was no more confused over his words than he was. What was he doing? He had been handed the perfect opportunity to set things straight between them, and here he was rattling off like some pathetic jealous loser. Unfortunately, she turned mean before he could rectify the situation.

"Better than hanging out with a two-timing jerk who couldn't tell the truth if his life depended on it."

He pointed a finger. "Now wait one damned minute. I never lied to you."

"You never lied to me?" Those blue eyes snapped as she poked him in the chest with her finger. "Are you kidding? You've done nothing but lie to me since the moment I met you. You lied about my car. You lied about where you live. You lied about the truck you drive. And you lied about my sister!" She balled up her fist and thumped him hard in the chest.

"I'll give you the car, but I didn't lie about anything else. I do live in Bubba's trailer—at least, for the time being—and you never asked me about the truck. And I haven't lied about Hope." Those blue eyes narrowed, and before she could let loose with more accusations, he held up his hand. "But you're right, I should've explained things to you before we—" He stopped, not sure what word to use. "Umm, before we..."

"Had sex," she stated.

It wasn't exactly the right phrase, but since he didn't have a better one, he let it slide. "Yes. I should've explained things before we had sex. But things just kind of got out of hand."

"Got out of hand?"

That wasn't right, either, but he forged on. "You know, in the heat of the moment, people forget things."

Those eyes narrowed. "Like the relationship between their past lovers and their present?"

"No!" Slate suddenly felt like a man drowning in his own damned swimming pool. "I told you, Hope and I were never lovers. We're friends. *Just* friends."

"Then why does the town think otherwise?"

Slate could've gone into his reasons for not setting the town straight, but he didn't want to come off as an arrogant selfish idiot—even if that was what he was. No, it was better to keep things simple. "They probably think that because we dated in high school."

Faith's eyes darkened. "But I thought you said you were just friends."

So much for simple. He ran a hand over the back of his

neck, squelching the desire to put a fist through the glass of the window so he could get some friggin' air. "We were friends. Friends who dated."

"I see," she said. Except it didn't sound like she saw what Slate saw.

"I know it sounds kind of crazy, but we sort of friend dated."

"Friend dated?"

"You know, two friends going to the movies and high school dances and Sutter Springs—"

Her eyes widened. "You took Hope to Sutter Springs?"

Oh shit.

"Well, not for what you and I did, darlin'. Hope and I just hung out up there and drank beer and howled at the moon and..."

"Kissed?"

He couldn't stop the telltale blush.

The slap she gave him rang his bell.

"You bastard!" She tried to hit him again, but he grabbed her wrist. Of course, it didn't stop her mouth. "How could you do that to me? To both of us? Or are you one of those beer-swigging jocks who likes a little twin action?" Her other hand cracked him across the opposite cheek. "Pervert!"

"Dammit, Faith!" He grabbed her hand. "It's not like that at all."

She stopped struggling. "Then what is it like, Slate?"

With his breath chugging in and out of his chest and his cheeks burning, his brain refused to give him one explanation that would fix the mess it had gotten him into. So he gave up on it altogether.

"It's like this." He jerked her up to the toes of her little red boots.

A surprised puff of air escaped her mouth right before he covered those glittery pink lips with his. Without thinking, he brought her hands too close to his head, and she grabbed fistfuls of his hair. He braced himself, waiting for the pain that was sure to follow. Except instead of yanking, her fingers relaxed, brushing the tips of his ears with a caress so gentle that it made him moan. Her mouth opened, and her lips slid in harmony with his. He released her wrists and spanned her waist, lifting her up to the counter as their tongues finally crossed the threshold and started a lazy waltz.

Her legs encircled his waist and pulled him close, the rigid fly of his Wranglers pressed against the center seam of hers. He tugged open the snaps of her shirt, then slipped a hand inside the gaping hole. With a twist, he unhooked her bra. Her whimper vibrated through his mouth as he filled his hands with the soft flesh of her breasts. She pressed more firmly against his fly, tightening her legs and brushing back and forth until Slate's knees trembled.

He pulled back from the kiss to catch his breath, but she looked so damned sexy with her head tipped back and her eyes closed and her mouth all parted and glistening, that he couldn't stay away for long. He gave her another deep kiss as he unhooked the buckle of her belt, flicked open the snap of her jeans, and slid down the zipper. But the jeans were too tight to slip his hand inside.

He had just started to lift her off the counter when the door shook.

"Hey, come on! Give a guy a break, would ya?" Another bang rattled the latch.

"It's taken!" Slate yelled back, his voice hoarse and raspy.

"Slate? Is that you?" Rye Pickett's voice came through the door.

"Slate's in there?" Another male voice joined in. "I thought he went home with Hope."

"I guess not," Rye replied. "Maybe he's sick or something. He's sure been in there a long time, and he don't sound so good."

Slate released his breath and dropped his forehead against the top of Faith's head. "I'm sorry, darlin'. It looks like we're going to have to finish this later."

He wasn't quite prepared for the fist that hit him full in the gut. He wheezed and stumbled back a few steps. "What was that for?"

"Slate? Who are you talkin' to?" Rye asked.

"What's going on, guys?" Kenny had joined the growing mob.

"Slate's in there."

"By himself?"

"I hope not. Because if he is, he's gone off his rocker, and it's too late to get another coach for the season."

Faith glared at Slate as she zippered her pants and buckled her belt. Her bra proved a little more difficult for her shaky hands.

"Now, darlin'." He helped her hook the bra back together and would've snapped her shirt if she hadn't jerked away from him. "Don't go getting your feathers all ruffled. This wasn't any big deal—"

A high-pitched squeak came out of her mouth, and he held up a hand. "I mean, it was a big deal, but just not a big enough deal to worry about." Her eyes almost popped out of her face, now the exact color of the deep red of her plaid blouse.

"Slate?" Harley's voice came through the door. "Son, are you all right in there?"

"Yes, sir," he hollered back, when what he really wanted to do was tell them to mind their own damned business and get back to their drinking and crazy line dancing.

"Is someone in there with you?"

Slate walked over to the window and gave it his best effort, but it refused to budge. He sent Faith an apologetic look before he spoke. "As a matter of fact, sir, Hope and I were just having a little conversation."

"Hope? Hope's in there with you? Oh, well, in that case, we'll let you two get back to it."

"But I have to go real bad, Harley," Rye grumbled.

"Use a bush, Rye. Hope and Slate need some privacy."

There was the shuffle of boots, then finally peaceful silence. Slate looked back at Faith, but refused to open his mouth. Not when every time he did something came out that turned her back into a wildcat. Falling back on his old standby, he leaned a shoulder against the stall, crossed his arms, and smiled.

It was a mistake.

With a low growl, Faith lowered her shoulder and hit him square in the solar plexus better than his defensive line. The air whooshed out of him and he crumpled over, a position that gave him a perfect view of those little red boots as they waltzed right out the door.

"Hey, Slate." Kenny's square-toed ostrich boots came into view. "I guess you and Hope made up."

Slate straightened and tried to act like he could breathe.

Kenny winked. "I guess you proved to her that nobody does sexual on-counters like a man."

If Slate didn't die in the next few seconds from lack of oxygen, he was going straight home.

To pack.

Chapter Twelve

BURL AND JENNA'S HOUSE WAS BIGGER than the house Faith grew up in and much more cluttered. The huge corner lot surrounding the aluminum-sided home and separate cinder block garage was filled with a new Cadillac, an old Cadillac, a beat-up pickup truck, a flatbed trailer, numerous motorcycles, and a rusted tractor. One of the only spots without some kind of vehicle on it was the rectangle of grass that grew in front of the wide front porch, although it was covered with a multitude of whirling lawn ornaments.

Faith pulled Shirlene's Navigator in behind the new Cadillac and turned off the engine. She couldn't say what had changed her mind about coming: Shirlene's constant badgering, the need for Hope's address, or the unquenchable curiosity about her birth parents.

But now that Faith was there, she couldn't quite bring herself to open the car door. A strange paralysis had claimed her limbs. And there was no telling how long she would've sat there if a pack of dogs hadn't come charging around the side of the house, barking and yelping. Two large hound dogs and two smaller wiry dogs raced over to the SUV.

Fearing that they would jump up on Shirlene's car and scratch it, Faith started to get out. Unfortunately, she swung the door open a little too quickly and it clipped one of the hounds in the head, causing the dog to squeal out in pain. Which in turn caused the other dogs to turn tail and run off.

"Ohmygod." She grabbed her purse and searched for her disinfectant wipes. But by the time she got one and climbed out of the truck, the dog was staggering away.

"Faith?"

Jenna stood on the front porch, an expectant look on her face. She lifted a hand in a hesitant wave as Faith closed the truck door. But instead of waving back, Faith took a deep breath and smoothed the wrinkles from her wool pants.

She'd gotten dressed in her conservative clothes that morning in a vain attempt to bring sanity back to her life. It was so much easier to blame the Wranglers and boots for the events of the previous day than it was to blame herself. Of course, the western clothes hadn't forced her to hold a man at gunpoint or tell a room full of women a bunch of bizarre lies. Or almost devour an arrogant cowboy in the men's bathroom.

Just the thought of the way she'd kissed Slate made her cringe.

But one horrible situation at a time.

Walking around the front of the truck, Faith wondered how to address the woman. Mrs. Scroggs seemed too formal and Jenna too familiar. And "mother" was completely out of the question. Maybe it was best not to call her anything.

"I think your dog is hurt." She pointed around the corner, the wipe still clutched in her hand.

"Oh, those ain't my dogs." Jenna smiled and moved to the top of the steps. "Burl has bad allergies."

"But they came around from the back."

She glanced over her shoulder. "Yeah, they sit back there in the shade sometimes."

"Do you know who they belong to? Because I think one might be hurt."

Her brow knotted. "I think one of them belongs to Tyler Jones, but I don't know which one. And the other three, I couldn't tell you."

Not sure what else to do, she held the wipe out to Jenna. "Well, if you see the brown and black hound dog, you might want to use this on his head."

Jenna stared at the wipe in confusion until Faith clarified.

"It's a disinfectant wipe."

"Oh." She reached out and took it, then stuffed it in the front pocket of her blue jean skirt.

Faith's mother had never worn blue jean skirts. Or bright pink shirts. Or beige cowboy boots with intricate pink stitching. Or long dangling silver earrings that got caught up in hair the color of deep rich soil—the exact color of Faith's before she got it highlighted.

As long as Faith could remember, her mother had always worn wool slacks and starched pastel blouses, and kept her gray-streaked hair short and her face makeup free. Unlike this woman, who had applied a variety of cosmetics to a face that looked too youthful to belong to a mother of a thirty-year-old—let alone two.

While Faith took in the familiar features, Jenna

appeared to be doing the same. She stood on the top step with the toes of her boots hanging over the edge as her gaze wandered over Faith with an almost hungry intensity.

Suddenly uncomfortable with the emotions that pushed up from somewhere deep inside, Faith looked away and studied the pinwheel petals of a plastic sunflower lawn ornament.

"Goodness." Jenna finally spoke. "Where are my manners?" She stepped back and pulled open the screen door. "Please come on in."

Faith shook her head. "I don't want to keep you. I realize you just got off work and it's close to dinnertime."

"Oh, shoot." Jenna swatted the air. "You ain't keeping me. Tonight's Burl's bowling night, and I usually just eat whatever's in the fridge and watch the daytime shows that I TiVo. Are you hungry? I've got leftover chicken and dumplings."

"Really, I can't stay. I just stopped by to see if you had Hope's address."

"Oh." Her face fell, and she let the screen door slam. "I guess you're in a hurry to get to California?" Without waiting for a reply, she continued. "I figure your mama told you where to start looking."

Faith nodded.

"But she didn't tell you about me." It was a statement rather than a question, so Faith didn't acknowledge it as Jenna moved over to the railing that ran around the deep porch. "Me and Burl really must've surprised you the other day."

"You could say that." Standing mere feet from the woman, Faith still felt surprised. And angry.

"I'm sorry." Jenna studied the brightly colored mums that bordered the porch. "If I had known it was you with Slate instead of Hope, I never would've barged in like that."

"So you would've gone on pretending you weren't my mother?" Faith knew she was being cruel, but she couldn't help it. She thought she had her emotions under control. Obviously not, although the pain-filled brown eyes that stared back at her didn't exactly make her feel good about the snide remark.

"Maybe that would've been for the best."

"Maybe." She turned away, needing some distance between her and the petite woman who brought out the worst in her. She stared out past the yard to the wide open field on the other side, wishing she'd never come to Jenna's—or to Bramble.

There was a squeak and a rattle of chains, and she glanced up to see Jenna take a seat on the faded cushion of the porch swing.

"But I guess it's too late to go back," she said, more to herself than to Faith. "'Course even if I could go back, I'd still be a young, stupid fifteen-year-old and probably make all the same mistakes."

"Fifteen? You were only fifteen?" Faith moved closer to the porch.

Jenna nodded and sent her a weak smile as the swing creaked back and forth. "Fifteen and in love. A dangerous combination."

Faith tried to conjure up an image of herself at fifteen. A short, skinny kid with acne on her chin and braces on her teeth. A scared, insecure ninth grader who refused to use the school bathroom because of the fungus she might catch or kiss boys because of the germs. Pregnant? It was too mind-boggling to even consider.

"How old was Burl?" she asked.

"Seventeen."

Seventeen. It wasn't much better.

She climbed the steps. "But how—I mean...I guess I'm wondering why you didn't just get an abortion."

"We talked about it. But both me and Burl were raised Christian, and it didn't seem right. So we decided to put the baby up for adoption."

"Baby?"

"We didn't realize I was going to have twins."

"The ultrasound didn't show that?"

"Never had one. Back then, it wasn't such a big deal, and Doc Mathers isn't one to spend a lot of time with pre-natal nonsense. So we were pretty surprised when two came out instead of one."

"So why didn't you put both of us up for adoption?"

Jenna's eyes welled with tears. "I guess because after I held both of you, I didn't want to let go. Of course, I couldn't keep you both, not when your mama was there waiting for the baby I'd promised her. But the other one..." She shrugged. "Well, me and Burl just figured it was fate—that God wanted us to keep one."

A tight knot formed in Faith's chest. "But why me?" It was a question that had plagued her for the last few days. A question she hadn't wanted to ask—but needed to.

Jenna released a deep sigh. "Both Burl's parents and mine were poor, so we knew how hard a life could be without money. And since we were both so young, unmarried, and still in high school, I figured our lives together wouldn't be much better. So I wanted to choose the strongest one. The one that could survive all the hardships ahead. Hope came out first all red-faced and squalling to beat the band, while you came out all soft and sweet. I figured the oldest and loudest would survive the best." She looked down at her folded hands as tears splashed over her knuckles. "I guess it wasn't the best way to decide, but it was the only way I knew how."

A tear traced down Faith's cheek, and she quickly brushed it away before she turned and placed her hands on the porch railing. The anger was gone, but the hurt still remained. Even if Jenna's decision made sense, it was still hard to accept the fact that she was the one given away.

"I was sorry to hear about your mama," Jenna whispered. "Was she a good one?"

Faith nodded, afraid if she opened her mouth she'd end up squalling to beat the band.

"That's good. Even though I helped pick out your parents, I still worried about that. Although she was a better mother than I was—when she found out I'd had twins, she wanted to adopt you both."

So her mother had known Hope was kept by her biological parents. Faith should've been angry about the deception, but all she felt was sorrow. Sorrow for a teenage mother burdened with adult decisions, and sorrow for the adoptive mom who only wanted to protect her child from the painful truth.

Fighting back the tears, she allowed her gaze to wander around the yard that was so different from the one she grew up in. Not different in a bad way, just different. Maybe it had been fate that two children were born instead of one. Fate that Faith didn't cry and Hope did. Fate that Faith grew up in a small brick house with no siblings and Hope grew up here with three. And fate that her search led her here to Bramble instead of Los Angeles, where she might never have gotten to meet the people who had made that difficult decision.

"Good Lord, would you look at me?" The porch swing creaked as Jenna got up.

Swiping her tears away, Faith turned and watched as Jenna pulled the disinfectant wipe from her pocket and dabbed at her eyes. She lifted a hand to stop her, but then let it drop. At least she hadn't put it in her mouth.

"I probably should be going," Faith said.

Jenna's face fell, but she quickly recovered and waved a hand. "And here I am yammerin' my fool head off— something I do when I get nervous."

Faith smiled. "So do you have Hope's address?"

"I wish I could help you out with that, honey. I really do. But she just moved into a new apartment, and I keep forgetting to get it when she calls. Of course, once we get to gossiping, everything goes straight out the window."

"How long has it been since you talked?"

"Just a little over a week. She usually calls on Sundays, but this past Sunday we were in Lubbock visiting Jenna Jay."

"So you haven't told her about me?"

Jenna's eyes flickered down to the toes of her boots. "No—but I'm going to. I should've told her a long time ago." She looked back up, her eyes sad and sincere. "It wasn't fair to either one of you."

It wasn't fair. But if Faith had learned anything in the last few months, it was just how unfair life could be.

"Say," Jenna said, her face suddenly hopeful, "why don't you come back on Sunday and have Sunday dinner with us? That way you can be right here when Hope calls. Besides, Dallas is supposed to come home from Austin. And I could try to get Tessa and Jenna to come back, too. That way, you would get to meet your brother and sisters before you head out to Hope's."

She'd had months to get used to the idea of having a sister and only days to get used to the idea of having a big family. Still, she wasn't about to pass up the opportunity to meet her siblings.

"I guess I could stop by for a little while," Faith conceded.

Jenna beamed. "Good. And besides, it will probably be best to give Hope a heads-up before you show up on her doorstep. She don't really like—"

"Surprises," Faith finished for her.

Jenna grinned sheepishly. "Pretty much. I just hope no one in town lets it slip before I talk with her."

"I don't think you have anything to worry about. Not when the entire town is convinced I'm Hope."

Jenna laughed, the sound so familiar it was almost creepy. "Bramble is pretty close-minded. But I have to admit, you two do look like two peas in a pod."

"But you knew."

Jenna's eyes grew misty again. "Yes. I knew."

It took a while before Faith could pull her gaze away from the soulful brown eyes.

"Well, I better get going," she said. But before she had taken more than two steps, Jenna stopped her.

"Faith." The word slipped from her mother's lips like a prayer. "Thank you for letting me tell my side of things. It felt good to finally get it out."

Faith nodded. She hadn't forgiven Jenna and Burl for

giving her away, but at least now, she knew why they had. And Jenna was right; it did feel good to get it all out.

"So I'll see you on Sunday," Jenna chirped happily as she followed Faith down the steps. "Of course, I'll probably see you even sooner than that." When Faith shot her a questioning look, she continued. "Homecoming's this weekend, and you're planning on going, ain't you? After all, you were Bramble's prettiest queen," she teased.

Unfortunately, Faith didn't see the humor in the joke. She'd forgotten about homecoming. Or maybe she'd shoved it out of her mind, along with the Hollywood sex lies and kissing cocky cowboys in men's restrooms. If she stayed until Sunday, there was no way she could miss the festivities. Not with the way this town felt about their Hope.

And not when Faith was responsible for cups and plates.

Chapter Thirteen

"...so I said to Kenny, I'm not puttin' up with that kind of crap from nobody. Not even a man who knows what to do with his tongue." Twyla yanked the comb through Faith's hair, uncaring of the tears that sprang to her client's eyes.

"I mean, where does he get off, anyway? My mama may worship the ground he walks on, but that don't mean I will." She paused and rested a hand on one denim hip as she waved the comb around. "And I'll tell you one thing, if he don't start treatin' me like the successful business-woman I am, I'm likely to find some other Texan to hang my hat on."

Since she had already relayed numerous stories about the other Texans she'd hung her hat on, Faith believed her.

"'Course, you got the best one." Twyla went back to tugging. "Good Lord, that man is somethin' to look at. I saw him at the diner this mornin'." She paused in mid-yank. "Funny, but he didn't smile and wink at me like he usually does. In fact, he didn't stay more than a second.

He just looked around, and then away he went. 'Course, I'm sure he's all flustered up about the game tonight.... Still, he usually smiles and winks."

Smiles and winks and makes women fall at his feet.

Faith gritted her teeth. And she was one of them. Of course, it had taken more than a smile and a wink, but not much more. The simple brush of his lips had just about done it. And now, try as she might, she couldn't get the image of his sweet lips out of her mind—or any of his other body parts, for that matter.

Twyla turned on a blow-dryer and continued to talk, even though Faith couldn't hear a word she said. No longer distracted by Twyla's sordid past, her mind wandered back to Slate.

It was probably stupidity at it finest, but she believed him when he said he and Hope hadn't been lovers. Although by the way he stammered and blushed when he talked about it, Faith knew there was more to their relationship than he was letting on. Enough for Faith to want to keep her distance.

The blow-dryer clicked off, and Twyla stepped back to examine her work. Faith wanted to examine it as well, but it was hard to see much of anything in the tiny section of mirror that wasn't covered with pictures of Twyla and all her cowboys. If Faith had enough hair to worry about, she might be scared. But, so far, all the woman had done was shampoo, condition, and blow-dry.

"Now comes the best part." Twyla scurried over to a large cabinet in one corner and pulled something out. At first, Faith thought it was the pelt of some wild animal. But then she noticed the white Styrofoam mannequin head peeking out from beneath the brown fur, and suddenly she felt the fajitas she'd had for lunch rise to the back of her throat.

"What is that?"

Twyla twisted it around to display the long, fat curls from all angles. "Isn't it just gorgeous? It's a Joni Tail."

"A what?"

"A Joni Tail." Twyla hurried over and set it down on the counter amid her instruments of torture. "Ever since you came home I've been worried sick about what to do with your hair." Her eyes narrowed. "Seein' as how you let somebody butcher it and all. At first, I was thinkin' about orderin' some of those hair extension things that all the famous stars use. And since Darla's so good with hot glue I was going to have her come over and help attach them. But then I was watchin' QVC the other night, and my eyes almost jumped right out of my head." She clapped her hands together. "Right there on the television I won in my last divorce was the answer to all my prayers. The Joni Tail."

"Twyla." Faith tried to get up, but the plastic cape was hooked around the back of the chair. "I don't know if this is a good idea."

"Of course it is, honey. You should've seen those models before. They all had ugly short hair just like you, and then with just a few bobby pins, they were transformed into the prettiest things you've ever seen in your life. I'm tellin' you it was just like a miracle. And thank the Lord for overnight shippin' because I might not have gotten it here in time for the parade otherwise."

"I-I don't know. The color doesn't even match my hair."

"It does now."

"What?" Faith ducked her head and moved closer to the mirror. "You dyed my hair?"

"Don't worry, honey. It's semipermanent. So it'll wash right out after twelve to twenty washes."

"Twelve to twenty?"

"Oh, please, Hope!" Twyla grabbed Faith's hand and held it to her ample chest. "Just let me try it. I promise if you don't like it, I'll take it right out. But I just know if everyone sees that I can make even your awful hair pretty, my business will double. Maybe even Shirlene will start coming in here, instead of flying all the way to Austin."

After standing up to Sheriff Winslow and an arrogant cowboy, Faith had started to believe she wasn't such a pushover after all. But staring into Twyla's pleading eyes made her realize that she was still a wimp at heart.

Thirty minutes later, Faith figured she wasn't a wimp as much as a sucker. Her head felt like a pincushion, and her neck strained under the weight of a mountain of curls and a towering tiara. But the hair was nothing compared to the dress she now wore, a pile of canary yellow satin that belonged on the front lawn of Tara—instead of a basement salon in the twenty-first century.

"Oh. My. God." Twyla clutched a hand to her chest, her eyes watering as she bit her lip. "You look just like you did on homecoming night over ten years ago."

Oh. My. God.

"But those red boots don't match," Twyla stated as Faith struggled to get the numerous stiff petticoats through the door of the tiny bathroom. "But I guess they'll be all right. Nobody will be paying any attention to them anyway. Not with the way your hair looks. Good Lord." She rushed over and jerked a hairpin out, popped it in her mouth, smoothed out a curl, and then rammed it home. "There. That's better."

"Well, well." Shirlene's drawl came from the doorway. "Would you just look at the Princess of Haskins County."

Faith's eyes narrowed as she turned to the grinning woman at the bottom of the basement stairs. After spending the last few days with Shirlene, Faith had started to think of the woman as a close friend. But a close friend wouldn't have convinced her how fun it would be to get her hair done before the big homecoming game. And as Shirlene continued to rub it in, Faith's gaze settled on a pair of Twyla's scissors.

"Well, you've sure outdone yourself this time, Twyla."

"Why, thank you, Shirlene." Twyla beamed. "She does look stunnin', don't she?"

"She sure does. As stunning as a yellow rose of Texas." With her green eyes sparkling, Shirlene turned and headed back up the stairs. "Get a move on, honey. I can't wait until people get a load of you."

Faith hurried after her with every intention of giving her a piece of her mind. But by the time she had corralled the full skirt and petticoats up the stairs, out the door, and into the Navigator, she was too tired to do much more than glare at Shirlene.

Shirlene laughed as she pulled away from the curb. "I don't know what you're scowling at, honey. This is going to be more fun than a barrelful of monkeys."

"Fun" wasn't the word that popped into Faith's head as she struggled to buckle the seat belt over the pile of satin. Although it started with an *F*.

The town hall was a two-story building made of pretty gray stone that, according to the bronze plaque between the two flagpoles out front, had been built in 1892. But as Shirlene and Faith stood in the shade of the maple trees waiting for the float to arrive, Shirlene informed Faith that the date was wrong.

According to her, William Cates, a metalsmith out of Lubbock, had been commissioned to make the plaque before the building had been completely finished. When bad weather delayed the completion by a few months—fourteen to be exact—the date on the plaque Cates delivered was no longer accurate. The mayor of Bramble refused to pay him. Irate at the injustice, Cates grabbed the man and demanded his money. Unfortunately, the sheriff at the time—who happened to be a distant relative of Shirlene's—didn't take kindly to people grabbing the mayor and shot Cates dead. Rather than put money out for another plaque, the townsfolk voted unanimously to keep the one they had.

After all, Cates had done a beautiful job. And what difference did a few months make?

If Faith was a tourist, the story would've been rather quaint and folksy. But standing in the late afternoon heat in a pile of petticoats, waiting for a float to arrive so she could display her "Gone With the Wind" attire and Joni Tail for all to see, she completely sympathized with the poor metalsmith whose fate rested on one tiny little mistake—attempting to do something nice for a town of loonies.

"Here she comes!"

Faith looked up in time to see the large red and silver semitruck bearing down on the fifty or so women who were decked out in formals, paste tiaras, and towers of teased and curled hair. The young girls didn't look so bad,

but a few of the older women were dressed even more out-
rageously than Faith. Poor Rachel Dean, who even with
her man hands had snagged the title of Bramble High
Queen 1971, wore a long, polyester dress and a short cape
with a fake-fur collar that looked like roadkill a good
week after the hit-and-run.

The semi's horn blasted, and Faith almost jumped out
of her boots as it eased up to the curb amid squeals of
delight and Shirlene's gasp of disbelief.

"Good God."

Faith stared at the flatbed trailer hitched to the truck.
Shirlene was wrong. There was nothing good or godly
about the horrendous sight. Nothing at all. It looked like
a satanic nightmare. A huge purple fantasy of the devil.

Although Twyla was right; Darla had to be good with
a glue gun to attach the thousands of purple silk roses
that covered the float and draped down over the tires to
the street. But the roses weren't the worst part. No, the
worst part was the gigantic gray spray-painted Styrofoam
revolvers that graced all three tiers of the float, their long
barrels pointing out like weapons of mass destruction.

"Get it!" Darla shrieked. "Guns and Roses!"

"Guns and Roses?" Rachel Dean looked puzzled.

"You know, that's the name of the band that sings the
theme song."

"Oh." Rachel stared up at the towering monstrosity.
"Why, isn't that clever."

"Well," Shirlene said. "It could've been worse."

"You've got to be kidding." Faith refused to take her
eyes off the float for fear it might turn into something
even more horrific.

"Yeah, you're right. Nothing could be worse."

But she was wrong again.

"Who gets to sit up top with the Colt Peacemaker?" one queen yelled.

"Who else?" another answered.

It took Faith a second to realize all eyes were on her. "Oh no." She backed up until she bumped into Shirlene. "I think someone else should have the honor."

"But, Hope, it has to be you," Darla said. "You're the most popular queen in Bramble history."

"Well, I wouldn't say that," Cindy Lynn mumbled.

Faith grasped the opening. "Of course, you're right. You should be up there, Cindy Lynn. You look stunning in that black velvet with those colorful…" She waved her hands at the yards of multicolored satin that billowed from her sleeves. "You should ride on top. Or better—" She looked at the group of young girls. "This year's queen should ride on top."

"Can't happen," Rachel Dean said. "Lou Ann gets the honor of drivin' the truck. Besides, you haven't been home in a while and people want to get a good look at you."

That was what Faith was afraid of.

"Of course it should be Hope," Shirlene stated. "Now, Hog, quit trying to be humble and get your little yellow behind up there on that Colt."

"On it?" An image of her straddling the barrel with petticoats flapping in the breeze flashed through her mind.

"I meant beside it." Shirlene patted her arm.

"Here, Hope." Darla handed her a small paper bag, and when Faith looked confused, she added, "It's candy to toss at the kids. Although you need to be careful how hard you throw it. Two years ago, Rachel Dean almost put Tommy Wilcox's eye out with a watermelon-flavored

Jolly Rancher. Which was ironic since his father is a rancher and wasn't at all jolly about it—him and Rachel Dean almost came to blows."

"I did not almost put Tommy's eye out," Rachel Dean defended herself. "I hit his cheek, and the scar is barely noticeable now."

"Okay, ladies," Cindy Lynn directed, "let's get this show on the road."

To emphasize Cindy Lynn's words, the new queen blasted the horn two more times. Then suddenly, Faith was being hoisted up on the float by some guy. And before she knew it, she was standing on the very top tier with a brown paper bag clutched in one hand and a barrel of a gun in the other.

"Just smile and wave," Shirlene directed from her safe spot beneath the trees. "The stadium's only a mile away."

The words soothed Faith until the truck jumped the curb and the platform wobbled, along with her towering Joni Tail. She grabbed on to the gun with both hands as the truck bounced back down to the street accompanied by Lou Ann's giggling apology. Then the speakers that were attached to the top of the cab clicked on, and the theme song blasted out.

"Welcome to the jungle, we've got fun 'n' games..."

A mile was a lot longer than it sounded, especially when the truck barely hit ten miles per hour. A block from the town hall, Sheriff Winslow's car pulled in front with lights flashing, and for a split second, Faith enjoyed closing one eye to take dead aim at the tail end of the squad car.

Within a few blocks, people appeared along the sides of the street, sitting on the tailgates of their pickups or reclining in camping chairs with cans of beer in holders. When they saw the float, they hollered out, but it was hard to hear what they were saying over Axl's screaming lyrics. She was surprised to see a lot of familiar faces, including Jenna's and Burl's. Jenna waved enthusiastically while Burl only lifted a hesitant hand.

Faith relinquished the death grip she had on the gun and waved back. When nothing bad happened, she plastered a smile on her face and continued to wave to the beaming crowd. But the thought of scarring a kid for life kept her from throwing the candy.

By the time they got to the stadium, she had listened to "Welcome to the Jungle" a few times, and still didn't know the words. Thankfully, the song cut off mid-scream when the truck jumped the curb again and stopped in front.

It looked like the entire student body was standing in the parking lot, the band in their purple and gold uniforms with tubas gleaming and the football players suited up with helmets in hand. Unable to stop herself, she scanned the crowd looking for Slate. The other coaches were camped out by the entrance to the locker rooms, but Slate wasn't with them.

"Look, the homecoming queen's got a gun," some smart-aleck teenage boy yelled.

Everyone laughed, and then the drum section tapped out the count as the band fired up the fight song. Faith released the barrel of the gun and would've attempted to climb down by herself if strong hands hadn't reached up and encircled her waist. It wasn't until her feet touched the rose-covered trailer that she realized that the hands didn't belong to the same stranger who had hoisted her up there.

"Hello, Scarlett."

The honey-drizzled voice sounded nothing like Rhett Butler.

It was sexier.

Faith tried to pull away, but her knees had been locked for so long, they finally gave out. She stumbled against Slate's chest, and his arms came around her, his hands gliding over the tight satin at her back. For a moment, she indulged. Gazed into his eyes. Breathed in his scent. Absorbed his heat.

His fingers tightened, and his eyes glittered in the fiery rays of the setting sun. For a second, she thought he was going to kiss her. Not just a peck, but an honest-to-goodness "Gone with the Wind" kiss, the kind that swept a woman off her feet and took her breath away.

And the funny part about it was that she probably would've let him. Because no matter how much she tried to tell herself it was wrong to lust after your sister's boyfriend, even if it was past history, she couldn't stop wanting him. And what really scared her was that it felt like so much more than lust.

It felt like deep, soul-twisting longing.

"Let me go." Faith released the stranglehold she had on his shirt.

He blinked; then his eyes darkened. "I'm trying," he whispered right before his hands dropped away. A smile slipped over those perfect lips, a smile that didn't resemble the charming grin she was used to. This smile looked forced and uncertain.

"Nice hair."

"You like it? It's a Joni Tail." She tried to keep her voice steady.

"It looks more like a phony tail to me." Slate jumped down from the float and then grabbed her waist to lift her down. But his hands didn't remain there for long. "And no, I don't like it—or the color."

"That's shocking. I thought you liked long dark hair."

He crossed his arms and stared down at her. "Not on you."

She didn't know what that meant, and she didn't care. She just wanted to get away from the man before she did something stupid—like dive on him and beg him to kiss her.

"Well, it's growing on me." She shrugged. "So who knows, maybe I'll dye my hair dark brown and grow it out."

His eyes narrowed as he studied her. "We need to talk."

"I don't think that's a good idea."

"Well, I do. Are you going to the dance tomorrow?"

"Yes."

"Good. I'll pick you up at six." He turned and took a few steps before she found her voice.

"Excuse me?"

He turned back around. "You want me to pick you up earlier?"

"No. I don't want you to pick me up at all."

One golden brow arched. "Too bad."

"For you." She didn't know what it was about the man that turned her from a passive woman into a belligerent liar. "I already have a date."

The other eyebrow joined the first one. "A date? As in a male escort?"

"That would be the kind."

His steely gaze wandered from the top of her head to the tip of her cowboy boots. "Have it your way, sweetheart."

As she watched him walk away, Faith tried to remind herself that it was for the best. Even without his past relationship with her sister, she and Slate weren't compatible. His life was here in Bramble, while hers was back in Chicago. But if that was true, then why did her heart feel like one of Darla's ugly purple roses crushed beneath the tires of the semi?

"Good Lord." Rachel Dean came up behind her. "What got into him? Slate don't ever get mad."

"I guess he didn't like my hair," Faith whispered, and was shocked when a tiny sob slipped through her lips.

"Awww, honey," Rachel's big hand came around her shoulder and pulled her close. "Don't worry none about that. Take my word for it, when men get you in bed, they ain't worried about your hair."

Faith cried even harder.

Chapter Fourteen

THE HOMECOMING GAME WAS A NIGHT from hell that began with Faith's rejection and went downhill from there. Before the game even started, Slate's best running back sprained his ankle when he broke through the "Beat the Cougars" paper banner and ran into Dawg, the mascot. The football player was taken off the field on a stretcher while Dawg only suffered a rip in one fuzzy gray knee of his costume.

The incident set the tone for the game, which was one freakish mistake after another. Their first punt was blocked and run in for a touchdown—the first of three touchdowns that would be scored in the first half. At half-time, Slate was so upset he yelled at his quarterback, who then went back out in the second half and threw three interceptions, which resulted in two more touchdowns.

Slate would've loved to blame the 35–17 loss on his team, but he hadn't exactly been the most attentive coach. Numerous times during the game, he caught himself looking back at the stands for the spot of bright yellow satin in the first row. It was a sad state of affairs when a woman took precedence over football.

Although that was nothing compared to the way he felt when he arrived at the homecoming dance the following night and discovered Faith *had* brought a date. If that's what you could call the gangly sixteen-year-old in the ill-fitting pants and dress shirt. He looked more like a slobbering puppy. And it didn't help that he was slobbering all over Faith. Of course, if Slate had been dancing with her, he'd be slobbering, too. The ugly hairpiece and dress of the night before were gone, replaced by her short sexy hair and a little red number she wore that clung to every curve of her body. Paired with those red high heels, she looked like a shiny candy apple just waiting to be bitten into.

And if the kid tried it, he was dead. Sixteen or not.

"Hey, handsome." Shirlene walked up and handed Slate a paper cup of punch. He started to refuse, but she flashed him a wink. "I added a little something."

He took a sip, and the warmth of whiskey slid nice and smooth down his throat. "You added whiskey to the punch or punch to the whiskey?"

She laughed and leaned back against the wall. "For you, punch to the whiskey." She shot him a glance from the corner of her eye. "You looked like you could use it."

"You got that right." He leaned a shoulder on the wall next to her and took another sip.

For a few minutes, they silently watched Austin and Faith gyrate in some weird rock dance to a country polka. Slate wasn't complaining. At least the kid wasn't touching her, although his eyes looked like they were about to bug out of his head.

"Tough game," Shirlene finally said.

"Yeah."

"Jared is a nice kid, but he stinks as a quarterback."

"Yeah, pretty much."

"Austin plays quarterback."

He glanced over at her. "I realize that. He was on the team the first week."

"Bad attitude?"

"To say the least." He watched as Austin took Faith's hand and spun her under his arm.

"Attitude aside, is he any good?"

Pulling his gaze from the dance floor, he asked, "What's your point?"

She pushed away from the wall. "My point is that if the kid is better than Jared, why isn't he still on the team?"

"Because he's a smart-ass who didn't want to follow the rules. And because he would rather be anywhere but here. And I don't need that kind of aggravation."

Shirlene laughed. "Maybe that's exactly what you need, Calhoun."

"What does that mean?"

"It means your life has been too cushy. Maybe you need to have things shaken up a little." Her eyes narrowed. "Or are you scared if things get shaken up, you might lose your cool? And if The Great Slate Calhoun loses his cool, maybe the town wouldn't think so highly of him. Maybe they'd think he was just like everyone else."

He downed the rest of his drink. "And I think you're nuts."

"So prove me wrong." Shirlene nodded out toward the dance floor. "Give the kid a chance. If I remember correctly, when you first came here you weren't exactly happy about it."

She was right. The first few months he'd been one

angry kid. Of course, his aunt and uncle had gotten the brunt of it. Luckily, his uncle Clyde had had the exact opposite of his mother's high-strung nature. He was calm and patient and rarely raised his voice. He allowed Slate to vent, and then he would take him outside and toss the football with him for hours. He wouldn't say anything, just toss the ball back and forth, back and forth, until the chill of twilight settled in and the smell of cooling earth drifted on the air. Until all the anger and resentment Slate felt for his parents fizzled out. They had done that almost every night until Slate went off to college. It had been a kind of therapy for him.

One he sorely missed when his uncle died.

"I'm not telling you how to coach your team," Shirlene said.

Slate snorted. "I don't know what else you'd call it."

She flashed a sly grin. "Okay, maybe I am."

"Well, join the club. Everyone in town thinks they know what will fix the team. Why should you be any different?"

"All right, I'll shut up. But if I can get the kid to apologize, will you at least listen to him?"

Slate looked at the dance floor where Austin and Faith were attempting a country swing. "He's not exactly doing things to get on my good side." He crumpled the paper cup and shot it at the tall trash can a few feet away. It ricocheted and landed on the floor, followed by Shirlene's bright laughter.

"So are you telling me you've got designs on Hope's sister?" she asked.

"Had, maybe." He walked over to dispose of the cup in the trash. "I don't have them anymore."

"You are such a bad liar, Slate Calhoun."

He glanced back at her. "And what if I do? It's not going to do me any good. Not when the entire town has her convinced that Hope and I are lifelong sweethearts."

"And whose fault is that?"

Damn, the woman was annoying.

But no more annoying than the punk kid who took Faith's hand and walked her right out the gymnasium doors. Slate might've charged after them if Shirlene hadn't stopped him.

"Don't go running off half-cocked, Slate. They're probably just getting a breath of fresh air." She hooked her arm through his. "Come on. Let's see if you've gotten any better since the last time I danced with you."

Slate hadn't. He wasn't a good dancer to begin with, and with his gaze riveted on the doors, he was downright pathetic. Smashed toes might've gotten rid of Shirlene, but it didn't deter the herd of females that lined up to take her place. His patience lasted for all of three songs, before he detangled himself from Cindy Lynn's arms and headed for the door.

Although he should've known it wouldn't be that easy to escape.

"What's your hurry, Slate?" Harley came huffing after him. "Me and the boys wanted to go over a few things with you. We were thinkin' that if you would've used Buford Cummins on the defensive line, we could've stopped those last few touchdowns."

Slate didn't even slow down. "Buford graduated last year, Harley."

"He did? Are you sure?" He shook his head. "Funny, I thought he was just a junior last year."

"Nope," Slate stated as he walked out the gymnasium doors.

Once outside, he checked every dark corner he came to. But instead of finding Faith and Austin, he startled two teachers who were married—just not to each other. After mumbling a lame apology, he headed for his truck. What was he doing? Faith wasn't about to do anything with Austin. The kid was barely out of diapers. Which probably explained why they had left so early. Austin had a curfew. It seemed like a logical explanation. At least it did until Slate walked past the stadium and heard Faith's laughter.

The gates were locked so he walked around to the side fence and ducked through the hole that had been there since he'd gone to school. On the way through, one of the broken chain links caught on his dress pants and ripped a good-sized hole in the leg. But he could've cared less when another peal of laughter rang out.

By the time he jogged up the ramp and rounded the corner of the stands, he was pissed, although his anger dwindled quickly enough. The stadium was dark, but not so dark that he couldn't make out the lone figure sitting in the front row of the stands watching the kid on the field. A kid who stretched up for an imaginary pass, then ran through the opposite end zone for a touchdown.

Faith clapped and yelled her approval. And if that wasn't enough, she jumped up and started a cheer.

"Said the little chicken to the great big hen. We ain't been beat since we don't know when. So ruffle up your feathers and stick out your tail." At this point, she stuck out her little tush. "'Cause we're gonna beat your team to—rickety, rackety, russ, we ain't allowed to cuss, but

I confess that Austin's the best so…yaaaaay!…" She waved her fists like pom-poms. "Us!"

"Yay us?" Slate walked up.

Startled, she stumbled in her heels and sat down hard on the bench, placing a hand on the deep V-neck of the dress. "You scared me."

"Sorry." He flopped down a few feet away. "So where were you a cheerleader, Us High?"

"No." She smoothed the hem of her dress, that had hiked up to display a tantalizing amount of thigh. "I wasn't a cheerleader."

"No kidding?" He couldn't help the grin.

Instead of replying, she looked back out at the field.

Slate inched down the bleacher. "I take it that young kid who is now doing backflips in the end zone is your date?"

The stubborn chin came up. "As matter of fact, he is."

"Going for the younger men, I take it?"

"They have less baggage."

He chuckled. "Yeah, I could see that. They also have less facial hair."

Faith sent him a very sassy look. "Which is nice. Facial hair can get a little scratchy."

"Funny, you never complained."

Those wide blue eyes blinked before she turned away. A stiff wind whipped the short strands of her hair, and she rubbed at her bare arms. With October just around the corner, the night was colder than it had been in a while.

Slate shrugged out of his jacket and held it out. "Here." When she only stared at it, he added, "It doesn't bite." He glanced back at the kid, who was now showing off his skills at climbing the goalpost. "And it doesn't look like you're going to get another offer."

"Fine." She went to grab the coat, but he refused to let go, holding it until she slipped her arms in.

When it was on, he reached out and pulled the lapels closed, the backs of his fingers brushing the bare skin just below her throat. She shivered, and her gaze snapped up to his. If her eyes hadn't been so wary, he might've kissed her. Instead, he released the jacket and leaned his elbows on the bleacher behind them, trying to act like his heart hadn't kicked into overdrive.

"So how did you meet Austin?" he asked.

"I almost ran him over with your—Bubba's truck."

He turned to her. "I take it you're serious."

"Very. Thank God the kid is agile and fast." She looked over at him. "You should let him back on the team."

"That's what I hear."

"Shirlene?"

"Yeah, she gave me an earful." He groaned. "Along with everyone else in town."

"I guess they're upset about losing the game." When he nodded, she continued. "Austin thinks Jared sucks."

"Right." Slate sat back up and ran a hand over his face.

"So are you going to give him a chance to apologize?"

"Sort of like you gave me?" He was getting grumpy again, but he couldn't seem to help it around the woman.

"I gave you a chance."

"You call that a chance?" He turned and stared at her. Faith shrugged, which really pissed him off. "Fine. I'll tell you what. You let me explain things to you—and I'm not talking about a few words in a bathroom with people banging on the door. I'm talking about a private conversation where you really listen to what I have to say—and I'll listen to what Austin has to say and consider giving him another chance."

Clutching the edges of the jacket, she swiveled around on the bench and glared at him. "That's blackmail."

He shrugged just as nonchalantly as she had. "Call it what you want; that's the deal."

"Hey, Faith." Austin was standing on the goalpost. "Watch this!"

The boy sat down on the crossbar, then flipped back and dropped to the ground on his feet. The sheer delight the kid took in showing off made Slate smile. At one time, he'd done the same thing—climbed the goalpost and cherry-dropped off the crossbar to Hope's cheers. The innocence of the moment almost made him like the kid.

Almost.

Faith clapped her approval before she turned to Slate. "Fine. But you don't consider taking him back—he's on the team."

"All right. But that doesn't mean I'll play him."

She hesitated. "But if he's good, you will?"

He heaved a sigh and stood up. "If he's good." He was willing to do anything to save himself from a repeat of the previous football massacre.

"And no touching," she added.

"Austin?"

She didn't laugh. "Me."

It would be hard, but she was probably right. Touching her screwed with his mind. Besides, this need he had to set things straight had never been about sex. It was about not wanting their relationship to end on a sour note when it had started on such a sweet one.

He stuck out a hand. "Deal."

She slipped a hand from the jacket. It was cold and dainty and made his heart rate increase even more. He might've held it for a bit too long and too tightly, since she had to use force to get it back. Still, he stood there staring down at her until she lifted her eyebrows.

"So are you going to talk to him?"

"Who?"

She looked confused. "Austin."

He mentally slugged himself. "Of course I'm going to talk with Austin." He pointed a finger at her. "Don't go anywhere. I'll be right back."

Feeling better than he had all week, Slate took the stairs down to the field two at a time and caught Austin before he reached the fifty-yard line. Even in the dark, it was easy to recognize his shock.

"Coach?" The dress shoes slipped out of his hands, but by the time he grabbed them back up, the surprise in his voice was gone. "So I guess I'm in trouble for breaking into the stadium."

"There is a rule—"

"So what are you going to do, kick me out of school?"

At the kid's belligerent tone, anger pushed up from deep inside of Slate, reminding him of the reason he'd given Austin the boot in the first place. The sullen kid was like a burr under a saddle, and Slate was the horse's ass. But if he wanted a chance to clear things up with Faith, he'd have to deal with the annoyance.

"I *could* get you kicked out of school, at least for a few days. But since it doesn't look like you were doing any harm, I'm willing to let it go."

"Gee, thanks."

Slate tried to unclench his jaw. "So I heard you might want to come back on the team."

"I never quit."

"Right. You were just the one who complained nonstop about the rules."

"Because some of your rules suck."

There wasn't much to say to that. Slate thought some of the rules sucked, too. They were antiquated, but they'd gotten the team ten state championships, and Slate wasn't willing to mess with something that worked. Although it hadn't been working lately. Still, if the kid couldn't follow the rules—Faith or no Faith—Slate couldn't let him back on the team.

"All right then, if that's the way you feel." He turned to leave, but Austin stopped him.

"I didn't say I wouldn't follow the rules. I just said they sucked."

He turned back around. "So are you telling me you want to give it another shot?"

Austin relaxed his stance. "Will you play me?"

"If you work hard and prove yourself, yeah."

"Okay, I'll give it a shot."

Slate released his breath and held out his hand.

Austin looked at Slate's hand for a few seconds before he gave it a firm shake. "So I guess I'll see you on Monday."

"No."

"No?"

"Tomorrow morning." Slate pointed down. "Here. With me. You have some work to do."

"But I thought the offensive coach is the only one who works with quarterbacks."

That was true, but Slate wasn't going to split hairs. "What? You think I don't know my stuff?"

"No. It's just that I've never seen you work with anybody before."

His answer completely blindsided Slate. Of course he worked with his players. He might not spend a lot of time with individual kids, but that was only because he was the head coach. He needed to look at the big picture—coordinate the assistant coaches, determine the game plans, and make all the major decisions.

Shit. The kid was right.

He placed his hands on his hips and stared down at the rounded toes of his dress boots. "Well, by tomorrow you'll be sick of working with me. So go home and get some sleep. You'll need it."

"Okay, but first I need to take Faith home."

Slate looked up. "I've got that covered."

Austin actually laughed. "I doubt that, especially with the way she feels about you."

"And just what does that mean?"

His smile flashed in the moonlight. "Faith doesn't like you."

Talk about losing his temper. He had the urge to start the kid's lessons right then. Starting with a full-body tackle.

"I'm taking her home," Slate ground out between his teeth.

"We'll see." Austin turned and ambled toward the stands.

Slate tried to remember to breathe as he watched him walk away. Maybe meeting him tomorrow morning wasn't the best idea. If he felt like whupping his ass after only five minutes, what would he feel like after a couple hours? Still, there was a tiny part of him that admired the kid's tenacity. For being a sophomore and a newcomer, he didn't back down. And while that rubbed Slate the wrong way, it was a quality that might just lead a team to victory.

If Slate didn't kill him first.

Chapter Fifteen

THE SEDATE BURGUNDY YUKON WAS NOTHING LIKE Bubba's big redneck truck. There were no flapping flags or bumper stickers, no football helmets or peeing little boys, no gun rack and no long bench seat that was perfect for kissing cocky cowboys.

Faith missed the stupid truck.

She glanced over at the man who sat in the gray leather seat next to her dressed in a button-up blue dress shirt and charcoal pants—but it was a testament to her insanity that she missed the cocky cowboy even more.

"Nice truck," she commented. "Is it yours? Or just another borrowed vehicle?"

Slate shot her a grin, and she smiled back before she could stop herself. "Mine. Why, are you missing Bubba's?" He glanced down at the console. "I sure am."

It wasn't right that she should be so pleased that his thoughts ran along the same lines as hers. It wasn't right, but it was true. For the last week, she'd been miserable. Now suddenly she didn't feel miserable at all. She felt... giddy. And she had no right to feel giddy with a man who hadn't been truthful about his relationship with her sister. Unfortunately, she couldn't seem to help it. Which was why she'd only shown token resistance when he wanted to take her back to Shirlene's.

"You were a little tough with Austin, don't you think?" Faith tugged his jacket closer around her, enjoying the deep, rich smell of man and spicy cologne.

"Tough? The kid didn't exactly make it easy."

She laughed at the thought of Austin staring down Slate. "He was just trying to make sure I wanted to go with you."

"I guess he had a right to be concerned. You didn't look exactly overjoyed with the prospect."

"I'm not," she sniffed. "But I made a deal. So the sooner we get it over with, the better." She turned to him. "So talk."

He shot a glance over at her. "Here?"

"You have a better idea? It's a good ten minutes before we get to Shirlene's."

"Ten minutes!" He stared at her in disbelief. "Not likely. I didn't give that belligerent kid a second chance for ten lousy minutes."

She crossed her arms beneath the jacket. "You didn't specify how long the conversation needed to be, and Austin isn't belligerent. He's just scared."

"Scared? Yeah, like a cornered badger."

"Fine. How long did you want to talk? Fifteen? Twenty? If the bathroom at Bootlegger's was any example, you don't seem to have a whole lot to say."

His gaze sizzled down her body. "I got sidetracked at Bootlegger's."

Faith tightened her arms and tried to control the

tremble that welled up inside her. "Okay, so where did you want to talk?"

In the red glow from the dash instruments, his eyes gleamed devilishly. "Sutter Springs?"

"Not a chance."

Slate nodded. "I guess you're right. With this damned console, it wouldn't be any fun anyway." He flipped on the blinker and turned off on a small paved road. It wasn't the road to Sutter Springs but it looked as secluded.

"So you mind telling me where you're taking me?"

"My house."

"Let me guess, you're building a mansion bigger than Shirlene's."

He laughed. "Not even close."

Slate's house *wasn't* even close to being as big as Shirlene's. But, to Faith, the southwestern ranch-style home they pulled up to was much prettier. Its smooth sand-colored walls and flagstone accents blended perfectly with the mesquite, cedar, and sage-filled landscape, giving it a homeyness that Shirlene's big mansion lacked.

"I've got a lot of work left to do," Slate said, his voice suddenly hesitant as the headlights shone on the small courtyard that led to the double doors. "Of course, with football season in full swing, I haven't had a chance to do much. But once the play-offs are over, I plan on spending every weekend working on it."

"You built this?" Faith knew Slate was building a house, but she had assumed he'd hired professional builders to do the actual work.

It was too dark in the car to tell for sure, but she could've sworn he blushed before he ducked his head away. "Well, I had a lot of help from Kenny and a few of the guys."

Shy uncertainty was so unlike Slate that she couldn't help but be completely honest. "It's beautiful."

His gaze snapped over to her. "You want to see the inside?"

Faith wasn't sure it was such a good idea—the console was a security blanket she wasn't ready to give up—but his sudden vulnerability caused her to ignore the warning. "I'd love to."

Before she could remove her seat belt, he'd grabbed a flashlight and was on her side of the truck. He helped her out, his hand on her elbow as she wobbled across the uneven ground in her heels. It seemed there were certain benefits to dating an older, more experienced man. Austin had left the door opening to her. Of course, the poor kid had been a nervous wreck for most of the night, no doubt wondering why an older woman had asked him to the dance.

"Watch your step. I still need to clean up a little bit." Slate led her along the flagstone path and under the archway of the courtyard.

The double doors had no hardware, and it took only a shove to get one open. The inside was more unfinished than the outside. The beam of Slate's flashlight swept over sawdust-covered cement floors and exposed insulation and electrical wires.

"As you can see I've got a ways to go." He highlighted the different accents in the room. "Kiva fireplace." He flashed the light up. "Tongue-and-groove ceiling." He guided her toward the kitchen that had light wood cabinets but no appliances or countertops.

"Bar." Slate waved the light at a large piece of plywood on top of the cabinets between the living space and the kitchen before tracking it over to the center of the floor. "An island will be here with countertop burners."

"Gas or electric?"

"I was thinking the electric kind with the smooth glass top. What do you think?"

"Electric's okay, but most people who love to cook prefer gas."

"Do you like to cook?"

"Yes. Although I haven't done a lot of it in the last few years. I've been too busy working."

There was a long pause. "Funny," he said. "But I don't even know what you do."

She smiled and moved over to the large window. "I'm a programmer for a computer software registration company."

Slate set the flashlight down in an exposed cabinet drawer, the beam aimed at the ceiling. "That's something I couldn't do—sit behind a computer all day. Do you like it?"

"No." It was a truth she'd shared with few people.

"All the time or only occasionally?"

"All the time." Faith looked out at the night sky with its blanket of stars. "My parents thought computer programming would be a good career."

"And what did you think?"

"I wanted to be a teacher."

"But weren't your parents teachers? I would think they'd have wanted you to follow in their footsteps."

She shrugged. "You're right; they probably would've been just as happy if I'd told them I wanted to teach."

"It's not too late, you know." His voice held a seriousness she rarely heard. "You could still be a teacher."

"Who knows; maybe I'll look into it when I get back."

"After California?"

"Yes. After that."

"So did you get Hope's address?"

She heaved a sigh. "No, but hopefully I'll get it tomorrow when she calls Jenna. Of course, even if I find out where she lives, I won't be going anywhere without a car."

Suddenly he was right behind her, his face and broad shoulders reflected in the glass. "Yes you will. If Winslow doesn't return your car, you can take my truck."

The offer surprised her, and she turned around. He was too close for comfort. With the window behind her and the cabinets on either side, there was nowhere to go. So she hugged the jacket closer and stared at the second button of his shirt.

"Yours or Bubba's?"

He laughed. "Mine. I don't want to be responsible for any hit-and-runs on the way."

"Thank you," she whispered, but refused to look up.

"Look, Faith, there are some things I need to explain." Slate released a low sigh, and his breath brushed over her face, sweetly scented with alcohol. "Things I should've cleared up a long time ago."

"There's nothing to clear up, Slate." She swallowed. "I made a mistake, and I don't intend to repeat it."

"A mistake? I didn't see it that way."

"That's because I've never been in a relationship with one of your family members."

"Okay." Slate stepped back to lean on the edge of a counter. "Let's get this straight once and for all. Hope and I were never in a relationship. Yes, we hung out together in high school, but so did a lot of kids. That's how a small town works—everyone hangs out with everyone else. And I guess people got used to seeing us together so they just assumed we were a couple."

Faith desperately wanted to believe him, but there were too many things that didn't add up. "But you dated…kissed."

"Yes, we dated, if that's what you could call it." He looked away. "And every couple months we'd try it again. I guess we both wanted to see if there were any feelings between us. But it never went further than a few kisses, and we never wanted it to."

"So why does the town still think you're a couple?"

"Probably because neither one of us ever set them straight." He paused before he continued. "Actually, I was the one that never set them straight. I liked having an invisible girlfriend, someone I could pull out when other women got too close."

Confused, she stared at him. "So you had other relationships?"

A grin tipped the corners of his mouth. "Do you want a number, darlin'?"

"No," Faith blurted out. "I just wondered how they could go on thinking you were together if you both dated other people."

"How can they still think you're Hope? It's just a bizarre phenomenon of the small-town psyche."

Even in the dimly lit room, she could read the truth in his hazel eyes. While she felt relief, she also felt scared. And she wasn't sure why. She hadn't been scared of him a week ago. Of course, a week ago, he'd been nothing more than a handsome stranger who had appeared in her life at a time when she wanted to rebel—someone she could live out her fantasies with and never see again.

But now, he was no longer a stranger. He was Slate Calhoun, a handsome cowboy with a ready smile and kind word for everyone he met. A bigger-than-life football hero who loved country music, his dog, and the people of his town. A man who had invaded her thoughts and her dreams, and who could so easily end up breaking her heart when it came time to leave.

Which was probably why it had been better when Hope was between them. Without Hope as an excuse, her heart was too exposed. Too vulnerable.

A blast of static broke the silence, and she turned to discover Slate bent over a radio that sat on a piece of plywood. He dialed through the stations until he landed on a slow country ballad, then adjusted the volume to a soft but audible level before he turned to her and held out a hand.

"Can I have this dance?" he asked. She started to shake her head, but he stopped her. "Just a dance, Faith."

"I don't think—"

He reached over and clicked the flashlight off, plunging the room into darkness.

"Come on." His voice was too close. "I have to be better than a young whelp." Slate slipped the jacket off her shoulders and set it down on the plywood.

She shivered, but not from the cold, as he stepped closer and encircled her waist with one hand while the other linked their fingers.

Faith had never been much of a dancer, probably because the men she'd dated preferred quiet dinners and nonparticipatory activities—the opera, ballet, or movies—to activities that involved physical skill. So the line dancing at Bootlegger's and the silliness with Austin had been the first time she'd danced in years. Which would explain her stiff limbs and awkwardness. What it didn't explain was the wild knocking of her heart or the heat that infused her body when Slate's hips casually brushed against her.

"Relax," he whispered. "I won't try anything too complicated."

Slate stayed true to his word, barely lifting his feet off the floor as he moved in a slow circle to the song that played softly in the background. Trying to keep some space between her and the pressed cotton of his shirt, Faith's body remained rigid as her feet shuffled next to his.

"I missed you." His breath tickled the top of her ear.

It didn't seem right that such simple words could cause such havoc in her mind and body. Her heart seized up, and her knees felt like they could give out at any second, as one part of her brain tried to rationalize while the other held on to the words like a lifeline.

"I know it's crazy," he said as he dipped his head closer. "Especially since we've only known each other for a week, but I can't seem to help it." His hand slipped from hers and joined the other one at her waist, pulling her so close there wasn't more than a whisper of space between them. "I can't seem to control this need I have to be with you...." His lips brushed her earlobe, and her world tipped dangerously. "To touch you."

"Slate," she breathed as her head dropped back. "We can't do this."

"Do what?" He kissed a fiery path down her neck.

"This." Faith tried to push him away, but it was a weak effort.

"Dancing?" He opened his mouth and sucked in the sensitive spot at the base of her neck, sending goose bumps skittering over her skin. "Because that's all we're doing, darlin'." He breathed on the wet spot. "Just a little dancing in the dark."

Put that way, it didn't sound so wrong. Especially when there wasn't a bed or truck seat within ten miles. And when this would probably be the last time they were together. And when just the thought of leaving him made her heart feel like it was breaking.

What could a few more minutes hurt?

Slate continued to sway in a slow, dizzying circle even though the song had switched to one with a faster beat—a beat that mimicked the thumping of Faith's heart.

"Mmmm," he hummed against her throat. "You taste good."

She felt the vibration of his mouth all the way down to her toes, and she stumbled. His hands tightened on her waist, lifting her hips up against the hard press of his rigid heat. And just that quickly, her resistance drowned beneath a tidal wave of uncontrollable desire. His head dipped, and their lips met in a hungry kiss, their tongues greeting in one slick slide. His mouth was hot and tasted of strong alcohol, and she grew light-headed on the intox-icating flavor.

Slipping a hand up her body, he covered her breast, molding and shaping it through the clingy material of her dress before he pushed aside the fabric and cupped her in the warmth of his palm. The strength of his fingers felt good, but she only savored it for a moment before she reached for his shirt.

That night at Bubba's trailer, Slate had done most of the touching—something she'd come to regret. She didn't plan on making the same mistake twice.

Especially if this would be her only opportunity.

The buttons proved much more difficult than snaps. Still, Faith stuck with it until the cotton separated to expose all that warm skin to her touch. Spreading her fingers wide, she ran her hands up his flat stomach and over his hard chest—just grazing his nipples before sliding up to his collarbone. Her fingers caught the edges of his shirt, pushing it off smooth shoulders. He released her waist, and the shirt slipped to the floor as her hands sloped down to the defined biceps that had starred in so many of her steamy fantasies. The muscles flexed beneath her fingers, causing her breath to catch and her heart rate to triple.

Leaning in, Faith kissed the indentation at the base of his throat. He tasted of salty sweetness, and craving more, she licked her way down. Beneath her lips, his chest rose and fell. Slowly, she kissed her way over the hard, flat hill of pectoral muscle to the tiny beaded center. She sipped at it, gently at first then harder when he moaned. His excitement urged her on, and she reached for his belt. Once the zipper was down, she slipped her hand inside the opening, surprised to find a pair of cotton briefs. She traced a finger down the double stitching and over the hard length beneath. Slate's breath halted.

"Damn, Faith," he croaked as she released him into her hand.

She had thought the skin on his neck was hot, but it was nothing compared to this smooth heat. She stroked him from the base to the very tip and back again. His head fell back, and his hips tipped forward. The more excited he got, the bolder she became. And it wasn't long before she eased to her knees on the cold cement floor and took him into her mouth.

A hiss came from his lips, but before she could find a good rhythm, he reached down and lifted her to her feet. She started to protest, but it turned into a squeak when his hands slipped under her dress and jerked down her panties. With a flex of muscle, he lifted her and moved over to the plywood counter where he set her down on the jacket. His hands came to rest on her knees, his thumbs tracing tiny circles on the inside of each one as if coaxing them to open.

"Are we still dancing?" she whispered.

The thumbs stopped moving. "Do you still want to?" The question held a trace of the same uncertainty she'd heard when they first arrived at the house. The cautious thing to do would be to say no and get out of there as quickly as possible. Unfortunately, it was already too late for that.

She reached out and ran a finger down the center of his chest. "Yes, I still want to."

He swallowed hard. "All right then." He reached for his wallet. A few seconds later, he nudged her knees apart and stepped between them. "I call this the Texas Slide." Once he was positioned, he thrust his hips and took her breath away.

Faith braced her hands behind her. But instead of rushing things, he took his time—pushing in deep, then pulling out slow. He shoved back the hem of her dress, and his hands grasped the very top of her thighs, his thumbs resting against the spot that throbbed for him. The combination of his rhythmic glide and heated fingers catapulted the slow burn of their lovemaking into a sizzling fuse. But just as she neared orgasm, he lifted his thumbs and slowed the tempo of his thrusts. She started to complain, but he kissed away her protests and soon resumed the hot strokes and dizzying rhythm. He repeated the sweet torture numerous times, until her legs trembled, and she actually thought she might pass out from lack of oxygen.

"Slate, please." She tightened her knees and hooked her ankles around his legs, refusing to let him pull out. She waited for his confident chuckle. But all she heard was the ragged sound of his breath and a groaned whisper.

"Thank God."

Then he hiked her legs up, his hands gripping her calves as he thrust hard and deep. Consumed by the sweet friction, she laid back and allowed her cowboy to control the ride—a ride that ended with simultaneous orgasms that left them both weak and winded.

"Damn." He collapsed over her, his head nestled in between her shoulder and neck.

Faith waited for the fear to settle back in. Instead all she felt was a warm cocoon of contentment. She knew it wasn't forever, but for now...it was enough.

Slate lifted his head. "You okay?"

"Besides a few splinters, I think so." She reached up to brush back the strands of hair off his forehead.

He caught her hand and pressed his lips in the center of her palm. "I didn't plan this, you know." His breath felt hot against her skin.

"I know."

Slate straightened, pulling her up with him. "But I'm not sorry it happened."

"Me either."

He released his breath and gathered her close to his chest. "In that case," he kissed the top of her head, "let's go back to Bubba's. My legs are about ready to give out."

Smiling, she brushed her lips over his chest. "So I guess The Great Slate Calhoun isn't as great as everyone thinks."

"Excuse me?" He pulled away and looked down at her. In the dark, she could only imagine his shocked look. "Are you telling me you're not through dancing, darlin'?"

"I think..." She hooked her hands over his shoulders. "That's exactly what I'm telling you, darlin'."

Chapter Sixteen

"YOU'RE LATE."

Slate crinkled his eyes against the glare of the early-morning sun and quickly spotted the young kid sitting on the field with his hands dangling over his raised knees.

"Mornin', Austin." Slate smoothed down his sleep-rumpled hair and slipped on his baseball cap. "And you're right, I am late."

"That's bullshit."

Slate thought it was bullshit, too. Bullshit that he was standing there with a sullen-faced kid, instead of back in Bubba's bed cuddled up next to Faith's warm little body. And that's exactly where he would be, if that warm little body wasn't attached to a kind heart and stubborn mind. Damn fool woman, threatening to withhold sex from him if he didn't meet with the kid. She needed to be reminded of just who she was messing with.

And he planned to do just that.

Once he finished with the kid.

"Well, bullshit or not, I'm here and you're here, so let's get this show on the road."

Austin gave him another glare before he ambled to his feet. "So what do you want me to do? Run a few laps while you watch?"

Man, he didn't know if sex with Faith was worth this. Steamy images of the night before popped into his head, and he tossed the football he'd brought out of the locker room to the ground.

"Actually, I need a little exercise myself." He eyed the kid. "So let's run a couple miles before we start."

"You and me?" Austin snorted. "You're kidding?"

The kid was really starting to piss him off. He nodded at the track. "Whenever you're ready."

Beneath the strands of shaggy brown hair, Austin's forehead knotted. "A race?"

"I was thinking more of a leisurely pace."

"Fine." He jerked off his sweatshirt to reveal a gold T-shirt with a navy blue bee on the front.

"You played for the bumblebees?" If he was forced to hang out with the kid, he planned to give as good as he got.

"Hornets."

"Ooooo, big difference." Slate jogged toward the track, calling over his shoulder. "All you need is a bigger flyswatter."

Austin jogged past him. "And I guess an asthmatic dog that slobbers is a better mascot."

"Much. A bulldog can hit a lot harder than a bee." Slate sailed by him.

"But a sting hurts more." Austin breezed around the outside.

"Dogs are loyal." It took a little work but he overtook the kid. "You ever had a bee for a pet?"

"No, but I've never had a dog, either." Austin easily pulled ahead.

"Are you kidding me?" Slate drew abreast. "You've never had a dog?"

"No. My dad doesn't like animals." He stayed even with Slate.

"I thought you lived with your mom and grandparents." Slate's words were punctuated with heavy breathing. Maybe running hadn't been such a good idea. Especially after a wild night of sex.

"I do." The kid didn't even sound winded.

Slate concentrated on keeping his breath steady. "So how come you can't have a dog now?"

"I don't want one."

"You don't want a dog?" He turned to stare at him. "What are you, communist?"

"No." The sullen tone was back. "And I'm not a dumb redneck, either, who lets their poodle wander around without a leash."

"A poodle?" His breath came out fast and hard. "I wish you Yankees would get it through your heads that Buster isn't a poodle. He's a Labrador retriever mix. A hunting dog. And how can a hunting dog hunt on a leash?"

"Whatever." The kid rolled his eyes. "Look, maybe I just don't want to get attached to something and then have to leave it when I move back with my dad."

The resentment Slate felt toward the kid dissipated beneath a much stronger emotion. One he hadn't felt in a while. Empathy. It may have been a good seventeen years ago but he remembered exactly how it felt when his mother and father divorced. The anger. The resentment.

The hurt. It all came back, leaving Slate chugging like a freight train under a heavy load.

He stopped and bent over at the waist, resting his hands on his knees.

"That was only one lap," Austin stated as he ran back to him.

"I'm just getting warmed up." Favoring the stitch in his side, Slate walked off the track and over to the end zone.

"Right." Austin smirked as he reached down and grabbed up the football to toss it in the air. "Did you do a little too much hick line-dancing last night, Coach?"

He probably had danced a little too much. Of course, the dancing that Austin referred to and the steamy dancing Slate was thinking about were two entirely different things.

"So I guess you struck out with Faith," Austin said, a joyous note in his voice.

Slate straightened. "Gentlemen don't discuss ladies."

Austin grinned. "Yeah, you struck out."

There was an overwhelming desire to set the smart-ass kid straight, except he wasn't so sure he was wrong. Slate had gotten Faith back in his bed, but for some reason, he didn't feel like he'd hit a home run. Probably because he knew the happiness he felt was only temporary. Sooner or later, she'd leave.

The football zinged toward him and would've hit him square in the chest if Slate's reactions hadn't been quick. It still stung when it smacked into his hands. He lifted his eyebrows at the smirking kid before he threw the ball back with as much, if not more, velocity. The kid caught it, but not before it knocked the wind out of him.

Slate grinned when the next pass was more of a lob. "So you're going back to live with your dad?"

"Just as soon as the school year is over."

Slate tossed the ball back. "So explain to me why I should waste a lot of time and energy on a quarterback who isn't even going to be here next year?"

Austin gripped the leather of the ball, threading his fingers between the laces. "Beats me."

"Beats me, too." Slate waited for the ball, but when it didn't come, he released his breath and placed his hands on his hips. "Of course, when I first got here I didn't plan on staying, either."

"You weren't born here?" Austin pulled back his arm and threw the ball.

Slate caught it and adjusted his grip before tossing it back. "Nope. I was born in Georgia."

"Same difference," the kid grumbled.

"I didn't think so. I was from a big city, so Bramble was like another world."

"So why did you move here?"

It was strange how hard it still was to talk about. "I was a little hot tempered, and my mother couldn't handle me after my parents got a divorce, so she dropped me off here to live with her older brother."

Slate must've put a little more zip on the ball because it hit Austin in the chest again. But the kid didn't even flinch as his brown eyes stared back.

"So your mom just dropped you off? She didn't stay?"

Slate shook his head and held his hands up for the ball.

Austin tossed it back. "But what about your dad? How come you didn't go live with him?"

"I guess he didn't want me, either." Damn, he hadn't

planned on being so truthful with the kid. Obviously, lack of sleep and strenuous exercise were not a good combination. Or maybe it was the soothing ball tossing that had his tongue so loose. Whatever the reason, he'd given more information than he wanted to. Especially to a kid who would soon be part of the team he coached. By this time next week, every person in school would know Coach's sob story.

Great.

"Well, my dad wants me," Austin blurted out as he fired the ball at Slate.

Slate's fingers stung like hell as he caught it. "Of course, he does. And my dad probably wanted me." He didn't really believe it, especially since he'd rarely spoken to his father since the divorce. But he couldn't tell Austin that. Not when his brown eyes looked so lost and confused. "It's just that sometimes people have to make hard decisions. Decisions that don't exactly work out for everyone."

Austin snorted. "You mean, don't work out for kids."

"Pretty much." Slate tossed the ball.

They didn't talk for a few minutes as the ball sailed back and forth between them. The sun had moved up farther in the sky, but the air remained autumn crisp. In the distance, a train whistle blew as it chugged by the outskirts of town, and a few minutes later, First Methodist's bell pealed in a vain attempt to lure folks away from First Baptist. A flock of startled quail took flight from the tall grass beneath a cluster of cedars on the far end of the stadium, while on the vibrant artificial field, two people tried to come to terms with the ball life had thrown them.

"I can't believe you had a temper." Austin finally spoke. "All I ever see you do is smile. Even when your quarterback just screwed the pooch by throwing an interception."

"Well, my aunt always said you catch more flies with honey than vinegar."

"And you believe that shit?"

Slate held the ball and sent the kid a warning look. "Watch your mouth."

Austin rolled his eyes. "Fine. You believe that crap? Because once in a while, you need to get mad. Otherwise how are people going to know how you feel? I just assumed you didn't care about winning."

Slate dropped his arm with the ball still in his hand and glared at him. "Of course I care about winning. I'm the damned coach, for God's sake."

Austin grinned. "See. Now I believe you."

The kid really got under his skin. Between him and Faith, Slate was starting to doubt whether or not he could continue to keep his cool. Although maybe the kid had a point. Maybe he needed to show his team a little more emotion. Maybe honey didn't catch flies as much as it just made a gooey mess.

And if anything was a perfect example of a gooey mess, it was his professional and personal lives.

"So are we just going to throw the ball for the next two hours?" Austin caught the ball and tossed it back. "Because I've got to tell you, Coach, I don't know if that's a good thing for my rotator cuff."

"You really are a smart-ass, aren't you?"

"Hey, watch your mouth."

Slate caught the ball and tucked it under his arm. "You hungry?"

Austin perked up. "You brought something to eat?"

"No." He tossed the kid his sweatshirt. "But I'll buy you breakfast, and we can go over the playbook."

"I know the playbook." Austin pulled the sweatshirt over his head.

Slate was more than a little surprised since the kid had only had it for a few weeks before he was kicked off the team. "You know it? Completely?"

"Enough to start winning games."

"I'm not playing you this week, so you can get that out of your head right now." He started walking toward the locker rooms, wondering why he was even messing with the kid. Especially when he had a warm, willing woman waiting for him. At least, that's who he hoped was waiting for him. Faith had more mood swings than his aunt during menopause. He just prayed the spike-haired angry Faith wasn't waiting for him when he got home. That Faith scared the hell out of him.

Austin jogged up next to him. "Of course, you'll play me. Because I'm your best bet."

"What you are is one cocky kid."

"A cocky kid who is going to win you games."

They argued for most of the ride to Josephine's. And by the time they got to the diner, Slate was actually enjoying himself. It felt good to say exactly what he thought for a change, instead of worrying about being Slate Calhoun, the easygoing coach. The diner was almost empty. Most of the town was at church while the rest were at home cooking up hot wings for the Dallas Cowboys game that afternoon.

Rachel Dean glanced up when they entered but didn't give her normal greeting. In fact, she completely ignored

Slate and looked at Austin. "You're that new kid from Iowa, ain't you?"

"Yes, ma'am." His manners were surprising. Especially since all Slate got was sass.

"Your mama's been in a few times, but I ain't seen much of you around."

Austin merely shrugged as he slipped onto a stool. Slate joined him, taking off his hat and setting it on the counter.

"Does Josie have leftover pot roast?" he asked.

"Nope." Rachel's eyes narrowed on him. "Remember, we was closed last night for the homecomin' dance."

Since there wasn't a soul in town happy with him over the outcome of Friday's football game, he ignored the scowl and flipped over his coffee mug. "Fine. I'll have ham and two over-easy eggs with grits. And coffee when you get a chance."

She sent him another dark look before she turned and grabbed the coffeepot from the back counter.

"I'll have scrambled eggs and bacon," Austin said, then closed the menu and placed it back behind the sugar container. "And an order of pancakes."

"You got it, honey." Rachel winked at him before going back to glaring at Slate as she filled his coffee cup. But once it was full, she continued to stand over him.

Slate glanced up. "Is there a problem, Rachel?"

"There sure is, Slate Calhoun." She slapped a big hand on her ample hip. "You had no business treatin' Hope the way you did at the homecomin' parade."

Slate glanced over at Austin, who was playing with the lid of the cream pitcher. "I don't think this is the time to talk about it, Rachel."

"Fine," she huffed. "But just know this. If you don't start treatin' that girl better, she'll never agree to marry you." She huffed off to the kitchen.

"You getting married, Coach?" Austin asked as soon as she was out of sight.

"No, I'm not getting married."

"Then who is this Hope everyone keeps talking about?"

Slate released his breath. He really didn't want to explain the situation to a wet-behind-the-ears kid from Iowa, but he couldn't see any way around it. And maybe Austin was the only person in town he could explain things to.

It didn't take him long to relay the story.

"So people think Faith is Hope." Austin went back to flipping the creamer lid.

"Yes."

"And they think you and this Hope still have a thing going. But now you like Faith."

There was a moment of sheer relief that finally someone understood the craziness. "Exactly."

The kid slanted him a doubtful look. "I gotta tell you, Coach, that's kind of low, hitting on two sisters. Especially twins. A friend of mine back in Iowa tried it with the Filmore girls, and they cornered him in the hallway after school and worked him over pretty good. Of course, he should've known better than to mess with big farm girls who toss bales of hay on the weekend."

Slate lowered his head to his hand and rubbed at his temples. "I'm not hitting on two sisters."

"Maybe not at the same time, but it's the same difference. No wonder Faith hates you."

He looked up. "Faith doesn't hate me."

"She doesn't particularly like you, either." Austin nodded at the cup of coffee. "You gonna drink that?"

Annoyed by the kid's honesty, Slate slid the cup over to him, then watched as he poured half the cream and a third of the container of sugar in the coffee. As much as Slate hated to admit it, the kid probably had a point. Faith might like his kisses and the way he brought her to orgasm, but that didn't mean she liked him all that much. And maybe that was what was making him so crazy. He didn't just want Faith's body to like him, he wanted... hell, he didn't know what he wanted.

Leaning down to slurp off the overflow, Austin looked up at him. "So does this Hope know you love her sister?"

"Love?" Slate almost fell off the stool. "Who said anything about love?"

Austin held up his hands. "Okay. Okay. I got you. You don't love Faith. I guess I figured you liked her a lot, since she was able to convince you to give me a second chance." He went back to slurping his coffee as Rachel came out of the kitchen carrying their food.

"Here, sweetie." She set Austin's plate down first. "You let me know if you need anything else." Slate's plate was flopped down so hard, the bowl of grits actually jumped before she sent him a glare and headed back into the kitchen.

Austin attacked his food, while Slate wasn't all that hungry anymore. The conversation with Austin had upset his digestive system. That just showed you what a wet-behind-the-ears kid knew about relationships.

Love Faith.

Yeah, right.

Like love could happen in only a week. Sure, he loved certain things about her. Like the way her nose crinkled up when she worried over things. The way she melted into his kisses. And the way she laughed. Or just smiled. The way she filled out a pair of Wranglers and the way she strutted in her bright red boots. He loved the feel of her skin and the peachy scent. The sleepy way her eyes had gazed at him that morning. And he loved—

Shit. He was in trouble.

"Hey, Slate!"

He swiveled around as Kenny Gene walked in the door followed by Harley and Rye.

Kenny flopped down next to him and pulled his Stetson off. "Twyla's cooking up some steaks. You want to come over and watch the game?"

"No, thanks. I thought I'd hang out at home." Although after his revelation, he wondered if it was a good idea for him to go back to Bubba's. If he spent any more time with Faith, he'd find other things he loved. Then before he knew it, he really would love everything about her. Which was probably as close to love as a person could get.

Harley stepped up and looked over at Austin. "Hey, son. I was glad to see you at the dance last night."

Austin nodded, but didn't lift his head from over the plate.

"Of course, it surprised all of us that you came with Hope." Harley smirked at Slate. "But I knew all along you were only pullin' a fast one."

Rachel Dean suddenly appeared. "What do you mean, Harley?"

Harley stuck out his big belly, and the buttons of his western shirt strained. "Well, it appears that Misty Jean and Ike were having a little dispute in the parking lot of the stadium, when they saw Hope and Slate getting in his truck."

Kenny shoved Slate in the shoulder. "You sly dog, you."

"It seems," Harley went on, "that our beloved football coach performed a little quarterback sneak." He thumped Austin on the back. "With a little help from a friend."

"A quarterback sneak?" Rachel looked confused.

Harley winked at Slate, who wanted to wipe the smile off the man's face with his fist. "I called Shirlene this morning, just to check on Faith. But surprise, surprise, she wasn't there."

"Harley," Slate started, but then realized he didn't have anything to say. Until Burl and Jenna fessed up, no one would believe him anyway. Besides, he couldn't very well call Misty Jean and Ike liars when Faith was still asleep in his bed.

"What?" Rye jumped in. "Cat got your tongue, Slate? Or maybe our little Hope."

"And speaking of cats"—Kenny grinned—"I guess one's out now."

The men all laughed.

"Well, isn't that the greatest thing." Rachel finally smiled at him. "I knew you two wouldn't be mad at each other for long."

"So when's the date?" Harley pulled a chair out from the table behind them and flopped down. "I figure football season is out."

"Of course it's out." Rye pulled another chair out. "We can't have our coach worrying about a weddin' when he's got games to win."

"There's not going to be any wedding," Slate said.

"No wedding?" Harley's eyes widened. "So you're just going to live with our little Hope in sin, Slate Calhoun?"

"Of course he's not," Rachel said. "Burl would never put up with that."

Slate groaned and turned his back to the group. In his desire to get Faith back in bed, he'd forgotten about her gun-toting, bad-tempered daddy. Now, thanks to Shirlene's big mouth, he would need to do some fast talking or wind up with a hunting rifle aimed at his heart.

"I was thinking December after the play-offs." Harley cleared his throat. "But seeing how y'all are already living together, we better move it up."

"Move it up?" Rachel Dean gasped. "The weddin' committee hasn't even met."

Slate jumped up and tapped Austin on the shoulder. "Come on, let's go."

Austin took one look at his face and dropped his fork. "Anything you say, Coach."

Slate flipped some money on the counter and grabbed up his ball cap before he nodded at Rachel. "Thank Josie for me."

"Now, Slate, don't go getting all bent out of shape." Harley tried to get up, but it was a struggle with his big belly. By the time he was standing, Slate and Austin were already at the door. "I realize football season is a hectic time, but you and Hope won't have to worry about a thing," he called after them. "We have everything under control—"

The door slammed closed behind them.

"Damned fools." Slate hit the handicapped sign with his fist on the way by, and it wobbled as his knuckles throbbed.

"Temper, temper, Coach," Austin teased, not realizing Slate was a split second away from hitting something besides a sign. And Austin was pushing it.

"So how come you didn't just tell them that Hope isn't Hope, she's Faith?" Austin asked, once they were in the Yukon.

"Seat belt," he ordered, then waited for Austin to comply before he answered. "We tried that, but those idiots only see what they want to."

"So they're planning the entire wedding without you and Hope's—I mean Faith's—approval?"

"Pretty much." Slate popped the SUV into reverse. He aimed for the bumper of Harley's Cadillac, but inches away, he applied the brakes.

"Wow." Austin shook his head. "That is crazy."

"You can say that again."

"Wow. That is crazy." Austin grinned over at him.

Slate didn't grin back, but it was a struggle. The kid was growing on him. Sort of like a flesh-eating fungus.

"Well, look at the bright side," Austin said. "They can't have a wedding without a bride. And from what I hear, Faith doesn't plan on sticking around much longer."

The thought should've made Slate feel better, but it didn't. As much as he was convinced that he shouldn't spend too much time with Faith, he didn't want her leaving. At least, not yet. In a couple days, he would probably feel different. Once he'd gotten his fill of those sweet full lips and that baby soft skin and those big blue eyes. The need to get his fill was probably the reason he wasn't pushing the townspeople to realize their mistake.

Which meant he was as crazy as they were.

God, he really needed to get out of this town.

"Hey, what is this shi—crap?" Austin pointed at the radio.

Slate reached out and turned up the volume. Jimmy Buffett came through the Bose speakers, singing about Margaritaville. His shoulders relaxed. He glanced over at the kid, who was squinting into the sun that poured through the windshield. He grabbed his straw hat from the dash and tossed it to him. "You ever been to Mexico, Austin?"

"No." The kid stared down at the hat for a few seconds, as if it were a rattler, before he slapped it on his head and slouched down in the seat like a true Texan.

Slate grinned. "Yeah, me neither."

Chapter Seventeen

"IT LOOKS LIKE THE GANG'S ALL HERE," Slate said as he pulled Bubba's truck into Burl and Jenna's front yard.

"The gang?" Faith moved away from the warm, cozy spot she'd occupied against his side and fear rolled through her stomach as her gaze wandered over the extra cars and trucks parked in the yard.

"Now, let's see," Slate said. "The green Malibu is Tessa's. The Ford Explorer belongs to Jenna Jay, and the pickup is Dallas'. It looks like the whole family came to meet you."

She tried to swallow but her throat had gone as dry as the strong wind that buffeted the truck windows. As if sensing her discomfort, Slate slipped his arm back around her and tugged her against his chest. His hazel eyes twinkled down at her as he reached up to smooth the hair off her forehead.

"You feeling a little nervous?"

"No."

"Good, because there's no reason to. The Scroggses are nice people." His lips brushed the spot between her eyebrows. "I'm especially partial to the youngest twin."

She pulled back. "But what if they don't like me?"

Those hazel eyes looked confused. "Not like you? What's not to like?"

The sweet words made her chest feel light, but they didn't soothe her nerves. "There's a lot not to like. Especially when they're expecting an identical twin."

"And you do look exactly like Hope."

"But I don't act like her. I don't cuss people up one side and down the other, or drink tequila shooters, or call hogs."

"And that's not such a bad thing, darlin'. Especially since I've been cussed up one side and down the other and it's not real fun. Besides, I prefer beer to Cuervo and hog calling has always sounded to me like nails screeching down a chalkboard."

Her brows tightened. "But don't you see, they're expecting an outgoing homecoming queen, not an introverted computer nerd—a nerd who isn't good with animals and has a very weird accent."

"Well, I can't really argue with you about the whole animal thing, seeing how Buster was passed out for two hours straight from the cold medicine you gave him this morning."

She cringed. "But I didn't realize that all dogs have wet noses."

"Well, it's nothing to worry about. He's a little slower than normal and ran into the screen door twice, but he'll snap out of it by tomorrow." He bit back a grin. "Although I think it might be a good idea to leave the medicating of animals to the vet."

"But that just proves my point. Only an idiot would do something so stupid."

"Or a person who didn't want an animal to suffer with a cold." Slate kissed the tip of her nose. "And as for your weird accent, it's kind of grown on me. There's something damned sexy about the way you say naughty things when I'm deep inside—"

She swatted him in the chest. "I'm serious."

"So am I." He grinned, but when she continued to frown he relented. "Okay, so you sound a little different. It's not a big deal. I sounded different when I first showed up, and people couldn't've cared less."

"But that's you." Faith waved a hand at him. "You're handsome, and charming, and clever."

The grin returned. "Handsome, charming, and clever?"

She rolled her eyes. "You know what I mean."

Releasing his breath, Slate sat back in the seat, his gaze pinned to the ugly cinder-block garage. "Yeah, I know what you mean—probably better than most people. And I wish I could tell you that everything was just great when I first came to live with my aunt and uncle. But I was pissed about my parents' divorce and having to leave all my friends and being forced to live in a small town with people I didn't know."

"Austin."

He nodded. "Yeah, I guess I was a lot like the kid. Except I saved my insolence for my aunt and uncle. I complained about everything—the size of my room, the walk to school, and even my aunt's cooking—which was some of the best stuff I'd ever put in my mouth. For the first month or so, things were pretty bad. But I guess that's just how it works when people are trying to get to know one another. You can't cut to the good stuff right away."

He reached down and lifted her chin. "I know you're scared, Faith. And I wish I could tell you that you'll walk in there and every person is going to love you at first sight. But, thankfully, the saying that blood is thicker than water has some truth to it. When someone is related to you, you have a tendency to overlook little imperfections and concentrate on the good things about a person, the things that make them a unique member of your team." He shrugged. "So I guess what I'm trying to say is, if they don't love you now, darlin', they will."

Something warm and wonderful washed over her, erasing most of the nervousness with a buoyant happy feeling. Suddenly, it didn't matter if her brother and sisters liked her as long as this man did.

Faith smiled up into his eyes. "Thanks for the pep talk, Coach."

"You're welcome." He gave her a quick kiss on the lips before he opened the door and helped her down. "Just remember, if you get too nervous, we can always leave."

Standing in the circle of his arms, she sent him a discerning look. "Back to Bubba's, I suppose?"

His eyes widened with innocence as the wind played with the strands of his hair. "Only if you insist, darlin', only if you insist."

Going back to Bubba's wasn't a good idea. The more time she spent in his bed, the more attached she became. But she couldn't bring herself to tell him no. Not after the endearing pep talk. And not when the thought of returning to his bed made her as dopey as Buster. She realized it probably wasn't the smartest thing she'd ever done in her life and, eventually, she'd probably pay for it with a broken heart. But for now, she was right where she wanted to be.

In Slate's arms.

"Hey, you two," Jenna called from the front porch. "There's a lot of folks waiting to meet Faith, so get on in here."

Slate gave her waist a reassuring squeeze before they walked around the front of the truck.

"What a cute outfit, Faith," Jenna said as her gaze wandered over the brightly colored blouse, jeans, and red boots.

Slate had driven her back out to Shirlene's to change clothes after he'd finished practicing with Austin. Shirlene wasn't the least bit upset that she hadn't come home the night before. In fact, her green eyes practically danced around in her head the entire time Faith and Slate were there.

The manipulative woman.

"Thank you," Faith said as she climbed the front steps. "I like yours, too."

Jenna shook her head as she held the door open. "Oh, this old thing. It was just the first thing I grabbed this morning."

But her blush told Faith that Jenna had spent a little more time than that picking out the conservative black and tan dress. She sent her mother a bright smile. But the smile evaporated when she stepped into the large living room and four sets of eyes stared back at her.

Faith took a step back, and Slate's fingers tightened on her waist.

"Hey, y'all," Slate greeted the group. "Ain't this a big surprise?"

"Not as big of a surprise as findin' out you have another sister." A tall young woman with a long blond ponytail stared at Faith from familiar blue eyes.

"Now Jenna Jay, don't be sassy," Burl warned. Dressed in his Sunday best, he smiled weakly at Faith.

"I'm not being sassy, Daddy." The girl flopped down on the floral couch. "I'm just statin' the truth."

"And statin' it mighty sassy." Burl took a hesitant step closer and gave Faith an awkward hug. His huge body dwarfed hers, the smell of his aftershave eye-stingingly potent. "We're glad you could come, Faith." He thumped her twice on the back.

"Try not to kill her, Daddy, until I've had a chance to greet her." Another woman stepped up. This one looked older than the blonde and a lot less sassy. Her face was a carbon copy of Jenna's, but her body was tall and thin.

"I'm Tessa." She gave Faith a heartfelt hug before she pulled back and gave her the once over. "Wow. You do look exactly like Hope—well, except for that hair. I was thinking about cutting mine...but maybe not."

Slate laughed. "It grows on you."

Tessa's eyebrows lifted. "It looks like a lot more than just my sister's hair has grown on you, Slate Calhoun."

There was a long uncomfortable silence before Jenna jumped back in.

"Now quit teasing, Tess, and let me introduce everyone. You've met Tessa. The sassy one is Jenna Junior, or Jenna Jay as we like to call her. And the lazy one who won't get off the couch is my youngest—Dallas. Dal, show a little respect, would you?"

The young, sandy-haired man unfolded from the couch, his blue eyes guarded. He was as tall as Burl but not as wide, his body filled with the lean muscles of youth. He moved like his father in a hesitant, cautious way.

He lifted a hand. "Hey."

Faith nodded her head. "It's nice to meet all of you."

"All of you," Jenna Jay snorted. "You mean 'y'all'?"

"She means everyone but you, smart britches," Slate teased. "I would've thought some of those college boys at Texas Tech would've kissed some of that sassiness out of you by now."

She glared back at him. "I'd like to see them try."

"What do you say, Dal?" Slate dropped his hand from Faith's waist. "You hold her down, and I'll kiss her."

Dallas grinned, a grin that completely transformed his face. "I don't see why not, Coach." Then he moved with an agility and quickness that surprised Faith and scooped his sister up from the couch as she fought like a wildcat.

"Put her down, Dallas," Jenna ordered, then pointed a finger at Slate. "And you quit stoking the fire, Slate, or I'll get out my wooden spoon."

"Yes, ma'am." He held his hands up as he leaned down to Faith and loudly whispered, "Take my word for it—you don't want to get on the bad side of Jenna's wooden spoon. My backside stung for a month after she caught me helping Hope sneak out her window." Noting Faith's expression, he quickly added, "We were all of fourteen, darlin', with three packages of toilet paper and a whole lot of trees to put it in."

Her brow knotted, and Jenna Jay laughed as Dallas deposited her back on the couch. "Hell, she doesn't even know what TP-ing is."

"Watch that mouth, Jenna Jay." Burl shot a stern look at his daughter.

"Of course, I know what TP-ing is," Faith blurted out, even though she didn't have a clue. All eyes turned to her, and she stuttered. "I-It's when you make a—"

Slate started to speak, but Dallas beat him to it. "It's when you make a mess out of somebody's yard by throwing toilet paper all over."

That wasn't what she was going to say, and everyone in the room knew it.

"Exactly." She sent him a weak smile.

"Is that fried chicken I smell, Jenna?" Slate asked.

"Oh, Lord, I forgot all about it." Jenna hustled into the kitchen, calling over her shoulder. "Come on, everyone. If we don't eat it fast, it'll get cold."

"I hate fried chicken," Jenna Jay grumbled as she got up off the couch.

"Good. I'll eat yours." Dallas hooked his arm around her neck, giving her noogies until she elbowed him in the stomach and got away.

"I'd stay away from fried food if I were you, little brother," she said. "From the looks of that belly, you're one drumstick away from looking like Harley Sutter."

"Real funny, Jay." He gave her a shove that knocked her into a curio cabinet. The figurines rattled, and Jenna yelled from around the corner of the kitchen.

"I swear if you two don't stop it..."

"Come on, Slate." Tessa took Slate's arm. "I'm dying to hear about the homecoming game."

Slate would've pulled Faith along if Burl hadn't stopped them. "Faith, I was wonderin' if you might want to see my garden."

Slate's hand tightened on her waist as he looked down at her. She knew he would've stayed with her if she wanted. But Burl looked so pitiful standing there, she couldn't refuse him.

"Go on with Tessa, Slate. I'll be there in a minute."

Once they were gone, Burl held the door open for her, and she stepped out on the porch. He followed, easing the screen door closed behind him. She waited for him to lead her down the steps and around to some vegetable garden she hadn't seen the last time she'd been there. Instead, he moved to the railing and looked down at the profusion of brightly colored mums.

"They're at their peak right now. In a few more weeks, they'll be nothin' but dried-up stems." He reached over and snapped off the head of a withered flower. "Still, fall wouldn't be fall without their color. They're like summer's last hurrah before the browns and blacks of winter set in."

Surprised by the sensitivity of such a large, mean-looking man, Faith didn't reply.

Burl turned back around, the head of the flower still held in his big hand. Like Jenna before him, his gaze took its time wandering over every feature until she blushed and looked away. The blush seemed to please him, and he smiled and held out his hand.

"Welcome to the family, Faith Anne."

She didn't hesitate to take it, which made the smile deepen on his sun-weathered face. "How did you know my middle name?"

"Because I picked it. Anne is my mama's name."

"You and Jenna named me?"

His blue eyes registered surprise. "I thought you knew. Hope. Faith."

It made sense, but until this moment she hadn't put the two together.

"It was part of the deal Jenna made with your mama," he continued. "Of course, we had to start all over when we found out there was two of you instead of just one. We had Anne Marie picked out for both our mamas. Then, when two of you came out, we decided to use those as middle names and choose new first ones. Poor Jenna stayed up most the night fretting over it. But by morning, she had it all figured out. The baby we kept would be Hope, because she hoped we could be good parents. And the baby we gave away would be Faith, because she had faith that God would bring you back to us." He shook his head. "And darned if He didn't."

Faith tried to keep the tears from falling but it was a complete waste of effort. She bent her head to hide them, but the tears dropped down to the cracked cement between her feet, making tiny little dark dots that wavered before her eyes.

"Oh, honey, please don't cry." Burl stepped over and thumped her on the back. "Don't you see, everything turned out just fine."

"What did you do, Burl?" Slate pushed out the screen door.

"I'd watch my tone if I was you, Calhoun," Burl said in a threatening whisper.

"I don't care if you like my tone or not. If you're responsible for those tears, I'm going to give you a lot more than just a bad tone."

Burl bristled. "You think so, do you? Because for the last week, I've wanted to give you something, and after the way you've been pawing Faith since you got here, I'm more than ready to do it."

"Then let's go—"

"Stop!" Faith yelled and held up her hands. "Slate, you're not going to beat up my father." She wiped at her eyes and looked up at Burl. "And you're not going to beat up my boyfriend."

"Father?" Burl's eyes widened.

"Boyfriend?" Slate tipped his head.

"Good Lord," she mimicked Jenna, and strode back through the door, leaving both of them standing there grinning like idiots.

Lunch, or dinner as everyone kept referring to it, was like no family gathering Faith had ever witnessed. Instead of the occasional soft conversation punctuated by the clink of silverware on plates, the long table was the center of nonstop chatter, loud laughter, and a staggering amount of food consumption.

Though Slate was right. Faith didn't quite fit into the family picture.

Jenna and Burl were almost too polite when they spoke to her. Jenna Jay continued to act belligerent. And it was hard to tell if Dallas liked her or not because he was so quiet. Tessa was the most congenial. Although by dessert, her conversation became more of an interrogation.

"So do you have a boyfriend back in Chicago?"

Faith fidgeted under everyone's stares. "No."

"So you don't date," Jenna Jay jumped in.

"Of course I date. I just haven't dated recently." She slid a quick glance over at Slate, who was no longer slouched in his chair. He looked back at her, his eyes intent.

"Why not?" Jenna Jay asked.

Faith pulled her gaze away from Slate and looked over at her sister. "Because my mother was sick, and I was too busy taking care of her."

Jenna Jay looked away. "Yeah, Mama told us about that. I'm sorry."

"We all are, Faith," Tessa chirped. "But when God closes a door, he always opens a window." She grinned. "And I guess we're your window. Although I wouldn't look too closely, if I was you, because we've got more than a few cracks."

Everyone laughed, which lightened the mood considerably. At least, it did until Jenna Jay put a damper on things.

"So are you living with Slate?"

"Jenna Jay!" Jenna yelled.

"It was just a question."

"And one that's not any of your business, smart britches." Slate sat back.

"I'll take that as a yes." Jenna Jay smirked.

"Not for long," Burl stated as he threw Slate an angry look.

Slate ignored it and covered Faith's hand with his. The outward sign of possession didn't go over very well with Burl, and he pushed back his chair and stood.

Luckily, before the fists could fly, Dallas pointed at the clock on the wall behind Burl's head. "Cowboys," he simply stated. And the entire table cleared, leaving Faith sitting all alone with her biggest fan.

Jenna Jay.

"Cowboys?" Faith tried not to fidget under the young woman's stare. "Is there a Western on?"

Jenna Jay rolled her eyes. "You're clueless. Completely clueless. You probably don't even watch football."

"Yes, I do," she defended herself. "I saw the homecoming game."

"And who won?"

Faith cleared her throat. "The other team."

"Which was?"

"Some kind of cat, I think."

"Brother." Jenna Jay picked at her thumbnail and seemed in no hurry to follow her family into the other room. "So you lived in Chicago?"

"Yes."

"I guess you think we're nothing but a bunch of stupid country hicks." Her blue eyes flickered up. They were as cold as glaciers.

"No." When Jenna Jay's eyes narrowed, Faith decided to be honest. "All right, maybe I did to begin with. I took one look at Bubba's truck and thought I'd driven into a town filled with a bunch of crazy rednecks."

Jenna Jay continued to pick at her nail, but a slight smile tipped her full lips. "Bubba's truck will do that. Although Bubba's from East Texas."

Faith laughed. "I thought Bubba's truck was Slate's."

She stopped picking and sat up. "You're kidding? And you still liked him?"

"Believe me, if you'd told me a week ago I'd be driving around with a cocky cowboy in a monster truck, I would've thought you were crazy. But if I've discovered anything in the last few days, it's that Texan men can be extremely persuasive."

Jenna Jay nodded. "Amen to that, sister. Amen to that."

The Dallas Cowboys game lasted longer than the movie *Titanic,* but without one good love scene—unless you considered the occasional butt pats the football players gave one another. But even without the love scenes and with no knowledge of what a safety or illegal motion was, Faith liked being sandwiched on the couch between Slate and her brother while they jumped and hollered every time their team did something they liked, and especially when they didn't.

Jenna, Burl, and Tessa sat on the opposite couch and did their fair share of yelling, while Jenna Jay sat on the floor and painted her toenails, acting as if she wasn't the least concerned about the game. But Faith realized it was all a pretense when the Cowboys' quarterback threw the ball to the opposing team, and Jenna Jay knocked over the bottle of pink polish on the green carpet as she jumped in aggravation. To Faith's mother, the mishap would've been a major catastrophe, but Jenna only helped her daughter clean it up—keeping an eye on the television the entire time—completely unconcerned that she now had a permanent pink spot on her floor.

When the game ended, so did the party. Dallas headed back to Austin, while Tessa headed back to Amarillo. Because she had Monday off from school, Jenna Jay wouldn't go back to Lubbock until the following evening. Slate and Faith remained for a couple hours after the game, eating leftovers and waiting for Hope to call. Unfortunately, by nine o'clock they still hadn't heard from her.

"She always calls on Sunday." Jenna sent Burl a concerned look. "Even last week when we was gone, she still called and left a message."

Burl didn't look any less worried, but he tried to calm his wife. "Nothing to fret about, honey. She'll probably call later on tonight."

"He's right, mama," Jenna Jay said. "Besides, I don't know what you're so worried about. I don't even call you every week."

Jenna sent her an annoyed look. "Something I've been meaning to talk with you about, young lady."

"Well, before you get started, Jenna"—Slate pushed his chair back from the table—"I think it's about time Faith and I get going."

"So soon?" Jenna looked at Faith. "There's still some apple pie left."

"No, thank you," Faith said. "But I would really appreciate it if you'd let me know when Hope calls."

"Of course we will." Jenna reached over and patted her hand.

"Well, I've been thinking about that." Burl pushed his empty plate away and switched the wooden toothpick to the other side of his mouth. "And I don't see any need for Jenna to call you." When Faith looked surprised, he added, "Because I don't think you should be staying anywhere but right here with us."

Faith glanced at Slate and couldn't help the blush that spread over her cheeks, which made Jenna Jay laugh.

"Burl's right; that's a perfect idea," Jenna gushed. "If you stayed here, it would be so much easier for you to talk with Hope. And it would sure put my mind at rest knowing if Hope called during the day, you would be here to answer it."

Slate stood. "Well, that's real nice of you, Jenna. But Shirlene has gotten real attached to Faith, and I'm sure she'd be devastated if we were to jerk her away like that. And you don't want to upset the boss's wife, do you, Burl?"

Burl got up from the table, his eyes pinned on Slate. "Why don't we call Shirlene, Jenna, and see how she feels about things? Slate is right. I certainly wouldn't want to upset the boss's wife."

"Now, you two quit mad-dogging each other and sit

down," Jenna ordered. "Nobody is going to call anyone until Faith tells us what she wants to do. After all, she's a guest here in Bramble."

They both sat back down and turned to Faith.

With all eyes on her, it was hard to speak. Especially when she didn't want to stay with Shirlene or Burl and Jenna. She wanted to stay with Slate in a tiny trailer with new sheets and a doped-up dog. But from the look on her father's face, that wasn't going to go over very well. And they did have a point. If she stayed there, she would have a better chance of talking to Hope. Besides, Jenna looked so excited at the prospect that she couldn't tell her no.

"All right." Faith tried to smile even though she didn't feel like it. "But I don't plan on staying longer than a few days. If we haven't heard from Hope by then, I'm leaving for California."

"In what?" Jenna Jay asked.

"If I don't get my car back, Slate said I could borrow his." Faith sent Slate a smile, but he didn't return it. In fact, he didn't look happy at all.

"You don't need to borrow a car from Slate," Burl said. "I'll drive you out myself."

"No, you won't," Slate stated. "I'll drive her out."

"During football season?" Jenna Jay sounded like she thought everyone had lost their minds.

"I don't need anyone to drive me out," Faith said. "I got here by myself; I can get to California by myself."

Slate jumped up. "Could I talk with you for a second, Faith?" He glared at Burl as he pulled back her chair. "In private."

Setting her napkin on the table, Faith got up. "If you'll excuse me."

Jenna Jay snorted.

This night was cooler than the night before. As soon as they stepped out the door, Faith shivered, although she wasn't cold for long when Slate directed her over to the porch swing and pulled her into his arms. The position was familiar and nice. She snuggled against him and took a deep breath of cool air and warm-scented man as he pushed the swing back and forth with his foot.

"Now I know you don't like to hurt anyone's feelings, darlin', but I think you need to tell Jenna and Burl that you don't want to stay with them. You want to stay with Shirlene."

She rubbed her nose against the sweet-smelling spot between his neck and shoulder. "Except we both know I won't be staying at Shirlene's."

He groaned when she took a nip at his skin. "You're right. I want you staying with me. But I don't think your daddy is going to like it too much if we tell him that."

Faith pulled back. "And you think he hasn't already figured that out? And even if he hasn't, all it will take is a phone call. You know Shirlene won't lie."

Tipping his head back, Slate said a very naughty cussword.

She giggled.

He glanced down at her. "You think this is funny, do you? I spent the entire game visualizing what I was going to do to you when I got you back to Bubba's, and it was all for nothing." The light that filtered through the living room curtains haloed his golden hair, giving him an angelic look. But she knew better.

"You did not spend the entire game thinking about me."

"Okay, so I only spent the commercials thinking about

you, but it's given me the same problem." He took her hand and guided it down to the fly of his jeans.

The feel of all that hard maleness beneath nothing but worn denim caused desire to pool between her legs, which increased when he leaned down and whispered against her ear.

"Do you feel how badly I want you?"

She tipped her head back for the kiss she knew would be waiting. It was wet and hot and a preview of things to come. And come. And come. But after only a few seconds, Faith pulled back from the kiss and rested her ear against the rapid thump of his heart.

"If you ask me to, I'll go in and tell them I'm not staying with them. But I won't lie—I think they deserve better than that. Especially since Burl is only being protective. And if you had a daughter, wouldn't you do the same?"

"Not when she's thirty."

"I don't think there's an age limit on fatherly-protectiveness." She lifted her hand from his lap and ran a finger along the open collar of his western shirt. "So you want me to go in and tell them?"

"No," he grumbled. "But I'm not happy about it. And I'm certainly not satisfied."

She traced her finger down his stomach and over his waistband to the fly of his jeans. "I can see that, but just because I'm staying with them doesn't mean we can't make sure you get satisfied."

"Here?" He pulled back to look down at her. "If Jenna Jay wasn't such a little terror, I might take you up on that, darlin', but that girl is probably looking out the window as we speak."

Faith glanced over her shoulder as she did a little

figure eight on his fly. "I wasn't talking about here. I was talking about stopping off at Sutter Springs on the way to Shirlene's house to get the rest of my things."

The swing dipped as he jumped up. Tugging her along behind him, he yelled in through the open screen door. "I'm taking Faith to get her stuff from Shirlene's! We'll be back in a minute!"

He had her in the truck and tucked against his side before the porch light clicked on and a smiling Jenna, a laughing Jenna Jay, and an angry Burl stepped out the door. Slate honked as he gunned the truck, the big tires churning up dirt on its way out of the yard.

Giggling, Faith did what she *had* been thinking about the entire game. She grabbed the top edge of his shirt and jerked.

The sound of popping snaps filled the air.

Chapter Eighteen

A COLD FRONT MOVED IN ON FRIDAY, and the temperature dropped by a good fifteen degrees, which was unusually cold for the first week of October. But Slate didn't notice the weather as he turned and looked up at the packed stands. Nor did he pay attention to the band that had just ended their pregame performance. His complete attention was focused on locating a certain mop of honey-streaked hair in the mass of purple and gold.

"Something wrong, Slate?" Travis asked as he followed Slate's gaze toward the stands.

"No. I was just checking out the crowd."

Travis nodded. "It's a packed house. Of course, it always is."

"Yeah, packed."

Packed with everyone but Faith.

He turned away. What difference did it make if she was there or she wasn't? He'd spent the last four years coaching games that she hadn't attended. One more wouldn't make a difference.

Except it did.

In the last five days, he'd gotten used to looking up and seeing her. On Monday, his heart had done a little crazy jog when he looked up during practice and saw her sitting up in the bleachers. Then she smiled and waved, and the jog turned into a full-out sprint. And suddenly, standing right there in the middle of the football field, he had the overwhelming desire to show off for her. To shimmy up the goalpost, just like Austin had done, and do a cherry drop to her applause.

Unfortunately, he wasn't so sure his thirty-year-old body would cooperate or his coaches wouldn't send for a padded truck. So instead, he decided to impress her with his coaching abilities. Which was difficult since most of his coaching abilities centered around observing. And you couldn't impress a girl by standing around watching. So he stopped watching and started teaching, going over the fundamentals and taking the time to talk and listen to each player. As he moved from defense to offense to special teams, he forgot all about showing off and began to enjoy himself. Suddenly halfway though practice, it dawned on him what had been missing from the football program the last four years.

Passion.

Passion for the game.

Like him, the team had just been going through the motions—killing time in a small town where there was little else to do. And that was his fault. Instead of teaching a love of the game, he'd only been concerned with winning. Winning, not for the kids, but for his own inflated ego. He'd been the elusive coach who stood on the sidelines and talked on a headset—a coach who, deep down, had resented the fact that these kids had the opportunity to succeed in a game where he felt as if he'd failed.

But by the end of practice on Monday, thanks to the petite woman huddled under a blanket in the stands, his love for the game was back, along with the strong desire to see his boys have fun. He must've succeeded. The excitement and enthusiasm was such that practice ran over by a good forty minutes, yet no one complained. Not the coaches or the kids.

Not even Faith.

Not the first day or the next four. Every day, she drove to the stadium in Burl's old pickup and sat on the hard metal bleachers until he was finished. Then she waited for him in the parking lot so he could follow her back home. Slate had tried on more than one occasion to whisk her back to Bubba's, but she wouldn't go along with it. It seemed Faith had a streak of honor a mile wide. She told Jenna and Burl she'd stay with them, and she was going to do it, regardless of how easily she melted into his arms. He didn't complain, not when she spent so much time sitting in the stands and not when he was invited over for supper every night.

But it was getting harder and harder to say good-bye. Especially when they sat out on the porch swing after dinner, and she fed him a dessert of warm kisses and steamy caresses. Every night, he left with a hard-on that could easily hammer in six-inch nails, while Faith waved good-bye with a happy sparkle in her eyes.

Slate would like to think he was responsible for that sparkle. But he knew some of it had to do with the new relationship she'd formed with her biological parents, and because she would soon have her reunion with Hope. Hope had called on Monday while Faith was at the stadium and left a message that she would call back this weekend.

Which meant Slate's time with Faith was running out. So where the hell was she?

The band struck up the national anthem, and Slate covered his heart and returned his gaze to the field where the color guard held the American and Texas flags. The song ended, and the uniformed kids had barely gotten off the field when a loud female voice rang out.

"Give 'em hell, Austin!"

Slate looked back to see Shirlene leaning over the railing, decked out in a down purple coat with a white fur collar. But his gaze only rested on her briefly before getting trapped by a pair of eyes as blue as any Mexican ocean.

Faith stood next to Shirlene, engulfed by a huge purple and white letterman's jacket. And not just any letterman's jacket.

Slate's.

His heart leaped up to his throat, and happiness gushed through his body like a midsummer flash flood. She hugged the leather sleeves close and sent him a timid smile. He swallowed his heart back down and grinned like he'd never grinned before. He didn't know how she'd gotten the jacket, and he didn't care. It was exactly where he wanted it to be—wrapped around his girl.

"Coach?"

It took an effort to pull his gaze away from Faith to the kid who stood next to him.

"You ready to win this ball game?" Austin asked with a cocky grin.

"Damned right, I am." Slate smacked the kid on the butt, then watched as he strutted out on the field with Billy Ray for the coin toss.

Suddenly, Slate's senses were on overload. The green of the field was more vibrant, the stadium lights brighter, the sound of the band clearer, and the yells of the cheerleaders more distinct. He could smell cheesy nachos and anxious sweat. Feel the cold wind nipping at the tips of his ears and the end of his nose, and the adrenaline pumping through his veins. He watched as the shiny coin hurtled up into the night sky, flipping end over end before it started its descent down to the artificial turf between the ref's cleats.

It felt like high school all over again. No, better than high school. All because a blue-eyed girl wore his jacket.

"You think Austin will be all right?" Travis asked, bringing Slate out of his moment.

Slate had spent quite a few hours debating the same question. Austin was only a sophomore and a newcomer to Bramble. But age and status didn't seem to matter when the kid got the ball. His talent was as obvious as his arrogance. He was quick on his feet and consistent with his passes. At least, he was in practice. But in a packed stadium beneath bright lights, it could be a different story.

"We'll have to see," Slate said as the coin toss went against them. Fortunately, Rutledge chose to receive, which Slate considered an advantage for Bramble. He always preferred to get the ball at the beginning of the second half.

But the Rattlers proved that it wasn't such a disadvantage. They moved the ball down the field and scored a field goal on their first possession, while on the Bulldogs' first possession, Austin was sacked three times for a loss of yardage.

"What's going on with the offensive line?" Slate asked

Travis, wishing he still had his headset so he could talk to his coaches in the booth.

"I don't have a clue," Travis answered.

Frustrated, Slate walked down the sidelines to where his offensive line stood sucking down Gatorade and looking not the least bit concerned.

"Is there a problem?" One by one, he stared them down until they looked away.

"No problem, Coach." Austin stepped up, looking no worse for wear after getting his bones crushed by the Rattlers' big defensive ends. "We're just warming up. We'll do better the next possession."

His offensive line shot glances at one another but refused to look at Slate or Austin.

"Fine." Slate spoke through his teeth. "But I expect to see some blocking out there."

The blocking didn't get any better, and Slate was forced to call quick little screen passes in an attempt to keep his quarterback from getting hurt. Not that Austin showed any signs of pain. The kid took the punishment without one word of complaint. After a sack, he simply rolled to his big feet, huddling the line back up with pats and words of encouragement.

Slate wished he was taking it as well. He was pissed, and when the whistle blew at the end of the half, he was already on his way to the locker room. He didn't even wait until every boy had stepped through the door before he started in.

"What the hell is going on out there?" He threw down his clipboard, and it slid across the cement floor and hit the lockers. Every sweat-matted head turned and stared at him as if he'd gone off the deep end.

"We spend a good week going over the fundamentals, and my offensive line folds like a piece of tissue paper?" He shoved a finger at them. "That's bullshit and you know it! I don't care who I put in as quarterback—it could be your worst damned enemy—it's still your job to protect them! Do you understand me?"

There were a few "yes sirs," but for the most part there was nothing but shocked silence. Even the coaches wouldn't look at him. The only person who would was Austin. With his head completely drenched in sweat, he grinned like a Cheshire cat. Surprisingly, this didn't annoy Slate as much as he thought it would. He only lifted an eyebrow at the kid before he moved on.

"All right. Now let's talk about the defense getting some coverage on their wide-out."

The second half looked like a completely different team. The defense recovered two interceptions and kept the Rattlers from scoring again, while the offensive line protected their quarterback long enough for him to throw four touchdown passes and run in for the fifth.

It was a great 13-to-35 win.

"I told you," Austin crowed in the locker room as he strutted to the showers, his long lanky body covered by nothing but a towel.

"So you did." Slate stood in the doorway of his office in his jeans and western shirt, having already changed out of his team polo. "Think we can do it again next week?"

"Of course."

"You want to tell me why you didn't get on your offensive line?"

He shrugged. "It's all part of initiating the new kid—you should know that. They wouldn't respect me if I couldn't take a hit and recover from it. But I have to tell you, I was glad you stepped in. That last sack hurt like hell." He looked down at the black cowboy hat in Slate's hand. "I forgot to give you back your hat the other day."

"Yeah, you did." Slate leaned a shoulder on the doorjamb.

"I'll bring it on Monday."

Slate twirled the hat around. "Nope."

"Aww, don't tell me we have to practice on Sunday again?"

"Nope."

Austin looked confused.

"The hat's yours. You earned it."

Austin looked surprised before he recovered. "Gee, thanks, Coach. Just what I always wanted—a hick hat." He rolled his eyes as he walked away.

Slate laughed and flopped his own hick hat on his head as he returned to his office to look over some game film with the coaches while the boys finished showering.

Twenty minutes later, a herd of excited boys was showered and dressed, but seemed in no hurry to head out the door. They clustered around outside his office until Slate finally stepped around his desk to see what the problem was.

Of course, it was Austin who spoke first. "We've been thinking, Coach."

He tried to keep the smile off his face. "That's good. I like a team that can think."

Austin smirked. "Well, that's good because we decided we don't like the weekend curfew."

Slate rested a shoulder on the doorjamb and pushed back his hat. "Really?"

Billy Ray cleared his throat but refused to look at him. "It just doesn't seem right, Coach, that we don't get to go out and celebrate after the game. I mean, if we win, that is. I guess if we lose, we probably should go home. But if we win, I think we should get to stay out longer."

"And what's the deal with not getting to have a girlfriend during the season?" Joey yelled from the back. "You've got a girlfriend, Coach."

He couldn't argue the fact. He did have a girlfriend, one he wanted to see before the night was over.

"Shut up, Joe," Austin said. "We'll talk about girlfriends another time. Right now we're discussing curfew."

Slate had to give it to the kid; he knew how to take the bull by the horns. "So how late are we talking about?"

"Three!" someone yelled out.

Slate lifted an eyebrow.

"Two!" someone else yelled, and Slate's other brow followed the first.

"How about twelve?" he offered.

"Twelve-thirty," Austin countered.

Slate bit back his grin and nodded. "Fair enough. But only on Friday and Saturday night and only if your parents agree to it. School nights, eight o'clock is still the curfew."

A wild cheer rose up, followed with a stampede for the door.

"You think that's a good idea, Slate?" Travis asked as they followed the boys out. "That curfew's been in place for a good fifty years."

"Maybe that's fifty years too long, Trav." He tugged down his hat, turned out the lights, and locked the door behind him.

His team didn't waste any time. The parking lot was almost empty when he and his coaches got to it. He firmed up some meetings to go over strategies for next week's game, then said his good-byes before heading around the side of the building to where he had parked Bubba's truck.

He'd brought the truck in hopes that once the game was over, he could convince Faith to go out with him to Sutter Springs. Unfortunately, now all his players would be out there. Besides, Faith had probably left with Shirlene to celebrate with everyone else in town at Bootlegger's. The thought didn't make him happy. He didn't feel much like spending the rest of the night with a bunch of wedding-crazed fools. For the last week, he couldn't set foot in town without being asked about cake flavors or fonts for invitations.

But if that's where Faith was, he was willing to endure it.

He pulled his cell phone from his back pocket and scrolled through the numbers, looking for Shirlene's. He was so preoccupied that he didn't see the woman who stepped out from around the corner of the locker room until she spoke.

"I hope you realize I'm practically frozen."

His phone clattered to the asphalt. All the emotions of the last week swelled up inside of him, and he couldn't form one coherent thought. All he could do was stare and absorb every precious square inch from the top of her windblown short hair to the toes of her sexy little red boots.

She stepped closer, and the sweet scent of shampoo and peaches filled his lungs. He closed his eyes for a second, savoring it.

"Thankfully, Jenna found this in the closet—" Faith flapped the sleeve of the jacket at him. It fell well past her fingertips. "Or I really would've frozen to death." She glanced down at all the patches on the sleeves. "From the looks of things, you were quite a stud. All-state. All-district. Two state championships—"

He wasn't sure what happened. One second he was standing in front of her and the next he had her in his arms and was kissing her as if his life depended on it.

It felt as if it did.

Faith filled a void inside him. A void he never knew existed until she walked into his life over two weeks ago. And now he couldn't stand the thought of life without her. It seemed too empty. Too desolate even to contemplate.

As always, she melted against him, the stiff leather-covered sleeves hooking around his neck as he pulled her up to her toes. Need took over finesse as he guided her back against the wall of the locker room, giving her one devouring kiss after the other. He wanted to eat her up until there wasn't a morsel left. Until he had completely consumed her so he would never be without her again.

"Slate," Faith mumbled against his lips as his hands slid inside the jacket and covered her breasts. "Slate." Her hands came up to his chest, but it still took a minute for him to realize she was pushing him away, not pulling him closer.

He pulled back and looked down at her, his breathing ragged.

In the shadows, it was hard to see her expression, but her words sounded amused, not angry.

"People can see us."

Reality slipped back, and he glanced around, realizing that even though the lighting wasn't very good under the eaves of the building, they were still in plain sight of the highway.

"Come on." He tugged her along as he retrieved his cell phone, then pulled his key out and unlocked the door. It was dark inside, but he knew his way well enough not to bump into anything as he took her hand and guided her around benches to his office. Once inside the room, he flipped off his cowboy hat and turned to her.

Reaching out, he pushed the jacket off her shoulders. It dropped to the floor with a muffled thump. He slid his hands down her arms, over the soft knit of her sweater to her hands. She shivered when his fingers closed over hers. She was right when she said she was almost frozen; her hands were like ice. He held them for a few minutes, trying to warm them.

"You're freezing."

"I know." She stepped closer to him. "Got any ideas on how to warm me up?"

"A few." Slate smiled. "You want me to tell you or show you?"

"Show me."

He gave her hands one final squeeze before he reached for the bottom edge of her sweater and pulled it up. It got stuck on her head, and she giggled in the folds before he stripped it off. She shivered again, but this time he could feel the goose bumps rise on her chilled flesh.

"Darlin', I think I'm going to need a little help warming you up." He rubbed her arms.

"I'm going to tell you right now, Slate Calhoun, that I don't go for any kinky stuff."

He smiled as he leaned down to give her a quick kiss. "Are you sure? Because I know some pretty good kinky stuff."

"That involves just you and me?"

"Just you and me and a hot shower." He unsnapped her bra, then filled his hands with her creamy, delicious flesh.

"Here?" Her voice quavered.

"I think you'll like it a lot better than Bubba's." He leaned his head down to take one nipple into his mouth. She gasped and slid her fingers up through his hair, holding him like she didn't plan on letting him go anytime soon.

"Mmmm," she hummed. "I might not need a shower to get warm."

"You might not need it, but I think you're gonna like it." He kissed his way to the other breast as he pushed her jeans down to the tops of her thighs.

"I like this."

"So do I." He guided her to the edge of the couch and eased her down.

When her butt hit the cold leather, Faith let out a squeal that ended on a moan when he knelt down in front of her and buried his face between her warm thighs. Her muscles tightened around his cheeks as he kissed her through the cotton of her panties.

"Slate," she breathed.

The sound of his name on her lips made his body tremble, and he breathed in her musky scent before slowly releasing his breath. She wiggled against his lips, and he repeated the inhale and exhale until her panties were warm and damp, and her moans were loud enough to be heard clear out on the highway. Then using his teeth, he tugged the cotton out of the way so he could reach the quivering flesh beneath.

It didn't take more than a few strokes of his tongue to send her careening over the edge, but he continued the gentle flicks until her hips settled back into the leather. With one last kiss, he sat back and reached for her boot.

"Wow." Her voice was thick and seductive. "You are a stud."

"Of course I am, darlin'." Slate tugged off the boot, then rolled off her sock before reaching for the other one.

"And extremely arrogant."

"Extremely." Taking the hem of each pant leg, he stood and tugged her jeans off. Her bottom came up off the couch, and she laughed when he almost pulled her to the floor along with her pants.

"By the way." Faith came to her feet and stepped into his arms, five-foot-nothing of sweet, naked sin. "Great game." She grabbed the edge of his shirt and gave it a yank until all his snaps popped open.

"You liked that, did ya?"

"The game or the snaps?"

He grinned, because as much as he wanted to be deep inside of her, he also loved just standing there holding her and swapping quips.

Slate leaned down and kissed one bare shoulder. "The game. I figured out a long time ago that you liked the snaps. Why do you think I kept wearing these shirts? But I gotta tell you, darlin', I got a limited supply."

Her warm lips found the center of his chest, and she licked her way up to the base of his throat, where her sharp little teeth took a nip. "Then I guess we'll just have to buy you some more." She sucked hard enough on his neck to leave a mark, and he pulled away.

"Be careful. The boys will eat me alive if they find a hickey on me."

"And what about all the hickeys you've left on me? I've had to wash out my turtleneck for the last three nights."

"Believe me, in the last few nights, I've wanted to do a lot more than just suck your neck." He bent his head and brushed a few kisses on the spot behind her ear, while his hands skated over her breasts. "And if it hadn't been for your father peeking out every two seconds, I would have."

"He just doesn't want to see me get hurt."

"Hurt?" He pulled back, and his hands dropped away. "I would never do anything to hurt you, Faith. You know that, don't you?"

Her hands froze against his chest, and a painful silence followed. "Yes, I know that. But sometimes people can't help but get hurt, Slate. Even when they go into a relationship with their eyes wide open."

It didn't take a rocket scientist to figure out what she was talking about. They had both stepped into the relationship knowing that Faith would be leaving soon. But knowing that wasn't going to make it any easier to say good-bye. Maybe Burl should've run Slate off with his shotgun. Unfortunately, by the time Jenna and Burl showed up, it was already too late.

He swallowed and tried to keep his voice level. "I've been thinking." He slipped a hand to her waist. "What if I drove you out to California to find Hope?"

Her stomach fluttered beneath his fingers. "During football season?"

"I would be back for the game, and I could talk on the phone to my coaches—"

She placed a finger over his lips. "No. But thank you for the offer."

He waited until she removed her finger before he continued with his craziness. "All right, then what if you were to move here?"

"Move here?"

"Why not? It doesn't sound like you have any family left in Chicago besides some snooty aunt, and I'm sure you could get a job doing something here with computers. Or better yet, you could go back to school and get your teaching degree. There's always openings at Bramble High for good teachers." He knew he was rambling but he couldn't seem to stop himself.

Luckily, she stopped him before he could start groveling. "What are you saying, Slate?"

Slate didn't know what he was saying. All he knew was he liked being around Faith—liked seeing her in the stands, cuddling with her on a porch swing, and making love to her anywhere he could.

"I'm saying . . . don't leave."

The breath she released fell hot and heavy against his chest right before she melted into his arms.

"I don't want to leave, either," she whispered.

His arms came around her. "Then don't."

"But, Slate, I need to meet Hope."

"I know you do. But if you quit your job, you'll have plenty of time to go see her. In fact, if you can wait another month until football season is over, I'll take you there myself. I had planned to take a couple weeks off, anyway." A couple weeks off in Mexico. But suddenly

Mexico didn't seem as wonderful as what he held in his arms. "And that will give Jenna time to talk with Hope—and Hope a chance to get used to the idea of having a twin sister."

"And until then I continue to live with Jenna and Burl?"

"No. You move in with me. I've been thinking about hiring people to finish the house anyway. This will give me an excuse."

"I don't think Burl is going to go for that."

"He won't have a choice, if that's what you want." His arms tightened. "Is that what you want?"

Her answer came with sweet quickness. "Yes."

His heart moved back down to his chest, and he released his breath as overwhelming relief filled him. "Okay then, we'll talk to Burl tonight."

She pulled back. "Not tonight, Slate. I want to stay with them for a few more days before we break the news."

"Okay." He kissed her head, then rested his cheek against it. "But I don't know if I can take the swing much longer."

"I thought you said something about a shower."

Slate smiled. "Well, there is that." He leaned back. "So, darlin', do you think you're as good with zippers as you are with snaps?"

"I don't know." Her fingers slid down his chest to the waistband of his jeans. "But I'm willing to try." She flipped open the button and slid down his zipper.

Slate tipped his head back and closed his eyes.

It turned out she was better.

Much better.

Chapter Nineteen

THE LOCKER ROOM SHOWER WAS TWENTY TIMES larger than Bubba's, with no holes in the walls and an abundant supply of hot water. Standing beneath the steamy spray, it didn't take long for Faith to get warmed up. Of course, Slate's soapy hands skating over her body didn't hurt, either. He made love to her against the cold tile and again on the leather couch when they went back to his office to get dressed.

By the time they were headed to Bootlegger's, Faith felt sated and content. Not just because of the great sex, but because her cocky cowboy had asked her to live with him.

And she had said yes.

Faith realized she was probably being foolish. Logically speaking, it made no sense for her to move to a town where she didn't have a way to support herself—a town where career opportunities had to be slim to none. Nor did it make any sense to move in with a man she'd known for only two weeks. But she'd been logical all her life, and not one of those logical decisions had made her as happy as this illogical one had.

Stupid or not, she was going to follow her heart.

And as much as she had tried to deny it, her heart belonged to Slate.

"Darlin'." He kissed the top of her head. "There's something I probably should mention before we get to Bootlegger's."

"Don't tell me. The sheriff still hasn't found my car." She couldn't stop her fingers from popping open a snap or two so she could caress the smooth skin beneath.

"Well, there's that. But there's something else you need to know."

"I refuse to do one more parade."

"Nope. There's no more parades until Thanksgiving. But it's almost as bad as a parade." His grip tightened on the steering wheel. "You might even think it's worse."

Faith pulled back and looked up at him. "Spit it out, Coach."

He sent her a cocky grin. "I love it when you get all sassy." When she scowled, he continued. "It seems the folks of Bramble have started planning a wedding."

"Really? Whose?" When he only stared at her, her eyes widened. "Ours?"

"Not ours, exactly. Mine and Hope's."

"You've got to be kidding. I knew they wanted you two to get married, but I didn't think they meant now. They haven't said a word to me."

"And they won't. The town's always been a little afraid of Hope's temper. And seeing how you already blame them for taking your car, they figure I'm the one who should break the wedding news to you."

"But why didn't you tell them you're not marrying me—I mean Hope?"

His eyes narrowed as he looked out at the highway. "Well, at first I tried to, but then I figured why waste my breath. You'd be leaving soon, and Jenna and Burl would eventually break down and tell the truth."

"So you did exactly what you've done for years. You let them believe something that wasn't true."

His face betrayed his discomfort. "Sort of."

"Not sort of, Slate. You did. In fact, both of us are guilty of letting the town believe what they want. But I think it's time we set them straight. I realize Jenna wants to tell Hope first, but if the entire town is planning a wedding, we need to stop them before things get too out of control."

"I think it might be a little late for that, darlin'. The invitations went out today."

Her mouth stayed open for a few seconds, before she snapped it shut. "Invitations? You mean they already have the date?"

"Two weeks from today. We don't have a game that weekend, so I guess they figured it was the perfect time."

She fell back in the seat, leaving a few inches between her and the body that seemed to suck out all her brain cells. "But it's just plain crazy. People can't just plan a wedding without consulting the people who are getting married."

"Well, now, they did kind of consult me."

"What?" She turned on him, wanting to beat him with the black cowboy hat perched on his head.

"Now don't go getting all riled up. I didn't think deciding on a few details would hurt anything." He shook his head. "Of course, I didn't really think the townsfolk would go this far, so my choices might've been a little careless."

He shot a hesitant glance at her. "You like purple, don't you, honey?"

"Purple! My wedding colors are purple?"

"And gold."

"The team colors!"

He nodded down at the letterman's jacket she wore. "You have to admit they look good on you."

"Good on me!" she squeaked. "My wedding dress is gold and purple?" If she hadn't been blindsided by the news of the wedding, it might've dawned on her that it didn't matter what color the wedding dress was; she wouldn't be wearing it anyway. But she just couldn't get past the horrific image.

"If I remember the Polaroid, it's purple with a gold bow."

"Oh. My. God!" Faith flopped back and crossed her arms over her chest. "This is crazy."

"Now, honey, it's not that crazy considering everyone in town knows we've been spooning on Jenna's porch swing for the last four nights. I guess they just figured they would hurry the process along a little."

"A little? A wedding is a little?"

Slate grinned at her. "Okay. A lot."

"So what are we going to do?"

"Well, since you're not leaving, I guess we'd better tell them the truth."

Suddenly, Faith didn't feel as strongly about telling them. "Tonight?"

"Why not? Everyone will be there. Including Jenna and Burl. Of course, we should probably warn them before we say anything." He reached over and pulled her back against his side.

She swallowed. "How do you think they'll take it?"

He squeezed her close. "Well, I figure pretty good considering they'll now have two hometown sweethearts to love instead of just one."

"But this isn't my hometown."

Leaning down, he kissed the top of her head. "It is now, darlin'." His voice held a smile. "It is now."

But ten minutes later, Faith wasn't so sure. The people she was about to inform that she was an impostor were the same people who painted their faces and bare chests purple and yelled obscenities at the referees. Certainly they wouldn't treat a person who had fooled them for two weeks any better.

Hopefully, they wouldn't treat her worse.

"Stop worrying," Slate ordered as he helped her down from the truck that was parked on the sidewalk. "It's not like we didn't try to explain things to them to begin with. They were just too stubborn to listen." His hand rode her back as they walked to the door. "And don't be surprised if they're still too stubborn."

He pulled open the door of the bar, and a wave of smoke drifted out along with loud music and the rowdy laughter of partying cowboys. The noise level seemed a lot higher than the other two times she'd been there.

Reading her thoughts, Slate grinned down at her. "The last two times we were losers."

Just inside the door, she paused and waited for her eyes to adjust to the dimly lit room. A country song blared from the jukebox, but the dance floor was empty. Everyone seemed to be clustered around the bar in noisy excitement.

Faith shot a questioning glance at Slate, but he only

shrugged. "Maybe they're deciding on wedding rings." When she glared at him, he laughed and took her hand. "Just kidding, sweetheart." He tugged her along behind him. "The rings have already been decided on."

"Great," she muttered as she followed him to the edge of the group. Whatever or whoever they were gathered around had to be pretty entertaining because it took them a good five minutes to notice her and Slate. But when they did, the entire group seemed to turn as one.

"Helluva game, Coach."

"Great game, Slate."

"We sure showed them, didn't we, Coach?"

"That new quarterback sure has an arm, don't he? Where did you say he was from?"

Before Slate could say anything, someone answered for him. "He's from Iowa. 'Course he was born in Texas."

"Well, that explains it then."

Faith couldn't completely stifle the giggle that welled up inside her, which drew everyone's attention. It was funny, but they didn't look at her the way they usually did. Their manner was hesitant and guarded and a few of the men pulled off their hats.

She glanced up at Slate, who looked as confused as she was. His eyes remained puzzled until he glanced over to the bar. Then suddenly, every muscle in his body stiffened, including the ones in his hand. Faith flinched from his tight grip, but before she could say anything, a voice rang out that caused her own muscles to freeze.

"Slate Calhoun! It's about time you showed up, you rowdy cowboy!"

With the loud bellow, the crowd stepped back, leaving a large empty space between them and the bar.

Faith's gaze tracked along the cement floor and up the chrome legs of the bar stool to the brown scuffed cowboy boots that hung from either side of the lower rung. Up a pair of tight Wranglers to a large shiny belt buckle. Up a white blouse with a ruffled collar to a face framed by the brim of a black felt cowboy hat and miles of rich brown hair.

Pushing off the stool she straddled, she jumped down to the cement floor in one smooth fluid movement. She was petite, though her stance was mighty. She stood there with her hands on her hips as if waiting for something or someone. Then suddenly, she dropped her hands and strutted toward them like a woman on a mission. It didn't take long to figure out what the mission was. Without hesitation, she flung herself at Slate, knocking both cowboy hats to the floor as she pressed her lips to his.

It was a toss-up on whose eyes were wider—Faith's or Slate's. Clinging to Faith's hand like a drowning man, he sent her a desperate plea for help. She might've done something if her entire body wasn't frozen with shock.

With the hat off, Faith had an unobstructed view of the woman's face. And except for the glorious hair that trailed down her back, it was like looking in the mirror. The familiar features held her transfixed as emotions swelled and ebbed.

Hope finally unlocked her lips from Slate's, and her heels slipped back down to the floor. "What? The cat got your tongue?" She laughed, a deep husky laugh that put a dreamy look on the faces of all the men standing around. "Well, let me tell you, I was pretty tongue-tied myself when I heard about the wedding. Were you planning on inviting me, cowboy, or did you plan on getting married without the bride?"

"Hog..." Slate started, but left the word hanging.

Hope sent him a seductive smile that Faith couldn't have duplicated if her life depended on it. "No need to explain. I think it's kinda cute." Her big blue eyes sparkled up at him. "And the answer is yes. I'll marry you, Slate Calhoun."

A cheer went up at the same time Slate's mouth dropped and all the blood ran out of Faith's head.

Hope patted his chest. "I guess I should've waited for you to ask me, but since you've asked me at least a hundred times in the past, I figured I wouldn't put you through it again."

A hundred times?

Faith's fingers slipped from Slate's.

He reached for her, but she took a step back. "Now, darlin', it's not what you think."

"Who's that?"

Faith looked away from Slate's traitorous eyes into duplicates of her own. Hope's eyes widened as her arms dropped from around his neck. For the last few months, Faith had tried to imagine how she would feel when she looked into her sister's eyes for the first time. But nothing had prepared her for the deep connection she felt, a connection that went past the physical similarities into the spiritual. It was almost as if she was looking into a piece of her soul. A piece that had split from hers and taken form.

It was wonderful and scary all at the same time.

Hope's eyes narrowed. "Who are you?"

"Now, Hope, honey." Jenna rushed up. "That's what me and your daddy was trying to tell you, but as usual, you was too busy talkin' to listen. This here is your twin sister, Faith."

"My what?!" She looked at her mother, then back at Faith.

Jenna shot a glance at Burl, who stood there looking scared. "Your twin sister." She waved a hand. "I know it's kinda hard to swallow, which is why I think we all need to go back to the house and talk about it."

If possible, Hope's expression grew even meaner. "I'm not going anywhere until you explain how I ended up with a twin sister at thirty years old."

Jenna cleared her throat. "Well, you had one your entire life, honey. You just didn't know about her."

"And why the hell was that?!"

"I guess because I didn't tell you." Jenna smiled weakly.

"Well, thanks a whole hell of a lot for that, Mama!" Hope jerked up her hat and started through the crowd. It parted like the Red Sea. When she got to the door, she turned back around and looked at Slate.

"Well, are you coming or not?"

Slate started to shake his head when Jenna stopped him.

"Please, Slate. Go on with her. She needs somebody to explain things to her, since I did such a horrible job of it. And you and her were always such good friends. She'll take it better from you."

He glanced down at Faith, then back at the door, then back at Faith again. Faith couldn't speak if she had wanted to, not when she felt like she'd just opened a present she had always wanted, only to discover it wasn't as great as she thought it would be.

"Please," Jenna begged.

Slate reached out and took Faith's chin in his hand.

"I'll be right back, darlin'. And as soon as I talk with Hope, I'll explain everything. I know it looks and sounds bad, but you've got to trust me, Faith. Please."

"Calhoun!" Hope called.

He gave Faith one last pleading look before he dropped his hand, picked up his hat, and followed Hope out the door.

When he was gone, the crowd swarmed back around Faith.

"I always knew you weren't Hope," Harley said.

"Me too," Twyla agreed. "The hair is all wrong."

"Didn't dance nothing like Hope," someone else joined in.

"Or sound like her."

"Of course, you can't help how your family sounds," Kenny said. "My second cousin on my mother's side was born with too much fat in her top lip so she always sounded like she was talkin' underwater—"

"Good Lord," Rachel Dean jumped in. "Don't start talkin' about your family or we'll be here all night. Besides, you heard Hope. The weddin's on. Which means, we still have a lot of work to do."

"A week! I need to order the silk flowers." Darla scurried for the door.

"And we need to finish painting the town hall." Harley followed her.

The bar cleared out. And Faith was left standing there, the ignored victim of a train wreck. Almost ignored. Jenna and Burl stood next to Sheriff Winslow at the bar.

"Well, I guess I'll have Tyler tow your car out to Burl's." The sheriff shook his head as he walked away. "Vole-vo. Don't know why anyone would name a car after those ornery varmints."

Jenna walked up and put her arm around Faith's shoulders, then hugged her close. "Don't you worry none about Hope, honey. Slate will get this all worked out. If anyone can get Hope to listen, it's Slate. Those two are as close as two tomatoes on the vine."

That was exactly what Faith was worried about.

Slate didn't feel close to Hope at that moment. He felt annoyed. And scared. Annoyed at Hope for acting like a crazy woman and scared that Faith would do something stupid like leave town before he got the opportunity to talk with her.

Damned fool women, letting their emotions get the best of them, he thought as he chased Hope across the parking lot. He didn't catch up with her until she was in her Chevy truck with the engine started. Jerking open the door, he hopped in the passenger's seat.

"It took you long enough," Hope grumbled before she peeled out of the parking lot.

He clung to the dashboard as she took the corner on two wheels. He hadn't planned on leaving Bootlegger's. All he wanted to do was calm Hope down long enough to give Faith the reunion with her sister she'd been dreaming about. But it looked like that plan was blown out of the water.

"Slow down, damn it!" Slate yelled. "You want to get us both killed?!"

It didn't surprise him that her foot only pushed harder on the accelerator. Hope never had listened worth a hoot.

"A twin!" The loud yell almost broke the windshield. "As if my life wasn't complicated enough! Now I have to worry about some ugly-haired twin!"

"It's not ugly." Slate reached down and fastened his seat belt.

"It's not ugly?" Her eyes stared at him with disbelief. "This coming from the same man who made me swear never to cut my hair."

He shrugged. "I didn't realize it would look so cute."

"Cute?" She rolled her eyes. "Great. Just great. I now have a cute twin sister."

Slate glanced over at her. "You're pissed because she's your twin? Or because she's cuter than you are?"

"She's not cuter than me!"

He grinned. After not seeing her for over a year, he'd forgotten how feisty Hope was. But as much as he had missed her, he would rather be back at Bootlegger's with Faith. Sitting next to Hope, he realized how much he preferred a short, sun-streaked mop of hair to a long brown mane. A hesitant smile to a brazen one. And a sweet disposition to a feisty one.

Although Faith could get pretty feisty when she was mad.

And if he knew Faith like he thought he knew Faith, she would be plenty feisty by the time he got back to Boot's. He couldn't blame her. If some guy jumped on her, Slate would be more than feisty. He'd beat the perpetrator to a pulp. Of course, Faith couldn't beat up her own sister.

Which left him.

He took his hat off and tossed it to the dash. "You want to explain what happened back there?"

Hope shot him another nasty look. "And here I thought that was what you were going to do—explain where the hell I got a twin sister."

He hadn't been referring to the twin part as much as the

kiss/marriage part, but he let it pass, figuring she deserved an explanation. It didn't take him long to get through the story of how she ended up with a twin and how that same twin had come to be in Bramble. Hope remained unusually quiet during the telling, not speaking until he was finished.

"So Mama and Daddy just gave her away?"

"From what I can gather, they didn't feel like they had much choice."

He still thought it was a lame excuse to give up a kid, and he waited for Hope's fiery temper to voice his opinion. Surprisingly, she didn't say a word as she turned up the road to Sutter Springs.

"I don't know if this is a good idea, Hope." He clung to the dashboard as the truck bounced over the ruts.

"Why wouldn't it be? We always talk up here."

It was true. But back then he didn't have a girlfriend to worry about. A girlfriend who just happened to be Hope's sister. "I still think it would be better if we went on back to Jenna's."

"I'm not going back there. I'm staying with you."

If he thought Faith would be upset about Sutter Springs, it would be nothing compared to how upset she'd be if Hope moved into Bubba's. "No, you're not."

She looked over at him. "Why not? You got a girl-friend?"

"As a matter of fact, I do."

"Please don't tell me it's my cute twin."

"The same."

She snorted. "Then why does the entire town think we're getting married in two weeks?"

"The same reason they've believed for the last fifteen years that we're sweethearts—they're crazy."

There was a long pause that made Slate uncomfortable.

"Maybe they're not so crazy," Hope said.

He swiveled in his seat and stared at her. "And just what is that supposed to mean?"

Hope stared at the road, refusing to look at him, which only made him more uncomfortable. "Just that we've been together for a long time, so we might as well be sweethearts."

Obviously, Hollywood had screwed with her mind. "Please don't tell me you've got a butterfly tattoo on your butt."

"A what?"

He shook his head. "Never mind. Look, Hope, we've been friends for a long time, and I want to continue to be friends with you. But we both know that's all we are. Friends. So I don't know where that kiss came from or the acceptance of a marriage proposal I never issued."

"That's a lie, Calhoun." She glared at him. "You used to ask me to marry you at least once a week."

"When we were kids!" He glared back. "And we both know it was all a joke—something we did to get the townsfolk all riled up. I never meant it, and neither did you."

"Well, maybe I've changed my mind."

"What?" His voice jogged as the truck hit a big pothole right next to the clearing at Sutter Springs.

"I said I've changed my mind." Hope pulled the truck around in the clearing and parked. Luckily, none of his players were there. At least, not yet. Now all he needed to do was get Hope to stop acting crazy and go back to Jenna's before someone did show up. Someone that would undoubtedly open their big traps and spill the beans about Coach being at Sutter Springs with Hope Scroggs.

"Well, you're not allowed to change your mind." It sounded pretty stupid, but he didn't know what else to say. Especially when he didn't believe her for a minute. Hope didn't like him in that way. She better not like him in that way. Not when he was crazy about her sister.

She turned off the engine. Once she'd released her seat belt, she leaned her forearms over the steering wheel and stared out the windshield. "I forgot how much I used to love coming up here."

The way she said it was so forlorn that his anger melted away, and he released a deep sigh as he unhooked his seat belt and slouched down in the seat.

"Yeah, I've missed it, too." He stared out at the moon that was a hair short of being full, bright enough to light the clumps of cedar and mesquite and the slow-nodding pumpjacks. "So what happened?"

There was a long pause, before she answered. "Hollywood wasn't what I expected."

He dropped his head back on the headrest. "I know what you mean. I was convinced I would be the best college quarterback in the country. But when you get out of Bramble, things sure look a lot different, don't they?"

She nodded, but didn't speak.

"So if it was so bad, why did you stay gone so long?"

Hope shrugged. "I guess I didn't want to disappoint a town that was convinced I was the next Sandra Bullock."

She sounded so defeated that he couldn't bring himself to ask any more questions, although there were a lot running through his head. All these years he'd pictured her in California living the high life while he was here coaching a team that couldn't win a state title if their lives depended on it. Instead, her life didn't sound like it had been all that good. And it turned out his wasn't all that bad. At least, it hadn't been bad in the last week. In the last week, it had been pretty close to perfect.

"Did you ever get to Mexico?" she asked after a while.

"Nope." Slate shook his head. "But I've got the plane ticket." Except now, he didn't plan on using it. Pretty blue eyes had replaced his desire for warm sandy beaches.

"Then how about tonight?"

He blinked, and his head came up. "Tonight?"

Her voice rose with excitement. "Why not? We could be cooling our toes in the ocean by the time the sun comes up."

After the weird way she'd been acting, he knew she wasn't kidding. But he still treated it like a joke. "And miss next week's game when I finally got me a quarterback? Not a chance."

Hope didn't laugh. She just turned and looked back out the window as the seconds blended into minutes. When she finally spoke, her voice was barely above a whisper. "I do love you, you know?"

The confession brought with it a deep sadness for the distance that now separated them much more than just mile markers on a highway. Five years had taken the innocence from their relationship and replaced it with the cold reality of life. He mourned its passing as he reached out and stroked the back of her head.

"Yeah, I know. I love you, too."

"But not enough to marry me."

"It's not about being enough. Our love is the friendship kind, not the marriage kind."

"It could be. Sometimes the best marriages are between friends."

He ran his fingers down through her hair. "What happened to the Hope who told me I kissed worse than Buster?"

She laughed and glanced over at him. "I was hoping you'd improved while I was away."

His eyebrows lifted. "Are you saying I haven't?" The sassy smirk she shot him was 100 percent Hope and made him feel a whole lot better. "Now there's the Hope I remember."

The smile faded. "So I guess your love for her is the marriage kind?"

It was funny, but he hadn't thought about marriage to Faith. His mind had been too consumed with other things—like convincing her to stay. But now that Hope brought it up, he took a moment to consider it. Of course, it was crazy. People didn't get married after only a few weeks of knowing each other. Marriage was a lifetime commitment.

He blinked as the images of a lifetime spent with Faith unfurled like Bubba's flags in a stiff Texas breeze. A lifetime of waking up next to a woman as beautiful as a Texas sunset. A lifetime of kissing pink glittery lips or spooning against a soft, warm body. A lifetime of cute little dark-haired girls and ornery little blond-headed boys.

A lifetime of happily ever after.

A smile split his face.

"What are you grinnin' about, Slate Calhoun?" Hope asked.

"We need to get back." He sat up and buckled his seat belt.

"I'm not going anywhere." Like the stubborn woman she was, Hope crossed her arms over her chest and refused to budge.

But Slate wasn't about to put up with any more temper tantrums from Hope. He was sorry Hollywood hadn't worked out for her, but he had his own happiness to consider. Happiness he wanted to get back to. He was out of the truck and had Hope's door open before she could do more than blink.

"I told you I'm not ready."

"Then you better get that way." He shoved her across the seat so he could take the driver's side.

She ranted and raved, but it didn't faze him—Hope had always had a bad temper. What did faze him was the noise the truck made when he turned the key. It rolled over, but refused to start.

"Ooops," Hope said, her anger completely gone. "I guess I should've gotten gas before we left town."

Unwilling to accept defeat, Slate tried over and over again to get the stupid truck started. Unfortunately, it was no use. The truck appeared to be as stubborn as Hope was. Which meant they would have to call someone. Someone who would have no problem relaying the information to the entire town of Bramble.

But he didn't care about the entire town.

He only cared about the petite blue-eyed woman he planned to marry.

If she ever forgave him.

Chapter Twenty

FAITH SAT IN THE DARK ON JENNA and Burl's sofa, waiting for a flash of headlights to pierce the green sheers that covered the front window. She'd been waiting for a long time. Long enough to replay the scene in the bar at least a thousand times. And long enough to let her imagination run wild with one sexual scenario after another—Slate and Hope passionately entwined in Bubba's truck at Sutter Springs, in the locker room showers, on the couch in Slate's office, beneath the sheets of Bubba's bed, even on Jenna's front porch swing.

For the umpteenth time, she got up and peeked out the window, but there was no one in the swing and no truck parked out in front. The moonlit yard looked the same as it did when she'd arrived home with her parents. Except now her Volvo was parked behind Jenna's Cadillac. Tyler had towed it out soon after they'd gotten home. Faith now had her car and her suitcases. What she didn't have was her boyfriend.

The trade-off didn't seem like a good one. She would gladly give up her car and her suitcases to be snuggled up against Slate on the porch swing. Unfortunately, Slate had someone else to snuggle up against now. Someone who was prettier. And cleverer. And sexier. Someone he'd asked to marry him a hundred times.

A few hours ago, a hundred had seemed like an exaggerated number. But not now. Not after three hours without a word. Now it didn't seem exaggerated at all. Especially when a truck finally pulled into the driveway and only one person got out.

A very petite cowgirl with a very cocky strut.

Faith released the curtain and stepped back from the window just as the front door opened and Hope stepped over the threshold. Moonlight gilded her long dark hair, and all Faith could think about was yanking it out by the roots and turning it into a Joni Tail. It would make at least two. Or she could keep it in one long strand to strangle her sister with.

Unaware of her twin sister standing in the dark, Hope didn't waste any time heading toward the bedroom—the same bedroom Faith had been sleeping in. And Faith didn't hesitate to follow her; she might not have enough courage to attack her, but she had enough anger to confront her. By the time she reached the room, the light was on, and Hope was rummaging through the top dresser drawer. She was so involved in her search that it took a while for her to glance up.

"Shit!" Hope jumped, and her hand bumped the dresser, causing the numerous golden pig trophies to wobble.

An apology almost slipped out of Faith's mouth, but she bit it back as she stepped farther into the room. "So I guess Slate failed to mention I was staying here."

Recovering quickly, Hope crossed her arms and sent Faith a sassy smirk. "It must've slipped his mind."

Slipped his mind? Faith wondered what else had slipped his mind. Like maybe Hope having a twin sister whom he'd just had sex with in the boys' locker room showers. Or the fact that he'd promised to come back and explain things to that same sister. She gritted her teeth as her eyes narrowed. But the look didn't seem to intimidate Hope. She only tipped her head and shrugged.

"You got a problem?"

"No." The wimpy lie just popped out.

"Good. Because I've known him a lot longer than you have." She waved a hand at the pictures that covered the walls.

After spending five nights in the room, Faith was familiar with each and every one. It had been hard enough looking at the happy couple when she'd been alone; with her sister standing there smirking, it was extremely painful. Each photo of Slate and Hope—football hero and cheerleader, prom king and queen, graduating seniors—seemed to taunt Faith. And if there had been a Sharpie close by, the grinning faces would be nothing more than black blobs.

With devil horns.

As if she could read Faith's thoughts, Hope's smile got even bigger. "As you can see, Slate and I are close." She toed off first one boot and then the other, a skill Faith still couldn't accomplish.

"So close you haven't seen each other for over a year." The great comeback had Faith smiling her own smirky smile as her sister's eyes narrowed.

"Well, I'm back now, sis. So you might as well hit the road, because Slate is mine." With a flick, she tossed her cowboy hat in the corner where it landed on the head of the giant stuffed purple bulldog.

It was hard to stand up to such confidence, especially for a wimp. But this was one battle Faith couldn't lose. Not when the outcome would mean a life without Slate.

"I'm not going anywhere. Especially since Slate has already chosen me."

With a snap that caused Faith to jump, Hope jerked her belt out of the loops. "Well, if that's so, then why did he spend the last few hours with me . . . at Sutter Springs?"

"Sutter Springs?" Faith squeaked. She felt like bursting into tears. And she might've if her sister hadn't turned so smug.

"And I have to say, Slate is still the best kisser this side of the Rio Grande."

Faith wasn't quite sure how it happened, but suddenly one of the throw pillows from the bed went sailing through the air and smacked Hope right in the face before it dropped to the floor at the toes of her hot pink socks.

The shocked look was quickly followed by a mean one. "Did you just hit me with a pillow?"

Faith's dropped jaw closed with a snap, but she refused to state the obvious. With a sizzling glint, Hope leaned down and grabbed the pillow. Faith braced herself. But instead of immediate retaliation, Hope walked to the door and closed it before turning back around.

"Why, you little fraud." Hope threw the pillow so hard it hit with a smack that poofed Faith's hair out. "You think you can just waltz in here and take over my life?"

"I didn't take over your life!" Faith jerked up the pillow and flung it back. But Hope easily dodged it, and it sailed into the dresser, knocking over two pig trophies.

"I don't know what you'd call it." Her sister grabbed the pillow. But instead of throwing it, she came at Faith.

"You've taken my room." Smack. "My family." Smack. "My boyfriend." Smack. "And my clothes." She smacked Faith right in the Mickey Mouse nightshirt she had borrowed from the top dresser drawer, knocking her down to the mattress. But anger made Faith a little more agile, and she bounced back up with a big pillow in hand.

"I didn't take your nightshirt. I borrowed it." She whipped the pillow around and hit Hope in the head. It was a pretty good blow. Hope must've thought so too because she stumbled back a step, and her eyes widened. But her surprise didn't last long.

"Well, I want it back!" She thumped Faith in the stomach, then whacked her over the head repeatedly. Obviously, a smaller pillow gave you an advantage. Still, Faith wasn't about to give up. She clocked her sister in the side while Hope continued to rant and swing her pillow with twice the accuracy. "And while you're at it you can give back the other things you took! Like my family! My room! And my boyfriend!"

"He wasn't your boyfriend!" Faith tried to regain her balance from a blow to the back of the head just as Burl knocked on the door.

"Girls? You okay in there?"

"Fine," Hope called as she sent Faith a warning look. "We were just going to bed."

"Oh...well...your mama and I were thinking you might want to talk."

Dropping the pillow, Hope pointed to the lamp. "I'm pretty tired, Daddy."

There was another pause. "Faith, you okay?"

"Fine." She sat down on the bed and clicked off the light. Once the room went dark, her father conceded.

"Well, good night then."

"Good night, Daddy."

"Good night, Burl."

They listened as he moved back down the hallway.

"Why don't you want to talk with them?" Faith asked once he was gone.

Hope walked over to the dresser. "Not that it's any of your business, but I'm still a little pissed." She pulled out the bottom drawer and rifled through it until she found what she'd been looking for. "How come you aren't? After all, you were the one they gave away."

In the moonlight that streamed in through the window, Faith watched as she undressed. It shouldn't have been a surprise that their bodies were as identical as their faces, but it was.

"I was pretty upset at first," Faith said. "But after talking with both of them, I realized they made the decision that seemed right to them at the time."

"Great. I have a logical-thinking wuss for a sister." Hope slipped the large shirt over her head and headed for the bathroom. In the moonlight, the purple letters and numbers on the back stood out like a billboard.

Calhoun 12.

The pillow Faith threw missed Hope completely. But it did knock a picture off the wall. Unfortunately, it was one of Hope with Shirlene, not Slate.

Flopping back on the bed, Faith stared up at the popcorn ceiling. The pillow fight had taken most of her anger. Now she just felt hurt. All the time she'd been conjuring up images of Slate and Hope together, a part of her had completely trusted him. A part that believed he would return to her and explain everything. And what was even crazier is that she still wanted to trust him. To believe that Hope had lied, and there was a logical explanation for why he hadn't come back. An explanation that had nothing to do with him realizing that he'd chosen the wrong sister.

"If you think you're sleeping here, you can think again." Hope stood in the doorway of the bathroom with her hands on her hips. "This is my room."

Hope was right. Faith had no business being there. And she could just as easily sleep in Tessa and Jenna Jay's room. But if she conceded the room, Hope might think she had conceded the man. And she wasn't ready to do that. At least, not until she talked with Slate.

"I have just as much right to be here as you do." She got up and reached for the covers at the same time as Hope.

Hope paused with her hand curled around the top edge of the sheet. "I'm warning you. If you know what's good for you, you'll get your skinny carcass out of here."

"I don't have a skinny carcass. And even if I did, yours is just as skinny."

For a few nerve-wracking moments, Faith waited for her sister to jump across the mattress and punch her wussy lights out. But instead, Hope heaved a tired sigh and climbed into bed.

"Whatever. I'm too tired to beat your ass tonight—I'll do it in the morning."

The relief Faith felt annoyed her, along with her inability to keep her eyes from following her sister's every move. Standing like an idiot at the side of the bed, she watched as Hope placed a throw pillow between her knees and then punched the pillow beneath her head twice before lying down. After weeks of trying to find some common traits with her twin, the nightly routine identical to her own should've made her happy. Instead she just felt more annoyed.

Climbing beneath the covers, Faith tugged the blankets up to her chin, flat refusing to duplicate anything her sister did.

"Please don't tell me you're a blanket hog," Hope grumbled.

"I don't think so."

"What do you mean you don't think so?"

"I've never stayed the night with anyone besides Sl— with anyone who complained."

"So I guess you were lucky enough to be an only child?"

"I don't know if I would call it lucky."

Hope snorted. "I would. I didn't get my own room until Daddy built the new garage and converted the old one to a room for Dallas. I've shared toys, clothes, beds, and cars ... and I don't want to share anything else. Especially with a woman who didn't even ask first."

Since she couldn't think of anything to say to that, Faith chose to keep her mouth shut. After a few minutes of silence passed, she glanced over, surprised to find those familiar eyes pinned on her. It was strange the pull they had; Faith couldn't have looked away if she'd wanted to. In those eyes she saw anger, confusion, and an infinite amount of pain.

"You love Slate?"

The question caused Faith's heart to beat faster. "I've only known him for two weeks."

"So you don't love him."

It would be so easy to agree and act as if the events of

the night hadn't left her heart feeling like a punching bag. But she figured if she was able to read Hope's emotions, Hope could read hers.

"Yes, I love him."

The sheets shifted as Hope turned away. "Me too."

It was a long time before Faith fell asleep.

A few hours later, Faith awoke to the gray tinge of dawn. She glanced over at the pillow next to her, but it was empty. She might've gone back to sleep if a horrible gagging sound hadn't come from the bathroom, punctuated with Jenna's soft voice.

Pushing back the covers, Faith slipped out of bed.

The bathroom door was cracked open and through it she saw Hope leaning over the toilet. Jenna sat on the edge of the bathtub next to her, talking softly as she held back her daughter's thick brown hair.

"...it will pass, honey. Believe me, I know. 'Course I didn't get sick in the mornings, it was the evenings that were worse for me. I swear I never threw up so much in all my born day—"

"I told you I'm—" Hope tried to interrupt, but instead went back to gagging.

Jenna smoothed back her hair. "I know what you told me, Hope Marie Scroggs. But I'm not fallin' for that story about Josie's red chili upsettin' your stomach, not when you was practically raised on the stuff. Besides, mothers have a sixth sense about these things. And from the moment you walked into Bootlegger's, I knew you was as pregnant as a barn cat in spring."

Faith's knees gave out, and she reached over and grabbed on to the dresser to keep from hitting the floor. The pig trophies rattled, but Jenna kept right on chattering, unaware that Faith was seconds from joining Hope at the toilet.

Instead, she swallowed hard and allowed the truth to sink into her numb mind. Suddenly everything fell into place. Hope returning to Bramble out of the blue. Her sudden desire to marry Slate. The reason Slate hadn't returned last night.

It all made perfect sense.

Perfect devastating sense.

As the sun cast its first golden rays through the window, her gaze settled on the pictures that lined the wall, and Faith finally saw them for what they truly were. Hope and Slate. Not two lovers—or even boyfriend and girlfriend—just two friends who shared a lifetime of memories.

Two friends who loved one another enough to make sacrifices.

Chapter Twenty-one

LESS THAN TEN MINUTES LATER, Faith was back in her Volvo heading out of town. Dressed in her beige pants and brown sweater, she resembled the woman who had first driven into Bramble more than two weeks earlier—minus the Passion Fruit lip gloss and red high heels. And minus the exuberant excitement she'd felt at meeting her sister for the first time.

Now Faith wished she had never met Hope.

It was a horrible thought, but one she couldn't control. It sat there on the edge of her mind along with the sharp ache that throbbed deep down in her chest.

If Hope had never shown up, Faith would still be back at Jenna's. She would eat the Raisin Bran Jenna had bought especially for her, and sip the orange juice Burl poured. Since it was Saturday, there would be no hurried showers or rushed good-byes. Just a lazy morning with hours to uncover family history and discover shared traits. Then a golden-haired football coach would come to call and take her for a ride in Bubba's truck. Or just sit on the porch swing next to her with his arm looped over her shoulder and his head resting on the top of hers as they enjoyed the beautiful autumn day.

For a split second, Faith's foot lifted off the accelerator before she remembered the blissful, utopian picture was only a daydream. There would be no peaceful morning spent with Jenna and Burl. No lazy afternoon in Slate's arms. Because, as much as she wished otherwise, Hope was home—sexy, vivacious Hope who strutted into town and completely turned Faith's perfect world upside down by pulling out a gun even bigger than the ones on Darla's bizarre nightmarish float.

A baby.

Not Slate's baby. Since Slate and Hope hadn't seen each other in over a year, that was an impossibility. But it didn't make any difference. Whether by Slate or some actor she'd met in California, Hope still had an innocent life growing inside her. An innocent life that needed a father. And who better to fill that role than the hometown football hero?

It made sense. Which was probably why Slate hadn't returned the night before. Hope's pregnancy had brought him to his senses and made him realize that a two-week fling didn't compare to years of friendship and love. And somehow Faith couldn't blame him for that. He had never told her that he loved her. He liked her, and he desired her. And, at one time, that had been enough.

But not now.

Now a baby had forced her back to reality. A reality that looked stark and lonely.

The Volvo's instrument panel binged, and Faith glanced down to discover she was almost out of gas. She didn't want to stop in Bramble, but with the next town being close to fifty miles away, she didn't have much of a choice. So she pulled into Jones's Gas Station and cut the engine. A young teenage kid came out of the garage wearing a blue short-sleeved uniform shirt, worn jeans, and a familiar crumpled cowboy hat. As he walked toward her, she stepped out of the car.

"Austin?"

"Hey, Faith!" He pushed the hat back in a gesture so like Slate's that it made her eyes water. Fortunately, his gaze was locked on her car, and he didn't notice. "Is this your car? I didn't know you drove a Volvo."

"And I didn't know you wore a cowboy hat."

He blushed. "Yeah, I know. Real lame, huh? Coach gave it to me so I figure I have to wear it." He glanced back at the car. "Man, if I'd known this was your car, I'd have called you last Tuesday when Mr. Jones was showing me around." When she looked confused, he pointed at the garage. "It was parked right inside."

The news didn't surprise her. After living in Bramble for the last few weeks, very little did.

She nodded at his shirt. "So you work here?"

"Yeah, well, if I want to get a car, I have to work—not that I plan on staying here very long—but Mr. Jones gave me a pretty sweet deal. I only have to work on Saturday and Sunday mornings and only if Coach doesn't want me to practice." A cocky grin split his face. "So, ma'am, can I help yew?"

The twang made her smile. "Yew sure can."

Austin unscrewed the gas cap and placed the nozzle in. "So where's Coach?"

She tried to keep her voice steady as she dug around in her purse for her credit card. "I don't know, probably sleeping. I'm sure he was pretty worn out from the game last night."

"Worn out?" He looked skeptical. "You're only worn out after you lose. When you win you have so much energy you can't contain it."

She blushed as her mind swept back to a steamy shower and a soapy naked man with so much combustible energy he'd brought her to three mind-blowing orgasms.

Taking note of her reaction, Austin leaned against the car and crossed his arms. "Okay, what's up? Did you two have a fight?"

She opened her mouth to deny it, but then snapped it shut. Hope was right; she was a wuss. Too wussy to tell Jenna and Burl good-bye. Or talk to Slate before she left. Or answer a young teenager truthfully.

"I'm leaving, Austin."

He pushed away from the car. "What? But why?"

"Because I need to get back to work."

His brown eyes were confused. "But I thought you and Coach..."

Faith shook her head and made an attempt at humor. "Didn't you hear? Hope and Slate are getting married."

"But he doesn't love Hope. He loves you."

The words made her heart rate quicken. "Loves me? He told you he loves me?"

"Well—no—not exactly. But he told me he likes you a lot."

Her heart settled back down in her chest. "And I really like him, too. But I need to get back to my life in Chicago."

His eyes implored her from beneath the propped-up brim of his crumpled straw hat. "It's not so bad here, you know—I mean it's not as bad as it used to be. It just takes some getting used to, is all." He paused and lifted a hand. "Come on, Faith. Stay. Who will go to bat for me with Coach if you leave?"

She gave him a weak smile. "You don't need me to go to bat for you. You're the star quarterback—the golden boy of Bramble."

"Nope. That's Coach's title. I'm just a nobody from Iowa."

Reaching over the gas hose, she pulled him into her embrace. "No, you're not. You're my friend."

The safety clip on the nozzle clicked off, and Austin pulled back. "So you're really leaving?" When she nodded, he looked away and stared out at the highway. "Why does life have to be so friggin' complicated?" When she didn't answer, he jerked out the nozzle and thumped it back in the pump before he reached for her credit card. "I'll get your receipt."

She let him go. He was right. Life shouldn't be so complicated. Or maybe it wasn't life that was complicated as much as relationships.

As she pulled out of the gas station, she made the mistake of looking in her rearview mirror. Austin still stood by the pumps, his gangly arms at his sides, and the crumpled hat high on his forehead. At the sight, her tears finally started to fall. And once the dam broke, there was no holding it back.

By the time she reached Josephine's Diner, tears were dripping from her chin. When she passed the football field, a sob broke free. And when the WELCOME TO BRAMBLE sign faded from sight in her rearview mirror, she was squalling to beat the band. She didn't fight the tears but let them fall, figuring sooner or later she'd run out of moisture.

It turned out to be later.

For close to two hundred miles, Faith sobbed as trucks and big rigs sailed past her with an occasional blast of a horn. Around Lubbock, she'd tried to distract herself with the radio, but country music was king in Texas, and the sad songs about lost love only made her cry harder.

On the outskirts of Amarillo, she was so weak and dehydrated that she had to pull off the highway into a Wal-Mart Super Center parking lot. For over an hour, she lay back in her reclined seat as squeaky baskets rolled past and hordes of Saturday shoppers pulled in and out on either side, in too much of a hurry to notice the prone, weepy woman in the car next to them.

Once the tears finally dried up, it was all she could do to drag her lifeless body into the store. Like a blurry-eyed zombie, she moved from one aisle to the next looking so confused that blue-vested employees kept asking if they could help her. They couldn't. Nobody could. She had just lost her new sister, family, friends, and boyfriend, all in one fell swoop.

She left the store with a box of Little Debbie Swiss Rolls, a pint of Ben & Jerry's Chunky Monkey, and a 2-liter bottle of Dr Pepper. In a room at a Courtyard Marriott, she overdosed on chocolate, ice cream, and caffeine while she watched more reality television than she had in her entire life. The large quantity of sugar sent her into highs of hysterical laughter and lows of uncontrollable tears. The laughter she could understand—watching washed-up celebrities hunt for girlfriends, go to rehab, or just go about their bizarre lives was pretty funny. But who would've thought that reruns of *My Big Redneck Wedding* would be such a tearjerker.

Finally, around two o'clock in the morning, her body gave out, and she slept. And she probably would've slept for most of the following day if someone hadn't come knocking at her door. Or pounding would be a better word.

She opened her eyes and stared at the dark room in confusion for a few seconds before she glanced over at the red digital numbers of the clock. 10:17. She closed her eyes again, but the pounding continued, followed by a sassy female voice.

"Open the damned door!"

Recognizing the voice, Faith sat up, just as a calmer female voice joined in.

"Faith? Please open the door, honey."

Her heart seemed to stop as she waited for a male voice. But it never came. Only the sound of a boot connecting with the door.

Jerking back the covers, Faith hopped up. She had never been at her best in the mornings, and the sugar hangover didn't help. She marched to the door with every intention of giving her controlling sister a piece of her mind. Unfortunately, she flung open the door too quickly, and a hard fist cracked her right in the bridge of her nose.

With a grunt, she dropped to the floor like a wet dishcloth.

"Well, shit." Hope rubbed her knuckles as she stared down at her.

"Way to go, Hope." Shirlene crouched next to Faith. "Oooo, that looks like a gusher." She hopped back up and headed for the bathroom while Faith tried not to think about the warm liquid that ran through the fingers she held to her nose.

"Well, excuse me all to hell!" Hope moved away from the scene of the crime and flopped down on the bed. "How was I to know she was stupid enough to jump in front of my fist?"

"I'm not stupid," Faith muttered, her words nasally.

"I don't know what you'd call it, running off like some damned fool and worrying everybody in town sick." Hope switched on a lamp, then grabbed the remote and turned on the television.

Faith took her hand away from her nose. "Everyone is worried sick?"

"Not everyone. Slate doesn't look upset at all. MTV? You watch MTV? It figures." She grabbed the box of Swiss Rolls and pulled out the last package as Faith tried to come to terms with the fact that Slate didn't miss her.

"Here." Shirlene squatted down and pressed a cold, wet washcloth over Faith's nose. "Pinch it, honey. I think you'll be okay once the blood clots. Hope's bark has always been worse than her bite."

"Keep it up." Hope spoke around a mouthful of chocolate cake and cream. "And I'll show you just how sharp my teeth really are."

"I'm shaking in my boots. Besides, I already know," Shirlene replied. "Or did you forget the time you bit me in the leg because I got on the back of Colt's Big Wheel before you?"

"It was my turn," Hope grumbled.

"It was always your turn." Shirlene stood up and helped Faith to her feet. "Move over, Hog, so Faith can sit down."

Hope snorted, but moved her legs. "Quit babying her. She's fine." She shot Faith a quick glance. "You're fine, right?"

"Fine" wasn't the word Faith would use for her condition. Still, she nodded. Her nose only throbbed a little, and the light-headedness probably had more to do with the sugar low than Hope's fist.

"In that case, let's blow this pop stand. I want to be back in Bramble in time for the Dallas game." Hope lifted the other roll in the twin pack, but Shirlene snagged it before she could take a bite.

"Is that why you're here?" Faith asked. "To get me to come back to Bramble?"

Hope rolled her eyes. "No. We just spent the entire day yesterday trying to track you down so we could have ourselves a little slumber party."

"Don't be snide, Hog." Shirlene joined them on the bed, folding her long legs in front of her and showing off her pretty blue stilettos. She took a big bite of the Swiss Roll and talked with her mouth full. "Besides, a slumber party might be fun. Of course, I'll need to make a tequila run."

"So how did you find me?" Faith pulled the washcloth back, then tentatively touched the bridge of her nose. When her fingers came in contact with a huge swollen bump, she shot a nasty look at her sister.

Shirlene grinned. "In a town as small as Bramble, it wasn't hard to find the last person you talked to. Although Austin wasn't exactly a fount of information. If it wasn't for his throwing arm, that kid would be a real pain in the patootie."

"But how did he know where I was?"

"He didn't. But he did say you stopped for gas, and all it took was a criminal mind to go from there." Shirlene glanced over at Hope as she polished off the last of the Swiss Roll, licking her fingers with fire-engine-red nails.

"What?" Hope glared back at her. "It wasn't that hard to figure out. While Shirlene distracted the kid by plopping her fake hooters in his face, I got your credit card number, which wasn't that difficult since Tyler refuses to get a new cash register and the number was right there on carbon for God and the world to steal. Although I would've thought a computer geek would come up with a better password than her birth date."

"Fake?" Shirlene stuck out her chest. "These suckers are one hundred percent genuine. You're just mad because your teacups wouldn't distract an escapee from the state pen."

"And lookee what yours attracted—a wrinkled geezer old enough to be your father."

"Lyle is not that wrinkled. At least, not where it counts."

Faith jumped into the conversation. "So you broke into my credit card account?"

Hope lifted the empty Little Debbie box and looked inside. "Which made me realize exactly how dull my twin sister is. Besides gas and a few hotels, all that was on there were bookstores and Chinese takeout. Good Lord, woman, get a life."

Faith gritted her teeth, then winced when a pain shot up through her head. "I have a life. A life I plan to get back to."

"Too bad, so sad. Because I didn't come all this way to go back home empty-handed."

Ignoring Hope, Shirlene leaned in. "So why did you leave Bramble without saying a word, honey? I mean, I didn't expect you to throw me a party in appreciation for my hospitality, but a simple good-bye and thank you would've been nice. And I'm sure Burl and Jenna feel the same way."

"It doesn't matter why, Shirl," Hope jumped in. "All that matters is that we get the little Disney princess back."

Faith hopped up. "I'm not a Disney princess! And I'm not going back! I can't go back, not when you're pregnant!" Shirlene and Hope's eyes popped wide, but neither reaction came close to stopping Faith's rant. "And not when the perfect solution to the problem is you doing what every person in town wants you to do—marry Slate. And please don't act like it's not what you wanted. Why else would you come back to Bramble? And why would you kiss Slate like you did? And why would you accept his proposal in front of the entire town? And why would you hate me so much!" She threw the washcloth, and it smacked Hope in the face. A face that started to get a very evil look.

"Why, you little sneak, you eavesdropped on me."

Before Faith could answer, Shirlene butted in. "You've got a bun in the oven, and you didn't even tell your best friend?"

Hope whirled on her. "I do not have a bun in the oven! It's just some crazy notion my mama got in her head when I got sick on Josie's red chili!"

It was Faith's turn to be shocked. "You're not pregnant?"

"Of course not!"

Refusing to believe her, Faith leaned closer and stared

into her eyes. The truth was there as plain as the anger on her face. "But it makes perfect sense—I mean, why else did you come back to Bramble and want to marry Slate?"

Something that looked a lot like a blush spread over Hope's face, but before Faith could get a good read, she quickly looked away. "How about because Bramble is my hometown and Slate is my boyfriend?"

"Now, Hope." Shirlene rolled her eyes. "Don't you think that's a stretch, especially when you've been gone for five years? Slate might have the patience of Job, but let's get real. Although I heard tell that he wasn't so patient with you on Friday night when you took him up to Sutter Springs and ran out of gas. Tyler said he was spitting mad."

Faith's gaze shot over to Hope, who suddenly seemed preoccupied with the washcloth. "You ran out of gas at Sutter Springs? But I thought..." Her eyes narrowed. "You lied about kissing him, didn't you?" There was a rush of blood in Faith's ears, and the next thing she knew, she was flying across the bed and attacking her sister. Unfortunately, her right hook barely grazed Hope's shoulder before Hope moved and Faith went sprawling to the floor.

"Geez," Hope said. "How can I have a sister who is such a wimp?"

Stunned, Faith staggered to her feet. "You lied!"

"Okay!" Hope yelled twice as loudly. "I admit it! What I did was downright mean. But what else did you expect? It's not every day that a woman finds out she has a twin sister. A twin sister who just happened to steal her identity."

"I didn't steal your—" She stopped because that was

as big a lie as her sister's. She had stolen Hope's identity and put very little effort into correcting the situation. Hope might've lied, but Faith wasn't blameless.

She released her breath. "You're right; I should've set things straight a lot sooner, and I'm sorry for that."

Surprised by the apology, Hope stared at her for a few seconds before she got to her feet. "Okay, so can we go home now?"

Home. Funny, but regardless of how many years she'd lived in Chicago, Bramble did seem like home. Probably because the corny saying was true: *Home is where the heart is.* And her heart was back in Bramble. Back with Jenna and Burl and Austin and all the crazy townspeople. But mostly back with Slate. Slate who never lied to her about his feelings for Hope.

Or his feelings for her.

"I can't go back."

Hope sent her an exasperated look. "You want to explain why not?"

Tears welled up in her eyes, further proof that she was a wuss. "Because he doesn't love me. If he loved me, he would've come after me. You said yourself that he wasn't even upset over me leaving."

"Of course Slate wasn't upset, honey," Shirlene said. "You could drop an atomic bomb on Bramble, and all the man would do is smile. Hell, he keeps his emotions more bottled up than a shook can of Coca-Cola." She reached out and patted Faith's arm. "But anyone with eyes can see he loves you. And I'll tell you something else. If I had a man like that loving me, I wouldn't be sitting in a motel room with nothing but a television and Little Debbie for company."

"Forget it, Shirlene." Hope started for the door. "If she wants to be a martyr, let her."

Shirlene grabbed a pillow and hugged it to her chest, then proceeded to chew on a bright red thumbnail. "We can't just give up, Hope. Not after we came all this way. There has to be some way to convince Faith that Slate loves her. And just going back isn't going to do it because getting those words out of his mouth would be like pulling teeth. Especially after she left him high and dry just like his mama did."

Faith cringed as Shirlene continued to think aloud.

"Of course, if anyone could get the words out of him, you could, Hope. If you could get him to fess up about his love for Faith, all we'd have to do is make sure she was somewhere close by so she could hear him." She straightened, and her eyes got a look that Faith had learned spelled trouble. "Or maybe you wouldn't have to be there at all—at least, not in body."

Hope shook her head. "Marrying a sugar daddy who doesn't spend enough time with you has left you as nutty as a PayDay, Shirl."

Shirlene jumped off the bed. "Not nutty, Hog. Just manipulative." She pointed a finger in Hope's face. "Remember that old movie of Jenna's we used to watch, the one with the twin daughters who were trying to get their parents back together?"

"The Parent Trap?"

"That's it." She watched Hope and waited expectantly.

It didn't take long for Hope's confused look to clear. "You mean switch?"

"Exactly."

With critical eyes, Hope turned to Faith. "It will never

work. She couldn't act like me if her life depended on it. Especially with that god-awful hair."

Shirlene joined in the perusal until Faith began to fidget. "The hair's not as big of a problem as her demeanor. Still, I think we can pull it off...if it was dark...and for a short amount of time." She smiled, a cunning smile that really worried Faith. "What do you say, honey? You want to go back to Bramble? Or do you want to go back to Chicago and spend the rest of your born days wondering why you gave away heaven without a fight?"

Put that way, it wasn't much of a choice.

Chapter Twenty-two

"Dammit, Austin," Slate mumbled under his breath as he walked down the sidelines, following the path of the ball that his quarterback had just thrown. The bright lights reflected off the brown leather as it floated down in the outstretched hands of his wide receiver, who then tucked it in the cradle of his arm and ran it over the goal line. The touchdown should've eased his temper.

It didn't.

With his anger boiling, Slate stood with the toes of his running shoes just on the edge of the sideline and tried to breathe as he waited for an elated Austin to finish bumping chests with his wide-out and jog off the field.

"Just what the hell do you think you're doing?"

The clear plastic mouth guard slipped out of Austin's mouth as he unsnapped his chinstrap. "Winning a football game." His calm voice really grated on Slate's nerves.

"Don't pull that cocky crap with me." Slate's hand tightened around the clipboard. "I gave you a play call, and you completely ignored it."

"Because it wouldn't have worked. The defense was

lined up for a blitz, which left VJ wide open. I took the opportunity that was handed to me."

"I don't give a damn what kind of opportunity is handed to you. If I call for a running play, I expect to get one."

The crowd roared as the extra point went through the uprights.

Austin jerked off his helmet. "Well, I expect to get a coach who doesn't have his head up his butt because he's too chickenshit to go after what he wants."

"What I want? I'll tell you what I want! I want a damned quarterback who knows how to take directions." He whirled around and yelled at Travis. "Get Jared's ass over here! He's finishing the game."

"That's bullshit!" Austin threw down his helmet and stepped closer to Slate.

Slate stared the kid down, even though he was a good two inches taller. "Bullshit or not, if you don't pick up that helmet and go sit down, you'll never set foot on this field again."

Austin might've argued if two of the offensive linemen hadn't jumped between them.

"Chill, Big Oz."

"Yeah, man, you want to ruin our chances for state?"

With a few choice cusswords, Austin jerked up his helmet and pushed his way over to the bench. Slate turned back to the game. But his temper didn't cool. He tried to calm down by thinking of clear blue waves rolling up smooth sparkling sand, but since Faith had left, the serenity of Mexican beaches was well out of reach. Especially when, not more than fifteen minutes later, Jared fumbled the ball and the other team ran it in for a touchdown.

Luckily, they were still up by ten points and only had three minutes left in the game. Still, it only took ninety seconds of that time for Jared to throw an interception. But the defense held, and they walked into the visitor's locker room winners. Funny, but Slate didn't feel like a winner. He felt worse than when his mother had brought him to Bramble, then sneaked off early the next morning before he'd even gotten out of bed.

Women leaving him seemed to be the bane of his existence. But at least Hope had enough guts to say good-bye. Which made her a hell of a lot better than the other two women he'd loved.

Loved.

Damn, he hated the word.

The bus ride home was quiet for a win. Slate sat in the front with the rest of the coaches and talked about strategies for the first play-off game. When they got back to the school, the boys trudged into the showers while Slate went to his office and changed into his boots and western shirt. It was more out of habit than anything else. He didn't feel like going to Bootlegger's to celebrate, nor did he feel like going back to Bubba's, where memories were as thick as flies and twice as annoying.

"You wanted to see me, Coach?" Austin stood in the doorway with the straw hat pulled over his wet, slicked-back hair.

"Come in and close the door," Slate directed.

Austin strutted in, closing the door behind him. "What? You don't want witnesses when you kick me off the team?" He flopped down on the couch and stretched his legs along the cushions. On his feet were shiny new lizard-skin boots with pointy toes. He couldn't bring himself to tell the kid that pointy toes were out. Of course, he glanced at the misshapen straw Resistol on the kid's head and realized that he didn't exactly follow fashion himself.

"Nice boots."

Austin cocked his head as he examined them. "It figures you'd like them."

"Are you telling me you bought boots you didn't like?"

He shrugged. "When in Rome."

If Slate hadn't felt so depressed, he might've laughed. Instead, he got up from his chair and moved around the desk. He leaned back on it, his hands clasping the edge. "You deserve to be kicked off the team, you know."

Austin glanced up at him. "For winning a football game or for calling you chickenshit?"

"How about for not running the plays I give you."

A good minute passed before Austin spoke. "Fine. I'll run your plays, even if they suck."

"Good." Coming up from the desk, Slate reached down and grabbed the front of Austin's hooded sweatshirt and jerked him to his feet, Slate's forehead brushing the brim of the cowboy hat he'd given him. "Now about you calling me chickenshit." His fist twisted in the thick cotton, pulling it taut around Austin's chest. "It might be wise if you didn't do that again. Especially since I haven't been in the best of moods."

Slate had to give it to the kid; his fear only lasted a second. "And the reason you've been in such a lousy mood is because you're too chick—pigheaded to go get her and bring her back."

Slate released his sweatshirt and stepped away. "Austin, I'm not going to discuss my personal life with you." He moved back around the desk and sat down.

"Then that's it?" When Slate refused to answer him, Austin threw up his hands. "Fine! Then you might as well throw me off the team, because as far as I'm concerned you *are* a chickenshit—just like my dad!"

After the door slammed, Slate fell back in his chair. The kid was probably right. He was a chickenshit. But he wasn't about to go chasing Faith down so he could grovel at her feet. He'd never groveled in his life. If people didn't want to stay, they didn't have to. It was their choice. And he couldn't change that. What he could change was how he dealt with it. Instead of sitting there feeling sorry for himself, he had a play-off game to win. Which meant he needed to go home and watch some game film.

It didn't take him long to finish locking up and then head out to the parking lot. The night was cold, cold enough for him to slip on his lightweight team jacket.

"Slate?"

At the softly spoken word, he looked up so fast he hurt his neck. A figure separated from the shadowy side of the locker room—the same spot Faith had stood in a week earlier. Except the woman who came toward him didn't walk with Faith's feminine glide; this was more of a boyish strut.

Hope.

"Hi, Hog." He tried to keep the disappointment from his voice. "What are you doing out here?"

"Waiting for you." Her voice sounded nasally and a little hesitant.

His eyes narrowed as he tried to make out her features in the shadow cast by the brim of her black Stetson, but all he could see was her stubborn little chin. If it wasn't for the two long braids, he might've doubted who he was talking to. Especially since she didn't sound like Hope. Or Faith, for that matter.

"You got a cold?"

"Yes—" She cleared her throat. "I mean, what's it to you?"

Hope was sure acting weird, and had been acting weird since Sutter Springs. He didn't know what had happened in Hollywood, but it couldn't have been good. And he felt bad that he had been so wrapped up with football that he hadn't stopped by to see her in the last week. She might've pissed him off with her inopportune timing and stubborn nature, but she was still a good friend, and he couldn't stay mad at her.

"Listen." He rubbed the back of his neck. "I'm sorry I haven't stopped by Jenna and Burl's. It's been a hell of a week." Instead of commenting, she shivered, and he shrugged out of his jacket. "Here." He hooked it around her shoulders, snapping the top snap. "You should be home in bed instead of wandering around without a coat."

"Thank you," she said in a way that had him bending down to look beneath the brim of the hat again. But before he could see more than the tip of a cute little nose, she ducked her head and quickly added, "And stop bossin' me around, cowboy."

"Well, someone needs to." He turned and headed for his Yukon. When he reached it, he looked back to find her still standing where he'd left her. "So do you need a ride or what?"

She hesitated for only a second before she hurried over, braids swinging. She hadn't worn braids since middle school, nor had she ever let him open doors for her. As she brushed past him to climb into the SUV, a scent filled his nostrils. A sweet, subtle scent that caused his gut to tighten. Peaches. Ripe, juicy peaches. Which was just crazy. He didn't know what Hope smelled like, but he was sure it had never been peaches.

After closing the door behind her, he took a deep, cleansing breath of cool night air. And by the time he slipped beneath the steering wheel, he was convinced the scent had been his imagination.

"How come you're not driving Bubba's truck?" Hope asked as he started the engine.

"I only drive it when I need to haul things out to the house," he lied. Hauling wasn't the only reason he drove Bubba's truck. He had liked driving it. Liked sitting up so high that he could see most of Bramble. Liked the flags of his state and country flapping and fluttering in the breeze behind him. Liked Buster having an entire truck bed to roam around in. But mostly, he had liked the long bench seat where a woman could stretch out or cuddle so close he didn't know where he ended and she began. A week ago, he'd been considering buying the truck off Bubba. But not now. Now, he hated the thing. Hated it with a passion.

"So what did you think of the game?" he asked, trying to change the subject.

"Uhhh, it was good."

Since "good" wasn't a word an avid football fan like Hope would use for a win, his gaze shot over to her. But the hat obscured most of her features. Except for those damned sexy lips.

Startled by the thought, he returned his gaze to the high-way and cleared his throat. "Good? After a couple teams in our division lost tonight, it looks like we're in the play-offs. I'd say that was more than good, Hog."

"I meant great," she mumbled as she looked around. "So where are you taking me, Calhoun?"

He eased his foot off the accelerator. "I thought you'd want to go home. Did you want me to drop you at Boot's?"

"I was thinking—I mean, I want to go to Sutter Springs."

Sutter Springs was not a good idea—not after their conversation last Friday night. But mostly because the place held too many memories of Faith.

"I'm pretty tired, Hope."

It was the truth. Since Faith had left, he'd gotten very little sleep. Coaching his team had helped keep his mind off her during the day, but at night, in the small dark room of Bubba's trailer, there was only him and a whole lot of hours filled with nothing but thoughts of Faith.

She shot a glance over at him. "I thought you might want to talk about Faith."

"Why the hell would I want to do that?" Slate took off his hat and tossed it to the dashboard. "And why would you want to? I thought you were pissed at her for stealing your life."

"I—she didn't steal my life."

"You're right. She stole mine," he muttered under his breath. Unfortunately, not low enough.

"Yours? What do you mean?"

He ran a hand through his hair. "Look, it doesn't matter. What happened between me and her is history. But I'm glad you don't hate her."

"You hate her?" The way she said it sounded so much like Faith, he glanced over at her. Damn, his mind was really starting to play tricks on him. Cuddled against the door, she even looked like Faith.

"What difference does it make what I feel about her? I'll probably never see her again." He nodded at Bootlegger's as they passed. "You sure you don't want me to drop you off? It looks like your folks are there."

She ignored the question. "Do you want to see Faith again?"

He snorted. "Are you kidding? Not in this lifetime... or the next."

The answer seemed to shut Hope up, and she remained silent the rest of the way through town.

When they got to the corner of Jenna and Burl's street, he finally spoke. "Look, Hog, I didn't mean to get you all upset. I'm glad you've forgiven Faith. She really wasn't trying to steal your identity. All she wanted to do was meet her sister."

He just wished that he hadn't gotten in the way.

"Where's your truck?" he asked as he pulled into the driveway.

"I left it at Shirlene's." Her voice was much more nasally. And a lot more quavery.

The quavery part scared the hell out of him, and he quickly parked and turned to her. "Shirlene's? Well, why didn't you have me drop you off there?"

"I-It doesn't m-matter." She blindly reached for the door handle.

Shit. He had never seen Hope cry in his life.

"Now, Hope, honey, it's nothing to get all upset about. I might be tired, but it's not going to take any time at all to drive you out there."

"N-no." She shook her head. It was strange but only her head moved; the hat and braids stayed stationary. "I don't want you to take me anywhere."

Then before Slate's mind could get around the weird thing he'd just witnessed, she jerked up the handle and jumped down. The pack of stray dogs that always hung around trooped around the corner of the house. Spying Hope, the lead hound ran toward her, but halfway there he skidded to a halt, turned tail, and ran back the way he'd come, the other dogs following on his heels.

Slate's eyes narrowed. Hope had always had a way with dogs, unlike Faith, who could almost kill them with kindness. His gaze returned to the woman who walked up the path to the front door. Gone was the strut with too much wiggle, and in its place was a feminine stride with just enough. Enough to send heat to Slate's crotch and adrenaline coursing through his veins.

He was out of the Yukon before she even reached the steps.

"Faith!"

The last of his doubt evaporated when she swung around, the hat and braids now sitting at a crooked angle on her head.

Slate wanted to race up and jerk the damned disguise off. Instead he slowed his pace and tried to steady the wild thumping of his heart.

"Well, well." He slipped his trembling hands in his back pockets. "*The Prince and the Pauper* comes to Bramble. Of course, you'll have to get a larger audience if you want to make it to Broadway." He didn't stop until the toes of his boots were inches from her scuffed brown ones. "Or did you have another purpose in mind?" He grabbed one fake braid and tugged the hat around. "Like maybe making a fool out of a dumb cowboy?"

Faith stared up at him. Even with her back to the

porch, the light was enough to see the tears brimming in her eyes. It took sheer determination to hang on to his anger. Especially when all he wanted to do was grab her up in his arms and absorb the heat of her skin. The subtle scent of peaches. The softness of each curve. But before he could make a complete fool of himself, he noticed the large bump on her nose and the faint yellow bruises beneath each eye.

He grabbed her arms. "Who hit you?" She flinched, and he loosened his grip, but it wasn't easy, not when blind rage tightened every muscle.

"What difference does it make to you?" Faith jerked free and ran up the steps.

Slate started to go after her, but tripped over one of Jenna's stupid lawn ornaments, cracking his knee on the edge of the cement porch step.

"Damn it!" Pain shot down his leg as he got to his feet and hobbled up the steps just in time to catch the screen door but not the solid wood one. It slammed in his face, followed by the click of the lock—more than likely the first time it had ever been used.

"Open this door, Faith!" He jiggled the knob. "I mean it. I'm not through talking with you!"

Unfortunately, it looked like she was through talking with him. Which pissed him off even more. What kind of game was she playing, anyway? Obviously, a game where he had no idea what the rules were. A crazy game that involved twisting his emotions into a knot, then refusing to explain herself. Well, he was through with her. Completely and utterly through.

"Fine. Don't talk to me. I don't want to talk with you anyway." He limped down the steps, then turned and pointed at the house. "You're crazy, you know that? Crazy! And thank God I found it out before we moved in together. At least now I won't be stuck with some schizophrenic woman who can't make up her mind on who she is or whether she wants to go or stay. In fact, let me help you out with that one." He waved a hand. "Go! Get out of here and go on back to Chicago! Along with all the other crazies!"

The lock clicked, and the door was jerked back open.

He hated the sense of relief he felt.

"Crazies?" she yelled through the screen. "Well, I have news for you, Slate Calhoun! Bramble is the craziest town I've ever been in! And you belong right in the middle of it—because you're the king of crazy!" She jerked open the screen door and stepped out on the porch, the hat and braids now pushed back on her head to reveal a set of highlighted bangs. "King Calhoun with his crumpled straw hats and his cocky smiles strutting around town like you're some kind of god while every man, woman, and child bows down to kiss your feet." She moved to the edge of the porch and shoved a finger in her chest. "Well, not me. I'm through kissing your feet or anything else for that matter. Because you're not a god, Slate Calhoun. You're just a mortal man who hides behind an emotionless smile so nobody can see how terrified you are of making a commitment."

"A commitment? I wasn't the one who made the commitment to stay and then ran off with my tail between my legs."

She marched down the stairs. "Are you calling me a coward?"

"If"—he glanced down at her Ropers—"the boot fits."

"Really?" She glared at him. "And what would you call your behavior? Brave? You didn't even have enough guts to come back and talk to me after you'd spent the night up at Sutter Springs with my sister."

He leaned down so their noses touched. "Since we ran out of gas and didn't get back until after three, I figured you'd be asleep."

"Well, you figured wrong." She pushed past him.

"And just where do you think you're going?" He followed her out to Burl's old pickup.

"To Bootlegger's to drink enough nasty shots to forget I ever met you."

Slate snorted, mostly because it was hard to talk when just the thought of Faith doing nasty shots with anyone but him made him want to beat something. Preferably the guy she would be doing nasty shots with—or the guy who'd given her the black eyes.

If Slate knew what was good for him, he would hotfoot it back to Bubba's and spend the rest of the night with his nose in a Mexican vacation brochure. Or better yet, he should hop in his truck and drive to Mexico right then. To hell with his job and the crazy people of Bramble. And to hell with the little bit of sass that glared back at him as she started the engine of the old Ford.

And that's exactly what he would've done if his body had listened to his logical mind.

Instead he grabbed on to the door handle. "You're not going anywhere until you explain why you came back and what you're doing in that getup."

"You figure it out." She backed out, barely missing the toes of his boots with the front tire.

If he had gotten more than ten hours of total sleep that

week—and if she hadn't tried to make a fool of him with her stupid little charade—and if his every nerve ending didn't tingle with the need to touch her—he might've let her go. But her hateful words coupled with the bird she flipped him on the way out of the drive were the final straws that broke the mild-mannered cowboy's back.

Slate Calhoun was really pissed now.

It took him longer than he thought to catch up with her. The woman drove like an Indy racecar driver, barely braking for corners and paying little or no attention to traffic signals. She blew through the stoplight at Elm and Main without a backward glance, which caused Slate to cuss a blue streak.

By the time he reached Boot's, Faith had already parked in his parking space by the front door. He jumped the curb and came to a stop behind the pickup, unconcerned that the ass end of his Yukon blocked the driveway.

He hopped out just as she did. "Just what in the hell do you think you're doing?"

"Parking." She slammed the door of the old truck with enough force to cause the rusty frame to sway.

"I don't give a shit about parking. I'm talking about the way you were driving. You could've killed someone."

"Really?" She smiled sweetly and tugged her hat down over her forehead before straightening those stupid-looking braids. "I guess I had a good teacher." She turned just as Kenny and Twyla stepped out the door.

"Hey, Slate." Kenny's grin got even bigger when he noticed Faith. "How you doin', Hope? You ready for the big day?" They both glared back at him, but he paid little attention. "We wanted to throw Slate here a bachelor's party tomorrow night, but he wouldn't have none of it."

He winked at Faith. "Said he wanted to save up his energy for the weddin' night."

Twyla giggled. "You better wear your ridin' boots next week, honey."

Faith turned to him with a look of disbelief. "You still haven't told them."

She was right. He should've explained things as soon as she'd left town—probably sooner—instead of burying his head in a playbook. But he'd jump headfirst off the water tower before he agreed with her. "What difference does it make? You're not the bride."

Her eyes narrowed. "You're damned right I'm not!" She pushed Kenny out of the way, jerked open the door, and stomped inside.

"The weddin's off?" Twyla looked crestfallen.

"Of course it's not off," Kenny said, although his grin didn't look quite as bright. "They just had a fight, is all. They'll be right as rain as soon as Slate apologizes for givin' Hope those two black eyes."

Slate growled and shoved past them.

"Now, Slate." Kenny followed behind him. "I think you need to cool off. Once is a mistake, twice is... well, I don't know what it is, but I can't let you hit her again."

Slate ignored him and headed for the bar, where Faith was already seated on a stool between Tyler and Rye. But one look at his face moved them quickly enough.

"Give me a nasty shot," she yelled at Manny, presenting her back to him.

Slate grabbed her shoulder and spun her around. "Don't give her a damned thing. She won't be staying long enough to drink it."

"The hell I won't—" But her words ended on a squeak when he jerked her up in his arms.

"Put me down!"

"No." He started for the door, then changed his mind. If she figured out some way to get away from him, he'd have a lot harder time catching her outside than he would in a small closed-in room. He turned toward the bathrooms.

Unfortunately, the town had finally become aware of their arrival and started to circle like buzzards to a fresh kill. But this time, he wasn't concerned with the town or his image. All he cared about was getting answers. Answers that would somehow fill the empty void that football and Mexico and all his friends had been unable to fill once Faith had left.

"Hey, Slate, you're supposed to carry Hope over the threshold, not the dance floor," Rachel Dean teased.

"Yeah, Coach. And that's after the weddin'," Rye yelled.

His jaw tightened as he maneuvered her through the crowd.

"Put me down," Faith hissed through her teeth.

"You want down?" He kicked open the door of the men's bathroom and dropped her like a hot potato. Ignoring the pounding of her fists on his back, he slammed the door closed and slid the lock home.

"Let me out of here!" She screamed loud enough to win a pig-calling trophy of her own.

Slate turned and then grabbed both of her wrists before she could land any more punches. "Not until I get the truth."

"Funny." She glared up at him. "But that's what I came back for."

His brows lowered. "And you thought you'd get it by dressing up in an ugly wig?"

"It worked, didn't it?" Those big blue eyes filled with tears before she blinked them away. "You hate me and never want to see me again."

"What did you expect me to say after you ran off without a word?" His voice reverberated in the small room. "Did you expect me to proclaim my undying love for a woman who didn't even have enough guts to stick around? A woman who tricked me into believing she was one woman who cared enough to stay?"

"And why would I want to stay, Slate Calhoun, when right after you asked me to move in with you, you raced off to Sutter Springs with my sister and never came back?"

"I came back, but you weren't there!"

"Yeah, you came back!" She leaned up until the brim of her hat touched his forehead. "The next day."

He stared into the angry blue of her eyes. Eyes he had missed more than he ever thought possible. Like the deep blue of Mexican waters, they beckoned him, offering peace and tranquility to a ravaged soul. Except he didn't feel so peaceful at the moment. Just angry and hurt. Mostly hurt. Hurt at the thought of her leaving and taking those tranquil blue eyes away from him forever.

"And you couldn't trust me for one night, Faith?" His thumbs brushed over the insides of her wrists before he released her. "That's all I wanted. One night of trust."

She blinked, and her lips parted as if to say something, but nothing came out.

The air left his lungs, and he couldn't seem to get it back. He felt like he had after running the track with

Austin, completely drained and fighting for breath. He looked at her one last time before he turned to the door and struggled to push back the latch.

"You were right. You don't belong here." His chest felt like it was caving in from lack of oxygen. "And it's a good thing we figured it out before it was too late."

Chapter Twenty-three

STUNNED, FAITH WATCHED AS SLATE DISAPPEARED INTO the crowd that had gathered outside the opened bathroom door. Shirlene's plan had backfired. Instead of Slate telling her he loved her, he was leaving. And there didn't seem to be anything to do about it. Not when he was right. Faith Aldridge belonged in Bramble about as much as Bubba and his truck belonged in Chicago.

Which meant that Slate would keep walking—right out of her life. And she would never again see those hazel eyes sparkle with teasing humor or his lips turn up in that cocky smile. Never again snuggle against his hard chest or spend a passion-filled night in his arms—

"No!" The word gushed up from deep inside her and ricocheted off the ceiling of the tiny room.

Faith Aldridge might not belong in Bramble, but Faith Scroggs did. After three weeks of living in Texas, the sweet conformist was pushed out by a determined rebel who wasn't about to let the only man she would ever love disappear from her life for a second time.

At least, not without a fight.

Striding to the door, she pushed through the people still crowded in the hallway.

"Step back, everybody," Kenny said. "Hope's on the warpath."

The men and women hurried to get out of her way. Still, by the time Faith got through the sea of townspeople, Slate was already halfway across the dance floor.

"Slate!"

He didn't even break stride, and she was forced to sprint to catch up with him. She grabbed the back of his western shirt, but he only pulled her along behind, the slick soles of Hope's borrowed cowboy boots sliding across the wooden dance floor.

"Slate, wait."

"Let go, Faith."

"No!" Her grip tightened, and her heels dug in. There was a loud rip as his shirt tore. And finally he stopped and turned to her, his eyes emotionless and terrifying.

"What do you want, Faith?"

She tried to smile, but her lips quivered. "You asked me that before, and the answer hasn't changed."

"I believe, at the time, we were talking about sex."

Someone in the crowd snickered, and Faith blushed, but she refused to back down. "You're right, we were. And I want that, too."

One golden brow lifted. "Too?"

It was so much easier to be tough when she wasn't looking into a pair of eyes the color of her world. Lowering her gaze, she stared at the pearl snaps of his shirt and tried to organize her thoughts into coherent words. But with her heart jarring up against her ribs and her palm sweating through the cotton of his sleeve, she couldn't be eloquent.

All she could be was truthful.

"I know you're upset because you think I didn't trust you. But it wasn't about trusting you as much as it was about trusting myself—or, at least, trusting my heart. All my life I've tried to make other people happy. I guess the need to please the people I love has always been stronger than the need to please myself." She took a deep, quivery breath. "And when I discovered Hope was pregnant"— there was an audible gasp, but too much was at stake for Faith to notice—"I figured leaving was the best thing to do—after all, an entire town couldn't be wrong."

"Hope's what—" Slate started, but Faith refused to get sidetracked.

"It doesn't matter. Because I don't care if my twin sister, who I so desperately want to love me, suffers a broken heart—or if the entire town thinks you two should be together—or if you and Hope really are more compatible. I don't care about anyone or anything. Because after thirty years, I am finally going to listen to my heart and go after what I want."

"Which is?" Slate asked, drawing Faith's gaze up to eyes that no longer looked so vacant and defeated.

She released her breath. "I want red shoes—lots and lots of red shoes."

"Shoes?" A woman right behind her spoke. "Did she say shoes?"

"And I want pink lipstick—a drawer filled with it. And tight jeans and…I want pets—a lot of pets. Like a Labradoodle who is sturdy enough to withstand my coddling."

"What the hell's a Labradoodle?" someone asked.

A sparkle entered Slate's beautiful eyes, prompting her

to continue. "And I want to be a teacher and live in a small town."

"Now there's something we can finally agree with," another person said.

"And I want a truck with a long bench seat for snuggling. And a front-row seat at Bramble High football games."

"The girl has good taste," a man piped up.

"But most of all I want to spend my days with a gifted coach—and my nights with a loving cowboy." Tears moved to the back of her throat, making it difficult to talk. "Even if that cowboy doesn't love me as much as I love him. I just want to be near him—to watch him coach his kids and build his home. And that's why I came back. Not for my sister. Or my parents. Or even for you." She rested a hand on her chest. "I came back for me—for my heart's desire."

There was a chorus of "ahs" and "ain't that sweet." But Faith wasn't interested in what the town thought; she was only interested in what the man before her thought. Thankfully, he didn't waste any time letting her know.

One second Slate was staring down at her, and the next he gulped a big breath of air and tugged her up in his arms.

"Well, that's just fine with me, darlin'." He pulled back and looked down at her, his eyes sparkling. "Because you're my heart's desire and have been ever since you kissed me and knocked off my hat." Then he gave her the world. "I love you, Faith."

"I love you, too, Slate." She tipped her head up for a kiss. But before his lips touched hers, a large fist came out of nowhere. And Faith watched in disbelief as Slate's head snapped back, then popped forward.

He wobbled in place for a few seconds before he regained his balance and held a hand to his eye. "What the hell, Burl?"

"What the hell!" Her father took a step closer, his eyes bugging from a face suffused with anger. "You hit my daughter, and you ask me what the hell? Jenna, get my gun from the truck!"

"No!" Faith finally recovered from her shock enough to step in between the two men. "He didn't hit me!"

Burl looked confused for only a second, before his eyes narrowed again. "Jenna, get my gun."

"Now, Burl," her mother said, stepping up. "You can't shoot Slate—at least not until after the play-offs."

"I don't intend to kill him," Burl said through his teeth.

"Oh." Jenna glared at Slate before she turned and pushed her way through the crowd.

"Didn't you hear me?" Faith asked. "Slate didn't hit me." She couldn't believe he would actually shoot Slate, but stranger things had happened in that town.

Burl pulled his attention away from Slate and turned it on Faith. His gaze halted on her nose, and his jaw tightened. "I'll get to you later, Little Miss. After the way you ran off and scared your mama and me, you'll be getting a piece of me soon enough. Now step out of the way."

Since Burl had never shown any kind of anger toward her, Faith almost obeyed. But her fear for Slate's safety overrode her usual compliance. "I'm not going to let you hit Slate again. Especially when he didn't deserve it in the first place."

"It's all right, darlin'." Slate moved her out of the way. "This is between me and your daddy."

"You're damned right it is," Burl growled. "My daughter

left without saying a word and then comes back with a broken nose. Why, I should beat you within an inch of your life and then shoot you."

Slate didn't say anything, nor did he look like he was going to back down.

"Stop this," Faith said. "Slate didn't hit me."

"Then who did?" both Slate and Burl asked at the same time.

Not wanting to throw her sister under the bus, she hedged. "It doesn't matter who did it, it wasn't Slate." Her eyes widened as Burl reached for the very large gun Jenna had returned with.

"Mama!" The word just sort of popped out of Faith's mouth. Jenna lit up like the floodlights on Bubba's truck. Unfortunately, it didn't make her side with Faith.

"Now, Faith, honey, don't worry your head over it. Burl will only wing him, and he deserves a lot worse for hittin' you."

"But he didn't hit me!"

"Now, nobody believes that." Her mother patted her arm. "Not with the way you love Slate. Lovesick women, regardless of how stupid it is, have a tendency to protect their men."

Faith opened her mouth, but before anything came out, Hope shoved her way through the crowd, followed by Shirlene.

"Does it look like your stupid plan worked, Shirl?" Hope hopped up on the dance floor next to Burl.

"Now don't go making judgments, Hog, until we have the facts." Shirlene looked at Burl. "Are we having a shotgun weddin'?"

"Slate hit Faith," Jenna explained.

"No, he didn't," Shirlene said, although it was hard to hear her over Hope's loud laughter.

When Hope finally stopped, she sent Burl a saucy grin. "Slate didn't hit her, Daddy. I did."

"You did what?" Burl yelled.

"Don't freak out. It was an accident—yow!" She rubbed her arm where Jenna had reached out and pinched it.

Jenna poked a finger in her face. "How many times do I have to tell you, young lady? We don't hit family."

"No," Hope fumed. "We just point guns at close friends."

Burl lowered the gun. "Sorry about that, Slate."

"No harm done, Burl. I should be able to see in another month or so." Slate tentatively touched his eye before he glanced over at Hope. "I should've known you were behind this charade, Hog."

"Well, you're wrong. The entire switching-places idea was Shirlene's."

Shirlene looked expectantly at Slate. "Please tell me it worked, Slate. Or I'll never hear the end of it."

Slate's gaze traveled to Faith. "If your plan was to get me to tell Faith that I love her"—he smiled a heart-melting smile—"then it worked."

A mutter of confusion broke out in the crowd.

"Love Faith? I thought he loved Hope."

" 'Course he loves Hope. He just told her."

"But that's not Hope, that's Faith."

"So he loves Faith, too?"

"Well, maybe he's hopin' for a little twin action before he gets married."

Faith couldn't keep the smile off her face as she looked up at Slate. "So are you going to tell them?"

He groaned, but turned to the crowd. "There's something I need to make clear to y'all. Something I should've made clear a long time ago." He cleared his throat. "I'm not marrying Hope. Hope and I are just friends." He glanced over at Hope, and his eyes narrowed. "Friends who need to have a good long talk."

Hope shook her head. "Sorry, cowboy, but I'm all talked out."

Slate frowned, but stayed on course. "And I realize I shouldn't have let y'all go on believing that we were more than that. I guess I didn't want to disappoint the folks of Bramble, seeing as how I pretty much consider y'all my family."

The look of contentment and pride on each face was easy to read as Harley stepped up.

"Why, you could never disappoint us, Slate. And don't you worry about the weddin' preparations. The pig centerpieces can go back into storage, the inside of the town hall looks great painted purple, and the silk flowers Darla can use on next year's homecomin' float. Of course, I don't know what we'll do with the weddin' dress."

A cocky smile slipped over Slate's face as he reached out and tucked Faith under his arm. "Actually, Harley, I've been thinking about that."

Chapter Twenty-four

"OH, SWEET LORD." Jenna stepped into the room, her eyes filling with tears. "You look so beautiful, honey."

"Thank you, Mama," Faith said. "It's the dress."

Jenna wiped at her eyes with the tissue she'd held in her hand ever since entering the church. "No, it ain't. It's the woman wearing it."

Faith turned back to the mirror and wondered if her mother wasn't right. She did look prettier than she ever had. The bruises were gone, the bump on her nose barely noticeable, her blue eyes sparkled, and her cheeks were flushed with excitement and a little bit of nerves.

Still, the dress didn't hurt. Instead of the nightmarish purple and gold creation Darla had made, Faith wore the simple dress her mother had been married in—a floor-length, antique-white gown with three tiers of aged lace and a wide satin ribbon that tied just beneath the bodice. On her feet, she wore off-white cowboy boots with inlaid red hearts running up the sides—a wedding gift from Slate, along with two tickets to an all-inclusive Mexican resort.

Of course, they couldn't go until after the Dawgs took state. And with the way her life had been going, Faith had little doubt that they would.

The door flew open, and Hope clomped in, cussing as she tripped over the purple satin hem of her dress. "This isn't funny, you know." She flopped down in the chair across from the mirror and hooked a leg over the arm, the stiff petticoats forcing the hideous purple satin almost to her chin. "This is the most god-awful dress I've ever seen."

"Hush now, Hope. We don't want to hurt Darla's feelings." Jenna closed the door.

"Which is the only reason I agreed to wear it." She tugged up the strapless bodice. "But I don't know why Shirlene couldn't have worn it."

"Because Shirlene is too busty, and Jenna Jay and Tessa are too tall."

"Are you saying I'm short and flat-chested, Mama?" Hope attempted to tug out a purple silk rose from her bouquet, but Darla's super-industrial-strength hot glue was tug-proof.

"Of course not." Jenna retied the ribbon on the back of Faith's dress. "But you're the maid of honor, so your dress needs to be different."

"Different?" She snorted as she leaned back on the couch and closed her eyes. "Oh, it's different all right."

With a look of concern, Jenna crossed the room and placed a hand on Hope's forehead. "Is your stomach still upset, honey?"

Hope sat up and pushed her hand away. "Would you stop fussing over me, Mama! I told you, it was only Josie's red chili that upset my stomach."

But Jenna didn't look convinced. "I know what you told me. But if there is ever anything you want to talk about, you know I'm here for you."

"Whatever." Hope rolled her eyes as Jenna headed for the door.

"I better take my place before Cindy Lynn has a conniption." She gave Faith one more watery look. "I'm so proud of you, honey."

"Thank you, Mama."

Once she was gone, Hope grumbled under her breath. "Crazy woman."

"Did you ever think that maybe she's just looking for an excuse to keep you here?" Faith said as she reached for her tube of Passion Fruit lip gloss.

"Fat chance," Hope stated. "Nobody in their right mind would want to live in this godforsaken place. I came back for a visit—only a visit."

It was a lie, and both of them knew it. Hope had come back for Slate. But Faith wasn't willing to point that out to her sister, not when she and Hope had formed a kind of truce. Although there would come a day when they would need to discuss it.

Just not today.

The door opened, and Shirlene stuck her head in. "Hey, Tweedledee and Tweedledum, it's time." Her head popped back out, and the door clicked shut.

The nervousness that had only heated Faith's cheeks before came to a quivering boil in her stomach. And her hand trembled as she reached for her own bridal bouquet of ugly purple silk flowers.

"I think they call it the weddin' jitters," Hope stated as she dropped her scuffed brown cowboy boots to the carpet. " 'Course, if you're too chicken, I'll be more than happy to fill in."

The comment was enough to stiffen Faith's spine. "Not a chance."

Hope shrugged. "Well, in that case, little sister"—she pointed at the door—"let's go get you hitched."

In the foyer, Burl and the rest of her attendants were waiting in line. Shirlene, Tessa, and grumpy Jenna Jay's shimmering gold satin dresses were actually pretty, especially when compared to Hope's. A little blond flower girl, a distant cousin of Burl's, stood behind Shirlene holding a long gold ribbon attached to the purple collar and tiny pillow around the ring bearer's neck.

Buster had never looked better. Of course, it had taken a few days for his skin to stop itching from the salon conditioner Faith had used on him during his bath. Luckily, the dog had a forgiving nature. His tail thumped against the carpet when he spied her.

Or maybe he was looking at Hope.

But at least Burl was looking at Faith. Dressed in a black tuxedo and matching felt cowboy hat, he looked handsome ... and unhappy.

"You look beautiful, baby." Burl held out his arm, and when she slipped her hand beneath his elbow, he covered it with his. "But I don't know if I'm ready to give you up seein' as how I just got you back."

Before she could reply, Hope jumped into the conversation.

"You know what they say, Daddy. . . ." She squeezed in front of them, forcing the flower girl and Buster to jump out of the way of her full skirt. "You're not losing a daughter, you're gaining someone to go huntin' with."

"Big deal," he grumbled just as Cindy Lynn shushed them.

The controlling woman held a finger to her lips as she and Twyla pulled open the double doors, and Elvis's "Can't Help Falling in Love" started playing through the speakers. Then one by one, Cindy Lynn directed the procession down the aisle, fluffing skirts and whispering directions to everyone but Hope, who warned her with one look.

Then finally it was Burl and Faith's turn.

"I love you, Faith," her father whispered right before they reached the threshold of the chapel.

"I love you, too, Daddy."

She tried to blink away the tears, but it was hard to do when the entire town looked back at her with big smiles that conveyed love and a whole lot of pride. Some she knew by name—Rachel Dean, Tyler Jones, Rye Pickett, Harley Sutter, Lyle and Darla. And some she only recognized as the postmaster, the librarian, and the cashier at the grocery store. It would take time to learn all their names. But she would. These were her folks. And Bramble was her home.

A smile lit Faith's face as her gaze drifted over the congregation, then along the line of groomsmen in their black tuxes and matching cowboy hats. Dallas, Kenny, Travis, and finally Austin, who looked right at home in the western-cut tux and hat. At last, her gaze settled on the man who waited at the end of the rose petal–strewn aisle. The tall, blond hometown hero who made her heart race and her knees tremble. The cocky cowboy who, from the moment he kidnapped her from Bootlegger's, held her heart hostage. Halfway down the aisle their eyes met and, as she slipped inside the deep pools of golden brown and cool green, she realized she'd made a mistake.

Bramble was her town.

Slate was her home.

It seemed to take an eternity to reach him. Then once his hand closed over hers, time slipped by too quickly. Before she knew it, the ceremony was over, and Slate's lips touched hers in a warm invitation. An invitation she couldn't ignore. Standing up on tiptoes, she flung her arms around his neck to deepen the kiss, and his cowboy hat hit the floor amid a chorus of hoots and hollers.

After a few sizzling seconds, Slate pulled back, and a brilliant smile lit his face.

"Hang on to that thought, darlin'." Jerking up his hat, he whisked her down the aisle, through the foyer, and out the door into the bright autumn day, where Bubba's truck sat next to the curb with beer cans attached to the huge bumper and *Just Hitched* written in white shoe polish on the back window between the peeing boy and the Cowboys football helmets.

Almost, but not quite, obscuring the gun rack.

The town followed behind them, but not fast enough. Slate had her up in the cab and the engine started before Harley hit the first step. The only one to reach them before Slate drove off was Buster. With purple ribbon dragging and empty ring pillow flopping, he bounded out the church doors and leaped from the top step into the bed of the truck.

"We can't really leave them, Slate." Faith stared out the back window as the crowd surged into the street. "Not when they've done so much work for the reception."

"Work? They loved every second of it." He leaned over the steering wheel and tried to struggle out of his jacket.

She reached over and held the sleeve as he pulled his arm out. "I realize that, but we still have to attend. Josephine spent all week cooking, and Jenna says the town hall has been completely repainted just for the occasion. Did you realize the centerpieces are handcrafted antiques?"

Slate laughed as he tossed his jacket to the other side of the seat. "I think Jenna stretched the truth a little." He tugged on his bow tie until it came undone. "But I'm not planning on skipping out on the reception. I'm just planning a little detour."

"A detour?" Her gaze followed his deft fingers as he opened three studs, and the crisp pleated shirt gapped to reveal the hollow of his throat and the hard planes of his chest.

His gaze slid over to her. "Is there a reason you're sitting all the way over there, darlin'?"

Considering she was only inches away, the question made her smile. "This detour wouldn't have anything to do with making love to me up at Sutter Springs, would it?"

The grin he sent her was pure mischief and all Slate. He slipped an arm around her and tugged her close, bestowing a kiss on the crown of her head. "Only if you insist, darlin'. Only if you insist."

Behind them, the townsfolk stood out on the highway.

Harley hitched up his pants. "I always knew those two would get together."

"Yeah, they're a perfect match, ain't they?" Twyla said.

"'Course it makes sense," Rachel Dean joined in. "Seein' how they was both Texas-born."

"Faith was born in Texas?" Kenny Gene asked.

"Just miles away."

"Well, that explains it then."

"It sure does."

The town turned to head for the reception as, with flags and Labradoodle ears flapping, Bubba's truck disappeared into the brilliant West Texas sunset.

Make Mine a Bad Boy

Acknowledgments

Like my character, Hope Scroggs, I am blessed with people who believe in me. And I can't thank them enough for all their love and support:

My loving husband, Jamie; my beautiful daughters, Aubrey and Tiffany, and their wonderful men, John Sedberry and Donny Sevieri; and my precious granddaughters, Gabby and Sienna. You are my heart, and I am so proud of each and every one of you.

My mother-in-law, Kay Smith, for all her encouragement over the years.

My L-Sisters—Lori Tillery, for dropping everything when I needed help; Lu Loomis, for always being the voice of reason; and Linda Chambers, for all the giggly dinners.

And speaking of giggles, my favorite night of the month is book club night, when I get to flop down on a couch and drink wine and munch on snackies while discussing books with the divine Dog-eared Divas.

Then there are the lovely ladies of LERA, the Land of Enchantment Romance Authors, the best Romance

Writers of America chapter in the world. It is an honor to be part of a group of such talented writers. Go, Team Romance!

And thanks to all my Defined gym-rats. If I need an expert, I can always find one there. Thanks, Jeff Fauver, for all your custom bike expertise. I hope your custom bike kicks butt in Sturgis.

Last, but not least, a special thanks to my agent, Laura Bradford, for all her business savvy and the great title. And to Alex Logan, my editor, for all her hard work. I'm so lucky to have such a great team!

Chapter One

IT WAS A DREAM. It had to be. Where else but in a dream could you be an observer at your own wedding? A silent spectator who watched as you stood in the front of a church filled to the rafters with all your family and friends and whispered your vows to a handsome cowboy you've loved for most of your life. A cowboy who kissed you as if his life depended on it, before he hurried you down the aisle and off to the reception, where he fed you champagne from his glass and cake from his fingers, before taking you in his strong arms and waltzing you toward happily ever after.

It was a dream.

Her dream.

"Hog, you gonna eat that piece of cake?"

And just like that the dream shattered into a nightmare.

Hope Marie Scroggs pulled her gaze from the dance floor and looked over at Kenny Gene, who was staring down at the half-eaten slice of wedding cake on her plate.

"'Cause if you ain't," he said, "I sure hate to see it go to waste." Without waiting for an answer, he speared the cake and crammed a forkful into his mouth, continuing to talk between chews. "That Josephine sure outdid herself this time. Who would've thought that raspberry jam would go so good with yeller cake?"

The fork came back toward her plate. But before he could stab another piece, his girlfriend, Twyla, slapped his hand, and the plastic fork sailed through the air, bounced off one of the ceramic pig centerpieces, and disappeared beneath the table.

"Kenny Gene, don't you be eatin' Hope's food! She needs all them noot-tur-ents!"

Hope didn't have a clue what Twyla was talking about, and she didn't care. All she wanted to do was recapture the dream. But it was too late. Too late to ignore the fact that she wasn't the one who whirled around on the dance floor in the arms of Slate Calhoun—the handsomest cowboy in West Texas.

But she should've been.

It should've been Hope dressed in her mama's three-tiered lace wedding dress. Hope who sipped from his clear plastic Solo cup. Hope who licked Josephine's Raspberry Jamboree Cake from those strong quarterback fingertips. It should have been her arms, looped over that lean cowboy frame, and her face tucked under that sexy black Stetson, awaiting a kiss from those sweet smiling lips.

Her.

Her.

Her.

Certainly not some damned Yankee who had come to Bramble, Texas, looking for her long-lost twin sister, only to steal that same sister's identity like a peach pie set out to cool. It wasn't fair, and it wasn't right. Not when Hope was the one who had done all the prep work. The one who suffered through all the cheerleading practices and home-coming parades and hog-calling contests, all to make her family and the townsfolk proud.

And then some citified wimp with ugly hair showed up, and their loyalties switched like Buford Floyd's gender, and she was expected to grin and bear it? To pretend that everything was just fine and dandy? To act like she didn't give a hoot that her life had just been spit out like a stream of tobacco juice to a sidewalk?

Her anger burned from the injustice of it all, and all she wanted to do was drop to the ground and throw a fit like she had as a child. If she'd thought it would work, she would have. But it was too late for that. The vows had been spoken, the marriage license signed.

Besides, she was Hope Marie Scroggs, the most popular girl in West Texas, and she wasn't about to let anyone know just how devastated she was that the dreams of her wedding day were being lived out by someone else.

Someone who, at that moment, looked over at her and smiled a bright, cheerful smile with white, even teeth that reflected the lights shooting off the huge disco ball hanging from the ceiling. How could some sugary sweet Disney princess have lived in the same womb with her for nine months? It made absolutely no sense whatsoever. Nor could Hope figure out why she smiled back—though it might have been more of a baring of teeth, because Faith's smile fizzled before Slate whirled her away.

"Your fangs are showin', honey." Her best friend, Shirlene, slipped into the folding chair next to her with a soft rustle of gold satin.

Since her daydream was already stomped to smith-ereens, Hope turned to Shirlene and lifted a brow at the mounds of flesh swelling over the top of her bridesmaid's dress.

"Better than havin' my boobs showin'," Hope retorted.

Shirlene didn't even attempt to tug up the strapless confection that put Hope's grotesque purple maid-of-honor's dress to shame. "Admit it. You've always been jealous of the girls." Shirlene flashed a bright smile at Kenny and Twyla as they got up and headed for the dance floor.

"The girls?" Hope's eyes widened. "Those aren't girls, Shirl. Broads, maybe, but not girls."

Shirlene laughed. "Okay, so you've always been jealous of the broads."

Hope shrugged. "If you had my teacups, you'd be jealous too."

"I don't know about that. I get pretty tired of lugging these suckers around."

"I'm sure Lyle doesn't mind helping out with that." She glanced around for Shirlene's husband. "Where is Lyle, anyway?"

"He's got a meetin' in the morning, so he wanted to get to bed early."

"A meetin' on a Sunday?"

For just a brief second, Shirlene's pretty green eyes turned sad before she looked away to fiddle with the purple ribbon tied around the fat ceramic pig, one of the same pigs that had been pulled out for every town celebration since they were made for Hope's fifteenth birthday. "That's the problem with marrying a wealthy man. They're so busy making money, they don't have time to make babies."

"Are you still trying?"

Shirlene shrugged as she retied the ribbon in a perfect bow. "Lyle thinks it's God's will."

"You could adopt, you know."

"I know, but maybe Lyle's right. Maybe this West Texas girl is a little too wild to be a good mama." Releasing her breath, she flopped back in the chair, causing her broads to jiggle like Aunt Mae's Jell-O mold. "Geez, we make a pathetic pair, don't we, Hog? Me a lonely, childless housewife and you a jilted woman."

Hope looked around before hissing under her breath. "I was not jilted, Shirl."

"I don't know what you would call it, Hog. Everyone in town was there when you agreed to marry Slate—regardless of the fact that he hadn't asked."

Hope's jaw tightened. "You know as well as everybody else that Slate proposed to me."

"Years ago. And we both know he was never serious." She hesitated and sent Hope a pointed look. "And if I remember correctly, neither were you."

Unable to look back at those perceptive green eyes, Hope stared out at the dance floor, where Slate continued to whirl her twin sister around. "I always planned on marrying Slate."

Shirlene snorted. "If I had a dime for every one of your plans, Hope, I'd be rich enough to lure the Dallas Cowboys away from Jerry Jones."

"As if you're not already."

"True." The contagious smile flashed as Shirlene reached over and picked up a champagne bottle. She filled a cup for each of them before lifting hers. "Here's to wild West Texas women—we might be down, but we'll never be out."

Finally giving in to a smile, Hope lifted her cup and tapped Shirlene's. "Damn straight." But before she could take a sip, the mayor, Harley Sutter, came chugging up and took the cup from her hand.

"No time for drinkin', Hope." He handed the cup to Shirlene and pulled Hope up from her chair. "Not when the entire town wants a dance with their sweetheart."

Since Hope had never been able to disappoint her hometown, she rolled her eyes at Shirlene and allowed Harley to pull her out to the dance floor. Unfortunately, the two-step had ended, and the band struck up one of those stupid wedding songs that only worked in a room filled with drunks. Still, she pinned on a smile and tried to act like she enjoyed impersonating a flustered chicken.

"Glad to see you so happy, Hope," Harley said as he flapped his arms above a belly that was more keg than six-pack. "You know what they say: 'Home is where the heart is.'"

Unless some Disney princess stole it right out from under your nose, Hope thought as Harley swung her right on over to Sheriff Sam Winslow.

"He's right, Hope," Sam said as he flapped. "Hollywood has had our sweetheart long enough. Though I bet they ain't gonna be real happy to lose such talent. That hemorrhoid commercial you did sure brought tears to my eyes. It had to be real hard to get such a look of complete discomfort." He swung her around. "But you sure nailed it, Hog. Myra raced out and got a tube that very night."

"A tube of what?" Rachel Dean stepped up.

"Hemorrhoid cream," Sam answered, before stepping away.

"Oh, honey." Rachel Dean clapped her man hands, then jerked Hope into a swing that almost snapped her spinal column. "I got hemorrhoids when I was pregnant. And I'm tellin' you right now, there ain't no cream on God's green earth that will help with that hellish burnin'."

Not wanting to talk about hemorrhoids or pregnancy, Hope gladly turned to her next partner, although her pinned-on smile slipped when she stared up into a pair of dreamy hazel eyes. As she struggled to regain her composure, the silly song ended and a waltz began.

"Could I have this dance, Miss Scroggs?" Slate asked.

The word *no* hovered on her lips. But, of course, she couldn't say no. Not unless she wanted him to know exactly how hurt she was.

"Only if you keep those big boots off my toes, Cowboy."

"I'll do my best." Slate flashed the sexy grin that made women melt. Hope didn't melt, but she felt thoroughly singed, or maybe just annoyed that she didn't get to claim the body that went with the smile.

His best turned out to be worse than Hope remembered. After only two steps, her toes were smashed under his boots, and she was forced to do what she'd always done when they danced: Take the lead. Except now he didn't follow as well as he used to.

"Listen, Hope," he said. "I realize this has been hard on you. You come back to Bramble expecting...well, I don't exactly know what you were expecting, but it sure couldn't have been a twin sister you didn't even know you had. Or a wedding that had been planned without you knowing—our wedding, no less." Slate chuckled. "Crazy townsfolk."

She looked away. "Yeah...crazy."

"But you want to know what is even crazier," he continued. "All it took was one look from Faith—or maybe a kiss that knocked my hat off—and I was a goner. A complete goner."

Hope wished that she was a goner. Gone from this man. And this room. And this town. If the pits of hell opened at that very moment and swallowed her up, it would be a relief.

But that didn't happen. So all she could do was guard her toes and try not to act like she gave a darn that her wedding plans had disintegrated just like her dreams of becoming a movie star. She was thankful when the slow ballad ended and Slate was pulled away as Harley bellowed, "Come on all you unhitched folks! It's time for the garter and bouquet toss!"

Hope tried to make a run for it, but the town pushed her forward, swarming around a chair that had been set up in the middle of the dance floor, a chair where her sister sat and waited for Slate to dip that head of sun-kissed hair and, using nothing but his teeth, tug the light blue garter down a leg identical to her own.

"I love a man who knows what to do with his mouth!" Rachel Dean yelled, and whooping and hollering broke out loud enough to shake the sturdy stone building.

With the town's attention focused elsewhere, Hope attempted to inch her way to the door. But she should've known better, especially when she had such an ornery best friend.

"Now don't be gettin' any ideas about leaving, Hog." Shirlene positioned her body between Hope and the exit. "Not when everyone expects you to get up there and catch that ugly bunch of silk flowers Darla hot-glued together."

"Ugly?" Darla clasped her hands to her chest. "Well, I'll have you know that I paid a pretty penny for those at Nothin' Over a Buck."

"Of course, you did, honey." Shirlene sent her a wink. "If anybody can stretch a buck, it's you."

The words seemed to pacify Darla, and she smiled

brightly as Shirlene slipped an arm around Hope and leaned down to speak in her ear.

"Now I know you want to go home and wallow in self-pity. But we both know that this town isn't going to let you get away with that. So just bite the bullet and get in there and do me proud." She gave her a loving pat on the back before she shoved her into the middle of the dance floor, and by the time Hope caught her balance, Shirlene had disappeared in the crowd of single ladies.

It was a pathetic group. There was Twyla, who had already been married three times. Rachel Dean, who came close, with two. The librarian, Ms. Murphy, who was smart enough to avoid marriage altogether, but still had to endure the crazy ritual every time someone had a wedding. Hope's two younger sisters, Jenna Jay and Tessa. And a couple other giggling girls.

Her twin sister stood to the side, holding her "Nothin' Over a Buck" bouquet and grinning like the seven dwarfs were all coming over to the castle for dinner. Of course, who wouldn't grin if she had just wrangled the best-looking man this side of the Mississippi while her sister was forced to fight for the leftovers?

Well, Hope wasn't fighting.

She was all fought out.

She didn't care if Darla's hot-glued flowers were made out of solid gold. She wasn't going to lift a finger to catch them. Not one finger.

"Ready?" Faith looked directly at her, and Hope experienced the same strange phenomenon that she always experienced when her twin sister looked at her. It was like looking into a mirror. Not just externally, but internally. Everything Hope felt was reflected right back at her. Hurt.

Confusion. Anger. Self-pity. It was all there in the familiar blue eyes.

Fortunately, Faith broke the connection by turning around and giving Hope something else to think about, like how to avoid the large bouquet of silk flowers that Faith launched over her shoulder.

Hope figured it wouldn't be hard, not when Twyla had perfected the wide-receiver dive that won her numerous silk-flower trophies and a bunch of good-for-nothing husbands. But as the bouquet sailed through the air, Twyla didn't move one underdeveloped muscle toward it. Nor did Rachel. Or Ms. Murphy. Or Jenna Jay. Or Tessa. Or any of the giggling girls. Instead, everyone just watched as the purple batch of flowers tumbled end over end, straight toward Hope.

She took a step back.

Then another.

But the bouquet just kept coming. If it hadn't been heading for her like a heat-seeking missile, she might've turned and run. But she wasn't about to take her eyes off Darla's creation, not when Hope's own maid-of-honor bouquet was a good solid five pounds of hardened hot glue. So, instead, Hope widened her stance and prepared to deflect the floral grenade with an arm.

It would've worked too, if her watch hadn't snagged the yard and a half of tulle netting surrounding the flowers, something Hope didn't realize until she lowered her arm and felt the dead weight.

Like a preschooler doing the hokey pokey, she shook her arm to try and get it loose. But the bouquet refused to budge. And after only a few seconds of crazy waving, she realized it was no use and let her arm drop. She expected a wave of catcalls and whistles, but what she got was complete silence.

Confused, she glanced up to find the entire roomful of people staring.

Except not at her.

Few things could pull the town's attention away from their sweetheart. Yet something had. Something that had nothing to do with ugly silk flowers and five pounds of hot glue. Something that so intrigued the town they had completely forgotten that Hope Scroggs existed.

A chill of foreboding tiptoed up Hope's spine, and her stomach tightened and gave a little heave as she slowly turned around.

Just that quickly, things went from bad to worse.

A man stood in the open doorway with his shoulder propped against the frame as if he didn't have a care in the world. As if he didn't stick out like a sore thumb from the other men, who were dressed in their Sunday best of western pants, heavily starched shirts, and polished cowboy boots.

This man looked like a desperado who'd come off a long, hard ride. Road dust covered his round-toed black biker boots with their thick soles and silver buckles, partially hidden by the tattered hem of his jeans, jeans so worn that they molded to all the right nooks and crannies, defining hard thighs and lean valleys. A basic black T-shirt was tucked into the jeans, stretching over miles of muscle and hugging the hard knots of his biceps.

But although he had a body that could tempt a Bible-banger on Sunday, it was his face that held Hope's attention, a face made up of tanned skin, hard angles, and a thin layer of black stubble. Come to think of it, everything about the man was black—including his heart. Everything but those steel gray eyes, eyes that scanned the room as if looking for something.

Or someone.

Hope ducked behind Kenny Gene and stealthily peeked over his shoulder, watching as the man pushed away from the doorjamb and weaved around the tables—fortunately, in the opposite direction. The smart thing to do would be to slip out the door before he saw her. And she might've done just that if his fine butt in those buttery jeans hadn't distracted her.

It was a shame, a darned shame, that the man was such a mean, ornery lowlife.

A mean, ornery lowlife who stopped right in front of…

Faith?

It made no sense, but there he stood, those unemotional eyes drilling her sister with an intensity that caused the Disney smile to droop.

"It seems I missed the weddin'," he stated in a deep, silky voice that didn't match his rough exterior. "So I guess the only thing left to do"—those big biker hands slipped around Faith's waist—"is kiss the bride."

Then, before Hope's mouth could finish dropping open, he lowered his head and laid one on her twin sister. Not a gentlemanly peck, but a deep wet lip-lock that left little doubt that a tongue was involved. It was that tongue that forced Hope's true nature to return from the depressed, self-pitying cocoon it had been hiding in since learning that Slate was in love with Faith. That lying, conniving tongue caused Hope's long-withheld emotions to spew forth in a geyser of liberating anger.

"Colt Lomax!" Hope screamed, loud enough to shake the tiles from the ceiling, as she shoved her way through the crowd. "Get your filthy hands off my sister!"

Chapter Two

COLT LOMAX HAD SPENT MOST OF HIS LIFE in Bramble, Texas, angry. Angry over his daddy dying at such a young age. Angry that his mama couldn't pull herself together after his daddy's death and take proper care of him and his little sister. And angry that he had to grow up in a small town filled with small-minded people who only saw what they wanted to see.

But it wasn't anger Colt felt when he pulled away from the kiss. It was confusion. Confusion over the fact that the woman he thought he'd just kissed was the same woman racing toward him with murder in her big blue eyes. And since the look was a familiar one, Colt figured he'd made a mistake. But before he could figure out the extent of his mistake, Slate Calhoun's fist connected with his face and rang his bell.

Now, he had always accepted responsibility for his mistakes, along with a fitting punishment. But one punch was fitting, two was overkill. So when the next punch came at him, Colt was ready and easily deflected it with a raised arm. Unfortunately, this fist belonged to Hope. Her skinny forearm thumped against his so hard that he worried about fractured bones. But that concern was replaced with another when the bouquet of flowers that hung from her wrist clipped her in the chin, dropping her to his feet in a crumple of shiny purple material and a pile of glossy brown hair.

If fear hadn't gotten in the way, Colt might've seen the humor in having Hope Scroggs spilled over his boots like a religious fanatic at the foot of an idol. But there was no humor in the pale, limp arm flung over the gray-speckled tile floor. No humor in the satin-covered chest that didn't appear to rise and fall.

"Gee, Colt," Kenny Gene said. "I knew you didn't like Hope, but did you have to haul off and hit her?"

Stunned and slightly punch-drunk, it took Colt a moment to react—a moment that found Hope in Slate Calhoun's arms.

"Just put her down here, Slate." Jenna, Hope's mama, directed Slate over to a table where a couple of the women scurried to clear off the plastic plates and utensils and a ceramic pig that almost brought a smile to Colt's face.

But it was hard to smile when you had just knocked out a woman. And not just any woman, but the Sweetheart of Bramble, Texas. He was surprised that they hadn't tarred and feathered him by now. Probably because they were too concerned over their little Hope.

Although not as concerned as Colt.

Slate carefully laid Hope down as Jenna soaked a napkin in water and ran it over her face. The rest of the town moved in to huddle around her, and it took a few well-placed elbows for Colt to make his way to the front of the pack.

"She ain't dead, is she?" Kenny tipped his black cowboy hat up on his forehead and leaned closer as the knot in Colt's stomach tightened.

"Of course, she ain't dead," Rachel Dean said, although her man-sized hands were clutched to her chest in a very unconvincing way.

With her purple gown spread out around her and the bouquet resting on her chest, Hope looked like a fairytale princess. Not the one who slept, but the one who had been poisoned. Miles of rich dark hair framed a deathly white face. A face as familiar to Colt as his own, from her high forehead to the stubborn chin—a chin that now had a nasty-looking red knot.

What the hell was the matter with these country bumpkins anyway? Someone should be calling 911 or running to fetch Doc Mathers, not standing around like a bunch of hicks straight off the farm. But before Colt could voice his thoughts, Slate leaned over her, presenting a picture all too familiar.

Now the fairytale was complete. Slate and Hope. Star quarterback and homecoming queen. Colt waited for the prince of Bramble to kiss the princess awake, but instead Slate tapped her cheek in a way that didn't look all that princely.

"Come on now, wake up, Hog."

The nickname sent a stab of anger through Colt. But it was nothing compared to what he felt when those long, dark lashes fluttered open, and a dreamy smile slid across those rosy lips.

"Slate," Hope breathed with what could only be described as awed relief.

Slate grinned down at her. "What? Did Hollywood

turn you into a citified wimp? You used to take a punch a
lot better than that, Hog."

Just that quickly, her smile slipped, and her gaze shot
around the room until it hit Colt square in the gut. Those
baby blues narrowed, and in one fluid motion, she swung
her legs over the edge of the table and hopped down
onto her scuffed brown cowboy boots.

"You hit me!" Hope yelled in a voice that made his
head ache. She swung at him, but he caught her wrist, the
bouquet of heavy-assed flowers cracking into his forearm
with a painful thud.

Her other fist flew at the opposite side of his face, and
he grabbed it too. With no hands left, her little cowboy
boots started in, attacking his shins with a vengeance. It
hurt like hell, but he wasn't about to let go of her hands,
not in a room filled with heavy ceramic pigs. Of course,
he didn't think about her knees until one came way too
close for comfort.

Colt turned to the side to avoid having his voice
changed three octaves and tried to figure out some way to
contain the wildcat. Luckily, Hope's daddy, Burl, stepped
up and placed a beefy arm around her waist, gently pulling her away.

"Settle down there, little girl, your mama's worried
you're gonna hurt yourself."

Hurt herself? Colt was the one with a multitude of
bruises. Not that anyone seemed to care. All eyes were on
Hope, who still ranted and raved like a lunatic.

"You lowdown son of a snake! You smelly piece of
Texas roadkill! You disreputable good-for-nothing motorcycle bum!"

It wasn't anything that he hadn't heard coming out of

Hope's mouth before, so he settled in and waited for her to run out of steam. He knew from experience that it could take awhile. But the rant was cut short when his baby sister pushed her way through the crowd.

"What in the world is going on here?" Shirlene sashayed over to Hope in her high heels and pretty gold dress. Next to Hope, she looked like an Amazon, a golden-haired Amazon with laughing green eyes. It had been only six months since he and Shirlene had met in Odessa to visit with their mama. Still, it looked as if his baby sister had grown even more beautiful since then.

As Shirlene set down the plastic cup of what looked like straight tequila, her gaze drifted down to the bouquet that dangled from Hope's arm. "Okay, so I see you caught the bouquet, but is that any reason to throw a temper tantrum? I mean, it's not like you're going to become Twyla."

"And just what is that supposed to mean, Shirlene Dalton?" Twyla huffed.

Shirlene lifted an eyebrow at the woman in the too-tight dress and piles of makeup. "Do I need to explain it, honey?" She turned back to Hope. "But it's only a bouquet, Hog. It's not like anyone's forcing you to get married."

"She ain't mad about the bouquet, Shirlene," Rachel Dean enlightened her. "She's mad because Colt knocked her out."

"Colt?" Shirlene turned and her gaze snagged him. "Colt!" In two steps, she was in his arms, and he had to say that it was nice to finally receive a warm welcome. "What are you doing here, honey?" she asked. She pulled back, all smiles, until her gaze settled on his lip. Then her face looked like a mama tiger that had just discovered her cub abused. "Who hit you?"

He tested his lip with his tongue and, tasting blood, used the back of his hand to wipe it off. "It's not a big deal. I made a mistake, is all." *More like numerous mistakes. The biggest was coming back to Bramble in the first place,* Colt thought.

"What kind of mistake?" Shirlene's eyes clouded with confusion. Colt knew exactly how she felt. He still wasn't quite sure what he had walked into.

"I think I can explain." Harley Sutter stepped up.

Harley was the mayor/judge/lawyer of Bramble, and as such, he had always taken it upon himself to be the town mouthpiece, a long-winded mouthpiece who could talk for days. Which was why Colt leaned back against the edge of the table and crossed his arms.

"It appears to me that this is a simple case of mistaken identity. Colt here—" Harley paused and gave Colt the disapproving look he'd always given him. "I thought you were in prison, son."

Colt tossed back his signature go-to-hell look. "I got out on good behavior."

Harley's eyes narrowed suspiciously before he rested his hands on a stomach that had seen too many nights of chicken-fried steak from Josephine's Diner and then continued. "Not being as perceptive as the rest of the town, Colt assumed that Faith was Hope." His gaze moved around the room. "Where is our little Faith, anyway?"

"Right here." The woman Colt had kissed stepped forward, and his eyes widened.

During the hoopla of the last few minutes, he'd convinced himself that, between lack of sleep and the hard ride, his mind had played a trick on him. But his mind hadn't tricked him at all. The blushing woman who stared back at him with innocent blue eyes looked identical to Hope—identical except for the short, honey-streaked brown hair that curled around her face.

"So you're Shirlene's brother," Faith said, without any twang whatsoever.

"Faith, this is my ornery brother, Colt Lomax," Shirlene made the introductions. "Colt, this is Faith Aldri—I mean, Faith Calhoun."

His gaze shot over to Hope, and their eyes locked for a brief second before she looked away. But a brief second was all he needed to read the turbulent emotions that swirled around in the endless blue eyes.

"It's nice to meet you, Colt," Faith said.

Since Colt had done a little more than meet her, he rubbed a hand over the back of his neck and stumbled through his mind for a way to apologize for cramming his tongue down her throat. "Nice to meet you, ma'am. And I'm real sorry about the confusion and all."

A tentative smile tipped the corners of her mouth, and she took a few steps closer. She looked so much like Hope that if he hadn't already been leaning against the table, he might've taken a few steps back.

"Apology accepted," she said in a voice so soft that he could barely hear her.

Colt cocked an eyebrow. She might look like Hope, but she sure didn't act like her. Hope had never accepted an apology from him in her life. Not that he'd ever given her one.

Those pretty eyes scrunched up. "Did you realize you're bleeding?" Before he could do more than nod, Faith jerked a couple napkins off a nearby table and dunked them in a cup. "I wish I had my disinfectant wipes, but this will have to do."

The first touch of the soaked napkins on his cut lip almost sent him straight through the ceiling tiles.

"Lord, woman!" He held a hand to his burning lip. "What the hell is on that?"

Her blue eyes widened before she glanced down at the napkin. "Water?"

"I think that would be Rachel Dean's Everclear, Faith," Slate said as he took the napkins from her hand. "But don't you worry, darlin', 150-proof liquor works just like your disinfectant wipes," his humor-filled eyes tracked over to Colt's, "just with a little more sting."

Faith shook her head, and the curls danced. "I'm so sorry...I thought—"

"Is someone going to tell me who hit my brother?" Shirlene cut in.

"I did," Slate stated.

Shirlene's eyes narrowed on him. But before she could let him have it, Rachel Dean jumped in.

"Only because he was kissin' Faith."

"More like devouring," Twyla added. "I got all hot and bothered just watchin'. 'Course after years in prison, a man must be pretty starved for female attention."

Something that sounded an awful lot like a growl came through Slate's teeth, and Colt braced himself for another go around. Although at this point, he would welcome a good fight. But his sister held up her hand before Slate could threw the next punch.

"So let me get this straight. Colt mistook Faith for Hope and laid one on her?" Shirlene asked. Without waiting for a reply, she started laughing like a crazy woman.

Always willing to laugh at a good joke, the town joined in. And, as annoyed as Colt was with the entire prison comment, he had to smile. The only person not laughing was Hope, whose eyes had turned as cold and icy as a North Dakota fishing pond in the dead of winter. And all that frigid hate was directed solely at him before she whirled and stomped off.

As usual, once Hope was gone, the townspeople didn't quite know what to do with themselves. Women looked at each other while men stuffed their hands in their pockets and studied the tiled floor. More than a few uncomfortable minutes passed before Harley took the bull by the horns.

"Well, what are we all standin' around for?" He nodded at Bud Mueller, who had always played a mean fiddle, and Bud hurried off, followed by the other band members. "Are we gonna let a little fight stop us from celebratin' Faith and Slate's weddin'?"

A chorus of *hell no*s rose up, and just that quickly, people dispersed, leaving Colt alone with his sister.

"Lord." Shirlene shook her head as she retrieved her cup and sat down at the table. "I leave for two seconds and miss all the good stuff."

"Believe me, it wasn't all that exciting." He sat down and grabbed a napkin and held it to his mouth.

"I guess after spending the last few years in prison, Bramble must seem awfully dull." Shirlene shot him a quirky little grin before she offered him her cup. When he shook his head, she pulled it back and took a deep drink. "I bet folks would be surprised to know you're such a teetotaler. Of course, folks would be surprised by a lot of things."

He sent her a warning look. "Things I'd just as soon you kept to yourself."

She ran a finger across her lips. "Sealed as tight as a drum."

Colt didn't need the reassurance. Shirlene could keep a secret. Which was a good thing, given their childhood.

Cradling the cup between her hands, she rested her elbows on the table. "So what brings you back to Bramble, big brother?"

"I missed my little sister."

She snorted. "I'd believe you, if it hadn't been eight years since you've been back."

"You got me." Colt winked at her before stretching the truth a little. "I'm on my way to Austin to deliver a bike and needed a bed for the night." Even though she was good at keeping secrets, there were still some things that she didn't need to know.

She sat up, splashing tequila on the gold satin of her dress. "One night? You're only staying one night?"

He hadn't even planned on staying that long. In fact, he hadn't planned on coming at all. One second, he was talking about a bike delivery, and the next thing he knew, he was passing by the WELCOME TO BRAMBLE sign on the same bike that should've been heading for Austin in a covered trailer.

"Hope is right," Shirlene huffed as she set down the cup and flopped back in the chair. "You are a lowdown motorcycle bum, Colt Lomax. The least you could do is stay a couple nights and keep your sister company."

"Lyle working a lot?"

"Too much."

Colt scowled. As much as he liked Shirlene's husband, the twenty-five-year age difference was still hard for him to swallow, especially when his sister didn't look all that happy. Of course, he could help with that. All he needed to do was stick around for a few days. Unfortunately, Colt had his own demons to deal with, and most of them resided right there in Bramble.

"I'll tell you what." He leaned his arms on the table. "How about if you come to Austin with me for a few days?"

"On the back of your chopper?"

He lifted one eyebrow. "I was thinking more of you meeting me there."

"Sort of like you meet me other places—you get there three days late and leave three days early. No, thanks. Besides, I don't want to go to Austin. I want you to stay right here with me in Bramble and do all the fun things we used to do as kids."

Fun things? Colt couldn't think of one fun thing he'd done as a kid. Still, not wanting to bust his sister's bubble, he held his tongue and let her continue.

"It will be just like old times, especially with Hope back in town. Except now, with Faith here, it will be double the fun. You're going to love Faith. She's Hope, but nice."

Colt laughed. "I gathered. So who is she?"

"Hope's twin sister, who Jenna gave away at birth."

The news surprised Colt. Not the twin part—that was obvious—but the giving away part. Jenna Scroggs had always been the perfect mother. The kind who baked cookies and played hide-and-go-seek and read books and bandaged scraped knees. The kind who was the complete opposite of Colt's and Shirlene's inattentive mama.

As if reading his thoughts, Shirlene nodded. "I know. It was hard for me to believe too. But I think people forget that she was only fifteen when she had Hope and Faith. She and Burl weren't married, or even out of high school. And you remember how hard it was for them back then. They were in the same boat as we were."

Not quite. Their boat had sailed, while he and Shirlene had remained behind.

"So how did Hope take the news that she had a twin?" he asked.

"Not well, especially when Slate ended up falling for Faith."

His gaze shifted to the dance floor, where half the town waltzed in a circle around the happy couple. While the sight gave him a certain satisfaction that justice had been served, a part of him almost felt betrayed. In a life where he had learned to count on nothing, Slate marrying Hope had been one of the few things he'd counted on. Which didn't explain his initial anger, or the kiss. But, years ago, Colt had given up trying to explain his behavior where Hope was concerned. Like Bramble, she brought out the worst in him.

Even knowing this, he still couldn't stop himself from scanning the crowd as he talked with Shirlene and all through the windy speech Harley made before the newlyweds headed out the door. He continued looking for her long after the drunks sobered up, and the ceramic pigs were boxed away, and the plastic dishes were rolled inside the ugly purple tablecloths and tossed into the trash.

Funny, but Colt hadn't taken Hope for the type to turn tail and run. But that's exactly what it looked like she'd done. And maybe she had the right idea. Maybe the best thing for him to do would be to hop on his bike and get the hell out of Dodge. He didn't know why he'd stopped here, but nothing good would come of it. Bramble was a part of his past, and he needed to keep it that way. Shirlene would be upset, but he would make it up to her by spending the holidays with her—anywhere but Bramble.

Outside, he found the night had grown chilly. It would be a cold ride to Austin, but he didn't mind. While most people found comfort in a cozy home, out of the elements, Colt preferred the open road. No ties or responsibilities, just miles of blacktop and freedom.

Parked up on the sidewalk, right beneath the town hall's flagpole and right next to the dedication plaque, sat the custom chopper he'd been working on for the last few months. It was a slick machine with a hot custom paint job and chrome exhaust and wheels that gleamed in the light from the overhead streetlight like high-polished mirrors. It wasn't as fancy as some, but Colt had never gone for show as much as go. This baby had a 124-cubic-inch motor and a six-speed transmission, and just hearing it rev made Colt proud as hell.

After slipping on his leather jacket, he started up the bike and circled around the courtyard of the town hall. The loud, unbaffled engine had people stepping out the doors to investigate, his sister one of them. When Shirlene saw him, she didn't look surprised. Obviously, she knew him too well.

"Remember I love yew, big brother!" she yelled, over the throbbing noise. He might've paid more attention to the devious gleam in his sister's eyes if the woman in purple satin hadn't caught his attention.

Hope stood next to the big maple tree, her dress crumpled and her hair limp. In the shade of the tree, he couldn't see her eyes, but he didn't need to. Her arrogant stance said it all. The unyielding strength of such a little bit of sass made him smile. Even after her lifelong beau had chosen somebody else, Hope would not be defeated. He admired that about her. Would always admire it. He touched a hand to his forehead in a salute to both of the women who had made such an impression on his life.

Then he twisted the throttle and shot off the curb, the thick 240 mm back tire bouncing down to the asphalt. Unfortunately, that was as far as he got before Sheriff Winslow's patrol car came barreling around the corner with lights flashing and siren blaring to cut him off.

Chapter Three

"HOPE, HONEY?"

"Shit!" Hope slapped a hand to her chest and turned to her daddy, who sat at the table in the dark dining room. With her heart thumping guiltily, she plastered on a smile. "Oh, hi, Daddy. I didn't realize you were still up."

"Your mama's snorin' gets worse when she drinks, so I had trouble gettin' to sleep. What are you doin' up?"

"Uhhh," she tried not to glance back at the front door she'd been headed to. "I was just checking to see if Jenna Jay, Tessa, and Dallas got home okay."

"Jenna Jay slept over at her friend's house. And Tessa and your brother are passed out cold." Her daddy shook his head. " 'Course, when I was younger I did the same thing—weddin's are a perfect excuse to tie one on."

Especially if the bride was supposed to be you, Hope thought. Unfortunately, every time that Hope had reached for a drink, she had been grabbed by one dancing fool or another.

Her father held up what appeared to be a half-eaten Ding Dong. "You care to join your old daddy?"

Unable to help herself, Hope glanced back at the door. "No, thank you, Daddy. Now that I know everyone's home safe and sound, I guess I'll head on back to bed. I wouldn't want to sleep through church tomorrow."

"I suppose you're right." Her daddy polished off the rest of the Ding Dong and then downed the last of his milk before he pushed back from the table. "Although if I want to get any shut-eye, I'll have to use my earplugs."

Since that would make escape much easier, Hope nodded. "That's a good idea, Daddy." She lifted a hand. "Well, good night." She hurried back down the dark hallway, but her father proved that he was still as quick on his size-fourteen feet as he'd been when he played high school football. Before she could close her bedroom door, his big frame filled the doorway.

"Your mama says you've been makin' lists again."

Damn. She knew she should've taken her trash out. Luckily, all that was written on the numerous crumpled pieces of paper were four words—*Hope's New Life Plan*.

Trying to make light of it, she chuckled. "You know I've always been a list-making fool, Daddy."

"And that's exactly what I told your mama—our little Hope Marie don't do nothin' without a list. But that didn't seem to make her feel any better. She thinks you're gettin' ready to run off again on some wild tangent." He paused and stared down at her for a few excruciating seconds. "Now I realize things didn't work out exactly like you had planned." He cleared his throat. "But me and your mama sure wish you'd stick around for awhile."

Touched, she stood on her tiptoes and gave him a hug. "I love you, Daddy."

"I love you, too, princess." He awkwardly patted her back, then turned and lumbered down the hallway.

Hope waited in the darkness of her room until she figured her daddy was ear-plugged and tucked in tight before she slipped out and headed for the front door.

The night air was cooler than she thought it would be. But she welcomed the stiff breeze that rustled the crisp autumn leaves of the elms and cottonwoods as she headed into town. As she walked, her father's words came back to her. No, her life hadn't turned out the way she had planned, and she couldn't figure out where things had gone wrong.

Her plan had made perfect sense. She would go to Hollywood and become a famous movie star while Slate stayed there and concentrated on his coaching career. Then, once she had fame and fortune, she would return to Bramble and marry the hometown hero, who would be more than happy to let her make the occasional blockbuster as long as she returned during football season.

Okay, so maybe she should've called more often. Or come back on weekends. But she had been terrified that Slate, and everyone else in town, would find out that while she'd shone on the performing arts stage at Bramble High, in L.A. she was just a mediocre actress with a thick Texas twang.

So she had stayed. Unable to accept defeat, Hope suffered through long, grueling auditions with rude, critical casting directors. She'd forked over hundreds for acting lessons and voice coaches and basically had tried to fit a country square into a Hollywood star. All while she hustled tables at any restaurant or bar that would put up with her taking off for auditions or jobs.

Not that she landed many jobs. Her biggest job had been the hemorrhoid commercial. And she'd only gotten it because the casting director was an extremely short guy who had trouble finding women his own size to date. She had to suffer through a boring dinner listening to the guy's many "accomplishments" before the commercial was filmed and she got the first check, a check that didn't stretch quite far enough.

Despite these challenges, she would probably still be in California if she hadn't completely lost her mind one night. Waking up alone in a cheap motel room had forced her into reevaluating her entire life plan and making a few minor adjustments. Like accepting the fact that she couldn't act and returning home to marry the man she was destined to be with—the kind of man who would never leave her or let her down.

When she returned to Bramble and was welcomed home like the prodigal daughter, Hope figured she'd made the right choice. After years of feeling like a piece of chewed-up gum on the sole of a flip-flop, it was an overwhelming relief to be back with people who loved and adored her—adored her so much that they had already planned her wedding. It seemed a little fast, but since that was why she came home, she couldn't very well back out. So she stepped up to the plate. Except, when she got ready to swing, she discovered someone else had hit the home run and won the game, someone who hadn't wasted five years trying to prove she was more than just a small-town girl. Someone who at that very moment was enjoying her honeymoon with Hope's only backup plan.

The thought riled Hope so much she forgot to pay attention to where she was walking and almost fell into the big pothole at the corner of Maple and Main. Sidestepping the hole, she hopped up on the sidewalk and headed down Main Street. Past the post office on the corner with the big red-and-blue mailbox out front—the same mailbox she and Shirlene had dropped their unfinished Popsicles into as kids, for which they had received a stern lecture from Miguel the Postmaster about federal crimes. Past the Halloween-decorated window of Sutter's Pharmacy, where she had bought her first tube of mascara. And past Duds N Such, where she and her sisters had browsed through racks of jeans while her daddy salivated over John Deere mowers.

With her old fuzzy slippers thumping softly against her heels, Hope continued down the street. Past the city park with its patchy grass that always needed more water and the small Catholic church that never quite caught on. Past Josephine's Diner, the pink-painted caboose where Hope had worked for years, serving up chicken-fried steak.

She didn't slow down until she reached the one-story brick building located on the other side of the town hall, a building that was completely dark—except for one tiny square of light.

The wind picked up, loosening a few strands of hair from her ponytail and rattling the chain against the town hall flagpole. A chill tiptoed down her spine, and she shivered. Given that she wore nothing but a skinny-strapped cami and thin cotton pajama bottoms in the middle of October, it wasn't surprising. Except the goose bumps that covered her bare arms didn't come from the outside temperature as much as from the cold knot that settled in the pit of her stomach, warning her of imminent danger.

And as she stood in front of the city jail, she knew exactly what that danger was.

Colt Lomax.

Just the name made her want to scream out a very nasty cuss word. She glared at the light spilling out from the small barred window. Why couldn't Shirlene just let her brother stop for a quick visit? Why did she have to have him arrested? The man was ornerier than a cornered jaguar, and prodding him only made him worse—something Hope knew from experience.

No, the best thing to do for a caged wild animal was to set it free.

Hope glanced around, then quickly headed down the path that led to the double-glassed doors of the jail. She didn't expect them to be locked, and she wasn't disappointed. No one in Bramble locked anything, probably because there wasn't anything in Bramble worth stealing.

Hurrying through the dark reception area, she made a quick stop in Sheriff Winslow's office and then headed down the dark hallway to the only jail cell.

Like any good Christian woman of Bramble, Hope knew the way. More than once, she'd come with her mama to deliver Bibles to the poor lost souls who found themselves behind bars. Not that Bramble had a lot of criminals. Most of the Bibles had gone to Elmer Tate, who slept it off in jail every time he got drunk rather than go home to his wife, who had a mean right hook. Despite his love of Jack Daniel's, Elmer was a nice man who would always drop the Bibles back at First Baptist so the women could redistribute them.

Being the town troublemaker, Colt had gotten his fair share of Bibles too. Though Lord only knew what he'd done with them.

At the end of the hallway, Hope pushed through another unlocked door and into the room that housed the jail. But how anyone could call it that was beyond her. Except for the bars, the cell looked like a country bed and breakfast. Up against one wall was a brass bed with fluffy down pillows, a wedding-ring quilt, and crisp, flowered sheets that matched the curtains on the window. The white porcelain toilet was sparkling clean and had an air freshener on the back and a fuzzy blue cover for the lid. The sink had a Dixie cup dispenser and small mirror hanging above it, a mirror Colt was using as he cleaned the blood from his lip.

The door clicked shut behind her, and he turned. And for a split second, Hope had the urge to run for her life. No wonder the folks of Bramble thought he'd been in prison. The man looked like he belonged behind bars—an unscrupulous outlaw who spent his days robbing trains and his nights stealing the hearts of loose women. Wind-tousled black hair fell almost to his shoulders, and the stubble on his square jaw looked even thicker than it had a few hours earlier. Those steely gray eyes stared back at her, the whites bloodshot from booze or lack of sleep, or possibly both.

Suddenly, she didn't feel cold anymore.

"Deliverin' Bibles, sweetheart?" The dark slashes of his eyebrows lifted. The sarcasm in his deep, smooth voice snapped her out of her outlaw fantasy and back to loser reality.

"As if reading the Bible would do your black soul any good." She pushed away from the door. "I'm here to get you out."

"A jailbreak? Funny, but I thought you were the reason I was here in the first place. Mean Colt Lomax beat up sweet little Hope Scroggs."

"Don't blame me, Lomax. I wasn't the one who got Sam after you. Not that you didn't deserve it, after hitting me." She felt only a second of remorse over the lie. She was well aware of what had hit her, but she just wasn't about to let Colt get off so easily. Not when he had hurt her plenty in her lifetime.

"A jailbreak, huh?" He took a few steps closer to the bars, and it was a challenge for her to keep from taking a step back. "So what's your plan? Dynamite? A bulldozer? A file pulled from those silken locks?"

"I was thinking more of a key." She held up the heavy key ring.

One corner of his mouth flirted with a smile. "A key. What an ingenious plan."

Ignoring his sarcasm, she walked over to the lock and started trying keys. It was a daunting task, considering there had to be enough keys there for every unlocked door in Bramble, so many that she had trouble remembering which ones she'd tried. Especially with Colt standing there watching.

"You're not kidding, are you?"

She glanced up into a pair of curious gray eyes. "I realize you skipped school more than you attended, but does it look like I'm kidding?"

Those eyes narrowed. "So what's in it for you?"

"What else? I get you out of my hair."

So quickly that she couldn't avoid it, he reached through the bars and snagged a lock of her hair that had fallen over her shoulder from the low ponytail.

"I guess a man could get lost in this." He rubbed it between his fingers.

The sight made her stomach do a crazy flip before she

jerked her hair back, leaving a few strands entwined in his rough biker fingers. "Stop screwing around."

"But I like screwing around." Those dark brows lifted. "Remember?"

Her face flushed hot. "Do you always have to be such a smartass?"

"Weren't those our roles in high school?" He pointed a finger at her. "Homecoming queen." He touched his chest. "Smartass."

"Loser, is more like it." She went back to the keys, but damned if she hadn't lost her place again.

Luckily, Colt had always been easily bored. After only a few minutes, he walked over to the bed, where he stretched out on Granny Lou's quilt and propped his hands behind his head. It was hard to take her eyes off all the miles of muscle that rippled the black cotton shirt and soft jeans.

"So are you cold?"

At his words, the keys slipped through her fingers and clanked to the floor as her gaze flashed back to his face.

"What?"

His head turned toward her, and those gray eyes slithered down to her chest. "Cold."

She glanced down to the beaded nipples that poked through the soft white cotton of her cami. She crossed her arms over her chest and glared back at him.

"You are a sick pervert, Colt Lomax."

He shrugged. "I only take what's offered."

Not wanting him to think she offered anything, she tugged the ponytail holder out and slipped it over her wrist before adjusting her hair over her chest.

"The hair should've been a dead giveaway," he stated.

She glanced over at him.

He had rolled to his side, his head propped up on his hand. "The mistake I made with your sister—I should've known you would never cut your hair."

Thankful to be off the subject of her boobs, Hope shrugged as she picked up the key ring and tried another key. "I thought about it once. I even went to a salon in L.A. with the intention of whacking it all off."

"What happened?"

"I chickened out."

There was a long pause before he spoke.

"I'm glad."

Her gaze shot over to him. She might've taken it as a compliment if she hadn't known better. "This coming from a man who used to refer to my hair as a matted possum pelt."

He flashed her a full-fledged smile. Since it wasn't something he did often, the blinding radiance took her by surprise. "And you think a skinned possum would look better?"

With her insides boiling, she went on the offensive. "As if I care what a lowlife motorcycle bum thinks. Why don't you get a job, Lomax, and quit being a blight on society?"

"Because I believe the fewer the responsibilities, the freer the man."

"And you are about the freest man I know," she said as she continued to try the keys. "Of course, you wouldn't be so free if you didn't have Lyle Dalton's money to spend."

"Is that where you think I get my money?"

She glanced up. "Isn't it?"

Seconds ticked by as he stared at her. Finally he relaxed back against the pillows and rested his hands over his chest. "You found me out, honey. Luckily, old Lyle doesn't seem to care."

The truth shouldn't have bothered her. But it did. Just another reason she needed to get him out of town as quickly as possible. Thankfully, the next key worked.

Twisting the lock open, she pulled back the barred door. "Come on. We don't have much time." She pulled the key out of the lock and moved over to the outer door. "Regardless of the wedding, the churchgoers get up bright and early on Sunday. But since you have never attended church, you probably don't know that."

"I go to church."

Hope turned to find him standing close behind her, his hand braced against the door that she'd just cracked open. It was one thing to have a row of bars separating her from all the testosterone-pumped maleness, and another to have it inches from her nose. Startled, she dropped the keys, and they slid out into the hallway.

"I call it the Church of Our Lady of the Highway." Colt released the heavy door, and it clicked closed as he tipped up her chin. "You should've put ice on it. It would've helped with the swelling."

"I did," she breathed, her voice betraying her quivery insides.

"By the looks of it, not long enough." He shook his head and gently brushed his thumb over the bump. "You never did have a lick of patience."

It took a second for Hope to find her voice. "Which is exactly why I want you out of this town as quickly as possible."

Colt leaned down, and his cheek brushed against hers in a slide of prickly heat. "Now why is that, I wonder?" His breath fell soft and warm against her ear, and everything inside her seemed to still in anticipation of what he'd do next.

Except he didn't do anything. He didn't have to. Just his mere presence was enough to make her head fill with thoughts that had no business being there. Naughty thoughts that involved the rugged outlaw in front of her and the soft mattress behind him.

She took a deep, steadying breath. But it was a mistake. While most guys in town doused themselves in whatever country-singer-endorsed cologne was popular at the time, Colt had always smelled like soap and detergent beneath a layer of grease and gasoline, a powerfully strong mixture that never failed to make Hope light-headed.

Although now the grease and gasoline weren't as strong as another scent—a raw masculinity lacking in his youth. It was this scent that drew her like a moth to a porch light on a hot summer night. But, refusing to get her wings singed, she slipped beneath his arm and stepped around him. In an attempt to slow her heart rate, she moved over to the sink and washed her hands.

"Still avoiding my touch, Hog?" he asked from behind her.

"At all costs." She tried to keep her voice even, but it still came out shaky and a little breathless. "And don't call me that. Only my friends call me that."

"And just where in the hell do you think they got it?"

Confused, Hope turned back to him, her hands dripping water on the rag rug in the center of the floor. If it was possible, he looked even more dangerous than he had only moments before.

"You're lying," she stated with a firmness that she didn't quite feel. "Slate made it up."

Colt studied her for only a few seconds before he tipped his head. "Of course, Slate. Who else would come up with such a sweet moniker for his girlfriend?" He rested a shoulder on the frame of the barred door. "So what does he call Faith? Frog ... or maybe just Wife."

The arrow struck with a reverberating thunk.

"I'd shut up if I was you," she growled.

His eyes widened with innocence. "What? Did I hit a sore spot? Is Hope Scroggs a little pissed at her twin sister for stealing her boyfriend?"

Forgetting about drying her hands, she headed for the door. Unfortunately, his big body blocked it.

"Get out of my way," she ordered.

Colt shook his head. "Not until you fess up."

"There is nothing to fess up to."

He crossed his arms over his chest, bringing her attention to the tattoos that covered his arm from shirt sleeve to wrist. "How about being so pissed off your head is about ready to explode? You're practically shaking from all the suppressed anger. So go ahead. Let it out. Scream and rant and rave about how your life has been ruined because Slate Calhoun, the hero of Bramble, found someone he liked better."

"Shut up!"

"Or maybe he didn't find anyone he liked better. Maybe he just got tired of waiting around for you?"

"The only thing I'm going to let out is how much I hate you! You have always been a burr on my butt, Colt Lomax, and you still are!"

Hope ducked under his arm and would've made it past him if he hadn't grabbed a hank of her hair.

"Let me go!" she yelled, but he had always been a poor listener. He wrapped the strands around his fist and reeled her in. Hope refused to give in that easily, and she stretched out and grabbed onto one of the bars. Unfortunately, the bar she grabbed onto was connected to the door, and as she was tugged backwards, the door slammed closed behind them with a loud clang.

Her hair was released.

"Did you . . . ?"

Colt's words hung there until Hope let out a high-pitched squeal.

"No!" She raced over to the bars and jerked on them, but they didn't budge an inch. Not one inch. She searched around for the keys before she remembered that they were lying on the floor on the other side of the door.

She whirled around to let him have it, but stopped at the sight of him pulling his shirt up. It was hard to talk when confronted with a washboard stomach that she could play with a spoon.

"What are you doing?" she squeaked.

"Going to bed." The shirt inched higher before she snapped out of her sexual haze and jerked it back down.

"Have you lost your mind? We have to find a way out of here!" She looked around the tiny cell for anything that would help her escape. But she could find no use for a Dixie dispenser, a pile of *Field and Stream* magazines, or a crocheted doll toilet paper cover. And what infuriated her even more was that he didn't seem at all concerned about the situation, probably because he'd spent so much time behind these bars that it was like home to him.

"We?" He bounced down on the bed and propped his hands beneath his head, fortunately with his shirt still on. "Since I'm not the one who locked us in here, I don't see how that's my job."

"No! You were just the idiot who caused me to slam the door in the first place!"

He shrugged. "All right, I'll give you that one. So you want me to get us out of here?"

"Forget it!" She paced the cell, her slippers flopping. "Lord knows, I wouldn't want you to hurt yourself."

"If you say so, honey." He tugged the quilt up. "But could you turn out the light before you come to bed?"

"I'm not coming to bed. I'm going to find a way out of here if it kills me!" She sent him her most determined look. He must've read it perfectly, because he released a long, heavy sigh.

"Well, hell." In one fluid motion, he was off the bed, had the light off, and her hefted over his shoulder.

"Put me down!" She kicked and swung at him, but she couldn't do much damage in the two strides it took to get to the bed. He tossed her down on the mattress, and before she could sit up, he bounced down next to her and clamped an arm around her waist.

"Now believe me, honey, when I tell you that I've always found your temper tantrums entertaining. But after riding for close to twenty hours, getting my bell rung, my shins kicked, and tossed into jail for no damned good reason, my patience is running a little thin. So I think the smart thing for you to do right now is to be quiet and go to sleep."

"I'm not going to sleep with you!"

"Then don't sleep—I don't give a damn. But you're not getting out of this bed until the sun shines through that window up there."

She made one more attempt at getting loose, but he only tugged her closer and flung one very hard thigh over her legs.

"You are the same arrogant jerk you were in high school," she huffed.

"And you're the same spoiled brat."

"I'm not spoiled."

He stuffed a pillow under his head, while his other arm remained firmly tucked around her waist. "I don't know what you would call it. You have an entire town doing your bidding."

Accepting the fact that she wasn't going anywhere, she relaxed and allowed her arms to flop over the corded muscles of his forearm. "Not the entire town."

"No, I guess you're right." And with that, he pressed his face into her matted possum pelt and went to sleep.

Hope lay awake, trying to figure out how she had ended up in bed with Colt Lomax. Again.

Chapter Four

HOPE SCROGGS WAS a cuddle bug.

Who would've guessed it? Certainly not Colt. Not after a lifetime of watching the sassy, independent woman strut around Bramble as if she owned the place. Which she pretty much did. At least, every heart in Bramble belonged to Hope.

Except one—one lone heart that wasn't stupid enough to give itself to such a stubborn wildcat. No, his heart didn't belong to her, but other parts of his body could be persuaded to. Especially when she was plastered against his chest like a nice custom paint job, miles of rich brown hair spilling down his sides like bronze metallic flames. How did such a small woman grow hair so thick and gorgeous?

He gently ran his hand through the tangled mass. He could bathe in it, wrap himself in the satin strands twice over and drown beneath the silken waves. Bringing it to his nose, he breathed deeply. The scent, faint but familiar, was a mix between earthy woman and sweet berries. As far back as he could remember, Hope always smelled like berries. Smelled and tasted.

Smoothing the hair back from her face, he studied her lips. They were about as perfect a pair as he had seen. Not too plump and not to skinny, with two cute little peaks that just begged for some lovin'. And since he had never been a man to refuse a woman's plea, he leaned down and brushed his lips over hers. Not a deep kiss, just a settling of firm flesh against soft.

"Mmmm." She hummed against his mouth, sending a sizzling shaft of heat straight to his crotch.

Liking the direction things were heading, Colt deepened the kiss. But just as he was about to slip into all that warmth, her eyes blinked open. Up close, they were bluer than he remembered—a mixture of cobalt and azure that would elude the most talented artist's airbrush. They stared back at him, all sleep-drugged and baffled. And for a moment, he got lost. Unfortunately, a moment was all it took for her to remember where she was...and who he was. When she did, she pulled away, taking all that wet heat and mind-altering blue with her.

"You!"

He figured she was about to tack on a few descriptive words. But before she could, her gaze shifted up to the sun shining in through the window. Her eyes widened, and she scrambled off the bed and started searching for her slippers.

"Why did you let me sleep so late? They'll be here any minute to give you breakfast."

Since it looked like the fun was over, he rolled to his feet. "Eight o'clock on the dot. And with my stomach touching my backbone, I'm sure looking forward to some homemade biscuits and gravy."

"No!" She stared at him as if he had lost his mind. "Don't you see? I can't be found in here with you."

"You could always tell them you came to save my black soul." He moved over to the toilet and unzipped his pants.

"If we could just find a hairpin—" She hesitated at the first splash. "Are you … ?"

At her shocked voice, he glanced over his shoulder into her bright red face.

"Draining the lizard? Emptying the fuel tank? Taking a piss—?"

"I get it!" She whirled around and started searching the corners as far from him as she could get.

He grinned. Sex would've been a lot funnier, but he had to admit that teasing Hope was pretty darned fun.

After using the bathroom, he washed his hands and rinsed out his mouth before he picked up the washcloth and cleaned away the blood that he'd missed the night before. The cut on his lip had started to scab over and in a few days wouldn't even be noticeable. He rubbed a hand over his beard. He could sure use a shave. He wondered how long Shirlene planned on keeping him locked up. Talk about a spoiled brat. Still, he had told her that he would stay the night, which was why he had gone along with Sheriff Winslow without a fight. If she wanted him to stay so badly that she had him tossed in jail, he figured he could at least give her a day.

One day wouldn't hurt anything.

He turned around to find Hope on her hands and knees, scouring every inch of the concrete floor. He had to give it to her. She was tenacious. Tenacious and damned sexy in the pink pajama bottoms sheer enough to see that she wasn't wearing any panties.

Offered such a nice view, he figured he had a few more

minutes to spare before he headed over to Shirlene's. He
flopped down on the bed and stacked his hands behind his
head. Hope had never had much in the boob department,
but what she lacked up top she made up for downstairs
with an ass so sweet and tight that it made his mouth
water. It was a darn shame her tenacity paid off as quickly
as it did.

"I found one!" She jumped up and held out what
looked to be a skinny silver straight pin.

He squinted. "Uh, I hate to disappoint you, honey. But
that's not going to work. A hairpin, maybe. A paper clip,
even better. But a little bitty straight pin, no way."

Her eyes narrowed. "Being as how you spent more
than a few nights here, I probably should take your word
for it. Except you never were good at setting goals and
achieving them."

"And just what goals would those be?"

"Any goals—sports—high school—college." She strutted over to the bars and squatted down, showing a hint of
butt crack that caused all the moisture to evaporate from
his mouth.

"The only things you put any effort in were motorcycles and women." She slipped the pin into the lock, and
with each wiggle, the elastic waistband inched down, then
back up.

Colt swallowed hard. What were they talking about?

"Not that the loose women in this town made you work
real hard," she continued, although he no longer could
comprehend a single word. Not with her pajamas playing peek-a-boo butt crack. She stretched even further and
revealed so much butt cleavage that a moan escaped his lips.

She swiveled around. "What's wrong?"

He cleared his throat—twice—before he could speak. "Nothing." He patted his stomach. "Just hungry, is all."

Sending him a skeptical look, Hope went back to lock-picking. "Is that all you can think about, Lomax—physical satisfaction?"

Pretty much. At least, that was all he could think about at the moment; the satisfaction of filling his hands with those sweet cheeks. Unfortunately, he had learned from past experience that giving into temptation was extremely bad for his health. Which meant he needed to get out of there before his body overruled his brain.

He sat up. "You about spent, honey?"

"No. I just about got it. All I need is a little more... Damn it!" She bent over and searched the floor, giving Colt a view that almost sent him to his knees.

Luckily, before he could start begging, she turned and flopped back against the bars, sending him a look that wasn't all that friendly.

"Is it too much to ask for you to get off your butt and help me out?"

He lifted his eyebrows. "You want me to help? Because I thought you had your heart set on doing it all by your lonesome."

Hope gritted her teeth. "The only thing I have my heart set on is getting you out of this town as quickly as possible and the hell away from me!"

"In that case." He rolled to his feet and walked over to the picture of the Texas state flag that hung on the wall. Reaching behind the frame, he felt around until he found the paper clip stuck in between the bricks.

"What are you doing?" she asked as he walked over with the stretched-out piece of wire.

"Granting your wish, honey." He winked at her before he knelt on the cold concrete and slipped his arm through the bars. It had been a lot easier when he was a skinny kid. Now that his biceps barely fit, it took a little more concentration. Which was close to impossible with Hope standing there tapping a foot.

"Are you telling me that you could've broken us out last night?"

"No." He wiggled the end of the paper clip in the lock.

"Don't you dare lie to me, Colt Lomax! Not when the proof is right in front of my eyes."

There was a click as the lock released, and he pushed the door open.

Straightening, Colt turned to her. "Now how could a no-account motorcycle bum break us out of jail when a spoiled control freak already had a plan?"

"Oooo!" Hope stomped her foot before she flopped past him. "You have always loved making a fool of me."

"Maybe because it's so easy to do."

"Easy for a troublemaker with mischief on his mind." She jerked open the outer door, her elbow jabbing him hard in the stomach. "And don't think I don't know that you were the one behind all those mean pranks that happened to me."

"I don't know what pranks you're talking about."

She bent over to pick up the keys. "The frogs in my bed. The garter snakes in my lunch box. The huge rubber pig on the homecoming semi. My bra hoisted up on the town hall flagpole. The live ammo in the prop gun of my senior play."

"Live ammo in a prop gun? You really think I'd be that devious?"

Hope glared over her shoulder as she stomped down the hallway. "I don't think so! I know!"

Colt followed her at a more leisurely pace, partly so she wouldn't see his grin and partly because he wasn't in any hurry. The night in Bramble hadn't been so bad after all. Although the company could've been a little sweeter. Of course, he had never liked things too sweet. He preferred his coffee black and bitter. His food spicy and hot.

And his women...

His gaze followed her cute little butt as it slipped into Sheriff Winslow's office, then back out again.

And his women warm and willing.

Something Hope would never be.

Outside the jailhouse, it was a nice autumn day. Not too hot and not too cool, with blue skies that stretched on forever. Summer in West Texas could be hot, dry, and brutal. But autumn made a man feel like hopping on a motorcycle and cruising down to Fredericksburg for some peaches or over to Austin for some good blues or down to San Antonio to mingle with the spirits of heroes.

Of course, in order to do that, you needed to have a motorcycle to hop on to. And looking around the parking lot, it didn't appear that he did.

"Where's my bike?"

The words were spoken more to himself than to Hope, who was already half a block away. It didn't take him long to catch up with her short legs and to step in front of her.

"Where's my bike?"

"How would I know?" She tried to sidestep him but he met her, steel toe to matted fur.

"So you were going to break me out of jail with no form of transportation?"

"I figured you could handle that part of the plan." She flipped a hand in the air. "Which was really crazy of me, considering you don't seem to be able to handle any part of any plan."

His eyebrows lifted. "I got us out, didn't I?"

"About four hours too late!" She whirled and started back down the street. As he watched those silly little slippers eat up the concrete, he realized she was probably right. He shouldn't have spent an hour alone with her, let alone four. Which didn't explain why he hurried to catch back up.

"Josie still make the best red chili this side of the Pecos?" It was a stupid thing to say, but with less than four hours of sleep and no coffee, it was the best he could come up with. It seemed to work, because she stopped and stared at him.

"Oh, no." She waggled a finger beneath his nose. "You're not eating breakfast here. You're finding your motorcycle and leaving, A-S-A-P."

"And just how do you expect me to find it when I don't know where the hell Sheriff Winslow put it?"

She thought for a moment before her eyes lit up. "Kenny drove it off."

"Kenny Gene got on my chopper!"

Since he had never been much of a yeller, Hope blinked. "How else do you think they were going to get it out of the middle of the street?"

He hadn't thought about that. He'd been too pissed off to do more than fantasize about getting his hands around his sister's neck. And Hope's. Agitated, he ran a hand through his hair, but he should've known better than to show any weakness around his arch nemesis.

"Aww, does the big, bad biker not like to share his toys?"

Damn straight, he didn't like to share his toys. Especially with some hick who didn't know the time and effort put into one of his bikes. But he wasn't about to let Hope know how pissed he was.

"So you think Kenny has it?"

"Probably." She started walking again. "Unless he wrapped it around a telephone pole." She shot a sly glance over her shoulder. "He was pretty drunk last night."

"Funny."

"I thought so." She grinned, showing off her crooked incisor. Besides her disposition, it was her only flaw. But Colt had never viewed it as such. For some reason, he found it endearing and extremely sexy.

"So are you going to give me a lift out to Kenny's?" he asked, in an attempt to get his rebellious mind on other things.

"Do I have a choice?"

"Not if you want me gone, you don't."

"Fine."

It was the first time Hope had ever conceded anything to him, and his enjoyment of the day increased tenfold—even if the concession had to do with getting rid of him.

And as they walked together down the uneven sidewalk, Colt took the time to look around.

Bramble had changed little over the years. There was the pharmacy, where he'd swiped more than his fair share of Fireballs and Bazooka bubble gum. The Duds N Such, where he drooled over a pair of lizard cowboy boots. And Josephine's Diner, where he worked every night after leaving Jones' Garage. But what *had* changed was his feeling about the town. What had once seemed as suffocating as a wet wool blanket now felt, if not welcoming, at least familiar.

"I guess they still have the Parade of Queens," he said as they walked along.

"According to Mama, every year."

"Minus the most popular homecoming queen."

Hope glanced over at him. "If you are referring to me, then yes. Although I hear my sister filled in for me this year."

He expected to see a thundercloud settle over her features. Instead, she laughed. It had been a while since he'd heard the deep, husky sound or felt the warmth it caused deep down in his belly.

"I have to say that's one thing I'll gladly give her," she said.

"Not the hog-calling trophies?"

"Are you kidding? I don't share my trophies with anyone," she mimicked his earlier response to Kenny riding his bike.

"I don't think hog-calling trophies are in the same league with eighty-thousand-dollar motorcycles."

She halted in mid-strut and stared up at him with eyes the same color as the sky above them. "Do you mean to tell me that motorcycle cost you close to a hundred thousand dollars?"

"It's worth that, and then some."

"Have you lost your mind, Colt Lomax?"

He grinned down at her and shrugged. "Some people think so."

"Hey, Hope!"

Startled, they turned and looked down the street.

Kenny Gene stood out in the parking lot of Josephine's Diner, a parking lot filled to the brim with dust-covered trucks and dinged-up American-made cars.

"Oh, hell," Hope grumbled under her breath, but it only took a second for her to recover and wave and smile like the true homecoming queen she was. "Hey, Kenny Gene! We was just talkin' about yew." She spread the Texas twang on thick as peanut butter. "You wouldn't know where Colt's motorcycle is, would yew?"

"Shore do!" he yelled back.

"And just where would that be, Kenny?" Colt asked.

"Well, hey, Colt! I didn't see you standin' there."

It wasn't surprising. Colt had always been invisible to the people of Bramble, especially when standing next to the town sweetheart.

"So where is it?" Hope asked.

"Where's what?"

Damn, Colt had forgotten how annoying the folks of Bramble could be.

"So where is my motorcycle, Kenny?"

"Oh, I can't tell you that. Shirlene would have my hide." His eyes narrowed. "Hey, ain't you supposed to be in the town jail?"

"I'm going to kill him," Hope said through her teeth.

"Only if you beat me to it." Colt stepped off the curb with every intention of grabbing Kenny up by his stiff western shirt and shaking the information out of him. Unfortunately, before he could, the mayor came out of Josephine's.

"Hope, honey, what in the world are you doing, standin' over there?" Harley waved his hand. "Come on over here and let me buy you some breakfast. At a time like this, we need to keep you well fed."

Confused, Colt looked over at Hope, but she didn't even spare him a glance as the bright fake smile slid back in place.

"Actually, Uncle Harley, Mama and Daddy are waitin' breakfast. So I need to get." As she backpedaled down the sidewalk, she spoke to Colt out of the side of her mouth. "Just keep walking, and when you get to the corner, run like hell."

Most people wouldn't understand her crazy talk. But after growing up in the town, Colt understood perfectly. One Bramble citizen was easily dealt with—two, almost impossible. Unfortunately, before he could follow her instructions, a brand-new black Lincoln Navigator came barreling down the street and zipped into the parking lot. The dust hadn't even settled before the door opened and a pair of bright turquoise stilettos slipped out.

"Well, good mornin', big brother." Shirlene strutted across the street in a tight pair of jeans, a huge concho belt, and a white blouse unbuttoned low enough to show off the hundred pounds of silver and turquoise wrapped around her neck. "I see you made it out of jail all right."

"No thanks to you." Colt crossed his arms and shot her an annoyed look.

"Now, honey." Shirlene batted those green eyes at him. "You aren't mad at me for forcing you to keep your promise, are you?"

He probably should be mad. The woman was too arrogant and controlling for her own good. But she had a point. He had promised to stay the night. And she was his baby sister, who he'd always had a soft spot for.

"Besides," she continued. "I knew you could get out anytime you wanted. In fact, what took you so long? I was hoping we could watch—" Those green eyes flickered over his shoulder and widened, but only for a split second. "Well, now, what do we have here?"

He glanced back to see Hope standing a few feet away, frozen in her spot. She looked all mussed and cute in her saggy pajama bottoms, her big eyes a little fearful at being caught by someone who knew how to put two and two together. For some reason, her fear prompted the need to rein in his sister.

"Quit being a brat, Shirlene, and tell me where you stashed my motorcycle."

Her gaze flickered back to him. "A brat? All I'm trying to figure out is why the Sweetheart of Bramble is wandering around in her pajamas with an escaped convict."

Colt really wanted to give his sister a good sock in the arm for bringing Harley's attention to the situation.

"What are you doin' with our little Hope?" Harley asked, not looking at all happy about the situation.

"Doing?" Hope finally entered the conversation, her voice sounding three pitches too high. "Nothing. We aren't doing a thing...I was just taking a walk and ran into him."

Shirlene tipped her head and smiled. "Sleepwalkin', were you, honey?"

With her hair all tangled and wild around her face, Hope did look like she just rolled out of bed. And she pretty much had—his bed. The thought brought a flash of heat to his crotch and, not wanting to embarrass himself, he tried to get his mind back on track.

"It doesn't matter what Hope is doing. Where's my bike?"

Shirlene flapped a hand, the morning sun refracting

off her huge diamonds. "Would you stop worrying about that bike? You'll get it back all safe and sound in a few days."

"A few days!" Both he and Hope spoke in unison.

As if on cue, Sheriff Winslow pulled up in his squad car and rolled down the window.

"You put the cell keys back, Shirlene?" When she only flashed her dimples, he turned to Colt. "Colt, I shore hope you ain't plannin' on causin' any more trouble. I'd hate to have to lock you up again."

"I sure hope so too, Sam." Shirlene threw Colt a sly look. "It breaks my heart to see my big brother behind bars. And I give you my word that I'll keep an eye on him. In fact, we were just headed over to Josephine's to have us a nice, hearty breakfast." She waltzed over to Hope and hooked an arm through hers. Hope put up a good fight, but in the end Colt's ornery baby sister prevailed and tugged her across the street.

Colt remained on the sidewalk with his arms crossed over his chest, debating whether or not he wanted to follow his sister or tell her and the entire town of Bramble to take a hike. But the truth was, with the bike delivery deadline a week out, he didn't have anywhere that he needed to be.

Still, he hadn't completely made up his mind until Hope shot him a wicked glare over her shoulder. A glare that grew even more poisonous when he couldn't help but grin. She turned back around, and he watched the wiggle of her butt beneath the thin cotton.

What were a few days?

Especially when it annoyed the hell out of the homecoming queen.

Chapter Five

THERE HADN'T BEEN anyone murdered in Bramble, Texas, since 1892, when the sheriff shot William Cates for attacking the mayor, after the mayor refused to pay him for the dedication plaque he'd made for the town hall.

But Hope was about to change that.

As she sat at the counter, awaiting a breakfast she hadn't ordered and didn't want, she eyeballed the knife Harley was using to spread the mound of whipped butter over his pancakes and calculated how long it would take to grab the knife, ram it through Shirlene's conniving heart, and get out the door before Sheriff Winslow could clear his gun from beneath the edge of the counter.

Of course, it didn't matter how quickly he cleared it. He didn't keep any bullets in it anyway. "Safety first" was the town motto. And people knew from experience that Sam wasn't someone who could carry a loaded weapon safely.

Still, the sheriff wouldn't need a gun to stop her. Especially when her truck sat at her parents' house. By the time she said good-bye to her sisters and brother, her mama made her bologna sandwiches for the trip, and her daddy checked the oil and the other fluids in the engine, the lynch mob would be in the front yard, amid her mother's whirling lawn ornaments.

So her murder plans would have to wait.

"...so I said to Mary Jean, you should be thankin' your lucky stars that Melvin ran off with your manicurist," Rachel Dean continued her nonstop chatter as she poured Shirlene a cup of coffee, coffee that smelled as good as it looked. "After two husbands, I can tell you men ain't all that."

Hope flipped her cup over and set it in the saucer.

"Maybe you just haven't had the right man," Colt spoke up for the first time since entering the diner. Not that it was easy to get a word in edgewise with the folks of Bramble. Especially Rachel Dean.

Rachel turned to Colt and studied him as if just realizing he sat there. A smile creased her weathered face, and she moved past Hope's empty cup, right on over to his.

"Well, it looks like you got yourself a golden tongue while you was in prison, Colt Lomax." She sent him a saucy wink as she poured his coffee. "And I can't say as I don't prefer it to that chip you carried around on your shoulder as a kid."

Since Colt had never taken criticism well, Hope waited for him to take offense. Instead, he gave Rachel a sexy, gray-eyed wink of his own before he took a sip of coffee and closed his eyes in euphoric satisfaction.

Annoyed that she wasn't experiencing the same enjoyment, Hope tapped a finger on the rim of her cup. But Rachel couldn't seem to take her eyes off Colt. Not that she could blame the woman, or any of the other women in the diner, who had lost interest in her food to stare at the man who exuded a raw, masculine sex appeal in his travel-worn clothes and dark scruffy stubble.

Like a regular at a local bar, Colt straddled the red vinyl stool, his knees almost touching the counter where his bare forearms rested. Tattoos snaked up the arm furthest from her, while the one closest boasted nothing more than hard, tanned muscle, covered in a sprinkling of silky black hair. The muscles led to a thick wrist and a hand scarred and calloused from tinkering with machines.

Hope watched as his hand lifted the white porcelain mug to his firm, unsmiling lips. But before he took a sip, the cup halted. She glanced up and found him watching her, his eyes bemused. Not wanting to appear guilty, she stared back. They gazed at one another for a few moments until his eyes lowered to her chest. His brows knotted.

"Rachel," he called, even though the woman wasn't more than six inches away. "You have a sweater or something for Hope to put on?"

Hope's eyes shot down to the front of her shirt, and she quickly crossed her arms as Rachel scurried to do his bidding.

Shirlene laughed. "If you didn't wander around half dressed, honey," she said as she stirred five packets of sugar substitute into her coffee, "your teacup handles wouldn't be showin'."

"Real funny, Shirl." But that didn't stop her from taking the ugly gray sweater and slipping it on—with the annoying help of one very cocky motorcycle bum.

"Nice to see you remember your manners, son," Harley said, before he leaned over the counter to whisper something in Rachel's ear. She nodded and moved back to stand in front of Hope.

"Manners is a nice thing for a man to have," Rachel said. "Neither one of my husbands had a manner one, although Homer always said a polite 'excuse me' after he burped or farted."

Colt choked on his coffee, but had the manners to whisper a quick "excuse me" before Rachel continued.

"But worse than that, in my opinion, is a man who don't take responsibility for his own actions." She lifted her nonexistent eyebrows at Hope, as if to convey some message Hope wasn't getting.

Nor was she getting any coffee.

"She's right," Sheriff Winslow chimed in from his spot further down the counter. "There's nothing lower than a scoundrel who won't own up to his mistakes."

Knowing the town could go on and on about something that had nothing to do with anything, Hope finally spoke up.

"Could I get some coffee?"

After topping off Colt's cup, Rachel held up the half-full pot. "You don't want this coffee, honey, it's been sittin' out too long." She dumped it in the sink and grabbed a pitcher of orange juice. "Now let me pour you a glass of OJ. All that vitamin C is much better for a body than caffeine."

"I don't want orange juice," Hope stated as Rachel set the glass down in front of her. "I want coffee."

Rachel's smile faltered, but only for a second. "Well, of course, you do. I'll just start another pot." Except she didn't move to start one; instead, she set the pitcher down and rested one big man hand on her hip and the other on the edge of the counter.

"Now I bet there's a lot of men out there in Hollywood who ain't got no idea how to treat a lady, especially someone as sweet as our little Hope." She leaned closer. "I bet you knew a few fellers like that, didn't you, Hog?"

The clink of forks on plates halted all at once, and Hope could've sworn the entire place leaned in. Even Colt's gaze settled on her.

She sent him a scalding look before she answered.

"A few."

"A few, like two?" Rachel asked. "Or is that a couple? I always get those two mixed up."

"A few is three," Cindy Lynn enlightened her from a table behind them. "And a couple is two. Like Ed and me are a couple."

"Unless she's at Bootlegger's," Shirlene mumbled under her breath. "Then her couple can expand to any man willing to give her the time of day."

"A few." Rachel's eyes turned worried. "That many, huh? Are you sure you couldn't narrow it down some?"

Harley leaned over from his end of the counter. "Well, now, I'm sure Hope doesn't want to talk about all the men she dated out in California. After all, there had to be a slew clamorin' for an opportunity to date the prettiest homecomin' queen we ever had."

Colt snorted.

"But what Rachel was askin'," Harley continued, "is if there was any one special. Anyone that might've made an impression on our little sweetheart."

With a pair of steel gray eyes pinned on her, Hope really wanted to come up with a name of someone really special. A name that would wipe the cocky smirk off Colt's whiskered outlaw face. But since she had been too busy in California trying to make ends meet, the only man she could come up with was her old roommate. Sheldon had only been a friend, but Colt didn't need to know that.

"Well...there was this one guy—"

"A movie star?" Twyla jumped in.

"Matthew McConaughey?" Cindy Lynn's voice almost wept with envy.

"Tommy Lee Jones?" Rachel Dean breathed.

"Sandra Bullock?" Kenny added. When everyone in the room shot him a surprised look, he smiled sheepishly. "Faith had an on-counter with her. I just figured it was worth a shot."

Hope didn't have a clue what Kenny was talking about, but then again, she never did. So instead of getting sucked into the craziness, she kept it simple.

"No, Sheldon is not a movie star."

"A pro quarterback?" Sheriff Winslow asked, and Hope couldn't help but smile at the mental image of Sheldon on a football field.

"No."

"A country western singer?" Cindy Lynn leaned around her poor whipped husband.

"Afraid not."

"Is he at least a Texan?" Harley said, and when Hope shook her head, he heaved a sigh and slumped back on the bar stool. "Well, I guess that settles that."

"It's not the end of the world, Harley," Rachel Dean said, as she slipped two plates down in front of Hope and Colt. "He can't be all that bad if our little Hope likes him." She pointed down at the plate and prodded. "Go ahead, honey, Josie made it just the way you like it—the eggs runny and the chili hot."

While Colt attacked the food like the starving convict he was, Hope stared at the two fried eggs swimming in a sea of brilliant red chili. The same red chili that had burned a hole in her stomach two weeks earlier.

God, she *had* become a wuss since leaving Texas.

She pushed the plate away. "I'm not feeling like chili today, Rachel."

Rachel only looked confused for a second before she jerked the plate back up, and then reached out and patted Hope's hand. "Take a few deep breaths, honey. It will pass."

"What will pass?" Colt turned to her, his fork poised in midair. "Are you sick?"

As Rachel walked off with her plate, Hope turned to Shirlene. "Is it my imagination, or has everyone completely lost their minds?"

Shirlene shot her a skeptical look. "You have been gone too long, honey. Since when have the people of this town had minds?" She took a couple bites of steak and eggs before she continued. "So what shall we do today? Everyone could come over to my house for a barbecue and margaritas. Or we could go out to Sutter Springs for a picnic. Or we could—"

"Find my motorcycle," Colt stated.

"I told you I'd get it back to you." Shirlene pointed her fork at him. "But is it too much to ask for a couple days? You would think that a man who owns—"

"Fine." He threw her a warning look. "I'll stay for a couple of days. But come Wednesday morning, I'm out of here."

"A week would be better."

"Don't push it, baby sister."

Her dimples flashed. "Wednesday it is."

It was hard for Hope to keep her mouth shut when she wanted to yell "No!" at the top of her lungs. She didn't want Colt to stay one hour longer, let alone three days. Unfortunately, there wasn't anything to do about it. Shirlene was too smart for her own good, and there wasn't any way that she would let Hope's objections go without a pisspot full of questions. Questions Hope wasn't about to answer...even if she could.

"Here you go, honey." Rachel set another plate down in front of her.

Hope stared down at the four saltine crackers and wondered if Rachel had sniffed too much diesel fuel from the clothes of her truck-driving husbands.

"What is this?" she asked.

"Crackers."

"I know they're crackers, but why are you giving them to me?"

"To settle your stomach." She winked. "Every mornin' for three entire months I ate nothin' but saltines and a little ginger ale. 'Course around lunchtime, I was right as rain and could swallow down an entire cow without stoppin' to spit out the hooves and horns. But until then, I couldn't look at real food or even smell it."

"What are you talking about, Rachel?"

"Oh, honey." Her eyes teared up. "I realize that at a time like this you'd just as soon not have a big bunch of people makin' a fuss over you. But we're family, Hope. And we love you. Even if you did run off to Hollywood and get yourself—"

"It's a mistake!"

Hope was still trying to piece together Rachel's words

when Faith's voice rang out through the diner. She swiveled around on the bar stool to find her sister standing by the door, looking all wild-eyed and sleep-tousled.

And annoyingly satisfied.

The satisfied part, no doubt, came from the handsome cowboy who stood directly behind her. Although he didn't look exactly happy to be there.

"It's all a mistake," Faith continued as she stepped into the diner in a cami and pajama bottoms very similar to Hope's. "Slate told me what you all think, and I take full responsibility for you thinking that because it was me who said it—although I didn't mean it the way it came out—I was just trying to explain to Slate why I had left Bramble without saying a word and I didn't realize everyone was listening and would assume what you've obviously assumed. But she's not." She held a hand to her chest. "Really."

There was an exchange of glances as if everyone knew what Faith was rambling about—everyone but Hope, Colt, and Shirlene. Shirlene seemed to fit the pieces together quick enough.

"Lordy." She fanned herself with one hand. "Things just keep getting more excitin' and more excitin'. Pretty soon I'll have to move just to get some rest."

"What are you mumbling about, Shirl?"

"I think you're about to find out, honey." She winked at Hope as Harley slipped off his bar stool.

Hitching up his pants, he moved over to Faith. "Now, I realize Hope's embarrassed about what happened, and being her sister, you want to keep her little secret, but you can't change our mind about something we heard with our own two ears."

"But you heard wrong!"

Hope had to give it to her. Faith could win a few hog-calling trophies of her own.

Harley's eyes squinted. "So are you tellin' us you lied?"

"Not lied, exactly. I just didn't explain things properly."

Slate stepped up and placed his arm around Faith. "Now, darlin', I know you want to set things straight and all, but I don't think now's the time or place. Why don't we go on back to Bubba's and continue where we left off before I went and opened my big mouth."

"No." She shook her head. "If I don't explain they'll continue to believe Hope's pregnant, and I can't let them—"

"What?" Hope came off the stool so quickly that her slipper got caught in the rung of the bar stool. And she would've hit the floor, just like Colt's coffee mug, if Shirlene hadn't reached out and grabbed Rachel's gray sweater and reeled her back in.

Rachel hurried around the counter, ignoring the broken shards. "Now, don't be gettin' yourself in a lather, honey." She fanned Hope with one hand, which created enough air to rival a ceiling fan. "It's not good for the babies."

"Babies?" Hope sat down hard on the bar stool and tried to keep from passing out.

"'Course, babies." Rachel fanned harder. "You're a twin, ain't you?"

"No." Faith raced over. "I told you, she's not pregnant. It was all just a misunderstanding. She threw up, and I just assumed she was pregnant."

Rachel nodded her head. "And that's a good assumption, honey. I threw up like the town drunk with both my kids."

"Except she's not pregnant."

"Says who?" Harley said.

"Says me." Hope finally came out of her comatose state and stood back up to glare at her twin sister. "I gather I have you to thank for this mess?"

Faith's eyes widened, and she nodded.

Damn. A double murder was going to be more difficult. But before Hope could let her sister have it, Slate pulled Faith toward the door.

"Come on, darlin', I think you've straightened things out enough for one day."

"B-but," she stammered and sent Hope one last beseeching look before she disappeared out the door.

Once they were gone, Hope turned to the group. "I'm not pregnant," she stated firmly. "It was just a little misunderstanding between sisters."

"So you didn't throw up," Kenny jumped in.

"Yes, I threw up, but only because I ate red chili the night before."

"But, Hope," Twyla entered the conversation, "you grew up on red chili—"

"I'm not pregnant!" Hope screamed so loudly that the glasses rattled on the shelf behind the counter.

The town exchanged looks before Shirlene spoke up, her green eyes twinkling almost as much as Colt's were.

"I don't know, honey. Throwing up and bad mood swings, I'd say that about clenches it."

Shooting a murderous glare at her best friend, Hope

slapped Rachel's fanning hand out of the way and jumped up from the stool.

"Where are you going, Hog?" Kenny yelled as Hope headed for the door.

"To get me a cup of coffee and a loaded gun!"

The folks of Bramble waited for Shirlene and Colt to follow Hope out before they hurried over to the window.

"So what are we gonna do?" Kenny asked as he watched Hope cuss Shirlene up one side and down the other.

"I'm not sure," Harley stated. "But we can't let our little Hope raise a passel of children by herself." There was a long pause as Harley twirled the end of his mustache. Finally his eyes narrowed, and he looked over at Rachel.

"Rachel, isn't your cousin, Bear, a private eye?"

"He ain't a private eye, Harley. He's a bounty hunter."

Harley nodded. "Well, I'd say that's even better."

Chapter Six

COLT MISSED THE open road.

Shirlene's guesthouse was more than comfortable, and her Mexican cook sure knew her way around a kitchen, but comfort didn't compare to freedom. Which was why, before Shirlene rolled out of bed on Tuesday morning, he stole the keys to the Navigator and headed out on his own.

On the way into town, he made a few calls on his cell phone, a phone Shirlene had retrieved from the leather bags on his bike, along with his aviators and extra clothes. He wasn't much of a talker, so the calls only lasted a few minutes. Just long enough to make sure things were going smoothly back at his custom motorcycle shop in L.A.

Colt had started Desperado Customs six years earlier in an old, abandoned warehouse. With his ability to hand-form sheet metal into unparalleled designs, wealthy customers had quickly lined up to own the hottest bikes on the street. His talented group of designers and mechanics didn't build a lot of motorcycles, but the motorcycles they built were unique enough to attract a huge cult following.

The majority of his followers couldn't afford his bikes, but they were more than willing to shell out twenty bucks for a T-shirt or twelve for a ball cap. He made as much selling that crap as he did selling his motorcycles.

After checking in with the shop, he fiddled with the radio until he found a station that played soft rock, which was about as far from country as he was going to get in this neck of the woods. He was singing along with a Bob Seger tune when he drove past Bramble High School.

The school was small and looked even smaller compared to the huge football stadium next to it—a tribute to the town's dedication to the sport. Colt hadn't played football. Not because he hadn't wanted to, but because school and work didn't leave room for much else. But, occasionally, he would sneak into the games after he finished working at Josephine's, to watch Slate Calhoun throw winning touchdown passes while Hope cheered him on with high kicks and straddles.

It was after those games that he got into the most trouble.

Up ahead, the faded and chipped sign of Jones' Garage stuck out like a sore thumb against the gray skies, and Colt lifted his foot off the accelerator.

"Hey, Colt," Tyler met him as he stepped from the SUV. "I see you got some proper boots."

Colt looked down at the black lizard cowboy boots he'd purchased in Lubbock; a foolish whim egged on by a sassy sister. Luckily, he'd drawn a line at the snap-down plaid western shirt.

"Yeah, well, you know how it goes." He placed his hands on his hips and stared over at the garage, a garage he knew like the inside of a carburetor. "So I guess if I was to wander around a bit, I just might run into a custom bike."

Tyler grinned as he took the cap off the gas tank. "You might. But I sure hope you don't."

Colt arched an eyebrow. "I thought we were friends, T-bone."

"Sure are." He lifted the nozzle and slipped it in. "Which is why I hope you stick around for a while."

"And you and Shirl are about the only ones who feel that way."

Tyler spit out a stream of tobacco before wiping his mouth with the back of his hand. "And whose fault is that? I've never seen anyone work so hard to make folks dislike him."

"I didn't have to try all that hard."

"Nope." Tyler leaned against the side of the Navigator and crossed his arms while the tank filled. "You just had to be your obstinate self. If the town said white, you said black. Couple that with spending most of your free time bullying the town sweetheart, and that about did it." He returned his attention to the pump. "It was your choice, buddy. Always your choice."

Had it been? Funny, but it hadn't seemed that way so many years ago, when he was forced to scrap for everything he got. Growing up, he'd always thought it was the town that held him back, the town that kept him from being what he wanted to be. But he wondered if Tyler wasn't right. Maybe it hadn't been the town that held him back as much as his own belief that he would never be more than "that poor Lomax kid." Of course, it made no difference now.

Changing the subject, Colt nodded at the excavated lot next to the gas station. "Planning on expanding?"

"I thought about putting a car wash there, but that out-fit on the interstate beat me to it." Tyler shook his head as he hooked the nozzle back in the pump. "'Course I didn't really have the money for it, anyway. Things have been slow around here."

Colt took his wallet out of his pocket and handed Tyler the cash. "Thanks, Ty."

Tyler nodded. "You still tinkering around with motorcycles?"

"Pretty much," he said. "You still making babies with Missy Leigh?"

Tyler's smile was genuine and proud. "Pretty much."

Grinning, Colt walked around to the driver's door.

Tyler followed him. "If you stick around until Friday, we've got a play-off game. Best darned quarterback since Calhoun."

"Sounds like fun, but I'll be long gone by then." Colt opened the door and climbed in. But before he pulled away, he backed the truck up and checked inside all three open garage stalls, while Tyler stood there laughing.

"Take care of her, T-bone," he yelled through the open window.

Tyler nodded. "Will do, Colt."

After leaving the gas station, Colt decided to take a quick cruise through town before he headed back to Shirlene's. He thought about breakfast at Josephine's, but Shirlene's cook had fed him enough red and green chili to last him awhile. That, and he didn't much feel like listening to the people of Bramble talk their nonsense. Although he had enjoyed them razzing Hope about being pregnant with twins.

Hope pregnant. He shook his head and laughed.

Crazy townsfolk.

Of course, he hadn't been laughing at first. He'd been too stunned to laugh. Over the years, he'd thought of Hope in a lot of different scenarios. But pregnant wasn't one of them. Probably because babies weren't something he spent a lot of time thinking about.

Not that he didn't like babies. He liked babies just fine. His sister had been a baby once, and she had been kind of cute. Still, it had been a full-time job making sure that she didn't roll off the couch or play around electrical sockets or ram pennies in her mouth. And as she got older, there were more responsibilities. Like getting her out of bed, dressed, and fed before school. And making sure she washed behind her ears and did her homework before she watched TV. And keeping all the boys away from her when she finally outgrew being a tomboy and turned into a hormonal teenager.

It had been a relief when she married Lyle and settled down.

But that didn't mean that Colt had stopped worrying about her. In the last couple days, he'd noticed that she was drinking more than usual. He figured it had to do with Lyle being gone so much. Lomax women didn't do well without their men—his mama was a perfect example. Which was why he planned on talking to Lyle about staying home more often and keeping his wife from drowning her lonely heart in a bottle of Jose Cuervo.

With his thoughts wrapped up in Shirlene, he barely noticed the woman who stepped off the curb to flag him down until he almost ran her over. He slammed on the brakes, and the tires squealed to a stop inches from her scuffed cowboy boots.

He didn't have to read her lips. Even with the windows closed, her voice carried.

"Oh. It's you."

With a thunderous look, Hope turned and stomped back over to her beat-up truck, parked next to the curb in front of the Food Mart. Biting back a smile, Colt pulled into a space and got out. Even with the gray clouds that rumbled overhead, the day somehow seemed brighter.

"You need somethin', honey?" he asked politely, although he had to admit a little gleefully.

Completely ignoring him, Hope struggled with the big box of groceries that sat on the sidewalk next to her truck, the same truck she'd had eight years ago.

He walked over and leaned against the open tailgate. "You sure you don't need any help? That's a mighty big box for such a little thing." He drew the word *thing* out into a nice Texas *thaaang.*

"I'm good," she growled between clenched teeth.

His gaze traveled over the swells of her bottom in the thin cotton dress. "No doubt about that, honey."

The box thumped down, and glass bottles rattled as she turned to glare at him. "Don't you have something else to do, Lomax? Like maybe find a hundred-thousand-dollar motorcycle so you can get the hell out of town and quit harassing me?"

"I hate to bring this to your attention, but I wasn't the one who flagged you down."

"I didn't flag you down! I flagged Shirlene down!"

With his arms crossed, Colt shrugged. "Well, one Lomax is as good as the other."

"A few days ago, I might've argued the point. But after all the stunts your sister has pulled recently, I'll have to agree with you on that one. I don't know why I flagged her down in the first place." She turned back to the box.

It would've been easy to leave her there. In Bramble, someone would show up to help her out. But *easy* wasn't in Colt's vocabulary. Besides, it wasn't like he had anything else to do.

Pushing away from the tailgate, he bodily picked Hope up and set her out of the way, taking only a second to notice the way his hands spanned her trim waist.

"Darn you, Lomax, I told you I don't need your help!"

"I know. But you're going to get it anyway." He picked up the box and hefted it into the back of the truck, next to the other boxes of food. "Burl training for the pie-eating contest?"

"Funny." She tried to shove him out of the way to close the tailgate, but he wasn't having it.

"So where are you taking all this?"

She glared at him for only a few seconds before she answered. "Out to Grover Road."

His eyebrows shot up at the mention of his old neighborhood. "I thought the church only handed out boxes at Christmas?"

"They do, but I thought they might need something to tide them over. So I called Shirlene, and she called Ed and told him to charge whatever I wanted."

It was so like Hope. Whether delivering Bibles or food for the hungry, Hope never let the people of her town go without. The realization brought with it a wave of warmth that settled all nice and cozy in his stomach. Although the look she sent him was anything but.

"So do you mind moving so I can get out of here before it starts to rain?"

On cue, a rumble of thunder drew their eyes up to the dark sky.

"You got a tarp?" he asked. When she didn't answer, he looked away from the nebulous clouds into annoyed baby blue. "I'll take that as a no." He reached back in and pulled the large box out.

"Give me that back! I don't need any help." She tried to take the box from him, but he held tight.

"I don't doubt that for a minute, sweetheart. But you ever tasted soggy cereal?" When she looked confused, he glanced up at the sky. "Because in about three minutes that's exactly what you're going be handing out to those kids if you don't let me get the rest of these boxes inside that SUV."

"Fine." She released the box and stepped out of his way. "But if you hadn't nosed in, I could've made it."

"Doubtful." He placed the box in the back of the Navigator and turned to find her standing there with another one. He went to take it from her, but she refused to let go.

"You really can't help yourself, can you?" He lifted a brow at her. "Now let go and let me do it."

"Or what?" Her blue eyes snapped, and he would've laughed at her stubbornness if the store owner's wife, Jeannie Mitchell, hadn't raced out the front door.

"Hope, I thought I told you to wait until Ed got off the phone before you loaded those boxes. You want to give those babies bad backs?"

Colt laughed, and Hope's eyes narrowed as she released the box. "I hope Kenny Gene is riding your motorcycle all over the countryside."

Mentally cussing Kenny, Colt loaded the rest of the boxes while Jeannie stood on the sidewalk and watched with a confused look on her face.

"I sure never thought I'd see the day when Colt Lomax did charity work."

"Actually, I'm just takin' these back to Shirlene's." He winked at her as he slammed the hatch. "But I figure you're the type of woman a man can trust with all his secrets."

Jeannie blushed to the roots of her bright-red hair. "Rachel was right. You have turned into quite a sweet talker since you've been in prison, Colt Lomax." Her smile got even bigger when he walked around and held open the door for Hope.

"Fake talker is more like it," Hope mumbled beneath her breath as she slipped inside, flashing a good amount of tanned legs before she jerked down the hem of her flower-printed dress.

Smiling almost as big as Jeannie, Colt slammed the truck door behind her.

Grover Road sat north of the town dump and south of the junkyard, although it looked more like an extension of both. Around a dozen trailers sat in the midst of rusted-out cars and trucks and piles of old mattresses. And each pathetic home looked the same, a rectangular box of aluminum siding with cracked windows, tires on the roof, and lopsided steps leading up to torn screen doors.

"It's weird, isn't it," Hope voiced his thoughts. "I mean, everything looks the same, except not. I don't remember the trailers being so small." She glanced over at him. "Did we really live here?"

Raw emotion rumbled through Colt like the dark clouds that had yet to produce rain, and he struggled with the strong desire to crank the wheel and head back to town. Instead he slouched down in the seat and tried to get his shoulders to relax. "I lived here a lot longer than you did."

She studied him for a few more seconds before she looked away. "Mama said to leave the boxes beneath the steps. Folks like it better that way."

He nodded in agreement. The one time the church ladies arrived with their Christmas charity box, he'd been so ashamed that he'd refused it, tossing in a few belligerent cuss words for good measure. Later on, when the other kids had fruit snacks for their lunches and Shirlene didn't, he'd regretted his bad behavior. But by that time, it was too late. Which seemed to be the story of his life. Hot temper followed by rash behavior followed by a whole lot of regret.

"Just pull in here," Hope directed him into a weedy lot.

"Does old man Smith still live here?"

"No, Mama told me he died a few years back."

Maneuvering the SUV around the junk and weeds, Colt parked by the door. "He was sure a mean old bird. Every time I moved, he called the sheriff out."

She glanced over. "And I'm sure sweet little Colt Lomax didn't do a thing to deserve it."

His gaze took in the filthy front window with the huge crack spidering across it. "Okay, so maybe I did occasionally deserve it, but the guy was a jerk."

Whether the guy was a jerk or not, dead or not, that didn't stop Colt from pulling out his wallet when Hope wasn't looking and slipping a hundred beneath the snap top of an oatmeal box. Not that the money would go to fix the crack Colt had made in the window, but it made him feel better.

"You think they'll find it before it rains?" Hope asked, as he slid the box under the sloping metal steps.

"It should be okay here until they do."

They placed boxes at eight more trailers, and Colt recognized a few more cracks in the windows and shelled out a few more hundreds, although at the last one, a pit bull almost chewed clean through his brand-new cowboy boot before he could get the box placed under the stairs.

"Nice boots, by the way," Hope yelled as they raced back to the truck. "Flashy but nice."

"You should talk." He jumped behind the wheel and slammed the door before the dog could get his head in. "Weren't you the one who asked for those hideous pink boots for Christmas that year? Whatever happened to those, anyway?"

"I lost them," Hope stated, before directing him to the next trailer.

It was funny, but he almost didn't recognize his childhood home—funny because nothing much had changed. The yard was still cluttered with beat-up vehicles and old motorcycle frames. And the trailer still had rust spots and dangling screens, along with a wooden door with a fist-sized dent in the middle.

"Damn," Colt breathed as he pulled in behind the old Ford truck without any tires, windows, or doors. "Does someone actually live here?"

"No." When he shot her a questioning look, she grinned. "I just thought you might like to take a walk down memory lane."

"Gee, thanks." He looked around. "Why hasn't anybody in town come out here to clean things up?"

"Probably because the one time Marty Clines tried it, you chased him off with a hammer."

"Still, they should raze the place."

"The place? Or your memories?"

His gaze shot over to her serious blue eyes. "Both." He reached for the gear shift. But before he could pop it into reverse, Hope had her door open.

"Come on, let's look around."

"I had eighteen years to look around," Colt stated. "And believe me that was plenty."

She leaned in the open door. "I dare you."

"Double dog?"

"Triple."

Never one to refuse a dare, he got out, leading the way down the worn path that led to the broken-down steps. But when he tried the door, it refused to open.

"You've got to be kidding!" He jiggled the handle in disbelief.

"Ironic, ain't it?" Hope stood at the bottom of the steps, smirking like all get out. The wind kicked up, sending the mane of hair flying around her upturned face and molding the soft fabric of her dress to her small breasts and flat stomach. "The only locked door in Bramble and it's Colt Lomax's."

She giggled, and then the giggle turned to out-and-out laughter. And no one laughed like Hope. She laughed like she yelled, loud and uninhibited with her head thrown back and her arms crossed over her stomach. But while her yelling could bust an eardrum, her laughter had a mellow huskiness that filled Colt with a warm contentment.

He didn't know how long he stood there staring at her, or how long he would've continued to do so, if her laughter hadn't suddenly died and her gaze lifted up to the skies.

"Gully-washer," she stated, but not soon enough for either one of them to escape the deluge of water that suddenly dropped from the sky without one drip of warning. One second they were completely dry and the next soaking wet.

Most women would've been squealing their heads off. But not Hope. Her laughter returned, and she did a quick little spin in her scuffed cowboy boots.

"Come on," Colt yelled as he took the steps in one leap, the racket of raindrops against aluminum deafening. He tried to shield her with his body and steer her toward the truck, but Hope had other plans and raced around the piles of junk toward the large elm tree.

When he finally caught up with her, she was struggling with the rusted door of the old Chevy. He wanted to jerk her stubborn body up and carry her back to the comfortable, heated seats of the Navigator, but instead, he reached out and added his strength to the door, then held it while she clamored in on the torn seat. Soaked to the skin, he climbed in behind her.

"Have you lost your mind, woman?" He slammed the door and scraped the wet hair back from his face.

"I just wanted to see if it was still here," she said, all out of breath. "Besides, a little rain never hurt anyone."

"A little?" Colt turned to her. The sight that greeted him brought a smile to his lips. "You look like a drowned rat." He reached out and smoothed back a rope of wet hair.

"And what makes you think you don't," Hope tossed back, her gaze locked on his chest. It remained there for only a second before she turned to the rain-drenched windshield. "I'm surprised no one has broken it out."

"Believe me, it was quite a temptation."

She glanced over at him. "So why didn't you?"

Staring at the water that rushed in tiny waves down the

solid sheet of glass, he only shrugged. "I guess because it was the only play equipment Shirlene had. She used to love climbing behind the wheel and traveling all over the world."

"I know," she said. "I traveled with her."

Hope was right. She had been there, sitting in the front seat next to Shirlene while Colt was busy taking apart some old piece of junk in the yard. Those were the days before her life got better. *Before high school cliques. And before Slate Calhoun,* Colt thought.

"Don't act like you didn't like playing in here too." She sent him a smug smile before latching on to the big steering wheel and turning it back and forth. "Where do you want to go? New York? California? Paris?"

Unfortunately, the thoughts of Slate and high school had soured his disposition and the rebellious, belligerent kid he thought was long gone reared his ugly head.

"Come on now, Hope, don't tell me you've forgotten what we used to play."

She stopped twisting the steering wheel, and her hands tightened on the hard plastic. But she refused to look at him.

Rain or no rain, he should've pushed open the door and climbed out. But Colt had never known when to leave well enough alone. Or when to leave Hope alone, for that matter. His gaze followed a drop of rainwater that trickled down one flushed cheek, over a stubborn jaw, and along her soft throat to disappear beneath the damp collar of the flowered dress.

"Come on, honey," he breathed as his arm stretched out along the back of the seat. "I'll show you mine, if you show me yours."

Chapter Seven

"I DON'T KNOW WHAT YOU'RE TALKING ABOUT," Hope said as her gaze remained locked on the water cascading down the windshield.

Colt slid closer, blocking her view with miles of wet black T-shirt. She now understood why men were so enthralled with wet T-shirt contests. Wet cotton made for some mouth-watering fantasies, especially when shrink-wrapped to the hard, chiseled body in front of her.

As her gaze got stuck on the tiny beaded nipples topping each perfectly sculptured pectoral muscle, her breathing grew uneven. The seat was big enough that she could move back. Except that a strange paralysis had settled over her, and she couldn't move if she wanted to, especially when his hand came to rest on the steering wheel and his other on the back of her neck. A chill spread through her body, which brought his droopy-lidded gaze sliding down her soaked dress.

"Sure you do," he whispered, as his breath wafted over her face. It smelled of mint toothpaste and cool rain. "You know exactly what I'm talking about—sophomore year behind the girl's locker room."

Hope closed her eyes and tried to get a handle on her suddenly topsy-turvy world, but lack of vision only made matters worse when a hot hand skated up her bare leg. Her eyes flashed open as she grabbed his wrist.

"Stop." She tried to sound firm, but only came out sounding needy. She cleared her throat. "I mean it, Colt." Except it didn't really sound like she meant it.

Those sensual gray eyes stared back at her from beneath lowered lids. "Come on, honey," he coaxed as his fingers caressed the spot right above her knee. "Just a little peek." He leaned over, and his cheek brushed against hers, not as prickly as it had been in jail, but prickly enough to cause more chill bumps. "I promise not to tell a single soul—I never did."

The man knew exactly what to say. Always had. If he took a notion, he could tempt a nun from her habit. Hope was no nun, but she could count on one hand the times she'd had sex in the last year. So how could she fend off a desperado like Colt Lomax? A naughty outlaw who had no scruples about cornering her in an old Chevy while water cascaded down the windows like the best carwash fantasy she'd ever had?

So she gave in. Just a little. Just enough to let her eyes close in surrender. Just enough to lean into the mouth that trailed kisses down her neck. Just enough to loosen the grip she had on his hand.

But she refused to let it go. She might be sex-deprived, but she wasn't stupid. Although that didn't seem to stop his fingers from moving. In fact, her hand just went along for the ride, clinging tight to his wrist as he stoked a line of fire up her thigh. He caught the damp material of her dress on the way up, baring her legs to the chill of the air and the warmth of his fingers. Fingers that hesitated for a brief heart-dropping second before skating over the satiny smoothness of her panties.

She moaned and pulled back, needing air in the worst possible way. Releasing his hold on her neck, he allowed her the freedom, his gaze settling on her mouth for a moment before dropping down to the quivering need between her legs. He stared for sizzling seconds—a full mind-blowing minute.

"I have to say," his voice came out even more husky than normal as a finger flicked over her most quivery part of all. "I might even like these better than the cotton heart ones you wore in high school." He inched the dress even higher, until part of her stomach and hipbones were bared to his greedy gray eyes. His gaze returned to hers, all heat and desire.

"You want to get real naughty, baby?"

When put that way, she did.

She really did.

So she nodded and waited. Waited for those wonderfully talented fingers to dip into her panties and put out the fire that burned out of control. Except instead of diving in, he removed his hands and settled back against the door.

"So show me," he stated, his eyes smoldering.

She knew what he wanted; she just didn't know if she could give it to him. Never in her life had she stripped in front of a man. Pathetic but true. She might be loud and controlling, but she had always been modest about showing her bits and pieces. Which is why she had never collected any Mardi Gras beads to hang off her rearview mirror, or sunbathed topless, or chosen nude acting roles.

And those things had only dealt with her bits. Her pieces were an entirely different matter.

If she'd been thinking right, she would've jerked down the hem of her dress and called it a day. But she wasn't thinking right. After spending the last few weeks feeling like the most undesirable woman on the face of the earth, beneath his hot gray eyes she suddenly felt like the most desirable. And even though she knew it was a big mistake, she couldn't seem to help herself. There was something about Colt Lomax that brought out the naughty girl in her—that made her want to take a walk on the wild side. Or dive smack dab into an entire pool of wicked.

She just refused to be the only one making a fool of herself.

"Only if you show me yours."

Surprise flashed in his eyes before they steamed back up.

"Lead the way."

Now that she was the main attraction, crazy things started popping into her head. *I wish I'd taken the time to shave this morning. Or trim. Or even fluff and spritz with some intoxicating perfume. I wish I owned intoxicating perfume. Something that would make up for the lack of hair sculpturing. Would a big bad biker prefer Brazilian or native? Or maybe somewhere in between—a wild Brazilian—*

"I hate to hurry you, honey," Colt's voice interrupted her rambling thoughts. "But if you don't show me something soon, what I have to show you might not be all that impressive."

Her gaze flickered down to the bulge beneath soft damp denim, and she blushed. When she glanced back up, a smart-aleck grin creased his face. Which annoyed her. She might not be an expert in the art of seduction, but she wasn't a naïve schoolgirl anymore. If he wanted to play wicked, she could oblige him as well as any other woman.

Hooking her thumbs in the elastic of her panties, she slowly inched down the material, her fingers cupping her inner thighs and her thumbs forming a V around her moist—getting moister by the second—center. She kept her eyes on him, while he kept his eyes lowered, the heat of his gaze burning through his dark, thick lashes. She lifted her hips off the torn leather and slipped the satin down her thighs. The springs of the old seat squeaked, but not loud enough to cover Colt's intake of breath.

She dropped her hips back to the seat, allowing the hem of the dress to fall over her lap as she struggled to get the panties over her cowboy boots. It wasn't easy. And after getting one boot out, she gave up and left the scrap of satin dangling off the top of the other.

"Next time it might be easier, honey, if you just don't wear panties." Colt's voice strummed across her.

"There won't be a next time."

His hot gaze lifted. "Then I guess we better make this good." The *good* came out all sexy and sizzling as his eyes lowered to the spot between her legs.

But before she lifted her dress, she took a quick glance around. The rain had ended as quickly as it came, leaving behind sparkling rivers that trailed down the steamed-over windows. If she couldn't see out, no one could see in. So she leaned back against the opposite door and slowly eased up the dress. The soft fabric brushed against the tops of her thighs, teasing the throbbing spot between her legs before coming to rest just above her hipbones.

Colt's breath hissed through his teeth, and Hope glanced up. He hadn't moved, but his body seemed tighter than before, his hands clenched in fists on the knees of his faded jeans.

"Spread them," he said in a breathy groan.

Slowly, she separated her knees, settling one bent leg up on the seat and allowing the other to loll against the steering wheel. He didn't touch her, but he didn't need to. His gaze stroked over her most private parts like hot, skilled fingers as his breath grew more uneven. Her breathing followed his, and soon the air grew thick with restrained desire.

"Now you." Her voice came out needy and desperate.

Without taking his eyes off her, he slid a hand to the button on his jeans and flipped it open. Tooth by brass tooth, the zipper eased down over the hard fist of denim to reveal black cotton stretched to the limits. With a few simple adjustments, he was released, and it was Hope's turn to greedily eat him up with her eyes. His penis was smooth and hard with tiny veins pumping through it and a broad tip that held a trace of moisture. Her mouth went dry, and her heart did a funny little two-step.

"Nice," she croaked.

"Thank you. You want to touch it?"

She glanced up expecting to see a cocky smile, but instead there was only serious heat. She swallowed and tried to remember why she wasn't going to let things go any further than a little naughty fun. Of course, the day after was never fun. Especially when you had to confront the man you had naughty fun with.

Except she wouldn't have to confront Colt.

He was leaving.

Tomorrow.

So basically all she had to do was hide out for one day. How hard could that be? Of course, sex was out of the question. But touching was well within the parameters of naughty without getting nasty. And with the way she was feeling, it wouldn't take much naughty to send her right over the edge. Except about the time she leaned in to accept his offer, a cherub face pressed against the steamed-up, water-splashed glass.

"Kid!" she screamed as she drew her legs together and shoved down her dress.

"Now, honey," Colt sat up and reached for her. "I've got that covered. I never play without a raincoat handy."

"I'm not talking about me getting pregnant, you idiot!" She slapped at his hands. "I'm talking about a real kid!" She waved a finger at the window. "A kid who just saw my pieces!" She fumbled around for her panties, but when she shoved her other boot through the hole, the satin ripped clean in half.

Colt looked back at the window behind him. The kid was gone, but the face imprint was still there.

"Shit!"

While Hope stuffed her ruined panties in her boot, he readjusted. Although he had a hard time getting his zipper up.

"Damn it, I thought you told me nobody lived here!"

"That's what Mama said. And they probably don't." She leaned up and wiped a circle in the steam. "It's probably some kid from another trailer."

"Well, why the hell isn't he in school?"

"How would I know? Do I look like the principal?"

Once he had his jeans zipped and buttoned, it only

took a second for his temper to cool. And only another for him to chuckle.

"Well, I guess that's what we get for being naughty."

"Real funny." Hope glared at him. "Now we have to figure out how to get out of here without him seeing us."

The smile slipped. "Afraid to be caught with the Bad Boy of Bramble?"

She shot him a smug grin. "No more than you should be worried about being caught in a compromising position with a woman expecting twins."

"Point taken." He made his own circle in the steam. "Well, it looks like he's gone now. No doubt scared by that hog-calling squeal of yours."

"You are just a hoot a minute, Lomax." She shoved open the door and cautiously stepped out.

The rain had completely stopped, although it still dripped from the overhanging branches of the elm. Shaking out her damp dress, Hope looked around, but all she saw were piles of dripping junk. She was about to tell Colt that the coast was clear, when a black dog came bounding through the hedge that separated the property from the lot next door, quickly followed by her twin sister.

"Hope?" Those sweet-as-blueberry-pie eyes blinked in confusion. "What are you doing here?"

She slammed the door in Colt's face, just as Buster slapped his muddy paws on her chest and bathed her face in dog slobbers. She pushed him down, and, having been taught at an early age that the best defense was a good offense, she threw the question back. "What are you doing?"

Faith blinked. "I was trying to get Buster to come in out of the rain when I heard you yell." She looked back at the car. "Is someone in there?"

"No."

"But I think I see—"

"A little rain won't hurt a dog," Hope cut her off as she reached down and pushed Buster away from the door where he'd started to whine. "So quit fretting about Buster and get back inside before you catch your death."

"But..."

"No ifs, ands, or buts." She flapped her hands. "Go on with you. Mama would kill me if I let you get even a sniffle."

Stubbornness obviously ran in the family because Faith didn't move a muscle, except for the ones around those innocent eyes that she squinted at the car. But fortunately, after only a few seconds she gave up and looked back at Hope.

"I'm sorry about the baby thing."

A simple *sorry* didn't come close to making up for the last few days of hell Hope had had to endure. Between pregnancy advice and people fighting over shower dates, Hope was about ready to blow this town regardless of whether or not she had money or a plan. But since an angry tirade would only prolong the conversation, she had little choice than to accept.

"Apology accepted." She tried to brush the mud off the front of her dress. "Well, you better get inside, and I better get going."

"But what about Shirlene's brother?"

Hope's head came up, but she refused to look behind her. "What are you talking about? Everyone knows I wouldn't be caught dead with Colt Lomax."

Faith leaned closer and squinted even harder. "Are you sure? Because that looks exactly like the man I met

Saturday night, and the one I saw with you and Shirlene at the diner."

Releasing her breath in one drawn-out sigh of frustration, Hope turned back to the car. Sure enough, the steam had evaporated enough to see Colt sitting there, as clear as day. He stared back at her with one dark eyebrow hiked up along with a corner of his sexy mouth. Wasn't the man even smart enough to duck?

"Well, good mornin'," he drawled as he stepped from the car and squatted down to scratch a wiggling Buster. "Nothin' like a little rain shower to liven things up."

Faith might be a little princess, but she was no dummy. Her gaze swept over Colt's rain-soaked body, then back to Hope, then over to the car, and then back to Hope. And just that quickly, the sun rose in those wide blue eyes along with the biggest, most disgusting smile Hope had ever seen in her life.

"Well, good morning, yourself." If people could pop from happiness, Faith was about to bust like an over-inflated balloon. "So what brings you here, Mr. Lomax?"

"Kindness and charity, Mrs. Calhoun," Colt said with a smile almost as big. "I'm helping Hope deliver food boxes."

Faith looked back at her. "How sweet."

Hope's desire to pick up the rusted crowbar at her feet and use it to wipe off both white-toothed smiles was almost too much to bear, especially when Colt continued to enjoy himself at her expense.

"That's a mighty pretty dress you got on, Mrs. Calhoun."

Since it was almost an exact duplicate of Hope's—minus the mud—she threw him a glare as Faith blushed and held out the soft fabric.

"Why, thank you, but please call me Faith."

Yes, please.

Colt shook his head. "Well, I'd love to, but my mama would have my hide if I showed such disrespect to such a fine married lady."

Hope wanted to show them both disrespect and leave their butts in the dust of Shirlene's Navigator. Unfortunately, the keys were in the pocket of Colt's wet jeans. Besides, before she left, Hope had to convince her sister that she had no reason to be grinning like a Disney princess after all the wicked stepmothers had been banished to another kingdom.

"I sure hope you weren't delivering boxes in that thing," Faith said with just a tad bit too much innocence.

"No, ma'am." Colt leaned an arm on the roof of the Chevy. "Even I couldn't get this thing to run."

She nodded, and Hope wondered if maybe she would leave it at that. But she should've known better.

"So if it doesn't run, what were you doing?"

Hope opened her mouth to reply, but nothing came out. Damn! Where was a brain when you needed it.

"We were just reliving old times," Colt helped her out. "I used to live here, and Hope lived next door."

Faith's eyes widened, and she turned to Hope. "I didn't realize this was where you and Shirlene grew up. You lived in Bubba's trailer?"

Colt's gaze snapped over to Hope's, and she explained to both of them. "Some guy named Bubba Wilkes bought it off Daddy for a hunting lodge, and now my sister and Slate are living in it while Slate builds his house."

Colt smiled and turned to Faith. "So welcome to the world of trailer trash, Mrs. Calhoun."

Faith didn't seem the least bit concerned about the negative connotation. "Thank you. I have to say, it was a little overwhelming at first, but now I love my little trailer. I'll be sad when we move out this Saturday."

"Slate's new house is finished?" Hope asked, suddenly consumed with resentment.

"Everyone in town chipped in to help." Faith's eyes twinkled with happiness. "It's been like a dream come true."

Yeah, my dream, Hope thought.

Faith nodded back in the direction of Bubba's trailer. "Why don't you come over and I'll make you some tea." She glanced back at the car. "That's if you're finished... talking."

"No," Hope said.

Colt's eyebrows lifted. "We're not done...talkin', honey?"

Hope's eyes narrowed as Buster came back over and sniffed around her boots. "No, I mean we don't have time for tea. We need to finish delivering the boxes."

"But I thought—"

"Try not to think, Lomax. Your brain can't take the sudden exercise."

He chuckled before demonstrating the manners that Hope had lacked. "Thanks for the invite, Mrs. Calhoun, but Hope's right. We need to finish delivering the boxes before we get another gully washer. But maybe next time."

"I'd like that. You're coming to the game on Friday, aren't you?"

"I'm afraid not," Colt said. "The open road calls."

"That's too bad." Faith sounded truly upset as she glanced at Buster, who trotted back to her. "Buster, what do you have?" She reached down and tugged something from his mouth, and Hope stared in horror as her sister lifted her tattered blue panties up. "What in the world?"

Colt's shout of laughter had Hope whirling and stomping off, and he was still laughing when he caught up to her.

"Real funny, Lomax," she fumed as she waited for him to pull the keys from his pocket.

"Come on, Hope. Lighten up." He chuckled as he fought with the wet denim. "You're not mad your sister caught us as much as you're mad about her moving into a house you wanted—with the man you wanted. You need to work on hiding your jealousy, honey."

"At least I'm not a kiss-ass." She kicked at a rusted tin can as she mimicked him. "Good mornin', Mrs. Calhoun. What a pretty dress you've got on, Mrs. Calhoun."

"I wasn't kissing ass. It is a pretty dress." He pressed the button on the key ring, but the locks clicking up could not drown out her grumble. She reached for the door handle, but the locks clicked back down before she could open the door.

"Don't tell me you're jealous of the compliments I gave your sister," he stated with the grin still in his voice.

"Not hardly." She jiggled the handle, refusing to turn around and face him.

"Are you sure?" He moved up closer, caging her in by resting his hands on the roof of the Navigator. "Because I'm sure I could come up with something to compliment you on. Although with all that mud, it's not going to be easy...or the wet doggy smell wafting off you." He grunted when she elbowed him in the stomach. "Now don't go gettin' all bent out of shape, honey. That wet, matted Rastafarian-looking hair isn't so ugly." This time he sidestepped the elbow, although he didn't remove his arms. "No, seriously. There are times when you don't look so bad...times when you look—"

He cut off suddenly. And when he spoke again, his voice held awe and deep-felt emotion.

"Beautiful. Breathtakingly beautiful."

Something inside her went very still at the words. Still and wobbly, all at the same time. Probably because Colt had never complimented her in his life, and she didn't realize how much those simple words would mean. Especially coming from his mouth. Slowly, she turned and lifted her eyes to him.

But, obviously embarrassed, he refused to look at her, his gaze pinned to a spot over the top of the Navigator.

"I've never seen anything like it," he continued as she blushed. "I mean I've seen parts before, but nothing like..."

Parts? He had to be talking about what she'd shown him in the car. And while it wasn't exactly what she wanted to hear, it was nice to know he'd been so impressed. Although she refused to think about how many other parts he'd seen.

"But seeing that beautiful V-twin housed in its original package..."

Okay, V-twin was a little weird, but coming from a mechanic, probably not so much.

"And those rocker boxes."

Boxes. Last time she checked, she only had one.

Confused, she finally spoke up. "Rocker boxes?"

His gaze flickered down for only a second before flickering back up. "Just look at it." His arms dropped as he pointed a finger over the top of the Navigator.

Hope had to climb up on the running board to see what

he was pointing at. An old rusty motorcycle leaned up against a dinged-up washing machine, and it didn't take a rocket scientist to figure out which one Colt was talking about.

"A motorcycle," she fumed as she turned to him. "You've been talking about a motorcycle?"

He looked back at her in shock. "That's not just a motorcycle, honey. That's a 1941 Harley Knucklehead."

Anger bubbled up inside her, and when his gaze snapped back to the rusty piece of crap, she jumped down and jerked the keys out of his hand. But it took her starting the SUV for Colt to finally snap out of his daze.

"Hey, what are you doing?" He reached for the door handle, and she quickly locked the doors. But she did crack the window.

"What am I doing?" She smiled sweetly. "I'm leaving you with the most breathtakingly beautiful piece of machinery you've ever seen." She popped the truck into reverse. "You knucklehead."

Chapter Eight

THE MOTORCYCLE WAS A CLASSIC. A perfect example of American ingenuity.

Named for the V-twin engine's rocker boxes that looked like lined-up knuckles on a fist, the Knucklehead was one of the fastest bikes of its time. With its wrap-around oil tank, teardrop gas tank, and rocker covers, it became the model for all Harleys that followed.

Colt didn't know how it had ended up in a pile of junk. All he knew was that it hadn't been there when he lived in the trailer. He wouldn't have missed a gem like this. Which meant someone had dumped it there. Someone who didn't understand the value of such a bike. And if that was the case . . . finders keepers, losers weepers. Especially since Shirlene's husband, Lyle, still owned the property that the bike sat on.

"So you gonna chop it?" Tyler asked.

"I'm not sure." Colt ran a hand over the cracked leather of the sprung saddle seat. "It's a beauty just like it is."

"A beautiful pile of shit." Tyler shot a stream of tobacco juice out the open door of the garage.

"That coming from a man who drools over old Ford pickups."

"I guess everyone has their weaknesses. And yours has always been motorcycles. But good luck getting this one to run."

Colt glanced up. "Are you doubting my skills, T-bone?"

"Nope." Tyler adjusted the wad of tobacco in his lip. "I'm just remembering that other Harley you brought in."

Colt shook his head. "No comparison. That was a screwed up piece of crap, and I was all of fifteen."

Tyler placed his hands in his back pockets and smirked. "Still, it never reached the corner."

"This one will reach the corner and then some," Colt said, just as the rusted bolt he'd been trying to get off the engine case broke off in his socket wrench. He removed the bolt, to Tyler's chuckle.

"Now that's a pretty motorcycle." Tyler nodded at the custom chopper he had wheeled into the garage just that morning. Like Colt had figured, his bike had been hidden in the back shed. Parked next to the old Harley, it gleamed like a jewel of shiny chrome and metallic blue paint.

"So I thought you were leaving today," Tyler commented, as he leaned against a stack of tires.

"I am. Just as soon as I get this thing running." Colt sprayed more Liquid Wrench on the next bolt before he applied the socket wrench, but after a few fruitless minutes, he figured he would need to pull out Tyler's acetylene torch to get it loose.

"So you're staying a few months, are you?"

He sent Tyler an annoyed look. "A day, at the most."

"If you say so."

"I say so."

The words came out sounding pretty childish, and Tyler grinned as he walked back inside to answer the ringing phone.

Once he was gone, Colt tossed down the wrench and ran a hand through his hair. Tyler was right; it was going to take more than a day to get the bike running. With the rust and corrosion, it might take most of a year. So instead of sitting on the greasy garage floor, dirtying up the only pair of jeans he'd brought, he should be making arrangements to have the Knucklehead hauled back to his shop in L.A. where he had all the proper equipment to fix it.

Except something didn't feel right about using modern tools on a classic piece of history. The Knucklehead shouldn't be thrust into the twenty-first century so brutally, but rather babied in the small garage where Colt had taken apart his first carburetor with nothing more than a screwdriver and a pair of pliers, welded his first frame with a hand-held gas torch, and sanded his first gas tank, using nothing but a strip of 220-grit sandpaper and a little elbow grease.

Not that he planned on staying there until the bike was completely restored. But he had a few more days before he had to be in Austin. A few more days to spend with Shirlene, and a few more days to try to get inside a pair of satin panties that were as blue as the Texas bluebonnets that lined the highway to San Antonio.

Just the thought of what that strip of blue covered left him hotter than a tailpipe after an all-day ride. Which wasn't good. He had no business playing such naughty games with Hope. Hope was trouble with a capital T. Or more like tempting with a capital T. A temptation he needed to ignore if he wanted to keep his life as carefree as it was. Hope carried way too much baggage. Not only was she the town sweetheart, but she still had her heart set on catching someone like Calhoun—a hometown hero deeply rooted in Texas soil. And Colt was about as far from that as a man could get.

Of course, she might have her heart set on a respectable Texas boy, but her body seemed to like wild motorcycle bums just fine. And since that was the case, what was wrong with him offering her a little comfort after losing her lifelong beau? They were both consenting adults.

"Hey, mister. That's my motorcycle you're messin' with."

Colt looked up at the shadowy figure slouched in the open doorway of one garage stall. Taking the sunglasses out of the collar of his shirt, Colt slipped them on and studied the young boy in the beat-up cowboy boots, holey jeans, and stretched-out Spider-Man T-shirt. His hair was a bright strawberry blond that shot out in all directions like he hadn't combed it in a week, and his face still held the remnants of breakfast. Or possibly supper. Colt placed him at around ten or eleven, although he didn't know enough about kids to be sure.

"Did you hear me, mister?" The kid took two steps closer. "That's my motorcycle."

"Really?" Colt got to his feet and stretched out the kinks in his knees. "And I assume you have the papers to prove that."

His sunburned brow knotted as his dirty chin tipped up. "I don't need no papers. It's mine."

"Then what was it doing on Lyle Dalton's property?"

"I don't know nothin' about no Lyle Dalton. I was ridin' it down the road, and it ran out of gas, so I rolled it up into a yard."

Colt's eyebrows shot up. "Riding it down the road?" His gaze returned to the motorcycle that looked as if it hadn't been started since Kennedy was in office. "Is that so?"

"Yeah. And I was about to come and get it. Except you stole it before I could. And now I see that you busted it up." He pointed one grubby finger at the broken off bolt. "That's gonna cost ya."

Colt couldn't help but grin, which made the boy's big brown eyes turn even angrier.

"Are you makin' fun of me?"

"No, sir." Colt shook his head. "Although that has to be the worst lie I've ever heard. This motorcycle hasn't run for a good forty years and was probably on my brother-in-law's property for the last five."

"That's a lie!" The boy doubled up his fists. "I found it at the dump, and I rolled it home a week ago!"

Colt's eyes widened. The bike weighed five times more than the kid did, but for some reason, he didn't doubt for a minute that the scrappy kid had achieved such a feat. Especially if he lived out on Grover Road. Tough times made for tough kids. And if that was the case, then the whole finders keepers thing worked against Colt.

Unless the kid liked money more than he liked machines.

"Calm down." Colt held up a hand. "I didn't realize the Knucklehead belonged to you. How about if I give you a thousand for it?"

The kid seemed to stare right through him with eyes way too observant for such a small fry. Then, before Colt could even sweeten the deal, the boy whipped out a cell phone from his back jeans pocket.

"How do you spell that? N-U—"

"K-N," Colt supplied, stunned by the agility of the thumbs that flew over the keypad. When the kid finished punching buttons, he held up the phone with a wide grin, showing off a chipped front tooth.

"More like thirty thousand."

Colt's eyebrows hiked up at the number flashed at him. "For a running bike with all the original parts, not a rusted piece of scrap metal I'm not even sure I can get to run."

The kid gave him another steely-eyed look before his gaze wandered over to the gleaming chopper. "You make that bike?"

"Yes, but I had a little help."

"How much they pay you for something like that?"

"Enough."

"You know Jesse James?"

Colt hesitated, wondering how much he should tell the kid. Figuring it didn't make any difference, he answered truthfully. "I do."

With boots that appeared to be too big for his feet slapping against the concrete floor, the kid moved around the custom bike, examining it from all angles. "I'll tell you what, I'll trade you, even steven."

Colt bit back a smile. " 'Fraid not, buddy. That one's already sold."

"I'm not your buddy," he stated as he flipped a leg over the bike.

"Oh, no, you don't." Within two steps, Colt had the kid off the bike and back on the floor.

"Don't touch me!" The boy jerked back, almost dropping his phone.

"Then don't climb on my bike without asking."

His bottom lip protruded. "Well, now I ain't gonna sell you my bike at all." Slipping the phone back into his jeans pocket, he grabbed the handlebars and used the slanted heel of one boot to kick at the kickstand.

Since the bike wasn't his, all Colt could do was watch. But it wasn't easy, not when he had to fight down the urge to jump in front of the bike and fight over it like he was fighting for a Tonka truck at a playground. Instead, he pulled his wallet from his back pocket and took out a twenty, which was about all he had left after dropping the hundreds out at Grover Road.

"I'll tell you what." Colt tried not to beg. "Take this as earnest money, and then, if I can get it running, I'll have it appraised and give your parents thirty percent of whatever the appraisal turns out to be."

The kid stopped kicking and turned to him, his eyes riveted to the money. "Ninety percent, and we got a deal."

Colt had to give it to the kid. He was a wheeler and a dealer.

"Fifty and that's final."

"Seventy, and I get to help."

"Oh, no. I don't need some kid running around getting in my way. Besides, shouldn't you be in school?"

"I'm homeschooled." The reply came almost too quickly.

Colt's gaze narrowed on the innocent-looking face. No kid on Grover Road had ever been homeschooled that he knew of. Of course, no kid had an expensive cell phone with Internet access either. Obviously things had changed in the last eight years. Still, he wasn't about to have some obstinate little kid bugging him nonstop while he tried to work.

"Sixty, and you stay the heck away from the garage."

"Fine," he grumbled as he stuck out one grubby hand. "But I get to ride it once it's finished."

"Not in my lifetime." Colt smacked the twenty into his palm. "Now get out of here and let me work."

The kid stared at the money for a few seconds before he stuffed it in his front pocket.

"You better make sure there are no holes," Colt advised, before he sat back down next to the motorcycle.

"There ain't," he said. Out of the corner of his eye, Colt watched as the kid felt around in his pocket.

While Colt went back to work on the bike, the boy meandered around the garage with his hands stuffed in his pockets before he came back to sit on the other side of the Knucklehead. "I'm named after him, you know."

"Who?" he asked without looking up.

"Jesse James—the outlaw, not the motorcycle dude."

Colt shook his head.

It figured.

He felt like he'd just been held up.

Chapter Nine

A WEST TEXAS football game was something to behold—
not necessarily the game itself as much as the insanity
of the fans who attended it. The Bramble High Football
Stadium looked as if a huge purple paintball had been
dropped from overhead, splattering sweatshirts and jack-
ets, hair and faces, and even bare man-boobs and beer
bellies with the dark, vibrant color. Of course, this wasn't
just any game. This was a play-off game, the first in a
series that could lead to a state championship and another
year added to the WELCOME TO BRAMBLE sign at the city
limits. Pennants flew, pompoms waved, and balloons
floated amid the chattering, excited folks of Bramble.

But since the game had yet to start, the town's attention wasn't on the field as much as it was on Hope, as she
made her way up the steps of the stadium.

"Hey, Hope!" Kenny Gene blasted his air horn, and
Hope's heart almost jumped out of her chest.

"Hope, honey, don't be sittin' too close to the field,"
Rachel Dean yelled from her spot right behind the band.
Her purple foil wig glittered in the stadium lights as she

pointed two huge foam fingers straight at Hope like a double-barreled shotgun. "Some of Jimmy Daniels punts can go a little haywire, and we don't want you goin' into an early labor."

"Early would definitely be the word for it," Shirlene said from behind her.

Hope glanced back at her best friend. As usual, Shirlene was dolled up like a blonde bombshell—hair curled and fluffed, makeup artfully applied, and enough gold and diamonds to warrant an armed escort. And everything she wore, from the sky-high heels to the down jacket, was a deep Bramble High purple. Hope, on the other hand, had done nothing more than run a brush through her hair and slap on a sweatshirt.

Purple, of course.

"Up here, girls," her mother yelled, shaking her cowbell to get their attention.

Hope didn't particularly want to sit next to her mama, not when her mama was still convinced she was pregnant and nothing Hope said would change her mind. Jenna Scroggs had been a smothering mother before, but it was nothing compared to what she was now. They hadn't even reached her row, when Jenna started in.

"Hope Marie, don't tell me you forgot to bring a jacket? If I told you once, I've told you a thousand times—don't forget your jacket. And now ain't the time to catch a chill."

Since the jacket Hope had worn to every game since she was fifteen was now being worn by the woman sitting next to her mother, all she could do was shrug, which wasn't enough for her mama.

"Burl, take off your coat and give it to Hope. I don't want her catchin' a chill."

"I don't want Daddy's coat," she said, a little too loudly. "I'm not cold. In fact, I'm burning up." She was burning up, burning up with jealousy over an ugly purple letterman's jacket with more than a few state championship patches on the leather sleeves.

"Leave her be, Jenna," Darla butted in from the next row up, where she sat with her husband, Billy Joe. "I thought I would boil alive with my first one. Tyson was like havin' my own little heatin' pad tucked right inside my belly. Billy Joe swears we saved hundreds on our utility bills that year."

"She's right," Billy Joe agreed. "I didn't even need no blanket when snuggled up next to her."

Shirlene laughed. And since her friend thought the situation was so amusing, Hope shoved her into the row so she would be the one to sit next to Slate's coat and closer to her overprotective mother.

"Temper, temper, honey," Shirlene whispered back at her. "You don't want to hurt the twins, do ya?"

"Shut up, Shirl." Hope sat down on the purple-and-gold blanket that her mother had spread all the way down the bleachers, even though the only children living in Bramble were Hope and Faith. After the wedding, Hope's brother, Dallas, had headed back to the University of Texas in Austin. Jenna Jay had gone back to Texas Tech in Lubbock, and Tessa had returned to her job in Amarillo. Lucky ducks.

"Hi," Faith spoke so softly Hope could hardly hear her over the crowd's building excitement.

"Hi, honey," Shirlene patted Faith's Wrangler-covered knee. "You all packed up and ready to move into that gorgeous new home of yours?"

"There wasn't really that much to pack."

"Well, give it a few months, and I'm sure you'll have as much crap as I do."

"Doubtful," Hope grumbled.

Shirlene shot her a snide look before she got even. "'Course, crap or no crap, Hope and I will be there bright and early in the mornin' to help you move into your dream home."

"Really?" Faith leaned over and looked at Hope with enough wide-eyed gratitude to fill Cinderella's castle.

"What are sisters for," Hope said as sincerely as a jilted woman could. But Faith wasn't so easily fooled, and after only a second of staring into Hope's eyes, she glanced down at Slate's letterman's jacket, and all that Disney happiness fizzled right out of her.

"Of course, if you'd rather not help, I understand."

"Hope not help out a member of Bramble?" Shirlene sounded horrified. "Why that's like asking a wide-mouthed bass not to swim." She shot a warning look at Hope. "Isn't that right, Hog?"

"I'll be there with bells on," Hope said, although this time she refused to look her sister in the eye. Fortunately, Faith didn't push it and instead turned to answer a question her mama had asked.

"Just you wait, Shirl," Hope spoke under her breath. "Your day will come."

"My day has already come and gone, honey. The town loved to gossip about all my sexual exploits before I married Lyle, but after the weddin' no one seemed the least bit interested." She opened her huge purple designer purse and pulled out a bag of microwave popcorn. "Of course, I can't say as I blame them. Married life is about as boring as it gets."

Hope took a handful of popcorn. "Lyle still out of town?"

"Yes. And I have to tell you, I'm starting to get worried."

Hope choked on a kernel, and Shirlene tapped her on the back while her mama leaned over with a concerned look. After catching her breath, Hope waited for her mother to sit back before she whispered, "You think he's cheating?"

Shirlene's green eyes widened. "Of course not. Why would a man cheat when he could come home to this?" She fanned French-manicured nails down the front of the tight purple sweater. "No, I think it's something worse."

"What could be worse?"

"Try *no money*."

"Dalton Oil's in financial trouble—"

Shirlene slapped a hand over Hope's mouth before glancing around. "Would you keep it down, honey? We don't want a riot on our hands, do we?" After releasing Hope's mouth, Shirlene dove into the popcorn, as if she hadn't just brought up her husband's financial ruin.

"So what makes you think there's a problem?"

"Last time I was in Austin shopping, I had two of my credit cards rejected."

Hope snorted. "With the way you shop, Shirl, that's not a big deal. You probably just spent over the limit."

"Over a hundred-thousand-dollar limit? I'm a big spender, honey, but not that big. Which means Lyle isn't paying them off like he used to every month—which means something isn't right."

"Why don't you ask him about it?"

"I have, and he just keeps telling me not to worry my pretty little head over it."

"I hate to bring this up, Shirl." Hope leaned over for another handful of popcorn. "But isn't that what you wanted when you married him? You told me you never wanted to worry about money again."

"I guess you're right." Shirlene nibbled a few kernels before she turned to Hope. "But what if I should be worried? What if the well ran dry—literally?"

It was a terrifying thought. Dalton Oil employed half the town. If it went under, Bramble would too. It had happened to other small towns when their main source of income fell prey to a weak economy. But Hope couldn't believe that could happen to her beloved town—not when oil was what made the world go round.

"It's probably not as bad as you think," Hope tried to rationalize. "Maybe Lyle just got too busy and forgot to pay the credit cards off. And now that you brought it to his attention, I bet it's already been taken care of."

"Probably," Shirlene said, in between bites, although she didn't sound convinced. "But when I go to Midland for your baby shower decorations, I'm definitely taking cash."

Another kernel got stuck in Hope's throat, but this time a blast of disbelief shot it back out, and it sailed down three rows to land in Sue Ellen's purple spray-painted hair.

"Baby shower?" Hope shook her head. "Oh, no, you are not throwing me a baby shower, Shirl."

"Why, of course I am, honey. What kind of a best friend do you take me for?"

Before Hope could tell her exactly what kind of friend she took her for, the announcer's voice blasted through the speakers.

"Please stand for our national anthem!"

"I mean it, Shirl," Hope said as she stood and placed

a hand over her heart. "This foolishness has gone on long enough, and I'm certainly not going to let the good people of this town spend their hard-earned money on things I'll never use."

"Who says you'll never use them. You want kids, don't you?"

Hope had wanted kids. Cute little blonde-headed mini-quarterbacks and petite, brunette starlets, but that plan had gone to hell in her sister's handcart. Now all she wanted was to cuss out Shirlene, along with an entire town of people who refused to accept the truth.

Unfortunately, she was forced to drop the conversation when the Bramble High ROTC took the field; if there was one thing the folks of Bramble didn't put up with, it was disrespecting the American flag. And after the honor guard marched off the field, the roar of the crowd grew deafening as the team tore through the paper banner.

Slate was the last one to step through the tattered remnants. Without a hat, his hair shone like liquid gold in the bright stadium lights. When he reached the benches, he looked up at the crowd, his eyes searching until his gaze caught hers. Suddenly she was back in high school, standing on the sidelines in her cheerleading uniform, awaiting a smile and a wink from the most popular boy in school.

Except this time, his gaze moved on quickly, and she became nothing more than an observer to the warm, loving smile that he sent her sister, a sister who reciprocated with a blown kiss that Hope could've sworn made Slate blush.

The cheers grew louder, and Hope jerked her gaze away, only to be caught in the stormy depths of a pair of eyes she hadn't planned on seeing again.

Ever.

The pain in her heart moved to her butt.

Colt Lomax stood at the bottom of the bleachers in a tight black T-shirt that made him stand out in the sea of purple like the black sheep he was. He casually leaned against the concrete wall that ran in front of the stands, one biker boot crossed over the other and a worn leather jacket hooked over his tattooed arm.

He didn't look at her with loving warmth. More like steamy lust. Steamy lust that caused her breath to hitch and her heart to thump wildly. This man would never blush if she threw him a kiss; more than likely he would catch it and place it somewhere really nasty.

The pervert.

Of course, he wasn't the only pervert in the stands. Every time she was alone with the man, she broke every moral instilled in her since birth. Even now her body heated from the message in those devilish silver eyes.

If you show me yours, I'll show you mine.

"Colt Lomax!"

Hope jumped guiltily when Shirlene stood up and yelled.

"Quit blockin' the view and get your cocky butt up here!"

His eyes remained on Hope for a brief second more before he pushed away from the wall and ambled up the steps. Without asking permission, he sat down on the end of the bleachers, sandwiching Hope between his broad shoulders and Shirlene's puffy down jacket.

Faith leaned over and smiled down the row at him. "I thought you were leaving, Colt."

"Change of plans," he merely stated, before he reached over to grab a handful of popcorn, his bare arm brushing against Hope's boob in the process. She pulled back, only to run into Billy Joe's knees.

"Pardon me," she choked out, before sitting back up.

Meanwhile, Colt munched the popcorn as if nothing was amiss, although when he reached for the next handful, Hope quickly crossed her arms over her chest. One corner of his mouth twitched, but he didn't say a word.

With Colt sitting there smirking, she thought it would be hard to concentrate on the game. But it didn't take long for her to get caught up in the thrill of competition, especially when the Bulldogs' lanky quarterback had an arm that would make pro scouts drool.

The kid's talent quickly turned the game into a rout, so much so that Hope's attention began to wander. Unfortunately, it didn't wander very far. In fact, no more than a few inches, to the man who sat with his arms propped on his hard thighs and his gaze riveted to the field.

His dark hair didn't shine like liquid gold in the stadium lights, but rather gleamed like Shirlene's polished onyx kitchen countertops as it spilled over the ribbed neck of his black T-shirt. A T-shirt that stretched over broad shoulders and lean back muscles, stopping just short of the waistband of his jeans. A very tiny bit of skin peeked out, just enough to make Hope swallow hard and shiver.

He glanced over. "Are you cold?"

Since she wasn't about to claim otherwise, she nodded and, within seconds, found herself engulfed in the folds of his thick leather jacket.

"No, really..." She tried to slip it off, but her mother jumped in.

"Don't be rude, Hope Marie."

Not wanting to cause a scene, she acquiesced and

slipped her arms into the smooth satin lining. It smelled of him—raw and dangerous, something she tried not to notice as her gaze returned to the game. But only a few seconds later, her eyes left the green of the field to stare down at the tattooed arm resting on one knee.

It was the first chance she'd had to study the tattoo up close—in the Chevy, her mind had been riveted on a different part of his anatomy. Still, the blue-ink design was so cluttered and detailed it took her a few minutes to figure out what it was.

A snake coiled around the corded muscles of his forearm, its opened-fanged mouth poised over the huge knot of Colt's biceps and its rattle curled around his wrist like the watch he never wore. Along the diamond-backed reptilian body, other tattoos jutted out. The front forks and tire of a motorcycle. A banner with "Desperado" written across it. A tombstone with his father's initials. The Texas state flag. A queen of diamonds playing card. A thorny rose. And at the very top, peeking out from beneath the tight sleeve of his shirt, was some kind of snarling animal.

A wolverine?

A javelina?

Hope leaned closer. But before she could figure it out, his arm moved from beneath her nose, and she glanced up into Colt's curious, gray eyes. Caught in the act, there wasn't much she could do.

"What kind of animal is that?" She pointed.

"A rattlesnake."

"Not that one. The one—" Before she could finish, he jumped up.

"I'm headed to the snack bar. Anybody want anything?"

"More than you can carry, big brother." Shirlene quickly

got up to go with him. Surprised that Shirlene would leave a football game for food, Hope glanced back at the field, only to discover it was halftime. Where had the time gone? There was no way she had been looking at Colt for an entire quarter. But as the band performed their marching routine, she realized she'd done just that.

Stunned by the revelation, she didn't pay much attention when Emma Jean flopped down next to her and started chattering up a storm.

"...and she's only been doin' this for a couple months, but I think she's got real talent, and I just know with your expert Hollywood advice she can go on to great things—possibly even a hemorrhoid commercial." Emma Jean pointed out at the field. "Look, there she is! Isn't that the cutest little outfit you've ever seen in your life? I wanted to get it in the school colors, but wouldn't you know it, it only comes in red, white, and blue—which is almost as good."

A little girl strutted out on the field in a white cowboy hat and a sequined outfit with a blue star on the front. She wore little white boots with huge blue tassels and red sequined cuffs around her wrists. Hope had to admit that she looked cute and was about to say so, when she noticed Emma Jean's husband, Chester, following behind her, holding two batons and a blowtorch.

"Oh, no." Hope shook her head. "I don't think this is a good idea, Emma. Especially if she's only been doing this for a couple months. I mean, I'll be more than happy to help her anyway I can—"

Before she could finish, the blowtorch flamed, and the batons were lit and handed to the little girl, who didn't look the least bit worried. Obviously, she'd done this before. But that didn't stop Hope from leaning forward in fear.

The band struck up "You Are My Sunshine," and flaming batons took flight. And darned if the little girl didn't manage to toss and twirl those burning sticks like a pro. Impressed and relieved, Hope stood and clapped and whooped as loudly as the rest of the crowd as the performance ended in a blur of whirling fire and a cute little hat-tipping bow. The batons were handed off to her daddy, who was beaming like any proud papa should.

Hope sat back down and sighed in relief.

It was a tad bit premature, because while Chester had brought something to light the batons with, he'd failed to bring anything to put them out. And while most people might snuff them on the ground, football turf was as sacred as the Shroud of Turin to the people of West Texas. So he stood there with the flaming sticks, uncertain what to do or where to go. Things might've turned out alright if the team hadn't come out of the locker room, forcing the band to leave the field.

Hope had never been in the marching band, but she'd listened to enough practices to know members did not get out of line for anything less than a natural disaster. And these kids had learned the lesson well. Without breaking file once, they marched right past those flaming batons as if they weren't there—eyes straight ahead and instruments held vertically in front of them as a drummer tapped out a beat.

Chester did his best to avoid bare faces and hands, and it was easy to see where his daughter got her baton-twirling skill. As the tuba section left the field, it looked as if a catastrophe had been avoided. It wasn't until the band members took the steps back up to the bleachers that Hope noticed the flaming poof on the cap of a trombonist.

"Fire!" Hope hollered at the top of her lungs and pointed down at the kid.

Everyone froze.

Everyone except Colt, who was headed back from the snack bar. Retaining the 64 oz. Big Slurp, he handed the tray of nachos off to Shirlene before knocking the hat to the ground and stomping out the fire with one big biker boot.

Hope might've commented to Emma Jean about his quick reflexes if her attention hadn't been caught by the giant of a man who had just entered the stadium behind Colt.

It had been years since she'd seen Rachel Dean's cousin Bear, and she had forgotten how appropriately he'd been nicknamed. Bear stood a good head and a half taller than the other men who were filing back into the stands with their nachos and drinks.

Except Bear wasn't carrying a cardboard tray of goodies. Instead, his huge paw was clamped over the shoulder of the short man that he pushed in front of him. A man Hope recognized immediately.

"Sheldon?" Hope spoke more loudly than she intended, her voice quieting the mutters that had started after the fire had been put out.

Bear looked up and grinned broadly, flashing an incomplete set of tobacco-stained teeth. "See, Harley," he yelled as he shoved poor Sheldon up the stairs. "I told you I would find the baby's daddy!"

Chapter Ten

"Too bad Sheldon didn't turn out to be the daddy," Kenny Gene said as he piled his paper plate high with food the women of Bramble had brought to feed the crowd that had showed up to move Slate and Faith into their new home. "Besides that sissy fit of tears he broke into when he saw Hope, I kinda liked the little feller."

Standing beneath a cedar tree behind Slate and Faith's just-completed house, Colt couldn't help feeling a little annoyed. He might not want to be part of the daddy-hunt, but it was a little ego-deflating that he didn't even rate above a man who wore orange pants and used more hair products than Twyla. If Sheldon was straight, Colt would eat Kenny Gene's hat.

He took another bite from his own heaping plate of food, while he continued to eavesdrop on the group of townsfolk clustered around the long table.

"Still," Sheriff Winslow wiped the barbecue sauce off his chin with the edge of the paper napkin tucked into the collar of his uniform shirt, "since Hope insisted we throw this one back, Harley says the hunt is still on." He glanced over at Bear, who sat at the end of the table in front of two heaping plates. "But this time, Bear, try to pick out one who doesn't act like Darla's nephew."

"I'll do my best, Sam," Bear said, over the sparerib he'd been annihilating.

At that point, Colt probably could've stepped in and tried to set things straight about Hope not being pregnant. It would be the right thing to do. But Colt had never done the right thing where Hope was concerned, and it seemed a shame to start now.

His gaze wandered through the crowd until he found her. She wore jeans today. Not tight Wranglers, but worn jeans with a relaxed fit that hung low on her hips, along with a long-sleeved navy T-shirt with the name of a California surf shop printed on the front, and a pair of flip-flops that showed off her pretty pink-painted toenails.

The October sun had reddened her nose and deepened the tan of her cheeks, a tan that had been brought to his attention in the front seat of the beat-up Chevy. And in the last few days, he'd thought of little else but the tiny triangle of pale skin Hope had revealed beneath her panties. Even now, he had to do a little covert adjusting at just the thought of Hope in the tiny bikini that had left that triangle. The kind of bikini with ties that took only a swift tug to undo.

Hope glanced up, and he got lost in the blue of her eyes. A blue that turned all dark and sensual, as if she, too, was thinking about their naughty fun. Of course, her eyes didn't remain sensual for long. It only took a few blinks before the passion turned to annoyance.

But her sass made Colt even hotter, and he tossed the remainder of his food into the trash bag taped onto the table, with the intention of joining the group of townsfolk that she was talking with. But before he could make his way through the crowd, a strawberry blond head of hair caught his attention, and he looked over to see Jesse stuffing his face with a hot dog, the ketchup dripping off the end onto his Batman T-shirt.

"Hey, Kenny," Colt said. "You know that kid?"

Kenny looked up from his plate at Colt and registered surprise. "Hey, Colt, when did you get here?" He glanced around. "What kid?"

"The one over by the hot dogs—Jesse."

Kenny's eyes landed on the boy, who had moved on to the chicken wings. "Sure, everyone knows Jesse. I bought Twyla one of them stand-up hair dryers from him that made her happier than a pig in mud."

Sam Winslow jumped in. "He sold me a wet vac that had more suction than a ten-dollar hooker—" He shut up when Darla walked past. "Anyway, that thing was well worth the thirty dollars I gave him."

Colt couldn't help but grin at the kid who was now munching on a wing. No wonder Jesse could afford the fancy cell phone. The kid was a real shyster.

"What does his father do?" Colt asked.

"He doesn't have a daddy," Sam said. "Just a mama that works nights at that truck stop on 87."

"I thought she worked cleaning rooms at a hotel in Lamesa," Kenny leaned over the table and snagged a cookie. "Least ways that's what Jesse's big sister told me when she picked up the money for that hair dryer—pretty thing, but not real friendly."

The thought of a single mom working two jobs made Colt reevaluate the deal he'd made with Jesse. Of course, knowing how prideful people on Grover could be, he couldn't just hand the woman a check. But once he finished the bike, he could jack up the appraisal.

"Would you look at our little Hope," Sam pulled Colt's attention away from Jesse. "It looks like she's back to her old self."

Sure enough, Hope was giving Harley Sutter an earful. At first, Colt thought she was ranting about her gay friend getting kidnapped. But when he walked over, he realized she was rattling off from a list that she held in one hand.

"...and the storefronts along Main need some paint. And we could use another stoplight to keep the out-of-towners from speeding—I was thinking right on Spruce, near Josephine's, since it might pull in more business. And what happened to that hotel chain building a hotel in Bramble?" She tapped the list. "Oh, and there's a pothole on the corner of Maple and Main that needs fixing."

Harley chuckled, and his mustache twitched. "Now that's the goddaughter I remember—always trying to take my job."

Hope snorted. "Not hardly, Uncle Harley. I just wanted to point out some things that need fixing."

"All things I've noticed for myself. But money has been a little tight the last couple years. And with Dalton Oil cuttin' back, it doesn't look like it's going to get better anytime soon."

"Cutting back?" Hope's eyes turned concerned.

Harley patted her shoulder. "Nothing to get upset about. Just a little tightenin' of the belt, from what I hear."

Since Desperado Customs also had to cut back on spending from time to time, Colt wasn't concerned about Lyle's company. But Hope wasn't so easily pacified.

"Will anyone lose their jobs?"

"Of course not. They probably won't hand out Wal-Mart gift cards for Christmas this year, is all."

Colt could tell by the look on her face that Hope didn't completely believe him. But she allowed Harley to change the conversation to the upcoming Halloween carnival and Thanksgiving Day Parade. Colt didn't really care about carnivals or parades. He only had a day before he left town, and he planned on spending it trying to get in Hope's panties. But it wasn't easy to distract a woman who was as single-minded as Hope. His own mind had about exhausted itself, when Slate and Faith showed up.

Faith led her husband by the hand, as if she was forcing him to do something he really didn't want to. And Colt figured out what that something was when Slate opened his mouth.

"I want to thank you for helping out, Colt." He glanced over at his wife. "If I'd known how many different configurations a couch could be put in, I would've bought a couple of beanbag chairs and been done with it."

"Shush, you." Faith swatted at him, and then laughed when Slate pulled her into his arms and snuggled her neck.

The open show of affection had Colt glancing over into Hope's hurt eyes. He couldn't really blame her. The guy had built a house with his own two hands. Damn, you couldn't get any more perfect than that. Hope had the right to be bent out of shape, and having it shoved in her face at every turn couldn't be easy…something that might play right into Colt's hands.

"You're welcome," Colt said. "But I probably should get going." He turned to Hope. "Since my ornery sister seems to have left already, did you need a lift?"

Without a moment's hesitation, she answered. "If it's no problem."

"No problem, at all." Colt tried to contain his smile, while Faith didn't even attempt to hide her enthusiasm for the idea.

"If you're riding on Colt's motorcycle, you'll need some boots," she offered, before she scurried back inside.

The cowboy boots were bright red and sexy as hell. Colt had a hard time keeping his eyes off them as Hope braided her hair and waited for him to pull the helmet and leather jacket out of the side bags he used when traveling.

"I don't need the jacket," she stated.

"Believe me, you'll feel differently after a few minutes in a fifty-mile-an-hour wind."

Surprisingly, she didn't argue, but slipped her arms into the jacket that he held out. Once she had it zipped, he handed her the helmet. It was too big, but it would have to do. She struggled with lacing the strap, so he brushed her hands aside and did it for her. But the feel of the soft skin beneath her chin distracted him so much that it took him a couple tries.

"It's a pretty bike," she said, her breath falling over his face, all warm and sweet.

But it wasn't her breath that left him feeling like he had just planted the American flag on the moon. It was on the tip of his tongue to tell her that he had built the bike, was involved from its conception to the last spit and polish. But before he could, her mouth quirked up in a smirk.

"Not eighty thousand pretty," she completely deflated him, "but pretty."

"I guess I'm just a sucker." He jerked the helmet strap tight before he walked around the bike to flip down the passenger foot pegs. Most choppers didn't have pegs or a small removable leather seat that fit over the back fender. But his client had a wife, although Colt wasn't sure for how long, after the woman spent a few hours straddling the hard metal.

Colt didn't plan on riding that long. Just long enough to get Hope somewhere less populated.

After climbing on the bike, he turned and helped her on. Then he flipped down the visor on her helmet before he took his aviators from the collar of his shirt and slipped them on.

"You ready?"

"Yes," came her muffled reply.

He turned the electric switch on the chrome analog dash and punched the starter. The engine roared to life, and the loud throb soothed his bruised ego as he settled back on the form-fitting leather seat and released the clutch. He eased the slick machine over the gravel drive and out onto the blacktop. Hope's hands rested on her knees, until the bike bounced over the edge of the asphalt, and then she quickly latched on to his waist.

He smiled.

Okay, so maybe a passenger wasn't such a bad thing.

Colt took his time on the side roads, cruising no faster than thirty. But when he turned onto the highway, he twisted the throttle, and the bike took flight. Hope slid back before her arms and thighs tightened, and she slid back up, the edge of the visor bumping against his head. Of course, a sledgehammer could've dropped from the sky and he wouldn't have cared, not with those sweet thighs locked around him. Heat emanated from the spot pressed against his lower back, taking the chill right out of the wind that whistled past them.

The pretty autumn scenery took a backseat to hot

images of tanned thighs spread wide and waiting. Desire knotted in his stomach, and his crotch started to throb more intensely than the engine. He tried to keep his mind on the road, but it was difficult with two soft hands inches from the brain he was now using.

Hope seemed to be falling right into his plans to get her into bed; now all he had to do was figure out what bed. He didn't think she'd go willingly back to Shirlene's guesthouse. Nor could he take her back to her house. Not when Jenna and Burl could arrive home at any minute. And a hotel was a good fifty miles away.

That left only one other place.

He expected Hope to start yelling and pounding his back when he turned off the highway—even an unbaffled motor was no match for a champion hog caller. But, strangely enough, she didn't show any signs of protest.

The road to Sutter Springs was unpaved, and it took all his concentration to finagle the bike around the ruts. Once there, he pulled under the big cottonwood and cut the engine. Before she could ask what they were doing, he quickly tried to come up with a feasible excuse.

"Since you're not used to riding, I thought you might need a little break."

She slipped off the back of the bike, taking those sweet thighs with her.

"Geez." She rubbed her butt. "You really need to come up with a better backseat."

With his eyes glued to the way the soft denim clung to the sweet hills, he couldn't comment.

Undoing the strap beneath her chin, she pulled the helmet off. "You would think with as much as the bike cost, they could add a little more cushion." She slipped off the jacket and placed it, and the helmet, on the seat. Then she stretched her hands over her head, showing off a strip of tanned stomach that finished off the moisture in his mouth.

Colt turned away, hoping to get some kind of control over his out-of-control libido. "Custom choppers aren't really made for passengers."

"Then who invented the little seat?"

"A guy who was hoping to get lucky."

"Well, you didn't get lucky, Lomax." She moved over to the shade cast by the shimmering gold leaves of the cottonwood tree.

Finally able to move without causing himself pain, he pulled out a rain poncho from one of the side bags and walked over to spread it out under the tree.

"So why are you still here?" she asked, once they were both seated on the poncho. "I thought you would be long gone by now."

Leaning back on his elbows, he cocked a brow at her. "I could ask you the same thing, especially when it seems painful for you to be around your sister and Slate."

"It's not painful," Hope snapped.

"Really?"

"Okay." She crossed her arms and looked away. "So it's a little painful. So what? I'll get over it."

He reached out and grabbed a blade of buffalo grass and placed it in his mouth. "I don't doubt it for a minute, especially since you've lived five years without him."

"That was different."

He shrugged. "Well, I'm not an expert, but true love seems like it would get a little antsy after five years."

"You're right. You're not an expert." Hope shot him a

snide look. "Did you ever even have a girlfriend—and I'm not talking about one-nighters."

He tipped his head. "You sure you don't want to talk about one-nighters? Because some of the best times I've had have been one-nighters."

He didn't expect her to take the bait. Hope had always had a selective memory. He only wished he could be as fortunate, but with those glossy lips in front of him, memories sizzled through his brain as if they had happened only yesterday.

"Never mind," she said as she turned and looked at the horizon. "I should've known I couldn't have a normal conversation with you."

"A few."

Hope looked back.

"I've had a few girlfriends, but nothing serious," Colt said, truthfully. "And what about you? And I'm not talking about gay roommates."

"Who said Sheldon was gay?" When his eyebrows hiked up, she conceded. "Okay, but he's also a very nice guy who helped me out when I first arrived in L.A. and who didn't deserve to be dragged halfway across the country by a crazy bounty hunter. I'll be shocked if he doesn't sue the entire town."

"He won't. From what I could tell, he has a major crush on Bear. Besides, Shirlene pampered the hell out of him and flew him home first-class." He pulled the blade of grass out of his mouth and tossed it away. "So what happened in L.A.?"

It hadn't been hard to figure out that Hollywood hadn't been kind to Hope. He had dated his fair share of women with stars in their eyes and had listened to countless horror stories of tough casting directors and endless auditions.

Most never made it past a few commercials or a couple lines in a B-movie. It wasn't anything to be ashamed of. But Hope wasn't one to own up to defeat. Which was why he was shocked when she answered so honestly.

"I sucked."

A snorted laugh popped out of his mouth and earned him a vicious look from her sky blue eyes.

"Don't get all feisty." He held up a hand. "I wasn't laughing at you. I was laughing at your choice of words."

"I don't know why," Hope said. "Those were the exact words you used after my debut performance in *Annie Get Your Gun*. Are you telling me you lied?"

"I might've stretched the truth a little. You weren't that bad." When she glanced over at him with a look of disbelief, he added, "I mean, some parts weren't so bad—the scenes where you didn't look terrified."

"I wasn't terrified. I was merely nervous. And who wouldn't be nervous when the gun in their hand held a live round?"

"Come on, Hope," he pressed, "be honest. The only reason you took drama your senior year was because Shirlene wanted to. And the only reason you ended up as Annie was because Shirlene got the flu and couldn't do it. Still, I might've believed you stumbled onto your one true passion if I hadn't been sitting in the audience that night. The girl I saw up on the stage looked like she was about to throw up—and not from happiness."

"I did throw up," she stated. "Right in the back of the wagon Daryl Watts loaned to the drama department."

He laughed, and this time she joined in. The sun had dipped even lower, low enough to spill beneath the aging leaves of the cottonwood, gilding her face and catching the natural highlights in the lock of hair that had come undone from her braid. *Cute* and *sassy* had always been the words that came to mind when he thought of Hope. But now the word *beautiful* joined the list.

And the realization caused him to sober.

Just as quickly, she stopped laughing and tipped her head to one side in confusion. "What?"

Since the entire beautiful thing was out of the question, he pointed to the speck of barbecue sauce just below her bottom lip. "You've got something right there."

She swiped at her chin. "Did I get it?"

Being a man of few words, he reached out and took care of it himself. At the first touch of her soft skin, his finger lingered, then took a detour up to her mouth. Her lips opened, and a hot, moist puff of air caressed his finger, sending a shaft of heat straight to his stomach...and lower.

Cradling her jaw in his hand, he tipped her chin up with his thumb and leaned in.

"I think we missed a spot," he breathed, before he lowered his mouth for a deep taste.

He expected some sort of refusal. Hope had never come easy. But instead, her mouth opened in sweet surrender, offering up spicy heat that, if he hadn't been sitting, would've brought him to his knees. He took full advantage, sweeping his tongue into the warm recesses and coaxing her tongue into a sensual dance of give and take. But soon the connection of mouth and hand were not enough, and he crawled closer, bringing her up with him as he came to his knees.

She accommodated their differences in height by hooking her arms around his neck and straining closer as his hands slipped down to the sweet blue-jeaned cheeks he'd spent the last few nights dreaming of. Or possibly the last fifteen years. The firm flesh filled his palms as he pressed her closer to the hardened fly of his jeans.

The snap and zipper of her jeans came undone without a hitch or argument, and within seconds, he had his hands beneath the denim. He stroked and teased each cheek until she quivered in his arms like the golden leaves overhead. And still it wasn't enough. Patience had always been one of his virtues, but he wanted her naked. And he wanted her naked now.

The T-shirt slipped easily over her head, but the front snap of her bra took more than a few tries. Finally it slipped open, and he pulled back to look at what he'd exposed.

Sweet Lord.

He'd been right. She did own a teeny bikini. Two tiny white triangles encased sweet dollops of crème topped with deep raspberry nipples.

"Don't you dare laugh, Lomax," she said in a shy whisper.

"Oh, honey," he breathed as he lifted two very shaky hands and slipped off the thin pink bra straps from her shoulders. "As God is my witness, these are the most beautiful things I've ever seen." His hands slid over each one, cradling the softness. "The most beautiful things..." Unable to resist, he dipped his head and gave one small beaded nipple a gentle kiss. "Beautiful..."

"Colt," she groaned, and her hand came to rest on the back of his neck, pulling him closer as her head fell back.

He swept his tongue over the rigid tip, circling it a few delicious times before pulling it into his mouth.

"I want you," she stated as her fingers restlessly fluttered through his hair.

"And I want you too, baby." He continued to sip and stroke. "More than you will ever know."

"No." Her fists closed around his hair, and she tugged hard enough to bring tears to his eyes. "Now. I want you now."

Well, if she insisted.

His mind struggled with the logistics.

Hard ground.

Rough tree.

Small bike.

The ground won out. But before he could do more than kiss his way up her neck, a noise broke through his lust. A noise he instantly recognized as a truck engine—undeniably Chevy.

Shit.

Easing back, he took a moment to absorb the glorious bounty of Hope's bare-chested surrender. The soft breasts and wet peaks gilded in golden sunlight. The curved waist and tanned stomach sloping down to the opened V of her jeans and the tantalizing peek of white lace. The sexual droop of those blue eyes as they stared back at him. It took every ounce of willpower he had to reach down for the bra and slip it back on.

"What?" She blinked back to reality, and saying goodbye to those lust-filled eyes was like a swift kick in the gut.

"Company," he croaked, desire still high in his throat.

"Company!" She grabbed at the bra as the truck engine grew louder.

"Look, honey," he tried to keep the desperation out of his voice. "Why don't we go on back to Shirlene's? I've got the guesthouse all to myself—"

"Not a chance, Lomax," she stated with so much vehemence it left no hope.

No Hope, at all.

Chapter Eleven

"Isn't this the most fun y'all have ever had?"

Faith and Hope exchanged dubious glances as Shirlene came out of the kitchen carrying a large tray of brownies and drinks. Dressed in cow pajamas with a tiara perched around her high ponytail, she looked like a little girl. A little girl with over-developed breasts and no clear idea of what constituted fun.

"I can't believe you both wanted milk over margaritas." She plopped the tray down on the glass-topped coffee table, sloshing milk and green liquid over the rims of the tall glasses. "It's like you share the same addled brain."

"Not hardly," Hope said, although it was weird that she and Faith had said "milk" at the exact same time.

"I don't know what you would call it." Shirlene took the margarita glass and flopped down on the couch next to Faith. "Not only do y'all speak at the same time, but you've got that whole twin dress-alike thing down pat."

...A twin dress-alike thing that had really started to annoy Hope. Every time she turned around, Faith was wearing the same outfit that she was. And every day it

became Hope's goal to screw things up by switching out-
fits a couple times before leaving the house, but damned
if she still didn't come face-to-face with her mirror image.
Thank God the woman had short hair. Although in the
last few weeks, it seemed to have gotten longer.

"Of course, I think it's absolutely adorable," Shirlene
continued, her eyes twinkling back at Hope. "I mean, just
look at you two."

Hope glared down at the flannel pajamas with the silly
flying pigs on them. "Adorable if you're seven."

Picking up a brownie, Shirlene sent Hope a wounded
look. "You mean you don't like the pajamas I bought you,
Hope?"

"Of course, she likes them," Faith hurried to smooth
things over. "She just…"

"She just feels ridiculous sitting here in a pair of
ugly pig pajamas with a dumb tiara on her head," Hope
grumbled.

"You don't like the tiaras I brought?" It was her sister's
turn to look hurt, except her look wasn't fabricated.

But even though she'd started to feel some kind of big-
sister sensitivity toward Faith, Hope refused to backpedal.
Not when at any time, Colt Lomax could come waltzing
into the house and have enough ammunition to amuse
himself for a good month. Not that she cared what Colt
thought. It was just that…she cared what Colt thought.
And had always cared what he thought. Be it about her
pink cowboy boots or her acting ability, Colt's opinion
mattered. It shouldn't, but damned if it didn't.

"No, I think they're dumb." Hope reached up to pluck
the tiara off her head, but Shirlene had french-braided the
thing right to her scalp.

"Now, honey, don't be such a party pooper." Shirlene lifted the plate of brownies and offered them to her. "Here, have some chocolate. I read it's good for mood swings."

"I'm not having mood swings, Shirl," Hope said as she tried to twist the tiara free. "Geez!" She gave up and flopped back on the couch, glaring at both of the grinning fools. "What was I thinking, accepting an invitation to a slumber party at your house, Shirl?"

"You were thinking about how much fun we used to have at sleepovers." Shirlene set the plate back down. "And you'd be having fun now, if you'd pull that corn cob out of your butt." Lifting the margarita glass, she took a big sip before she winked. "Come on, Hope, let loose and get a little wild."

Get a little wild? Oh, Hope had gotten a little wild, which was exactly why she sat there as tight as a brand-new pair of boots. Because a little wild was no longer enough. She wanted to go hog wild with a certain dark-headed, nimble-fingered motorcycle bum. A motorcycle bum who was only yards away. So close that her mind kept bringing up images of smoldering eyes, tight wet T-shirts, and warm, skilled lips.

Reaching out, Hope snagged a brownie off the plate and bit into it. The rich chocolate melted between her tongue and the roof of her mouth, but it did nothing to alleviate her cravings.

"So?" Shirlene pulled her bare feet up on the couch and tucked them under her. "What should we do now? Watch a chick flick? Paint our toenails—which Faith looks like she desperately needs? Or play a little Truth or Dare?"

Since Truth or Dare was the last thing Hope wanted to

play, she quickly tried to answer, but ended up choking on a chunk of brownie as Faith took the bait.

"Truth or Dare? I've always wanted to play that game."

"Then Truth or Dare it is," Shirlene said, before looking at Hope, who had finally dislodged the brownie. "Since Faith hasn't played, I'll go first. Start me off, Hog."

Resigned, Hope flopped back on the couch. "I don't know why I have to ask, you always choose Dare."

"I do not, so quit stalling."

"Fine. Truth or Dare?"

"Dare."

Hope rolled her eyes and wondered why in the world she had chosen such an annoying woman as her best friend.

Reaching for another brownie, Hope tried to think up a good dare. It wasn't easy. Not when Shirlene loved dares as much as her outlaw brother. She could have Shirlene strip off her cow pajama top and race around the outside of the house three times, but Shirl had never much minded getting naked. Nor did she mind making a fool of herself. In fact, Shirlene was up for just about anything.

Well... maybe not anything.

"All right." Hope smiled evilly. "I dare you to attend First Baptist every Sunday for the next month."

That got a rise out of her friend, and her size nine feet hit the Oriental rug beneath the coffee table with a thump.

"You know full well, Hope Marie Scroggs, that it has to be something I can do tonight—not next Sunday or the Sunday after. Besides, if folks caught me at church, they'd figure hell froze over and start sinnin' up a storm."

While Hope tried to come up with another dare, Faith spoke in her quiet voice. "How about not drinking for the rest of the night?"

Hope choked on the drink that she'd just taken, and milk rushed up her nose. But since this time it was at Shirlene's expense, she didn't mind so much.

"Oh, no, honey." Shirlene held up a hand. "That's not a good dare."

"It's not?"

"Oh, no, you want to suggest things like stripping naked and singing 'Copacabana' at the top of your lungs out in the front yard, or making me wear my panties on my head—stuff like that."

"Actually, I think that's a brilliant dare," Hope said. "In fact, that's the dare. No booze for the rest of the night." She reached out and picked up the margarita with every intention of downing it herself. But the thought of mixing chocolate, milk, and lime didn't sit well, so instead, she emptied it in the potted plant that sat on the end table next to her.

"That was a waste of fine liquor," Shirlene stated, with the first frown Hope had seen all night.

"I doubt that." She smiled innocently. "In this house, I'm sure the plant will thrive."

Shirlene's green eyes snapped. "Okay, Miss Smartie Pants, you're up. Truth or Dare?"

It was a conundrum. Hope had quite a few truths that she wasn't willing to share. Of course, if she chose Dare, she had little doubt she would be racing around outside without a shirt on. Normally that wouldn't be a big deal, especially with Lyle out of town. But now there was a guest in the guesthouse. A guest who needed no encouragement in that direction. Especially when he thought her small breasts were the most beautiful things he'd ever seen.

Heat infused Hope's body at the mere thought of those appreciative gray eyes, and she had a hard time getting out the answer.

"Truth," she said, but when she noticed the devilish glint in Shirlene's eyes, she quickly added. "But it's Faith's turn to come up with the question."

"She came up with the dare."

"No. She suggested the dare. I was the one who gave it."

Shirlene flopped back on the couch. "Fine. But make it good, honey."

Only a few seconds passed before Faith spoke. "Do you hate me for marrying Slate?"

Damn. Hope had been willing to answer anything but that. Well, maybe not anything. There were a few questions that could be worse—much worse. Still, this one was pretty bad. She studied one pink flying pig on the knee of her pajamas as she searched for the truth. Did she hate her sister? She hated spinach. Hated raisins cooked in anything. And pretty much hated Cindy Lynn. Or, at least, strongly disliked her. But what she felt for her twin sister wasn't close to any of those things. In fact, since coming home, she hadn't had much of a chance to figure out how she felt about Faith. Not when she'd been too busy trying to keep all her emotions bottled up, including her desire for a certain biker.

She looked over at the woman who sat across from her. A sweet little Disney princess in flannel pig jammies who wore her emotions on her face like a downtown L.A. billboard. A woman who, at every turn, had offered her friendship and love, even after Hope had ignored her and hit her in the nose and pretty much treated her like a stray dog with fleas.

How could she hate someone like that? Especially when it wasn't Faith's fault that Slate fell in love with her. If it was anyone's fault, it was Hope's. She was the one who left Slate on his own for five years.

And if she truly loved him, why *had* she left him for so long?

She released her breath in one long huff. "No, I don't hate you."

"You don't?" Faith leaned up on the couch and gave Hope one of those laser stares. "Because sometimes it feels like you..."

"Are an ass," Hope finished for her. She looked her straight in the eyes, even if it did give her the willies. "Look, I guess I've just been feeling sorry for myself, and I took it out on you."

It was a lame excuse, but once the words were out, Hope realized they were the truth. She had been feeling sorry for herself, and Faith was the easiest scapegoat. A Disney princess scapegoat who wasn't to blame for a backup plan gone south.

A brilliant smile lit Faith's face. "So Slate *was* just your backup plan."

Hope's gaze snapped over to Shirlene, who was smiling broadly. "Don't look at me, honey. I didn't tell her that."

But if Shirlene hadn't told her that, then who had?

"And I'm not a Disney princess."

Hope's eyes swept back to her sister, and her mouth dropped open. "How did you...?"

"Just a guess," she said brightly, before she reached for a brownie. "So is it my turn now?"

Shirlene needed no further encouragement to jump back into slumber-party mode. "Truth or Dare, honey?"

Faith looked away from Hope, who was still trying to decide if her sister had just picked her brain as clean as a shucked ear of corn. "Well, since I'd rather not run around the house naked, I guess Truth," Faith said.

Shirlene looked thoroughly disappointed. "I should've gotten y'all chicken pajamas. Especially since Faith doesn't look like the type to have any good secrets." She tapped a fingernail to her chin as her devious mind worked. "All right, honey, tell us something you haven't even told Slate."

Since Shirlene was right, and Faith wasn't the type to have any juicy secrets, Hope figured it would be something like she put an extra pinch of salt in Slate's beef stew. Or used milk on his cereal a day after the expiration date. Or used his razor on her legs.

But her sister surprised her again.

"I think I might be pregnant." Her entire face lit up like she'd just found the other glass slipper in her pocket. "I mean, it's only been a few weeks since we kind of forgot to use protection, but I just have this feeling. And I know it's stupid. I mean, who feels like they're pregnant after only a couple weeks? And that's why I haven't mentioned it to Slate—because it *is* so stupid." Finally realizing the other two occupants of the room weren't exactly bubbling over with enthusiasm, her smile wilted. "I guess I should've chosen Dare."

As usual, Shirlene was the first to snap out of it. "Why, honey, that's wonderful news." She shot a glance over at Hope. "Isn't it, Hope?"

"Yeah." Hope tried for a smile, but it didn't quite reach her mouth. "Wonderful."

Shirlene lowered her eyebrows at her before she turned back to Faith. "So, honey, why haven't you just gone and gotten one of those tests? Now you can pretty much tell if you're pregnant as soon as the swimmer hits the pool."

"I was going to, but I haven't had a chance to drive to Odessa, and there was no way I could get it here without the entire town knowing. You know how crazy they will get when word gets out."

"Yeah." Hope couldn't help the snide reply.

"Now, Hog." Shirlene flapped a hand. "That's all water under the bridge. Although don't you think it's rather ironic? I mean, the town thinks you're pregnant and actually it might be Faith."

"Real ironic, Shirl."

But Shirlene chose to ignore her sarcasm as she hopped up from the couch. "Come on, girls. Faith has just given us our next fun activity."

Hope had had all the fun she could take for one night. Still, she followed Faith and Shirlene down the long hallway and through the master suite to the master bathroom. Though some people might find the room gaudy, it reminded Hope of Shirlene. Bold and beautiful. The walls were covered in golden-hued tile that had been cut and refigured into intricate patterns that ran along the double sinks and into the glassed-in steam shower. On the floor, darker-toned tiles formed a multi-pointed star that encircled a spa-sized tub with a Tuscan chandelier hanging overhead.

"I'm not hopping in the tub with you two," Hope stated. "It's big, but it's not that big."

"Don't be silly," Shirlene said as she opened one of the cabinets next to the vanity. "We'll get naked in the Jacuzzi later." She pulled out a small box, then another one, and then another, until eight boxes were lined up on the counter.

"What in the world, Shirl?" Hope walked over and picked one up. It only took a glance to figure out what it was. The physical display of her friend's desperation brought a lump to her throat, and she set the box back down without saying a word.

"Now stop acting so morbid." Shirlene waved a hand at her. "Especially when I'm almost an entire year younger than both of you and have plenty of time to get pregnant."

"You're trying to get pregnant, Shirlene?" Faith asked, her eyes suddenly wide and concerned as she studied the boxes. "If I had known, I never—"

"Shush up. Just because I can't get pregnant doesn't mean I can't be happy for people who do." She tore open a box and pulled out the plastic-wrapped device. Using her teeth, she tore open the package and pulled out the flat white stick. "Okay, so here's how it works. You pee on this lower part, then we wait a few seconds and see if a blue line shows up."

"That's it?" Faith accepted the stick from Shirlene.

"That's it. Of course, the first few times I did it, I wasn't sure what I was looking for—" She stopped. "In fact," she grabbed another box and opened it, "it probably would be best if we had something to compare it to. You know, positive versus negative."

Faith nodded. "I think that would make me feel better."

While Shirlene opened another package, Hope sat down on the ledge that ran around the tub.

"Don't go gettin' all comfortable, honey." Shirlene tapped the stick on her arm. "You're up."

"What?" She jumped up and immediately started shaking her head. "Oh, no, I'm not peeing on some stick for a comparison. After what the town's put me through,

I refuse to do anything that deals with babies." And she would've stuck to her guns, if the pained look that entered Shirlene's clear green eyes had only been an act.

"Fine!" Hope grabbed the stick and headed for the toilet, slamming the door behind her. No more than thirty seconds passed before she was back out.

"Here." She shoved the stick at Shirlene, who shook her head.

"I'm not touchin' that thang. Put it down on the vanity." She looked at Faith. "Go on, honey. If grumpy Hope can do it, so can you."

But suddenly Faith was hesitant.

"What if Slate doesn't want a baby? I mean, we haven't really talked about it. I mean, we talked about kids but not about having them so soon. And what if—"

Hope didn't know why she stepped up. Maybe she just wanted to shut her up. Or maybe she just couldn't stand to see her sister so upset.

"Are you kidding me? Slate has loved kids ever since I can remember. Just look at how much he loves coaching. Besides, wasn't he the one who forgot the contraception in the first place?" When Faith nodded, Hope herded her toward the bathroom. "So what makes you think he didn't plan it? Besides, I didn't pee on a stick for nothing."

Once Faith stepped into the bathroom and closed the door, Hope turned to Shirlene, who sent her a soft smile.

"You're a good person, Hog."

"Not really." Hope walked over and sat down on the edge of the tub. "Inside I'm seething with jealousy."

Sitting down next to her, Shirlene rested her pile of blonde hair on Hope's shoulder. "Me too, girlfriend. Me too."

Luckily, Faith took a lot longer than Hope did, which gave them both plenty of time to feel sorry for themselves. By the time she came out, they had ditched the baby blues and were engrossed with the precautions on the back of one box.

"Who would shove this thing up their butt?" Hope asked.

"I guess someone who thought they were going to have a butthead for a kid," Shirlene replied, and they both fell against each other laughing as Faith stood holding the test like it was a lit stick of dynamite.

"Just set it on the counter, honey," Shirlene directed, after she caught her breath. "It doesn't take more than a few seconds."

Faith bent over the vanity. "So what am I looking for again?"

"A blue line," Shirlene said before pointing to the next warning and giggling against Hope's shoulder.

"So if there is a blue line, I'm not pregnant?" She leaned closer.

"No, that means you *are* pregnant."

"Does it start with a blue line and then fade out if you're not?"

Sending Hope a look that said Faith might be a few eggs short of a dozen, Shirlene got up and walked over to the vanity.

"See that blue line?" Shirlene pointed down to the stick on the counter, and Faith nodded. "That means you're knocked up. Congratulations, honey."

"But that's not mine." Faith lifted the stick she still held in her hand with an identical bright blue line. "This is."

Chapter Twelve

STAYING AWAY FROM the main house wasn't easy. Not when one slumber party fantasy after another kept popping into Colt's brain. The only thing that kept him from becoming a Peeping Tom was his sister. There was no way he wanted to catch her doing anything kinky. That was the nice thing about fantasies. You could invite whomever you wanted to the party. And at his sleepover, all he wanted was a matched set of twins. Twins wearing nothing but tiny see-through panties and a few strategically placed down feathers from their pillow fight. Of course, both twins looked exactly alike, right down to their butt-length hair.

With his hands tucked beneath his head, he stared up at the ceiling in Shirlene's guesthouse and let the fantasy play out.

Ooops! One twin took a direct hit from the other one's pillow and bounced down to the bed, sweet breasts jiggling. Thrown off balance, the other twin fell on top of her in a tangle of tanned limbs and silky hair. Amid girlish giggles and fun, bare skin brushes bare skin and lips might . . . accidentally collide. And once that happens, an innocent curiosity might get the best of them and they might—

A knock on the door jerked his attention back to reality, although it did nothing to soften the raging hard-on that stretched out the black cotton of his boxer briefs. Nothing short of a dip in Lake Michigan in late winter would do that. Rolling to his feet, he searched around for his jeans, wondering why someone was knocking at his door at one o'clock in the morning—and not knocking as much as pounding.

"Hold on," he called as he pulled up his jeans and hurried to the door, zipping them as he went. As he crossed the small sitting room, he banged his big toe on a chair leg and was still cussing when he opened the door. But the f-bomb fizzled when he saw who it was.

Hope stood in the darkened doorway with straggly pieces of hair framing her face and a tiara perched lopsided on her head. The flannel pajamas with the scary flying pigs were as far from see-though panties as a person could get, although the prospect of getting his hands on a flesh-and-blood woman made up for his disappointment in attire. Unfortunately, before the spider could welcome the fly into his web, she hauled off and punched him right in the nose.

"Damn it!" He pulled back and covered his throbbing nose with one hand. "What the hell was that for?" While he checked for blood and broken cartilage, she shoved her way past him and started ranting and raving in her hog-calling voice.

"How about for being a good-for-nothing, incompetent idiot!" She waved her hands around as she paced. "Don't worry about a thing, honey! I've got everything under control, sweetheart! I'm all suited up!"

Having worked herself up into a frenzy, Hope whirled around and came back at him with clenched fists.

But he wasn't about to be a punching bag without an explanation.

"Hold up there, wildcat." Colt grabbed her wrists and held her back. It wasn't easy. She was as mad as a hornet. But he couldn't figure out why. There was no way she could've tuned in to his twin fantasies. Although when she stopped struggling, he read more fear in those blue eyes than anger. And since fear wasn't something he'd seen in Hope's eyes often, he started to get worried. His worry tripled when those pretty blue eyes blinked as if fighting back tears.

His grip on her wrists loosened. "What happened, honey? Is Shirlene hurt? Faith?"

Her eyes narrowed as two words came out of her mouth. Two words he couldn't quite make out over the buzzing in his ears—a buzzing that grew louder as he stared down at the woman in front of him.

For a second, he wondered if he was dreaming—if he had nodded off during the twin fantasy and would wake up in the morning, sighing in relief. But then a foot stomped down hard on his toes and the dream bubble burst.

"Are you listening to me? I'm pregnant!"

The sudden increase in volume had him dropping her wrists and pressing his fingertips to his temples. Or maybe it was the words that had his head throbbing.

"Well, aren't you going to say anything?" she asked.

Lifting his head, he looked into those fear-filled eyes

for one brief moment before he turned and walked over to the mini bar. After switching on the light above the cabinet, he started searching. Wine. No. Vodka. No. Whiskey. Most definitely. He poured a good two fingers and downed it in one gulp before he poured another one and did the same.

"Great," she spoke from behind him. "My child's father is a drunk."

He might've poured himself a third if the entire "child's father" thing hadn't brought the whiskey back up his throat. With a hand braced on the bar, he swallowed hard as his eyes stung like hell.

"Now you see how I felt," Hope said. "Except you didn't have to find out the news while two women stared back at you."

Colt turned around. "Shirlene and Faith?" What girls did at slumber parties took a mean curve. "But why would you . . ."

"Faith thought she might be pregnant, so your sister pulled out her entire drugstore of pregnancy tests. I was supposed to be the constant in her little experiment." Her laughter held no humor whatsoever as she flopped down on the sofa. "Some constant."

"But those things aren't foolproof. Are they?"

"Ninty-seven percent accurate." She looked up at him. "One percent less than your raincoat."

"Shit." Colt ran a hand through his hair as he paced over to the sliding glass doors that led out to the pool. The pool was closed for the winter, but it didn't matter. He couldn't see anything beyond his own disbelief. He turned back around. "Maybe you should take another one—just to be sure."

"I did. After Shirlene and Faith fell asleep, I used up her entire inventory. I've now been told I'm pregnant by blue lines, green dots, and one very annoying word." She swallowed hard. "Pregnant."

The air left his lungs in one long rush, and his knees finally gave out, and he flopped down in the closest chair. There were a thousand things to say, too many for him to dissect at the moment, so he chose to say nothing. He just sat there with the whiskey churning in his stomach and his eyes pinned on the swirls in the rug beneath his bare toes.

Pregnant? He could understand getting the news after being in a serious relationship, but one quickie in a hotel room didn't seem worth the burden that had now been placed on his doorstep. Of course, most of the blame was his. He was the one who had gone looking for her after Shirlene had called, worried because she hadn't heard from Hope in weeks. He had been the one who rented the hotel room close to the club where she worked so he wouldn't have to make the long trip back to his house on Hermosa Beach so late at night. And he had been the one unable to control his desires long enough to consider the consequences of fumbling around in the dark with a condom that had been in his wallet for a good month and had endured more than its fair share of road time.

"Aren't you going to ask if its yours?" Hope spoke almost as softly as her sister. Colt looked up. In the dim light put out by the mini bar, she looked small and child-like, all curled up on the couch in those silly pig pajamas with the crooked tiara.

"It's mine," he stated without hesitation.

They stared at one another for a few seconds before

they both turned away. The front door stood open, and only the occasional chirp of crickets broke the thick, heavy silence. He didn't know how long they sat there, both lost in their own thoughts, before he finally spoke.

"So what do you want to do?"

She fiddled with one of the buttons that ran down the front of the pajamas. "I don't know, but I don't think I can get an abortion. What do you want to do?" she shot back.

The question shouldn't have taken him by surprise, but it did. Probably because the shock had yet to wear off. A baby. His baby.

He swallowed and tried to think. Do? What did he want to do? A variety of things popped into his head. Drink the rest of the whiskey and move onto the vodka and wine. Sue the condom company. Stomp over to Shirlene's and yell at her for asking him to check on Hope in L.A. in the first place. Hop on his bike and pretend this never happened.

Except it had happened, and there was no way to pretend otherwise.

So what did he want to do?

He didn't have a clue. The only thing he knew for certain was he didn't want to have a baby. He wasn't ready for something like that. Like Hope said, he was an irresponsible motorcycle bum and proud of it. A motorcycle bum who spent half the year in a garage and the other half touring the country on a custom chopper that only had room for one. One lone rider, who stopped when he wanted. Not when a woman needed to take a pee, or a kid screamed for release from the confining contraption he'd been buckled into.

That was the way it was and that was the way Colt liked it.

There were a few times he felt lonely, but certainly not lonely for a baby. But now he didn't have much of a choice. There was a child—his child—therefore he needed to give Hope an answer. Or if he couldn't come up with one, he needed to at least be honest about that.

He ran a hand through his hair. "I don't know. I haven't ever really thought about babies."

"And you think I have?" Her words held a lot of anger, no doubt because he'd taken so long to answer.

Feeling a little tense himself, his gaze snapped over to her. "Come off it, Hope. That's all you and Shirlene talked about when you were growing up. Weddings and babies."

"With Slate! Never with some motorcycle bum who can't keep a foolproof condom in his wallet!"

Just like that, the situation turned nasty.

He tipped his head. "Funny, but you didn't seem to be too worried about that in the Motel 6."

"Because you seduced me!"

"Seduced you?" He arched a brow. "Was that before or after you sucked my tongue down your throat?"

"You ass!" Hope jumped up. "I should've known it was useless to come here expecting you to take any kind of responsibility for your actions." She started for the door, but he got up and blocked her way.

"Oh, I take full responsibility for my actions. I had no business taking you back to my hotel room, but I'll be damned if I take full responsibility for what happened after. You were just as hot as I was for it, baby. And don't you ever forget it."

"How can I? I'll carry that mistake around for the next eight months!"

The word *mistake* caused his temper to flare. "And that's what really chaps your ass, isn't it? It will be hard to pretend to the people of this town that you hate my guts with my child growing in your stomach."

"Your child?" She tapped her chest. "You mean, my child."

"So now you're going to claim immaculate conception?" He snorted. "The people of this town are stupid, but I don't think they're going to fall for that."

"Well, they certainly won't think you're the daddy! Sandra Bullock won out over you!"

"Then why are you here?" Colt finally released all his anger and frustration. "If you're going to walk around pretending I'm not the father, what the hell are you doing asking me what I want to do? If that's the case, you can damn well figure it out on your own."

"I hate you, Colt Lomax! I hate you so much!" She shoved him out of the way. "And I will figure it out on my own. I don't need anything from you."

The door slammed closed behind her, and Colt stared at it as he whispered, "No. And you never have."

Chapter Thirteen

IN THE TIME it took her to cross Shirlene's lawn and slip back into the dark house, Hope's anger had turned to a hard knot of anxiety. Needing to do anything to prevent complete hysteria, she felt her way to the kitchen, where she rifled through the drawers until she found a pen and pad. Switching on the lights over the breakfast bar, she sat down on a stool and started writing.

Reasons I'm Not Pregnant
1. *My period is always late.*
2. *I'm not sick in the mornings.*
3. *My breasts are not tender.*
4. *I feel exactly the same as I did two months ago.*
5. *—*

She paused for only a brief second before writing the next sentence, pressing so hard it tore the paper.

It was only one time! One measly time that I haven't even given a second thought to!!!!

But even as she dropped the pen and flopped her head

down upon her folded arms, Hope realized it was a lie. She'd given more than a second thought to that night in L.A. As much as she'd tried to forget it, it had been carefully preserved in her brain like a Turner Classic, waiting for just such a moment of weakness to be pulled from the vault and replayed in all its digitally mastered glory.

"See ya, Sweetie," Phoenix, one of the strippers at Tittly Wink's, called out before she climbed into her brand-new Porsche.

"See ya." Hope waved as she hurried across the parking lot to her old beat-up Chevy truck. In her haste to get back to her apartment after the long night on her feet, Hope hadn't even taken the time to remove her blonde wig, something she didn't realize until the cold breeze blew the short strands across her face.

"Got any change?"

Hope almost jumped out of her black sports bra when a man materialized out of the darkness.

"Geez, Marty." She held a hand to her chest. "You scared the crap out of me."

"Sorry, Hope." He pushed back his long, greasy dreadlocks with a dirty, sun-damaged hand. "I figured you saw me."

She probably should have. In his flowered board shorts and parka, he was hard to miss.

"It's not a big deal," she said as she searched through her purse for some change. Unfortunately, all she came up with was a linty orange Tic-Tac. Even Marty looked disappointed as he stared down at her open palm. But his eyes lit up when a ten-dollar bill suddenly appeared over Hope's shoulder. Grabbing the ten, Marty popped the

Tic-Tac in his mouth and offered up a "God Bless You" before hurrying off.

Hope turned to thank the man who offered the bill for his generosity, and ended up looking into a pair of cool, steel gray eyes she remembered well.

"Living dangerously, honey?"

After five years of walking through a parched desert of surfer dudes and arrogant actors, the familiar twang blended with the husky male timbre poured over her like a cool West Texas rain shower. But she only had a moment to drink it in before the implications of Colt Lomax finding her working at a dump of a strip club smacked her right between the eyes.

If Colt knew, so would the entire town of Bramble.

Hoping it was all just some weird coincidence, Hope tried to bluff her way through it.

"Did you need something, sir?" She mimicked the hard tones of all her California neighbors.

His eyes narrowed. "Yeah, I need something all right. I need you to tell me what the hell you think you're doing!"

She swallowed hard and tried to keep her eyes off the chest muscles that strained against the black cotton of his T-shirt. Muscles that had gotten much more pronounced in the last eight years.

"Doing? I don't know what you're talking about. You must have me confused with someone else." She went to walk past him, but he grabbed her arm.

"Cut the shit, Hope."

"Hope?" She stared down at the sexy tattoo on his arm. "I'm afraid I don't know anyone by that name. My name is...Pumpkin."

The name popped out before she could stop it. Damn Shirlene and her theory that the best stripper names were made up using the name of your first pet. What was the matter with her? What if he remembered Pumpkin? Her pony had been very cute and very memorable.

"Fine. We'll play it your way." He jerked a twenty out of his pocket and slipped it in the front of her sports bra. His eyebrows lifted at the extra padding. "I think that's the going rate, isn't it?"

Before she could say a word, he bent down and hefted her over his shoulder.

"What do you think you're doing?" she yelled, as she pummeled his hard butt with her fists.

"I'm collecting my lap dance."

"But I'm off work!"

"Consider it overtime."

His long strides made it much harder to land a punch, although that didn't stop her from trying. While she flailed her arms aimlessly, she looked around for one of the many bouncers who worked at the club. Unfortunately, they were all inside, having their usual after-hours drink with the boss. And while she had been searching for change to give Marty, all of her dancer buddies had left. Which meant there was no one to stop Colt but Hope.

She gave it her best shot, but the guy's butt and legs felt like they were made of wrought iron. During one wild screaming tangent, the wig came off and her hair swept down to tangle in his legs.

"Nice hair, Pumpkin," he gloated.

And since the jig was up, she gave in.

"Colt Lomax, you good-for-nothing piece of Texas roadkill, put me down!"

"Now, there's the sassy little Hope I remembered. I thought I'd lost you forever."

"You're going to lose your teeth, if you don't put me down," she yelled so loudly, her voice echoed down the alley they passed. But he only laughed and kept going.

She didn't have a clue where he was taking her, but it took him long enough to get there. He walked a good half block with her screaming and fighting all the way. In another neighborhood, someone would've called the police. But here, calling the police was like inviting an anteater into an anthill.

Finally, he turned into a parking lot, and she glanced up at the brightly lit sign. "Oh, no. If you think I'm going into a hotel room with you, Colt Lomax, you can think again."

Except in a matter of minutes that was exactly where she found herself, bouncing on a flimsy mattress while Colt stood over her, looking none too happy. "Have you lost your mind?" She scrambled off the bed on the opposite side.

He swept his jet black hair off his forehead before resting his hands on his hips. "Funny, but I was about to ask you the same thing."

She tried not to fidget under the intense look, but it was hard when her heart thumped so loudly in her ears. "I wasn't the one who kidnapped a person and is holding them hostage in a cheap hotel room."

"No, you're just the person dressed up like a hooker and working at a strip club."

"I'm not dressed up like a hooker." Hope tried to defend her clothing, but even she knew it was a losing battle.

"Really?" His gaze ran over her, starting at the hem of the short black skirt and moving up her bare quivering belly to the low neckline of the sports bra, where two squares of toilet paper now hung out. "What would you call it?"

"A waitress's uniform."

The stiffness eased from his shoulders. "Waitress?"

She placed her hands on her hips, mimicking his stance. "What difference does it make to you, anyway? You never have approved of anything I wear. My cheer-leading skirt was too short, my pink boots too bright, my homecoming gown too low. What are you, my daddy?"

His steel eyes flickered. "I liked the uniform you wore when you worked at Josephine's."

Her hands dropped. "You've got to be kidding. That ugly thing came down past my knees."

"It was decent."

"Decent? This coming from a man who dated Marcy Henderson."

The grin was real this time. "I guess Marcy didn't exactly dress decent, did she?"

The smile did something to her stomach. Something she tried to ignore. But it was hard to ignore the fact that this was a man who knew her—had known her ever since she was born. Colt might be annoying as hell, but he was as close to home as she had gotten in more than a year. And she missed home. Missed it more than she had realized until that moment.

Flopping down on the end of the bed, she unbuckled the skinny black straps of one of her high heels and slipped it off to massage her aching toes. "Talk about a hooker. That girl screwed anything with pants on. And why you dated her, I'll never know."

His hands dropped from his hips, and he moved around the end of the bed and took a seat next to her. "Because I was a horny young kid, and she would screw anything with pants on."

Rolling her eyes, Hope switched feet and unbuckled her other shoe. "I'll tell you one thing, the running shoes I got to wear at Josephine's sure beat these to hell and back." The shoe slipped to the floor, and she rubbed her sore arch and groaned. "Lord, that feels good."

"Here." He reached out and grabbed her foot.

"You are not touching my feet, Lomax." She tried to pull her foot back, but he refused to let go. And once those strong fingers started to move, any resistance she might've had was completely snuffed out.

"Scoot back," he ordered, and she quickly complied.

Once she was stretched out with her head tucked against a pillow, he lifted her foot to his lap and started in earnest. For a motorcycle bum, he knew his way around a foot. His thumb dug into her arch while his fingers massaged the instep. And when he stretched her toes back, she moaned and dug her head back into the pillow.

"Feel good?" he asked.

She could only nod. Although his next words brought her out of her physical utopia.

"So why are you working there?"

A thousand smartass remarks filled her mind, but instead she told the truth. Foot massages would make one hell of an interrogation tool.

"I need the money."

"It's hard to believe you couldn't find a better place to work." He pulled on her pinkie toe, and she died and went to heaven.

"Don't tell me you haven't spent your fair share of time in strip clubs—tonight being a perfect example. Of course, you got there a little late, didn't you?"

There was a moment of hesitation before he spoke. "I wasn't there for the strippers."

She leaned up on her elbows and stared at the ebony hair curled around the strong column of his neck. "Don't tell me you were there for the eight-dollar Dr Peppers."

He glanced back at her. "I was looking for you."

"Me? But why?"

Still holding her foot, he shifted around on the bed. "Shirlene has been worried about you, so I told her I'd look you up."

Hope's stomach dropped, and she tugged her foot away from him.

"So now you know." She tipped up her chin with as much defiance as she could muster. "Now you can call Shirlene—and whoever else you want to—and tell them that Hope Scroggs isn't a budding actress after all...just a barmaid at a sleazy strip club in L.A."

She expected some snide remark, but instead he just stared back at her with emotionless eyes. And somehow that seemed worse.

"Go home, Hope."

She shook her head. "I can't."

"Damn it!" In one swift movement, Colt came up off the bed. His eyes were no longer cool and emotionless as he strode around to stand over her. "Why can't you ever just let things go? You don't belong here. You've never belonged here. You belong back in Bramble—back with Slate Calhoun. So accept it and get your ass back there!"

Hope sat up on the bed, her own anger bubbling to the

surface. "That's easy for you to say. But I don't see you going back."

"Because I was never the town favorite. I was that poor Lomax kid, remember? And who the hell in their right mind would want to deal with that every day of their lives? But you are Hope Scroggs, loved by every man, woman, and child—"

"And that's the point. I can't go back there when they believed in me—when they think I'm the next Sandra Bullock. How can I possibly live with myself if I disappointed them?"

Tears welled up in her eyes, and she tried to push them back. It was bad enough that Colt had discovered her working at a strip club; she didn't want him thinking she had turned into a crybaby too. Except her body refused to listen to her brain, and the tears splashed down her rouged cheeks like her apartment's drippy faucet.

"Admit it, Hope," Colt sat down next to her. "It's not about the town as much as it is your own stubborn pride."

"B-but I thought I had it all figured out," she sobbed. "I m-made numerous lists."

"You and your damned lists." Releasing an exasperated sigh, Colt slipped an arm around her and tugged her close. "Sometimes things can't be planned, Hope. Sometimes things just aren't meant to be."

His show of kindness only made her cry harder. Tucked against his chest, she sobbed out all her anger, hurt, and frustration from the last five years. When she was finally spent, she remained there—a lifeless piece of quivery female.

After a while, his hand lifted from her shoulder and stroked her hair. "How did you manage to get all this up in that wig?"

"It wasn't easy," she said, her voice clogged with tears and snot.

A chuckle rumbled through his chest. "Pumpkin. I had my doubts until you mentioned that orncry old pony."

"He wasn't ornery."

"I don't know what you'd call it. He bit me every time I tried to pet him."

"Probably because he knew a mean kid when he saw one."

He laughed. "Probably." He continued to stroke her hair, and she continued to let him. How long had it been since someone had touched her like this? It seemed like a lifetime. And she didn't want it to end. Unfortunately, her nose started to drip, and no amount of sniffing would keep it contained. So she grabbed the toilet paper that hung from the sports bra and loudly blew her nose. She didn't realize how it must've looked until she glanced up into twinkling gray eyes.

"So that's what that's for."

"Very funny." She tried to tear off the used piece but only succeeded in pulling out more. Like a line of silk scarves from a clown's sleeve, the paper kept coming and coming as Colt's eyebrows hiked further and further up his forehead. Completely humiliated, she dropped her hand.

"It's not my fault that men tip better if you're blonde with big boobs."

"No, I guess not." He gathered up the toilet paper, then slipped his hand beneath the bra to get the rest. When his knuckle brushed her nipple, she sucked in her breath and jerked back.

"Sorry," he said as his hand popped out with the wad

of tissue. Except he didn't look very sorry. Those gray eyes gleamed with a devilish light. "Here." He tipped up her chin and wiped beneath her eyes. "You look like you've been in a fight."

"I have."

"Now, honey, that didn't even come close to some of the zingers we've had in the past. Remember the time I told you that you kissed like a three-year-old?" He chuckled. "I thought you were going to tear my head off and spit in my neck."

"I think you have that memory a little screwed up, Lomax. I was the one who told you that you kissed like a three-year-old, and you were the one who got upset."

His eyes filled with smoky heat. "Well, maybe we should see if I've improved."

"I don't..."

The words dropped along with her stomach as his mouth dipped toward her. He didn't move fast. In fact, she had plenty of time to stop him—to tell him that she had no need to test his kisses. Except she didn't want to stop him. It was insane. But she had always been a little insane where Colt Lomax was concerned. And as soon as those warm lips touched hers, she gave herself up to that insanity.

His lips swept over hers with a raw sensuality that held nothing back. No one kissed better than Colt. It was as if she was a goblet of water and he was a parched man in the desert. His hands cradled her face as his lips took deep thirsty pulls. Then, as if not completely quenched, he changed angles to drink some more.

She answered him with deep, thorough kisses of her own, her hands fisted in the cotton that stretched over his chest. Releasing her lips, his hands slipped to the back of her neck as he kissed his way toward her ear. Her breath fell out in heaving gasps as she fought for the oxygen he'd taken. This outlaw. This desperado who had stolen her will to fight. But the sports bra stopped him cold.

"How the hell do you get this thing off?"

She smiled at his impatience, although it faded at the thought of him seeing her breasts. They had never been her best attributes, and she wasn't about to show them to a man who had found so many flaws. But that didn't mean she didn't want to feel those big biker hands on her.

So she leaned over and turned off the lamp before stretching the bra up over her head. His hands were on her before she even got her head through the stretchy Lycra.

"Jesus," he sighed as he filled his hands.

He gently squeezed before he slid his palms up the sides and over the rigid peaks. As he stroked and teased, he leaned over and gave her another deep kiss, pushing her back to the mattress. Once he had aligned his body to hers, he pulled away from her lips and trailed hot, wet kisses down her neck and along her bare shoulders, before using that talented mouth and tongue on her breasts. Beneath his lavish attention, Hope felt as well-endowed as any one of her dancer friends. And luckier, much luckier, that Colt was the one doing the lavishing. Of course, she forgot all about what he was doing to her breasts when his fingers skated up one trembling thigh and slipped beneath her skirt.

It took all of three flicks to send her skyrocketing.

"Did you just…?" Colt's breath fell soft against her nipple. "Damn, baby."

Her orgasm seemed to incite his passion, and his

foreplay became more frantic, his need more evident. He left her for a time to strip off his clothes. There was little light in the room, so she could only imagine the articles being removed. The popping of cotton stitches. The thud of a heavy boot. The metal zing of a zipper. And then he was back—hard biceps cradling her hips—a solid wall of muscles pressed against her lower legs.

He didn't remove her skirt but merely pushed it higher as his breath fell hot and moist against her panties, panties that were no match for his deft fingers. Once they were gone, his familiar voice reached through her sexual haze.

"Let me turn on the light, Hope. I want to see you."

"No." She waggled her head on the pillow. Light might wake her from this dream, and she wasn't ready for that.

Not yet.

Acquiescing, his fingers traced up her bare thighs, then back down again before they stopped at her knees to press them apart. She waited, listening to the sound of his breath as it fell rough and heavy from his lungs. Anticipation grew, and she jumped when his hot, wet mouth settled over her.

He was gentle at first. A sweep of tongue. A sip of lips. But slowly he settled into a tempo that brought her back to the edge again. Her thighs closed around his head, and her hips lifted. But before she could take flight, he pulled away. Not that it was easy to unclench her fingers and squeeze past her thighs.

"Easy, baby," he said. "I'm not going to leave you hanging."

Then he moved up her body, and she felt the hot length of him, nudging for entry. Opening her legs wider, she angled her hips and welcomed him home. Although at the first deep thrust, reality broke through her sexual haze, and she pressed a hand to his chest.

"I'm not on birth control."

He leaned down and kissed her, his lips tasting musky and sweet. "No worries. I'm already suited up, honey."

On the word *honey,* he drove deep, taking her breath and reality with it. He stretched her to the limit, filling a space deep inside. A space she'd forgotten existed. With each thrust, the emptiness and loneliness of the last five years receded.

She tried to savor everything at once. The deep, satisfying stretch. The brush of his hips on each thrust. The strength of his arms braced beside her head. The sound of his breath as he neared climax. But it was too much for her mind and heart to absorb, so she closed her eyes and sank into her own universe of pleasure.

Soon after, Hope fell into a dreamless sleep. And when she awoke, Colt was gone. No good-bye. No note. Just the indentation of his head in the pillow next to her, along with the scent no other man could duplicate.

Chapter Fourteen

COLT DIDN'T KNOW where he was going when he left Shirlene's. All he knew was he needed to ride. So that's what he did. Without glancing at mile markers or highway signs, or worrying about putting mileage on a bike that wasn't his, he rode. Rode until his butt ached and his back throbbed. Rode through the frigid, appendage-numbing cold of the dark night to the cool dampness of the early morning. The only time he stopped was to get gas, use the bathroom, and down an energy drink before heading back out to the long stretch of blacktop that gave him solace when nothing else could.

When he finally arrived in Austin, he pulled into a restaurant, where he drank numerous cups of coffee in an attempt to defrost. Unfortunately, once his body had thawed, his mind still remained frozen, and he found himself watching the other occupants of the restaurant in a dazed kind of trance.

An older couple complained about the service and haggled over the bill. A young man sat and punched the keypad of his phone, using just his thumbs, while across the table his girlfriend did the same. A woman struggled to keep her two toddlers from ripping open the little jam containers and tipping over creamers while she tried to pacify her crying baby in the high chair. It turned out to be an impossible job, and finally she sat back in the booth and let all hell break loose.

Her gaze swept over to Colt, and they stared at one another for a few seconds, both defeated and at a loss for what to do.

Finally, Colt got enough gumption to call the man who had bought the custom bike and set up a time for delivery.

Travis Mossman's house was nothing short of spectacular: A sprawling estate on Lake Austin with a three-story main house and a scattering of outbuildings that included a boathouse, two guest cottages, and a huge garage that stored a variety of vintage cars and motorcycles.

If Colt hadn't been comatose, he might've been impressed, if not with the estate, at least with the nice collection of Harleys, Indians, and one Victory. But with no sleep and the effects of the coffee wearing off, his mind could barely stay focused on Travis as he walked around the bike Colt had brought, and looked at it from all different angles.

Compared to the classics, it wasn't all that impressive. Still, Colt was glad he'd taken the time to stop at a car wash and clean off the road grime. The chrome and custom paint sparkled in the sunlight that spilled in through the open doors of the garage.

"Impressive." Travis ran his hand over the custom paint job, admiring the tribal-blade graphics that ran over the tank and fenders. "I knew just by talking with you that you knew what you were doing—which is why I gave you *carte blanche*—but this is more than I expected. The detail is amazing."

Colt liked the man and was glad he had his approval. Over the last few months, they'd built a long-distance relationship, their discussions moving from bikes to the trials of growing up in small Texas towns. On the phone, Travis had come across as an honest, upstanding kind of guy who you wanted to count among your friends. And meeting him in person only confirmed this belief. His blue eyes were direct, his smile genuine, and his handshake firm. He was a few inches taller than Colt and about twenty pounds lighter, his body slim and fit. Even with the silver threaded through his dark hair, Colt didn't figure he was much over forty-five.

"Thanks," Colt said. "I've got a good group of guys working with me."

Travis finally looked up from the bike. He studied Colt for a few minutes before speaking. "Tough ride?"

Rubbing a hand over his day's growth of beard, Colt figured he probably should've hosed himself off at the car wash as well. "Yeah."

"I thought you were going to trailer the bike from L.A."

That had been the plan until the night at the Motel 6 threw him off course—was still throwing him off course.

"I wanted to test it on the highway before delivery." It was a lame excuse, but Travis didn't question it.

"So how did she do?"

"She'll go the distance."

Travis looked back at the bike, and for a moment, his eyes glazed over as if he was out on the road right then, instead of standing with both feet on the pristine epoxy floor.

"I look forward to that." The way Mossman said it made it seem like a dream more than a reality.

"Grandpa!"

Colt turned to watch as two bright-eyed kids raced across the immaculate lawn. Since there was no one else around, Colt figured he'd made a mistake in calculating Travis's age. Obviously, the man took as good care of himself as he did of his vehicles.

"Whoa there, partners." Travis reached down and lifted the little blonde-headed girl into his arms before he placed an arm around the bigger boy. "Colt, I'd like you to meet my grandkids, Lily and Daniel. Lily and Danny, this is Mr. Lomax."

The little girl shyly tucked her head into her grandfather's neck, while the boy stretched out a hand.

"It's nice to meet you, sir."

Travis smiled proudly as Colt gave the small hand a shake.

"Nice to meet you, Daniel."

Once the introductions were out of the way, Daniel didn't waste any time relaying his message. "Mima says lunch is ready, and you need to pull your head out of your tailpipe and come and eat before she gives it to Rufus."

"She said that, did she?" Travis's blue eyes sparkled with suppressed laugher. "Well then, I guess you better run back in and tell that ornery woman I'm on my way, and I'm bringing Mr. Lomax with me."

Once the kids were racing back across the manicured lawn, Colt held up a hand. "I really appreciate the offer, but I need to be getting back."

In truth, he didn't know where he was getting back to. The long road trip should've cleared his mind, but instead he felt more confused than ever. Hell, he hadn't even arranged for transportation after dropping off the bike. The original plan had been to take a cab to the airport and fly back to L.A., but the original plan had been shot to hell when he veered off the interstate and ended up in Bramble. Of course, his trip to Bramble hadn't really changed things. Even if he hadn't gone, Hope would still be pregnant with his child.

His child.

The words left him feeling like he had the first time he'd been knocked off a surfboard, struggling underwater with no clue which direction to swim in to find air. Unaware of Colt's dazed state, Travis pressed his offer.

"Nonsense, after that long trip, you might as well stay the night. We've got more guest rooms than relatives, and Sissy loves company about as much as she loves to harp at me."

"Thanks, but I can't." Colt pulled out his cell phone. "I'll just call a cab and wait out here."

For the first time since meeting him, Travis's tone carried a hint of the tough businessman he was. "Being from Texas, you should know Texans never pull out a checkbook on an empty stomach. Besides, once we've eaten, I have no problem driving you wherever you need to go."

Once Travis put it that way, Colt didn't really have a choice. So he nodded and followed him up to the house. Even with the high ceilings and massive windows, there was a cozy charm to the home that made a person feel immediately comfortable and welcome. Or maybe it wasn't the house as much as the people who lived there.

Sissy Mossman, as hospitable as her husband, was a sturdy cowgirl with flaming red hair that reminded Colt of his sister's before she had gone blonde. Though she wasn't as pretty as Shirl, there was a softness to Sissy's hazel eyes that Colt found soothing as he sat at the long dining room table and ate lunch.

"Would you like more salad, Colt?" she offered.

"Yes, ma'am." He didn't really want more, but he had always had a problem saying no to motherly women, and Sissy Mossman was as motherly as you could get. As they ate, she wiped mouths, refilled milk glasses, and cut up food into small bites for her grandchildren.

"Such nice manners, but *Sissy* will do just fine." She passed the bowl down.

"Yes, ma'am," popped out before he could stop it. Travis and Sissy laughed, which set the kids to giggling.

The kids were well-mannered and pretty cute. Daniel reminded Colt of Jesse, although he carried a youthful innocence in his blue eyes that Jesse was lacking. Youthful innocence was something kids lost early out on Grover Road. Still, both boys had the same interest in motorcycles, and Daniel spent most of the time asking questions about the customs Colt had built. Comfortable with the topic, Colt didn't mind answering his questions, but the conversation soon dwindled when it moved to monster trucks—a subject he knew little about.

The little girl, on the other hand, just sat there and stared at him with eyes the color of Texas sage and as big as the dinner plates they ate off of, which was why he was so surprised when she suddenly appeared at his side.

"You got whiskers."

Startled, he choked on the bite of chocolate chip bunt cake he'd just placed in his mouth. After forcing the chunk down with a few swallows of water, he nodded.

"Are they scratchy?" she asked.

He glanced over at Travis and Sissy, but they just smiled back like a couple of idiots. So he improvised.

"Would you like to feel them?"

She nodded, and Colt leaned down so she could slide a tiny soft hand over his jaw. When she giggled, he couldn't help but smile back at her and wink. That was all it took. Without a word, she climbed up on his lap and remained there while he tried to finish his dessert. Her small, crayon-scented body didn't make him all that uncomfortable. Shirlene had sat on his lap when she was little. He had just forgotten how nice it felt.

When the kids were excused from the table, Sissy ushered him into the living room, where a fire took the chill off the autumn day. Between the deep couch cushions, the full stomach, and the crackling cedar, Colt had a hard time keeping his eyes open, let alone keeping up the conversation.

"So you grew up in Bramble?" Sissy asked, as she took a seat on the couch next to her husband. The arm he hooked over her shoulder seemed as natural an action to him as breathing.

"We went through Bramble," Travis said, before turning to his wife. "Remember, honey, it was when we made that trip up to Roswell so Travis Jr. could see the aliens. Hell, that must've been ten years ago."

"Closer to twenty-five," she stated. "T.J. couldn't have been more than ten. And of course, I remember. How could I forget? You left our youngest daughter at the gas station."

"Now that wasn't entirely my fault. I thought she was still sleeping in the back of the camper. How was

I supposed to know she had gotten out when I wasn't looking?"

Sissy glanced over at Colt and shook her head. "Poor little thing, by the time we realized she was missing, we were halfway to Roswell. Luckily, the nice man working at the gas station took care of her." She glanced over at Travis. "What was his name? Smith? No, Johnson?"

"Jones," Colt supplied, surprised at what a small world it was. "Tinker Jones. I grew up with his son, Tyler. He runs the gas station now while his father and mother travel around in their motor home."

"Jones. Of course." Sissy smiled at the memory. "By the time we got back, he had taken Shelly over to this cute little train caboose diner and gotten her an ice cream. With three older brothers to contend with in the back of the camper, I think she was happy to get the short reprieve."

"That would be Josephine's," Colt said. "And it's still there, crooked stovepipe and all."

Sissy smiled. "That's what I love about small towns. They never change. It's like a time capsule that you dig up every time you go home. But instead of things, it's places that bring back all the happy memories."

Happy memories? He had never thought of Bramble in that way. But in the last few weeks, more happy memories had surfaced than bad. The taste of good red chili burning its way down your throat and the icy cold of a drugstore chocolate ripple ice cream cone. A rainy afternoon spent inside an old Chevy and the feel of the late afternoon sun on your neck on the way to Sutter Springs.

No, the memories weren't all bad. And Sissy was right; in a big city, things were constantly changing. Buildings coming down and more going up. Businesses failing and others taking their place. But in Bramble, things had stayed constant. And there *was* something nice about that.

"I think I told you about growing up in a small town just east of San Antonio," Travis continued. "Not more than a grease spot on the highway. And I tell you, I couldn't wait to get out of there and shake the dust of that town off."

"The dust," Sissy asked. "Or the girl?"

"Now, honey, I think that we've been over this. I was young and stupid."

"You sure were."

Travis looked over at Colt and rolled his eyes. "Anyway, the point I was trying to make is that no matter how much money I have or how big my house is, I'll always be that small-town boy."

Sissy leaned up and kissed his cheek. "And six grown kids and five grandkids later, I'm still your small-town girl."

Six? If the thought of one kid left Colt stunned, six with five grandkids was downright mind-boggling. How did a man get six kids? A faulty condom was a start. But six faulty condoms constituted a learning disability.

"I never thought I'd go back to my hometown to live," Travis continued. "But lately, I've been thinking about buying some land there and building a house."

"You have?" Sissy turned to him. "Why haven't you said anything?"

"I thought you would think it was stupid. I mean, we have three houses already."

"Oh, honey." She leaned her head on his shoulder. "I think it's a wonderful idea. And with our mamas and daddy getting older, we can be right there to help out if they need us."

While they continued the conversation, Colt leaned his head back on the couch and studied the cracking fire. He thought he'd only closed his eyes for a second, but when he opened them, the light had changed in the room, and Travis was the only one there.

As he sat up, Travis lowered the edge of the newspaper that he was reading and looked over at him.

"Sleep well?"

Colt rubbed a hand over his face. "I didn't mean to sleep at all. What time is it?"

"Around three." Travis nodded at the coffee table. "I've got your check right here. But before you head out, I thought you might want to talk a little."

Thinking it was about the bike, he said, "I sent you all the specs, and if you have any questions, all you need to do is call me."

"I'm not talking about the bike, Colt." He folded the newspaper and set it aside. "I'm talking about what has you strung as tight as a fiddle bow. And don't give me any bull that nothing's wrong. The man I've talked to on the phone for the last few months is not the same man who blew in here looking like the wrath of God. Hell, you no more than glanced at my collection—talk about a bruised ego." Travis flashed a grin. "Normally, I wouldn't push my nose into someone's business, but I feel like we've known each other for years. Not just from the phone conversations and e-mails, but through your designs and our mutual love of bikes."

Colt ran a hand through his hair. He had felt the same connection, which was one of the reasons that he had wanted to personally deliver the bike. He had wanted to meet Travis Mossman—to see the man behind the voice. But that was before his life had taken an unexpected curve. Still, the man deserved some kind of an explanation for his sudden wild appearance. And a rough road trip wasn't going to do it.

Especially when Travis asked, "So who's Hope?"

"How do you know about Hope?"

"You talk in your sleep. Luckily, the grandkids are outside with Sissy or they would've gotten an earful." Colt actually blushed as Travis continued. "Since I already know you're not married, I assume she's a girlfriend."

What would you call the mother of your child? Girlfriend didn't seem like enough. Of course, in Hope's case, it was too much. Except there was nothing else to call her.

"Yes."

"And you got her in trouble?"

Damn, how much did he talk in his sleep?

Colt blew out his breath and fell back on the couch cushions. "I guess you could say that."

"So what are you going to do about it?"

"I don't have a clue."

"I've shoveled enough bullshit in my day to recognize it when I see it. You know what to do, you're just too afraid to say it out loud. Afraid if you do that someone will hold you to it."

"If you're talking about marriage, you can think again."

Travis leaned over, his forearms on his knees. "I wasn't talking about marriage, but it's obvious you've been thinking about it."

Had he? Colt hadn't thought that he'd been thinking

about anything, but perhaps a part of his brain had been working without his realizing it. An illogical part of his brain. Marriage to Hope was out of the question. They could barely have a conversation without fighting.

"So you don't have feelings for the girl?" Travis continued his interrogation.

"What do you mean?"

Travis shot him a look that pretty much called him out on the idiotic question. Colt tried to backpedal, except there was no place to backpedal to.

"I...she's...there is this...Hell, I don't know."

The grin on Travis' face was downright annoying, and the glare Colt sent him must've said so, because he quickly held up a hand.

"Believe me, I'm not laughing at you...okay, so maybe I am. But it's nice to know I'm not the only idiot when it comes to women. I think it must have to do with being born in a small town. With everyone butting into your business, you get it in your head that when you grow up you'd rather go it alone."

Colt snorted. "I wouldn't exactly call a wife, six kids, and five grandkids going it alone."

The grin deepened. "No, I guess you wouldn't, but before I got married that was exactly what I had convinced myself I wanted to do. I left town and traveled around the country, until I ended up back in Texas working on an oil rig and pretending like I was having the time of my life. And then I ran into the girl I'd left behind. I tried to act like the big shot I wasn't, but she looked straight through me and called me a liar right to my face. God, how I hated her. It took me a good year of trying to convince myself I didn't need her before I realized she was exactly what I needed. Of course, by that time, she'd found somebody else."

"So the girl wasn't Sissy?"

"Of course she was. A little thing like a fiancé doesn't stop a Texan when he's made up his mind. I begged like a two-year-old in a candy store—a whole lot of tears and a whole bunch of promises to be the best husband she'd ever want. Of course, if she didn't love me, I guess no amount of begging would've gotten her to leave that idiot and marry me."

Colt had been so wrapped up in the story that he hadn't realized they'd come full circle. All the way back to marriage.

"I think your situation was a little different than mine. Hope doesn't love me. And I sure as hell don't love her."

Travis glanced behind him before he spoke in a low whisper. "Just between you and me, I didn't exactly love Sissy either." When Colt sent him a surprised look, he quickly continued. "To be honest, my head has always been a little behind my heart. I suppose my heart knew, even when we were dating in high school, but my head didn't realize how much I loved her until about six months into the marriage."

"So why did you marry her?"

He released his breath. "Because I couldn't stand the thought of her marrying Michael Beaudine."

Jealousy was something Colt could identify with. Growing up, he'd been jealous of just about everyone in town. But as an adult, he felt as if he'd conquered the emotion. The image of Slate and Faith's wedding popped into his mind. Okay, so maybe he hadn't conquered it. Of course, it wasn't jealousy that had caused him to belligerently kiss the bride as much as a bruised ego at the thought that Hope had fled from his bed straight into Slate's arms. And now he wondered if his ego had been responsible for his sleeping with Hope in the first place: The poor Lomax kid finally gets the homecoming queen.

Except it hadn't felt like his ego.

It had just felt right.

"Listen," Colt got to his feet, "I need to be going."

Travis stood. "Had enough of my advice, have you?" When Colt didn't reply, he only smiled. "Well, marriage or no marriage, I don't doubt for a minute that you'll take care of your own. From the way you talk about your sister, I'd say you've had some practice."

"A little," Colt hedged. He reached for the check on the table, then pulled his wallet from his pocket and slipped it inside. When he glanced back up, the smile was gone from Travis's face, replaced with a look that made Colt suddenly wary.

"Listen, Colt," he said, "I probably don't have any business bringing this up. Being a business man yourself, you realize how quickly gossip can get out of hand." He paused as if carefully considering his next words. "But I think you should be aware of the rumors that are going around about Dalton Oil."

The haze that had settled over Colt's mind lifted, and he became alert.

"What have you heard?"

Travis released his breath. "That the gulf oil well Lyle invested in didn't produce, and he's having a hard time paying back his loans. Companies are already talking about getting their hands on Dalton—companies I wouldn't wish on my worst enemy." When Colt didn't comment, he continued. "Look, I've only met Lyle a few times, but he struck me as an honest man. If he decides he needs some investors, I know of a good company that might be interested—C-Corp. And if there's anything else I can do…"

"I need a ride to the airport." Colt finally spoke.

With a nod, Travis reached down and picked up a set of keys off the coffee table.

"A man's got to do what a man's got to do."

Chapter Fifteen

NEVER ONE TO wallow in self-pity for too long, Hope spent the following week on the list of things that needed to be done in town while she clung to the thin thread of hope that pregnancy tests were as faulty as condoms.

The pothole was her first project. It wasn't hard to talk some of the highway construction guys into stopping by for a free lunch at Josephine's. Then, while they were filling up on biscuits and gravy, she used a little country charm to convince them to fix the hole at the corner of Maple and Main on their way back to work.

The next day, she lit a fire under Harley and had him call the hotel chain to find out if they were still considering building a hotel in Bramble. After spending a good half hour trying to bridge the language barrier between India and Texas, he was transferred to the corporate office where he spoke to a vice president who beat around the bush more than Uncle Harley before he informed them that Slumber Suites had decided Bramble was a bad risk.

The news was discouraging, but it didn't slow Hope down. On Thursday, she stopped by the hardware store to see if Ralph would donate some paint for the storefronts. Unfortunately, he had already donated ten gallons of purple paint to paint the town hall for Faith and Slate's wedding. Hope had just stepped out of the hardware store on her way to go talk to Rye Pickett to see if they had any paint left over when Bear's big black Dodge truck pulled up.

After Sheldon, she thought the town would give up on their craziness. Obviously, she'd been wrong. But at least this time, the man Bear had with him didn't look terrified. In fact, he looked quite pleased with himself.

"Hey, Texas!" Her agent, Ryan Seever, hopped up on the sidewalk and engulfed her in a hug. After she had inhaled a lungful of his expensive cologne, he pulled back and gave her one of those smiles that only convinced people who didn't know him. "So this is where you've been hiding out."

Hope barely acknowledged the greeting before she turned her narrowed gaze on Bear. His beady eyes widened with fear, and he took a few steps back, stumbling over a crack in the sidewalk.

"Now, Hog, I didn't force him. This here feller wanted to come see you."

"That's exactly right, Bear." Ryan reached out and slapped the mountain of a man on the back. "I take full responsibility."

Since Ryan had never taken responsibility for anything, Hope grew even more suspicious about his presence in Bramble. But she wasn't about to question him, not when they had started to draw a crowd.

Traffic had slowed to a snail's pace, and people were stepping out of the businesses up and down Main Street to stare at her and Ryan like they were bugs beneath a microscope. The women looked hopeful, as if waiting for her and Ryan to declare their undying love, while the men just looked mean. When riled, Texans could be extremely unpredictable. And even if she and Ryan hadn't ended on the best of terms, she didn't want to see the man riddled with buckshot because they thought he'd deserted Hope and his baby.

Another lowlife was responsible for that—a lowlife who she hoped was getting pelted with golf ball–sized hailstones on whatever highway he was traveling down.

Pinning on a smile, Hope hooked an arm through Ryan's and steered him down the street. As they walked along, she made the introductions.

"Hey, y'all, this here is my Hollywood agent, Ryan Seever, who just stopped by to see how I was gettin' on. Isn't he the sweetest?"

The entire Hollywood agent thing seemed to work. The women looked thoroughly depressed and the men seemed disappointed that they didn't have an excuse to whip out their guns.

But it didn't take long for Ryan to change their expressions. Always the charmer, he greeted the townsfolk as if he and Hope were walking the red carpet. And by the time they had reached Josephine's Diner, he had the men laughing at his jokes and the women convinced they were all movie starlets just waiting to be discovered.

Even Rachel Dean fell under his spell when she brought their menus and water to the corner booth. Hope couldn't blame her. Ryan had done the same thing to Hope when she first landed in L.A. It took her years to read through the layer of charming fluff and get to the egomaniac center.

"A Hollywood agent," Rachel beamed. "Now ain't that somethin'. I guess you've met plenty of stars. You know that Angelina Joe Lee? I like her movies and all, but if that skinny little gal didn't have those lips weighin' her down, she'd blow clean away in a puff a wind."

Despite the Botox injections that left his skin scarily tight, Ryan's smile actually looked real.

"I couldn't agree more, Rachel. I think the days of skinny leading ladies are behind us. People want their heroines made of sturdier stuff." He winked at her. "Now, I bet a woman like you would make a great action hero and could take down an entire third-world country of terrorists without even blinking an eye."

Rachel blushed to the roots of her salt-and-pepper hair. "Well, I don't know about that. But I've taken down a few steers in my day. And one time, when my first husband got a little too drunk for his own good, I had to wrangle him into a kitchen chair and duct-tape him until he sobered up." She stared off and shook her head. "Although I feel real bad about that. The hair on his wrists and ankles never did grow back."

Knowing the conversation would only get crazier, Hope jumped in. "Could you get us a couple of diet Dr Peppers, Rachel?"

"Shore thing, honey." She gave Hope a direct look. "I guess this ain't the one, either." When Hope shook her head, Rachel's shoulders drooped and she walked away, muttering to herself.

When Rachel was gone, Hope turned back to Ryan.

"Okay. What are you doing here?"

Shaking his head, Ryan stared out the window. "Unbelievable. It's like Mayberry on crack."

The accurate description almost had Hope smiling. "I mean it, Ryan. Cut the crap and explain to me what caused a man who delights in traveling first class to ride across country with Bear."

He flipped open the menu and scanned it. "Surprisingly, it wasn't really that bad—and since someone forgot to pay their cell phone bill, it was the only way to get a hold of you." His eyebrows shot up. "Frog legs? People actually eat frog legs?"

"Only when they're in season," she said, dryly. "So why would you want to talk to me, when you dropped me as a client?"

Setting down the menu, he released his breath in a long sigh. "Fine. I made a mistake. I was thinking leading lady, when I should've been thinking..." he waved a hand at the window, "reality star." A smile flashed. "I have a job for you."

Since it wasn't something she'd heard often, it took her a moment for his words to sink in. "A job on a reality show? You mean like the ones who run around half-naked, drinking from tree-bark bowls and foraging for beetles to eat? I think I'll pass."

"You would be lucky to get on that show." He pulled out his cell phone and started texting while he talked. "But no, it's not quite as intense. All you'll have to do is what you've been doing for the last few years."

"Fail?"

He didn't even crack a smile as his thumbs flicked over the small screen. "Exactly. Except you'll get paid for it. It's tentatively called *Hollywood Dreams,* and it will follow the story of five different people who are trying to make it big in Hollywood. The producers are looking for unique actors who have their own distinct personality. And I immediately thought of you. I sent them the audition tape you did for that criminal show, and they loved it."

Hope's eyes narrowed. "The one where I played the corpse?"

"That's the one."

"But I couldn't get my eyelids to stop twitching."

Ryan shrugged. "They obviously know talent when they see it."

She reached out and jerked the phone out of his hands. When he looked up, she shot him a skeptical look.

"Okay," he said as he leaned back in the booth, "so maybe they're not looking for talent as much as entertainment. And what could be more entertaining than a feisty little Texan with a cute country twang? The audience is going to eat you up like *crème brûlee*."

He leaned up and started rattling off the details of production dates and offers, but Hope wasn't listening. Her mind had finally settled back on the one thing she didn't want to think about. The one thing that kept her from jumping up and down with excitement over the fact that her goal of becoming an actress was within her grasp.

Fate was more than cruel; it was downright devious.

"...so they loved the tape, but they want to meet you in person. When I found out where you were hiding out, I called them back and scheduled a meeting for the end of next week. I figure that will give you plenty of time to tie up any loose ends you have here."

Loose ends? She had more than loose ends. It seemed her entire life had come unraveled.

"So when do you think you can leave?" he asked, just as Rachel walked up with their drinks.

"You feelin' okay, sugar?" Rachel's gaze dropped to the hand Hope rested on her stomach—a hand she hadn't even known was there. "You want me to get you some of them saltines?"

Hope shook her head. "I'm okay," she said, although she did feel slightly nauseated. But crackers weren't going to help.

The bell jingled over the door, and both she and Rachel turned to look at the three men who stepped in. It was clear that they were strangers to the area. Instead of finding a place to sit down, they stood just inside the door, waiting to be seated. They wore business casual attire—creased pants, lightly starched shirts, and high-polished laced shoes. If Hope's mind hadn't still been on Ryan's offer, she might've given the three men's presence in Bramble more thought. Instead, she turned back around as Rachel went over to greet them.

"I could be pregnant, Ryan," Hope stated. The words came out much easier than she expected.

Ryan had gone back to tapping out messages on his phone and didn't even glance up.

"Did you hear me? There's a good chance I'm pregnant."

He held up a finger; then, after punching the screen one more time, he set the phone down and looked at her. "Bear might not be a big talker, but I got that much out of him. And he was terribly disappointed to learn I hadn't seen you in over six months." A grin tipped up one corner of his mouth. "I take it the father is still on the loose?"

"Long gone."

"Good." A sly smile eased over his face. "There is nothing more appealing to an audience than a single mom who is struggling to feed her child." The smile turned blinding. "The producers are going to love it."

Ryan might not have a sincere bone in his body, but he knew the business inside and out. And if he thought the producers wouldn't care that she was pregnant, Hope believed him. What she couldn't believe was that all her prayers had suddenly been answered and all she could do was sit there and stare at him. Was she crazy? This was her chance, her chance to become—if not an awarding-winning actress—at least rich and famous. And she would be a fool not to take it.

"I have an appointment on Monday, but I can leave anytime after that." She forced the words out of her suddenly dry throat.

"Good." Ryan patted her hand. "I think this is going to work out well for both of us." He slipped out of the booth. "I need to go to the bathroom and make a few calls." He motioned at his drink. "While I'm gone, do you think you could get me a cappuccino or maybe some carrot juice? Carbonation sucks all the elasticity right out of your skin."

Her gaze wandered over his taut, spray-tanned face.

"I'll see what I can do."

But once he was gone, Hope didn't wave Rachel over. Instead, she just sat there staring out the window.

Bramble Elementary had just gotten out. Kids raced by with backpacks flopping, while other children meandered at a slower pace, stopping to kick an aluminum can down the gutter or peer in the window of Duds N Such while moms waited on almost every street corner to greet their children with warm hugs and bright enthusiasm for whatever they pulled from their backpacks.

Moms who didn't look terrified at just the thought of motherhood.

"...as far as I'm concerned we shouldn't have any problem whatsoever taking over Dalton."

The words cut into Hope's thoughts, and she quickly turned her head to stare at the bald spot of the man who sat in the booth directly behind her.

"I agree. The guy is so deep in debt—" The dark-headed man in the ivory dress shirt, seated on the other side of the booth, stopped talking when he noticed Hope peeking over his friend's shoulder.

Caught eavesdropping, Hope's eyes widened. But she recovered quickly. "Mercy sakes." She jumped up and glanced down at her bare wrist. "Would you look at the time? It seems my breaks are over before they even start." She gave them all a sassy wink. "Now you boys don't go anywhere, and I'll be right back to take your orders."

They looked more than a little confused as she hurried across the room and slipped behind the counter.

"You change your mind about them saltines, honey?" Rachel asked as she poured some coffee for Rossie Owens.

"Actually," Hope grabbed an apron off a hook by the door that lead to the kitchen and tied it around her waist, "I had a spurt of energy. And since you're so busy, I thought I'd help you out."

Rachel's face scrunched up as she looked around the near-empty diner. "Well, that's real nice of you, honey. But I think I've got it covered."

"Now, I won't hear any more about it." Hope steered Rachel around the counter to the bar stool next to Rossie. "You just sit right down there and take a load off those bunions of yours."

"Well, they have been hurtin' a little today." Rachel sighed as she took a seat.

"You tell her, Hog," Rossie said. "She works way too much for her own good."

As Rachel blushed, Hope moved back around the counter and quickly filled three glasses with water. But before she lifted the plastic tray, she grabbed a handful of napkins from the dispenser and shoved them in her bra. She adjusted each cup, flipped open two snaps on her shirt, and then picked the tray back up.

When she turned, both Rossie and Rachel were staring at her like two dogs looking at a rabid cat. She flashed them a weak smile before she walked back to the table, adding a little extra wiggle to her hips.

"So where you boys from?" She laid the accent on nice and thick as she handed out the water.

"San Ramon," the balding guy said, with an appreciative gleam in his eyes. Since it appeared that he was the most talkative of the bunch, Hope tucked the tray under her arm and moved over to his side of the booth.

"San Ramon? Ain't that in Mexico?"

They laughed, all except for the dark-headed unfriendly one.

"California," the skinny man with glasses finally spoke up.

She widened her eyes. "Don't tell me, y'all work in movies. 'Cause you're sure good-lookin' enough."

There was more laughter before the balding man answered. "We work for Pacific Coastal Energy."

Hope's smile dropped, but only for a second. "No foolin'? Is that like Red Bull? I tried one of those drinks once and stayed up for most of the night with more energy than a cat on a hot tin roof. You plannin' on sellin' that stuff here? 'Cause I know a few lazy cowboys who could sure use a little energy."

The balding man started to speak, but the dark-headed man cut him off. "We're just passing through, ma'am."

"Well, I hope you enjoy your stay in Bramble." She took out the pad and pen from the apron pocket. "So what can I get y'all?"

It was a good thing that Hope could take orders in her sleep, because her mind was a whirl, trying to piece together the information she'd just learned. She didn't have a clue why executives from Pacific Coastal Energy were thinking about taking over Dalton Oil, but she wasn't about to let it happen.

"I'll have that right out," she said as she headed back to the counter.

In no time at all, she had placed their orders with Josephine, stripped off the apron, and headed for the door. On the way out, she ran into Ryan, coming back from the bathroom. But she didn't stop to talk.

Hollywood would have to wait. Her Mayberry was in trouble.

Chapter Sixteen

"MR. DALTON," LYLE's secretary's voice came over the intercom speaker. "Hope Scroggs is on line two. I tried to tell her that you were still in a meeting, but this is the sixth time she's called in the last hour, so I thought it must be important."

Suddenly alert, Colt dropped the document he'd been trying to decipher and sat up so quickly that he almost toppled headfirst out of the leather conference chair. He didn't know why, but he suddenly felt as if he'd just been caught ditching class. And for a second, he had the strong urge to jump up and run like hell.

Which was just plain juvenile. Especially since there was no way Hope knew that he was at Dalton Oil's corporate office in Houston. And even if she did, so what? He was an adult who could go where he wanted to go and do what he wanted to do.

Still, that didn't stop Colt from pressing a finger to his lips when Lyle picked up the phone, which resulted in a bemused look from his brother-in-law.

"Hey, Little Bit," Lyle said, although his haggard face didn't match the jovial tone. "What a nice surprise—"

Before he could even finish, Hope cut him off. Colt couldn't make out what she was saying, but it wasn't hard to detect her anxiety. An anxiety that quickly changed Colt's fear of discovery into something much more terrifying. With his heart banging against his rib cage, he leaned over the conference table with every intention of jerking the phone out of Lyle's hand and finding out just what had Hope so upset. But before he could, Lyle spoke up.

"Now, Hope, honey, just because you overheard some guys from Pacific Coastal talking about buying—okay, taking over—Dalton Oil that's no reason to think we're going under. Companies try to buy out the competition all the time. That's just good business."

Colt flopped back in the chair and released his breath as Lyle continued to talk.

"So stop worrying your little head over things like that. Right now, the only thing I want you thinking about is names for those sweet babies." After a long pause, Lyle pressed the receiver closer to his ear. "Hope? You still there, honey?" There was a muffled reply, and Lyle quickly ended the call. "Well, I better get back to work so Shirlene can have some spending money. Say 'hi' to your mama and daddy for me."

After he hung up the phone, Lyle leaned back in his leather chair and rubbed his eyes. "I sure hate to lie to that little gal. But I can't chance her letting it slip to someone in town. Not when panic will only make things worse."

The intricate details of business had never been Colt's strong suit—he much preferred using his hands to his mind—but from what he'd ascertained in the last week, things couldn't get much worse for Dalton Oil. Due to bad investments and dropping oil prices, the company was as close to bankruptcy as a company could get, and it was only a matter of time before they went under. Still, Lyle looked so haggard and defeated, Colt couldn't bring himself to point that out.

"And I'll tell you one thing," Lyle continued. "If I ever run into the cowardly dog that got Hope pregnant, he'll rue the day he defiled our little sweetheart."

Colt was already ruing the day. Unfortunately, there was no way to go back and undefile. Which was why he was using the excuse of Dalton Oil's troubles to hide out, like the cowardly dog he was.

Rising up from the chair, he walked over to the floor-to-ceiling windows and stared out at the Houston skyscrapers.

"So Pacific Coastal showed up in Bramble," Colt mused.

"I figured it was only a matter of time before the vultures started to circle."

Colt turned back around. "Pretty soon they won't be circling—they'll be picking our bones." When Lyle didn't say anything, he continued. "I realize you want to keep the company in the family, Lyle, but instead of letting a group of money-grubbing sharks get their hands on Dalton by paying off the debt with seventy cents on the dollar, we should be looking for an honest company who might be willing to buy us out with a fair deal."

Lyle released his breath and slumped back. "You're probably right. It's just damned hard to let go of a business that has been in the family for close to a hundred years."

Figuring he'd made his point, Colt turned back to the

window and stared at the rows of lit windows. "Doesn't anyone go home in this town?"

"Time is money."

"If that's the case, then we should've made a bundle in the last week." When Lyle didn't say anything, Colt glanced over his shoulder. His brother-in-law was watching him with a look that made Colt extremely uncomfortable.

"Damned if you haven't surprised the hell out of me, Colt Lomax."

"I have a tendency to do that to people," Colt said, dryly.

Lyle chuckled. "I meant it as a compliment. I don't know what I would've done without your help this last week."

"I didn't do all that much."

"I disagree, but even if you hadn't lifted a finger, it was nice having family around—someone who cares about Bramble as much as I do."

Not wanting Lyle to get the wrong idea, Colt enlightened him. "I didn't do it for Bramble, Lyle. I did it for Shirlene." He turned back around. "And if you want the support of your family, why haven't you told my sister? I understand you not wanting the town to know about the company's trouble, but Shirlene is your wife."

Lyle swallowed. "I planned on telling her this weekend when she flew out, but then she started talking about Hope and Faith being pregnant..." His shoulders drooped. "If you could've seen that great big smile pinned on her face the entire time she talked about the baby shower she's planning, it would've broken your heart—especially knowing how much she wants a baby of her own." He looked up at Colt. "And damned if I could add to her misery."

Colt had never paid much attention when his sister had talked about having kids. Somehow the news that she wanted a baby so desperately made him feel even guiltier now for not wanting his.

"Still, I wouldn't want to be around when she finds out you've been keeping secrets from her," Colt said. "And the news will be out soon enough."

Instead of commenting, his brother-in-law just sat there, staring out at the glittering cityscape. For the first time since Colt had known him, he looked all of his fifty-six years and then some. His face looked drawn and his eyes were bloodshot from lack of sleep.

"I have to fix this, Colt," he said in a wary voice. "Not just for the folks of Bramble, but for the other employees of Dalton Oil and their families." He covered his face with both hands. "I couldn't live with myself if I let them down, especially since I'm the one responsible."

Colt had never been much of a touchy-feely kind of guy, but he couldn't help walking over and resting a hand on Lyle's shoulder.

"You haven't let anyone down. In fact, I've never seen a man work so hard to save a company." He gave him a couple awkward pats. "But there's nothing else you can do for now. So why don't you go home for the weekend and relax a little? Take that sister of mine out dancing at Bootlegger's. Or just kick back at the house and fill up on some of Cristina's cooking."

Lyle dropped his hands and shook his head. "I never was any good at dancing—or kicking back. Besides, you're right. Instead of sitting here waiting for the buzzards to land, I need to find a company worthy of Dalton. Didn't you tell me that Travis Mossman mentioned a company that was interested in us?"

"C-Corp." Colt walked back over to his chair and pulled up a file on the laptop. "It's a relatively new company. They started with farm equipment, then somehow ended up with land just south of San Antonio that was rich in natural gas. Two brothers own it." He glanced back up. "You want me to give them a call?"

It took Lyle less than a second to nod. "But if they're planning on sending anyone out to look things over, you might want to tell them to stay out of Bramble. Hope won't fall for my cock-and-bull story again." He grinned. "She's sure a firecracker, isn't she? You won't find another person in all of Texas who's more willing to fight for Bramble than our little Hope."

Colt glanced over at him. "I don't know about that. If it hadn't been for you and your family, Bramble would've turned into a ghost town long ago."

The smile dropped. "Which is why I can't give up, Colt."

"I know." Colt nodded.

A moment of awkward silence passed before Lyle leaned up and straightened the papers littering the tabletop. "And what about your own company? I guess you'll be headed back to L.A. soon."

It made sense. Colt had spoken with his office manager just that morning, and she'd informed him that his desk was piled high with project designs and part orders that needed his immediate attention. But for some reason he couldn't bring himself to leave the state of Texas, even if Hope had made it perfectly clear that she could handle things just fine without him.

When Colt didn't answer, Lyle cleared his throat. "I guess you wouldn't consider going back to Bramble for a few days? It would sure make me feel better knowing you were there, watching over the town."

"Watching over the town?" Colt's eyebrows lifted. "You do realize I'm the same delinquent that broke most of the storefront windows on Main Street."

Lyle laughed. "Do whatever you want to the windows, Colt, just watch out for my gal."

It was late by the time they finished working. Since Lyle had recently sold the penthouse, they were both staying in a hotel downtown. But while Lyle took a cab back, Colt decided to walk. He needed the fresh air to clear his mind of all the information and numbers that ran through it.

The streets were crowded with men in business suits and women in nice dresses and heels on their way to dinner or to get a drink. Colt could've used a few stiff drinks himself. But as always, he stifled the urge.

At the corner, he ran into a group of women dressed in skimpy costumes. There was a blonde vampire. A brunette French maid. And a very nasty-looking Little Red Riding Hood redhead who gave him a bold once-over as he stopped to wait for traffic. As he stared back at her, it took him a moment to make sense of the costumes. With the turbulent events of the past week, he'd forgotten all about the holiday. Now he remembered Shirlene talking about selling tickets at the Halloween carnival.

The annual event was a big deal in Bramble, and one of the few things Colt had enjoyed growing up. He loved the caramel apples. Got a real kick out of watching the mayor get soaked in the dunk tank. And anticipated a good scare in the haunted house. The only thing he hadn't enjoyed was watching Hope dressed up like a witch and passing out kisses for a dollar. Every horny guy for miles around would line up in front of the booth, awaiting a brush from those soft lips.

Everyone but Colt.

It became as big a challenge as the ring toss to see if he could resist pulling a dollar from his pocket and stepping in line. Of course, he never did completely resist. Sooner or later, he'd made sure that he took much more than a dollar's worth.

The light changed, and Colt waited for the ladies to step off the curb before he followed behind them. Halfway across the street, Little Red turned and blew him a kiss from her scarlet-painted lips.

He acknowledged the gesture with a smile, even though storybook characters had never been his thing.

Colt had always preferred witches.

Chapter Seventeen

"YOU'VE GOT TO be kidding me!" Hope's gaze narrowed on her twin sister, who wore the exact same costume as she had on—from the pointed black hat and purple sparkly wig to the purple-and-black–striped tights. The only things different were their boots. Faith's boots were black, while Hope wore the red ones she'd yet to return to her sister.

"Did you buy your costume in Lubbock?" Faith asked, as she came around the back of the carnival fishing booth.

"No. I've had it for ten years. Which makes it even freakier." Hope gave her sister's witch costume one final glare before going back to taping string on the end of the skinny dowel rods that they were using as fishing poles.

"It is freaky, isn't it?" Faith picked up a dowel from the box and started helping Hope. "It's like we have a telepathic connection. Sometimes I know what you're thinking without you even opening your mouth. Like at Shirlene's house."

"That was nothing more than a coincidence."

"I don't know about that. Since then, I've done a little research, and there are dozens of articles online about twins being connected mentally. And you have to admit it's strange the way we keep dressing alike."

Hope snorted. "*Strange* isn't the word I'd use—more like ridiculous. What woman in her right mind wants to dress exactly like someone else?" At the long stretch of silence, Hope glanced up into Faith's big, innocent eyes.

I can't help it. I like everyone knowing we're sisters.

"As if people couldn't figure out we're sisters without the clothes," Hope said, as she reached for another dowel. She had just pulled one out of the box when Faith grabbed her arm and squealed.

"You did it! You read my mind!"

The dowel clattered to the floor as Hope turned to her sister.

"What are you talking about?"

"I didn't say a word about me liking people knowing we're sisters, and yet you knew what I was thinking."

Hope's brow knotted. "But I heard..."

"Exactly." Faith smiled as if talking mice had just finished her trousseau. "That's exactly how it works with me; like you're in my head, talking. Go ahead, think of anything. In fact, make it something I wouldn't know about in a million years."

Since she really wanted to prove her sister wrong, Hope searched through her mind for something really obscure to throw at her. Faith concentrated on her for only a second before her face scrunched up in bewilderment. And Hope couldn't help but smile triumphantly.

But the smile faded quickly enough.

"Pumpkin?" Faith tipped her head in confusion. "Colt likes pumpkins?" Suddenly those eyes flashed open wide. "Colt and you? He's the father—"

Hope slapped a hand over her sister's mouth just as Shirlene came sashaying up to the booth in a gypsy costume, complete with black wig, silk scarves, and enough jewelry to sink the *Titanic* long before it reached the iceberg.

"So which witch is which?" Shirlene teased.

Since Hope had just spilled the biggest secret of her life to a woman with a face that was as easy to read as a first grade primer, it took a moment to collect herself. Dropping her hand from her sister's mouth, Hope sent her one stern warning look before she turned to her best friend.

"Real funny, Shirl," she said, with just the right amount of sarcasm.

"Well, that settles that." Shirlene pointed a red nail at Hope. "Wicked witch." She pointed at Faith. "Good witch. Although the good witch looks like someone just landed a house on all her munchkins. You okay, honey?"

Hope knew if she didn't get Shirlene out of there quickly, she would find out what a good-for-nothing piece of roadkill her brother really was.

"Of course, she's not okay, Shirl." Hope pulled a folding chair over and pushed her sister down, tugging the brim of the witch's hat low enough to shadow Faith's stunned face. "She's pregnant." She patted her sister none too gently on the shoulder. "Now you just sit right there and rest, Sis, while me and Shirlene go on back and finish getting the prizes ready."

A suspicious look settled over Shirlene's face, but after only a few brief seconds, she followed Hope behind the cardboard waves that Hope's mama had made.

"I'm mad at you, you know," Shirlene said, as she

flopped down in one of the chairs, her numerous bracelets and necklaces jangling.

Fearing Shirlene was much more perceptive than she'd thought, Hope moved over to the box of prizes and tried not to act guilty.

"For what?"

"For avoiding me for the last week."

Hope heaved a sigh of relief and sat down in the other chair. "I wasn't avoiding you. I was just busy, is all. Besides, if anyone should be mad, it's me at you for suggesting the stupid experiment in the first place."

"And just how was I supposed to know you two are Fertile Myrtles?" Shirlene said. "Especially when my best friend fails to tell me she's been doing the dirty deed with some guy out in California. The last I heard you were living with Sheldon."

Hope grabbed a bottle of bubbles and wrapped a rubber band around the cap, which would make it easier to attach the paper clip fishhook to when the kids tossed it over the waves.

When Hope didn't answer, Shirlene spoke up. "Don't tell me you changed his sexual preference."

"No. It wasn't Sheldon. The reason I didn't tell you is because it was just a one-night stand."

Shirlene shot her a skeptical look. "Since when does Hope Scroggs have one-night stands?"

"I can be as slutty as the next person," she defended herself. It was a lie, and the look on Shirlene's face said as much. There was only one man who brought out the major slut in her. An untrustworthy bum who didn't have two pennies to rub together or a responsible bone in his body.

"And I'm gathering it wasn't your spray-tanned agent." Shirlene snagged a bag of Tootsie Rolls out of the box and opened them.

"No. Ryan has only one love affair going and that's with himself."

Shirlene unwrapped a candy and popped it into her mouth. "So why is the man still here? I hear he's staying with Harley and signing people up with his agency right and left. He even has Twyla dreaming of her own reality television show."

The news didn't surprise Hope. It seemed Ryan felt as if Bramble was a sea of reality shows just waiting to make him millions. Fortunately, he had a flight out tomorrow morning. She would be glad to see him go. Not only because she didn't want him spilling the beans about the reality show until she got it, but because his presence reminded her that it wouldn't be long before she would have to return to California.

"So what are you going to do?" Shirlene asked, and Hope didn't need to be a mind reader to know what she was talking about. She stared down at the huge cardboard box of toys and did what she'd been doing since the slumber party—clung desperately to a false sense of hope.

"Maybe I'm not pregnant. Maybe I have an infection or something that threw the tests off."

"I guess it's a possibility." Shirlene offered Hope a Tootsie Roll before opening another one for herself. "Are you going to see a doctor?"

"Monday in Midland."

Without a second's hesitation, Shirlene asked, "You want me to go with you?"

Knowing how difficult a trip to the obstetrician's

would be for her friend, Hope shook her head. "Thanks, but I can handle it." She reached out and took her hand. "If I could trade places with you, you know I would."

"I know, honey." Shirlene squeezed her hand. "But as my mama always says, all things happen for a reason."

The words of wisdom didn't make Hope feel any better, and if the forlorn look on Shirlene's face was any indication, they hadn't worked for her either.

She was happy when Shirlene popped the candy in her mouth and changed the subject. "So when do you have to work the kissing booth?"

"Not until later. Cindy Lynn wants to make sure everyone is here."

"Well, can you blame her? Everyone in town believes the slow economy has to do with you not being here to dish out your good-luck kisses."

"Did somebody mention kisses?" Slate's voice came over the ocean waves, and when Shirlene and Hope got up, they found the two newlyweds kissing.

With so many other things to worry about, it didn't bother Hope as much as she thought it would. In fact, she couldn't control the desire to do a little devilish teasing. Without hesitation, Hope walked around the cardboard waves. "How could you, Slate?" She tried to blink up a couple of tears before her sister gave it away. But Faith surprised her by turning on Slate and socking him in the arm.

"Yeah, watch it, Calhoun!"

Confused, Slate glanced down at Hope's red boots before he apologized to Faith. "Sorry, Hog." He reached for Hope, but she held up a hand.

"Don't be mauling on me, cowboy."

He glanced back at Faith, and his forehead knotted. "This isn't funny, y'all."

But it was. So funny, all three women burst out laughing.

The kissing booth turned out to be twice as profitable as the fishing booth, but not nearly as much fun. After Hope sat down on the hard stool, a line formed clear out the gymnasium door and into the foyer. It wouldn't have taken so long if all the townsfolk expected was a peck on the cheek, but everyone had something to say—whether Hope wanted to hear it or not.

"Don't lift your hands over your head or the baby will be born with the cord wrapped around its neck."

"You date anyone else out in California? Maybe a Dallas Cowboy who stopped by Disneyland in between games?"

"Get out of bed on the right side, you'll have girls. Get out on the left, and it's boys for shore."

"What about one of those Texan actors? That Owen Wilson feller? Ethan Hawke? Matthew McConaughey?"

Hope tried to hold it together, but the craziness started to take its toll. And after what seemed like the five-hundredth kiss, she started grabbing the money, giving a quick peck and moving on to the next person, leaving the previous one still trying to get his words in edgewise.

Around nine o'clock, Kenny Gene stepped up to the booth, although she didn't know it until he lifted the white sheet and grinned back at her. He hooked the sheet over one of the pointed bull horns attached to his hat.

"Get it? Bull-sheet."

Hope had to admit it was clever, but she still thought Josephine's extra-crispy fried chicken leg deserved the best costume ribbon. Especially since the crumpled butcher paper looked so painful to walk in.

"So, Hope," Kenny grinned. "I was thinkin' that along with a kiss you might let me rub your belly—you know like one of them fat Buddhas? That way I'll get triple the luck."

Hope grabbed the dollar from his hand and slapped it in the cashbox before she leaned over and gave him the quickest kiss of the night. He started to complain, when Ryan came flapping up in a black cape and plastic vampire teeth. The costume was appropriate. If anyone could suck blood out of a person, it was her agent.

"Bella, Edward vants to suck your blood," he slurred as he flipped the cape around her and pressed the cold plastic fangs against her neck. When she shoved him back and sent him a warning look, Kenny jumped into the conversation.

"She ain't sellin' blood. She's sellin' kisses. And I thought your name was Ryan."

Ryan slipped the fangs out of his mouth. "Kisses?" He flashed a blinding smile. "God, I love this town." Before Hope could stop him, he pulled the wallet out of his back pocket and flipped it open. "Do you take debit or credit?"

Hope rolled her eyes at the gold American Express card shoved in front of her face. "Sorry, cash only," she said.

His smooth brow knotted. "You're kidding!" When she only stared back at him, he shrugged and slipped the card back into his wallet. "Then I guess you'll have to trust that I'm good for it."

"Sort of like you were good for the residual checks on my commercial?"

"Now, Texas," he tossed her an innocent look, "I couldn't help it if one of those checks got lost in the mail. And you did end up getting all your money."

She arched an eyebrow. "Yeah, after I almost got kicked out of my apartment."

Ryan held up a hand. "Fine." He flipped the wallet back open. "I've got an emergency hundred in here that I'm more than willing to give to your little charity. It's the least I can do for my new star client."

"You gonna give a hun-nerd dollars for a kiss from Hope?" Kenny jumped back into the conversation. "I hate to say this, but I just got one and a dollar's pushin' it."

Ryan pointed a finger. "Kenny Gene, right?" When Kenny nodded, he continued his brown-nosing. "Love the costume, man."

Annoyed, Hope reached out and jerked the hundred out of his hand and placed it in the cashbox. "Thanks, man." She slipped off the stool, ready to end her time in the kissing booth.

"Hey," Ryan said. "What about my kiss?"

"You'll have to trust that I'm good for it," she said, as she looked around for her witch's hat.

"Now, Hope," Kenny refused to keep his mouth shut. "That ain't very fair."

"What's not fair, Kenny Gene?" Rachel waddled up in her extra crispy costume.

"Hope's Hollywood agent just gave her a hun-nerd for a kiss, and Hope ain't even gonna give him a peck on the cheek—hell, for a hun-nerd, she should at least slip him the tongue."

"A hundred dollars?" Twyla joined the group in a saloon-girl cancan costume that was more appropriate for an adult party than for a kid's carnival. "Why, that's twenty haircuts."

"Fifteen six-packs of beer," Rye Pickett stated, as if he hadn't failed out of math four years running.

"Around forty cans of Spam," Rachel added.

"Forty?" Kenny looked truly shocked as he shot a glance over at Hope that said there was no way one of her kisses was worth forty cans of Spam.

Giving up on finding her hat, Hope stepped around the back of the booth with every intention of leaving the insanity far behind her. But Ryan was there, waiting with a devious twinkle in his eye and a pitiful whipped-puppy look on his face. No wonder he had become an agent; he was a worse actor than she was. Still, he had the town suckered.

"Oh, come on, Hope," Kenny pleaded. "Give the poor feller a break."

Realizing there was no way around it, Hope gave in. Besides it was for a good cause. All the money from the kissing booth went for new band uniforms, and Hope felt somehow responsible for the singed poof on the trombonist's cap, although it had been Colt who stomped it flat.

With the thought darkening her mood, she might've jerked Ryan over a little too hard for his kiss on the cheek. But her sympathy died when the sly dog swiveled his head and planted a kiss right on her lips. Surprisingly, they were as cold as a vampire's, cold and rather clammy, with the distinct flavor of Frito pie. But before Hope could pull back and give Ryan a piece of her mind, he was gone— like completely removed from her line of sight.

And it took only a second to locate him, dangling from a fist attached to a tattooed arm. For an instant, Hope felt relief. The instant right before she remembered that the man standing before her with a choke hold on Ryan's throat was the same man who had run off like a lizard with his tail on fire. A man who hadn't called or tried to contact her in over a week.

"Put him down," Hope yelled.

Colt glanced over at her, and his eyes narrowed. "You know this man?"

"Know him," Rachel Dean teased. "After a kiss like that, I'd say she knows him pretty well."

"Yeah," Twyla joined in. "You sure he ain't the daddy of your babies, Hope?"

"She's got a point, Hog," Kenny said. "Who else but a man in love would offer a hun-nerd for one kiss?"

There was a moment when Colt's grip tightened so much that Hope wondered if he was actually going to snuff the life right out of Ryan. But then his fingers relaxed, and Ryan slithered to the floor. Colt glanced back at Hope for one brief second before he tossed something to the floor and walked away. Rushing over, Hope knelt down to ask Ryan if he was okay, but the words got stuck in her throat when her gaze drifted down.

There on the high-polished wood of the gymnasium floor was one crumpled dollar bill.

Chapter Eighteen

COLT SHOULD LEAVE. He was pissed. And when he was pissed, he always did stupid things. Things he would regret later. Except his feet weren't listening to his head, and he continued to lean in the doorway of the auxiliary gym and glare at the vampire who had just offered Hope a bite of his caramel apple.

Colt hadn't known what to expect when he returned to Bramble, but it certainly wasn't another man. For some crazy reason, he had been convinced there was only one man in Hope's life to worry about—Slate. Now he had to reevaluate his entire way of thinking, and it didn't exactly sit well.

A gay roommate he could laugh off. A heterosexual Hollywood agent was not so funny. Especially when Colt wasn't buying his story. No agent Colt had ever met would waste his time driving hundreds of miles just to check on one of his clients. That was what cell phones were for. Which meant the man was here for a different reason. A reason that had Colt's temper boiling and his stomach knotted in a tight fist, a fist that tightened when Ryan leaned over to whisper something in Hope's ear.

Just that quickly, Colt realized he'd been wrong. He wouldn't regret wiping the fake blood off the man's chin with his fist. Not now or later.

"Hollywood agent, my ass," he growled under his breath. But obviously not low enough.

"I know what you mean, sugar buns. I couldn't believe it either."

It took an effort for Colt to pull his gaze away from Hope and over to Marcy Henderson. Now here was something Colt regretted already. He had no business latching on to Marcy like a spurned teenage boy. But there he stood, staring into a pair of eyes that held the same sexual invitation that had been there for as long as he'd known her.

"Hope has always stretched the truth," Marcy continued in a high-pitched voice that grated on his nerves. "But after talking with Ryan, I realized she wasn't lying after all. Ryan is an honest-to-goodness Hollywood agent." She placed a hand on her chest, drawing Colt's attention to the ample breasts that swelled above the low neckline of her tight sweater. "In fact, he offered me a part in one of those horror movies. 'Course I never was much of a screamer… least ways, not out of bed."

She paused as her gaze slid over Colt. "It's sure hot for October, don't you think, sugar? I swear I'm about ready to incinerate." Leaning over, she pressed her breasts against his folded arms. "What say, we go on back to my trailer and have us a nice cold beer? If I remember correctly, you always did like a cold one… followed by a lot of heat."

He had to admit the breasts felt nice. Unfortunately, they were accompanied by the overpowering smell of cheap perfume. Still, when he glanced up and noticed

Hope watching, he seized the opportunity as any spurned teenage boy would.

"Well, that sure sounds like fun, honey." His hands slid around her waist as he sent her a smoldering look. "But I've had a hard week, so I think I'm going to head back to Shirlene's and get some sleep."

"Sleep?" She looked thoroughly confused at the mixed signals he was sending her. "Since when do you sleep, Colt Lomax?"

Noting that Hope had gotten up from the table and was now walking off, he released Marcy. "Since I turned thirty." He tried to soften the rejection with a wink. "But how about if I drive you home?" It was the least he could do after using her to appease his wounded ego.

"No, thanks." Marcy shot him an annoyed look as she smoothed down her pink sweater. "I might be over thirty, but I ain't dead yet." With a flip of her fifties poodle skirt, she strutted over to a group of cowboys, who seemed more than happy to see her.

Once she was gone, Colt glanced around, but Hope was nowhere to be found. It was probably for the best. With the way he felt, he didn't need to confront her tonight. He slipped out the door and walked down the short hallway to the main gym. The carnival was winding down, and most of the booths had closed. But still people were reluctant to call it a night and stood around talking, as their children raced up and down the bleachers, hyped up on the sweets they'd consumed.

Colt weaved his way through the crowd on his way to the doors without much notice, which was why he was surprised when the tall, lanky kid who played quarterback for Bramble High stopped him.

"You're Colt Lomax, right?" When Colt nodded, the kid introduced himself. "I'm Austin Reeves."

Colt took his hand and gave it a brief shake. No wonder the kid could handle a football with such ease; his hands were the size of dinner plates. "I hear the Bulldogs are headed for state. Congratulations."

He grinned. "Thank you, sir. We've got a great team of guys." He held out a folded orange napkin. "The witch wanted me to give you this."

"The witch?" Colt took the napkin and glanced around. Hope stood just inside the doors that led out to the courtyard. Except she now wore a witch's hat that placed half her face in shadow. But he had no difficulty seeing the daring smile before she turned and disappeared through the doors.

Thanking Austin with a nod, Colt followed after her, flipping the napkin open and reading it as he went. When he got outside, Hope was already hurrying across the courtyard—her purple hair and black dress fluttering in the cool October breeze before she slipped inside the main building.

The note had said she wanted to talk. Obviously, she didn't want to be overheard by anyone in town. Or maybe she just didn't want her boyfriend to find out. The thought annoyed him, and he quickened his step, jerking open the door and taking the stairs to the second level two at a time.

When he reached the designated classroom, his gaze was caught by a cuss word scratched into the metal of one of the lockers that lined the hallway. The locker hadn't belonged to him, but the angry word did. The awkwardly written letters brought back a flood of memories—memories of a loner who had never quite fit in.

The room was dark when he stepped inside. The only light spilled in from the hallway. But even that disappeared when the door eased shut behind him. He took a few steps into the room, only to bump into a desk.

He muttered an oath as he stepped back and rubbed his thigh. He waited for Hope to laugh, but all he heard was the tick-tick of a clock. And all he could see was the shadowy outline of desks.

Obviously, Hope wasn't finished leading him a merry chase.

But Colt was finished. The long week in Houston, coupled with his anger, had left him too tired to keep up with a wildcat. So he turned back to the door with every intention of calling it a night, except that just as he reached for the doorknob, it was pulled open by a witch—minus the hat.

"Look, Hope, I don't have the time or the patience for any more of your games," Colt stated. But even as he said it, he stepped back to allow her entry.

"Funny, but I was just going to say the exact same thing." She strode into the room with her normal sass, and he couldn't help reaching out to stop her before she smacked into the same desk as he had.

She wasn't exactly grateful for the help. With something that sounded like a snarl, she jerked away from him. "Don't touch me."

He held up his hands. "Don't worry, sweetheart. That's the last thing I want to do."

"So what do you want?" She headed back to the door, and he watched her feel around for the light switch.

"What do I want?" He sat down on the top of a desk and crossed his arms. "I thought this conversation was going to include what you wanted. Child support. A new minivan. A house to keep your Hollywood boyfriend in the style he expects."

Giving up on the light switch, she turned to him. "As if I would waste my time asking for those things from a motorcycle bum. Lyle's money has you living in some kind of a dream world, Lomax. At least in high school, you accepted who you were."

"Accepted? Did I have a choice? This town gave me my role, and I was expected to play it."

"And you're still doing a great job. Colt Lomax the big, bad boy with the nasty chip on his shoulder who runs off at the first sign of trouble." She turned and walked to the front of the class. Obviously, her eyes had adjusted to the darkness, because she didn't run into anything. Unlike Colt, who banged his shin on a desk leg after no more than two steps. He bit back a cuss word and hobbled over to the opposite side of the teacher's desk.

"I came back, didn't I?"

"Yeah, a week later!" She pulled off her wig and tossed it down on the desk.

"What do you want from me, Hope? You want me to be the big hero—the one who saves the day with a game-winning touchdown? Because if that's the case, you've got the wrong man. I'm not ever going to be Slate." He stepped around the desk. "It's too bad that Faith had to show up. If she hadn't, you would now be married to the only man who's ever been good enough for you." He paused. "Of course, that doesn't explain your relationship with your agent. Come to think of it, maybe I should be asking for a paternity test, seeing as how you seem to get around more than Marcy."

The slap that she gave him rang his bell. He was so dazed and confused that it took him a moment to realize she had headed for the door. She already had it opened by the time he reached her.

"Oh, no, you don't." He slammed the door closed and spun her around. "You wanted to talk, so talk."

"Why, you bastard!" Hope pushed at his chest. "Get your hands off me."

"After seeing you with your agent, I thought you liked being pawed."

Hope stopped trying to pull away. "You should talk! If I'd known you still haven't grown up enough to avoid women like Marcy, I never would've had sex with you in the first place. Now, not only do I have to worry about being pregnant, but I also have to worry about what I might've caught."

"Worried about being pregnant?" He stared down at her, trying to make out her features in the darkness. "Are you telling me that you're not sure?"

He couldn't see her face clearly, but he could hear her swallow.

"I refuse to believe it until my doctor's appointment in Midland."

"You sure as hell sounded positive when you busted into Shirlene's guesthouse, screaming at the top of your lungs." He took a step back and ran a hand through his hair. "Do you know the hell you put me through in the last week?"

"You think it's been easy for me?"

"From my vantage point, it looks like you've been whooping it up with your Hollywood boyfriend."

"He's not my boyfriend."

"So what is he to you?" he couldn't stop himself from asking.

"None of your business."

He didn't know what annoyed him more: her refusal to define her relationship with her agent or her refusal to accept she was pregnant with his child. Whichever it was, it had his back up and his temper high. Before she could utter more than a startled squeak, he jerked her up and kissed her.

After their hateful words, the heat of Hope's response took him by surprise. She held nothing back, answering his passion with a raw energy that left him slightly dazed. Her sweet tongue dipped inside his mouth, demanding attention, and he gave it, sucking and stroking until her moan resounded in his ears. Pulling away from the kiss, he sipped a path to her ear.

"What is he to you, Hope?" Colt whispered. "Can he cause you to tremble like this?" He sucked on a tender spot, and when she quivered in reaction, his hand slipped down and cupped her through the thin black dress. "Or ache like this?"

Her hands slid up from his chest, and he had just started to enjoy the feel of her fingers caressing his scalp when they closed around his hair and yanked so hard that he saw stars. Before he could recover, she opened the door and slipped out. He went after her, but she hadn't lettered in track for nothing, and by the time he caught up with her, she had reached the gym.

Colt grabbed her arm and cut to the chase. "When's your doctor's appointment?"

Hope turned on him, her eyes narrowed. "Why?"

"Because I want to be there."

She smiled smugly. "Sort of like you were there for me this past week?"

"When?" he repeated. But before she could answer, Hope's mama yelled across the gym.

"Colt, quit teasing Hope. She needs to help me get these boxes in the car."

Colt had always respected Jenna, but he refused to release Hope until she answered him. As if sensing his determination, it didn't take her long to give in.

"Nine on Monday."

Colt nodded. "I'll pick you up at seven."

Across the gym, a group of townsfolk watched as Hope jerked her arm away from Colt and hurried over to help her mama.

"It was the most pathetic thing I've ever seen in my life." Rachel scratched at a spot under her arm where the crumpled butcher paper of her costume had started to itch. "Hope stuffin' her bra full of napkins in an attempt to attract those foreigners' attention just broke my heart clean in two—which is why I sent Bear straight back to California. We need to find that daddy before Hope hooks up with some loser."

"I couldn't agree more, Rachel," Harley said, his mustache drooping from the time spent in the dunk tank. "But I don't think we can wait any longer. We got babies to think about, and we sure don't want people talkin' about our little Hope. Which means we need to give up on findin' the real daddy and start lookin' for a home-grown boy to do the job."

"You mean like a step-daddy?" Kenny asked.

"That's exactly what I mean."

"But who?" Sheriff Winslow jumped in as he watched Colt turn and walk out of the gym. "Hope is real picky about her men."

"I don't know," Harley said. "But if we keep our eyes open, it will come to us."

Chapter Nineteen

"HOPE SCROGGS?"

Instead of the female obstetrician Hope expected to see, Jimmy Higgins walked into the room with her chart, flashing a set of teeth that could no longer eat corn on the cob through a picket fence.

"How the hell have you been, honey?" He gave her a big hug as if she wasn't as naked as the day she was born beneath the thin cotton gown.

Struck speechless, all Hope could do was stare back at him.

"Danged if you don't look exactly the same as you did in high school." He pointed a finger at her. "Remember when we had Crazy Fifties Day and we won the jitterbug contest? Never could figure out why you chose me as a partner when you were dating Slate. But I guess he won out in the long run." He winked at her. "Congratulations, Mrs. Calhoun, you're going to have a baby."

Suddenly, having Jimmy for a doctor took a backseat to the news. After seven positive home pregnancy tests, the chances of her not being pregnant had been slim to none. Still, she had clung to that one tiny thread of hope like a lifeline. And now, just that quickly, "Bucky" Higgins had clipped the thread, and she went tumbling head over heels into the black abyss. Luckily, Bucky had finally noticed the other person in the room and didn't see her inappropriate reaction.

"Colt Lomax?" He glanced back at Hope, then back to Colt, and still the light didn't go on. "I guess Slate is busy coaching that state championship football team, huh? Well, it's good to see you, man. I saw your name in *Street Chopper Magazine*—"

"The baby is mine," Colt stated. Even in her comatose state, Hope wanted to reach out and slug him.

Bucky's eyes widened, but he quickly collected himself. "Well, didn't I just put my foot in it?" He walked over to the sink and set down the chart before turning on the water.

"I guess I shouldn't be surprised," he continued as he scoured his hands with soap. "You two were always like vinegar and oil. And all it takes is a little shakin' to get things mixed up. And it looks like you two got shaken up pretty well." He chuckled. "Colt and Hope married. Now isn't that just a kicker?"

Drying his hands on a paper towel, Bucky turned around and finally took note of their solemn faces.

"Would you look at me, runnin' off at the mouth like an idiot? You're not here to visit. You're here to find out about your baby." He cleared his throat and reached for the chart. When he spoke again, he sounded more like a doctor, instead of a babbling idiot. "So, using the information Hope wrote down on the questionnaire, I have her at six weeks with a due date of June tenth. Right before it gets too hot for a little extra weight."

He winked at Hope, but all she could do was stare back at him.

June tenth. Only five days before her own birthday. It seemed entirely too close.

"So have you experienced any morning sickness or dizziness?" Bucky set the chart back down.

She shook her head, even though at the moment she felt a little sick and light-headed.

"Good. Some women breeze right through pregnancy without a hitch. And I don't doubt for a minute that our sassy little Hope here will be one of those." He walked back over, and, taking her hand, eased her back on the table before he spread the sheet over her legs. "You two living back in Bramble?"

She started to explain the situation, but then realized she couldn't explain the unexplainable. So she was somewhat relieved when Colt kept it simple.

"Yes."

Bucky nodded. "If Doc Mathers ever retires, I might just move back there myself. It's a good place to raise a family. Although I need to pay off my student loans before my wife and I even think about kids. Kids are expensive." He lifted one of her feet and placed it in a stirrup before he moved to the other side.

"Before you leave, make sure to get the maternity packet from Katie. It gives you all the information you'll need—what exercise is good, what vitamins you'll need to start taking, and what food and drugs to avoid. And, of course, if you have any questions, don't hesitate to call me. After all, we're like family." He hooked the low stool on casters with his foot and pulled it toward him before he disappeared from sight.

Until that moment, Hope had been too busy thinking about the baby to pay much attention to what Bucky was doing. Even when the sheet started to lift, it took her a second to react. Fortunately, Colt's reaction was much faster. He reached over and jerked down the sheet, and at the same time, used a boot to shove the stool clear across the room.

"Whoa there, Bucky. What do you think you're doing?" Colt stepped in front of the table.

By the time Hope got her feet out of the stirrups and peeked around, Bucky wore the same look on his face that had been there thirteen years earlier when she'd dragged him out on the dance floor so she would have a chance at the trophy instead of no chance with Two-Left-Feet Calhoun.

"A p-pelvic examination," Bucky sputtered.

"If that includes looking at Hope naked—I don't think so, Buck."

"But I'm a doctor."

"And I'm a biker who's about ready to kick some MD ass."

Hope waited for Bucky to take offense, but she'd forgotten how good-natured the man was. After only a few seconds, a grin spread across his freckled face.

"Fair enough, Colt." He got up off the stool. "Doctor or no doctor, I wouldn't want a man looking at my wife either. We have a woman on staff, and if you're willing to wait, I'll have her come in."

"We'll wait," Colt said, without giving Hope a chance to speak. Not that she could have. Between Bucky and the baby, she was pretty speechless.

The other doctor wasn't as nice as Bucky, but Hope

didn't care, as long as she wasn't someone Hope had done algebra homework with. When she was finished, she helped Hope sit up.

"Everything looks fine, so unless you have any questions, we'll see you in another month."

"A month?" Colt took a step forward. "Isn't that a little long to wait? And what do you mean, unless something comes up? What would come up?"

The doctor walked over and started washing her hands at the sink. "I mean, if she should experience anything out of the ordinary—cramping, bleeding, or—"

"Which is exactly why I think a month is too long. Anything can go wrong in a month." Colt shook his head. "No, we'll be back next Monday."

The doctor looked at Hope and winked as if they shared some special secret about the idiocy of men. "Of course, if you'd like to come back in a week—"

"A month is fine." Hope finally found her voice, although it shook as much as her hands, clutched in her lap.

"Very good," the doctor said.

Once the door clicked closed behind her, Hope just sat there, unsure of what to say or do. And Colt didn't seem much better. With his hands shoved deep in his pockets, he wandered around, looking at the charts on the walls.

"You okay?" he asked.

"Yeah," she lied. "But we shouldn't have told Bucky."

Colt glanced over at her. "You still think we can keep it a secret?" He looked back at the diagram of fetal development. "It. Is that what you call something the size of a lima bean?"

"I don't know." She got up off the table and proceeded to get dressed, no longer concerned about Colt being in the same room. Not that he paid any attention. His gaze was riveted on the lima bean.

"Have you thought about names?" he asked.

She swallowed. "No."

"Well, until we do, I'm going to call it Pumpkin Seed."

Her heart, which had been beating so quickly, seemed to freeze up in her chest as her gaze snapped over to him. "I don't think we should name...it. Not until we figure out what to do."

He turned away from the poster, his brow knotted. "What do you mean?" The confusion cleared, and his eyes narrowed. "We're not getting an abortion."

As if it was the most important thing to do at the moment, she carefully folded the gown. "No, but that doesn't mean I'm going to keep...it."

His gray eyes filled with disbelief, but before he could reply, the cute little nurse poked her head in, and the conversation was put on hold while she gave them the maternity packet and directed them back to the receptionist's desk, where Colt paid the bill, using a credit card.

A credit card paid for by Lyle Dalton, no doubt, Hope thought. The idea of his using someone else's money on their child angered her, although she was no angrier than he seemed to be. As soon as they pulled away from the parking lot, he started in.

"So that's it? You want to give Pumpkin Seed away?"

"Stop it!" She turned to him, the seatbelt cutting into her shoulder. "Stop calling it Pumpkin Seed!"

"It's not an 'it,' Hope! It's something!" He ran a hand through his hair as he returned his gaze to the road. "It's something."

"I know it's something. But it's something inside my

body. My body!" She thumped herself in the chest so hard that it hurt.

"And because of that, I don't have a choice. Is that what you're saying?"

Realizing she was being a raving idiot, she fell back against the seat and took a deep breath. "No, that's not what I'm saying. I'm saying, we need to consider all the options and make an intelligent decision. A decision using all the facts."

"Like what? The fact that you hate my guts?" He glanced over at her, his eyes shielded behind the dark green lenses of his sunglasses.

Hope started to say that she didn't hate his guts. That as much as she wanted to, her emotions didn't come close to hate. But she stopped herself. That kind of revelation would only cause more hurt and pain. And it was already painful enough.

"How about the fact that neither one of us has a job?"

"I have a job."

She shot him an annoyed look. "Riding around on a motorcycle bought by someone else is not a job, Colt. It's a pastime. Which means, if I don't get this reality show, I'll be living with my parents. And Mama and Daddy have no business helping me raise a child after they just sent their last one off to college."

"Reality show?" Colt glanced over at her. "Is that why your agent showed up? He wants you to go back to California for a job?"

She nodded. "Ryan thinks I've got a pretty good chance of getting it. I guess I'll find out when I fly back next week."

There was a long pause before Colt spoke. "So that's

what this is about. You finally have a chance to achieve your dream, and you don't want my baby screwing it up."

Hope pressed her fingers to her throbbing temples. "Can't we have one conversation where we aren't at one another's throats? This isn't about me or you, Colt. It's about an innocent life that deserves the best we can give it."

"So what's the problem? If you become a big reality star, you'll have plenty of money to spend on a baby."

"It's not just about the money. It's about giving our child a nurturing home—a home with two loving parents." She turned away. "Given your childhood, I thought you would understand how important that is."

"I survived," he growled.

"Exactly." She turned back to him. "But I don't want my child to just survive. And I don't want my baby being raised by a nanny because I'm working day and night, or being neglected by a father who can't unglue his butt from a motorcycle seat. I want my child to feel safe and secure, surrounded by a loving mother and father."

Colt's gaze narrowed on her. "You've already decided, haven't you?"

He was right. All the time that she thought she was just walking around in a daze, her mind had already been working on a plan—a plan that made perfect sense.

"She'll love the baby as her own," she whispered.

He pulled up to the stoplight and turned to her. "She?" He studied her for a second before his eyes widened. "Faith? You're going to give Pumpkin Seed to Faith and Slate?" When she shook her head, it didn't take long for the logical answer to come. Colt fell back against the seat and released his breath in a slow, painful sigh. "Shirlene."

Leaning as far toward him as the seat belt would allow, Hope tried to justify her decision. "She wants a baby so desperately, Colt. If you could've seen all those home pregnancy tests she'd hoarded, it would've broken your heart. And with us, all it took was one time with one faulty condom." She looked out the windshield, but saw nothing. "And maybe that's why it happened. Maybe it's God's plan. I'd be like a surrogate mother. It would even have her genes."

Colt just sat there with a hand hooked over the steering wheel and his gaze riveted to the stoplight. It changed to green, but still he didn't go, not until a car honked behind him.

"Have you told her?" he asked, once they were moving again.

"No. She's been disappointed so many times, I want to be sure."

He nodded. "Good. I think you should wait until you're further along."

"So you think that's what we should do?"

"We?" He glanced over at her. "Am I now in the equation?"

Suddenly exhausted, Hope leaned her head back against the headrest and closed her eyes. "If you can figure out another option, Colt, I'm willing to listen."

It seemed like they drove for miles before he finally spoke.

"No. I can't think of a thing."

Chapter Twenty

A STIFF WIND blew through Jones' Garage, making the concrete floor Colt sat on feel even colder than it was. Still, he wasn't ready to go back to Shirlene's. Not even for a blazing fire and a steamy cup of coffee. He needed the comfort of being wrist-deep in crankshafts and carburetors, pistons and rods.

Working on a motorcycle was almost as soothing as riding one, and after the doctor's visit, Colt needed all the soothing that he could get. He wasn't freaked out about the confirmation of Hope's pregnancy. Even without it, he'd come to terms with her having a baby. What upset him the most was the idea of giving that baby away. Which was crazy. As much as he might want to deny it, Hope was right. He was a motorcycle bum. A rich motorcycle bum, but a bum just the same. A bum who enjoyed his freedom and the open road. A bum who had no place in his life for a child.

So why did he feel as if someone had kicked him in the solar plexus with a steel-toed boot? Probably because, while staring at the diagram of the different stages of fetal development, the baby had suddenly become something more than just a big mistake.

It had become a small miracle.

His miracle.

Pumpkin Seed.

The words were more than just a silly name to tease Hope with. They held part of the past and a piece of the future. And damned if he didn't struggle with the thought of giving Pumpkin Seed away, even if it was to his own sister. A sister he would walk through fire for. A sister who wanted a child more than anything else in the world.

"Hey. Where's your cool chopper?"

Colt glanced up from the Knucklehead to see Jesse standing in the doorway of the garage, looking more ragged than usual. Today he wore a plain white T-shirt. At least, it had started out white. Now it looked worse than the rag sitting on the floor by Colt's knee. Jesse's hair was sleep-mussed, but his eyes were alert as they tracked around the garage.

"I delivered it," Colt said. "Where's your coat?"

"I ain't cold." Almost as soon as the words were out, he shivered.

Shaking his head, Colt pointed to the leather jacket hooked over a tire jack. "Put it on."

"I ain't—"

"Put it on," he ordered, before he turned back to the bike. He thought the kid would continue to argue, but instead, a few minutes later, he appeared on the other side of the bike with the jacket hanging off his bony shoulders.

"You ain't fixed it yet?"

Great. All Colt needed was another person thinking he was incompetent.

"No, I haven't fixed it yet."

Jesse flopped down on the other side of the bike, but he leaned in close enough for Colt to see his freckled face between the teardrop gas tank and the front tire. "I ain't gonna wait around for the money forever, you know."

"Speaking of which...what did you do with the money I gave you?"

"That ain't none of your business." Jesse swiped at his nose.

"It is if you want to see any more."

His face grew more belligerent than usual. "I gave it to my mom."

"Is this the same mom who homeschools you, even with two jobs?"

There was a long pause before the kid answered. "My big sister homeschools me while my mom works."

Kenny had mentioned that Jesse had a sister, so it seemed feasible. "Then you should be home studying instead of hanging around here."

"It's recess."

Colt couldn't help but laugh. "Fine, but don't touch anything. I don't want you messing anything up."

The kid snorted. "Like I could make this bike any uglier."

The morning went by quickly. Colt probably should've sent the kid home, but the kid's constant questions about motorcycles took his mind off his own problems, although after about an hour Jesse's questions brought him full circle.

"You got kids?"

Colt swallowed. "No."

"How come?"

"Because," he hedged.

The answer didn't suffice. "Because you don't want any?"

It was funny how kids could get straight to the heart of things. He hadn't wanted kids. At least, he thought he hadn't. But now he wanted one. One tiny little seed.

"No, I want kids." He stopped working and wiped his hands off on the rag. Through the opening in the bike, he watched Jesse's face scrunch up in thought.

"How many?"

He got to his feet. "I don't know."

"Four's a good number."

Shaking his head, Colt walked over to the soda machine. "Yeah, four is a nice even number." He dug through his pocket for some change.

"You got a wife?" Jesse came over to stand next to him. Colt hadn't realized how small the kid was until that moment. As he studied him, he readjusted his first age estimate. The kid couldn't be more than eight or nine— too young to be wandering around by himself.

"No, I don't have a wife." His gaze narrowed. "How old are you?"

"Old enough." He punched a button on the machine as if the money Colt had put in was for him. When the grape soda rolled out, he grabbed it up. "My sister's real pretty."

Colt crossed his arms and glared down at the kid. "Stop stalling and answer the question."

He popped the top. "Twelve."

Colt lifted an eyebrow.

"Ten." He took a deep guzzle, then burped loudly. "And Mia's really nice. Well, sometimes she's nice. When she ain't yellin' at me about doing my homework."

"Speaking of homework," Colt searched his pockets

for more quarters, but only came up with three linty nickels and five pennies, "I think it's time for you to get back to yours."

"I ain't ready."

"Too bad." Colt moved toward the office. "After I get some caffeine, I'm driving you home."

Shooting him a belligerent look, Jesse tipped up the can and guzzled the drink.

"Hey, Colt," Tyler greeted him as he stepped inside the small office. "How's the bike coming?"

"Not well." He handed him a dollar. "Could you give me some quarters?"

"So you still think it's going to make it to the corner?" Tyler opened up the cash register and exchanged the money.

Colt wasn't so sure anymore, but he refused to voice his doubt. "It will take some time, is all. But right now, I'm going to drive Jesse home."

Tyler laughed. "That kid is a pistol, isn't he?"

"More like a pain in my butt."

Unfortunately, by the time he and Tyler got back out in the garage, the pain-in-the-butt kid was nowhere to be found and Colt's leather jacket hung back over the tire jack.

"Looks like he had other plans," Tyler said.

Colt pulled the keys to Shirlene's Navigator out of his pocket with every intention of going after the boy, but before he could, a long motor home pulled up in front of the station.

He glanced over at Tyler, who had a big grin on his face.

"The old man got in last night, but he swore me to secrecy. Said he wanted to surprise you."

Colt felt a lot more than surprised as Tinker, Tyler's daddy, stepped down from the driver's side. A wall of unexplainable emotions welled up inside him, and something that felt a lot like tears filled his eyes. Luckily, he had a strong wind to blame them on.

"If I hadn't just had my eyes checked," Mr. Jones drawled around the huge lump of tobacco in his mouth, "I would think they was playin' tricks on me."

"No, sir." Colt stepped forward and stretched out his hand to the man who, despite a balder head, had changed very little over the years. "A sharper set of eyes I've yet to run into."

Tinker walked past the hand and enfolded Colt in a bear hug. "You ain't gonna get away with that, Colt Lomax. Not after you practically lived in my garage."

Tinker Jones had gotten shorter, or maybe Colt had gotten taller. But it didn't matter if he'd shrunk a good three feet, it was comforting to be enveloped against a body that smelled like Ben-Gay and Josie's fried onions.

"How you doin', boy?" Jones whacked him twice on the back before he eased away. His kind eyes pierced right through Colt. And with raw emotion clogging Colt's throat, it was difficult to get the words out.

"Good, sir."

What was the matter with him, anyway? Yeah, Mr. Jones had been like a father to him, but that didn't mean he had to get all weepy-eyed. He was Colt Lomax, the kid who never cried, even when he had something to cry about. But damned if he could get a handle on the feelings that welled up inside him.

"Come on. Let's get out of this wind." Mr. Jones ushered Colt in front of him. "Hell, no wonder I don't want to live here. The summers are too hot and the winters could blow you plum away."

"Well, you better not head out on the road until after the holidays or your grandkids and Missy will have my hide," Tyler said, as he started to follow them back into the garage. But his father stopped him by tossing him the keys to the RV.

"Ty, I was hopin' you'd give her a once-over. After thousands of miles of road, she might need a little pamperin'."

Tyler's gaze locked with his father's for only a second before he nodded. "Sure thing, Daddy. I just made some coffee; you and Colt help yourselves."

Once they were inside the office, Mr. Jones took the lopsided chair next to the cluttered desk and pointed to the chair opposite. "So what's goin' on with you?"

"Same old." Colt remained standing, leaning a shoulder on the doorjamb in as casual a manner as he could muster. "Business is good, but I spend a lot of time on the road."

"I'm not talkin' about business, boy. I figured you were doin' all right when you had that big old motor home delivered to my doorstep."

"I didn't—"

Mr. Jones held up a hand, a hand that had guided Colt toward the straight and narrow, even when he fought against it. "Don't give me that, boy. Who else would be pigheaded enough to think he owed me something? Besides, I never entered no sweepstakes for an RV."

Colt pushed away from the doorway and walked over to the front windows. "I do owe you. You were the one who gave me a job at twelve when no one else would. The one who taught me all about engines. And the one who bought my books when I started those satellite college courses. Some stupid motor home doesn't repay that."

"Any debt you owed me was paid in full, son, the moment you succeeded. That's all a man ever expects from his kids." The chair squeaked. "So let's dispense with the bullshit and get onto the reason you look like someone shot your best huntin' dog."

Colt laughed. "I never owned a hunting dog."

"No, I guess you didn't. You had enough on your plate without addin' an animal. This isn't about Shirlene, is it?"

"No," Colt said, even though his sister played a part. After years of trying to give her everything she needed—or wanted—he had finally stumbled upon something he couldn't bring himself to give away. Not even to her.

"Then I guess that leaves Hope."

Colt whirled around and stared at the old guy. "What?"

"Not what." His bushy white eyebrows lifted. "But who. And you heard me the first time."

"I heard you, but that doesn't mean I understand what she has to do with my hangdog look—not that I have a hangdog look—but if I did, she wouldn't have anything to do with it."

Tinker shook his head. "You still playin' that game, boy? Because at thirty-two, it has to be gettin' old."

"I don't know what you're talking about, old man."

A grin split Tinker's face, showing off the wad of tobacco. "Sure you do. It's the game where you act like you don't like Hope."

Oh, that game.

"After growing up with three brothers, I know it ain't easy for men to put their feelings in words," Tinker continued. "Which is why we do stupid things to get our girl's attention—like poppin' wheelies and doin' handstands."

Since Colt had never done a wheelie or a handstand for any girl, he quirked an eyebrow.

"I busted out three teeth showing off for Martha on my bike. Most embarrassin' day of my life." He shook his head at the memory. "'Course, you chose pranks over showin' off. The pig snout on the homecoming semi. The live ammo in that there stage gun."

"I did not put—"

Tinker held up his hand. "Not here, nor there. What matters is what you do now. And if you tell me you've hoisted her bra back up on the town hall flagpole, I'm going to warm your butt just like the last time."

Colt hadn't hoisted her bra. It was worse. He'd gotten her pregnant. Now instead of dealing with a few moments of humiliation, she got to spend a lifetime wallowing in it. And he was to blame.

Again.

Moving over to the chair, Colt flopped down and ran a hand over his face. "I got her pregnant."

Until that moment, he had placed equal blame on Hope, but now he realized that most lay at his doorstep. He was the one who knew how old the condom was, and still he had gone ahead. And maybe, subconsciously, he had wanted her to get pregnant. All in an effort to get Hope to notice him.

God, he wished he had just done a handstand.

The chair squeaked as Mr. Jones leaned back. "I figured as much when Tyler told me about the baby. Of course, he's convinced, along with the town, that it's somebody out in California who did the deed. The blame fools don't even seem to know that's the same place you live."

Colt looked over at him. "So you want me to stand up and touch my toes or lean over the counter?"

"I reckon you're a little too old for a whuppin'. Besides, that kind of mistake takes two people. Two people to mate, two people to create."

"One person to hate," he mumbled under his breath, but not low enough.

"And who would that person be?"

"We both know who it is. And I can't blame her. Not after everything I've done to her."

Mr. Jones sat back and laughed.

It wasn't quite the reaction Colt expected. "I'm glad you find it so amusing," he said, without humor.

"It's amusing that men can be so damned stupid where women are concerned, especially when women wear their hearts right out on their sleeves for anyone who takes a notion to see. Men are just too busy worryin' about their own egos to take the time to look."

"Meaning?"

"Meaning, that girl has had a thing for you since you were both knee-high to a grasshopper."

"I think you've got me confused with Slate."

Those bushy brows lowered. "Don't go callin' me senile, boy, or I'll change my mind about that whuppin'. I know who Slate is, and I know who you are. And that girl didn't like Slate for anything more than a boy to soothe her ego after you'd bruised it to hell and back."

Colt stared at Tinker with disbelief. "But he was the town hero."

"So?"

"So she was the sweetheart. It made sense."

" 'Course it did, which is why an entire town played into it. But whose fault was that, Colt? You didn't exactly give them another choice."

It was the same thing Tyler had told him, and Colt had started to wonder if maybe they didn't have a point. The thought rumbled around in his head while Mr. Jones swiveled in the chair and started rummaging around in one of the desk drawers.

"Since Tyler has always been a bit of a packrat, I fig-ure it's got to be around here somewhere—here it is." He lifted a small rectangular photograph from the drawer. He studied it for a few seconds before swiveling back around and holding it out for Colt. "I took it with the new camera Martha had gotten me for my birthday that year. I guess you must've been around fifteen, which would've made Hope…"

"Thirteen," Colt supplied, as he took the picture.

It had been taken from the doorway of the office. It was a close-up of two young kids: a dark-headed boy, who sat cross-legged in front of a motorcycle, his gaze intent on what he was doing, and a brown-headed girl, who sat just beyond. The angle caught his profile, the large nose and unruly hair that fell over his forehead. But it was the girl's face that was the focal point of the photo. A pretty little girl with a sprinkling of freckles across her button nose and a blush of womanhood across her high cheeks. She stared intently, not at the engine of the 250 Yamaha, but at the boy who worked on it.

In those eyes, Colt saw something that shook him to the core of his being.

"Tell me now that she didn't like you," Mr. Jones said. "And every time I looked out, that's exactly what I saw."

Colt stared at the picture, afraid to take his eyes off it. Afraid it might change if he did.

"What do you want, Colt?" Mr. Jones asked. "It's an easy question, boy."

It was an easy question. At least, it had been an easy question a month ago. Then he could've answered with one word: freedom. Freedom to go where he wanted to go and do what he wanted to do. But looking down at the picture, he realized that freedom didn't come close to holding the same allure as a pair of adoring eyes the color of a West Texas sky.

"It doesn't matter what I want." Colt started to hand back the photo, but found he couldn't quite bring himself to do it. "This was taken a long time ago. She doesn't feel the same way anymore."

Mr. Jones eyes narrowed. "But what if you're wrong, son?"

Chapter Twenty-one

"MARRY ME, HOG!"

Hope turned to the carload of teenagers who slowly drove past her as she walked down Main Street. With a roll of her eyes, she addressed the kid who hung out the back window with his hand over his heart.

"Call me when you're old enough to shave."

The kid rubbed his baby soft chin. "That could be years."

"I'll wait," she hollered back.

The boy grinned and blew her a kiss as the car picked up speed.

"What's the count?" Hope's mama, Jenna, stepped out the door of the Feed and Seed and took the can of purple paint Hope had been delivering for the storefront.

"Jonas Murphy was twenty-one, so I guess that makes Anthony twenty-two." Jenna held out a Styrofoam cup to Hope. "It's decaf."

Hope accepted it and took a heavenly sip before answering. "Either way, it's absolutely ridiculous."

"Now, I agree that the flowers and gifts have gotten

a little out of hand—last night your daddy couldn't even find the remote with all the boxes of candy and vases of flowers—but not every girl can claim twenty-two marriage proposals. That has to be some kind of a record."

"A record I have no desire to have." Hope sat down on the bench under the window, and her mother set down the can of paint and joined her.

"It just shows how much the people of this town love you, Hope Marie. They just don't want you raising that baby all by yourself."

At the mention of the baby, Hope's chest tightened and tears threatened. She tried to hide the reaction by taking another sip of coffee, but when she glanced back up, her mama was studying her with a concerned look.

"It's okay to be scared, honey," her mama said. "Having a baby is a scary thing, especially when you haven't planned it."

The week before, Hope would've agreed with her mother. She had been scared about being pregnant and raising a child by herself. But after her decision to give the baby away, she wasn't scared as much as...in pain. She felt as if a huge anvil had been placed on her chest. And day by day, it grew heavier and heavier, until she wondered if her ribs would hold beneath the pressure.

It made no sense whatsoever. She had thought it all out and made dozens of lists, and all the pieces fit perfectly together. But if that was the case, then why did it feel so wrong?

"Was it hard?" she asked around the lump in her throat.

Thinking Hope was asking about motherhood, her mama jumped right in.

"Yes, it was hard. At fifteen, I didn't have a clue what

to do with a colicky baby or a husband who would rather be out with his friends. And I couldn't blame him, not when he had the responsibility of putting a roof over our heads and food in our stomachs."

"So why did you keep me?"

Her mama stared off across the street. "When two babies came out instead of one, I guess I took it as a sign— a sign that God wanted me to have one for my own."

Hope set the Styrofoam cup down on the sidewalk. "Were you ever sorry?"

"Sorry for giving Faith away? Or sorry for keeping you?"

"Both, I guess."

Seconds ticked by before her mama finally spoke. "I wish I could tell you that I regretted one but not the other. But the truth is, there were times I wished I had Faith with me and times I wished I didn't have you—like when all my friends were going out and I was stuck at home because your daddy was working swing shift and I couldn't afford a babysitter. Or when we didn't have money to get me a new pair of jeans or a pretty new shirt because we had to buy diapers. Or when I couldn't buy you a new Easter dress for church."

She shook her head. "Of course, those thoughts blew in and out of my young brain like the unpredictable West Texas rain—they were gone as quickly as they came. All it would take is you snugglin' close to me, your breath all sweet and warm against my throat, and I figured I'd made the right choice after all. Then I'd start feeling bad about Faith."

This time Hope couldn't fight back the wall of depression that seemed to engulf her. Tears welled up in her eyes, and her voice shook. "But how did you live with all those conflicting emotions?"

Noting her tears, her mama reached out and pulled her close. "Awww, honey, you just take things day by day. That's how all folks do it. And it all worked out. You both turned out to be intelligent young women any mother would be proud of."

Hope pressed her face against her mother's neck. "I don't see how you can be proud of me."

Pulling back, her mama stared down at her in disbelief. "How could I not be proud of you, Hope Marie? You have always been a perfect child—slightly stubborn and controlling, but a hard worker, a loving daughter, and a good human being. What more could I ask for?"

"How about my having enough smarts to stay away from the wrong man," she sniffed.

It was the first time Hope had even come close to acknowledging her condition, and her mama's eyes filled with relief.

Reaching out, she smoothed the hair off Hope's forehead. "I'll reserve my opinion about the father of my grandchild until I get to meet him. All things have a way of working out in the wash."

Hope got to her feet. "That's doubtful, Mama, given that my machine is broken."

Her mother chuckled as she stood. "Well, I guess I better get back inside and make sure Marty's not playing those silly games on his phone instead of taking inventory. If his daddy catches him at it again, that boy is going to get his ears boxed but good."

The bell on the door jangled as her mother opened it. "I'd tell you to go home and take a nap—you look tired, honey—but you never have listened worth a hoot." The door jangled closed behind her.

Once she was gone, Hope wondered if her mama wasn't right. She was tired, so tired that she wanted to curl up on the bench and sleep—sleep until the nightmare of the next eight months was over.

"Uhhh...hey there, Hope."

The deep, slowly spoken words pulled her attention over to a large farmer in a faded pair of overalls. Hope had always had a soft spot for Ethan Miller, so she flashed a smile and quickly got to her feet.

"Hi, Ethan. What brings you to town?"

His face was sunburned, but it got even redder as he stared down at the scuffed toes of his boots. "Uhhh... well, I... brought you somethin'." He tugged on the leash that he had wrapped around one platter-sized hand, and a baby pig trotted out from behind his legs.

"This here is Sherman. Uhhh...he's house-broke and don't eat much. Though he does like an occasional roll in the mud."

Other men had offered Hope live gifts, but she had been able to reject them with a few teasing jokes. But Ethan wasn't a person who understood teasing, not when the kids in school had been so cruel about his size and awkwardness. And Hope hadn't become his champion all those years ago to hurt his feelings now. Even if a baby pig was the last thing she needed.

"Thank you, Ethan." She accepted the leash and knelt down to let the pig bump her with his snout. "He's adorable."

A grin appeared for a brief second before he continued. "Uhhh...so I was thinkin'." He paused and swallowed hard. "That's if you don't have your sights set on someone else..."

When he took another pause, Hope searched for anything to keep him from continuing. Accepting a pig was one thing, but a marriage proposal was something else entirely. Fortunately, before he could do more than utter another "uhhh," Colt walked up.

She hadn't talked to him since the day of the doctor's visit. And suddenly she felt as shy and embarrassed as Ethan. Or maybe just guilty about being the type of woman who was willing to give away their child.

"Nice pig," Colt said, but he merely glanced at the pig before his intense gaze settled back on Hope.

Disconcerted, she scrambled to her feet. "Sherman. His name is Sherman."

"Hey, Sherman." Colt leaned down and scratched the pig's back until it snuffled with delight and rooted against his legs. With a laugh, he straightened and reached a hand out to Ethan. "How you doing, Ethan? Your mama still make the best chocolate chip cookies this side of the Pecos?"

"She shore does, Colt," Ethan replied without hesitation. "But I would've thought that you got your fill of them all those nights we worked late at Josephine's."

"Not even close. If it wasn't for your mama packing food for me, I wouldn't have had the energy to stay awake." Colt glanced between the two of them. "I didn't interrupt anything important, did I?"

"No!" Hope jumped in before Ethan could start stammering again. "Ethan just brought me a present."

One dark eyebrow hiked up as Colt looked down at the pig.

"Well, I guess I better get on back." Ethan nodded at Colt before looking over at Hope. "Uhhh...bye, Hope."

"Good-bye, Ethan. And thank you so much for Sherman."

"You're shore welcome." He ambled back down the street.

When he was gone, Hope flopped down on the bench and stared at the pig, which had tipped over her cup of coffee and was now licking the liquid off the concrete.

"Is coffee good for pigs?" Colt asked as he took a seat next to her.

"It's decaf." She hooked the end of the leash over the arm of the bench.

After watching the pig polish off the last drop, Colt glanced over at her. "Another marriage bribe?"

"Yes, but thankfully Ethan didn't get to the actual proposal." She turned to him. "You washed dishes at Josephine's with Ethan? How come I never saw you?"

"Probably because I showed up after you were gone." He grabbed the leash and pulled Sherman away from the blob of gum that the pig was trying to get up off the sidewalk. "And I didn't do dishes, I cleaned the toilets."

Confused, she stared at him. "But I thought your mama cleaned—you helped her?"

He looked away, and she watched his Adam's apple rise and fall. "I didn't help my mother, Hope. I did it for her because she was too drunk to do it herself."

Drunk? Hope didn't have a lot of memories of Abby Lomax, but what she did have weren't of a falling-down drunk. Mrs. Lomax had been quiet and soft-spoken with hair as jet black as her son's and eyes as green as Shirlene's. She moved slower than Hope's mama and wasn't much of a housekeeper or a cook. But once she had helped Hope and Shirlene make Kleenex dresses for their Barbies and, another time, paper chains for their Christmas trees. Although, now that Hope thought about it, there was that time Mrs. Lomax had taken a nap by the front steps. And the time she came outside while they were playing in the Chevy in nothing but her bra and panties. And it did explain why she looked so tired and sick in the mornings. And why Hope had never been invited to spend the night.

Hope tried to think of something to say, but there was nothing to say. Especially when staring into those beautiful gray eyes. She knew a lot of Colts—the Cocky Colt, the Teasing Colt, the Spiteful Colt—but the honest, sincere man sitting next to her, she didn't recognize.

But before Hope could make sense of his behavior, her mama came out of the Feed and Seed looking worried and flustered. "Your daddy just called. They've laid off a bunch of people at Dalton."

"What?" Hope jumped up, and Colt had to grab her to keep her from tripping over the pig's leash. "Daddy? Did they lay off Daddy?"

"No," her mama shook her head. "But they laid off fifty others."

"Fifty." Hope felt her knees give out. Luckily, Colt still held on to her.

"Jenna, why don't you take Hope on home?" He pulled the cell phone from his back pocket. "I'll call Lyle and find out what's going on."

"I'm not going home." Hope pulled away from him. She had let Lyle get away with his lies once; she wasn't about to do it again. "I'm staying right here until I get some answers."

"And it looks like you're not the only one." Her mama

nodded at the cars that had started to fill the parking lot of Josephine's Diner.

Colt sighed and ran a hand through his hair. "Fine." He handed the leash to her mama, who looked surprised to find a pig on the end of it. "But I don't want you adding to the panic, Hope. If the town is going to pull out of this, we need to keep cool heads."

"This coming from the biggest hothead in Bramble."

He flashed her a warning look as they started across the street. "I mean it, Hope. People will be hysterical enough as it is."

The diner was packed by the time they walked through the door. And Colt was right; there was mass hysteria. Everyone seemed to be talking at once. Harley's mustache was bouncing. Sheriff Winslow's mouth was flapping. And Rachel Dean looked like she hadn't come up for air in a good hour.

"Get their attention, Hope, and keep it," Colt instructed, as he punched a button on his phone.

Hope looked around at the panicked townspeople. "And just how do you suggest I do that?"

"I'm sure the Sweetheart of Bramble will think of something. All I need is five minutes to talk with Lyle and figure out what's going on, and I don't want a lynch mob forming before I do." Without waiting for a reply, he headed back out the door.

Hope stared at the mayhem for only a second before she let out the hog call that had won her five trophies and an honorable mention. When it stopped resounding from the walls, every person in Josephine's had turned to her. But now that she had their attention, she didn't have a clue what to say.

"Hi, y'all." She smiled brightly.

"Sorry, Hope," Harley held up a hand, "we don't have time for pleasantries. Dalton Oil just laid off fifty workers."

"Oh." She chewed on her lip as she struggled to come up with something to say to that. When they started to turn away, she blurted out the first thing she could think of. "Well, I guess that's much more important than the identity of my baby's father."

Rachel hurried out from behind the counter. "Now, honey, I'm sure Harley didn't realize what you wanted to talk about. Of course, we have time to listen to our sweetheart." She patted the red vinyl of an empty bar stool. "Now you just come right on over here and tell us all about that lowlife who did you wrong."

Hope sent everyone a weak smile as she made her way through the silent crowd. "Are you sure? Because what I have to say can wait."

"Of course, she's sure," Twyla pushed her way to the front of the group once Hope was seated. "So go ahead, Hog, give us all of the dirty details."

With every eye pinned on her, Hope cleared her throat. But nothing came out.

"Oh, you poor thing," Rachel said. "Let me get you some water."

Thankful for being handed another stall tactic, Hope waited patiently for Rachel to fill a glass, and then took her time drinking every last drop.

Once the glass was empty, Darla jumped back in. "So who is it? Someone you met in California?"

"Yes." She glanced out the side window where Colt was talking on his phone. "In fact, I ran into him at the place I worked."

"I knew it!" Twyla almost jumped out of her skintight Wranglers. "The daddy is a movie star."

"A movie star?" Rachel stared at Hope with confusion. "But why didn't you just say that in the first place, honey. It sure would've saved us a lot time."

Suddenly stuck between a lie and a hard spot, Hope could only stammer. "Well, I...I..."

Darla jumped back in. "No doubt, she was worried that her name would be splashed all over those rag magazines."

Rachel's confusion cleared. "You're right. I remember when Daryl's two-headed hog got on the front cover. There were so many phone calls and people stoppin' by unannounced that the poor man was forced to sell it to a travelin' carnival, just so he could get a wink of sleep. And I know for a fact he's regretted it ever since. Daryl loved Mizty and Bitzy like they was his own kids." She patted Hope's knee. "But there's no need to worry about that, honey. If anyone can keep a secret, we can."

"She right, Hope," Cindy Lynn leaned in closer. "Is it Matthew McConaughey?"

Fortunately, before Hope had to answer, Colt stepped back in the door, his hair tousled and windblown. He was dressed like he always was—in a black T-shirt and faded jeans. But there was something different about him. Something that Hope couldn't quite put her finger on.

"I just got off the phone with Lyle Dalton." Colt's deep, smooth voice pulled everyone's attention away from Hope. With every eye on him, he continued. "He's right in the middle of some important negotiations and can't fly back, but I know he's doing everything he can to fix this."

"He's a little late, ain't he?" Joe Mitchell said, and a grumble of agreement went through the crowd.

Colt turned to look at the older man. "I can understand you being upset, Joe, seeing as how all three of your sons work at Dalton. But you've known Lyle all his life—gone fishing with him and enjoyed his hospitality on more than one occasion—so if anyone knows how hard the man works or how much he loves the folks of Bramble, it should be you."

Joe looked away, then nodded. "I suppose I do," he confessed.

"Seeing as how you just got out of prison, how do you know so much about it, Colt?" Rye Pickett asked.

Colt didn't even blink. "Because I spent last week in Houston at the corporate offices, going over the books with Lyle."

Hope sat up straighter. Colt had been in Houston helping Lyle? For a moment, she was angry that he had kept such a secret. But looking around the room at the panicked faces, she quickly understood why.

"I'm not going to lie to you," Colt said. "Dalton Oil is in financial trouble. Which is why Lyle's negotiating with another company to buy Dalton. Meanwhile, he's assured me that everyone laid off will receive a severance package to tide them over until they get another job."

"A job where?" Rye Pickett asked. "If Dalton don't get bought, there ain't gonna be no jobs."

It was a good point, and the crowd's grumbling grew louder. But before panic could set back in, Hope slipped off her stool and walked over to stand next to Colt.

"Dalton Oil has been around for longer than most of the people in this room," she stated. "So let's not go and put the cart before the horse. If Colt says Lyle is doing everything he can to set thing straight, I believe him.

Besides, this isn't just Lyle's problem. If Dalton Oil is going to survive, then we all need to work together."

"But how can we help, Hope?" Kenny Gene pushed his way to the front. "Most of us don't know nothin' about business."

Colt's gaze swept over the crowd. "We can start by not panicking. And we can rally around the families who did have a member laid off." His voice rose, strong and sure. "And we can do what all good Texans do when their backs are against the wall."

"What's that?" Harley asked.

Colt winked at Hope before giving the group one of his rare smiles. "We fight."

Chapter Twenty-two

LOST JOBS, OR a town's complete financial ruin, weren't enough to keep true Texans from a football game. Especially a state championship. So on Friday afternoon, the entire town of Bramble loaded up their cowbells, face paint, and pompoms into chartered buses and caravanned down to San Antonio, where they checked into a Best Western to prepare themselves for the game the following day.

The Houston team pitted against Bramble High turned out to be the size of pro football players with helmets covered in award emblems for basically being a bunch of badasses. In the first half, the Central High Cougars scored three times while the Bulldogs scored only once. Still, the Dawgs held them to field goals and went into the locker room at halftime down by only two.

When her daddy and mama got up to go to the concession stand, Hope's gaze drifted down two rows to where Colt sat with Shirlene. The stiff breeze played in the silk of his dark hair, fluttering it around his strong profile and the flipped-up collar of his worn leather jacket. He turned to laugh at something Shirlene said, and his gaze caught hers, impaling her in smoky gray.

It was funny how one piece of information could change an entire image. The knowledge that Colt's mama had been an alcoholic was all it took to make the pieces fit together. Colt's anger and delinquent behavior. His desire to leave Bramble and all its bad memories. His passion for the open road and a carefree lifestyle. Everything made sense now.

"It's so admirable the way Colt has stepped up to help out the town."

The softly spoken words pulled Hope's gaze away from Colt to Faith's wide blue eyes.

"Slate said that Colt is even trying to get other businesses to relocate to Bramble—just in case there are more layoffs," her sister continued.

Hope had heard the same thing, and was more than surprised that Colt had so many business connections. It was a shame that Hope wouldn't be around to see if any panned out. She started to question her sister about the businesses when Faith pulled her crazy mind-reading thing.

"So when are you leaving?" she asked.

After glancing around, Hope sent her sister a warning look. "Would you keep it down?"

"Why? Are you planning on skipping town without telling anyone?"

That was exactly what Hope planned on doing. Things would work out so much simpler if she left the following week, and Shirlene just ended up adopting a baby in eight months. Hope would tell people eventually, but for now, the town had enough to worry about.

"It's for the best," Hope said.

"For who? You're miserable about giving up your baby to Shirlene."

It was hell having your brain picked clean, and even worse having all your emotions put into words.

"I assume you have a better plan," Hope said, keeping her eyes on the field and her miserable emotions to herself.

"You can marry Colt."

"What?" Hope's gaze snapped over to her sister, who looked as if she hadn't just dropped a bomb of atomic proportions. "Have you lost your mind?"

"You tell me." Faith leaned closer and stared back at her sister.

The image that flashed into Hope's brain was like a Disney storybook ending, complete with a dark-headed prince, a set of laughing twins, and a princess who looked ready to pop with happiness.

Stunned, Hope looked away. "You *have* lost your mind."

"Why?" Faith lowered her voice. "If Colt's the father of your child, it only makes sense."

"Sense to someone who lives in a fairytale. Believe me when I tell you that the last thing that Colt wants is to be saddled with a kid and a wife."

"But maybe he just needs the right motivation to change," Faith said, her big eyes pleading. "Maybe you two just need to spend more time together, talking things through."

An image of the note Austin had given her on Halloween night popped into Hope's mind, and her gaze narrowed on her sister. "You." She pointed a finger, and

Faith's eyes got as big as saucers. "You're the one who sent me that note—not Colt."

"Okay, so I admit it." Faith held a hand to her chest. "But only because I truly believe that you and Colt belong together—"

Hope slapped a hand over Faith's mouth as their parents maneuvered their way along the row. She might've squeezed a little too tightly, because her sister's eyes watered. But Faith deserved a lot more than that. And although Hope was forced to keep her words to herself, she couldn't help sending her sister a telepathic warning: *Stay out of my business, you little conniving matchmaker.*

The answer came back loud and clear. *No.*

In the third quarter, the Cougars ran one in for six, but the extra point was no good, and the Bulldogs answered with a sixty-yard drive down the field that resulted in a field goal. With the score fifteen to ten with less than twenty seconds on the clock, things didn't look good for Hope's alma mater. But she should've known that Slate and his team had worked too hard to give up easily. Third down and thirty yards from the end zone, Austin threw a perfect spiral straight into the hands of his wide receiver, who raced over the goal line to win the game with only seconds to spare.

The people from Bramble were a small portion of the forty thousand in attendance at the Alamodome. But size didn't diminish the volume level as pandemonium broke out on the field and in the stands. The townsfolk jumped and screamed and hugged and smeared face paint from one end of the bleachers to the other. Rachel Dean squalled like a baby. Harley howled up at the bright afternoon sun. Shirlene's broads fairly jumped out of her tight sweater as her feet left the ground. And Faith squealed like her prince had just slain the biggest dragon.

Hope was kissed and hugged and passed around like a jug of moonshine at the end of Prohibition. But even as she reveled in the victory, her mind kept returning to a happily-ever-after that included two loving parents and a couple of smiling babies.

"Cowboy, you still suck at dancing," Hope stated, as Slate clumsily maneuvered her around the dance floor of the San Antonio honky-tonk where the town of Bramble had chosen to celebrate.

"And, darlin', you still try to lead." Slate twirled her under his arm and ended up bumping her head with his forearm and catching a piece of her hair on the pearl snap of his cuff.

Untangling her hair, she steered him back into the two-step. "You're right, which is why we will never amount to much on the dance floor."

He sent her a cocky grin. "But you still love me."

"Yes." Hope laughed. "I still love you." Looking up into those familiar hazel eyes, she said what she'd wanted to say all through the celebration dinner at the Golden Corral. "I'm proud of you, Slate Calhoun."

Those eyes widened before he reached up and yanked on her hair.

"Ouch!" Hope glared at him as he flashed a smile.

"Just checking to make sure you're Hope Scroggs."

Rubbing her scalp, she grumbled. "That's the last time I give you a compliment, cowboy."

"Good." Slate made the turn and stepped on her toe. "You don't want me to get a big head, do you?"

"As if your head isn't already the size of Texas."

His smile almost blinded her. "Well, whose wouldn't be? I mean, I've got the prettiest wife this side of the Mississippi—a baby on the way—a state football title— and the Sweetheart of Bramble, Texas, proud of me. What more could a man ask for?"

Releasing a loud country yee-haw, Slate picked her up and swung her around, with no consideration for the people who danced around them.

"Put me down, you crazy fool," Hope said as she clung to his neck and laughed.

But he didn't pay her a lick of attention. No telling how long he would've kept going if Colt and Faith hadn't danced past. Slate released Hope so fast that she almost landed on her butt as he reached out and tapped Colt on the shoulder. When they stopped, Slate took off his black Stetson and pressed it over his heart.

"What do you say, Mrs. Calhoun? Can I have this dance for the rest of my life?"

It was one of the corniest lines Hope had ever heard, but Faith didn't seem to realize that. Grinning as if she'd just been awakened from a thirty-year nap, she slipped into his arms. "I think that could be arranged, darlin'."

Hope watched as they waltzed off to a country swing. She waited for the pain of loss to return, but instead all she felt was a rising wave of relief. Relief that Slate had been smart enough to figure out their relationship long before she had.

"So do you want to dance or throw a fit because Faith took your best beau?"

Hope shot Colt a skeptical look. "Since when do you dance?" When he only shrugged, she let him off the hook.

"How about we wait for another waltz? It looked like you could count to three, but a western swing is a little more complicated."

"I think I can handle it." Colt grabbed her hand before she could get off the floor.

"You sure, because I can't lead you through—"

"Shut up, Hope."

And before Hope could continue to argue, she was being whirled around like a top—their arms twisting and untwisting in so many configurations she had trouble keeping up. His style was a cross between the Dallas Push and the Houston Whip with an added spark that was solely Colt—cocky dipped in a whole lot of wild. But not one time did he bump her head or catch her hair or lose the beat of the music as his boots shuffled around her. His grip was firm but not too firm, and he never jerked or pulled, only directed with a sureness that left her light-headed and breathless. When the song ended, he reeled her in to his hard-muscled chest and dipped her low.

Panting like the winner of the Kentucky Derby that had been ridden by a competent jockey who knew exactly how hard to push, she stared up at him in stunned disbelief.

"Where did you learn to dance like that?"

The look he sent her was one of complete indifference. "My mama liked to dance."

As he released her from the cuddle wrap, Hope's eyes welled up. The entire pregnancy weeping thing was really starting to annoy her. Every time she turned around, tears threatened. And she was getting darned sick of it. Unfortunately, there was nothing to do about it, especially when she couldn't shake the image of Colt dancing with his mama in the tiny front room of their trailer.

Luckily, a two-step started, and Colt swept her into the quick-quick-slow before she could make a fool of herself. His two-step was even better than his swing. His steps perfectly matched hers, with the dexterity to pull her into promenades and spins without losing track of the beat. The few times she tried to take the lead, Colt twirled her around until she was so dizzy all she could do was cling. And after a while, she relinquished all desire to lead and let Colt take her where he would. He took her to a heaven of dizzying polkas, and smooth two-steps, and slow, tranquil waltzes.

It was midnight when the folks of Bramble started to load back up on the buses to return to the hotel. Hope headed to the bathroom, surprised at how disappointed she felt that the night was over so quickly. She had just locked the bathroom stall, when someone jostled the handle.

"It's taken," she said. And after a little more jostling, whoever it was slipped back out the door.

Unconcerned by an obvious drunk's behavior, Hope finished using the bathroom. But when she tried to get out, the door wouldn't budge. Since it wasn't the first time she'd had trouble getting out of a bathroom stall, she spent a little time jiggling and jimmying until she realized that whatever was holding the door had nothing to do with the latch.

Hope thought about crawling underneath. But after working in a strip club, she knew the disgusting stuff that could end up on a bathroom floor. So instead, she yelled at the top of her lungs until a waitress came running in and unbuckled the slender belt that had been looped between the handle of Hope's stall and the hinge of the one next to it.

By the time Hope washed her hands and came out of the bathroom, she wasn't the least bit surprised to find Colt waiting.

"Faith said you weren't feeling good." He pushed away from the wall that he was leaning against. "You okay?"

"I guess the buses are long gone," she said through gritted teeth.

Colt's eyes widened fractionally before he nodded. "But I don't mind giving you a ride back to the hotel."

For a moment, Hope had to fight back the strong desire to chase the bus down so she could strangle her sister with her own belt. But once she got her anger under control, she tossed the belt into the nearest trash can and grabbed Colt's hand.

"Let's dance."

That's exactly what they did. They danced until they were sweaty and thirsty, then downed some water and danced some more. They couldn't have a conversation without fighting, but on the dance floor they had found a perfect harmony.

"I never would've believed it," she leaned her head on his chest and listened to the steady thump of his heart as the band struck up the last song of the evening.

He adjusted his hands around her waist and pulled her closer. Close enough that the fly of his zipper brushed her belt buckle. "Believed what?"

"That Colt Lomax is the best darned dancer I've ever danced with."

"Better than Bucky Higgins?" He rested his cheek on the top of her head.

"No comparison." She smoothed a hand over his shoulder and down to his biceps. His bare skin was hot and moist, his muscles hard and exciting. "Why didn't you ever ask me to dance?"

His fingers slipped beneath the hem of her T-shirt and stroked along the waistband of her jeans, sending a tiny shiver up her spine. "Maybe because you were always dancing with Slate."

"Liar."

She could feel his grin against her head. "Okay. So maybe I was afraid you'd say no."

"I wouldn't have."

"Now who's lying."

She laughed. "Okay, so I probably would've said no, but only because I would've thought it was some kind of trick."

"Smart girl."

Pulling her head back, Hope hooked her arms around his neck and fingered the silky hair that curled up on his shoulders. "Bad boy."

A smile tipped one side of Colt's mouth as those beautiful gray eyes stared back at her. "Sometimes bad can be really good."

His hands slipped under her shirt, and his fingers trailed lightly up and down her spine. She probably should've pulled away; their caresses had moved beyond dancing to something much more dangerous. But he was right—sometimes bad could feel really good. As they continued to sway to the music, she allowed his hands to wander along her flushed skin as she stared back at the man who was so different from the belligerent boy who wore a scowl a mile wide.

Although the eyes were the same. The same hungry gray. And now as then, she couldn't bring herself to look away. In the stormy depths, she'd found a reflection of her own soul. A soul that wanted so desperately to be loved, not for the image a town had concocted, but for itself.

The music continued, and their boots slowly swept back and forth against the wood floor. When they couldn't take the truth in each other's eyes a moment more, Colt dipped his head and kissed her. The first heated brush of his lips had her trembling, and his fingers tightened as he pulled her closer. Standing on tiptoes, she aligned her body to his. And with every step they took, a wonderful heat built beneath the friction of blue jeans. A moan vibrated between their lips—a hum of need and desire. Colt broke away first, his eyes two glittering coals beneath the fringe of dark lashes. He stared down at her mouth for only a second before he unhooked her hands from around his neck and pulled her from the dance floor.

Outside the bar, the night was cool and windy. He tucked his leather jacket around her and sheltered her body as they hurried across the parking lot to Shirlene's SUV.

Inside, she tried to think past her thumping heart and aching center. But once he'd slipped the seat belt around her, he kissed her again until there was nothing left in her head but desire.

No telling how long they would've remained there if a cold wind hadn't blown into the SUV, causing her to shiver. Colt pulled back and gave her one more heated look before he slammed the door and moved around to the driver's side. He slipped behind the wheel with the ease of a man who could master any mechanical vehicle and quickly backed the truck out.

Once he was out of the parking lot, he reached over and took her hand, bringing it to the console between them. She thought the space would cool her down, but the man was as gifted a hand holder as he was a kisser. With their fingers linked, his thumb caressed her palm with a back-and-forth stroke that left her nothing more than a quivering puddle on the heated leather.

They didn't talk on the ride to the hotel, nor did Colt waste any time getting there. He weaved in and out of traffic and on and off freeways like a NASCAR veteran. When they arrived, he whipped the truck into the first empty space and was around to her side before she could even unhook her seat belt. Not that she could've unhooked it with her hands shaking so badly, but he didn't even give her a chance to try before he released the clasp and had her in his arms.

Pressing her back against the truck, he gave her another deep kiss and pulled her up against the ridged fly of his jeans. Then, before she could do more than moan, he released her and was guiding her across the parking lot toward the hotel.

The lobby was empty except for the same desk clerk who had worked the previous night. He greeted them, then discreetly turned away. Before the elevator doors had closed completely, Colt had her back against the wall. This time his hand slipped beneath her shirt and wasted no time. With a twist, her bra was open and her breast covered in one hot palm.

"Colt," she breathed against his shoulder. "Someone could see us."

"I don't give a shit." His calloused thumb brushed over her nipple. And just that quickly, Hope didn't give a shit either.

Of course, she did when the doors opened, and Rachel

Dean was standing on the other side in a large floral muu-muu with her thin gray hair rolled up in sponge curlers and a full bucket of ice in her hands.

"Hey, Colt." She smiled at him as if his hand wasn't stuck under Hope's shirt. "The ice machine on my floor was clean out of ice and, with these damned hot flashes, I need a big glass of ice water handy at all times." She stepped into the elevator and punched a button. "Y'all just gettin' in?"

"Yes," Hope croaked as she tried to shove Colt away, but he didn't seem in any hurry to comply. Although his hand did slip from her breast to her hip.

"Well, I tell you one thing," Rachel continued, seemingly unaware of what was taking place right in front of her. "You can sure cut up a dance floor, Colt. Surprised the hell out of the entire town, seeing as y'all couldn't get along for more than two minutes without the fur flyin'. 'Course dancin' doesn't have to involve talkin', which is how I got roped into marryin' my second husband. Good dancer—bad talker."

The doors slid open, and Hope squealed as Colt scooped her up in his arms and walked off the elevator, moving right past an open-mouthed Rachel.

"And just what do you think you're doin', Colt Lomax?" she yelled after them.

"Taking Hope to bed," he called back.

Rachel's deep, manly laughter followed them all the way to his room.

Chapter Twenty-three

By the time Colt kicked the door to his room closed, the sweet agreeable woman he'd danced with was replaced with the spitfire he grew up with.

"Have you lost your mind, Lomax?" Hope's fist connected with his shoulder, the bony knuckles worse than any frogger he'd received in grade school. "What possessed you to tell Rachel Dean that? By morning, everyone will know you brought me to your room." She went to sock him again, but before she could, he tossed her down to the king-sized bed.

"And so what if they do? It's not the first time we've been caught in a compromising position. And you know as well as I do that the people of Bramble can't put two and two together without a calculator." He sat down on the edge of the bed to pull off his boots. "Although, I have to admit, it was strange that Rachel noticed me before she noticed the homecoming queen."

One of Hope's cowboy boots dropped to the floor by his foot.

"Not so strange, given your performance at Josephine's

the other night," she said as she toed off the other boot. "I think the town is starting to view you as their champion."

He laughed and was surprised when Hope didn't join in. He glanced back to find her sitting cross-legged on the bed, her eyes confused.

"What do you mean put two and two together?" she asked.

It would've been easy to hedge around the question. But after talking with Tinker Jones, Colt had come to a few conclusions: 1. An old photograph wasn't something to pin your hopes on. 2. It was time to cut through the bullshit and start being honest.

He propped his knee up on the bed as he turned to her. "About this thing we have for each other."

"A thing? What are you talking about? I've never had a thing for you."

"Really? And what would you call this?" His gaze dropped to her unclasped bra that stuck out of the neckline of her black shirt.

Those blue eyes stared back at him for only a second before her chin grew stubborn. "A mistake." She started to scoot off the bed, but he caught her.

"A mistake we can't seem to stop making." He took her chin in his hand, tipping it up. "And why is that?"

Her throat convulsed as she swallowed. "I...I don't know what you're talking about."

"And I think you do. I think you're just too stubborn to say it." He smoothed a strand of hair off her forehead. "Admit it, Hope. You have a thing for a lowlife motorcycle bum, a lowlife motorcycle bum who isn't afraid of overprotective townsfolk or big linebacker daddies. Who isn't afraid to take what he wants." He leaned down and brushed his lips over hers. "Even if it's from the Sweet-heart of Bramble, Texas."

She blinked before staring back at him with wide blue eyes. "Are you saying you want me, Colt Lomax?"

"I'm saying I want you, Hope Scroggs." He bit at her plump bottom lip, and then licked it better. "Have wanted you ever since I can remember. And you want me, which was why you kept showing up wherever I was, begging for something I was more than willing to give you." His tongue swept over her earlobe, and he felt the tremor that ran through her body all the way down to his soul.

"Very funny theory, Lomax," she breathed.

"No, it's not funny," he whispered. "Not funny at all."

Similar to their dancing, their lips effortlessly slipped into a slow sliding waltz that quickly progressed to a hungry salsa that had them both fighting for air. Easing her back to the mattress, he took her wrists in his hands and pulled her arms above her head. He liked the feel of having Hope stretched out before him, a compact feast spread out for his taking. And he took—took deep kisses and soft nips and long, wet forages that left him hard and begging for more.

When his mouth was no longer enough, he released her wrists and slipped a hand over one perfect breast. Through the cotton of her shirt, her nipple stood proud and hard. He gently brushed his thumb back and forth until she moaned into his mouth and arched her back up off the mattress. He pulled away from the kiss and lowered his mouth to her breast. At the first touch of his lips, her fingers scraped through his hair and encased his head, holding it firm while she rode his thigh.

Her enthusiasm incited him, and he stripped off her

shirt and went for naked flesh. Her breasts were plump and soft. And while he cradled and stroked, he sipped at each sweet peak until her fingers tightened against his scalp.

"Colt."

His name on her lips had him returning for another deep kiss before his hand slipped down to the button of her jeans. Once the zipper was down, he slid two fingers past the elastic band of her panties. The wet heat that greeted him was pretty much his undoing; the need to take things slow was obliterated by the need to be deep inside her. He might've taken her right then, if her jeans had cooperated. But the tight denim refused to slip over her hips, and he was forced to get to his feet and grab each pant leg. As he tugged, she giggled.

"You think this is funny, do you?" He cocked an eyebrow at her.

"Hilarious." Hope answered with a cocked brow of her own. "I thought the Bad Boy of Bramble would be a little more skilled at removing women's clothing."

He sent her an annoyed look as he tugged, but the jeans refused to budge, which sent Hope into another peal of laughter.

"I could use a little help here," Colt stated, although he couldn't help but smile at the picture she presented. Miles of wild hair played peek-a-boo with sweet naked breasts. At that moment, his entire world was contained in the tiny, five-foot-nothing body stretched out before him, and there wasn't a damned thing he could do about it.

Her laughter subsided, and with a sassy grin, she pushed her jeans over her hips.

It was the first time he'd seen her completely naked and, in the gold lamplight, she was as beautiful as he knew she would be. Though small, her body was perfectly proportioned, from the high breasts to the soles of her petite feet. Her legs and arms were lean and toned. Her stomach smooth and flat with an inny belly button he had wanted to lick since the rainy day in the old Chevy. But it was the small strip of hair between her legs that grabbed his attention and held it.

"You're so damned beautiful," he croaked, his voice thick with passion.

Her gaze lifted to his and, in those deep blue eyes, he saw gratitude and something he couldn't quite put his finger on. Something that made his stomach light and his heart seize.

As he stripped out of his clothes, her eyes turned hot and steamy. His stomach tightened, not only with desire, but with the strong need to be the only man to light this fire in her eyes. But she soon started a fire of her own when she scooted across the bed and took him in hand. His knees buckled, and he would've landed on the floor, if he hadn't reached out and grabbed onto the headboard.

Inching closer, she slipped her legs on either side of his, offering up a delectable view of all her hidden places—but the view was interrupted by a flash of heat that blinded him when she leaned forward and took him in her mouth.

His world tipped on its axis, and he didn't know if he was still standing or flat on his back. Her lips slipped down toward the base of his shaft before sliding back up with enough suction to cause his eyes to roll back in his head. The entire time, her hand kept up a nice steady stroke, while her other hand did a number on his balls. But seconds from orgasm, she lifted her head.

"Am I doing this right?"

He blinked and tried to figure out where he was. "Huh?"

"Am I doing this right?"

He was brought back to earth by a pair of insecure blue eyes. Since Hope had never been insecure about anything, he ignored the raw need that pulsed between his legs and tried to reassure her.

"Oh, baby. You are doing it just right." He cradled her chin and leaned down to give her a kiss. "In fact, so right that if I don't get inside you pretty soon, I'm going to be the first man to expire from lust."

Her smile flashed bright. "Really?"

"Really." Colt lowered a knee to the bed and followed her down.

Once there, he took his time sipping from her lips while his fingers stroked over her breasts and down her sweet body. When her hips pumped up to greet him, he dipped inside the wet heat and flicked her clitoris with his thumb until she begged for release.

Pulling back, he reached for his wallet on the night-stand. But just as he slipped the condom out, she stopped him.

"Don't you think it's a little late for that?"

He glanced back at her, and she shrugged.

"I mean, if you have something—"

His brain finally broke through his passion, and he shook his head. "No." He tossed the condom back down on the nightstand and rolled back to her side. "I don't have anything. I just forgot, is all." He smoothed her hair back. "I didn't hurt you, did I? I mean, this won't hurt you, right?"

She ran a finger over his chin. "Except for a few razor

burns, I think I'll be okay. Although if you don't get in me soon, I might just expire from lust."

He moved over her, cradling her head between his forearms. "Well, we can't have that. Now can we?"

"No, we can't—" She sucked in her breath as he entered her.

He knew how she felt. He had never been inside a woman skin on skin, and the pleasure was so intense that he almost lost it right there. He took a few seconds to name the parts of a motorcycle engine before he slowly started to move. As with dancing, their bodies quickly got in sync, and the slow strokes soon quickened to deep thrusts that had him seconds away from a mind-blowing orgasm. He tried to slow things down, but his stubborn Hope wasn't having it. Her legs locked around his waist, and her nails sank into his shoulders.

"Harder," she breathed. "Harder."

Complying, Colt rode her hard and fast until he reached a point where he didn't care if she joined him or not. Luckily, right before he went over the edge, she tightened around him, pulling him in after her. The orgasm crashed over him like a California wave at high tide, sucking him down into a maelstrom of intense sensation. When he finally surfaced, blue eyes sparkled back at him with what could only be described as pure feline satisfaction.

"You're heavy," she said as she smoothed the hair off his damp forehead.

He rolled to her side and stroked a hand down her stomach. "You okay?"

"Yes. But next time I better get on top."

He shot her a surprised look. "Next time?"

A quirky little smile tipped her mouth. "You don't think you can tell a woman you want her, and have wanted her for most of your life, and then kick her out after only once, do you? I thought a lowdown good-for-nothing biker would have more stamina than that."

His face cracked open with happiness. "Well, honey." He brushed the back of his fingers down the center of her chest and then around each breast, stopping to give each sweet peak a gentle caress before moving on. "I guess if I'm forced, I can find the strength somewhere."

The phone woke Colt out of the first sound sleep he'd had in months. He thought about ignoring it, especially when the woman in his arms wiggled her smooth naked butt against him. But then the numbers on the digital clock caught his attention, and he realized they had slept away half of the morning. Which wasn't shocking, considering they hadn't gone to bed until after four.

Carefully moving his arm out from under Hope, he leaned over her and grabbed the receiver. "Hello."

"Hey, big brother," Shirlene's voice came through loud and clear. Almost too loud and clear. "The buses are getting ready to pull out. But, lo and behold, no one can locate Hope. You wouldn't know where she is, would you? Burl and Jenna are about ready to call out the Texas Rangers."

He glanced down at Hope, who still slept like the dead.

Shit. This wasn't going to be good. But he couldn't see any way around it.

"She's with me."

There was a long pause where he didn't hear a sound, almost as if the mouthpiece had been covered, before she came back on.

"Burl's on his way up."

"What?" Colt scrambled for the covers, as if that was going to make a difference when Hope's daddy plowed through the door.

Shirlene laughed. "Just kiddin'. Burl and Jenna's bus already left."

As his heart tried to find an even cadence, he gritted his teeth. "Shirlene, I'm going to bust your butt when I get a hold of you."

"Now is that any way to repay a loving sister who lied through her teeth for you? If I hadn't told Burl that Hope spent the night in my room last night, your ass would be grass right now, big brother. Especially after Rachel Dean said she saw you two together last night." Another pause. "Hope is alive, isn't she? I would hate to think of my best friend lying in a bathtub wrapped in a shower curtain, waiting to be dumped in the San Antonio River."

"Funny, Shirl." Relieved that he wasn't going to have to deal with Hope's pissed-off daddy, Colt leaned back against the pillows and stroked his fingers through Hope's hair. "So are you heading out on the bus?"

"Actually, I thought I'd head over to Houston and see if I can get that workaholic husband of mine to take a couple nights off." There was another pause before she spoke. "It doesn't look good, does it, Colt?"

Even though he spent most of his life sheltering his sister from life's brutal realities, he answered her truthfully. "No. Even if Dalton gets bought out, I don't see how they'll avoid more layoffs. Which is why we need to entice other companies to make their home in Bramble."

"Companies like Desperado Customs?"

At one time, he would've laughed at the absurd notion

of returning to a town he'd wanted so desperately to leave. But he wasn't laughing now.

When he didn't answer, his sister continued. "Look, Colt, I've tried to keep my nose out of whatever has been going on with you and Hope all these years. But Hope is my best friend, and she's going through a hard time right now. So if you're just using her for a little entertainment while you're in town..."

Colt's fingers hesitated in the silky strands of Hope's hair, and for the first time, he owned up to his true feelings. "You should know, Shirl, I've always cared about Hope."

"I know, but you can still hurt someone you care about."

It was a truth that he and Shirlene had learned at an early age. Their daddy had cared about them and he died, leaving behind a woman who couldn't think through the pain. And consequently, she had hurt Shirlene and Colt by not being able to control a disease that almost destroyed their family.

The sound of a horn honking came through the receiver. "My cab's here," Shirlene said. "So I guess I'll see you back in Bramble, big brother."

"Only if I don't see you first, little sister."

The phone clicked, and he leaned over and hung it up.

Settling back against the pillows, Colt looked down at the woman who slept on her stomach next to him. Light filtered in through the crack in the curtains and fell over one bare shoulder and the smooth tanned skin of the arm that dangled off the edge of the bed. The heap of wild brown hair completely covered her face, and he reached out and smoothed it back. Her mouth lay open against the pillow, and without the thick hair to mute them, Colt could hear her soft snores. The sound made him smile, and he slipped back down in the bed and snuggled next to her, curling an arm around her waist.

Against the white of the sheet, the blue ink of his tattoo stood out. It had taken two years to complete and numerous painful hours beneath a tattoo artist's needle. The rattlesnake had been the first—a coiled symbol for fate and its ability to strike at any moment. The chopper and the banner with "Desperado" written across it came after the sale of his first custom bike. The Texas state flag on a night he'd missed home. And the tombstone with his father's initials and the date he'd been killed in the car accident were done on a night when he'd missed being a father's son. Shirlene had picked out the queen of diamonds playing card when she met him in Vegas one weekend. And, since she had talked him into a diamond bracelet the same night, it seemed fitting. As was the rose, a tribute to his beautiful mama and a relationship filled with its share of thorns.

But the tattoo that held Colt's attention was the one of the snarling hog with the tiara hooked over one ear. A hog with wide eyes staring out over a cute little snout. So obviously different from the others, the tattoo had been a conversation starter on more than one occasion. Although not one person had ever gotten an answer for why he had tattooed a mean-looking, tiara-wearing pig on his arm.

Probably because Colt didn't have one.

He hadn't been drunk or drugged or even slightly road-weary when he had drawn the design for the tattoo artist. But once it was there, he wished it gone. For instead of a humorous joke, it became a painful reminder of something he wanted but couldn't have.

He wanted Hope. Not just her body, but all of her. He wanted her quick wit and hot temper. Her strong moral beliefs and loyalty. Her stubborn streak and kind heart. He wanted her hero worship and her smiles. And he wanted her babies.

But mostly, he wanted her love.

He didn't delude himself that she felt the same way about him as she had when she was thirteen. But one thing was certain, Hope desired him. If he could only figure out a way to keep her in his bed, there might be a chance that the Bad Boy of Bramble would end up with the homecoming queen after all.

Chapter Twenty-four

"ALL RIGHT THEN," Cindy Lynn said. Since she didn't have the little wooden mallet she normally used when presiding over meetings, she tapped one purple acrylic nail on Shirlene's onyx countertop. "Darla will be responsible for decorations."

Just the thought of the silk-flower and hot-glue nightmare that Hope's and Faith's baby shower had just turned into should've sent Hope screaming from Shirlene's beautiful mansion like the hounds of hell were after her. The only reason it didn't was because she had more important things to worry about.

Like the financial stability of her town.

The future of her baby.

And the complete loss of her mind.

"Now who would like to volunteer to be in charge of the games?" Cindy Lynn asked the group.

"Me!" Twyla madly waved her hand and, before Cindy could even call on her, started rambling. "I've got this really cute poopy-diaper game where you melt different kinds of mini-candy bars in Pampers and then everyone has to open up the diaper and try to figure out what candy bar poop is in it."

"Oh, I played that one," Rachel Dean talked around the little spinach quiche she'd just popped in her mouth. "And it's harder than you think. The only one I got right was the Baby Ruth. But only because it looked just like my little Johnny's after he'd eaten corn."

Faith choked on her iced tea, and Hope slapped her on the back a little harder than she should have. But she was still mad about her sister's deceitful matchmaking tactics.

"I'm not lookin' at baby poop," Darla spoke up.

"It's not baby poop, silly." Twyla flapped a hand. "It's chocolate candy bar—" She stopped in mid-sentence, although her mouth still hung open, as if she wanted to finish but just didn't have enough air to do it. Wondering what had caused her reaction, Hope glanced behind her, and her own breath caught.

Colt Lomax walked into the kitchen from the garage. He was talking on his cell phone, completely unaware of the women sitting across the room at the breakfast bar. Women who were all transfixed by the hot body clad in running shorts and a tight black T-shirt. And Hope couldn't blame them. Not when she couldn't pull her own gaze away.

"I'm not planning on firing anyone, Juan. The people who don't want to transfer can stay in L.A." He pulled open the refrigerator and took out a container of orange juice. Then, holding the phone to his ear, he opened the cap and chugged the juice, straight from the bottle. A drop dripped down his whiskered chin, then plopped to the strip of hard chest above his shirt's V-neck. He swiped it off, causing Cindy Lynn to release a sigh that made

Hope want to reach over and rip out her high, tightly curled ponytail.

With the plastic bottle inches from his mouth, Colt turned to them. His surprised gaze swept over the group until it landed on Hope. Then it wasn't surprise as much as heat that settled in his steel gray orbs.

A smile tipped up the corners of his mouth. A wicked smile that spoke of sweaty sheets and carnal knowledge. Hope tried not to react, but it was impossible, given that less than forty-eight hours ago she'd been surrounded by sweaty sheets while he used that carnal knowledge to give her five amazing orgasms.

Which was dumb. Stupid. And completely insane.

She had no business falling in bed with Colt Lomax—five orgasms or one. No business whatsoever. Hadn't she learned anything from the past? Every sweet kiss and caress he had given her had been followed by some mean-spirited prank. Yet all it had taken for her to forget were a few sentences: *I'm saying I want you, Hope Scroggs. Have wanted you ever since I can remember.* Not "I love you. I need you. I can't live without you." Just "I want you." And that had been enough to send her mind over the deep end and her libido off the scales.

Stupid. Stupid. Stupid.

But even knowing how stupid it was, Hope had to fight back the urge to slip off the bar stool and walk straight into those well-defined arms. And the feeling only intensified when he hung up the phone without even saying good-bye.

"Hey." The word was simple, but the deep, sexy underlying tones made her panties moist. Like steam off a Jacuzzi, heat rose from the spot where the soft material of her dress puddled in her lap.

"Hey," she squeaked.

"Y'all look mighty pretty today," he said.

There was a chorus of "thank yews," even though his gaze never left Hope. Trapped in those beautiful pools of gray, all she could do was sit there and stare back. Until Faith coughed and broke the connection.

After one sexy wink of an eye, Colt recapped the orange juice and slipped it back in the commercial-sized refrigerator. "Shirlene failed to mention she was havin' a group of lovely ladies over this afternoon. If I'd known, I would've cleaned up."

"Well, I don't know about the rest of the women here," Rachel Dean said as she rested her chin in one man hand and looked Colt up and down as if he was a big stick of butter. "But I don't mind a bit."

Colt flashed a smile at her before he asked, "Where is my ornery sister, anyway?"

"She had a phone call," Cindy Lynn piped up, her gaze glued to Colt's legs. Unable to stop herself, Hope shifted on the stool and kicked her hard in the shin. "Oww!" She threw Hope a dirty look as she leaned down to rub the spot.

"Sorry," Hope said. "I was just trying to cross my legs." She looked up to see Colt grinning like an idiot.

"Well, I guess I better let you ladies get back to what you were doing."

"Baby showers," Darla supplied. "We're plannin' baby showers."

"Really?" He shot a glance over at Hope.

In between orgasms, they had talked about a lot of things. The town's troubles. Music and books. Politics and religion. Colt's adventures on the road and Hope's adventures in Hollywood. Colt's passion for motorcycles and

Hope's passion for the town of Bramble. But the baby was one topic they had avoided.

"I'm sure it's nothin' that you would be interested in, Colt," Cindy Lynn said, still devouring him with her eyes.

To keep herself from slapping Cindy Lynn upside the head, Hope picked up a little cheesecake cup from the plate in front of her and popped it in her mouth.

"Oh, I don't know about that." Colt strolled over, and the thick cream cheese lodged in Hope's throat. "I think people might be surprised at what I find interestin'."

And then right there in front of the biggest gossips in Bramble, he reached across the counter and curled his fingers under Hope's chin, his eyes sparkling with devilry. "You missed some, honey." His thumb brushed across her lips in a long, heated stroke before he brought the digit back to his mouth and sucked it clean.

Heat infused Hope's body as he sent her another sizzling smile before he turned and strolled out of the kitchen. With her lips burning and her mind tumbling, she sat frozen to the bar stool, waiting for the shock to wear off and the questions to start.

But she'd overestimated the IQ of the planning committee.

"So do I get to do the poopy-diaper game or what?" Twyla asked.

Hope sat through another fifteen minutes of craziness before she had had enough. Slipping off the bar stool, she sent everyone a bright smile. "Excuse me, y'all, but I have to go to the bathroom."

Rachel waved one oversized hand. "You go right ahead, sugar. My bladder felt like the size of a pea when I was pregnant."

Hope continued smiling until she rounded the corner into the living room. Then, once out of sight, she dashed to the front door and slipped out. She had barely knocked on the door of the guesthouse when it was jerked open and she was pulled inside against Colt's damp, naked body, straight from the shower.

"I was hoping you'd come callin'." He nibbled along her neck, causing her legs to turn to jelly.

She ran her hands up through his thick hair and pulled him closer, relishing the feel of his hungry mouth against her neck and his hard chest against the tight nipples that pressed through her sweater. But when he reached for the edge of that sweater, she stopped him.

"So who were you talking to on the phone? Did you get a business to move here?" When his desire-filled eyes didn't clear, she tugged on his hair. "Come on, Lomax, don't keep me in suspense."

"At a time like this," he took her hand from his hair and pressed it to his hard-on, "is that all you can think about?"

She gave him a few lingering strokes that turned his eyes to liquid heat before she answered. "Not all, but we'll get to the other things I'm thinking about later."

The passion-filled eyes sparkled back at her. "In that case . . . yes, Desperado Customs is opening a shop here."

With a squeal, she threw herself back against him. "You did it! You came through!"

"Now, hold up, Hope." His face was serious when he pulled her away. "A small motorcycle custom shop isn't going to save the town if C-Corp doesn't buy Dalton."

"I know that, but it's a start." She cocked her head to one side. "Desperado? Isn't that the name you wrote in permanent marker on the back of that jacket you owned as a teenager?"

Although it was hard to tell in the shadowed entryway, it looked as if he blushed. The sight of such a tough guy blushing made her heart melt, and to hide her reaction, she leaned up on her tiptoes and kissed him. The depth of the tenderness she felt for this man took the sexual heat to a new level, turning the kiss into a greedy mating of uncontrollable need.

His hand slipped beneath her skirt, and she didn't hesitate to hike up a leg and give him full access. But when his warm fingers came in contact with wet heat, he groaned and pulled away from the kiss.

"You were sitting there the entire time without any panties?" he asked in a desire-roughened voice.

"Didn't you tell me it would make things easy if I left them off?" She leaned in and ran her tongue over his nipple.

Tipping his head back, he groaned up at the ceiling. "God, I love a woman who listens."

Before she could move to his other nipple, his hands dipped beneath her skirt and lifted her up. Her legs came around his waist, and he pressed deep inside her. The hard penetration took her breath away, but no more than the sweet thrusts that followed. His biceps flexed as he brought her hips forward, then back. With his hands gripping the flesh of her bottom and the tips of his fingers teasing the sensitive area deep inside the crevice, it didn't take long for her to go tumbling over the edge of an amazing orgasm. She tightened her legs and moaned out her release, while Colt followed right behind her.

Once their breathing had returned to normal, he

carried her into the bedroom, where he laid her down on rumpled sheets. Easing down beside her, he leaned over and gave her a quick kiss.

"I've missed you."

"Hmmm," she sighed. "I've missed you too."

He slipped a hand beneath her sweater. "I tried calling you all day yesterday, but your phone was busy." His hand skated over the lace of her bra.

"Ryan keeps calling me. He's worried that I won't be on the plane tomorrow." She drew a heart in the middle of his chest hair, but before she could do something really stupid like add initials, Colt grabbed her hand.

"You're leaving tomorrow?"

His question brought her out of her sexual haze and slammed her back to reality. A reality she'd been avoiding. She *was* leaving tomorrow. Leaving this town. Leaving her family. And leaving this man, who stared down at her with a look in his gray eyes that made it difficult to speak.

Her hand dropped from his neck, and she sat up. "First thing in the morning."

He followed her, his bare chest inches from her shoulder. "Why didn't you say anything?"

"I told you about the reality show." It was a lame answer, and she knew it. But it was better to keep things as uncomplicated as possible.

Unfortunately, it was too late for that.

He stared at her for a second longer before he rolled to his feet. "Yeah, I guess you did." Completely unconcerned with his nudity, he walked over to the sliding glass doors and stared out. "So if you're leaving tomorrow, what are you doing here?" He glanced back at her. "Or was this just a quickie before you left town?"

Before she could do more than sputter, he laughed, the sound harsh and brittle. "I thought things had changed, but I see that they haven't. You're still the same scared little girl, searching for the town's approval. And I'm still that poor Lomax kid, just waiting to be acknowledged."

Now angry, she jumped up from the bed. "Fine, you want me to acknowledge you? I'll run into town and scream at the top of my lungs that the baby is yours. But you better be ready for what happens next, Colt Lomax. Because if you thought shooting out the stained glass window of the First Baptist Church with a BB gun pissed them off, it will be nothing compared to how they'll react when they find out you impregnated me. And I don't think you'll like their solution. Not when it will include being chained to a town and a woman you couldn't get away from fast enough."

His eyes darkened. "Who's running now, Hope? Because it sure as hell isn't me."

Stunned, Hope stared back at him. But before she could open her mouth to find out what he meant, the front door crashed open. And Colt barely had enough time to grab a pair of jogging shorts and slip them on before Faith raced into the bedroom.

When she saw Hope, she seemed more relieved than surprised. "It's Shirlene. Something's wrong. She came out of the bedroom screaming at the top of her lungs for everyone to get out."

Their anger forgotten, Hope and Colt exchanged looks before they headed for the door.

By the time they reached the main house, the ladies of Bramble were gone. Only Shirlene remained, her tall frame pulled into a tight ball in one corner of the couch.

When they came through the back doors, she glanced up and her green eyes glittered with unshed tears.

"The craziest thing happened, y'all." Shirlene swallowed hard as a tiny droplet trickled down her cheek. "Lyle up and died on me."

Chapter Twenty-five

THE NEWS THAT Lyle Dalton had suffered a heart attack while celebrating the buyout of his company spread like wildfire through Texas. And business associates from all over the state converged on Bramble for the funeral. Besides oil men, there were land developers, technology leaders, media moguls, ranchers, and politicians. Even the governor stopped by for a short eulogy—one of many that were made during the two-hour church service.

When the service ended, a long line of limos, rental SUVs, and trucks headed out to Heavenly Haven Cemetery, where Pastor Robbins said a few last words before an honor guard gave a three-volley gun salute for the years that Lyle had served in the military. After the last shots echoed into the cloudy November sky and the flag was folded to the bugler's poignant rendition of "Taps," the crowd dispersed to give the family a chance for final good-byes.

Hope wandered over to a nearby oak tree to watch as Lyle's midnight blue coffin was lowered into the ground. Shirlene and Colt stood at the front of the group, both dressed in somber black. And although the style was the complete opposite of his faded jeans and T-shirts, Hope couldn't help but admire the figure Colt cut in the expensive suit.

After learning of Lyle's heart attack, Colt and Hope had worked together to get Lyle's body flown home from Houston, notify family and friends, and help with the funeral arrangements. And although they spoke cordially to one another, their argument in the guesthouse remained between them. It seemed that no matter how many bridges they had crossed since Colt returned, it would never be enough—something that brought an intense wave of sorrow to Hope's heart as she watched Colt pull Shirlene close and kiss her forehead.

"I always hoped that you would marry that boy," a gruff voice behind Hope said.

Startled out of her thoughts, Hope turned to find her daddy standing there. Unlike Colt's suit, Burl's black suit was faded and ill-fitting, the jacket stretching tight across his large linebacker shoulders and coming up short on his thick forearms.

Sending him a weak smile, she glanced over at Slate, who was talking with Harley, his arm hooked protectively around Faith. "You and the entire town, Daddy."

"I wasn't talkin' about Slate," he stated. "I was talkin' about Colt."

Her gaze snapped back to her father's deep blue eyes. "What?"

Looking down at his scuffed cowboy boots, he shrugged his shoulders. "Yeah, I guess it was a pretty crazy thought, seein' as how you two are a little like a lit match to dynamite."

Hope snorted. "That's putting it lightly, Daddy."

He grinned. "There were a few times I thought you were going to kill the poor boy."

"The poor boy? I wasn't the one flattening *his* bike tires, or putting gum on the door handles of *his* vehicle."

Her daddy chuckled, a sound that had always warmed her. "And maybe that's what got me to thinkin' about you two. Colt reminded me of myself when I was younger."

"You did things like that to Mama?"

"Worse. There was this one time that I—" He blushed. "Anyway I was pretty ornery. And there was nothing I liked better than gettin' your mama all riled up for a good fight."

Hope stared at him. "But I never heard you and Mama fighting."

"Probably because by the time you got old enough to know what was going on, we had learned to keep our fights behind closed doors." A smile creased his weathered face. "You remind me so much of your mama when she was younger—she was the feistiest little spitfire you'd ever want to meet." He shook his head. "'Course she still is, when I forget to put down the toilet seat."

Hope grinned, but it faded when he continued.

"Now the crazy woman has got it in her head that you're thinkin' about givin' up the baby." His eyes, which were so much like her own, filled with a sadness that broke Hope's heart. "Thinks it has something to do with us givin' Faith away."

"Oh, Daddy," Hope moved into his waiting arms, burrowing her face against the familiar Dial-soap scent of him. She had cried so much in the last couple weeks, she thought she was all cried out. But as her tears soaked her daddy's suit jacket, she realized she'd been wrong.

"I thought I had it all figured out," she sobbed. "I'd

move to Hollywood and give the baby to Shirlene and everyone would be happy. But even if it makes perfect sense, I can't do it. I just can't give P-pumpkin Seed away."

Her daddy awkwardly patted her back. "Well, sometimes things don't have to make sense, honey. Sometimes they just have to feel right."

She pulled back and stared at him as he continued.

"And I'm not talkin' about fickle emotion. I'm talkin' about the kind of feelin' that settles right down in your soul—the kind that tells you you've made the right decision, even if it don't make no sense at all."

Since that was exactly how Hope was feeling after deciding to keep the baby, she figured her daddy was on to something. "And, I suppose, it wouldn't make any sense at all to give up a chance of fame and fortune in Hollywood to stay in a small Texan town with very few job opportunities?"

"Nope, that sure would be foolish." He winked at her. "But I'd rather be a happy fool than a miserable wise man."

Sighing, Hope rested her head back on his broad shoulder. "Damn, I wish I'd talked to you a few weeks ago, Daddy."

"I'm always here, baby girl."

They didn't say much after that. Instead, they stood silently and watched as Lyle's relatives dropped blood-red roses into the grave. Hope knew most of them from one gathering or another, except for Lyle's first wife, who had divorced him and moved to Houston when Hope was still a child. The woman was much older than Shirlene, but just as stunning, in a black suit that fit her tall svelte body to perfection. Her two grown sons had gotten her height and dark hair, while the teenage daughter was fair and short like Lyle. They didn't completely snub Shirlene, but they didn't exactly appear friendly either. Once they tossed their flowers in, they walked toward their limo without a backward glance, leaving Colt and Shirlene standing by the casket alone.

After giving her daddy one last hug, Hope started toward them. But she was delayed by Rachel Dean, who wanted to know if Hope thought Shirlene would like lasagna better than enchiladas. By the time she had assured Rachel that either one would be appreciated, Colt and Shirlene were no longer standing by the casket. Colt had moved over to talk with a distinguished-looking man and a redheaded woman, while Shirlene had walked to the far end of the cemetery.

When Hope reached her, she was standing in front of an old, crumbling headstone, a single long-stemmed rose clutched in her hand.

"Did you know my great-great-great-granddaddy was the very first sheriff of Bramble?" Shirlene said, as Hope came up to stand beside her. "Colt was named after him— not him exactly, but the man's favorite gun."

"I think you might've mentioned that," Hope said in a voice as soft as her sister's.

"I guess I did, didn't I?" Shirlene glanced over and sent her a smile that lacked her usual warmth and sparkle before she turned and headed along the row of headstones. Hope followed behind her to the gravestone on the very end, Shirlene's father's stone. There were no decorative scrolls, hearts, or pastoral scenes etched into the simple slab of stone, just the words *David Michael Lomax— Devoted Husband and Loving Father* carved above dates that spanned a mere twenty-four years.

Unconcerned with her expensive suit, Shirlene knelt down and rested the rose against the base. When Hope joined her on the cold ground, they both started clearing out the weeds that had cropped up around the stone.

"I don't remember him," Shirlene said as she worked. "When I was little, Colt would tell me stories of my daddy cradling me in his arms and singing to me, or carrying me around on his shoulders. But now I wonder if Colt didn't make it all up. He's willing to do just about anything to make me happy." She tossed the weeds off to the side before glancing over at Hope. "Even give away his unborn child."

Shocked, Hope fell back on her bottom. "Colt told you?"

"Faith. But I wouldn't be too angry at her. She can't help it if her face reads like a bestselling novel." Then, before Hope could figure out how to break the news to her friend that she'd changed her mind, Shirlene reached over and slugged her hard in the arm.

Placing a hand over the stinging spot, Hope glared at her. "What was that for?"

"For being stupid enough to come up with such a harebrained idea in the first place. What were you thinkin', Hog?"

"I was thinkin' about how much my best friend wanted a baby," she grumbled.

"And I appreciate the gesture." Shirlene scooted back to rest against Hootie Smith's grave marker with the scary-looking angel on top. "But I'm not one of your charity cases, Hope."

The anger fizzled out of her. "I wasn't doing it just for you, Shirl. I wanted my baby to have the best of everything—money, a big house, a mama who didn't have to work, and a dad—" She stopped and looked away.

"Man, Hollywood really screwed you up, Hog." Shirlene leaned her head back on the robes of the angel and closed her eyes. "The Hope Scroggs I knew wouldn't be worried about the things she couldn't give her child. Instead, she'd be figuring out how to get them. Besides, with the way you and my brother have been going at it, it doesn't look like you'll be without a daddy for very long."

"We have not being going at it!" When Hope realized how loudly she'd spoken, she glanced around. But most of the people were on the other side of the cemetery. Still, she lowered her voice and leaned in. "And even if we were, it didn't mean anything." She sniffed. "It was just... great sex."

Shirlene rolled her eyes. "And don't I feel sorry for you. Geez, Hope, pull your head out, would you? Colt has had a thing for you ever since I can remember."

"A thing?" Hope's heart skipped a beat. "He told you that?"

"He didn't tell me anything." Her gaze shifted over to the plain headstone with the single rose. "In case you haven't figured it out, we Lomaxes have trouble communicating our true feelings. Instead, we bury them beneath a tough exterior...or a quick wit. Unfortunately, some emotions refuse to stay buried and end up bubbling out in destructive ways—like rocks through windows or a smartass mouth."

When Shirlene looked back at Hope, her green eyes were even more sad. "Colt isn't going to tell you he loves you, Hope. Not because he doesn't, but because he can't. His only example of love came from a woman who couldn't stand up after one o'clock in the afternoon, let alone show her children any kind of affection. It wasn't so bad for me, at least I had Colt to shower me with love, but all he had was an ornery little sister."

Trying to think above her thumping heart, Hope leaned closer. "But if he loves me, then why did he pull all those pranks?"

"Maybe he was trying to get your attention."

She snorted. "Live ammo in a prop gun got my attention, all right."

"About that, honey..."

Hope's gaze snapped back to Shirlene, who suddenly looked like she had when Hope's mama had caught them smoking behind Shirlene's trailer. Shocked, Hope reared back and cracked her shoulder on Samuel Murdock's stone cross.

"You? You put the bullet in the gun? But why?"

Shirlene shrugged. "It wasn't enough that you won every award and contest there ever was. You had to go and take my part in the school play too? It just didn't seem fair."

Put that way, Hope couldn't very well argue the point. "I wish you hadn't gotten the flu, Shirl. It would've saved me a lot of grief." She looked across the cemetery to where Colt stood talking to Sheriff Winslow. "But if Colt cared about me, why did he leave town?"

One perfectly shaped eyebrow lifted. "Maybe because the girl he wanted had already made her choice."

"But I..."

Hope snapped her mouth closed. Shirlene was right; she had chosen Slate, if not in words, then in her refusal to correct an entire town's belief. And she was doing it again. Letting the town run around looking for a daddy, all because she was too scared to stand up for what she wanted, too scared of disappointing people who refused to see their sweetheart with a bad boy. Even if a bad boy was exactly who Hope wanted—had always wanted. A bad boy who had grown into a good man with a kind heart.

Unfortunately, her revelation might have come too late. In an attempt to shield her heart, she had said and done things that Colt might never forgive.

Hope turned her tearful eyes to Shirlene. "What am I going to do now, Shirl?"

With her head resting against Hootie's angel, Shirlene looked up into the overcast skies. Her smile was weak as she spoke just above a whisper.

"Funny, but I was going to ask the same thing."

Chapter Twenty-six

Since most folks wanted to be home on Thanksgiving with a twenty-pound bird and a forty-six-inch TV, the Bramble Thanksgiving Day Parade was always held the Saturday before. The weather had finally turned the corner to winter, and frigid winds snapped the flag in front of the town hall and sent tumbleweeds—along with a few cowboy hats—careening down the cordoned-off street. It had been a while since Colt had attended a parade, but he knew the routine and picked out a spot along the parade route to park Shirlene's Navigator.

"This look okay to you?" He glanced over at Shirlene, and his heart tightened.

The woman who sat in the seat next to him might look like his sister in her tight jeans and flashy jewelry. But the lack of spirit in her eyes and the somber droop of her lips were nothing like his baby sister. And Colt didn't know what to do about it. Shirlene had always been the optimistic one in the family—the one who saw the glass as half full instead of half empty. And being the half-empty guy, he counted on her to keep his world balanced, so the reversal of their roles had him floundering like a trout on a hook.

The cold wind smacked him in the face as he climbed out of the SUV, and he zipped up his leather jacket to his throat before he walked around to the back.

"Good Lord, Shirlene, you think you brought enough?" He tried to tease a smile out of her as they unloaded the Navigator.

She paused and stared down at the thermos of coffee as if she didn't know what it was or how it had gotten in her hand. "I guess I did overpack, didn't I? Lyle always called me his 'Material Girl.' I guess he was right."

Colt's hand tightened around the aluminum of a chair as he tried to keep the concern from his voice. "There's nothing wrong with being prepared. If it hadn't been for you packing my lunches every night, I would've starved in high school."

"Doubtful." She reached in for the blankets. "I'm sure you would've found some girl to feed you."

"Yeah, but not a one of them would've known how to make peanut butter and Frosted Flake sandwiches."

"Losers," she said, and then carried the blankets and thermos around to the front of the truck.

Once they were seated with the blankets tucked around them and the coffee poured into thermal mugs, Colt didn't have a clue what to say. Sympathy had never been his strong suit. He thought about bringing up his meeting with Lyle's lawyers, but then figured that that would only depress his sister more. Although Lyle had sealed the deal with C-Corp, his personal finances were still in turmoil. And Colt wasn't sure, after paying debts and lawyers, if there would be any money left for Shirlene. Not that it mattered. His little sister would never go without.

"I hope you aren't going to get sick of me," Colt finally said. "With the custom motorcycle shop going up on the property next to Jones' Gas Station, I'll be in Bramble more often. So you don't have to worry about anything. I'll be around to take care of you."

Shirlene nodded. "And I appreciate that. But I think you've got other things to worry about. Like Hope's baby."

His gaze shot over to her. "How did you—" He stopped when the truth dawned on him. "So I guess Hope told you about her plan."

His sister nodded, and Colt actually felt sick to his stomach. For some strange reason, he still clung to the belief that Hope would change her mind—about Hollywood and the baby. Obviously, he'd been mistaken.

Aware of how much pain he was about to cause his sister, he took a deep breath before he turned to her.

"I love you, Shirlene. You know that, right?" When she nodded, he continued. "Your happiness means the world to me. But even knowing how happy a baby would make you, I can't give you mine. I love Pumpkin Seed and I'm keeping her."

Pushing the blanket down, Shirlene gifted him with the smile that had been absent for way too long. "Well, join the club, big brother, because Hope couldn't do it either. So I guess I'll have to be the best darned aunt little…Pumpkin Seed will ever have."

He blinked. "Hope couldn't do it?" And when Shirlene shook her head, all his pent-up emotions broke free, and he jumped from the chair and pulled his sister into his arms.

"I'm going to be a daddy, Shirl! I'm going to be a daddy."

Shirlene hugged him back. "And the best darned daddy in the state of Texas."

"So I guess you don't need no wife?"

The belligerent voice caused Colt to pull back from Shirlene and look over at the young boy standing in the familiar grubby jeans. At least today, he had on a coat.

Jesse's hostile gaze ran over Shirlene before he looked back at Colt. "Unless you want one that ain't so old."

"Old?" Shirlene's eyes narrowed on the kid. "Who you callin' old, pipsqueak?"

Colt bit back a grin. "Shirl, I'd like you to meet Jesse. Jesse this is my sister, Shirlene Dalton."

"Sister?" Jesse's face brightened before he held out one dirty hand. "Nice to meet ya, Shirl."

Shirlene cocked a brow at Colt before she replied. "Nice to meet you, Jess."

"Jesse."

"Ms. Dalton."

The young face scrunched up with annoyance before he turned back to Colt. "So anyway, since you ain't tied up with this one, I thought you'd like to meet my sister." Jesse glared at Shirlene. "Besides being younger, she's a whole lot prettier," he added.

Ignoring the look of outrage on his sister's face, Colt nodded. "I would love to meet your sister. But more importantly, I'd like to meet your mother."

"Well, you can't." Jesse shoved his hands in the front pockets of his jeans. "She's at work. But my sister is right over there."

He pointed across the street to where a teenage girl with glasses stood behind a stroller with a blanket-bundled baby inside and a toddler holding onto one of the curved handles. When the teenage girl's eyes narrowed on them, Jesse suddenly acted like a cat with a firecracker attached to its tail.

"Then again, maybe another time." He raced across the street before Colt could stop him.

"Where did you meet that ornery kid?" Shirlene asked as she sat back down and adjusted the blanket around her.

"He came to the garage." Colt watched as the girl lit into Jesse, her gaze flickering across to Colt and back again before she whirled the stroller around and headed down the street. Jesse took the hand of the toddler and followed at a slower pace, glancing back only once to wave at Colt.

"He lives out on Grover Road," Colt said.

"Figures." Shirlene snorted. "Ornery kids come from Grover Road."

As the kids disappeared around a corner, Colt looked back over at her and grinned. "They sure do."

Colt had about a million questions to ask his sister about Hope's decision to keep the baby. But about that time, Sheriff Winslow's patrol car came around the corner of Elm with siren blaring to start the parade. And figuring he had plenty of time for answers, Colt leaned back against the SUV to watch the parade. It turned out to be better than he'd remembered. Even without helium balloons or Broadway numbers, Bramble's beat out Macy's for sheer entertainment.

In the first few minutes, Sheriff Winslow snagged the gaping pocket of a lodge clown with the bumper of his patrol car and dragged him halfway down the parade route before Rye Pickett grabbed one of the clown's big red shoes and pulled him lose. Then some idiot put the

Four-H Club in front of the Jazzercising Ladies from Shady Meadows Retirement Village, and those old gals put on quite a show, trying to keep the green tennis balls on the ends of their walkers away from the huge steaming piles left behind by the horses. The marching band never broke stride, not even when Ms. Murphy's toy terrier attacked a band girl's flag and was whipped around for a full minute of "Love Shack" before he let go.

Luckily, Rossie Owen's grandson, Jimmy, was one hell of an outfielder and had no trouble reaching up and snagging the tiny dog before he hit the ground.

Finally the football team arrived, crowded onto a flatbed trailer covered in ugly purple flowers and huge Styrofoam guns that pointed out in all directions.

"What the hell?" Colt breathed, unable to take his eyes off the hideous float.

"It was the homecoming float," Shirlene stated as if that explained everything. And it did. For as long as Colt could remember, the homecoming floats had been damned hideous.

"Hey, Shirlene!" Austin Reeves, who cockily straddled the Colt Peacemaker, yelled to her from the float.

"Hey yourself, Austin!" Shirlene waved back. "I guess you think you're a stud now?"

"Pretty much!" Austin waved his straw cowboy hat over his head and released a big cowboy yee-haw, which had his teammates laughing and the crowd cheering.

Austin reminded Colt of a dark-headed Slate, a conquering hero who had the town by the tail. And Colt couldn't fault the kid for that. Nor could he fault Slate for enjoying all the glory that came with being a winning football coach in Texas. Standing with the rest of the coaches in the back of the pickup following the float, Slate smiled and waved like the golden-haired boy he was.

As the truck passed, he looked down at Colt. At one time, the situation would've been demeaning—the exalted hero looking down at "the poor Lomax kid." But now Colt realized that they were two different men who filled two different spots on this big rotating ball. And neither spot was any better or any worse than the other.

He nodded, and Slate nodded back.

A split second later, Colt's gaze got caught on Harley Sutter's convertible Cadillac, following the truck. Hope sat on the trunk of the Cadillac with her feet on the backseat, tossing out candy to the kids who raced along beside her.

Even after the news about the baby, Colt had thought Hope would be long gone by now—off to Hollywood to accomplish another one of her goals. But instead, there she was, looking much as she did twelve years earlier when riding atop the homecoming float. Her face was flushed with cold, her long hair blew out behind her, and her smile was bright as she waved to the whistling crowd.

"She's something else, isn't she," Shirlene said.

"Yes." Colt straightened and tried to restrain himself from running out into the street and jerking her from the car, a good half a block away, so he could ask her about her decision to keep the baby.

"Faith looks as pretty as a picture and that fat little pig sitting between them is a riot. But, if you notice, everyone's eyes are on Hope."

Since Colt hadn't even noticed Faith, or Sherman sitting next to Hope, he had to agree with his sister.

"It's a strange phenomenon," Shirlene continued.

"One I still haven't figured out. Somewhere between reciting Bible scriptures in church and winning ribbons at the county fair, Hope became something more than just a member of the town. She became a shining beacon of everything this town stands for and all its dreams for the future."

Colt pulled his eyes off the Cadillac and turned to his sister, although he couldn't think of a thing to say. His mind was too consumed with the truth Shirlene had spoken, a truth he hadn't understood until now: Hope's life hadn't been any easier than his. In fact, it had been harder. While he had had the weight of a mother and sister on his shoulders, Hope had the weight of an entire town.

"Do you love her?" Shirlene asked.

The question didn't shock him as much as he thought it would.

"I'm not sure I know what love is."

"Bullshit, Colt Lomax. You know exactly what love is, you're just too afraid to give yourself over to it. Too afraid you'll end up like Mama. But what you refuse to see is that love didn't put Mama on the road to self-destruction, Colt. Mama did that all by herself. And while it's always been easier to blame our crappy childhood on a twist of fate, fate doesn't control our lives..." She leaned up. "We do."

How in the hell did his little sister get so smart? And so pushy? Colt wondered.

"It might be too late," he said. "She's got her heart set on making it big in California."

Shirlene snorted. "Does that look like a woman who has her heart set on being anywhere but right where she is?"

Colt stared at the laughing woman who waved and

yelled out greetings to everyone she passed. The sight evoked the same wealth of emotions it always had, but this time he took his baby sister's advice and accepted love for what it was: a perfect emotion in an imperfect world.

"And what if she thinks I'm not good enough for her?" he said, more to himself than Shirlene.

"You'll never know until you try," Shirlene shot back. She paused. "And by the way, if you ever tell her the things I said about her, I'll deny every word."

Colt might've laughed if the Cadillac hadn't finally reached them. Everything inside him stilled when Hope's gaze caught his.

After searching for it for the last few weeks, it was finally there in the deep-blue depths of her eyes—something he only thought he'd see again in an old photograph. And just that quickly, Colt's heart jumped up to his throat as if he was free-falling from a fourteen-thousand-foot drop, and he wished he had a cowboy hat to wave over his head as he yelled yee-haw.

He wasn't aware of moving out to the curb. Or stepping into the street. He wasn't aware of anything but those eyes, which mirrored the same emotions churning deep inside of him.

"Colt?" Hope's voice penetrated his love bubble. "What are you doing?"

Finally becoming aware of his surroundings, he realized he was jogging next to the car. A younger Colt might've cared about looking like a fool in front of the entire town of Bramble, especially when some smartass yelled out, "Hey, Colt! If you're supposed to be a clown, you forgot your pooper-scooper!"

But this lovesick Colt couldn't have cared less.

"I need to talk to you," he said as he ran.

"Now?"

It was a good question, since they were in the middle of a parade.

"Yes. Right now."

She nodded as she leaned up over the front seat. "Stop the car, Kenny."

"Now, Hope, you know I can't do that," Kenny said. "Harley gave us strict orders to keep it at ten miles an hour. No more, and no less."

"I don't give a shit what Harley said, Kenny," Colt said as he placed a hand on the side door. "Stop the damned car."

"Please, Kenny," Faith joined in. "Colt needs to talk with Hope."

"No, sir, I ain't stoppin'." Kenny shook his head. "Not when it sounds like Colt wants to punch my head in."

"Well, if he doesn't punch your head in, Kenny Gene, I sure as heck will," Hope yelled, loud enough to draw the attention of the clown following the car in a little battery-powered Jeep. The hugely exaggerated foam cowboy hat and thick face paint couldn't camouflage the handlebar mustache or the mayor's big belly, swelling over the small steering wheel.

"Now, Colt," Harley said. "You sure have earned my respect in the last few weeks, but I still can't let you disrupt the parade with any more of your delinquent shenanigans."

"I need to talk with Hope," Colt said through gritted teeth.

Harley drove around in tiny circles behind the Cadillac. "Well, we only have less than a mile until we get to the school. You can talk to Hope then."

Except Colt didn't want to talk to Hope when he got to the school.

"Now, Harley. I need to talk to her now."

"What is going on here?" Rachel Dean pedaled up on her unicycle in face paint and a curly red wig, her man hands waggling in front of her. Colt had to give it to her. For a large woman, she was extremely skilled on the one-tire bike.

"Colt is bothering Hope again," Harley explained, as he tooted the horn of the little red Jeep and fired off a couple rounds from his cap gun.

"He is not bothering me!" Hope turned around and yelled at him.

"Now, Hope," Harley said. "I realize you've always had a soft spot for the underdog, and no one is more of an underdog than Colt Lomax—being how he was falsely accused and sent to prison and all. But I won't condone any more pranks."

For a moment, Colt thought about lifting Hope from the car. And if she hadn't been pregnant, he might've tried it. But the car was going a little too fast and the soles of his cowboy boots were a little too slick for him to chance it.

Sheriff Winslow pulled up behind with lights flashing and leaned out of his window. "Is there a problem?"

"No problem, Sam." Rachel backed up and then went forward as she tried to keep the same pace as the car. "Colt is just pullin' another prank on Hope."

"I'm not pulling a prank! I want to ask her something, is all."

"Well, go ahead and ask her, son," Harley said. "At this point, no one's stoppin' you."

"Fine!" For a runner, he suddenly felt extremely out

of shape. His heart was beating like the base drum up ahead, and his head reeled from lack of oxygen. But it didn't seem to matter anymore. All that mattered was the woman who looked at him with big questioning eyes.

"Hope," he started.

"Yes?" She scooted along the backseat as close as she could get to him. The baby pig snuffled and followed her, his snout pushing beneath her arm until his head rested on her lap.

Colt cleared his throat, but before he could speak, he stepped in a steaming pile left by the Four-H Club and almost took a header.

"Colt!" Hope grabbed his coat and held on while he got his footing. And once he was keeping pace again, she prompted. "So you were saying?"

He took a deep breath and dove in. "Marry me, Hope."

Up ahead, the horn of the semi truck pulling the float blasted, drowning out his words.

"What?" Hope leaned closer. "What did you say?"

"He said, 'Larry needs soap,'" Rachel supplied on her way around the car.

"Larry?" Kenny Gene questioned. "Is that Larry Lines who lives south of Big Springs? Because he empties septic tanks for a livin', and soap ain't gonna get rid of that smell."

"He didn't say 'Larry needs soap,'" Harley jumped in. "He said, 'Ferry the boat.'"

"Well, what in the heck does that mean?" Rachel asked, on her way around the other side.

"I said, marry me Hope!" Colt blurted the words out as loudly as one of Hope's hog calls. It was quite a feat, considering he was still running. There was a long,

painful silence before everyone around them burst out
laughing.

"And you said you wasn't pullin' no prank!" Rachel
executed a jerky figure eight. "Why that's the biggest
joke I've heard in a while. Hope Scroggs marrying Colt
Lomax." She shook her orange corkscrews while Kenny
banged on the steering wheel.

"Whoo-wee, Colt, that was a good one. Especially
when Hope must've had a hun-nerd marriage proposals in
the last week, and she ain't accepted a one." Kenny glanced
back, and his eyes scrunched up at the corners. "Come to
think of it, the only one you did accept was Slate's."

"Kenny, Slate didn't ask Hope to marry him," Harley
clarified. "Hope asked Slate to marry her, but it was too
late because Faith had already beat her to it."

The words caused Colt to stumble, and he had to hang
on to the car or end up face-planted in the asphalt. When
he righted himself, he expected to see Hope looking as
confused as he was. But instead her face was painfully
pale.

"You asked Slate to marry you?" It was difficult to
talk around the huge lump in his throat.

"No." She shook her head. "I didn't ask him."

"No, she's right," Rachel jumped in again. "She just
accepted his non-proposal."

Stunned, Colt tried to keep up, not only with the car
but with the conversation.

"You came back to marry Slate?"

Her mouth opened, and then closed, then opened again.
"I was confused . . . after that night I didn't know . . ."

"Did you know about the baby then?" The words felt
like sawdust in his mouth.

"No!" She shook her head. "I swear I didn't, Colt."

But it didn't make any difference. All along, he thought she'd come back to Bramble to attend her sister's wedding, when in reality, she had come back to Bramble to marry Slate—right after she'd screwed the poor Lomax kid.

His feet slowed, and the car pulled away from him.

"Colt!" Hope called back to him. "It wasn't like that! It was a mistake!"

It was a mistake, all right.

A mistake to think that the Sweetheart of Bramble would ever love him.

Chapter Twenty-seven

"COLT!" HOPE YELLED as loud as her hog-calling lungs would allow.

But he didn't pay any attention as he walked away, his back straight and his dark hair waving in the wind. And with a sinking heart, she realized he wasn't coming back.

Not now.

Not ever.

"What are you doing?" Faith leaned over. "Go after him."

"It won't make any difference." Hope blinked back her tears. "There's no way I can ever explain."

"So you're not even going to try?"

Hope shook her head as she turned back around. Sherman rooted against her, and she hugged him close as the tears dripped in cold streaks down her cheeks.

"Well." Faith sat back and released her breath in one long agitated huff. "I guess I didn't realize my sister was such a chicken shit."

Hope's head came up, and her eyes narrowed. "A what?"

"A chicken shit," Kenny Gene supplied.

Just that quickly, anger joined pain, and Hope shot

Kenny a mean glare before she turned on her sister. "Oh, you should talk. You ran off with your tail between your legs as soon as I hit town."

"Only because I thought you were pregnant and needed a father for your child." Faith glared back at her. "But you're right, I was a chicken shit, but at least I let you talk some sense into me. Unlike you, who is just going to sit there and let the father of your child walk right out of your life without your doing one thing to stop him."

Kenny stretched around. "Colt ain't the father of Hope's baby, Faith. The entire town is bettin' on Matthew McConaughey."

"Shut up, Kenny!" They both yelled in unison.

Shrugging, Kenny turned back around.

"In case you don't remember," Hope continued, "I *did* accept Slate's proposal."

"Non-proposal," Rachel Dean clarified before she quickly unicycled away.

Exasperated, Hope spoke through her teeth. "I accepted Slate's non-proposal."

"So what?" Faith shrugged as if her twin sister hadn't wanted to marry her husband. "You were just on the rebound after Colt. Besides, when you had the chance to have Slate all to yourself, you didn't take it. Instead, you came and got me."

"Except I wasn't exactly happy about it, and everyone in town knows it."

"Of course, you weren't. Your safety net had been jerked out from under you by a sister you didn't even know you had." Faith reached out and took her hand. "But you don't need a safety net, Hope. All you need is enough guts to take a chance—to just step out on the wire."

Suddenly Hope realized it wasn't such a bad thing to have a twin sister after all. "But after everything I've done, how am I going to make him believe that I never loved Slate like that? That it was always him?"

"I don't know," Faith said, and Hope's shoulders slumped before her sister continued. "But aren't you Hope Scroggs, and isn't this Bramble, Texas?"

"Meaning?"

Faith smiled with so much evil devilry that it would've made a Disney villain proud.

Anything Hope wants...Hope gets.

It took more than a few seconds for her sister's thoughts to sink in. But once they did, Hope didn't waste any time screaming at the top of her lungs.

"Kenny Gene! If you don't stop this car right now, I'm going to jump out and hurt myself and the twins too!"

The car jerked to a stop and, as soon as it did, Hope handed off Sherman to Faith and hopped out. Unfortunately, Colt was already a good half of a mile down the street. She thought about running after him, but she didn't have more than a few minutes before he reached Shirlene's SUV.

"Uncle Harley!" she yelled.

He zipped over in the Jeep. "What, Hope?"

"As your goddaughter, I've never asked for much."

"No, honey, you ain't."

"Well, I'm asking now. I need your car."

Harley pulled off his big old hat and scratched at a spot on his forehead, leaving streaks in the white face paint. "Now, honey, why would you want this little old car when you can ride in my big old Cadillac?"

Hope glanced back at Colt's sweet behind. "Because

the man I love is getting away, and I've got to go after him."

Harley's eyes widened. "Now, are you sure about this, honey? Colt might be a converted convict, but, I hear tell, he doesn't have a pot to pee in or a window to throw it out of."

"I don't care," she said. And it was the truth. She didn't care if they had to live out on Grover Road in a tiny trailer with a leaky roof. As long as she was with Colt, she'd be happy. "Please, Uncle Harley."

Since she rarely used the word *please,* it only took Harley a second for his mustache to twitch up in a smile. "Well, in that case, honey." He waved Kenny Gene over. "Kenny, come help me out of here. Hope needs to go get her man."

It turned out to be harder to drive the little car than Hope had anticipated. Of course, her coat and the ugly purple maid-of-honor dress that Cindy Lynn, the parade coordinator, had insisted she wear didn't help matters. She ran up on the sidewalk more than a few times, scattering people like a bunch of startled chickens. But that didn't stop them from hurrying after her. Nor did it stop word from traveling. By the time she reached Colt, she had most of the town running behind her, quickly followed by the people in the parade—including the band, the football float, the coach's truck, and the mayor's Cadillac.

"Colt!" Hope tooted the horn.

His steps faltered, but he refused to stop.

"Colt, wait!" She sped up and circled around him. He adjusted his stride, but didn't stop, forcing her to talk and drive at the same time.

"I didn't come home to marry Slate. I came home

because I was heartsick and confused. I thought I was over the bad boy of Bramble who gave me sweet kisses, and then five seconds later ran my bra up the flagpole."

"Tiniest little bit of lace I've ever seen," Rachel Dean said, as she wheeled her way up.

Ignoring her, Hope continued. "But all it took was one look from those beautiful gray eyes and I was thirteen again, begging for whatever scraps you'd toss my way. And when you left that morning without saying a word, I couldn't deal with the rejection. So I did what I've always done to save face—I came running back to Slate. Except Slate had moved on and found someone else."

Making another circle around him, she glanced up at his face. But it didn't look any more understanding than it had a few seconds ago. His eyes still stared straight ahead, and his jaw was still as tight as one of Harley's western shirts. Still, she continued, like the rambling lovesick fool she was.

"And at first, I was mad. Slate was my backup plan, someone I counted on to be there when my life didn't work out the way I wanted. And when he wasn't there, I pouted like the spoiled brat I am. It took a while to realize what a mistake it would've been to marry Slate when I love someone else. And even if that someone doesn't love me, I still should've had enough guts to let him know how I feel—to let the entire town know how I feel." She took a deep breath and yelled as loudly as she could. "I love you, Colt Lomax!"

Hope thought the revelation would make him stop—or at least falter—but Colt kept on going as if he hadn't heard her. Completely defeated, she took her foot off the pedal and let the little Jeep coast to a stop. The town slowed with her, although their mouths kept going.

"Who does Hope love?" Twyla asked.

"Colt, you idiot," Cindy Lynn jumped in.

"Hope loves Colt?" Kenny said. "Well, ain't that a shocker."

"Not really," Rachel Dean said, as she pedaled up. "Not after seeing his hand up her shirt in the elevator."

"Come to think of it," Ms. Murphy huffed her way into the group, "there were all those suspicious times I caught them in the bibliography section, supposedly doing research for book reports."

"And there was that one time that I caught them beneath the bleachers," Sue Ellen offered. "And it didn't look like kissin' was the only thing going on."

"Well, well." Harley hooked his thumbs in his clown suspenders. "It seems we've solved the mystery of who impregnated our little Hope." He pointed at Sheriff Winslow, who had pulled up in his squad car. "Go get him, Sam."

"No!" Hope tried to stop him, but the siren drowned out her voice. And before she could even climb out of the Jeep, Sam had pulled up in front of Colt. She figured Colt was going to put up a fight, but instead he turned and walked back toward her, although he looked as angry as the sky above him.

"Now what exactly is goin' on here?" Shirlene said as she sashayed into the group.

"Colt asked Hope to marry him," Kenny stated with a broad smile on his face. "But then someone opened their big mouth and told him about her accepting Slate's proposal."

"Non-proposal," Rachel injected, as she whizzed around the group.

Shirlene got the gist and took over. "And I guess my big brother tapped into his stubborn streak and refuses to listen. Well," she shrugged, "I guess there's only one thing left to do." She glanced around the crowd until her gaze landed on Hope's daddy. "Burl, go get your gun."

"What?" Both Hope and Colt stared at Shirlene, but she only stared back with an innocence that didn't bode well.

"What else do you expect us to do? Our little Hope is knocked up, and if my ornery brother is the one who's responsible, then he needs to step up to the plate—or should I say the altar."

"Shirlene," Colt spoke through his teeth, "what the hell do you think you're doing?"

Her head tipped. "Are you saying that Pumpkin Seed isn't your baby?"

"Pumpkin Seed?" Rachel asked, as she continued to ride the unicycle as if she was competing for a Guinness world record. "Who's Pumpkin Seed?"

"Colt and Hope's baby," Faith supplied, as she struggled to control a wiggling pig. "Isn't that right, Hope?"

At that moment, Hope had a choice. She could deny it and spend the rest of her days without Colt, or she could accept what the town had given her and run with it.

Tipping up her chin, Hope took two steps closer to Colt. So close she could see the tiny specks of green in his gray irises.

"Yes. The baby's Colt's."

"Get my gun, Jenna," Hope's daddy said, not sounding the least bit angry.

Colt's eyes narrowed. "That's it? You're going to let your daddy force me into marrying you at gunpoint?"

She swallowed hard. "If that's what it takes to keep you, Colt Lomax, I sure as heck am. Especially considering you already asked me."

"I asked you before I knew about Slate."

"Well, too bad. You can't take it back now."

Hope tried to stare down his angry glare, but her nerves got the best of her and her knees started to shake uncontrollably. Especially when her mother returned with the gun and handed it to her grinning father.

"You can put the gun away, Burl," Colt said, his gaze never leaving Hope. "I'm not marrying Hope at gunpoint. No one can force me to do that."

Hope pressed her lips together and tried to act like her heart wasn't breaking. "I didn't expect that they could." Tears continued to form in her eyes until her vision was nothing but a watery blur. Which was why it took her a moment to realize that Colt was no longer standing in front of her.

"Hope Marie Scroggs."

Her gaze dropped down to the man who knelt on one knee. She brushed the tears from her eyes and looked again. But he was still there, his beloved gray eyes staring straight at her.

"I love you. And because of that love, I couldn't stay here and watch you marry Slate. So I left. But it didn't help. Because wherever I roamed, my thoughts were never far away from the Sweetheart of Bramble. I know I probably don't deserve you, but damned if I care. Marry me, Hope."

Unable to speak with the emotions clogging her throat, Hope flopped down on his knee and covered his face in kisses. When she pulled back, he was smiling.

"Yes," she breathed. "I'll marry you."

The townsfolk let out a rousing cheer. But the cheer fizzled when Rachel's cousin, Bear, shoved his way through the crowd, pushing a handsome man in front of him.

"I did it! I found him!" Bear beamed with pride, tobacco juice seeping from his wide grin.

For the first time in Bramble history, the townsfolk were struck speechless. Everyone just stood there staring as if they couldn't quite believe their eyes. Of course, it didn't take long for Kenny to find his voice.

"Well, hey, Matthew. Welcome to Bramble."

Epilogue

IT WAS A DREAM. It had to be. Where else but in a dream could you stand in front of a church filled to the rafters with all your family and friends and whisper your vows to the handsome outlaw you've loved for all your life? An outlaw who kissed you as if his life depended on it before he strolled you down the aisle and off to the town hall, where he fed you strawberry soda from his Solo cup and Josephine's Raspberry Jamboree Cake from his fingers, and sweet kisses from his lips before taking you in his strong arms and waltzing you toward happily-ever-after.

It was a dream.

Her dream.

"Hey, Hog!" Kenny Gene waltzed by with Twyla. "Is it true that you and Colt are buildin' a house out by Sutter Springs?"

"'Course it's true," Rachel Dean said, as she tromped by in the arms of Rossie Owens. "You can't expect a Hollywood movie star to live with her mama and daddy forever. Especially when she's got a husband and a couple babies on the way."

Hope ignored the conversation and snuggled back into her dream.

"Maybe I should start referring to the baby as Pumpkin Seeds." A deep, familiar voice rumbled above her head.

With a sigh of contentment, Hope pulled back and stared up at her handsome husband, who looked as sexy as a movie star in his crisp white tuxedo shirt. The black bow tie had long since been stripped off and the first few studs opened, so it was no trouble at all to slip her hand inside and touch all that smooth warm skin.

Preoccupied with the hollow at the base of his throat, it took her a while to answer. "I'm not having twins."

"And just what makes you think that?" Colt adjusted his hands on her waist so his thumbs could gently stroke her rounding belly. "Seeing as how the ultrasound isn't until next week."

"Call it woman's intuition—or just a strong feeling." Her fingers trailed along the edge of his collar, over his broad shoulder, down his hard biceps to his tattooed forearm. With his sleeve cuffed almost to his elbow, she was able to trace a fingernail along most of the rattlesnake. "Have I told you how sexy I think your tat is?"

"You might've mentioned it." There was a trace of humor in his voice.

"Of course, I could do without the pig."

The words were barely out of her mouth before Colt reached down and tipped her chin up. His eyes were heartbreakingly serious.

"Never. I'm never getting rid of my Homecoming Hog. Not in this lifetime or the next. And we better get that straight right here and now, Mrs. Lomax."

His words brought a brilliant smile to her face and a happy flutter to her stomach. She stretched up on her toes and gave him a kiss that ended the conversation for a good while. When she pulled back, she cradled his face in her hands, the two-carat diamond engagement ring flashing like the disco ball overhead.

"You spent too much money on the ring," she sighed.

Colt placed a kiss in her palm. "Please don't tell me, you *still* believe I'm broke."

She had, until she googled *Desperado Customs*. Then she sat in stunned silence staring at page after page of information about a certain motorcycle bum who had made it big.

Hope lowered her hands to his shoulders. "I'm sorry. I should've believed you. I guess I just didn't want to think you had made it when I had failed."

"Failed?" He shook his head. "Didn't you hear what Rachel Dean said? To the people of Bramble, you're a movie star—a movie star wealthy enough to pay for our house."

"A house way too big for just three people?"

"Three people," he sent her a sexy wink, "with more to come."

She tipped her head and shot him a sassy look. "So you plan on keeping me barefoot and pregnant, Colt Lomax?"

"Not barefoot." Colt glanced down at the pretty pink boots he'd given her as a wedding present.

"Well," she shrugged, "I can't say as I mind having a houseful of kids, as long as in between having babies I can go back to school to prepare myself for my next contest."

"Hog-callin' or pie-eatin'?" he said with a devilish grin.

"How about politickin'?"

For an answer, he swept her up in his arms and headed for the door.

"Colt Lomax, what are you doing?" she asked, not the least bit upset to find herself snuggled against his warm chest.

"I'm taking you to bed, Hog. If I'm going to be married to the next mayor of Bramble, I need to get while the gettin's good."

She giggled as the townsfolk took note of their departure.

"Hey, now," Harley yelled. "We aren't finished yet. I still need to make my speech."

"I'm sure it will keep, Harley," Colt said as he weaved around the tables.

"But you haven't throwed the bouquet." Twyla hurried after them, holding out the ugly silk arrangement.

Noticing Shirlene standing in one corner, Hope reached out and snagged it, heaving it as far as she could. The bouquet sailed through the air straight at Shirlene, who was forced to reach up and catch it or end up clocked in the head with five pounds of hot glue.

"Oh, no." Shirlene immediately dropped the flowers and shook her head.

"Too late, Shirl," Hope said, and sent her an evil smile. "You already caught it."

"She's right," Faith added, as she leaned over and picked up the bouquet. "Besides, who knows what waits for you just around the corner?"

"Trouble." Shirlene jerked the bouquet out of her hand. "No doubt, nothing but trouble."

Then Colt swept out the door, and Shirlene and Faith

were swallowed up by the herd of townsfolk who followed behind them. Beneath the town hall flagpole, an old Harley Knucklehead waited with a new custom seat Colt had made especially for two and a string of plastic baby bottles attached to the rusted back fender, along with a sign that read "Hitched Just In Time."

While Darla handed out the small bundles of birdseed and the townsfolk tried to figure out how to get the hot-glued pieces of tulle open, Colt slipped Hope's helmet on and snapped it beneath her chin.

"You sure you wouldn't rather drive away in my Escalade?"

Hope adjusted the helmet. "An Escalade when I just married a motorcycle bum? Not a chance."

Colt flashed her one of his smiles, which recently seemed to be getting more and more frequent, and then helped her into his leather jacket. It took some sweat and more than a few kicks to get the Knucklehead started, but finally the engine caught and throbbed to life as Colt hopped on and twisted the throttle.

Once he was satisfied, he helped her on and secured her hands around his waist before leaning back to ask, "So what's the plan?"

Snuggled up against his back, Hope contemplated the question before she rested her chin on his shoulder and whispered in his ear.

"To live happily ever after."

As the motorcycle eased down the sidewalk and off the curb, the townsfolk hurried after them, the unopened birdseed bundles still clutched in their hands.

"Well, who would've thunk it," Rachel Dean said as

she dabbed at the corners of her eyes with the sleeve of her Sunday-best dress.

"Makes sense," Harley replied, hitching up his pants. "Shoulda known our little Hope wouldn't fall for some foreigner from California."

"Though Matthew was awful understandin' about the mistake," Cindy Lynn said. "And he is from Austin."

"Austin's nice," Kenny Gene stated. "But there's no place better than Bramble."

There was a chorus of "sure ain't" as the Bad Boy of Bramble disappeared into the night with his sweetheart.

About the Author

Katie Lane is a firm believer that love conquers all and laughter is the best medicine. Which is why you'll find plenty of humor and happily-ever-afters in her contemporary and Western contemporary romance novels. A *USA Today* bestselling author, she has written numerous series, including Deep in the Heart of Texas, Hunk for the Holidays, Overnight Billionaires, Tender Heart Texas, The Brides of Bliss Texas, and Bad Boy Ranch.

Katie lives in Albuquerque, New Mexico, and when she's not writing, she enjoys reading, eating chocolate (dark, please), and snuggling with her high school sweetheart and her Cairn Terrier, Roo.

You can learn more at:
KatieLaneBooks.com
Twitter @KatieLaneBooks
Facebook.com/KatieLaneAuthor

**Don't miss another sexy series from Katie Lane,
The Overnight Billionaires**

Available now

And get into the Christmas spirit with Katie Lane

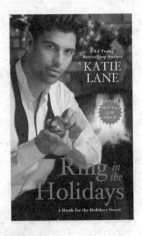

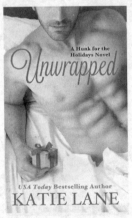

Available now

Looking for more Western romance?
Take the reins with these cowboys from Forever!

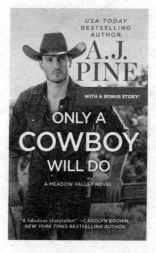

ONLY A COWBOY WILL DO
by A.J. Pine

After a lifetime of helping others, Jenna Owens is finally putting herself first, starting with her vacation at the Meadow Valley Guest Ranch to celebrate her fortieth birthday. Colt Morgan, part-owner of the ranch, is happy to help her have all the fun she deserves, especially her wish for a vacation fling. But will their two weeks of fantasy lead to a shot in the real world, or will their final destination be two broken hearts? Includes a bonus story from Melinda Curtis!

Discover bonus content and more on read-forever.com

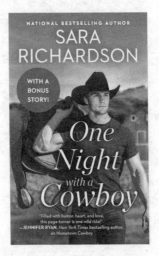

ONE NIGHT WITH A COWBOY
by Sara Richardson

Wes Harding is known as a devil-may-care bull rider—but now, with his sister's pregnancy at risk, Wes promises to put aside his wild ways and take the reins on their ranch's big charity event. Only he didn't count on his co-hostess—and little sister's best friend—being so darn distracting. One kiss with Thea Davis throws his world off-balance. But with her husband gone, Thea's focused only on raising her two rambunctious children. Can Wes convince her that he's the man on whom she can rely? Includes a bonus story by Carly Bloom!

Find more great reads on Instagram with
@ReadForeverPub

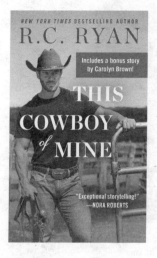

THIS COWBOY OF MINE
by R.C. Ryan

Kirby Regan just quit her career in Washington, D.C., to buy her family's Wyoming ranch. But when a snowstorm hits while she's out hiking in the Tetons, her only option for shelter is a nearby cave. She didn't realize it was already occupied... by a ruggedly handsome cowboy. Casey Merrick doesn't mind sharing his space with a gorgeous stranger, as long as they can both keep their distance—a task that begins to seem impossible as the attraction between them heats up. Includes a bonus story from Carolyn Brown!

BLACKLISTED
by Jay Crownover

In the small Texas town of Loveless, Palmer "Shot" Caldwell lives on the edge of the law. But this ruthlessly hot outlaw follows his own code of honor, and that includes repaying his debts. Which is exactly why icy, brilliant Dr. Presley Baskin is calling in a favor. She once saved Shot's life. Now she needs his help—and his protection.

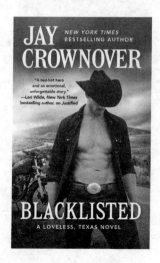

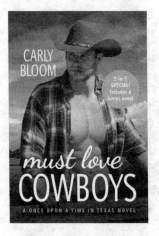

MUST LOVE COWBOYS
by Carly Bloom

Alice Martin doesn't regret putting her career as a librarian above personal
relationships—but when cowboy Beau Montgomery comes to her for help,
Alice decides to see what she's been missing. She agrees to help Beau improve his reading skills if he'll be her date to an upcoming wedding. But
when the town's gossip mill gets going, they're forced into a fake romance
to keep their deal a secret. And soon Alice is seeing Beau in a whole new
way...Includes the bonus novel *Big Bad Cowboy*!